The Coming of the King

Maria Albert

DESCENT of KINGS Book 3

Dreamspinner Press

Published by
Dreamspinner Press
5032 Capital Circle SW
Suite 2, PMB# 279
Tallahassee, FL 32305-7886
USA
http://www.dreamspinnerpress.com/

ISBN: 978-1-62798-194-1
Digital ISBN: 978-1-62798-195-8

Printed in the United States of America
First Edition
October 2013

Acknowledgments

A warm welcome to all my new readers and welcome back to those of you who have been on this journey from the start! Special thanks to Rachel, Ariella, and Joylyn, my beta readers, first fans, and staunch supporters, and to all the folks at Dreamspinner, for enabling me to fulfill my dream.

Particular thanks to Elizabeth North and Lynn West for coordination and production, Paul Richmond for his beautifully rendered cover art, and Andi and Ian, for their invaluable editing expertise, witty banter, and endlessly enjoyable repartee.

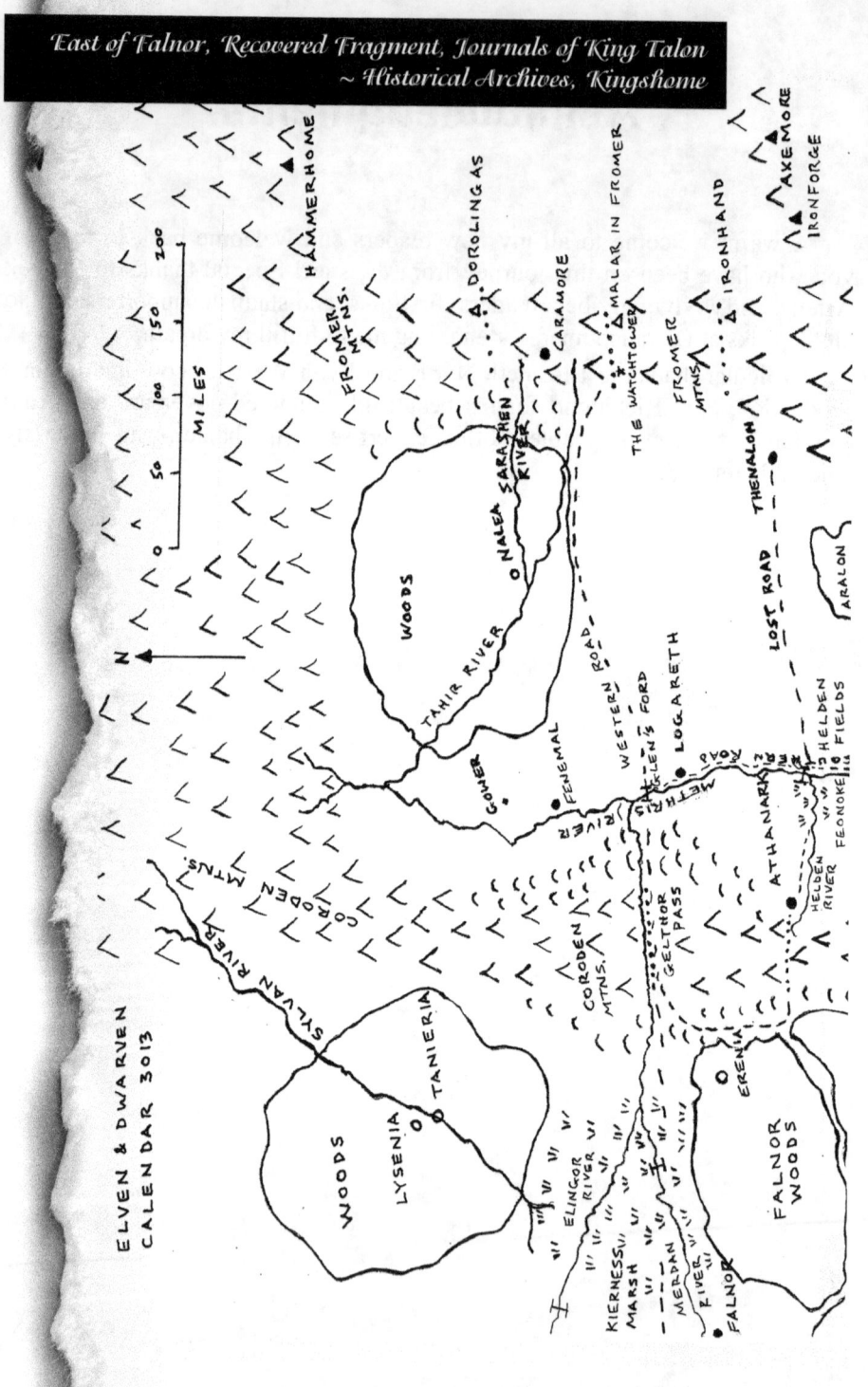

Acknowledgments

A warm welcome to all my new readers and welcome back to those of you who have been on this journey from the start! Special thanks to Rachel, Ariella, and Joylyn, my beta readers, first fans, and staunch supporters, and to all the folks at Dreamspinner, for enabling me to fulfill my dream.

Particular thanks to Elizabeth North and Lynn West for coordination and production, Paul Richmond for his beautifully rendered cover art, and Andi and Ian, for their invaluable editing expertise, witty banter, and endlessly enjoyable repartee.

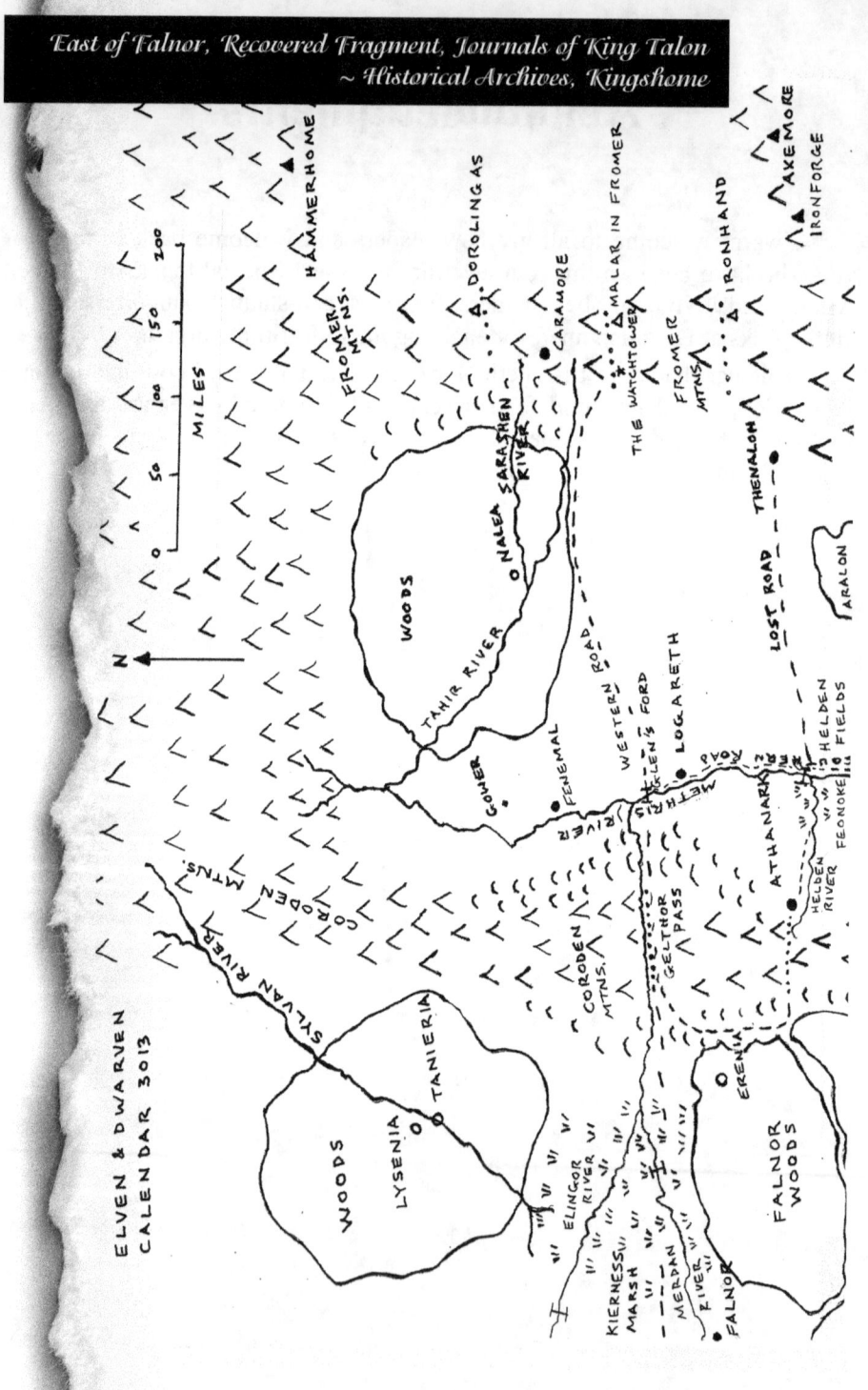

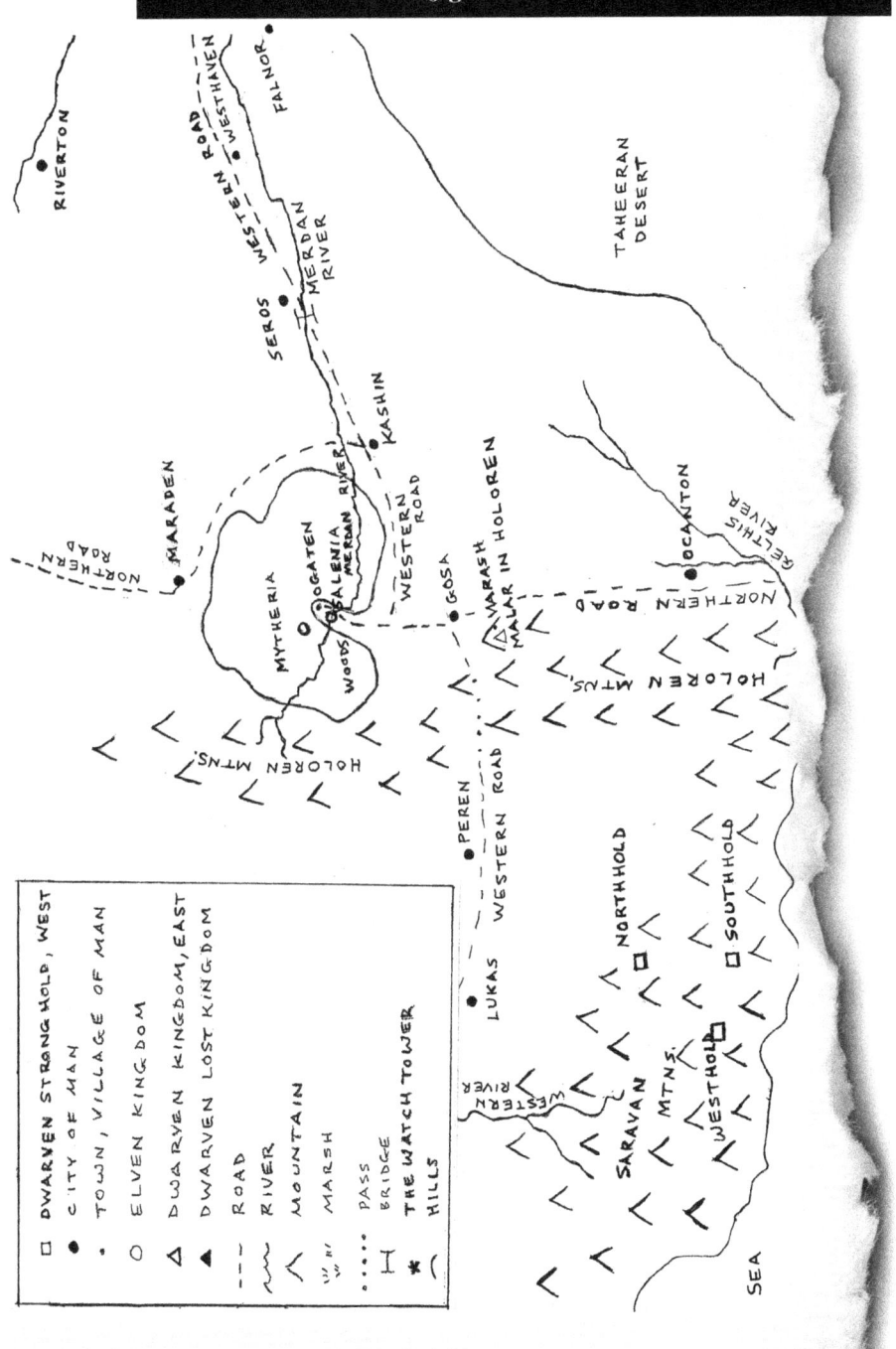

Chapter 1
Test of Courage

TARRELL scanned the common room of the inn a second time, more carefully than before, but he still didn't see Rion. He'd just come down from their room. He'd left Rion here, with their five guards, but he wasn't with Rarnak and the Ogaten brothers, or anywhere else visible. Rion shouldn't be walking about unprotected. They were still new to this City. Over the hundreds of miles they'd traveled from Athanark to Gosa, they'd faced ogres, obearn, Elves, and even a nightwhore, but Rion's prophecy had come true: they'd made it without losing a single man, though they'd had a number of terrifyingly close calls.

They'd paid off the rest of their guards the day before. Tarrell and Rion had hoped one or two more of their men would have wanted to stay on with them, at least until they were settled, but their guards were all well paid and eager to spend their earnings. They'd parted company at The Painted Turtle, where Tarrell and Rion planned to stay with their few remaining guards until they found a permanent place to live and set up their shop. Unfortunately, the food at that inn had been deplorable. Knowing they'd need to be in an inn for at least a week, if not more, Tarrell refused to pay those prices for such poor fare. So far this new inn, The Lost Eagle, appeared far more promising. But where was Rion?

"Master Tarrell?" a man asked, approaching him solicitously, an expression of concern on his face. "My name is Janus. I'm the innkeeper. My son Jasper told me you arrived a short while ago. He said you came from Athanark?"

"Yes, that's right," Tarrell said, listening with half an ear as he scanned the room again.

"I thought you should know: there's a man who's been here the past few days, asking after merchant caravans from there. I've seen him in here, but also in the street outside, hanging about, talking to unsavory people. He's tall and dark haired, lean, with a mean, scarred face. I don't like the looks of him, and I thought you should know, so you might be on your guard," the innkeeper said.

Tarrell turned to him. "Thank you, I appreciate that. If you'll excuse me, I'll tell the men."

Tarrell approached the table where they were seated.

"Got us all settled in, Tarrell?" Rarnak asked, knocking back a small metal cup of oushka.

"Never mind that. Where's Rion?" Tarrell asked, concerned.

Rarnak grimaced. "Out in the street, being sick. I tried to tell him he shouldn't try the oushka, but he wanted to show himself as much a man as any of us."

"You let him go alone?" Tarrell asked, worried.

"Tarrell, I know you're his guardian, but you can't treat him like a boy anymore. Rion's sixteen now, he's come-of-age, and he's more than proved himself a man on this trip. A man doesn't like anyone to see him heave from drink, especially not a young one," Van said, with all the wisdom of his seventeen years. He was the youngest brother, only a year younger than Tarrell.

"Someone's been searching for us, someone who looks dangerous and knows where we're from. It must be us. How many other caravans would be coming all the way from Athanark to Gosa? I don't know what's going on, but I don't want him left unguarded, even for a moment," Tarrell argued anxiously.

Tarrell turned to head for the door but saw a man enter the inn. He looked exactly as the innkeeper had described: tall, lean, and dark haired, with a scar running from temple to chin down the left side of his face. He headed for a vacant table toward the back wall and sat and began casually surveying the room. His eyes slid quickly from Tarrell when he realized he was being watched. Tarrell felt a sudden chill. The man had hard, dark, dead eyes: a predator's eyes.

"That's the man the innkeeper described. He just came in. The one in brown with the scarred face, at the far table. Rarnak, you come with me. You four, don't let him out of your sight," Tarrell ordered.

Tarrell and Rarnak went outside. Rion was not in front of the inn. They checked the narrow alleyways on either side of it. The one on the left smelled particularly rank, of vomit. There was a puddle of it on the ground that had yet to soak into the dirt of the alley, but Rion was not there. Chillingly, there were a number of fresh-looking footprints in the dirt all around it. Tarrell felt fear then.

Something glinted on the ground, and Tarrell picked it up. It was a brass button, with a little torn piece of blue fabric. The fear turned to dread. He showed it to Rarnak. "This is from Rion's shirt."

Tarrell examined the alley floor more closely and saw small, wet-looking dark spots, as if something had splattered and soaked into the dirt. He touched one, rubbed the grains of dirt between his fingers, and saw red. "Blood," he said, his hand shaking, as the dread turned to terror.

He ran back to the inn, into the common room, Rarnak at his heels, right to the table where the dark-eyed man still sat. The man tensed. "Where is he? If you've hurt him you'll wish you'd never been born!" Tarrell threatened, his voice shaking, as he drew his sword and pointed it at the man's throat.

"I've wished that many times, but my wish has yet to be granted. Who are you and whom have you lost?" the man replied coolly.

"You know who we are! You've been asking after us for days! Now, tell me where he is, or I'll start loosening your tongue with my blade," Tarrell said, moving the point of it closer to the villain's throat for emphasis.

Tarrell realized patrons had been scrambling from nearby tables, and the Ogaten brothers had joined Rarnak at his back. Though his eyes had left the man only for an instant, suddenly a blade appeared in the man's hand, coming from under the table. It was only a knife, but before he could react, as fast as an eagle seizing a mouse, the man struck Tarrell's blade. Remarkably, with a twist, the sword was yanked from Tarrell's grasp, and in the next instant, an arm snaked about his torso and the stranger's knife was pressed to his throat. Tarrell was stunned by the speed and skill of the attack and bit back a cry of despair. Rion! He'd failed Rion!

"This is not the place to discuss such things. The City Guard will likely come soon. Let us adjourn to the street. Your guards may follow: they know better than to try to harm me while I hold you hostage," the man threatened, his voice cold, deadly. Tarrell was astonished by the strength of the lean man as he was dragged helplessly toward the door.

The stranger brought Tarrell into the alley on the right. "Now then, first you answer my questions and then I answer yours. Where is Jargas who traveled with you?"

Tarrell saw that Ron, Ara, and Rarnak had followed, but there was no sign of Gar and Van. Tarrell realized they must be going for their bows, which were in their room. He needed to stall, to give them the time they needed to get them. "What business is it of yours?"

"The trail to find your missing friend grows cold while you bandy words about," the man said coolly.

"I'll not betray one friend to you to save another," Tarrell replied, his voice full of pain. It was a desperate lie. Jargas could overpower this man; he would be safe. *Rion, what's happened to you?*

"Ah. But Jargas is my friend also, and we would save much time if he were here and saw me. He would vouch for me. And then I could help you find the one you've lost," the man enticed.

The stranger's words rang surprisingly true to Tarrell's ear, as memory stirred in the back of his mind. There was something familiar about this man. Then he heard the deep rumble of Jargas's voice back in Athanark, describing him, and felt a small measure of relief. But he had to be sure. "What name do you go by? Not your given name. What name did Jargas first know you by?"

"Hunter," the man said, without hesitation.

Tarrell cursed. He called out to his anxious guards, who had been watching but dared not approach. "This is Hunter, a friend of Jargas and also of Talon, the man who tested you in Athanark. Sheathe your weapons." When they did so, Hunter released Tarrell, although he did not yet sheathe his own blade.

Tarrell turned to Hunter. "Forgive me. I thought you had taken Rion. He's missing and he's only just turned sixteen. I am his guardian, Tarrell. He was in the other alley. I found where he knelt, and a piece from his clothes, and blood."

He looked up at the sound of running steps from the street, accompanied by the almost musical jingle of hundreds of metal links rising and falling in symphony—the City Guard in Gosa wore chain mail, unlike their counterparts in most of the other cities they'd traveled through on their journey. They thundered into the inn. "The City Guard will help us," Tarrell said in relief.

Hunter shook his head, sheathing his blade. "No. If you value the boy's life, do not involve them. I will find him for you and recover him alive, if he yet lives, where they could not."

They headed for the door to the inn, but the City Guard they had heard emerged, swords drawn. "All of you, hands in the air," their Captain ordered when he spotted them.

"Is there some problem, Captain?" Hunter asked innocently as the others complied with the command.

"Raise your hands or lose them!" the man threatened, and this time Hunter obeyed, though he did not appear cowed.

"You there, why did you draw your sword upon this man?" he asked Tarrell, apparently having gotten their descriptions from whomever had summoned them.

"It was a mistake, Captain. I have already apologized to him for it. I thought he was someone else," Tarrell explained.

"You, what's your story?" the Captain asked Hunter. His voice was more harsh and his eyes narrowed; it was obvious he disliked the look of him.

"I was sitting at a table quietly when this man accosted me with bared blade. I convinced him to step outside, so if there were any bloodshed, no other innocents might be harmed," Hunter said, deftly grouping himself in the category of innocents, but his attempt was doomed to fail, considering his appearance.

"Convinced at the edge of your knife! We don't take kindly to that sort of thing here in Gosa," the Guardsman said.

"Please, Captain. I would be happy to pay whatever fine you might impose for violating the peace," Tarrell said, hoping a bribe might work. They were wasting time. "We have important business to take care of. The innkeeper can vouch that we are honest merchants. We only just arrived in your fair city, and we have rooms here."

The Captain eyed them shrewdly, assessing them, looking from Tarrell, in his fancy merchant's clothes, to Hunter, in his travel-worn and dirty ones. "All right then. For disturbing the peace and brandishing weapons, thirty gold each, or thirty days in a cell," he said, leering at Hunter, obviously suspecting he could not pay.

Tarrell saw Hunter tense. "Since the fault was mine, I will pay both fines," Tarrell quickly volunteered, emptying his lean purse into his hand and counting out sufficient coin. "Sixty gold," he said, returning two gold, ten silver, and six copper to his purse.

"See that you don't cause any more trouble," the Guard ordered, glaring at Hunter. Then he and his men marched off, past Gar and Van, who were standing by with their bows strung but slung over their shoulders. Tarrell realized they must have come after the City Guard arrived and seen he was safe. They talked in low voices to Ron, in that odd language they used to communicate with one another when they did not wish to be overheard, eyeing Hunter suspiciously.

FARAD listened to the Men speaking behind him in Thenalonese with half an ear, as he kept a wary eye on Tarrell and the departing Guard. He was as fluent in Thenalonese as he was in Amontirin, Common, and Dwarvish.

The tension left him at their words; these were honest Men, truly in search of their friend. His own quest, to find Jargas, would have to wait. If it cost him his sanity or his life, so be it. He could not leave an innocent in peril.

He must do all he could to help these Men find their missing friend, though he knew it was all too likely it would only be to avenge the one taken and to bring his body home. He would behead the corpse first, of course, though he would never reveal that he was the one to have done so. These Men would not understand why such a horrible desecration and mutilation was necessary. They could not know that if he left the body intact, it could be used by the Enemy against them. The Enemy would turn their friend into one of His minions, a Revenant, an undead monster in His thrall. "Show me what you found and tell me what you know, and describe what Rion looks like and what he was wearing."

Tarrell led him to the other alley. "Rion's grown some since we first met, but not much. He's small for his age. As I told you, he just turned sixteen, but he's still a head shorter than I am and about twenty-five pounds lighter: he's still got a boy's build. He's got light-brown hair and blue eyes in a fair-featured face. He was wearing a bright-blue shirt with brass buttons down the front, black pants, and black boots. His cloak's still inside."

Farad found the signs of a scuffle easily, and studied the button and scrap of cloth that Tarrell handed him intently. "Tell me, can the boy fight? Was he armed?"

Tarrell nodded. "He can fight. I trained him."

Farad eyed him appraisingly.

Tarrell said defensively, "I'm not a merchant by choice. I was a swordsman, a good one, too, before I nearly lost my arm. Your friend Talon did the best he could: by all rights I should be dead, but I can still use that hand to write and for other things. I've been training myself to fight with my left. Rion had a dagger with him, but the sword I gave him a few weeks ago for his coming-of-age is in our room."

"Then, from the tracks, I think this blood might not be his," Farad said, but Tarrell's obvious relief at hearing so was short-lived, as he continued, "Although, having injured one of them, he may also now bear injury. Tell me, did he carry a purse with him?"

"He had only a few coins in the purse at his side, but the rest of his coin is hidden within concealed pockets on the inside of his shirt. He's so slender that even with a loose shirt a full purse would otherwise be impossible to effectively hide. He had our new clothes designed especially for that in Athanark. We each carry half the coin hidden within our clothes."

Farad nodded. "Stay here, visible, in the common room. Wait for a request for ransom, but do not pay it. Have some of your men stay hidden. Do not go anywhere with those who come. Stall them. If they leave, send your two stealthiest guards to track them, if they are up to the task. I will return as soon as I am able."

"Let me go with you, or one of the men," Tarrell urged.

"No. I must do this alone. You must trust me, as Jargas and Talon would. Do you know where I might find Jargas, once I return?"

"He left us here, just outside the City, at the crossing of the Western Road with the Northern Road. He was returning to his home in the Holoren Mountains. He said it's twelve leagues southwest of here. That's all we know."

Farad was concerned. Jargas felt much farther away than that, from the bond they shared, but Farad did not feel him clearly. It was as if something was muddying their connection, but it did not have the dark taint of the Enemy's hand. "Thank you. I will not go to him until I see Rion returned to you." One way or the other, he thought grimly, but he did not voice his concern.

Farad left the alley quickly. The boy would have been taken for his coin, and might yet be ransomed, if the villains did not find the hidden coin. If they had found it, he would be dead, his body left in the nearest alleyway, probably stripped of his fine clothes. Farad checked the alleyways first, relieved when he didn't find Rion.

He thought of the anguish on Tarrell's face. Rion was so young, painfully young, with blue eyes. The face of Alarad, Farad's youngest brother, flashed unbidden in his mind's eye. The smiling face, with the worshipful eyes the blue of the sky. He tried to stop the memory, but he could not. He bit the inside of his cheek so hard he tasted blood as a second image followed the first, as it always did. Farad saw Alarad as he'd found him: the tortured, mutilated, defiled body, those beautiful eyes gouged out. He felt desperately for the coppery strand that bound him to Jargas, muted though that bond was, and held it carefully, drawing both calm and strength from it. His breathing steadied.

Now he would seek those he had spoken to this past week. He would find Rion, alive. He must find him alive.

RION felt a whimper rising in his throat and bit his tongue hard against it, the self-inflicted pain forcing the sound away. They were going to kill him. They were keeping him alive only long enough to get the ransom. Tarrell would pay it, he would come, he would do anything they asked to save him, but they would kill him anyway. And kill Tarrell. They'd told him they would. They'd laughed when they told him. Rion's eyes filled with tears, which he blinked away angrily. They would not see him cry.

His fingers could no longer work at the knot in the rope that bound his wrists behind his back, around the post that went from floor to ceiling. His hands were numb now, and his arms were losing all feeling as well. It was a blessing for his right one: the pain was fading.

It was his fault Tarrell would die, all his fault. He had so desperately wanted to show himself a man, but he was only a boy: a proud, foolish, stupid boy. Talon had chosen his guards well. Any one of them could have fought off his attackers, but he had left them all inside. It wasn't fair, to have survived such a journey, ogres and obearn and Elves and wizards, only to die like this, just when he'd thought himself safe!

They'd come at him while he was on his knees, retching. He had seen the danger and drawn his knife, and used it, but that had only made it worse. He'd only been trying to get past them, to get back into the safety of the inn. He'd known he couldn't hope to fight them all. By the time they were done, he had barely been able to breathe from the blows to his chest, and he was sure his right arm must be broken.

When they found his purse almost empty, he had known he would be killed if they found the rest of his coin, so he'd talked swiftly and convincingly, explaining that his guardian Tarrell carried their coin and they could ransom him. He had hoped they might spare him more beatings, as well as his life. But he'd cut the one with the missing fingers, and that one took great delight in kicking Rion whenever he walked past, and in describing how he would kill him.

Rion felt another whimper rise and could not stop it this time. He heard coarse laughter come from the darkened depths of the storage room, and then the one with the missing fingers was looming up over him in the faint light of the single lamp.

"What's the matter, boy, lonely? Want some company?" The cruel man aimed a sharp kick at the back of his left knee, and Rion cried out and started sobbing from the pain. He could not help himself. The man laughed and drew back his boot, slowly, to kick him again, enjoying the terror on Rion's face.

"Please don't hurt me!" Rion begged, hating himself for it, as he saw the boot coming for his face this time. But it was yanked suddenly away. There was an odd gurgling sound and a thud as the man fell back, clawing desperately at his throat.

A tall, dark shape suddenly loomed over Rion's tormentor. A hand reached down and yanked a wickedly barbed knife from the man's throat. The man convulsed as blood sprayed everywhere. He thrashed for a moment and then went ominously still. But the shadowy man grasped the hilt of the horrible, bloodied knife with both hands and stabbed downward, plunging the knife in over and over. Then he slashed at the throat so savagely that the man's head was completely severed from his body. Rion heard loud, panting breathing and watched, riveted in horror, as the knife was wiped on the corpse. Then the monstrous dark figure turned and approached him, blade in hand.

Rion screamed in terror, straining at the ropes that held him fast to the post and crying out in agony as he wrenched his wounded arm.

"Rion, it's all right! I'm not going to hurt you. My name is Hunter. I'm a friend of Jargas, and of Talon. Tarrell has sent me. I've come to rescue you." The voice was ragged and harsh sounding.

Rion whimpered, trembling uncontrollably.

Hunter's voice took on a softer tone. "Rion, come, you were so brave before. Even at the end you tried to be. I was watching you. I had to plan my attack carefully, because there were so many of them." He reached behind Rion, and Rion realized he must be cutting the ropes, but he could not feel anything until his arms suddenly fell free and his hands struck the floor. Rion cried out as a bolt of agony shot up his broken arm all the way to his shoulder.

"I'm sorry. I didn't mean to hurt you. I know they hurt you, but I didn't realize your arm was injured. They won't ever hurt anyone again," Hunter said grimly.

"You... you kept stabbing him. He was already dead and still you...." Rion's voice petered out as he shrank back from the brutal man, staring at him with horrified eyes.

"He hurt you, Rion. You were helpless and he hurt you. He enjoyed hurting you. I... I could not stop myself." Hunter sank to his knees by Rion's side. "Please, you must understand. I am no monster. I am not like them. My parents, my brothers...." His voice broke. "My whole family has been killed by people like this, by things worse than people. That is why I had to behead him, all of them, so that.... Forgive me, of course you could not know or understand. But please don't be afraid of me. I would never harm you. I could never harm you."

Rion stared at Hunter wide-eyed and saw him sway and almost fall over. Rion somehow caught him with his left hand. His fingers had been tingling, but now they felt wet and warm and sticky where they touched Hunter. Rion realized to his horror that he felt Hunter's blood. "You're injured!" he cried in shock.

Hunter nodded. "I had to act too soon. He was hurting you, and I could not wait any longer. I threw my knife when I needed to keep it, and I took a blade from the third I slew."

"Come into the light," Rion said, pulling him up with his good hand. The pins and needles had turned to agony, now, as feeling returned to his numbed hands. He started to walk for the single oil lamp, but his left leg unexpectedly buckled under him and he would have fallen, had Hunter not steadied him.

Under the light, he got a good look at Hunter for the first time. He looked past the horribly bloodied clothes and realized he was indeed the man Jargas had spoken to Talon of, what seemed like so long ago, in Athanark. He had the height and build of Talon, and some of his features were similar as well, but he appeared older. His face was hard and scarred, and his eyes were terrible to look upon, cold and hard and dead, exactly as Jargas had described. But Rion stared in wonder, for there were streaks from tears on his cheeks. "You cry for me," Rion said, amazed.

Hunter looked into Rion's eyes and said in a voice raw with pain, "And for those I have lost. Perhaps even for myself. Do you wonder that eyes like mine can still cry? I wonder. I have not cried since… since I burned the last of my brothers upon the pyre." His voice was soft now, little above a whisper.

"You're bleeding. I need to find bandages," Rion said practically, looking about for something he could use.

"I'll live. I always live. It is my curse. We should go. There should have been one other."

Rion gasped. "The ransom! He was going to tell Tarrell where to go. It was going to be a trap. They were going to kill him. The one you just killed, he said I'd be there, that he'd make me watch, and then he'd kill me, too, but he'd take his time. He said he'd have some fun with me first and…." He started trembling wildly again.

Hunter hugged him tightly, careful of his injured arm. "You are safe and Tarrell will be as well. Your five friends yet guard him, and Tarrell won't do anything foolish. I've warned him against paying the ransom."

"He does not think of himself when I am in danger. I won't have him hurt again saving me. The last time was too terrible."

"Come. We must go to the inn and show Tarrell you are safe, if not entirely well. The last man will not escape my wrath for long," Hunter said. He knelt down and picked up a quarterstaff, which one of the dead men had carried, and handed it to Rion.

The hand that took it shook and Rion's voice quavered as he spoke. "The man who wielded this broke my arm with it, so I'd drop my knife."

"You were lucky," Hunter said sincerely. "I know you don't feel very lucky right now, Rion, but they could have killed you first and ransomed you anyway. They were playing it safe doing it the other way, in case Tarrell insisted upon seeing you before paying."

Rion swallowed, hard, then took the staff to use as a walking stick, hobbling to the door at Hunter's side. Once on the street, they stuck to the buildings and alleyways as much as possible. The eyes of the few who noticed them were quickly averted, and people gave them a wide berth. They hid from a City Guard patrol Hunter spotted, when Rion would have called out to them.

"I'm covered in blood. I killed four men, Rion. I would be hanged for it."

Rion was appalled. "But they captured me and beat me and were going to kill me," he protested.

"But the City Guard is supposed to deal with such people. Never mind that they would not have found you in time, if at all, or would have done it so clumsily you would have been first to die, so you could not bear witness against them," Hunter said, his voice sounding as worn as he looked.

"And Talon said it would be safe to settle here," Rion said hopelessly. "Is there nowhere safe?"

Hunter sighed. "Rion, this city is safe, at least relatively so. It is a City of Man, far from the danger that is coming. As long as you are careful or guarded or both, once you know Gosa and its dangers and can avoid them, it will be safe. It won't be the first city to be overrun. It is far enough west that it will be one of the last, once the Elven Kingdoms are destroyed."

Rion stared at him, wide-eyed with horror. "The Elves? Destroyed? Aras and Thorn and Brook and all their people? Who could destroy the Elves? Why would anyone do such a horrible thing?"

"Curse my loose tongue. Memory is too raw in me. I am in the light, now, but I suffer still. I have said things I should not have. Do not worry. Talon will not let the Elven Kingdoms be destroyed. Pay me no mind," Hunter reassured him, as they approached The Lost Eagle. "Ah, we are here at last."

Rion started to enter, but realized Hunter was not following. He looked at him, puzzled. Hunter was staring at the sign over the door of the inn. It was of an eagle circling a mountain. There was anguish on Hunter's face, and Rion saw a tear fall from his dead eye. "Hunter?" Rion asked, and touched his arm gently.

"Forgive me," Hunter said. His voice was broken and gravelly. "It is only that we enter a dead House. The last of the Eagles is dead, though their blood still runs in my veins. Their blood runs everywhere," he said, looking at his blood-soaked shirt and laughing. It was a terrible laugh, a laugh of torment without end.

Rion was scared for him then. "Hunter, please. I'm afraid to go in alone. I need you to come with me."

Hunter swayed, and the weakness appeared to frighten him, for suddenly he appeared alert again. "None will harm you while I live," he swore. He seemed to draw strength from somewhere, and he steadied as he approached the door. "Stay behind me."

They entered the inn. Rion saw Tarrell and Rarnak and a man whose face was known to him, though he didn't know his name: he was the last of those evil men who had taken him prisoner. Tarrell's face held a look of fear and despair.

"Tarrell!" Rion cried, and Tarrell's eyes widened as he turned toward the doorway and saw them. Rion could imagine how awful he looked, bruised and bloodied and limping.

Tarrell drew his sword then, but the man had turned to run, and he escaped the blade that came for him by sending Tarrell reeling into Rarnak. The villain headed for the door, obviously thinking to dart past the two of them, drawing his knife. But Rion grasped the staff by one end with his good arm and swung it in a wide, strong arc. It cracked against the man's shins, and he crashed to the floor. Rion fell too, knocked off his balance from the impact.

Rion struggled to right himself on his good elbow. Hunter interposed himself protectively between them, but then Rion saw Hunter sheathe his dagger, unused. The man was lying still, too still.

Rarnak ran up to the fallen man, his sword drawn, and turned him over. The man had impaled himself on his knife when he fell, skewering his own heart.

Tarrell hurried to Rion's side. "Rion!" he cried. He hugged Rion, and Rion cried out in pain and almost fainted. Tarrell let go, looking at him with an anguished expression.

"It's all right, Tarrell. It's just you mustn't hug me like that. My arm is broken. But I'm all right, really."

When Rion turned to Hunter, he caught his breath. Hunter was watching them. And he was smiling. A real smile, not a grimace or a rueful one: a smile of happiness. Rion grinned back at him, and Hunter looked startled, like a fawn caught unawares in a meadow. But unexpectedly, his smile broadened and Rion saw joy light his face. For a moment, his face no longer appeared hard, nor his eyes terrible or cold. He looked as warm as Talon had, when he'd smiled. "I have saved you," Hunter said softly.

But then the City Guard came, Ron and Ara with them. Hunter's smile vanished, replaced by tension and weariness, and Rion swallowed, but remembered that smile just the same.

FARAD realized he should have left as soon as he saw Rion was safe, but he had been riveted by his reunion with Tarrell and unable to turn away. Knowing it was too late to flee now that the Guard was here, he took a single step toward the door anyway, but stumbled. He glanced down at the blood that coated his clothes and realized that a good portion of it truly was his own, this time.

He sank weakly and wearily into one of the unoccupied wooden chairs, drawing again upon his bond with Jargas for strength as he had only moments earlier, outside the inn, when he had faltered. Jargas was strong enough to aid him without endangering himself by it.

Farad would not allow himself to be arrested and imprisoned ever again. Apparently he would have to fight some of the Guard before he could continue his quest. It helped rather than hindered that they wore chainmail. For some unfathomable reason, his Power to shift objects with his mind always had worked best with metal.

He surreptitiously examined the corpse of the Man who had come to ransom Rion. He truly had impaled himself upon his own dagger without assistance, thanks to Rion's timely attack. Farad had not had to use his Power to make him stumble, or to twist the knife, as he had with Balgar. He forced the memory of his time in Malar in Fromer down, lest it overwhelm him, knowing he would need all his wits for what was to come.

He was pleasantly surprised when the innkeeper spoke in support of them, even of him, when he knew the Man hadn't liked the look of him from the moment he first saw him. The Guard who had come were not the same ones as before and were willing to listen. The two Men called Ronamark and Aramark defended themselves for running toward the inn with swords drawn. They explained about Rion being taken and the Man who had come to ransom him and said they'd been watching from either end of the street to follow the Man when he came out. But when they saw Rion miraculously appear from the shadows of an alleyway, they knew the Man still in with Tarrell would react like a cornered animal and be a danger to everyone in the inn.

After speaking with Rion, Tarrell, and the other witnesses, even hearing his own abridged version of events, to Farad's relief the Guard determined that, as the Man had wronged them and then fallen upon his own blade, he was to blame for his own death and the brothers had been justified in their actions. They removed the body without undo fuss and left the inn.

Farad had to bite his tongue and clench his hand into a fist to keep from demanding they behead the body or doing it himself. He would visit the City's morgue later and do it, when it might be safer to do so. He knew the way. He had already been there, to check for Rion amongst the City's dead.

He had to leave, now. He had already tarried too long. He desperately needed to see Jargas. He stood, but then had to brace himself heavily upon the table to keep from crumpling to the floor. First, he apparently needed to bandage his wound. Mountainous as Jargas's Power was, it could not save him if he allowed his life to drain away with his blood. Idare help him, his captivity and illness, both in the Dwarven Kingdom of Malar in Fromer and the Elven Kingdom of Tanieria, and his long journey in search of Jargas thereafter, had already weakened him greatly, before this latest injury. He was utterly spent, on the verge of collapse, even with Jargas's aid through the bond they shared.

Farad started to topple sideways and stiffened in shock when a strong arm encircled his waist and his full weight was effortlessly supported. Gaunt as he was, he was an Amontir and had more the weight of an Elf or a Dwarf than a Man, though his people had no idea why that might be so. Few ordinary Men would have such strength and never would he normally have allowed such proximity or physical contact by a stranger to discover so. From what had been spoken to the Guard, the Man's name was Ronamark of Ogaten, though Ronamark was a Thenalonese name. Rion had simply called him Ron.

Farad gripped Ron's wrist, seemingly for added support, but channeling his Power outward, until it permeated Ron so he could view his core, as always, prepared for the worst. Safe, he was safe; this was not a minion of the Enemy. But surprisingly, in spite of his appearance, not a Man either, or at least, not fully. He had the form of a Man, but the core of both Dwarf and Man, similar to that of Jargas, though Jargas was part Amontir as well. Ron's core was darker than Jargas's because of it, but still considerably brighter than the cores of those they had once called Lesser Men. They had discovered long ago that Dwarven cores were much more like their own than those of ordinary Men.

"Forgive me my touch, when I did not first obtain permission, but you were in need of aid," Ron apologized politely.

Odder still. The words were spoken in Common, yet the formal phrase was an Elvish one, one of the few Farad knew. Who was this person, who looked like a Man, had the core of a Dwarf, and spoke as if he was a friend of the Elves?

"Ara, please help Ron bring Hunter to our room. He certainly won't be able to manage the stairs on his own," Farad heard Rion say. He sought the slender young Man and saw him being assisted up the stairs by his guardian, Tarrell, with the aid of the staff he yet carried. Another Man, a stranger, was following closely behind, with a satchel in his hand, and the universal air of compassion and competence that a trained healer of some actual skill exuded. Farad was shocked and dismayed that he was in such a pathetic state that he had not even noticed the healer enter the room.

He and Ron and Ara followed the procession up the stairs. The innkeeper explained solicitously to Tarrell as they climbed the stairs that he'd sent his son to fetch Healer Deverill, as soon as he'd seen Rion returned injured.

RION tried to reassure Van and Gar, who had been guarding their rooms, that he wasn't badly hurt, in spite of how he appeared. The brothers and Rarnak waited outside their door and Rion heard Van ask Ara what had happened as both he and Hunter were led to the bed. Ron left the room as soon as he saw Hunter safely situated upon the bed.

To Rion's surprise, after introducing himself, the healer washed his hands thoroughly in their water basin, then again in something he poured from a large metal flask he'd taken from his bag. He dried his hands on a towel he had also pulled from his bag before turning to him.

Rion insisted the healer treat Hunter first. "He wouldn't let me bandage him," Rion said to Tarrell, worried. "It would have been hard, with only my left arm, but still… it's all my fault, Tarrell. I've made such a mess of everything," Rion said, his eyes welling with tears.

Tarrell hugged him gently, obviously mindful of his injured arm this time, now that he knew of it. "It's all right, Rion. You cannot blame yourself for this. None of us should, though we all feel awful it happened. But we need to put it behind us. I am so very proud of you."

"Proud? But I let myself get caught. And I cried, I even begged." Rion's voice was dark with shame.

Hunter spoke from beside him. "I told you, Rion, I watched you. You were strong when many men would not have been. You have nothing to be ashamed of. And when I freed you, you came to yourself again. You forgot all about your own injuries and tried to help me. You are a jewel among men, Rion. Never let anyone, least of all the dead, make you feel less than you are."

Rion gazed at him in wonder. Hunter had called him a man! And once again, he saw more to his eyes than coldness and death. "When I first saw you, I could not believe you were kin to Talon. He shines so brightly. But you shine also, when the night leaves your eyes. I am grateful to you, Hunter, and I will miss you as much as I miss Talon, I think, when you go."

Hunter looked at him in surprise. "When next I see Talon, I will have to ask him about your meeting, for I knew nothing about you when I came here."

"Then I will tell you of it before you go," Rion promised.

"And you mentioned Aras. I would hear of him, as well, for Talon travels with him and holds him deeply in his heart, and he is unknown to me," Hunter said, a hint of frustration and even anxiety leaking into his voice that Rion was sure he would not have wished for him to hear.

Rion grinned at the memory of Aras. "Aras I can tell you much of, for Tarrell and I spoke long and often with him, and he is not nearly so secretive as Talon. Talon's heart is in good hands with Aras."

Rion realized the healer had been taking advantage of their exchange and had been cleaning and bandaging Hunter's wound as they spoke. Rion knew from experience that it was best to distract a man in pain, particularly when his wounds were being tended to, and he was relieved to be able to render even that small assistance to Hunter, after all he had done.

When Healer Deverill was finished, he went back to the water basin and washed his hands in the water he had used before, scrubbing the blood off. But then, to Rion's surprise, he poured that water into the bucket by the water stand, rinsed the basin with fresh water from the pitcher, dumped it as well, and then rinsed it a second time with the contents of the flask. Then he washed his hands all over again and poured more of the contents of the flask over his hands, drying them on a second towel, which he pulled from his bag.

Finally he turned to Rion. "It is your turn, young master." He undressed Rion and examined him. Tarrell's face was lined with concern, as pained as if the brutal bruises all over Rion's chest and back and limbs were his own.

"I must ascertain the extent of the damage, and to do so, I must feel for what I cannot see upon the surface. Unfortunately, I cannot do so without causing you further pain, but I will be as swift and gentle as I can," the healer explained apologetically.

"I understand," Rion said, trying to be brave, hating the knowledge that he might cry out in pain when Hunter had borne his own so stoically.

TARRELL watched as the healer poked and prodded everywhere, working swiftly and efficiently. Rion winced in pain everywhere the man touched, but he did not moan or cry out. The healer nodded in satisfaction at every touch, until finally he was done.

"You are quite fortunate, young master, that those who sought to harm you did not do far worse. It does not appear as if any of your injuries are on the inside, where I would not be able to tend to them. Though I know the pain is severe, what damage there is—the many bruises and few cuts—will heal within a few days, even those on your leg. But your arm is broken, and that will take longer to mend. Four weeks for the bone to knit and four more until it is truly strong again."

The healer took two small flasks and a metal cup from his bag. Eyeing the stream of liquid carefully to gauge the volume, he poured a portion of one after the other into the cup. Then he handed it to Rion. "Drink this, all of it. One part is medicine for the pain. It takes a while to work to its full capacity, but once it does, it is quite potent. It will last for half the day or more. And the other is for the swelling in your arm. It is best if you gulp the mixture and swallow it quickly. Unfortunately, the taste is rather unpleasant," he said with an apologetic smile.

From the way Rion's eyes widened as he drank, the alacrity with which he swallowed, and the shudder that racked him, Tarrell realized it must be truly vile.

After Rion finished, the healer smiled in satisfaction. "Now, we will give the medicine some time to work," he said, as he pulled out a bundle of cloth bandages and a small flask and began applying the liquid from the flask, meticulously cleaning the small cuts Rion had acquired before bandaging them.

There was a knock on the door and Ron called through it. "Is it all right for the innkeeper to enter? He has two more pitchers of water he wanted to bring in. He said he was sure Healer Deverill would need them, though the pitcher in the room had been full."

The healer grinned as Tarrell told the innkeeper to enter. Ron held the door as the man entered the room, a pitcher in each hand.

"You know me well, Janus! You've saved me the trouble of having to ask for them, as I was about to. Thank you," Healer Deverill said sincerely.

"Is there anything else you need? No matter how revolting or strange, we'll fetch it for you. You know you have only to ask," Janus said eagerly.

The healer smiled warmly and scolded gently. "Now Janus, don't alarm my patients. I thank you for the offer, but I've all I need with me."

The innkeeper's face flushed, and he turned to them. "Your friend is in good hands. Deverill is blessed by Jarnath. He's the best healer in all the Lands of Men, even if his methods are sometimes bizarre. If it weren't for him, my son Jasper would have died, or if he'd lived, been so crippled he'd never have risen from his bed again. He was struck by a runaway wagon when he was only a wee lad, trampled by the horses and run over by the wheel. You'd never have guessed it from looking at him now. You've seen him. He's a fine strapping lad, with only a slight limp and his scars to show for it."

He turned back to the healer. "I'll leave you to it, then. But you're not to leave without staying for dinner, this time, and you'll bring home the pie Janessa has baked for you as well. I've told you before, my eldest won't wed unless it's to you, and the others are eager to see her settled so they can begin finding husbands as well. You cannot let talent such as yours fade into the mists of time, Deverill. You need good strong sons to carry your legacy when you're gone, may Jarnath take you none too soon, and my daughter's more than willing to provide them for you." He clapped the healer on the shoulder and then left the room, as the healer shook his head, smiling ruefully.

"Forgive the interruption. Janus has become a good friend, but he's a father first and foremost, and I'm a stubborn and willful man who's set in his ways and yet to cave to their onslaught." He bent to his task, pulling a large metal bowl and a nested sack from the bag. He poured the entire contents of the sack, a white powder, into the bowl, and then brought one of the new water pitchers over and began slowly mixing a stream of water into the powder, until it reached a paste-like consistency.

"You're not going to make me eat that, are you?" Rion asked, eyeing the bowl suspiciously.

The healer chuckled. "No. It's healer's plaster, for your arm. After I set the bone, I'm going to bandage it, then coat some more bandages with this. It hardens to an almost rocklike consistency. It will protect your arm from further injury and allow it to heal properly, ensuring that the bones remain in alignment."

Tarrell had never heard of such a thing. He had expected the man to splint Rion's arm. He was concerned the healer might not know his craft, in spite of what he had witnessed so far and the innkeeper's effusive praise, but then Hunter spoke.

"So I was right in my thoughts, when I saw the care you took with the cleanliness of your hands and my wound. You are Dwarven trained," Hunter said, clear admiration in his voice, bordering almost on reverence.

"No, sad to say, I've not had that honor. But my grandfather was, and he taught the skills to my father, who taught them to me. And I yet maintain the trading relations grandfather first forged with Malar in Holoren, which is how I get my more esoteric and exotic supplies."

He turned to Rion. "Now then, Master Rion, I must realign the bones in your arm, so that it will heal properly. It will hurt terribly when I do so, even with the medicine I have given you, and you will most likely pass out from the pain. Bite down on this, as hard as you can," he said, handing Rion a small wad of leather.

Rion swallowed, took the leather and put it between his teeth, and then bit down upon it as instructed, clamping his jaw.

Tarrell watched as the healer's own jaw clenched as he pulled and twisted with steady and sure hands. All the color left Rion's face as he screamed, muffled by the leather, and then fell limp.

"It's all right, he is only unconscious," the healer reassured them swiftly. "It was merely more than his abused body could bear. It is better this way. I did not want to say so in front of him, and alarm him without need, but it is a bad break. A man has two bones below the elbow, not one, and both are broken. I was not certain I would be able to get both realigned, so that he might fully heal." He smiled in satisfaction. "But I have done so. I need one of you, someone with steady hands, to hold the bones in place while I wrap his arm in cloth and then encase it in the plaster, to immobilize it in this position."

"I will do so," Ron volunteered.

"Then place your hands on the outside edges of my own," the healer instructed. Tarrell noted the healer did not release his own hold until he was satisfied with Ron's.

The healer began wrapping Rion's arm in the cloth bandages, having Ron reposition his hands as needed as he worked, until Rion's lower arm and much of his hand was fully covered. "Do not be so grim. Your friend will recover fully. He was very fortunate his injuries were not worse, I think. The medicine for the pain I have given him will help him sleep as well, and he must sleep to heal. You must see to it that he rests. He should stay in bed for at least three days, or at least try to keep off his leg as much as he can, both so it has a chance to heal and so he does not risk a fall that might damage his arm, in spite of the cast."

The healer wetted additional bandages in the plaster, a strip at a time, and began winding the gooey strips around Rion's arm and hand, overlaying the other bandages, working with practiced efficiency, while everyone watched.

"Four weeks from now, you'll be able to remove the cast. I would be happy to assist you, or you'll need a saw and someone with a steady hand to do so," the healer said.

When he was done, he washed the white residue from the bowl and then washed his hands again and repacked his bag, leaving the two flasks of medicine from before and a tiny metal cup, scarcely larger than a seamstress's thimble, out. He turned to Tarrell. "The larger one with the red wax about the stopper is for pain. Fill the little cup almost to the edge and give him a drink, twice a day, once tonight and once in the morning, and continue to do so until the bottle is empty. The smaller one with the blue stopper is for swelling. That he'll only need four doses of, spaced at the same intervals as the other."

FARAD saw that Tarrell thanked the Man and paid him, and he was relieved to see he paid for both their care, as he had hoped Tarrell might. His own purse was empty. He'd spent his last few copper in Kashin, the city to the northeast immediately preceding Gosa on the Western Road.

The healer had given him medicine for the pain as well, but he would not take it. He could not allow his wits to be dulled by it.

Farad allowed the healer to leave without questioning him about Malar as he would have liked to. He did not want to reveal his interest in it, or his relation to Jargas. After a lifetime of secrecy in the protection of his people, he was reluctant to speak of one of them to a stranger, even one he had trusted enough to tend to him, whose core he had tested.

Farad rose wearily from the bed. He could not stay here. He had no coin for lodging or food. He needed to find Jargas. He grabbed the bedpost to steady himself, locking his knees to keep from falling. Making it to the door to the hall seemed an insurmountable journey, let alone descending the stairs. How could he possibly walk and climb twelve leagues or more into the Holoren Mountains?

READING his intention, Tarrell stepped in front of Hunter, blocking his path. "You are not going anywhere until you are healed. You are weak and injured because of us, you have saved Rion's life, and he has already become fond of you. Also, you are Talon's friend, and we owe him much. I'll not see you brought to further danger because of us, when I might keep you safe. And I will not see you leave without Rion having a chance to say good-bye." He was afraid Hunter would argue with him and go anyway.

But Hunter sighed and lay back down. "It might be nice to sleep in a real bed for a change, as other men do," he said simply. Tarrell had seen many emotions cross his face, but how could one know what a man such as he was truly thinking?

Tarrell tucked the blanket gently about Rion. "It hurt less being injured myself, last time, than it does now, to see him so." He looked at Hunter again, when he did not comment, and saw to his surprise he was already asleep. Tarrell was strangely moved: Hunter trusted him to keep him safe while he slept. He pulled the chair over to the bed and sat in it and watched over them both.

TARRELL jerked awake with a start. He had not meant to sleep, but he had not slept well the night before, and the stress of losing Rion and waiting for news throughout the endless day had worn him to a thread. From the dim light seeping in through the crack around the shutters of the window, it appeared it was scarcely dawn. He knew they had not been vulnerable while they slept: at least two of their five guards would have been watching the room.

He stretched and rose quietly. Hunter and Rion still slept soundly. In sleep Rion still looked like a child, innocent and vulnerable. But even in sleep, Hunter's face had a hard look to it, and not merely because of the scar.

Hunter's eyes opened, as if he had sensed Tarrell's gaze upon him, even in sleep. "It is yet early, I think. You should rest longer. All is well," Tarrell said softly, lest he waken Rion. Hunter nodded and closed his eyes again.

Tarrell washed his face and hands, foregoing a shave. He changed his clothes quickly and slipped quietly from the room. Gar and Van stood alertly by the door.

Tarrell smiled at them. "Do you think your brothers would mind if I woke them early? I would like to have them accompany me into the City."

Van grinned. "If you're smiling, it means Rion's doing all right. Ron only went to bed a short while ago. That will teach him to spend our coin while we're hard at work making more."

Gar said, "I've found a pitcher of water over the head works best to wake him when he's had too little sleep and too much drink."

Tarrell shook his head. "I'm not so gullible as that anymore. I don't believe a word of it," he said, laughing.

Tarrell knocked on their guards' door and Ron answered. When he went in, Ron and Ara were already dressed in their livery, but Rarnak was just waking.

"Ron, I'd like you and Ara to come shop with me in the City. I plan to buy some clothes and a new bow and quiver for Hunter. He seems to have lost the ones Jargas described."

"If we're weapons shopping, we should all change," Ron said. "If they see us in uniform and you dressed as you are, they'll fleece us for sure. Do you have anything less conspicuous to wear, Tarrell?"

Tarrell shook his head. "Rion's the one who forces me to dress so fancy," he said, glancing down at the rich brocade of his maroon shirt in distaste. He far preferred his old guardsman's livery to the merchant clothes Rion had purchased for him in Athanark.

"Why don't you borrow some of Van's clothes, then? You're of the same height and build. Trust me, I don't think you'll regret it," Ron urged.

Tarrell was glad for an excuse to wear something other than his merchant clothes for a change. He didn't feel right spending Rion's coin on himself, to buy clothes that suited him better, for when he wasn't trying to impress customers. Rion kept trying to convince him that the half of the coin he carried was his, but he didn't deserve any of it. Rion had been Oberas's apprentice, not him. He had been Oberas's guard. He should not benefit from the death of the one he'd sworn to protect.

He looked at the clothes Ron held out to him. The brothers referred to the clothes they'd brought with them, before they'd gotten their livery, as their drinking clothes. He pulled off his merchant clothes and sighed in contentment at the feeling of the worn and comfortable clothes as he put them on.

He and Ron and Ara went downstairs. He had planned to head out immediately, but the common room of the inn smelled enticingly of grilled meats, roasting potatoes, and freshly baked breads, and when he saw the gusto with which the room's patrons consumed their meals, he headed for a table. He was famished. He'd not eaten a bite the day before.

The innkeeper himself came up to them, instead of one of his daughters, asking about Rion and Hunter in concern before speaking to them about food. Tarrell reassured him they were both doing well.

A short while later, he and the two brothers were eating with equal enthusiasm. They'd definitely made the right decision, coming to this inn, in spite of the near tragedy the day before. The food was amazing and the innkeeper obviously truly cared about his guests.

Rarnak came down only a short time after they started eating and joined them. He'd spot Gar and then Van, so they could eat as well, in shifts.

Once they were done, Tarrell and Ron and Ara headed out into the City.

IT WAS nearly noon when Tarrell shifted the clothing package under his arm, as they entered the fourth and last weapons shop. They'd had much better luck buying clothes for Hunter than a bow, so far. The clothes were brown, something a forester might wear.

The first two weapons shops had not had any bows at all. The third one, The Golden Arrow, had little but bows, but they were all short bows, which apparently were favored here in the west. Tarrell remembered hearing Hunter used a longbow, an overly long one. He might have to settle for a short one.

This shop, The Blade and Bow, was deplorable: dark, dirty, cluttered, and completely unorganized. Tarrell picked up a sword and laid it down in disgust. There was a layer of rust on the blade, and it looked like it hadn't been sharpened in the past ten years. If there was a decent bow here, they'd have to hunt for it. Any they found would no doubt be warped and useless. A grubby man watched them from the shadows, but didn't offer his assistance.

Ron was in the back corner and gestured to Ara and he came over. Tarrell came over, too, wondering what Ron had found. Ron was facing away from the proprietor and grinning from ear to ear. Tarrell had never seen him with such a smile; Ron was always the serious one.

Ron held a bow in his hands. It was poorly strung or warped or both. It appeared to be a longbow, of exceptional height, except the curve of the wood was wrong. It might once have been red: reddish spots showed under the blanket of filth that covered it. There were seven arrows as well, long and surprisingly straight, with no rust on the metal tips, but the fletching was bedraggled and worthless. There was no quiver. Ara grinned back in delight, as if they held a great treasure.

When Ron spoke, his voice belayed the look on his face. "Well, it's long enough, at least. He'll hate the look of it, though. Maybe that will teach him to be more careful with his own, next time." Ron turned, the smile gone from his face.

Ara turned as well, appearing equally dour. "He still hasn't paid us for the last one he broke. I say we just buy him a quarterstaff and be done with it, if all he's going to use it for is to crack someone across the back with it again."

"No, then he'd kill him, and we'd have to bribe the Guard and lose even more coin. Besides, how can we hunt for our dinner with a staff? Maybe we can sell him to the Dwarves to work in their mines. Then we'd have some coin for mead and be rid of him besides," Ron said.

"No, we can't do that. For better or for worse, he's our brother. So, I suppose we'll have to buy it for him," Ara said with a heavy sigh.

"I guess you're right. You there, shopkeeper. How much for this, then?" Ron asked, holding the bow out carelessly.

"Ah, for such an unusual bow as that, ten gold," the proprietor said.

Tarrell hid his surprise. He'd named a price two thirds less than what the other shop had asked for their short bows. The brothers' act had already reaped benefit.

Ron laughed in the proprietor's face. "Ten gold? For this? Do we look like we work for a rich merchant to you, that we can afford ten gold? We hunt for our dinner. We don't dine in fancy inns, drinking oushka, surrounded by pretty wenches."

Tarrell fought to keep a straight face.

"But sirs, this bow comes from far Aralon! They make the finest bows in the land!" the shopkeeper whined.

"Aralon? Never heard of it. So it's foreign, eh? No wonder it has such an odd look to it. I say we go to The Golden Arrow. We shouldn't have been put off by the gold in the name. They must have lots more for us to choose from. I bet they won't try to rob us," Ara suggested.

"Sirs, please! Did I say ten gold? Eight would be a fair price," the shopkeeper said, his tone wheedling.

"Eight?" Ron scoffed, as if the shopkeeper were truly mad. "We'll have to replace the fletching on the arrows, if we can use them at all, and there's only seven of them to start with, not a full dozen, and no quiver, and he wants eight!"

Tarrell had to leave the shop then. When he was safely on the street and out of earshot, he burst out laughing. Some passersby glanced at him strangely, noted the sword at his side, and skirted around him. Ah, Rion should have seen the two of them! They were wasted as guards! He'd had no idea of their hidden talent. He waited, eager to hear what they'd finally paid, and why they had wanted the warped bow at all, other than for its height.

A short while later the two brothers came out of the shop grim-faced, bow in hand, but then their faces burst into wide grins as they joined him.

"You almost made us stop the haggle, leaving so abruptly like that, but we hoped you might not get into too much trouble without us for a moment or two," Ron scolded him.

Tarrell grinned. "I had to leave, or I would have ruined it for you. I could no longer keep a straight face, listening to the two of you. A rich merchant and oushka indeed! I can see why you had us dress as you did. I had no idea we traveled with two such skilled traders."

Ara grinned. "We've been watching more than your backs while we guard you and Rion. You don't think we want to remain guards forever, do you? There's no future in it. With the coin the four of us have made on this journey, and the two before, we plan to start a business of our own. Ron and I will trade, and at first Van and Gar will be our guards. Van eventually wants to open an inn. He'd make a good innkeeper: he's friendly and good with people. Everyone's always loved him. Gar's always wanted to own a stable and breed his own horses. You saw how well he's trained his own and ours. Who knows where we might be, ten years from now?"

"We'd suspected you've been saving your coin for something, but we had no idea you were making such plans for the future. But tell me, how much did you pay for it?"

"Five gold. Five! It's worth at least a hundred, if not more. How he knew, I've no idea. I almost fainted when he said it. I hadn't thought he'd realize, but he was right: it's from Aralon. The imbecile! He should be flogged, storing a bow like this as he has. Strung! Fortunately, he strung it backward, so he hasn't harmed it."

"Aralon!" Tarrell said in awe. "Those arrows were in such poor shape, I never would have known it, but you're right: they're long enough, and the arrowheads are the same. I remember the shape, now that you've mentioned it. Rion bought two dozen arrows from Aralon in Athanark and gave them to Aras. He paid twenty-five gold per dozen, and he got an excellent price for them."

"The Horsemen don't part with their arrows lightly, and they never part with their bows. They name them. If one breaks, they bury it, and to break one is almost unheard of. They are passed on from father to son as some men pass down swords."

"How do you know so much about them?" Tarrell asked.

"Our grandfather rode with them—the Horsemen, I mean. His name was Aramark too. I'm named after him," Ara said proudly. "It's not something anyone usually ever gets the chance to do, ride with the Horsemen, but grandfather was from Thenalon, and they were still allies.

"There were ogres in the Fromer Mountains back then, and monstrous beasts, great hunting cats called pumar, bigger than wolven, with vicious razor-sharp claws and six-inch fangs. Something banded them together against Thenalon, the ogres and pumar. They came pouring out of the mountains one winter and attacked without warning. No one had ever seen anything like it, ogres leaving their mountains. It was like an army.

"They killed every farmer that didn't make it to the City in time, and burned their farms. Who ever heard of ogres using fire? But then they started savaging the City walls and heaving great flaming trees over the wall into the middle of it, even before they breached it.

"My grandfather, his three cousins, and two others were all Guards there. Their Captain saw the City would be lost without aid. He sent the six of them off to ride to Aralon. No one thought they'd get through, but my grandfather and his cousins worked as a team, as we do."

Ara's face grew grim. "It didn't save them. He was the only one who made it through, in the end. He gave the message to the Lord of Aralon. Thenalon had a treaty with Aralon that was over two hundred years old. It was the first time they'd called upon it since it was written, but Lord Halon honored it.

"Grandfather insisted on riding back with the Horsemen, though he could scarcely stay in the saddle. His own horse was spent, and he'd lost all his weapons, so they gave him one of their chargers, Windfire, and one of their bows, and he rode with them to the City.

"If you've heard the stories, you know they arrived too late. It was horrific, what they found: the great stone wall shattered in dozens of places and the City burning, so many dead, and others terribly maimed, with limbs torn off or half-eaten or crushed or burnt, and hundreds of the women… but that's the story. They retook Thenalon and rebuilt it, of course. We left there not six months ago, but it's a shadow of what it must have been.

"Grandfather was given the bow to keep, and Windfire, though he renamed him Windsong. But he couldn't stay in Thenalon, and he didn't really fit in Aralon. He had these terrifying dreams, of fire and death and darkness. He told us he needed to go west to try to escape from them. He said it felt like something hunted him in his sleep. He could only sleep in the daylight, and even then, his dreams were haunted.

"He finally reached the riverbank near what's now called Ogaten. Grandfather was worn to the bone and wasted away to almost nothing. He said the night he camped there he heard the Elves singing, though he didn't know that's who it was, and he listened to the water rushing past and fell asleep. He told us it was the first time he didn't have his nightmares of fire, and he decided that's where he would spend the rest of his days. That's where he could be at peace.

"The next morning, when he awoke, the Elves were all around him. The Elves were intrigued by him. They told him they had heard him calling to them. He didn't know what they meant. We still don't. But they actually talked to him, instead of trying to chase him away.

"He told them he wanted to build a mill by the river. He said his father had been a miller, and he understood why now: it was all about the water and the grain, not fire and bows. And he told them his story, of the terror and the fire. He cried then, for the cousins he'd lost and the City and his family and everyone else who had died and suffered so horribly. And the Elves wept with him. And they told him they would take care of him. Then one of them touched him and he fell asleep.

"When he awoke, he was sound again, his body was fit and healthy, and he discovered he was bearded. And there was a mill by the river, exactly as he had imagined it. He was able to figure out later that he'd slept for almost two months. They'd built the mill for him, so he could spend the rest of his days safe and at peace. And Grandfather never once had problems sleeping after that. He said the darkness had left him.

"The Elves had him grind their grain, at first. Then when some farmers discovered him, they brought their grain to him, instead of to Gosa. They made more coin selling flour than grain. And the town sort of sprang up around him, though a distance away to the north. The mill is actually within the Elves' Kingdom, in Salenia, and they wouldn't let anyone else settle right there on their river, though there's a stream that runs from it past the town. *Oga* means mill and *ten* is town, in Thenalonese," Ara added, speaking both foreign words gutturally.

"Grandfather made sure everyone treated the Elves with respect, mostly that they left them alone. The Elves still visited with him and spoke with him, when there were no other people about. Even Father is friendly with the Elves, and of course, so are Uncle Donara and our cousins."

Ara laughed. "I'm sorry! I didn't mean to go on so long. You'd asked a simple enough question, and here I've given you an answer like Thorn might have!"

Tarrell had kept silent in awe through Ara's story, but he spoke now. "But the Fall of Thenalon was a hundred years ago! Yet you said your grandfather himself told you the story. How can that be? It's been rumored those of

Aralon are longer-lived than other Men, but your grandfather was Thenalonese. Or are you of Aralonese blood as well?"

Ron gave Ara a quelling look, though he'd remained silent throughout the story. Ara looked sheepish and suitably chastised, his enthusiasm notably dampened.

Ron said solemnly, "Ara did not speak as carefully as we usually do, but I trust you, Tarrell, and so I did not silence him when I otherwise would have. It is true that Aramark the Elder was Thenalonese and Grandmother came from Maraden, to the north of Ogaten. Grandfather was eighteen when Thenalon fell a century ago. He did not marry for decades thereafter, and he passed only some few years ago. He lived nearly twice as long as the oldest Man might. We attribute the gift of his long life to the grace of the Elves."

"I will never speak to anyone of it, not even Rion, unless you allow it," Tarrell promised.

"Thank you, Tarrell," Ron said sincerely and then added gravely, "Between the arrows you bought and this bow we have found, I wonder if Aralon has fallen?"

Ara shook his head in denial. "That I cannot believe. More likely a lone Horseman or two has met with an untimely end. A scout or envoy, perhaps."

"We should tell Hunter," Tarrell stated seriously.

"Why tell Hunter?" Ara asked.

Tarrell took a deep breath. "Because he is a Captain of the Watch, and Talon as well, and that's the sort of thing they are on the lookout for. Rion told me they were. He wondered if I knew anything about the Watch, so I told him what little I did."

Ron and Ara stared at him in surprise. "Hunter cannot be," Ara denied. "A Knight, perhaps, but not a Captain."

"Why not a Captain?" Tarrell asked, puzzled.

"Because he was injured saving Rion. And his scarred face and his eyes. They don't get injured and their Captains can't be killed. Talon I might believe it of. I do believe it. I saw his swordwork. That would explain much. If you told me he was Lord of the Watch, even that I would believe," Ara avowed.

"What's the Lord of the Watch?" Tarrell asked curiously.

"Their King," Ara replied.

Tarrell said in surprise, "Talon *is* their King. Rion told me."

Ara said sharply, "How in the world could Rion possibly know that? No one knows who their King is! It's their most closely guarded secret, and those people live for secrets. We only know of them at all because Grandfather fought beside four of them in the war."

"What Rion told me… that's why I was so surprised you plan for the future," Tarrell said. "I cannot. Something terrible is coming from the Dwarven Lands. The Enemy the Watch has been looking for is coming. That's why Talon sent us so far, so we could be safe, for a time anyway. He said Athanark would not stand for long, that the wolven-riders were only the beginning. Rion told me all he said, and all he's learned since, from the Elves in Erenia, I suppose.

"And their Captains can be slain, though I'm not as surprised as you. They are only Men after all, even if they are more skilled than most. When Talon left, he took with him a sword of one of the Captains he knew: Beryl. He'd been slain and his sword recovered. Aras told us about it. Aras talked a long time with us that night. He was frightened, but I know he was trying to hide it from Talon."

"Aras? But he's an Elf! Elves don't know fear," Ara said in surprise.

Tarrell grew thoughtful. "Perhaps. But Aras is not like the others we've met, or like what I'd heard of Elves." He smiled fondly, lost in his memories of Aras for a moment. "He's more like a love-starved puppy than some aloof and malicious creature of moonlight." Then he grew solemn, almost grim. "Don't speak of any of this to Hunter. I don't think Talon realized what Aras knew or might have guessed that he would share with us, and he couldn't have known what the Elves would reveal."

The brothers nodded.

"We must get back to the inn," Ron said. "But first, we must go back to The Golden Arrow and buy a quiver. I saw one that would go well with the bow and these arrows."

They headed back to the other shop and purchased the quiver Ron had favored over the rest.

When they were done, they walked in silence to the inn, each lost in his own thoughts. They entered the inn in a pensive mood, so that when Van and Gar, who were guarding the door to Rion and Hunter, saw them, they immediately asked what was wrong, and had to be motioned to silence, lest Hunter overhear them.

Tarrell entered without knocking and was surprised to see both Rion and Hunter were awake. Hunter was bathing and Rion had already done so. His hair was wet and tousled and he was struggling to pull a comb through it, left-handed. Tarrell smiled at him, fondly. "You have two choices, I think. You can either cut it short again, or I can try to braid it for you, like Jargas's."

Rion scowled at him and threw the comb onto the floor.

Tarrell looked at him in concern and picked it up, then sat beside him. "Rion, forgive me, I was only teasing. What's wrong?"

"Stop talking to me as if I were a child! I am not!" Rion yelled, and leapt from the bed and left the room in a limping run, slamming the door behind him so strongly the doorframe shook.

Shocked, Tarrell headed for the door, but Hunter's voice stopped him. "Do not follow him. Let him alone for a while, Tarrell. Van will go with him as he did before. He's the youngest brother. He understands somewhat. He's been helping Rion."

"What is going on?" Tarrell asked, worried and hurt.

"Rion has barely survived something terrifyingly brutal and traumatic, Tarrell. He has only just become a man, and he has been shaken to his core. You did not mean to harm him with your words. But he is small and his face hairless, and you compare him to a hulking giant with a full beard, someone who would not have suffered as he has. Rion has been held a helpless captive, tormented and beaten and told he was going to die, and that you were going to die because of him. You, who he loves more than his own life. And all of this when he had finally thought himself safe.

"It is why I have stayed, why I will stay longer. I am trying to help him. I know what he is going through. Although he was not held so long, nor tortured, nor injured so grievously that he should not recover from it fully, he does need help to do so."

Hunter stood up from the tub and began toweling himself dry. Tarrell did not mean to stare, but he could not look away: Hunter's body was a map of pain. He bore scars everywhere, terrible scars, from blade and tooth and claw and even fire. He had survived so much! Tarrell swallowed. He understood the eyes better now. He did not want to see Rion's beautiful warm eyes, so full of love and joy, turn to pools of blue ice.

Hunter wrapped the towel around his waist, glared at the crumpled clothes on the bed in distaste, and frowned. Tarrell suddenly remembered the package in his arms. "Hunter, this is for you. We thought you could use some new clothes, to replace the ones you destroyed helping us."

Hunter's expression betrayed his surprise, and he took the package from him, opening it. He fingered the soft fabric and sighed. "Thank you. You show me too much kindness, for I have hurt Rion too, without meaning to. I told him things he should not know."

"Then I would know what you said to him," Tarrell said, phrasing it as a request, not a challenge.

"I tell you only because he should not have to be the only one to know what is to come. He might go mad with such knowledge, unshared. I told him that the Elven Kingdoms will be destroyed, and that Gosa will be one of the last Cities of Man to fall," he said, as he pulled on his new undergarment.

"Why would you say such a thing?" Tarrell asked, wide-eyed.

"Because it is true. But still, I would not have said it, were it not for my own imprisonment and the scars it has left, the ones you cannot see. I do not think properly, now. My rage overtakes me and my control flees. I do not see the consequences of my actions or words, until too late. Jargas released me from my Madness, but I need him to help me more, if I am to be fit enough to fight. Even now I am a fool to have bared myself to you," he said, glaring and pulling his new pants on angrily.

"But you must be able to fight, because you are a Captain of the Watch, as Beryl was. Is Talon truly Lord of the Watch? Is he your King?" Tarrell asked, then immediately regretted it. He could not believe he'd voiced his question out loud to a man such as Hunter, particularly when he was already angered.

Hunter went absolutely still for a moment and Tarrell fought panic, for his instincts urged him to flee or fight, lest he be slain.

"Yes," Hunter said. From under the pile of dirty clothes he pulled out a gleaming silver armband and snapped it about his bicep, and then pulled his new shirt on over it.

Tarrell swallowed. He had expected denial or hesitation or ridicule, if death had not come. But he had not expected that simple admission.

Hunter continued. "Though how you could possibly know, I've no idea. Although I suspect Rion was the one to tell you. He is remarkable. I have known few others of his caliber. I also told Rion that Talon would not let the Elven Kingdoms be destroyed. But Rion did not believe it, because I do not believe it.

"There is little hope for us, now. We are out of time. The Enemy is at our door. There are but three Dwarven Kingdoms left, and though they now stand united, they will be destroyed as easily as the others. Then the forests will burn and the Elves will perish and Men will awaken too late to the fight.

"The world is ending. It is a cruel world and perhaps it should end. But then, there is Rion, and you, and the brothers, and Rarnak, and those like you, those I might still find reason to fight for. So I search for Jargas, that he might help me, for I can stand alone against the darkness no longer."

Tarrell stared at him, speechless. What could he possibly say?

"But it will not happen today, or even this year. It won't take two hundred fifty years, as it did to subjugate our Kingdom and all the Dwarven ones. I fear it might be over in less than two."

Tarrell thought about Ron's words and his and his brothers' plans.

"But, as the world will not end today, and as I must eat to live and live to fight, I go now to lunch. We may convince Rion to come too, I think. He will feel bad for yelling at you. He may try to pretend everything is well, or force himself to smile, or he might not. If he asks you to forgive him for it, do so, as if you could do nothing less. Do not make light of it or dwell upon it. Do not say more about it. Talk of trading, of positive things, as if the future were not in question."

Tarrell nodded, reeling from all he had heard.

Gar still guarded the door when they left the room, and Ara was with him now. They'd watch the room even with no one inside, for their trade goods were there. Gar darted a pensive glance at Ara, as if they'd been speaking and Gar was waiting to hear more. Tarrell sighed. Perhaps he should not have said anything to Ron and Ara. But didn't they have the right to know?

Tarrell went downstairs with Hunter, although he had no appetite for lunch. They saw that Rion was already at a table with Van and Ron, and they were talking. He and Hunter approached the table.

"There you are! We've been waiting for you. I wondered that it took you so long to get dressed, Hunter," Rion said cheerfully. His voice sounded strained and hollow to Tarrell's ear, and when he turned from Hunter to Tarrell for a moment, Rion could not meet his eyes and looked quickly away.

Elsa, one of the innkeeper's daughters, came over and they ordered their food. When it came, Tarrell began to eat mechanically, although he thought it must taste good, from the enthusiasm Ron and Van showed.

Rion was struggling with his meat, unable to cut it effectively with one hand. Tarrell chose his words carefully. "I well remember how difficult it is to cut using only one hand, and all the times you helped me at the table while I was recovering from my own injury. Would you like me to return the favor and assist you?"

Rion scowled at the plate, and then at Tarrell, and held his knife out to him. "Of course. I would help you feel man enough that you can still wield a blade, even if it only be at the table."

Tarrell paled. "How can you say such a thing to me?" he whispered, hoarsely, and pushed away his chair, stumbling blindly from the table, shaking.

RION watched him go, eyes widening in horror, appalled by what he had said, and he dropped the knife as if it had burnt him. His eyes filled with sudden tears. "I hurt him," he said, his voice filled with disbelief. "How could I have wanted to hurt him, when he only wanted to help me, when he gave his arm for me, when he has lost so much for me? How could I say something so cruel? I did not mean to, I did not want to."

"If you did not want to hurt him, but you know you have, you must apologize to him for it," Hunter said solemnly.

"How can I talk to him now? He must hate me, as much as I hate myself," Rion said, distraught, as tears began rolling down his cheeks.

Van spoke up. "He does not hate you, Rion. He loves you still. You will see. He will be able to forgive you your words. Brothers sometimes say such things to each other. All brothers, even the best of brothers, hurt one another. You are a man now, and part of being a man is to accept the consequences of your actions and to assume the responsibility for correcting your mistakes. The longer you wait, the harder it will be for you to do, and the more pain you will cause him while he waits."

"If you will excuse me," Rion said, as he got up and left for their room, grateful that Tarrell had not headed outside.

Ara and Gar watched Rion in concern when he approached. Ara said, "Rion, what's wrong? You look devastated and Tarrell looked ill, but he wouldn't talk to us."

"I hurt him and I've come to apologize to him for it." Rion was relieved that they didn't ask any more. He knocked lightly on the door, but there was no answer. He took a deep breath and opened the door, walked into the room and closed the door behind him.

Tarrell was lying on the bed. His right arm was over his face, across his eyes. His sleeves were rolled up, and Rion saw part of the jagged scars that covered his right arm, from the wolven bite that had nearly killed him.

"Please go away," Tarrell said, his voice low and pleading.

Rion winced. "Do you really want me to go?" Rion asked softly.

Tarrell sat up suddenly. "No, Rion, I didn't know it was you. I thought it was Ara. I didn't think...." He trailed off, as if he was afraid to speak, concerned he might say the wrong thing.

Rion walked over to him and traced the wet path of a tear along Tarrell's cheek with his fingertip. "You've been crying."

Tarrell swallowed and nodded. "As have you," he said, and then looked as if he feared his own words.

Rion took a deep breath and then spoke in a rush. "Tarrell, I never meant to hurt you. I mean, I meant to, but I don't know why. I didn't want to, I.... Tarrell, please forgive me for what I said! I know you can never forgive me for what you've lost protecting me, although you already have. I still don't understand why you don't blame me for your injury, when I blame myself."

"Of course I forgive you your words! You have forgiven me for letting you come to harm, when I am your guardian and even now still your guard, when I cannot forgive myself for failing you. Rion, I desperately want to hug you, but I'm afraid to. I couldn't bear to try and have you pull away from me. My heart is still too wounded." Tarrell looked at him, eyes pleading.

Rion wrapped his arms tightly about Tarrell and held him, weak with relief. "I will try not to be such a beast," Rion said, his voice muffled by Tarrell's chest.

"I will forgive you when you are. And I will be more careful with my words, as well," Tarrell swore. "Hunter has explained much to me, as have the others. Even before you were hurt, I was not doing as right by you as I should have been."

They stood holding each other for a long moment, then Rion pulled back a little awkwardly, embarrassed. He changed the subject, to fill the silence. "Thank you for the clothes you bought for Hunter. It is something I planned to do. I would like to buy him a bow, as well. I cannot believe he is without his own, but I dared not ask him what might have happened to it. He is so like Talon in some ways, yet so very different. I like him, I will miss him, and I want to be friends with him, but he will not let me get too close. And he still frightens me. I hope Jargas can help him, somehow."

Tarrell nodded. "I like him and will miss him, too, but he frightens me as well. I hope you won't get angry with me for it, but Ron and Ara and I already bought a bow for him." Tarrell told him what they'd found and where.

Rion grinned, hearing about the brothers' remarkable haggle. "I would be curious to see this bow! So, Ron and Ara may soon become competition for us? It is fortunate Talon chose such a large city for us to settle in, then! I hope they stay here.

"I am glad they won't be guards anymore, although they will be hard to replace. I worried about them the most, the entire time we were on the road. Ron reminds me so much of Hardred, and I miss Hardred and Alnas so much! And the brothers' love and loyalty for one another is so like that of my father and Uncle Farion that it has been both painful and wonderful to see, for my memories of them both. I was terrified one or more of the brothers might die on our journey. I could never have forgiven myself for it, if something had happened to any of them."

Tarrell nodded. "I would not want to risk them again in such a crossing. Come, I will have Ara show you the bow. I am still curious about it as well."

They left the room, and Ara and Gar were relieved to see them both looking so well. Rion said, "Ara, we would like to see the bow."

"Of course! Come." Gar stayed to guard their room, while Ara took them to the room he shared with his brothers. He unwrapped the bow from the cloak that had concealed it.

Rion could not hide his dismay. "Tarrell did not do justice with his words as to how awful it looks!"

Ara laughed. "Just wait until we clean it up and wax it."

"And restring it, I hope," Rion said, inspecting it skeptically.

"String it properly. I'd not replace that string, ever, if it is one of theirs. I would have no need to. I do not think it can ever break. Let me show you how it should be strung, so that you might see some of its hidden beauty." He placed his foot through the bow and string, bent the bow gently, and removed the string from one end, and then he turned the bow around and carefully pulled the end down, muscles straining with the effort, and reattached the string. Rion and Tarrell admired the beautiful wide arc that was revealed.

"It's a recurve bow, and the fool had it strung as a longbow! Their power and accuracy are unparalleled. This one is overly long, especially as most other horsemen use a short bow. It's a full six feet in length, but Hunter has the height for it and the strength of arm, I think, for few others might be able to use is. It feels to be a hundred-pound pull or more. Grandfather's was not nearly so strong. I will show you." Ara drew the string back slowly, to his cheek, his bicep bulging with the strain and the bow trembling. He held the string still for a moment, and then slowly released the pressure on it until the string was taut and straight again. Then he unstrung the bow carefully, and rubbed his upper arm, laughing. "Much as I might wish to keep it for myself, I could never use it properly."

Tarrell reached into his purse and handed him two five-gold coins. "So you are not tempted. I had not yet reimbursed you for it."

Ara was clearly surprised. "But I told you, we only paid five for it."

"I know. The other five is your profit, which you earned by your talent for bargaining. I do not offer you thirty or more, the price he first should have named, or the hundred or more you told me it is worth, only the asking price he spoke. Put it toward your new business."

Ara grinned and accepted it. "I will also take it for the work we will do to make it and the arrows right again."

"The arrows! I forgot. I must try to find eagle feathers for you. Talon said Hunter fletches his arrows with eagle feathers," Tarrell said.

Ara's eyes widened. "Perhaps we should mend only the bow, then, and let him repair the arrows? No, I am sure we can do it almost as well as he might."

"Come, Rion, let us get back to our lunch, for I am suddenly hungry again," Tarrell said.

Rion grinned and joined him.

The others were almost done eating, and appeared glad to see Rion and Tarrell smiling again, except for Hunter, whose visage revealed none of his thoughts. Rion's and Tarrell's smiles quickly fled when, to their dismay, they saw their plates were gone.

Ron laughed. "Don't look so distraught, though well you might be. It was delicious. Elsa is keeping your food warm in the kitchen for you. We told her you had unexpected business to attend to, but should be back shortly."

Van grinned. "You should have heard her, Tarrell. 'Oh, of course! Anything for Master Tarrell,'" he piped up in a ludicrous falsetto, batting his eyelashes exaggeratedly. "It must be the clothes. I'm much prettier than you, Tarrell. Someday I'll have a wench look at me like that."

Tarrell blushed and Ron scoffed. "Only as you do now, nightly, in your dreams! He's wearing your clothes at the moment, idiot."

Van tried to kick Ron under the table, but he deftly dodged.

FARAD excused himself abruptly, as he lurched clumsily to his feet. He stumbled from the table and all but ran out onto the street, his eyes immediately going skyward, desperately seeking the sun. He breathed deeply, staring into the blazing glory, burning the images of his dead brothers away with the glare but forcing himself to look away far sooner than he wished, before he permanently damaged his eyes.

He could not stay here much longer: seeing and hearing the four brothers was torture to him. A smile, a glance, a word, and memories would flood over him of his own lost brothers, always followed by images of their torture and deaths.

TARRELL watched Hunter's receding back in concern as Hunter left the inn. "Ron, why don't you and Van go relieve your brothers, so they can get some lunch? Then I would have you work on the bow as quickly as you can. I do not think Hunter will be staying for much longer. I will go out and buy the eagle feathers alone. Dressed as I am, it will be safe enough."

"But first we will eat, for you wouldn't want to bring a frown to Elsa's fair face," Rion insisted.

Tarrell started to object, but then Elsa was there with their lunch, her smile warm and her eyes bright. "There you are at last! I've kept it warm for you, Master Tarrell. Here, let me refill your stein for you."

Tarrell smiled at her a bit shyly and she beamed at him. She left, with obvious reluctance, to wait upon some of the other patrons.

Ron pushed his empty plate away. "We're done. We'll have Ara and Gar join you for lunch, but then Ara and I will shop with you, for we will not leave you unguarded, and besides, we know what to look for in the feathers we seek. It shouldn't take so long that we can't finish the arrows and bow tonight."

Tarrell reluctantly agreed.

THEY were fortunate, found what they needed far more easily than they had hoped, and returned to the inn more quickly than they had expected to. Hunter had not yet reappeared.

The brothers spent the rest of the day restoring the bow and refletching the arrows.

Hunter missed dinner, and Rion was edgy and irritable. Tarrell did not think Hunter would leave without telling Rion good-bye after what he had said. He fervently hoped he would not.

The four brothers ate dinner in their room, all working on the bow and arrows, while Rarnak guarded the other room.

"We should either start trading tomorrow or begin searching for a permanent place to live," Tarrell said to Rion tentatively.

"I hate it here," Rion said petulantly, with an unaccustomed scowl. "I wish we'd never come."

"Rion, Hunter won't leave without saying good-bye," Tarrell assured him, hoping it was true, guessing at least part of the reason for Rion's foul mood.

"I don't care if he does," Rion said with feigned indifference, but his tone of voice betrayed him.

Finally, Tarrell saw Hunter enter the inn, his eyes flicking back and forth across the common room. They lighted on Rion and Terrell, and he came over to them. "Where are your guards?" Hunter asked critically, in concern.

"Rarnak is guarding our room and we gave the brothers the night off. Don't worry. We are safe here, and we don't plan to go outside. Have you eaten?" Tarrell asked.

Hunter shook his head and Tarrell waved Elsa over.

Hunter gritted his teeth. "I don't have coin to pay and you already purchased lunch for me," he protested.

"But it is our treat," Rion said. "Dinner for our friend, and oushka! Bring a flask."

"No, only a stein of mead. I should not drink oushka tonight," Hunter argued.

"Mead, then, please. For three." Rion looked intently at Hunter. "You said you would stay, but you are leaving tomorrow."

Hunter nodded.

"Tonight after dinner, Tarrell will rewrap your wound for you, and again tomorrow, before you go. Although it would be better to give it more time to heal," Rion added carefully.

"I cannot heal here," Hunter said, and Tarrell knew he meant more than heal from the blade wound.

Hunter ate quickly. Rion and Tarrell accompanied him to their room, where Tarrell tended to his injury. Then Tarrell left the two of them alone, to check on the brothers' progress.

"IS HE going to be all right?" Rion asked, his voice heavy with concern.

"Who, Tarrell? I thought you smoothed things out. Or has something else happened while I was out?" Hunter asked.

"We did. I meant Talon. The war." Rion swallowed. "In Athanark, he sounded like he thought you might lose, but I didn't know then that he would be one of those fighting. I did not know then that he was part of the Watch, that he was your King."

Hunter breathed deeply. "Rion, you must not tell anyone else. I know you already told Tarrell. It would be incredibly dangerous for Talon, were people to know. I have killed before, to keep his secret. I have kept his secret, and his father's before him, for over one hundred twenty years, since I came-of-age."

"But you cannot be one hundred thirty-six years old!" Rion denied, stunned.

Hunter gazed at him with tired eyes. "I am not. I am one hundred forty-six. Amontir come-of-age at twenty-five, not sixteen, as other Men do. But neither do we die at sixty. There was a time when I might have lived to be two hundred fifty, before the war. Yet now I am the eldest surviving member of our kin, and my remaining time is to be measured perhaps in days, if I am yet fortunate, not in years. But, again, I have told you too much," he said with a sigh.

"I cannot help myself, Rion. I do not know what Power it is you hold. I feel none within you, but you make me want to share all I know with you, as if somehow it is important that you know so much. You feel you must know, and you make me feel you must as well."

"I won't tell anyone! About Talon, or about what you said. I wish I could help the two of you, but I can't even hold a sword, now. I understand how Tarrell must feel. No, I'll have the use of my arm again, and it's not as if I need it for my livelihood. I'm a trader. If someone cut out my tongue, then I'd understand. Hunter, what's wrong?" Rion asked, in sudden fear.

Hunter's eyes widened in horror. "You must not say such things! Never say such things!" he demanded, grabbing him by the shoulders and shaking him.

"You're hurting me!" Rion cried out in pain and fear.

The door swung open with a bang and Rarnak was there. "Let him go, Hunter!" His hand was on his sword hilt, but he'd not yet drawn the blade.

Hunter released Rion, his eyes now squeezed tightly shut, his hands clenching into fists. "Leave me, quickly, go!" Hunter commanded, and Rion stumbled out of the room, shaking.

Rion ran to the brothers' room and told Tarrell what had happened. Tarrell went back to their room with him. Rarnak was outside, listening at the door. Rion pressed his ear to the door as well. There was a voice inside, low and rhythmic.

Rion instinctively tried the door and was disturbed to find it was not locked. He opened the door a crack. Hunter was sitting on the floor cross-legged, staring into the oil lamp, which was on the floor in front of him. He had removed the glass hood from it, and was gazing at the naked flame. The language he was speaking was not one Rion had ever heard spoken before, though he thought it might be the one he'd started teaching himself, along with Elvish, from Talon's book. He pulled the door softly shut. "We'd better tell the others what's happened."

They went to their guards' room. Tarrell said, "Hunter isn't well. I believe it's best we not disturb him. I think he has need of our room for the rest of the night. I'd like to have one of you guard him. And if it's all right with you, Rion and I will sleep in here tonight."

Ron said, "Of course. Remember, Tarrell, you're the one paying for our room. Who are we to keep you out? You must be more strict with your next guards, or they may take terrible advantage of you. You and Rion are too kindhearted by far."

Rion sighed. "I don't think I'll be able to sleep, in any case."

"Please try, Rion," Tarrell urged. "It's bad enough you've been walking up and down the stairs when the healer told us that you should be staying in bed until your leg has a chance to heal."

Rion glared at him.

"Rion, Tarrell's right. You know he is," Van said. "He should have said something to you long before this, but he's kept silent about it."

Rion swallowed. "I'm sorry. You're right, Van. Tarrell, I know you're only doing what's best for me. I…. Hunter grabbed me, and his eyes… he scared me. I felt…." He hesitated.

"I know, Rion. But you're safe. We won't let you be hurt again, I swear we won't," Tarrell averred. "You know that Hunter did not mean to hurt you.

He is ill. Please, try to get some sleep, all right? We'll make sure Hunter doesn't leave before we can give him the bow and we'll make sure you get a chance to say good-bye to him."

Rion nodded. He took off his boots and lay back on the bed, his mind racing, though he was very tired. He drank some of the medicine the healer had given him, relieved he'd put it in his purse and brought it down to dinner with him, though he'd forgotten to take it then. He wouldn't have wanted to enter their room and risk disturbing Hunter. He hoped the elixir might help him sleep, as well as relieve the pain in his arm and leg and that from his bruises.

TARRELL was relieved to see Rion fell asleep quickly. He'd been through much and needed to sleep in order to heal.

Tarrell watched the brothers work. After the second time he fell asleep in his chair, Ron finally convinced him to go to bed as well.

RION awoke with a start, sitting up quickly. Ron yawned and reassured him. "Good morning, Rion. Don't worry. Rarnak and Van took shifts and kept careful watch on your room all night. It's barely dawn and Hunter is still inside."

Rion slipped his boots back on. It felt odd, having slept in his clothes.

Tarrell sat up and pulled on his own boots. They left their guards' room and went to the door to their own.

"The two of you are certainly up early," Rarnak said. "Hunter's been awake all night. He hasn't stopped that odd chanting."

The door to their room suddenly opened, and they all jumped and then looked sheepish.

"It's convenient you are both here, Rion and Tarrell," Hunter said. "I must say good-bye to you. I cannot stay. I apologize for keeping you from your room, but I had need of it. I am not well. I am sorry I frightened you, Rion."

"I know, and I know you must go. But before you do, we have something for you," Rion said. "The brothers worked on it all day and all night. We hope you like it. Please come to their room. It will only take a moment."

Hunter eyed them warily, but then nodded. He entered the other room with them.

Ron held the bow out to him. It was not strung. It shone a rich, deep red; it was a beautiful weapon, worthy of a King. Ara held out the quiver of arrows.

Hunter's eyes widened and his hand trembled as he accepted the bow and his fingers traced the fine curve of it. "It is of Aralon, like my own, the one I buried by the River," he said reverently. "But this is a Lord's bow! How did you get this?" he asked in confusion. His fingers traced a mark on the wood, and his face paled. "It is Lord Halon's. I saw this buried with him. How could you have it here now?"

Ara paled and swore. "Lord Halon! Grandfather rode with him. The shopkeeper's a tomb robber, or knows one. That weaselly little slime! I apologize, Hunter. I did not recognize the mark for what it was, the Lord's sign. I'd wondered why the bow was red, not white. I didn't know what it meant. We did not mean to give you a cursed bow. We must see it safely back to Aralon, so it might be buried again beside him. May his spirit and Grandfather's forgive us for our stupidity."

Hunter shook his head. "No, I will see it returned. For now I have great need of it, may Halon forgive me for it." He examined the arrows curiously and removed one from the quiver. An expression of pain crossed Hunter's face, fleetingly, as he ran his finger lightly along one of the distinctive new eagle feathers.

"Now we know why the fletching was so ragged," Ara said. "We had to refletch the arrows. Tarrell said Talon told him you always fletched your own arrows with eagle feathers."

"You have done fine work. It is much appreciated." Hunter turned to Rion and Tarrell. "And you have fed and clothed me as well. I do not travel so ill-equipped now toward the danger I face. Thank you, all of you."

He stared intently at Rion. "Remember my words of the dead, Rion. Never give them such power over you." Then he looked away, through the open doorway, toward the stairs.

"I must go. I must make Jargas's village by nightfall. I cannot be alone on the road at night. I shall miss you all," he said, looking back at them. "You especially, Rion. Be well." Then he abruptly turned back toward the stairs and left the room, disappearing quickly and silently down the staircase.

"I'll be back in a moment," Ara said, and headed downstairs as well.

"I hope Jargas can help Hunter," Rion said softly. He did not know why the night held such terror for Hunter. He sighed. He wondered if he had made the right decision. He had decided not to tell Hunter about Circe's message for Talon. He had been so unstable, so troubled already, he was afraid the effect his warning might have had upon him. There would be some other way to warn Talon, he hoped.

Tarrell said, "Come, we should have some breakfast. We've still much to do, to settle in here."

They went downstairs and were surprised that Ara was not in the common room.

ARA called out to Hunter, who was now half a block ahead of him. He'd been running to catch up to him, but Hunter's stride was incredible. Ara had already nearly lost sight of him half a dozen times.

Hunter stopped and pivoted about, eyeing him both curiously and warily.

"I must talk with you," Ara said as he caught up to him.

"I need to hurry, Ara," Hunter argued.

"I realized you meant to try to walk to Jargas's village by nightfall. His village is twelve leagues southwest of here, in the Holoren Mountains. Even you cannot make such a journey in so short a time, especially as you are yet injured, without a horse. I offer you mine," Ara said sincerely.

"You have all already given me too much. I cannot take your horse," Hunter chided. "Why would you even offer it to me?"

"Because Grandfather would be dead if it weren't for you, and my brothers and I would never have been born. I've heard the stories often enough. My given name is Aramark. I'm the grandson of the man you and Lord Halon rode with, when you retook Thenalon."

Hunter looked at him levelly. "Whatever you thought you heard, I misspoke."

"No, you said, 'I saw this buried with him.' I know every detail of that battle. There was a Hunter that rode with them. He was young, he was only a Knight of the Watch, not a Captain, not yet banded, and he rode with three others. They were...."

"No! Do not say their names to me, not even their traveling names, even in the daylight!" Hunter demanded, but his voice was full of desperation, rather than anger.

"I am not here to torment you," Ara soothed. "I'm trying to help you. Please, take my horse. He's fast and strong. Gar trained him. He'll serve you well. We know the darkness is coming. We saw when we visited Thenalon, to bury Grandfather's bow. It's why we stayed there longer than we should have, and why we left Athanark when we did.

"Grandfather told us we must ever aid one of the Watch if we were to recognize him as such, that we must give him anything he might need. I offer you a fast horse. You may have my purse as well. I offer my sword to your service. I would kneel to you and swear oath to you, but there are people about."

Hunter sighed. "Were my need not so great, I would not accept your offer of a horse, Ara. But you are right: I cannot make it to Jargas by nightfall otherwise, and I fear last night was the only one left to me. Lead me to your horse and I will take him, gratefully. But I will not accept your coin, or your sword. And you must not tell the others about any of this. You must promise me."

"I swear myself to silence, as I swear myself to your service, if ever you are in need of me. Call for me and I will come."

Hunter nodded, wearily, and followed Ara back to the stable yard at the inn.

Ara saddled his horse. "His name is Aragar," he said to Hunter. Then Ara patted Aragar affectionately and said, "Take good care of Hunter. You belong to him, now."

Hunter led Aragar into the street, mounted, and rode off, without another word.

Ara watched until he disappeared from view and then headed into the inn. Ron and Gar were downstairs at a table with Rion and Tarrell, eating breakfast. He knew Rarnak and Van would be guarding their rooms.

"There you are! We saved you a plate. We were just about ready to start looking for you. You shouldn't wander off like that alone, after what happened," Ron scolded.

"I'm sorry I concerned you," Ara said meekly, instead of arguing the point as he normally would have.

He sat and began to eat, listening to his brothers and Rion and Tarrell talking with only half an ear, his mind on the stories his grandfather had told him of the War. He sent a silent and heartfelt prayer to Elmoth that Hunter might make it to Jargas safely.

Chapter 2

Into the Fire

ELVEN High-Prince Aras brought Guard Captain Leonas and Captain of the Watch Lunahr into the gardens around the Palace with him, where they might still be observed by the King's Guard that protected them, but not overheard. They had found no trace of former Lord of the Guard Ahrnad after his attack upon Lunahr, the young Lord of House of Eagles of the Amontir, who was formerly their prisoner and was now their reluctant guest. As a tool of the Enemy, Ahrnad, who had only recently been second in command of their combined armed forces and privy to all their strategies, could cause unspeakable harm to them all.

Aras desperately wished that Dewalaren was still here, or that they were yet linked. He feared the Man others knew as Talon, Prince of the Amontir and Lord of the Watch, was walking into danger without his protection, that the wizard Arcanus, who had nearly slain him once out of fear and desperation, might attack him again, or worse, that Incuban might find him. All Dewalaren's people were in grave peril, and he had entrusted his young cousin's safekeeping to Aras while he was drawn elsewhere.

"Ahrnad is up to some treachery," Aras told his two new friends, greatly troubled. "I do not relish waiting for him to strike. But there are other dangers that it is time I face. Our search for Ahrnad is hampered by the Hill People attacks. Arcanus warned us not to take the War into the Hills, thinking us safer here, and my father follows his counsel still. But this War must end."

"If I were myself, I could try to mediate between you," Lunahr said in frustration. "But I cannot leave the woods of Nalea. Arcanus has bound me here with his magicks. I wish I knew why the Hill People attack you now, after so many years of uneasy peace."

Aras was relieved to hear Lunahr say he would like to mediate, because he had conceived a desperate plan, and he would need Lunahr's help if it were to have even the smallest chance of succeeding. "The day of their first major attack, one of the Guard said that they thought with me and my father dead they could have an easy victory."

"But there must have been some other catalyst," Lunahr argued. "This War is too convenient to our Enemy, too well timed. I sense his hand at work here too."

"I agree. The trouble started after my father fell. I've been thinking that perhaps Ahrnad may have done some ill to them as well," Aras said. "If so, we might be able to end the War, but we must act quickly, before more blood is spilt. Each death breeds more hatred. I need your advice and aid, Beryl, for you can still help mediate between us from afar, even if I must be the one to carry the message." Aras was careful not to use Lunahr's given name in front of Leonas, when Lunahr himself did not even suspect he knew it.

Aras turned to Leonas, the young Guardsman on special detached duty to him. "I will need you to stand beside me, Leonas. I will be walking a dangerous path, and I do not want to walk it alone. But I must tell you both a story first, so you might understand why I plan to take the risks I feel are necessary, for all our sakes. Once you both hear, I need to learn your thoughts and know that I have your support, for I cannot do this unless both of you help me."

Lunahr nodded wordlessly. Leonas said, "I will do anything for you, Highness. You need only ask."

Aras smiled and shook his head. "In this thing I will ask, your loyalty to me will be the thing you need to overcome, in order to serve me, Leonas."

Leonas looked confused and concerned.

"For now, Leonas, you must listen. I will give you chance to speak your concerns later. In fact, I will command it of you," Aras said softly.

"Then speak, Highness. I do not mean to hinder you."

Aras was silent for a long time as he gathered his thoughts and his courage to give voice to them. He looked up then, but his eyes were not focused on either of their faces as he began to speak, his voice soft but intent.

"I know where the Hill People City lies. I have visited it before, many, many times, although the last time was long ago." He spoke more to Lunahr, at first, who had not lived amongst them for long and did not know as much of his history as Leonas. "When I was a boy, there were no others of my age here. There were no other children of any age. There should never have been children here. Men know only of the Seven Elven Kingdoms, four Wood and three River. Only your people, Beryl, know of Nalea.

"Father told me you thought us a lost Eighth Kingdom, when first we revealed ourselves to you, until we showed you we are instead the Army and the Navy of the Seven. The Watch did not understand. You still do not. How can you, when we have told you so little? Father has not wanted you to know. We have kept so much from you."

Aras sighed. "But I was speaking of children. We Elves are not as Men. We have few progeny, if any. Elves live to be a thousand years old. If we bore children as Men do, the world would soon be filled. My father had also been childless, for the length and breadth of his reign. It is said, 'To be a King is to be alone,' but he denied himself even a Queen.

"My father inspires loyalty and awe and, unfortunately, fear, but neither friendship nor love. But finally Ithelia came, she who was to be my mother and his Queen. They married soon after they met, and I was conceived almost immediately. I was born and she saw me grow for a time. She left when I was barely eight years old." He shivered and saw Leonas look at him in sympathy.

Aras knew the High-Queen had been well loved: she had influenced the people of Nalea as easily and thoroughly as she had manipulated their High-King. Leonas would believe, as did all the rest, the whispered rumors, that his father had killed her. Only Aras knew the truth. His mother lived hidden away on the Isle of Gryph, plotting her revenge against Arcanus and Incuban, the two she blamed for the destruction of their Homeland and the extinction of her entire race: the Elves of the Air, the Aerie. "My people miss her still," Aras said softly.

He took a deep breath and continued more strongly. "So, when I played and explored, it was always alone. As I grew older and bolder, I wandered far from the City, deep into the woods.

"One day, when I was twelve and ranged farther than ever before, I came to the end of our woods and saw the hills and the cold mountains of stone that tower over them. I was surprised, for I had not thought there could be a world without trees. At first I thought it a lonely and sad and dead place, those hills. Then I saw they were rocky but also green with smaller plants and alive with animals, and I grew curious.

"I left the woods and walked upon the hills and then found more hills beyond them. Far into those hills I found a beautiful valley and saw trees again, although far younger than our own woods.

"I explored those trees and grew to know them, returning home and coming back again many times. It was my own special, private place. My father never asked where I went. I do not think he even noticed I was gone.

"I had many to watch over me, and many teachers, of course. Often I was with the healer Jarnath, asking questions and learning his talent, or with Meloneth, learning songs and melodies, or with Etheria, learning to draw and paint, or outside the Lords' Grove looking wistfully where I could not enter until my coming-of-age, when I turned forty-nine and might attune to a Tree, and give it a name, if it accepted me.

"But then, unexpectedly, my father noticed me again. He said it was time that I be taught by him. So I learned to mediate and to judge, to command our forces and rule the people of the Seven Kingdoms. But it was no hard thing, for we are at balance with one another and the world. We are not as Men, always struggling for power of station, thinking we are lesser for the lack of it. True Power comes from within. The High-born have ruled always, he taught me. Father has always ruled here and kept careful guard, wary of the return of war."

Aras did not say that in their Homeland they had been ruled by the Council, a carefully selected body of the High-born. Here, in their new land, each of the Seven Kingdoms was ruled by a King, the descendent of one of the surviving Council members. Their position was no longer elected but hereditary. And they were all ruled by his father.

Lunahr must not know such details of their history, lest he seek to learn more. He never should have even spoken of the Homeland to them. It was highly probable Leonas did not know their dark and shameful history, unless someone had told him in secret. It was forbidden to speak of it.

"War was not something that was ever openly spoken of, though I had heard whispers of it many times. It was why all those around me were soldiers, warriors. War is in the very name. I found the courage and boldly asked Father what war was and was astonished when he answered me.

"Father told me of the other races of the world, Men and Dwarves and even of the ogres, for the latter once banded together and burnt Thenalon, a City of Man only one hundred seventy miles to the south of us. I was horrified to hear a city had been burnt, but did my best to conceal my fear. Father said that when the next war came, we would be fighting one or more of the other races and they would likely use fire against us. His rage, when he spoke of it, was terrifying.

"Father said he was going to teach me how to fight, with bow and sword and knife, so I might slay our enemies by his side. He would teach me to move silently, without being seen and without leaving tracks, as the King's Guard do. He would prepare me so that I would excel in my training, so that none might doubt that when it was time, I would be worthy of taking up the rule of our people after he was gone." Aras fought the pain of it. It was his own father who had questioned his worth, not his men, his people. His father was the one who had needed to be assured. That he had failed miserably to do so, as he had failed his father so many times before and since, was a source of everlasting shame.

"So I listened and I practiced and I trained as if I were already a cadet. I missed my valley, for it was two years until I saw it again. I was fourteen when my training ended, and I was left to my own devices, and set out for my valley again." He did not mention the training accident that had abruptly ended his training in disgrace and nearly ended his life. Marlaenus would have been slain, had he not diverted his attack. It was only his own incompetence and clumsiness that had resulted in Marlaenus injuring him so gravely. Thanks to Jarnath, they had both survived.

It was his friendship afterward that had caused Marlaenus's death. He and nine others all had died for their friendship, purposefully sent on hazardous duty into the hills and mountains beyond them by his father, with the intent that they die there, all to punish him. He had discovered the truth too late to save them, but he had saved eleven others, smuggling them safely to Salenia, where they might hide in plain sight and live out the rest of their days.

Aras learned that all who might befriend him would be in deadly peril. He distanced himself from Meloneth and even from Jarnath—especially from Jarnath. It was a testament to their people's love of Meloneth and Jarnath's abilities as a healer that they yet lived. Their people did not worship either of them as Gods, as Men did, in their ignorance, but they valued them both highly.

Aras forced himself to continue. It was hard to speak of the rest. He had never shared this before with anyone, not even Jarnath. "But I found my world changed. When I entered my valley, I was horrified, for half the trees were gone and wide flat fields filled with plants like the gardens of home, only far larger, covered the ground where the trees had been. And there was a stone building and many smaller buildings, the latter made from logs from the trunks of the missing trees. I was angry but also afraid, for there were strange people in my valley, with dark hair and eyes."

He bit back his first thoughts, that they were Aerie, like his mother as he had seen her without her masking spell, that he could not hope to survive against so many enemies and how he had all but collapsed in relief when he had seen their rounded ears. "But their ears were misshapen, oddly rounded, and they wore brightly colored clothes, and they laughed and they sang, though try as I might, I could understand none of the lyrics of their songs. I realized then that these must be Men. There were children as well as men and women, loud and many, laughing and singing and dancing and playing together. They were different and strange, but also wild and beautiful. They were not what I expected Men to be like at all, from my father's words. So I watched. I needed to understand.

"I stayed many days, and I thought I might talk to one, but when I heard them speak or sing, their words were strange to me. So, then I went home, to find if anyone knew the tongue of Man. I asked Mereth, one of our messengers, if he knew the language of Men, and to my surprise he told me there were many tongues of Man. But, he said, there was also a tongue Men used most with one another to facilitate trade, and that even the Dwarves spoke it. He told me our people had learned it as well. It was called Common.

I asked him to teach it to me and he did. It took many months to learn the odd grammar and vocabulary and guttural pronunciation, for he had many other duties to perform and the language was so different from the language I knew."

Aras fought back another wave of pain. Mereth's thoughts had been quite loud and vivid, though Aras had not meant to hear them. Mereth had been astonished by both the intensity of his study and his ability to master the language, for he had heard the King's Guard muttering that their High-Prince was an incompetent fool, completely inept in his training and unworthy of his station.

Aras forged resolutely ahead with his story. "When I learned all he knew, I returned to the valley. I had just turned fifteen. And I saw to my surprise that much more had changed in so short a time. Change for us is measured in decades or centuries, if at all. But the village had grown to be a City now, with many more fields cultivated around it, although they had not felled many more trees, I saw to my relief. The buildings were more numerous, and no longer of logs but of stone or planks of wood. Man worked so quickly! There were no horses, but there was more than one corral, to my surprise containing herds of deer.

"I thought to approach the Men now, but everywhere I saw signs of war. I wondered who their enemy might be. I still wonder. The men now all carried swords, and even the women bore knives and sometimes swords, though neither carried bows. I thought it was perhaps better to stay hidden and listen before I approached, but to my frustration and dismay, their words were still strange to me; they did not speak Common. Still, I watched and listened. As the days passed, I grew bolder and went closer, but always stayed hidden.

"I found they did not love their trees as we love ours, except the children, perhaps. Before, when I had watched, the children had often played in the woods and climbed the trees. But now, the adults with the swords would not let them stray so far from their City.

"Then, one day, I saw one of the children, a girl with long, thick hair black as the night sky and eyes the rich, warm brown of forest loam. She moved almost like one of us: silent, quick, and strong. And she glanced back often, as if she feared she might be followed. She went deep into the woods, and I kept pace with her, hidden in the trees. She looked about, then reached into the hollow under a tree and drew something out. I could not see it, and stepped forward to get a better view. Because of it, my eyes were on her hands, not my feet, and a twig cracked under my foot. She looked up, startled, and there was terror in her gaze.

"I stepped out of my hiding place and held out my empty hands to show I was no danger to her and said in Common, 'I will not hurt you. I would be your friend.' Her eyes filled with wonder then, and I realized how different and strange I must seem to her, with my long golden hair and green eyes and pointed ears. Then she smiled at me, with all the warmth of the sun, and I smiled back at her. I glanced down to see what she had retrieved and saw that she held a knife, though not as if she meant to use it. I looked back into her eyes and her face flushed darkly.

"But I had made a mistake. I had been away too long, watching her ever-changing world, and had forgotten to return to my own. My father had finally noticed me gone and sent the King's Guard to search for me. I later learned it had taken them many days to find my trail, for they did not know in which direction I had gone and had all of our woods to search. Even once they found trace of me, they lost my trail often, for my father had taught me well. But it was that moment that they finally discovered me. Six of the King's Guard slipped out from the trees, with bows drawn and arrows pointed at her.

"I cried out for them not to hurt her and she dropped the knife and turned and ran. Then the Lord of the Guard, it was Ahrnad, even then, said to me, 'We do not harm children, even children of Men. But we would protect our High-King's son.' Then he told me I must go with them, that my father summoned me. But I commanded them to wait.

"It was the first time I had ever commanded the King's Guard, and I do not think they expected it, but they obeyed me. They waited. I picked up the knife and placed it carefully back in its hiding place and covered the tracks the girl had left in her haste when she fled. I backtracked her trail nearly to the edge of the wood, where her tracks suddenly disappeared, as if her panic had fled and her caution returned. It had seemed important that she not be discovered, so I was glad I could do her that small kindness. I wished to talk to her but I knew it must wait. So I returned with the King's Guard, who had followed me the entire time, of course.

"They took me back here, to Nalea, and they reported to my father as to where I had been. My father grew enraged, for I had told no one that Man was so near. I had seen him infuriated before, I had seen others quail, but I had never felt the full force of his anger directed at me. I was terrified of him. I realized years later that he was afraid for me as well, but then I saw only his rage. He made me swear to him that I would never cross the hills and return to the City. My heart grew heavy, but I had no choice but to swear.

"I have kept that promise all these years since. And now I regret those lost years, for we might have met in friendship, had I been more bold and acted sooner, or had I defied my father. But we instead grew to be wary neighbors, and now enemies."

Aras swallowed. "Tomorrow, I go to break that promise, for he forbids me still, but I must go. The one other time I disobeyed my father's wishes, we both almost died. But there is so very much more to lose. The more blood that is spilled, the weaker we become, before the war to come. Yet still, I am afraid. So I will take you with me, Leonas, and I wish I could take you as well, Beryl.

"But I will at least bring your counsel with me, Beryl. The Watch has dealt with many different tribes and towns and cities of Men. Neither you nor Talon knows this tribe, you said before, but perhaps you might know others like them?" Aras was as careful not to use Dewalaren's given name before Leonas as he had been about Lunahr's. It was so hard to keep so many secrets! He had always hated secrets; he had lived his whole life in secret. Dewalaren lived in secret also. It was one of the many reasons Aras loved him. Dewalaren understood, when others could not.

"I would know how best to approach them and what I should avoid. What symbol of truce might I use to signal to them that I come in peace to talk? At least some of their elders must know Common, mustn't they?"

Lunahr looked at him intently. "It is true that many Men speak Common. Sometimes, though, it might only be a single person who is speaker for the tribe or village. In larger cities, especially ones where traders come from other lands, Common is used more widely, but the City you described is so isolated, they will likely be more like a smaller settlement in that regard.

"As for a symbol of truce, a white cloth held in one hand, or sometimes tied to a pole, is a universal symbol of peace among Men. The Watch has seen that life is often hard, especially for those who live isolated from their fellow Man. Food and even water can be scarce. Because of that, it is customary to offer food and drink, usually bread and clear water, when one wishes to parlay with the leader of the tribe or village. It is also important to do so, because among many tribes, once you eat and drink with each other, you are considered a guest and under their protection unless you do something to break that trust. But Aras, much blood has already been spilt on both sides. I do not think this will work," Lunahr added, sounding troubled.

"But I must try! Something must have started this. If I can find out what happened, then I can take action to fix whatever is wrong. I could heal the breach." Aras reasoned.

Lunahr took a breath and plunged onward. "Aras, if they choose not to honor your symbol of truce, they could easily decide to kill you. And aside from what that would cost you, and those who love you, think what it would cost them. Your father would be terrible in his vengeance."

Aras swallowed. "But they kill us now, and we kill them, and I cannot see a future other than more and more death on both sides. If there is another path, I would take it."

Aras turned to Leonas. "Leonas, my friend, what is your counsel? I go now to face your enemy. You have fought them, even slain them, I think, and they would have slain you, save for Talon's timely blade. They have hurt your friends, even killed some of them. Where is your heart in this? Do you seek vengeance for the fallen, or do you hope, as I do, to prevent more injury, more death?"

LEONAS'S heart went out to his High-Prince, whose life of privilege had been such a lonely one that he had sought friendship from a people not his own. But he feared Aras's childhood memories clouded his judgment, and he could not allow Aras to go into danger. "Highness, I do not know why they hate us, but I have seen their eyes, and I know they do. They wish only death for us. They will not be moved by any words of peace by one of us. If you go to their City, you go to your death. You ask me to choose between my loyalty to you and my need to protect you, but I cannot! My loyalty is from my love of you, but my need to protect you is from the same. Either choice is disaster."

He looked into Aras's eyes and despaired. "But I see now that I have no choice, for you have taken it from me. For you are afraid, and you fear that alone, you might have even less of a chance to succeed, but you still will go regardless of the danger. I see it in your eyes. So then, I will go with you, that I may somehow barter my life for yours."

LEONAS'S words frightened Aras, for he had not looked into the eyes of any of the Hill People he had fought. His focus had been upon their wrists, where his arrows must strike, when he and Dewalaren had succored Leonas and the others of his patrol. But surely there must be even one amongst them who might listen?

Leonas continued. "I do not lust for vengeance, but I cannot see them with a child's eyes, as you do. I see only their dark deeds." He sighed. "But they fight well, and they cry out for their fallen, and they rescue their wounded in peril of their own lives, and they retrieve their dead so they might be laid to rest. Perhaps they are more like us than they are different. Perhaps it will be enough," he said, though there was grave doubt in his voice.

Aras's heart was heavy with dread. Again, as in the woods before the wolven attacked, he feared he was making a choice that would lead to disaster. Yet that had turned out well even after disaster, so perhaps this might as well.

He took a deep breath and turned to Lunahr again. "Someone must know what has happened if we... do not return. I have written my father a letter, telling him all I told you and what I planned. If I do not return, you must give it to Jarnath, so that he may give it to my father for me."

LEONAS realized then that Aras had not expected to be dissuaded from his course. Beryl hugged Aras and then, to Leonas's surprise, hugged him as well. Elves disliked being touched by Men, yet Beryl was so like one of them in form and feature and temperament, Leonas did not mind. Even his scent hinted at distant forests and strange soils and a trace of something else he could not name.

Beryl stepped back and looked intently at them. "I would have you both know my given name, before you go. I should have told you long before this. My name is Lunahr." From the expression of concern and dismay upon his face, Leonas realized he did not think they would live to speak it. "Good luck, my friends. I will not say good-bye, for I already fear this may be the last time I will see either of you again," he said, his voice catching at the end, as if he fought back tears, though he looked at them steadily and hid his distress well.

Leonas wanted nothing more than to reveal Aras's plan to his father before he left, so that he might stop him, but he could not betray the trust he had been given. And he feared Aras would go anyway, that he would sneak away, without even Leonas's poor protection.

ARAS was touched that Lunahr had entrusted him with his given name. He loved him for it, both for the faith he had shown in him, and because now it was one less thing he needed to keep from Leonas.

He should not love Leonas as a friend also. He endangered Leonas with his love of him. It was no longer as when he was a child. His father would not seek to harm Leonas. But Arcanus would use him as a weapon against him, in a heartbeat, were he ever to learn of him. Incuban would do far worse, but Aras had been careful not to reveal even his own existence to Incuban yet. He wished again that Arcanus had not forced his hand, that he had not discovered him either. He was not ready to face his mother or her two enemies, not yet.

"We cannot act from here. I will convince my father that it is best for us to return to the Guest House, which can be ringed with King's Guard just as easily, saying Lunahr is uneasy in such close proximity to him, for fear of an accidental meeting, and the King's Guard are certainly enough on edge with him here. There is a secret way from the Guest House, long ago forgotten by everyone, which I found playing there as a child. I keep it secret still. Leonas, you and I will exit that way, while you remain inside, Lunahr, under protective guard. They will think all three of us still there."

Lunahr and Leonas looked at each other in dismay, and Aras realized they had both hoped that the King's Guard might stop him when they could not.

A short while later, Aras was easily able to sway his father, for the King's Guard was indeed apprehensive with Lunahr so near their High-King.

Aras had secretly been acquiring medicines for such a journey when he visited Jarnath and the wounded in the Healers' Hall, so he would not have to ask the healers for things he could not explain needing. If Jarnath had even an inkling of what he was attempting, he would try to stop him.

THAT night, under the cover of darkness, Aras and Leonas left the Guest House, and slipped silently amongst the trees, passing unnoticed between the King's Guard patrols, which Aras had helped coordinate; he knew their weak points. The patrols were stretched thin, for lack of the wounded men and the exponential increase of patrols within their woods. The enemy was getting more aggressive. Aras sensed there was desperation behind the increased ferocity and decreased intervals between their attacks, though he knew not why.

It felt odd to be traveling so poorly armed. He wore only his dagger and twin swords, and Leonas also carried his dagger and sword, but at his insistence, neither of them had brought their bows. He was not foolish enough to leave the relative safety of Nalea completely unarmed, but he hoped to appear less menacing to those he wished to communicate with peacefully. The Hill People wielded blades but did not use bows. The only time they might have encountered them at all was at the wrong end of his people's arrows. They would know they were a weapon that could be used at great distances and might never allow them close enough to speak were they so armed.

Aras confidently led them over the ground his feet knew so well. Thirty-four years had passed, but it was as if it were only yesterday.

He and Leonas easily spotted the Hill People sentries, scouts, and patrols on the bare and rocky hills and avoided them effortlessly, passing unchallenged all the way to the valley. They arrived as dawn was breaking.

Aras was surprised at what they found. He had thought the city of the Hill People would have grown to fill the valley by now, but it was only slightly larger than before. It brightened his heart to see the remaining trees from before were still preserved. He wondered if the knife was still hidden amongst them. He thought of the black-haired girl and the sweet smile he could still picture so clearly, and on impulse led Leonas to the spot he'd seen her last, every tree that had marked the location still vivid in his memory, though they were older and the trunks broader and taller than before.

The hollow was still there, beneath the tree, exactly as he remembered it. But when he reached inside breathlessly, his fingers encountered something entirely unexpected. It was half buried in the soil of the hollow, as if it had lain there undisturbed for many years. He pulled it out and brushed the dirt off and fingered it curiously: it was a necklace of carnelian. After a brief hesitation, he resolutely tucked it into his shirt and wordlessly motioned to Leonas to continue their journey.

They reached the edge of the wood and again viewed the City. But the light was brighter and they were closer, and now he saw something was terribly wrong.

It was summer, and the fields here should have been lush and green and filled with the bright colors of ripe vegetables ready for harvesting, as his own people's were. But everywhere he looked there were only thick brown masses of dead plants. The irrigation channels still flowed with water from the stream—there was water here, not drought—but all the crops were dead.

It was there, on the edge of the wood, while their attention was on the fields, that they were discovered. Suddenly, there was a cry from behind them, and the sound of swords being drawn.

Aras spun about and raised his weaponless hands in the air, the white cloth Lunahr had advised him to bring in his hand. "We come in truce, to speak with your Chief," he called out clearly in Common.

There were four men before him, and they looked from his hand to his face with dark, suspicious eyes and upraised swords. Then one of the men's eyes widened as if in recognition and abruptly narrowed in hate. *"Yehorog! Taka rog!"* he yelled and his sword flashed toward Aras.

Aras jumped nimbly backward and the sword slashed empty air where he had been. "We come in peace! We do not wish to fight!" Aras cried desperately. He did not draw his own blades, but he heard Leonas draw, and the clang of metal on metal behind him.

"Kata nu paten!" another voice barked in a commanding tone.

Something cracked hard against the back of Aras's head, and he felt an explosion of pain and then nothing.

WAKEFULNESS was slow in coming and with it came pain and memory of disaster. The Hill People had done nothing Aras had expected. Leonas and Lunahr had been right. He'd been a fool to come! He and Leonas would die for his mistake, and the men here would soon follow them, once their crime was discovered. Aras realized in dawning horror that he might well have condemned not only the men of this city to death, but the women and children as well. His father might well not allow the progeny of any of the Hill People to live, if his own son was slain.

Aras opened his eyes slowly and began taking careful stock of both himself and his surroundings. His head felt as if it had been cracked in two. He could not tell if it was bleeding. He was lying on a smooth floor made of neatly joined planks of wood, his arms tied behind his back around what felt to be a thick wooden beam. His hands felt numb, and his arms ached as if he'd lain this way for a long time. He realized then that he must not be bleeding, or at least not too badly, or he would have already died. He did not seem to be injured elsewhere, though it was difficult to tell for certain. He realized in dismay that his swords and dagger were gone, as well as his pack.

He pushed himself up with his right elbow and closed his eyes against the ensuing wave of nausea, but that only made it worse. He opened his eyes again, bracing his back against the beam, refusing to slide back down as his body begged him to. He focused his gaze upon the floor and began counting every growth ring on the plank of the murdered tree below his face, able to read only part of the story of the proud life that had been so callously and abruptly ended. As his own might soon be.

The dizziness had not quite passed, but he resolutely looked up again, far more slowly and cautiously this time, shifting his head in minute increments. He was in a large, windowless room made entirely of wood: walls, floor, and ceiling. Wooden beams like the one he was bound to were interspersed evenly throughout the room, from floor to ceiling. There was a single door, which was closed. The only light came from a small oil lamp set on the bare floor in the middle of the room. The room was empty of any goods or furnishings. It might be a meeting room or a storage room.

He realized he was completely alone and his heart raced. Where was Leonas? There was memory of the sounds of clashing swords, of pain, then nothing. Was brave Leonas alive or dead, free or captured? If a captive, should he not be tied here to one of the beams beside him? Aras feared the worst: that his foolish plan had cost his friend's life and that he would perhaps soon follow him.

The door opened without warning and a woman entered his prison. Her black hair fell past her waist, contrasting dramatically with the ankle-length sleeveless red dress, which billowed about her with every brisk stride. She was leanly muscled and barbarically beautiful. She was not alone. The man with the sword who had attacked him was there beside her, with the three others he had seen. All five of them glared at him with hate-filled eyes as they approached.

"We come in peace, under white cloth of truce, to speak with your Chief," Aras said, in Common, his voice coarse, his mouth dry.

The woman's eyes narrowed as she approached. She stood looking down at him, her eyes cold and cruel. "Those without honor have no voice to speak their poisoned words. They only have voice to scream," she threatened in Common.

Her tone and words chilled him, but gave him frantic hope as well. "You can understand my words! I come to you under cloth of truce, with water and bread of peace." He must make her understand!

The cold hatred in her eyes flared to burning fury. "Water and bread! You poison our fields, kill our farmers, and then bring us bread!" She laughed, but it was joyless and horrible to hear. She pulled out a knife from her belt, slowly, deliberately, and began weaving it sinuously before his eyes. "I will cut the lying tongue from your head last, for first I will hear you scream."

She grabbed Aras by the shirt and he saw no compassion or mercy in her intelligent eyes, only the long, tortuous death she planned for him. He was truly terrified. He could not die here, like this! He tried to focus his Power upon her, but gasped as pain stabbed through his head like a pike, and he fought another wave of dizziness, far worse than the first.

She held the blade before his eyes, turning it slowly, taunting him with his doom. He looked in wide-eyed fear of what was to come, at the red-tinted copper glint of the blade, as if it had already been dipped in blood, at the black of the hilt that fit her hand so well. Suddenly he recognized it, the double shock of recognition almost paralyzing him. It was the blade from thirty-four years ago, but it was also the stunted twin of the sword Dewalaren wielded!

"Would you hurt one who came to you as friend? I have your necklace!" he cried desperately, clinging to the faint hope that his words might bring doubt and talk instead of torture and death. Could this truly be the same girl, now a woman grown, he had seen so long ago? She was not nearly as old as she should look, were it her—her face was unwrinkled and her hair not graying with age—but neither was she as young as one of his people would be. He studied her face carefully. It could indeed be her.

The woman stared at him just as intently. "No, you cannot be. He never claimed my token."

"I had not returned until now. I claimed it today. It is in my shirt." His eyes widened with dismay, as he realized he did not feel it against his skin. "It was, I swear! It must have fallen out, when I was brought here. Please you must believe me! For the sake of both our peoples you have to listen!"

She said something to the men around her. The one who had first attacked responded to her and pulled forth the red necklace with obvious suspicion and reluctance.

She gaped at it in disbelief, reached for it, and held it tightly against her heart. Then she stared intently at him again and shook her head. "No. It cannot be you. You are too young."

He swallowed. "I am an Elf. We do not age as Men do." Nor did she, it would seem, though she certainly appeared older than he did.

Her voice was hard. "That was many years ago. If you had come then, I would have welcomed you. But now you poison our fields and kill our farmers and our warriors with your Demon Weapon."

"We did not poison your fields, I nor my people, and I have no demon weapon," Aras denied.

She gestured and one of the other men pulled two arrows from a bag that was slung over his shoulder, which she held out for him to see. "Do you deny these are yours? You wielded ones like these many days ago, when you attacked our warriors, although some bore feathers of white and others gray."

Aras saw the two arrows were fletched in gray like his own, but both bore the mark of the King's Guard upon them. The Guard's symbol was distinctly different. Neither he nor anyone else in that battle would have used them. "I carry a bow and use arrows similar to these, but these bear the mark of the King's Guard, the Army. They do not patrol our borders. Only the Guard, the Navy, do. The King's Guard has only walked these hills once, thirty-four years ago, to bring me home. Yet these are new. Where did you find them?"

"In the bodies of the women you killed, in our fields, the night you poisoned our land, killing our crops and deer. I bring them to return them to you. One for each eye," she said coldly.

Aras felt ill then with fear as his eyes widened in dawning horror. Ahrnad! He knew how to find this City. He'd been here before. And he had apparently come again and worked great evil here.

Aras spoke desperately. "Please! I have walked into danger to try to end this War between our peoples. I see now it has been falsely begun. We share a common Enemy. He has brought you to the edge of famine and laid the blame on us so that you would attack us. Now we fight you, for you attack us in our own Wood, in our home. He plays us one against the other to weaken us both, ere he strikes. How can I convince you I speak the truth?"

"If you are the one who came to the woods those many years ago, what did you do when I left?" she asked, coolly.

"The King's Guard had come to take me home. I commanded them not to hurt you and after you ran, I told them they must wait. I remembered watching you approach, as if in secret, as if in danger. I saw you pull the knife from under the tree. And I saw terror in your face when I discovered you, but then your eyes softened, and I realized it was because I was not the one you feared. Then you smiled at me. I thought if the knife were left on the ground, it might mean danger for you. So I put it back in its hiding place and followed your tracks and concealed them as I walked to where I saw you mask your own. I helped you as much as I could, before I left. I meant to return, but I was forbidden. I am still forbidden, but I come now anyway."

"You did not know me. Why keep me safe?" she asked shrewdly.

"Because it was my fault you were in further danger. You dropped the knife because of the King's Guard, and they had come for me, so I was responsible for your safety," Aras said without hesitation.

"Your words are those of one who knows honor, or once has known it," she admitted grudgingly and eyed him shrewdly again. She said something in her own guttural language to the men beside her.

Aras followed the two men with his eyes as they left the room, regretting it instantly when he made the mistake of turning his head as well, when they would have left his field of vision. If only Jarnath were here to tend to him! No, he would never wish Jarnath to be brought to danger because of him, though his very existence endangered the healer he yet loved as a father.

Aras watched the door anxiously, both curious and afraid. What had she told them? Where had they gone?

A few moments later, the door opened again and the two men returned, with four others surrounding them, all well armed, alert, and angry looking. The two men were dragging someone between them. They dropped him roughly to the ground at the base of the post to Aras's right. His head lolled limply as they tied him to it, a cascade of silver hair masking half his face, but not enough so that Aras didn't recognize him.

Aras's heart pounded. It was Leonas! He had thought him dead. He was limp and appeared lifeless as they tied him to the beam. But they would not tie him to it if he were not alive, would they? Unless they only wished him to believe Leonas yet lived. He watched intently, unable to hear his friend's thoughts, if any, for the pain lancing through his head. There! He breathed! Aras felt weak with relief at the simple rise and fall of his friend's chest.

"Leonas! It's me, Aras! Can you hear me?" he asked, in Elvish. Everyone learned Common as part of their training, but if Leonas was badly injured, he might not recognize Aras's voice and think he was being tricked and not respond.

At the sound of his voice, Leonas bolted upright, fully alert, his body tensing for action, and Aras realized he had only been pretending to be unconscious. The woman seemed both surprised and impressed as she spoke a few incomprehensible words to the men.

"Highness! I saw you fall, I thought you slain!" Leonas cried and there were tears in his eyes.

"I see the two of you are friends," the woman said, a hint of speculation in her voice as she moved so that Aras could see both her and Leonas without needing to shift his own position. She was eyeing them both appraisingly.

"I feared he was dead," Aras readily admitted in Common, his voice shaking with emotion.

The woman looked at them both coolly. "I thought to kill this one, for he is useless to me if he cannot speak, but I see now he is awake also. Can he speak this tongue?"

"I can speak it," Leonas replied to her directly in Common, eyeing her suspiciously.

"Good. Then you will be able to beg as well. I need only one prisoner. The other will die. I will let you choose between you who lives and who dies. But you must choose quickly, or I will choose for you."

Aras and Leonas looked at each other, stricken. "I will die," they both said simultaneously, without hesitation.

Aras shook his head and regretted it immediately, for the pain. "No, Leonas. It is my fault you are here. I asked you to come. I forced you to. You must...." His voice broke and then he continued on bravely, "You must take care of Beryl for me." He would not speak Lunahr's given name here.

"Highness, no!" Leonas said in Common, turning to the woman. "He is our High-Prince. He is a far more valuable prisoner than I am. I am only one of the Guard. I knew the danger I faced when I came. I will gladly give my life if I know it will save his. So if you would hear me beg, I beg only for him, that you will not harm him and that you will listen to him, for he has risked much in coming to you. And I beg for your sake, as well, for if he dies, his father will bring our combined Army and Navy to crush you, and we are thousands strong. He will obliterate this City and everyone who dwells here."

Aras said proudly to the woman, "As High-Prince, I claim the right to die for one of my people. Leonas is here because I commanded him to follow. I will not have him die for his loyalty."

Aras turned to Leonas. "I command you to silence. You will not speak again until after I am dead." His voice was suddenly firm with power as he spoke not with the voice of a friend, but that of the High-Prince. Aras feared that Leonas had already spoken too skillfully and that he would be chosen for death, for he was right. As a hostage, Aras was a far more valuable bargaining chip than Leonas could ever be.

Leonas drew himself up straighter and exhaled loudly. "Then my last words are treason, for I cannot keep silent and let you die." He turned back to the woman. "I am ready. Kill me slowly or swiftly, it matters not to me.

Only… if you would grant a dying man a last request, I ask only that you not make him watch." Leonas met her eyes bravely.

Aras desperately implored the woman before him. "He speaks out of his love for me, as I for him. How can my death or his end this War? And it must end, or both our peoples will perish! I can see your life in these hills has made you hard. But I have friends such as you who are hard but kind, and strong but compassionate. Do not mistake coldness for strength! Can you not remember the clear-eyed girl you once were, who smiled at me in friendship those many years ago?"

Unexpectedly, she smiled at him then, a smile of triumph. "You have passed my test! You have both proven yourselves men of honor." She looked at Aras shrewdly. "I did not know I held the son of my enemy's King as hostage. But I think you are to play a different role, now. I will meet with you under cloth of truce, and we will break bread together, and I will hear your words. And we will have to eat the bread you offered, for we have none."

She reached behind Aras and cut his bonds with her knife and then Leonas's as well. Aras rubbed his wrists with dead hands, dazed, for hope had suddenly sprung from despair. To his relief, tiny needles of pain almost immediately shot into his hands as the feeling began to return. Leonas rose upon unsteady feet and then knelt in front of Aras, who was still seated upon the floor. "Forgive me for my traitorous words, Highness."

Aras placed his tingling hand upon his shoulder. "Should I forgive you for loving me, or for offering your life for mine, even as you had warned me you would ere we left? There is nothing to forgive. Rise, my friend," he said, and they stood together, Aras's hand still firmly upon Leonas's shoulder.

Leonas flicked a concerned glance at his face but then kept his expression impassive as he bore Aras's weight upon his shoulder, obviously realizing belatedly that the gesture was not only one of camaraderie but also a mute cry for assistance.

Aras released his hold as soon as he was upright, focusing all his will upon walking and not vomiting as agony ripped through his skull like fire, his head swam dizzily, and his stomach churned. He hoped it might only be the pain from his injury that so debilitated him, that he did not have a concussion from the blow. He could ill afford to be incapacitated at such a crucial juncture.

They were led outside by the woman, surrounded by the eight guards. Aras was concerned to see it was nearly dusk. He had been unconscious for a long time, indeed.

They were led to another building, long and low. Here there were colorful cushions and rugs on the wooden floor, brightly hued, intricate tapestries on the walls, and a long, low table. The woman sat cross-legged on a cushion on the floor at the table and waved for them to be seated, and Aras sank slowly downward gratefully, Leonas's hand not straying far, in case he needed further assistance.

Four young women entered with copper basins and sponges and bathed Aras's and Leonas's faces and hands with scented, oiled water and then rolled up their sleeves and massaged their sore arms, wrists, and hands. They both withstood the soothing yet intrusive ministrations without complaint. Aras was relieved when the tingling in his hands finally stopped. He only wished the pain in his head might ease as well. He could scarcely think.

Finely crafted plates of brass were brought, and cups, but no food or water.

One of the young women produced Aras's pack from a wooden chest against one wall. She handed it to Aras. Aras looked at the older woman who had spoken to him before for permission to open it, and she tilted her head in the briefest of nods. He opened the pack and saw at once that it had been searched. He produced a loaf of raeta and one of the pouches of water he had brought and laid them on the table between them. "We bring you bread and water and ask that you eat and drink with us under cloth of temporary truce, so that we might find a more lasting peace between our peoples," Aras intoned in Common.

The dark-eyed woman spoke solemnly. "My name is Shadala. I am Chieftess and Healer of the Urwani and speak for them."

She gazed intently at Aras and he replied, hoping it was the right thing to say. "My name is Aras, son of High-King Laedrin of Nalea. As High-Prince, I speak for my people." He did not say he spoke for his father, because he knew he did not.

Shadala turned to Leonas, surprising both of them. "My name is Leonas, Guardsman, on special assignment to the High-Prince as guard and companion to his friend, Beryl. I am also companion and friend to the High-Prince. I can speak only for myself."

She nodded, satisfied.

Aras unwrapped one of the raeta loaves. "This is *raeta*, the field rations we eat. A loaf this size can sustain one of my people for seven days. We can split this loaf here amongst us, but I also have eleven more. If your people are hungry, I offer the rest to you, as a sign of friendship." He held out the pack to her. "You may take a piece from any of the loaves within or the one before us, and I will show you it is safe to eat."

She waved her hand toward the one he had already unwrapped. He broke off a piece and ate it without hesitation. When she broke off a piece the eight guards tensed. The one who had attacked him appeared ready to protest, but he remained silent. She ate the bread, chewing and swallowing deliberately, and then offered it to Leonas, who also ate a piece.

"We accept this offer of truce," she said solemnly. "We also accept your gift to my people." She turned to one of the four young women and intoned something in her guttural language, and the pack containing the bread was borne swiftly away.

"You do not speak of it, but I see you with a Healer's eyes. Your head pains you."

"It does," Aras admitted.

"Then may I minister to you and your friend with a Healer's hands, ere we begin? For pain can cloud judgment and we need clear heads for this task."

"I would be most grateful," Aras said sincerely.

She touched his face gently and an empathic scowl of pain creased her brow, as if she were Jarnath and could truly feel his injury as if it were her own. Then she touched the back of his head and they both hissed in pain. Leonas half rose from his seat, and the guards immediately tensed, the most aggressive of them calling out angrily in accusation.

Shadala snatched her hand away and barked angrily at the guards, who immediately stilled and then resumed their original positions.

Aras froze as well, from shock, rather than the Power of her voice, though Power there was. When Dewalaren had cried **"Hold!"** using the full force of his Power to stem the panic during the test of Rion's guardsmen in Athanark, he had felt such a wave of Power, Power akin to his own yet less intense. Now, as then, it washed harmlessly over him, but it was unmistakable. He had wondered before how the dagger might have come into her possession. Now he realized that, remarkable as it seemed, Shadala and perhaps some of the others here might in fact be kinsmen to Dewalaren.

"Aras?" Leonas asked warily.

"I am fine," Aras assured him.

"Forgive me. I had not realized the severity of your pain or the effort it has cost you to speak," she said, contradicting his words. "A lesser warrior would yet be incapacitated. Now that I am better prepared, I can assist you without harming myself," she said in Common. Then she spoke to the others in her native tongue, possibly repeating what she had said, for the men seemed less hostile, and even marginally impressed. The four young women appeared even more so. Only then did he realize they were also armed, as he saw one of them surreptitiously sheathing a dagger she had drawn in defense of her Chieftess.

Shadala drew forth a small tin of ointment from a pouch concealed within the folds of her dress and dipped her finger into it and applied it on the sore spot on the back of his head. He felt the area quickly grow numb, but the numbness did not spread to cloud his mind. Then she pulled out a small metal bottle sealed with wax, opened it, and handed it to him. "You must drink, all of it. It will settle your stomach and also alleviate the dizziness," she promised.

Aras accepted it and drank without hesitation, though he would have liked to drink it slowly, so he could try to analyze what was inside. He did not want to appear as if he did not trust her.

"While we wait for it to take effect, I will tend to the cuts and scrapes upon you and Leonas," she said. She tended to both of them, laying a hand to his stomach and then his head, before she examined and treated his minor injuries. He felt a familiar healing warmth emanate from her hand and fought to hide his astonishment. He had been right! She indeed shared Jarnath's gift!

To Aras's intense relief, under the combination of the elixir she had given him, the ointment, which was apparently some sort of anesthetic salve, and her own healing hand, the effects of his injury vanished as if it had never been. He was certain he would even be able to use his Power again, if there was need, though he dared not attempt to do so unless the need was dire. He could not risk that she might sense it and feel endangered by it.

"Already I see a benefit your friendship might bring to us," Aras said. "The medicines you use are unknown to me. Perhaps I can teach you some new medicines as well."

Her eyes were suddenly intent upon his face, flaring with an emotion he could not name. "Then, as Prince, you are also Healer? Does your sister then lead your warriors into battle?"

"I have no sister. And, as I am High-Prince, I cannot be named healer," he said. He saw the light fade from her eyes, and belatedly realized it had been the light of hope he had seen. He quickly added, "But I have been taught the skills of a healer, by our wisest one, and I was told by him that I have the hands of a healer, and have used them with such skill before. And I brought my medicines with me, for I thought I or my friend might have need of them, and I have learned not to walk into danger ill supplied."

"Then ere we speak, I would have you help one your people have harmed, if you can. For he is dear to me and he is dying. And if he might instead live, my own mind would be more clear of pain and I might hear you better." She called out to one of the young women, in the voice of command. The woman left the room and returned moments later with his pack. It was empty of the raeta now, but the healer's pouch was still inside.

"Come," Shadala commanded. She rose, and Aras rose quickly as well, as did Leonas. They left the building they had been in, trailed by the eight guards and four young women, and walked to another building. There were a number of guards at the door, and they stiffened in outrage and glared at Aras and Leonas in fury, with hands on their swords. There was a chorus of voices raised in anger, and more than once Aras heard the word *Yehorog*.

Shadala spoke with a voice of harsh command, though without the wave of Power, in her own strange tongue. The guards let them pass, but they glared at them with hate-filled eyes and joined the others, following them when they entered the room. Inside, it was similar to where they had been, except the room was much smaller and there was a bed in addition to the low table and wooden chests and tapestries. There was also a fire pit in the center of the room, beneath a hole in the roof, with a low-burning fire and a pot hung on a metal hook over it.

A man lay on the bed, much younger than Shadala. His features resembled hers strongly, his cheekbones and jaw and eyes. He would have been handsome, but his brown eyes were open but unseeing and shone too brightly, his face bore the reddish tinge of fever, and he was moaning and thrashing weakly. A young woman was tending to him, pressing a wet cloth to his face and murmuring soothingly to him. She turned as they entered and Aras silenced a gasp of surprise. She could have been Shadala herself, frozen in time from decades before, save she was perhaps a handful of years older than the girl he had met in the woods.

She cried out in rage and fear when she saw them, and stood protectively between them and the bed, questioning Shadala in a sharp tongue. Was she Shadala's daughter? Was the man who was dying Shadala's son?

Shadala did not speak harshly to the young women. She instead held her by the arms and talked intently with her. The young woman shook her head violently and Shadala shook her gently and spoke again. The young woman's eyes filled with tears and she began to weep. Shadala hugged her tightly and said to Aras, "You may see to him, now."

Aras stepped carefully around them and walked over to the bed. He laid his hand upon his patient's brow. The man was burning with fever, exactly as Dewalaren had been, in the wolven den. Aras examined him carefully and saw a clean white bandage about the left side of his chest.

"He is my brother's son, Veran, Warrior Captain. This is his sister, Falara. The day my people first saw you, and named you, you attacked sixteen of them with your Demon Weapon. Four you injured with sticks with gray feathers and twelve with sticks with white feathers. The four injured with gray-feathered sticks sickened and died from their wounds. I was powerless to aid them. Their deaths were long and painful: it took them four days to die, it stole their reason from them, and they burned with fire until it consumed them. The other twelve were spared and recovered quickly from their injury. We still do not understand why you condemned those four to such a horrible death, but let the others live.

"Four days ago, Veran was wounded by a Demon Stick as well. Many others were, but none of the others have sickened. We have all been consumed by rage as we have watched him succumb to the fire of illness, knowing that tonight he is fated to die. But now you are here and speak words of peace, so we hope you might lift the curse from him."

Aras swallowed hard, his heart heavy with guilt and grief. If that is what they believed, it was truly a wonder that he was not already dead. "I did not choose death for any of those I injured. I did not want to kill them. I tried only to injure them so they would drop their weapons and flee, and they did so. When I left, we were not at war with your people. I had hoped, I still hope, that we might yet find peace. But peace is harder with each death, with each family member and friend that grieves and thirsts for revenge. I had used the gray-fletched arrows before and they must have been unclean. The white-fletched arrows were not tainted. I do not know what is wrong with Veran, but I will do my best to discover it."

Aras realized then to his horror that he had also shot Hunter with one of those arrows. He feared the older cousin Dewalaren loved as dearly as he loved Lunahr might have unintentionally died by his hand before ever reaching Tanieria. But he could not allow himself to be distracted by that now, with so much else held in the balance here. First, he must try to discover why Veran was not recovering. "Do you have the arrow that wounded him?"

Shadala nodded and brought it to him. It was one of the Guard's arrows. He had feared that this too might be Ahrnad's work, that the arrow might have been poisoned, in spite of the similarity to the previous injuries, but Ahrnad would never lower himself by using the weapon of the Guards he despised. Aras studied the arrowhead intently and saw that the tip of one of the barbs was missing. He pointed to it. "The tip of this part of the arrowhead broke off when the arrow was removed and must still be in the wound. That may be why the wound festers. I must remove that piece, if I can, and then clean the wound and use my medicines." He swallowed. "I will need a knife to do so and I think it would be best that Falara not watch this."

He wished for his own pallenteum knife, but he had let Lunahr use it and still had not cleansed it yet, and it would have been impossible to replace with one of the same caliber.

Shadala studied him keenly. Then she spoke to the guards and to Falara. The guards reluctantly began to leave, save for the one who seemed to hate him above the rest, and Falara appeared to refuse to go as well. Shadala spoke to her far more harshly in a voice of command, and the young woman screamed back at her. Shadala commanded the reluctant guardsman, and he called out, stopping three of the others, who came back. He uttered two words and all four men seized Falara. She fought like a pumar, clawing and hissing and growling, but they carried her from the room, Shadala following them, to close the door firmly behind them, bolting it from within. Then she returned to them.

Shadala reached out, ran her fingers through Veran's wet hair, and kissed his brow. Aras knew Veran's skin must burn like fire against her lips. Tears filled his eyes, and when he spoke, his voice was filled with anguish. "I am sorry. I do not ask your forgiveness. I understand now why your people's eyes are filled with hate, for we must seem only bringers of torture and death to you."

Shadala looked at him in surprised approval. "You cry as if it is your own kinsman who lies dying. You truly see with a Healer's eyes and feel with a Healer's heart. We should not dwell in the past, when you now bring us hope for the future. I trust you will do all you can to save him."

Aras took a deep breath and nodded. He must not fail. "Leonas, boil some water for me, this much," Aras said, showing him a closed fist as he gestured to the fire. Leonas squirted the required amount into the pot from his water pouch and began heating it.

Aras took a pouch from his healer's kit, this one containing anosar, one of his people's rare and precious elixirs that would promote healing and restore strength. "This is for strength," he said simply, and squirted the clear liquid into the Man's mouth, massaging his throat until he swallowed. He ensured Veran drank only three small sips. Any more would be far too dangerous, even for one of his people.

Belatedly, he realized a Man should perhaps consume a smaller dose. But he sensed Power in this Man, akin to Dewalaren's or Lunahr's or Shadala's or that of a Lord of his own people, so he hoped no ill would come of it. He wished Jarnath were here beside him, guiding him. Jarnath would not make mistakes.

Aras washed his hands in water from one of his pouches, and then again, in alcohol. Then he unwrapped Veran's wound. It had started to heal, but poorly. The skin around the injury was puffy, red, inflamed, and puckered, and it was leaking a foul-smelling yellow discharge. The infection and resulting fever as the Man's body vainly tried to combat it could well prove deadly. Aras pulled three powders from various pouches, and separated out the proper amounts of two of them into a small bowl. He called Leonas over and instructed him to mix them into the boiling water, stirring them until they thickened to a syrup-like consistency and then allowing the mixture to cool until it might be safe to drink. Leonas set about to do as he commanded.

"I will need the use of a knife," he said to Shadala. He thought she might return his own and was astonished when she instead handed him her red blade, intoning something over it as she did so.

He studied it intently. It truly was cousin to Dewalaren's blade. He must find out where and how she had acquired it, and learn all he could of the history of her family line, but later.

Aras sterilized the knife with the alcohol. "I must find the broken tip. It will cause him pain, and the wound will bleed anew, but it must in any case. We must drain the infection from it."

She nodded solemnly. "I have done so before, to little avail. I have used all my talent and all the medicines I know, but it has not been enough. Do what you must. I swear no harm will come to you or your friend, regardless of the outcome, as long as you truly seek to help him."

Aras was moved by her trust. He knew that in her position, if this was Dewalaren or Lunahr lying here so gravely ill, he would not have found it so easy to trust or to forgive. He cut carefully into the wound. Veran moaned louder and struggled feebly. Before Aras could ask her to, Shadala clamped her hands about her nephew's shoulders, so that he would lie still.

"Thank you," he said as he felt around in the wound carefully with the tip of the blade. He found nothing. He must risk using his Power and hope it did not cause her alarm.

He closed his eyes and slowly extended his Power into the blade. The effect was as instantaneous and as devastating as if he had been struck by lightning. He nearly dropped the knife as his mind was bombarded with a host of images, betraying the twisted history of the blade:

THE sklabos colier *and* catena subdere, *slave collar and chains of subduing, forged by Escolier from pyrenteum, the metal he invented to bind the powerful* Houerfashang *he had created, those he should have loved as sons and daughters, fated instead to be controlled and contained, to serve as pleasure slaves at the often merciless whims of their morally corrupt masters;*

Pyrfier, a collared and chained Faeren slave boy, Escolier's greatest work, sexually and physically abused with sadistic and methodically violent brutality, driven well beyond the brink of madness by his master, the respectable deviant Potereth, one of the elite Council of their lost Homeland;

The escape of Pyrfier and reforging of the manacles that once imprisoned him into a weapon of revenge;

The death screams of millions yet resonating through the pyrenteum, as the former bindings turned weapon incinerated all those who had betrayed the mad Faeren man-child, and every other man, woman, child, plant, and creature upon their lost Homeland, as the continent vaporized and the oceans surrounding it turned to steam;

The terrible weapon stolen by Escolier, as Pyrfier basked in the lie of his creator's love as they were drowning;

The weapon reforged by Escolier into a knife meant only for healing, never again for harm, in his grief and guilt, powered by the tainted gem-battery containing the life essence of all who had perished when their Homeland was destroyed;

The healing knife gifted to his new children, to the first King of Amontir, and every King thereafter, ending with Albinar, so they might ever heal their people and protect them from all harm, in Escolier's desperate need for penance, absolution, recognition, attention, companionship, worship, and Power;

The theft of the King's Knife by King Albinar's younger brother Ebonar, who in thrall to Pyrfier slew his own beloved brother;

The reclaiming of the King's Knife by Ebonar's son Idare, who gifted it to his cousin, his murdered uncle's middle son, Alanar, as they and their people fled from Pyrfier's madness;

The death of Alanar, his body broken in battle, beyond the Power of the King's Knife to heal, without the Power of the gem-battery imbedded in the King's Ring to power the intricate crystal mechanism of healing within;

The line of children and adults who had held the Knife since, descendants of the ten Great Houses of Amontir Alanar led, their blood mixing with that of the Urwani who had succored them, until the blade finally passed to Shadala, who yet awaited with all her people the coming of their lost King.

ARAS blinked, uncomprehending for a moment, until Leonas's concerned face coalesced before his eyes and the strange babble of sound became recognizable as words spoken in a familiar voice. "Highness! Highness, are you all right?"

"I'm fine," Aras assured Leonas distractedly. They were Amontir! All of them, not only Shadala, but nearly the entire tribe, this City: three quarters of the men, women, and children were of Amontiri blood! Incuban could not possibly suspect the truth, that hundreds of Dewalaren's people yet lived, or he would not have sent Ahrnad to murder some and bring the rest to the brink of starvation. He would have instead descended with his entire Revenant army and engulfed them.

He turned his dazed gaze to Shadala, but she spoke before he could. "I did not realize, until I saw your eyes, your face, the understanding, the horror, the grief. You saw the visions of the history of the blade as if you were a War Chief born, yet you have the skills of a Chieftess and Healer. You truly are both, as you spoke it to me. I would not have believed one who was not of my people might have such Power, but I was right to trust you with the Knife.

"There will be time to speak of it later, but I fear Veran's breaths are numbered. Please, if you can suppress the images that haunt the blade and draw upon the hidden Power of the Knife, you might yet heal the son-of-my-heart. I have tried, but my Power, though the strongest of any of us who yet live, save perhaps for that of my brother, is not strong enough to work the magic of the Knife. None since Alanar have been able to do so. We had believed only the King's heir might."

"I am not your King's heir, though it is my great honor to know him, and I will gladly introduce you to him, when he returns from his quest," Aras swore.

Shadala's eyes widened in shock and hope and she opened her mouth as if to speak, but remained silent.

Marshaling his hopes and fears and thoughts, Aras set about mentally constructing a shield that might protect him from being overwhelmed once more by the fell history of the blade while yet allowing him to wield his Power through it.

Once more he extended his Power into the blade. This time it was carefully channeled to no ill effect, the images safely diverted by the shield. He painstakingly probed the wound, pressing deeply for the shard of metal. Veran's own body guided him to it, crying out against the invader that had poisoned it. It was child's play to feel the most minute resistance to the blade, to work the tiny fragment from deep within the wound to the surface. Veran's body was eager to expel it, desperate to heal, yet so terribly weak, it was a wonder he yet lived. Only his iron will kept him alive, even as his body failed.

Aras saw the small, dark fleck amidst the purulent discharge of the septic wound. He wiped the blade clean with a fresh bandage and then thoroughly cleaned the wound with alcohol. He applied the green powder he had opened before to the wound, and it sizzled and bubbled in the fresh blood.

He requested the elixir he had Leonas prepare, and he tilted back Veran's head and made him drink the liquid, which was dark red and viscous now. It looked like blood. "The powders come from plants," he assured Shadala. "I will show you how to collect them, and prepare them, once our people are at peace. They are for the fever."

She studied him intently, her eyes filled with hope and with challenge. "It will not be enough. He will die without the aid of the King's Knife."

Aras feared she was right. But he also feared the taint of the blade's history might endanger him, were he to truly activate it. Yet if Veran died, many of his people might soon follow. Veran moaned, scarcely a whisper of sound upon his tortured breath, deciding the matter for him in an instant. He could not watch another suffer and die without doing all he could to help.

Taking a deep breath, Aras extended his will into the Knife once more, this time channeling the Power upward into the hilt, rather than downward, into the blade. The crystalline mechanism was so elegant and ancient, so intricate yet simple, so beautiful and innocent looking, yet so powerful. This Knife was not a thing of evil, in spite of the dark history of its components.

He pressed the flat of the blade against the wound and activated the hidden mechanism with a thought. The effect was instantaneous. Aras could feel every bone and muscle and tendon and nerve in Veran, the blood coursing through artery and vein, the very air within the blood and more.

He gasped in wonder as the infection washed away, as polluted blood was cleansed, as severed muscle and torn flesh knitted together whole once more, as if never damaged. He listened in joy as Veran's proud heartbeat, all but stilled, grew strong again, as he breathed regularly and deeply. He drew the Knife away from his shoulder and wiped the area clean from unmarred skin that fairly glowed with health. There was no sign he had ever been injured.

"Veran!" Shadala said, calling his name and stroking his face, but he did not awaken. Worry clouded her face as her eyes lost their focus and then focused upon his face once more. "He broke his bonds to us, to Falara and me and Haran and Goturan, and erected a shield against us, when he realized he was dying. He feared what we might do to save him. His core flares brightly once more, but the shield is yet there. It is not something we speak of to others, yet you are as one of us, you know of what I speak. He cannot feel or hear me. Why does he not awaken?"

Aras was relieved that she sounded only concerned rather than suspicious. "I felt the healing Power of the blade. It is like that which you wield, or my mentor, Jarnath. Such a healing drains the healer, but also, there is a small, harmless price, a toll the patient must pay for undergoing such a healing. Veran's body is in shock from the grave nature of his previous state and the speed of the healing which has restored him. He will likely sleep for the night, or perhaps even the night and the day, but he will awaken. And once he sees he does not endanger you by it, I am sure he will allow you all to renew your bonds to him." Aras returned the Knife to her, though he ached to keep it, to study it, to learn how to replicate the fantastic mechanism within.

"Come, we must talk more, that we may begin to understand one another. Falara will watch over Veran." They left the building, and the guards glared at him with hate-filled eyes. Falara struggled against them anew, her comely face twisted with anguish and hate. Shadala spoke to her and the guards in her own tongue, her voice warm with joy. The guards released her as Falara's eyes widened in shock and hope, as did the eyes of those around her. She and the guard who had tried to kill him ran inside.

Shadala spoke again, a long dialogue. The remaining warriors listened intently. They went inside the room and emerged almost immediately. Then two of them left, moving quickly, as if on an important mission of some sort.

"All will be well now," Shadala assured him. "Come."

She led him and Leonas to the building they had left before, with the tapestries and table. Aras noted two beds had been added to the room, near the wall, and wondered why.

They sat again and Shadala said, "First, I would teach you our way, for your own is far different. I am Chieftess and Healer, as I have said. My brother, Haran, is War Chief. His son, Veran, is Warrior Captain and Falara, his sister, is Healer in Training. When my brother and I die, Veran and Falara are to become War Chief and Chieftess and Healer. Then, if either of them have both a male and female child, they will in turn become War Chief and Chieftess and Healer. If they do not, the line is broken, and another pair with Power must be chosen to be trained. It is our way.

"The men you see here are all commanded by Veran, and they follow him and fight for him. For all he is so young, he is a fine Warrior Captain, intelligent, brave and strong but also compassionate. He has saved many of them from death at the hands of your people. He was wounded saving Goturan, the man who attacked you with his sword. They are like brothers. But all his men love him and would die for him. Instead, they have been watching him die, unable to aid him."

Aras said in dismay, "Then he is also your Prince!"

Shadala nodded. "And, if he were to die, Falara could not become Chieftess and Healer. But your way sounds much different. Tell me of your people."

Aras had wondered before why Shadala had not used her Power at its fullest to heal her nephew, though it would likely have cost her own life. He realized now that her death would have also cost her brother his position as War Chief, and more, that Veran's sense of honor and obligation to his people would likely not have allowed him to live, were his aunt to have died for him and his father to have lost his position. Shadala had been in an untenable position, and he knew it must have been agony for her.

Aras swallowed and spoke. "As I have said, we are Elves, not Men. We do not age as Men do, or even as your people. We do not age much at all. I am barely an adult, to Elven eyes. Elves come-of-age at forty-nine. I came-of-age only a few short months ago. I understand coming-of-age for most Men is sixteen. I suspect it might be twenty-five for your combined tribe. I know that although I have lived forty-nine years, I would look to be only eighteen or so, to most Men's eyes. While Men live to be perhaps sixty, and I believe your people might live to be two hundred fifty, here on these soils Elves live to be one thousand."

Shadala looked stunned.

Aras continued. "My father is High-King. If he was to be killed, I would become High-King. He is the one who commands our Army and our Navy. We usually call them the King's Guard, and the Guard, now. There are also Lords under him; they are not related to us by blood, at least not directly, but they are all High-born. They all have Power akin to yours, although perhaps stronger. Our healers are also not related to us, nor are they High-born, save for the one who taught me. In these customs, our peoples differ. But I have seen that, in many other ways, we do not. We both love our people and would see them fed and protected. We love our kin and our brothers-in-arms. You love your hills and valley as we love our Wood and our River."

She nodded, her face thoughtful.

"Tell me," Aras asked, "what does *Yehorog* mean?"

A hint of a rueful smile flashed across Shadala's lips and then was gone. "That is the name our warriors gave you, after the attack and the sickness. The name means Yellow Demon. But my brother Haran and I once knew you by a different name. I did not know your given name, those many years ago, so I named you Akarhad, or Fair One. My brother would be dead now and I would not be Chieftess, had you not acted with wisdom and honor and hidden my tracks and returned the King's Knife to its hiding place. Someday I will tell you that story. But now, I would hear about this Enemy and this other War you speak of."

Aras told her some of what he had learned, from his father and Jarnath, and from his journey with Dewalaren, though he was careful not to name him or to say too much, not yet. He also told her of Ahrnad and his madness and all he had done.

Shadala told him the destroyed harvest had hit them particularly hard, because they'd had poor harvests the past two years and had used all their reserves, and this one would have been bountiful again. Now their herd of deer was dead, their valley was stripped of forage and animals to hunt, and they were on the brink of starvation.

Aras told her that his people could sustain them both until their fields or new ones might grow food for them again, that it was their duty because of Ahrnad's treachery, for he had done great harm to them.

Shadala said, "Know now, Akarhad, you chose wisely when you came to me today. For this morning my brother, Haran, set out with our army of warriors to destroy your City. And our army is hundreds strong. You must have taken a different path or you would not be here. Our other raids these past days have only been to test your strength and we have discovered you will fall against us, once the forest that shelters you burns.

"My brother's heart is consumed with grief and rage, for he thinks that tonight his son will die, and so he has chosen that tonight all the sons of his enemy will die. They planned to circle around and lie in wait across the river, to attack you from the south, where you would least expect danger to lie. They were to have struck tonight, setting fire to your woods while your people slept."

Aras turned desperately to the door and saw to his dismay it was already dark outside, but Shadala continued to speak.

"Do not be alarmed. They were not to have struck so early as this. They had planned to wait until you were at your most unguarded and vulnerable, deep into the night. Haran had unfortunately broken his links to me and Falara, so I was not able to communicate with him directly. But when we left Veran's lodge, I sent two of our swiftest warriors, those who saw Veran with their own eyes, with a message for my brother. I told him that his son Veran lives, that he has been healed by the son of his enemy's King, Akarhad, the one to whom he owes Life Debt. I have told him you are under the protection of House of Gryphon, as our guest, and that he must not strike against your people this night. You may stay here tonight, and no harm will come to you or your people."

Aras felt weak with relief over the knowledge of catastrophe only barely averted.

Shadala's eyes lost focus for a moment. "My brother's daughter calls to me. All is well with her brother, but she has need of me. She has suffered greatly these past days. As his twin, she is lost without her bond to her brother. They have been bonded from the womb, since before birth. You must rest now. We have prepared beds for you both, so that you might sleep here," she said, indicating the beds Aras had noticed earlier. "We will speak more tomorrow. May you sleep under bright stars."

"You also, Shadala, for you have given me hope for peace," Aras said.

She smiled at him, a quick bright flash, and then left. She reminded him of Dewalaren. He did not think she smiled easily or often.

Aras turned to Leonas, almost overwhelmed by all that had transpired and all they had learned. He dared not even think about the darker truths he had learned about their people, about their destruction. "We thought their parties of forty were their strongest attacks! My blood runs cold to think that they planned to attack us tonight with so many warriors, with fire, that they sought to burn us to death while we slept!"

Leonas nodded and said with the ghost of a rueful smile, "It is fortunate for us all you refused to listen to my wise counsel and to Lunahr's."

"I did not think so, when I awoke and thought you dead and she threatened to torture me with the Knife," Aras said, still terrified by the memory. "The necklace is all that saved me, at first." His thoughts went to Lunahr. "I worry about Lunahr, alone in the dark tonight without us. I wish we could let him know we are safe. I fear he will not have slept at all today."

"Lunahr will be all right," Leonas assured him, though he sounded less than convinced himself.

"I worry about Talon's kinsman, Hunter, also," Aras admitted, speaking both Dewalaren's and Farad's traveling names. He would not reveal their given names, even to Leonas. "I wounded Hunter with one of the reused arrows, to save Talon, when Hunter thought Talon a Resemblant. I fear now that Hunter may have sickened and died ere he reached Tanieria, because of my tainted arrow."

"You could not have known, and your worries might be for naught," Leonas reasoned. "Come, Aras, you must rest, for Shadala has commanded it of you, and for all we are speaking words of truce and are now being treated as guests, we are still technically her captives. I'm sure you've realized our weapons and my pack have yet to be returned."

"You have forgotten yourself and used my name," Aras said, smiling.

Leonas smiled back, a look of mischief in his eyes. "I only did so to see you smile, Highness," he said and laughed at Aras's vexed expression. "Goodnight, Highness." Leonas stretched out on one of the beds.

"Goodnight, Leonas, my friend. Sleep well," Aras said, lying down upon the other. But he could not sleep. His mind was yet abuzz with all he had learned.

LUNAHR paced the floor of the Guest House anxiously as the day passed and night fell, and still there was no sign of Leonas or Aras. He accepted the food that was brought for the three of them and buried it beneath one of the potted plants, so it would look like they had all eaten. He could neither eat nor sleep. Several times he went to his room and stared longingly at the instruments there, but he could neither sing nor play nor compose, although for the first time in what seemed forever, he wished he could.

The Guard outside still thought Aras and Leonas inside. Lunahr's concern for his friends grew, the more time that passed, although he knew such a process as the one they undertook would take a while, even if it were working. But for all he knew, they were already long dead.

He would go mad with this waiting! The darkness of the night shrouded the House, pressing heavily against him. It was far less likely that they would travel at night. They would not return until the morrow, if they were to come back at all.

Time crept by as the night deepened around him. Lunahr felt the beginnings of dread. He tried to fight the panic, but it seized him more strongly. Belatedly, he realized his fear was no longer only for his friends. The Grove! Something was wrong! The Trees were calling to him, in fear. No, they could not... but then, in his mind's eye, he pictured a great wall of flame, and he bolted for the secret exit Aras and Leonas had used.

He slipped past the Guards unseen and silently raced for the Grove. As soon as he entered, the Trees began shaking, the leaves and needles rustling violently, not just his own Tree, but all of them, as if in a great storm. He drew his sword and searched for danger, but the Grove was empty of enemies. Yet something was terribly wrong. He sheathed his sword and laid his hand upon Aranahr.

There was no peace this time at the touch. There was an image of fire, of the forest burning, of the River, and he heard screaming. Lunahr knew it was the trees that screamed, as they burned. He burned with them, as he had in the dungeon, while the Elves were torturing him for his attack upon Laedrin.

Lunahr tore himself away from Aranahr and the pain vanished. He was shaking as he scanned the trees outside the Grove wildly. He saw nothing, smelled no smoke, but it was not the Grove, nor was it the forest around them. It was the trees near the River. The Woods of Nalea were burning!

He was horrified, but not only for the trees that burned. If Aras's words of peace had worked, the Hill People would not burn the forest. He feared both his friends dead.

He ran. He must go to the Palace, he must tell the High-King. They must save the trees if they could. He knew of a way, if Laedrin would only listen and allow it, if Lunahr was not Guardian of the Trees in name alone.

Lunahr ran to the Palace unchallenged and up the stairs, but the entrance was blocked by four of the King's Guard. To his dismay he recognized one of the King's Guard from the dungeon, one of the men whom Aras had imprisoned.

"I must speak with the High-King," Lunahr said, his voice urgent and commanding. But the Elf's eyes narrowed.

"I think not. You do not have the High-King's ear, as you have the High-Prince's," he said, his voice dripping with venom.

Lunahr kept the panic from his voice, forcing calm, and drew himself up. This time his voice held the power of a Lord, as he said, "The High-King has named me Lord of the Grove, Guardian of the Trees. For their protection I must speak with the High-King. Let me pass."

The King's Guard wavered then, and he thought they would indeed let him through, but at that moment, Lord Alwen came from within the Palace. "You! What are you doing here?" he asked, eyes narrowed, and the King's Guard glared at him again.

"I have business with the High-King, as Lord of the Grove." Alwen would not believe him if he told him the woods burned. But his position held no sway over Alwen.

Alwen laughed in his face, coldly. "You have been granted a title. That is all. The High-King would do anything for his son. But you play a dangerous game, I think, playing them off each other. We keep the High-King informed. He will soon recognize you for what you are again."

Lunahr spun and ran down the stairs, heart pounding. He dared not try to use the King's Voice upon them. He was too terrified to safely channel his Power. The result would be catastrophic. He could not get past them, and Alwen's words had struck a mark; if Aras was dead and Laedrin found out he had known of his mission and not intervened, his own life would easily be forfeit. He ran to the Healers' Hall. Jarnath was his only hope.

Fortunately, Jarnath was there, tending to the many wounded who lay there. Lunahr called him away from his patients. "Jarnath, you must help me. The woods are burning near the River, and I can't get past the King's Guard to see Laedrin. I need to warn him. He must send the King's Guard to the Grove to guard it, for I fear Ahrnad might see the fire and think to use it as a diversion, to cause further treachery. He might strike at the Grove or at the High-King when they are most vulnerable. They must both be guarded. And I need to enlist the aid of the Guard, before the fire becomes too great, but I do not even know the way to the River."

"What of Aras and Leonas? Why do they not help you?" Jarnath asked, eyeing him suspiciously.

Lunahr licked his lips. "They cannot help me. They are not here," he said, and his voice broke.

Jarnath's eyes bored into his. Lunahr had no choice but to tell him. His voice came out a whisper. "They went out this morning, in secret, to the Hill

People City, to try to make peace. And now the forest burns. I fear their plan has failed and they have been slain."

Jarnath gaped at him in horror and then said with grim resolve, "Laedrin must not discover Aras is gone. I will give him only the message of the fire and Ahrnad. You must alert the Guard. The Guard House is to the left, once you exit the Healers' Hall, six hundred yards from here. Go now, quickly."

Lunahr ran again, ignoring the pain in his chest from his cracked ribs as he ignored the pain in his heart.

The Guard looked at him with curiosity and concern, rather than hostility. "I need to speak with the Commander of the Guard, or with Daras, Leonas's commander, or anyone who will listen to me. I am Beryl, named by the High-King Lord of the Grove, Guardian of the Trees."

"I know of you. I am Captain Gaius, friend to Leonas. Daras is the Commander of the Guard. What is your business with him?"

"The forest by the River is on fire. I need to mobilize the Guard to fight it, before the City burns." He fought to keep the rising panic from overwhelming him.

Gaius's eyes widened; he barked out an order, and an alarm was struck, a clear ringing bell that was picked up and toned throughout the City. "Follow!" he commanded and began running, heading for a small stone building to the right. They burst in, and Lunahr saw an Elf already halfway to the door

"Gaius, who sounds the alarm?" the Elf demanded.

"I do. Commander Daras, Lord of the Grove Beryl reports the forest by the River burns. He comes with warning," Gaius reported.

"And to help," Lunahr added. "I know your trees seldom catch. This is no small blaze, it is deliberately set, already large and terrible, but I have fought such a fire once before. Water will not be enough to combat it, but I can guide you, if you will listen to my counsel."

"Tell me," Daras commanded.

Lunahr's mind flooded with memory of the forest around Alridge ablaze and the City itself burning, as well as the horrific images Aranahr had shown to him. "There is already a wall of flame. I know three methods of fighting such a fire, by shovel, axe and even flame, but we must strike quickly if we are to have any hope of success. Bring every Guard who can wield a shovel or axe, and all of those you can find. I will show you what to do."

"Gaius, you stay with us," Daras commanded, and then he was out the door. Lunahr was heartened by how fast the Guard mobilized under Daras's command. Rank upon rank had already assembled at the alarm and armed themselves with shovels and axes. Lunahr knew from his time in Riviera that every Reservist was trained to fight fire, but those of the Guard were specifically charged with the duty of protecting their Cities.

The first patrols began marching double-time to the River within minutes of his warning, he, Daras, and Gaius leading them. Lunahr could scarcely breathe for the pain of his ribs by the time they neared the River.

They could smell the smoke on the wind now, long before they saw the darker curtain block out the stars. Then they saw the first glow of flame against the branches of the trees. Lunahr heard horrified gasps as they drew nearer. Night was no longer dark. Trees flamed everywhere. He sensed fear rise up around him, from these brave Elves who faced death daily at the hands of the Hill People. Fire was a primal terror for them, especially a large, wild, uncontrolled one such as this.

"We must fall back two hundred yards from the flames," Lunahr said to Daras. "We must dig a wide, deep trench parallel to the fire, and pile a wall of dirt behind it, to starve the fire of its fuel, for there is fuel even in the soil, both in the ground itself as well as the dead leaves and needles upon it. The trench must be wide enough so the fire cannot cross it."

Daras nodded. "It is exactly as we have trained." He gave the order, which was echoed down the line. Lunahr eyed the fire critically. So far the fire spread from the ground and as such could yet be stopped. He was frustrated that with his broken arm, he could not wield a shovel to aid them. But he patrolled the break line with Gaius, making sure the trench was deep and wide enough. They used ropes to retrieve those in the trench, since the wall of earth was perilous to climb.

The trench was ready, and the fire was already close, when they fell back over the earthen wall. They pulled back one hundred yards from it. Then Lunahr felt his heart clutch in fear. The wind from the River was blowing stronger, now, and the fire flamed ever higher. As he watched, it engulfed the tops of the trees, and he saw the flame leap from the branches of one tree to the branches of another. The fire had crowned, and now it spread from treetop to treetop. It would leap over the ditch!

He yelled to Daras, pointing, "The flame will leap the trench! We must fall back two hundred yards and dig another trench, then cut every tree at least twenty feet behind it, to rob the fire of its fuel."

Daras stared at him, horrified. "Cut trees that do not burn? We cannot! We can chop the burning trees to save them from their pain, but not the others."

Lunahr pleaded then. "But you must! Do you want the City to burn? These trees are not like the Trees of the Grove. But even if they were, like any honorable man, they would bravely die to see their brothers live! And they lie in the path of the fire. They are already doomed to die."

But he could see that Daras could not do it, and the men around him who heard looked at him with horror-filled eyes. They were already fighting their terror of the flame. They were in agony over the torture and death of the trees.

They could not do something so against their nature. And he realized in despair that they had too few axes and too few hands for the task in any case. And they would never set fire to these trees. They could not light a backfire. They would have to fall back to the City. There was some open land there. Perhaps they could save at least a portion of the City and the Trees of the Grove.

ARAS was awakened from his sleep by a hand on his shoulder and he leapt to his feet, astonished that anyone had been able to approach him without him knowing. It was Shadala. Aras saw Leonas awoke also. "Is it Veran?" Aras asked, fearing from the look upon her face that somehow something had gone wrong and he had died.

She shook her head. "No. He is still asleep, but his heart beats strongly. He will live. The news I bring is about your own people."

Aras's eyes widened. Had Haran attacked them anyway, against Shadala's order of truce?

"Haran has sent me word. They have not attacked, but his scouts report that someone else has set fire to the forest on the north bank. The woods are burning and a great wall of fire heads for your City."

Aras paled. "Then I must go back now, and help my people fight the fire, or all will be destroyed! Please, you must let me go."

"I will do more than allow you to leave. I will go with you, as will my people. We are skilled in the ways of fire. We will help you. Come quickly."

They were met at the door by a number of guards, one of whom handed their weapons and packs to them, while the one called Goturan handed Shadala a great horn that shone the too-bright silver of pallenteum in the moonlight. She blew upon it, and a loud, pure, haunting note rose from it. People began pouring forth from every building in the City. They gathered around her, torches and lamps in their hands, women armed with swords, and even children, many of them armed with knives, and some armed men, those few guards that remained in the City.

SHADALA called out to her people in a loud, clear voice, in Urwani, her heart burning with shame that she could not do so in Amontirin. None would understand her, save for Falara. They had lost their language, as they had lost so much, so many people, so much history. Only the tapestries, the Book of Houses, and the King's Knife yet remained. But Akarhad knew their King. He had promised to reunite them with him. They had successfully evaded the merciless Enemy who had driven them from their home two hundred fifty years ago. But he had found them again, and yet sought to destroy them. She would die before she would see him work his evil upon Akarhad's people or her own once more.

"I call to you now, as your Chieftess, to fight the ancient Enemy of our people, the Amontir. We have been tricked into fighting the wrong foe. Akarhad, Warrior Captain, son of his War Chief, one of great honor, has opened my eyes. His people did not poison our fields and slay our herd, nor kill our farmers. The Enemy has done these evil deeds, and cast the blame upon Akarhad's people so we would fight a war against them, and weaken them, for the Enemy is cowardly and does not fight with honor.

"Akarhad has given bread to your children. Akarhad has aided me in saving the life of Veran, your Warrior Captain. He does not die tonight! Akarhad has offered food to all of us, through his people, so that we may survive until we can grow our own food again. He offers the swords of his army to fight our common Enemy. But now we must offer our warriors and our farmers in aid to him.

"The treacherous Enemy has set fire to the woods around their City, so that they might burn to death in their beds. And they would burn the food that is offered to your children with it! We must take up axe and shovel and go to his aid. I call for one hundred farmers and craftswomen, mothers and wives and daughters, to join me. We march to join the army and battle this great evil, to save our own City, our Houses, and our children. Who will aid us?"

A wall of women stepped forward, as well as all the guards, and many of the children, both male and female.

She held out her hands. "One hundred women. The rest must stay with the children, as must the guards, for we may yet face our ancient Enemy this night. Each woman, bring shovel and axe. We must move quickly."

Within minutes, they were surrounded by an army of women with shovels and axes in hand, though half of them bore two shovels and no axe.

"Now you must lead me, Akarhad, for I do not know the way to your City, as you know the way to mine."

"It is this way," he said, and he began to run, his friend Leonas at his side, the army of women streaming behind them.

They left the hills and entered the woods, running along the riverbank. They smelled the burning trees long before they saw them. Akarhad and Leonas set a fast pace, but she and the other women kept up with him. They gradually lost sight of the moon and the stars, for the smoke in the air, but there was light, horrible orange-red light.

ARAS stared in horror at the destruction before him. The forest along the opposite bank was a blackened, smoking ruin for hundreds of yards north of the river, and a solid wall of flame stood between him and his home. This was not something they could fight! This was the horrific story his mother had told him so long ago, of the War of Flame, the Night of Fire, come to life again, to destroy their world. He had thought himself inured to flame, but he could scarcely breathe for the terror clutching his heart, and he heard Leonas moan in fear beside him.

Then suddenly they were surrounded, as the Hill People army closed about them. A man with features similar to Veran and Falara and Shadala spoke angrily to Shadala, in the same language she had spoken in her City to inspire her people to aid them. He must be her brother, Haran, their War Chief.

He gestured angrily at Aras. Shadala spoke back coolly, but with such authority in her voice that Aras would have known her for a Queen, by the tone of her voice. But her brother did not appear to be listening.

Aras heard the name Akarhad and Falara and Veran from Shadala and was frustrated that he could not understand any of their words. The argument rose in crescendo, as the men and the women of the City shifted uneasily, looking from one to the other. Then, her hand a blur, Shadala drew the King's Knife and flung it into the ground at her brother's feet, a hair's breadth from them. She ripped open the top of her red dress and barked five more words in challenge and stood silently, with the tops of her breasts exposed. Aras knew she had challenged her brother to plunge the Knife into her heart. The men watched silently, without moving, though their eyes shifted downward from her exposed chest, but the women fell as one to their knees in silent supplication.

The War Chief looked from his sister to the women, to the dagger at his feet. He pulled it from the ground and his hand was shaking. Aras did not dare move. Then to Aras's relief, he reversed the blade and handed it to Shadala, uttering a few words. He then turned to Aras and glared at him, but incredibly, removed his sword, scabbard and all, and held it out to him, and spoke in words he did not know.

Shadala rose, pulling the top of her dress closed once more, half a dozen women handing her pins to seal it. "Haran closed his ears to all my words, even words of his son. So then I reminded him that he owes Life Debt to you, as I owe Honor Debt to you, from those many long years ago. I told him that, if he would not repay his debt, I could not repay mine, and I would not live without honor, and he must slay me. Of course, then he could no longer be War Chief, without me as Chieftess. He now offers his sword and his army's in service to you. He had no choice. If you accept, say '*Haka ta lo fen.*' If not, '*Raka ta.*'"

Aras licked his lips and looked at the two of them intently. "How do I say that I accept, but only for as long as the fire burns? That after that, his debt and yours is paid? But that then I would want him and his warriors to be brothers-in-arms, our allies, if they wished, against our common Enemy? But more, we would want them as our friends?"

Shadala smiled in approval and told him to repeat each sentence she spoke carefully. Then she told him what to say and he did so, as Haran's eyes widened first in surprise and then in growing respect. He strapped his sword back on, with a nod and a grunt.

"Can anyone else speak Common, Shadala?" Aras asked.

"My brother knows only a few phrases. Falara and I are Speakers for the City."

"Then I'll need you to translate. First, we must cross the River. And then, I think we must get in front of the fire to stop it, but I don't know how." His attention was again on the flames and he felt the fear try to overwhelm him, but he forced it back.

Shadala said confidently, "Fire holds no fear for our people. Fire is a comfort, a friend. We know how to tame it to our will."

She called out and the women handed the fifty axes to the men and fifty of the one hundred fifty shovels. From the back of the army, planed logs were raised, and the river was spanned. "They had already prepared the war bridges for tonight's attack. Come, we must cross."

Once on the opposite bank, Shadala pointed to a weaker spot in the flames. "We break through here. Then we will face it."

As they headed inland from the riverbank there was a sudden cry off to the right, and they stopped. Something man-shaped and of like size was carried to Shadala by two of the men. Aras's eyes widened. It was the body of one of the Guard, not burned, but with an arrow in his heart. The markings of the King's Guard were on the shaft. Aras realized that to have lit such a large fire without having an alarm sound until it was too late, Ahrnad must have slain an entire River Patrol, perhaps more.

"Come, we must hurry. You may bury your dead later," Shadala said.

"No, wait! Leonas, carry him. He will be proof to our people that Ahrnad set this fire, not your people, Shadala."

They pressed forward, and Aras felt the oven-like heat as they continued on.

LUNAHR stared at the trench in dismay as the flame leapt over it, from treetop to treetop. The ground fire had stopped, for now, but as soon as flaming branches fell, it would be lighted again. Even as he watched, he saw ten separate new fires begin. Then, across the mound of earth, something rose, many things, swarming up and over as if the very earth were disgorging some new terror. There were dozens, of them, no, even more: hundreds of dark shadows and the glint of metal.

Lunahr despaired, for he realized it was the Hill People, come to lay waste to all before them, aiding their fire in its work. But this was not a single patrol, or two or three, but an entire army. And he could not even wield Loruthanar to defend himself.

Around him, fear turned to anger, and the Guard dropped their shovels and reached for their bows. But as the attackers drew closer, Lunahr could see faces by the orange light of the fire, and his jaw dropped in shock, for he recognized two of them.

"It's High-Prince Aras and Leonas! Daras, order them to hold their fire! The Hill People come in truce, to fight the fire!" he yelled frantically in Elvish. He saw now that their hands held axes and shovels, not swords.

"Hold your fire! It's the High-Prince!" Daras yelled, echoing his words, and others who had seen also cried out the same simultaneously. Word was passed over the roar of the flames, even as Lunahr and Daras and Gaius ran to them.

"Aras! Leonas! When I saw the fire, I had feared you were dead!" Lunahr cried. Then he saw that Leonas carried a body, one of the Guard.

"Highness!" Daras said. Then he cried, "Vanyr!" looking down at the face of the dead Guard. He gaped in horror at the shaft. "But that is an arrow of the King's Guard!"

Gaius had eyes only for Leonas.

Aras yelled over the roar of the fire, "The Hill People, the Urwani, come in truce to help us save our Wood. They did not set the fire! Ahrnad did!"

"We will talk later!" Lunahr yelled over the roar of the flame in Elvish. "For now, Aras, we could desperately use your aid. If you could help us dig a second trench, two hundred yards from the first, and help us fell every tree twenty feet beyond, we may yet rob the fire of its fuel and stem this blaze."

Aras relayed Lunahr's instructions to Shadala in Common, and she told Haran in Urwani. He spread the word, and the army and women surged forward. The Hill People and the Elven Navy stood face to face for an uneasy moment, and then they both bent to the work of digging the trench, side by side.

Lunahr worked at Aras's and Leonas's sides, unwilling to let them out of his sight, helping what little he could, directing the work, until he was sure everyone knew their tasks. "*It will work, it must work,*" he thought. Then all thought fled as he stared with haunted eyes at the trees around him. His body convulsed in shudders as his eyes focused here and there on one or another tree that burned. He felt the fire consume him. He felt the axe hew him. He screamed as he died for the third and fourth and fifth time.

ARAS saw Lunahr fall and ran to him. He was writhing on the ground as if on fire. Aras knelt beside him and grabbed his shoulders. Lunahr's skin was burning hot to the touch, but the heat from the fire was not so close yet. He should not be hot!

Lunahr's eyes were wild and he was shaking. A violent shudder passed through him. "He is dead! She burns! Help me! They are screaming! I hear them, I feel them. We are dying!" Aras touched his face, reaching out with a silver vine toward his core, but he drew back in agony. Lunahr's core was on fire, it was burning! He could not touch it, he could not help him. He realized in horror that Arcanus had bound Lunahr to the trees, and as they were dying, he would perish with them. Apparently the closer the trees were to the City, the more attuned to them he was, or he would have fallen long ago. But Lunahr's Tree, Aranahr, might yet save him!

"Lunahr, you cannot stay here. I'll have them bring you to the Grove," Aras said desperately.

Lunahr shook his head, "Guarded… King's Guard… won't let us in," and then he screamed again in agony and his body convulsed.

Aras lifted him in his arms and ran to Daras and Leonas. "I have to get Beryl to the Grove! He is dying! Leonas, you speak with my voice. Commander Daras, you must listen to him and follow his orders as you would my own. He will relay instructions between you and Shadala."

Lunahr convulsed again as Aras and Leonas watched in helpless agony.

"Gaius, go with the High-Prince," Daras ordered. "You must see him safely to the Grove."

Aras ran then, Gaius at his side. "Gaius, I do not need a guard. Instead, run to the Healers' Hall and summon Jarnath. Bring him to the Grove. Tell him to bring anosar and thasheera. I left my own behind. Hurry, he is dying!" Gaius ran.

Lunahr struggled weakly in Aras's arms, "No, I must stay. I must help save them!"

Aras heard the despair in his voice and feared for him. "Lunahr, you have! The fire is not out yet. Those before it still burn and those beyond are cut, but it will work. The fire will be stopped and the rest of the Wood will be saved. The City and the Grove will be safe. But you will die if you stay, for your bond to the trees.

"I do not give you leave to die. You are a Lord of the City and I am your High-Prince. I need you. And Aranahr needs you. You will hurt him, likely even kill him, if you die. And Dewalaren and Farad would never recover."

Lunahr stopped struggling and Aras knew a moment's relief, but then Lunahr went limp in his arms and Aras feared he was too late. He refused to believe it, and to his relief felt Lunahr's body yet pulsed with life and his core yet burned from within as well as from without. He continued to race for the Trees that might still save him.

At last he could see the Grove. The King's Guard almost did not recognize him. They had drawn their bows against him. Aras realized he was covered in soot and ash, that his hair was likely black with it, and they must at first have though him a wild Hill People warrior. But he called out to them and commanded them to stand aside, his voice ringing with Power in his need for instant obedience, and they drew back.

Once in the shelter of the Trees, Aras laid Lunahr with his back against his Tree and placed his hand against the strong trunk and begged. "Aranahr, please, help Lunahr! I fear he is dying. Lend him your strength. Ease his mind. He has saved all he could. He should not suffer for those that are lost. Please, I beseech you."

Aras felt a cool breeze in his mind and heard needles rustle softly. A great calm came over him as he felt a river of strength run into his palm, up his wrist, into his arm and through him. It met another river flowing up from Lunahr into his other arm. There was a great, ancient voice, and it was singing to him, of life and hope and joy and peace. He and Lunahr became part of the song, and it was ageless and endless.

ARAS heard the last sweet strains of deep melody drift away as if on the wind, and he remembered again who he was and where he was. He breathed deeply and opened his eyes and saw the face of his brother, Lunahr, whom he held in loving embrace. Lunahr was looking up at him, smiling in joy. Aras realized that the sun shone brightly overhead and the air smelled fresh and clean. Though they still were covered in soot from the fire, they no longer smelled of it; they smelled only of pine.

It was as if his body and Lunahr's were one. He knew Lunahr felt no more pain, that his arm and ribs had been fully healed. In hope and wonder he touched Lunahr's core. The fire was gone, but he was distressed to find that it yet bore the taint of the Enemy, though the darkness inside had been temporarily sealed away behind a pallenteum tree.

They stood and released one another from their embrace, and he could no longer feel Lunahr's body as if it was his own. They thanked Aranahr and headed for the edge of the Grove. They saw a sea of faces surrounding the Grove, but it was as silent as a tomb in spite of their number, and Aras realized he did not heard the sound of a single voice or the clank of metal or the rustle of fabric or a lone bird's call.

They left the shelter of the Trees, looking in wonder at the hundreds of people around them. Jarnath and Leonas and his father were there, and as they exited the Grove, Aras saw them stumble, as if they had been leaning against an invisible wall that was suddenly gone. In that moment there was sound again, and Aras heard a tumult of voices raised in excitement and relief and joy.

Gaius and Daras, Shadala and Haran, dozens of the King's Guard, hundreds of Guard, and Hill People warriors and women all let out a great cry. "Hail High-Prince Aras! Hail Lord Beryl! Akarhad! Aras! Beryl!" The two of them stood, arm in arm, overwhelmed, as everyone surged around them.

Aras let go of Lunahr and went to his father. To his shock his father hugged him tightly in front of all his people. There were tears in his eyes as he said, "My son, my son! You are returned to me a second time!" And then, incredibly, he let go, turned to Jarnath, and waved him forward.

Jarnath hugged him as well, tears in his eyes. "You drive me mad, Aras! First Beryl tells me you are slain by the Hill People, then you return and summon me, but no one can enter the Grove! You will have me go to the grass before my time."

Aras laughed, for the sheer joy of holding him. "No, never that! Forgive me, Jarnath!"

Leonas was hugging Lunahr tightly, and then Gaius held Leonas in a warrior's embrace as reverent hands reached to touch both Aras and Lunahr.

To Aras's relief, his father and Haran declared the War ended, through their interpreters. His father swore they would make reparations for the wrongs done to the Urwani. The High-King declared a great feast for the following day, so that the Hill People might bring their entire City to share in it.

THE next day, when the Hill People came, Veran was with them, awake and aware, as hearty and hale as if he had never been injured, his sister Falara glued to his side. All the progeny of the City were there as well, and Nalea rang with the laughter of children for the first time in all its long history.

Chapter 3
Where the Heart Is

JARGAS stood on the path to his village. The first of the houses would be just over the rise up ahead. He had already greeted six sentries. He was amazed that Jarina had not come running down the path barefoot, leaping into his arms, already, for all that she was a woman grown and Chieftess besides. He saw the houses then, and they were exactly as he remembered them. And there she was, running toward him, her long black hair streaming behind her, her face alight with joy, her clothes a riot of color, as if she had partially tamed a rainbow and wrapped it about herself. Then she was in his arms.

He caught her as he always did, and spun her about, as if they were children still. "At last, you have come back to me! You will never leave me again!" she demanded and pouted for a moment, but could not hold it, and grinned again.

"I will leave again, my sister, but when I next travel, I will take you and most of our people with me, from both the Kingdom and the Village. We are marching to War, and I find myself heir to a second Kingdom, though I want it not."

Jarina sighed. "I have known that there will be War, and I know much more. Our link, even with us so far apart, has been very strong." She looked at him oddly then, and he saw something he had never seen in her face, something he could not identify, it was so alien to her. "But I am not the only one you now share your thoughts with. I would know who else has earned such trust, that you would do so without even warning me."

He stared at her in surprise. "Jarina! You surprise me! You are jealous of Hunter?"

"Jealous? No, I am not jealous," she said softly, and he knew it to be true. "I am afraid. His thoughts are so dark, and I find them sliding down our bond toward me. I have had to seal myself off from you to keep him at bay. That is why I could not feel you near until you were almost at my doorstep."

Jargas said in concern, "Hunter is not someone to be feared, Jarina. I cannot pity him, for he is not someone who is pitiable, but I feel great sadness for him. If my link to Hunter is somehow a danger to you, I am sorry, my sister, but then I would break your link to me, for to break mine to him would do great damage to him: his sanity is tied to our link, his life is tied to it. He is neither well nor strong any longer. He has been through many terrible trials. I had hoped that you might help me to succor him. You live in such joy and he in such sorrow. But I would not cause you grief or pain, even to aid him.

"He is kin to us, Jarina. I have found our grandsire's people. I know now who we are and what I must do because of it. Come, we must speak with our father. I bring him news of his kin in Fromer, as well as other news."

They walked through their village and continued onward past it, up the path, until he saw the massive steel Door to the Mountain and knew he was truly home. The Door Guard bowed to them as they approached, and they nodded to them. The Guard signaled for the Door to be opened, and it swung wide. Jargas entered the great caverns with the same reverence he had always felt. His love was not diminished at all by the grandeur and splendor he had seen in Malar in Fromer. If anything, he valued the graceful simplicity of the walls of his own Mountain all the more, for seeing those others.

The rock here was little altered from when his Father's people had found it centuries ago. Only in some of the chambers, such as his father's Throne Room, the Study, and the Library, could their artistry be seen to any great degree. The air was cold and clear and sweet, the scent of the rock like perfume to him. The rock of Malar in Fromer had not smelled like this. Nothing smelled like the rock of home.

Jargas entered the Throne Room. His father was not there, but he had not expected him to be; he seldom stood on such ceremony. Only when conducting business of the Mountain, or the few times foreign dignitaries had visited them, had his father used that room. But the door to his Study was just beyond, and the main door to it led from the Throne Room.

His father was there, in the Study, leaning upon the thick carved-stone table in the room's center. There were maps spread there, of the Dwarven Lands that once were, before the Enemy came, before he leveled Kingdom after Kingdom, before he laid the lands to waste and slaughtered all who once dwelt there.

His father scowled without looking up. "I told you before, Sarnon, I'm not hungry, nor am I likely to get hungry. If you keep interrupting me, I'll miss dinner as well, and I'll be sure to let Jarina know it was your fault I've not eaten since yesterday."

"Then I'll dine with you to be sure you do," Jargas said.

Rongas looked up in astonishment, a broad grin spreading across his face. "Jargas!" He strode over to him. Jargas knelt before his father, and Rongas hugged him tightly. Even then, his father had to tilt his head upward to gaze into the eyes of his son. Jargas stood some inches over seven feet, while his father was on the tall side for a male Dwarf: four and a half feet tall.

Rongas scowled at Jarina and scolded her. "Why didn't you tell me he was coming? A fine welcome I've given him!"

"Forgive me, Father. I could not sense him until he was already here," Jarina said contritely.

Jargas saw his father's expression change to one of concern. Jarina was not smiling, and his sister was seldom without a smile.

Their father glanced from his daughter's serious face to his son's. "Your news must be grave from the expressions upon your faces. Do our kin reject us? You do not bring the axe back with you." Jargas was still in his worn and dusty traveling clothes and yet carried his pack and staff.

"No. The King, Balgar, grandson of the one whom your grandsire parted with, accepted the axe and through it our alliance. But his Kingdom was a poor ally. There were dealings dark and foul there. Had Balgar still lived, I would have urged you to reconsider our alliance, Father. But fortunately Balgar was killed, and his son Valar now rules, much to the betterment of the Kingdom. Valar has also accepted our alliance, under much better terms. And not only have we regained your kin, Father, but we have regained Mother's as well. At long last, I have discovered not only the secret of Mother's people, but the very identity of our grandsire as well. May I hold the band, Father?"

Rongas watched him with interest as he removed the jeweled armband from about his bicep and gave it to Jargas. He had worn it ever since his wife, Jahira, had gifted it to him. The metal gleamed like blood-dipped copper in the lamplight, and the inlaid ruby cabochon shone brightly.

Jargas now knew that the metal was called pyrenteum, a metal that only the wizards knew the forging and crafting of. Pyrenteum had all of the properties of pallenteum and more: it would not tarnish, nor dull once an edge was made, nor break, but in addition, it was impervious to fire. The King's Band, King's Knife, King's Ring, and Rowanar's legendary armor were all crafted of pyrenteum. Farad had revealed much to him, in their travels. He now knew the band was the original King's Band, lost two hundred fifty years ago with Crown Prince Rowanar and the ten Houses and three hundred kinsmen he had led. Dewalaren, who went by the name Talon—the currently acknowledged Amontir King, though he yet bore the title of Prince—wore a replica of the King's Band made of pallenteum. That band was also considered the band of the House of Obearn, for that band had also been lost.

Jargas turned to Jarina. "And the Ring you wear, Sister." Her eyes widened in surprise, but she slid it from her thumb. It was a man's ruby ring, fashioned of the same odd metal, too big to wear upon her ring finger, the stone identical in size and shape and color and clarity to the one set into the band. Jargas placed the King's Band on his right wrist, opposite the band of House of Gryphon, which he wore on his left, and the King's Ring about the first knuckle of his right pinky, as far down as it would go. Then he told his father and sister the story of his journey to Malar in Fromer, of the rescue of Prince Valar, and of his father, the evil King Balgar, and his misdeeds.

He spoke of the imprisonment and torture and rescue of his mother's kinsman, Hunter. He would not speak Farad's given name aloud to his father, not without Farad's permission. He told them of the treachery that ensued after the rescue, and the story of the history of his maternal grandsire's line, the Amontir, that he had learned: of madness and betrayal, regicide, and the destruction of their Kingdom. He spoke of the three symbols of the King split between the brothers and the three Princes' flights across the mountains as they desperately tried to lead their people to safety, a journey that ended in tragedy for each of them. He finished by saying. "So, I have discovered that I am the grandson of Crown Prince Rowanar, the murdered King Albinar's eldest son. I am the true Heir to the Throne, the rightful King of Amontir."

Jarina looked at him, intrigued. "What do you mean to do, then, Brother?"

Jargas said grimly, "Claim the throne I do not want and bring the armies of Malar in Holoren, Malar in Fromer, and the Varash to fight their War. For whether we fight it in the Fromer Mountains or in the Holoren, we will ultimately have to fight. The Enemy seeks to destroy the peoples of all the known lands.

"Hunter is going to report to their King, or Prince, as they call him, for he yet bears only the King's Sword, not the King's Ring and the King's Knife. Hunter seeks to have all the Captains of the Watch summoned for a great War Council at Caramore, their fallen city. He says they can wait no longer, that they must abandon the search for the Knife and the Ring, for they are out of time. He feels they must strike now, with the combined might of the three Dwarven Kingdoms he has forged an alliance with, Malar in Fromer, Dorolingas, and Ironhand. He hopes that the King's Sword might still be able to kill the Enemy, if it has Power enough. He feels they must prevent the Enemy from crossing the Fromer Mountains at all costs.

"I did not tell him we have the King's Ring. I am certain this is the Ring they are seeking," he said, indicating the one he now wore. "Hunter has told me the location of their last secret refuge, the Watchtower. I was to come to present myself formally to the Prince either at Caramore or the Watchtower, if I was too late for the War Council, to have our House recognized by him.

"Hunter left me before I stumbled upon Prince Talon in Athanark. Hunter does not know that the Prince has already welcomed me as Lord of a lost House. But they both think our House is Gryphon. I have told you how I deceived them and why. It is at Caramore, at the War Council, if I am able to arrive in time, that I will declare myself King."

Jargas looked intently at his father. "Neither Hunter nor the Prince knew of the Three Strongholds and the twenty-nine Dwarven Kingdoms of the West they contain. They believed those twenty-nine Kingdoms lost with the other hundreds that fell in the Dwarven Lands. Talon still does not know, but Hunter does now. I told him.

"Malar in Holoren can provide close to five thousand men and the Varash at least two hundred more. I propose that we send messengers to the Three Strongholds of the Kingdoms of the West, announcing our intent and asking them to join us. Although each of those Kingdoms are only a shadow of the lost eastern Kingdom they were born from, they yet might provide in total another ten thousand or more men to our cause. And if any should wish to seek revenge against the Enemy, it is they. If their armies could march with our own and join with the three remaining Kingdoms of the Dwarven Lands, it might turn the tide of battle in our favor. Father, I'd like you to send emissaries to each of the Three Strongholds, outlining the situation and requesting their aid. I'll discuss the details of the message I am thinking of with you later, if you find merit in the idea."

Rongas nodded thoughtfully and then a wide grin spread across his face. "Thirty-three Kingdoms! If thirty-three Dwarven Kingdoms were to march together, band together, fight together, no enemy in the world, be he wizard or madman or both, could stand against such a force! The very mountains will tremble with the thunder of battle!"

Rongas turned to Jargas and Jarina. "Come, children. We must have a war council of our own. A march such as the one you propose must be carefully planned, provisioned, and coordinated. Speaking of provisions, I'm famished and you look to be. Sarnon!" Rongas bellowed, and his steward came in.

"YES, Majesty?" Sarnon said as he entered, knowing what was to come the moment he saw the King's face.

"Where's my lunch? I've eaten neither breakfast nor lunch, and it's nearly dinner time! Do you want me and my children to starve?" Rongas roared.

Sarnon gave him a long-suffering look and said dryly, "Forgive me for failing you, Majesty. Perhaps you should replace me with someone who might better anticipate your needs."

Rongas chuckled heartily. "What, and give you an easy life? Besides, it's taken me two hundred years to train you and I drove twenty to drink before finding you! You cannot escape me that easily."

"I live to serve, Majesty," Sarnon said, his voice dripping with sarcasm.

Rongas roared with laughter as he left.

Sarnon smiled, as soon as his back was turned to the King. He was one of the few who ever dared turn his back to Rongas.

He was glad Jargas had returned. Rongas had been increasingly more distracted, poring over maps and old texts. Today was not the first day he'd gone without eating: it was one of many. Sarnon had begun to worry about him.

He walked to the kitchens and told them the King was wanting to be fed, but he had Jargas and Jarina with him. They quickly pushed aside the tray they'd been keeping warm for the King for the past four hours and instead pulled one of the goats they'd been roasting for dinner from the spits and put a new one on. The one they'd recovered was yet mostly rare, the way the Prince liked it, and big enough to satisfy him, with enough left over for his father and sister. The new one would be just about cooked enough for him by dinner. They diverted two loaves of bread, a wheel of cheese, and a full cask of wine from dinner, along with two trays of vegetables and a cake.

"Do you think this will suffice, since there's only two hours until dinner?" Dervan, one of the cooks, asked in concern.

Sarnon eyed the meal critically. "Aye, that should do it. The King can always yell for more if there's need. The Prince is looking lean. He mustn't weigh more than five hundred pounds now. I don't think he's been eating as well as he's used to." The cooks and servers shook their heads in sympathy.

Sarnon led the servers to the Study, where the King and his children were already deeply embroiled in discussion of war.

THREE days later, shortly before dusk, Rongas, Jargas, and Jarina were meeting in Jarina's lodge, planning the integration of the Varash warriors with the forces of Malar while they waited for the armies of the other Kingdoms to arrive. Kesh, one of the Varash warriors currently acting as door guard to Jarina's lodge, in tandem with another man and two Dwarves, came inside during their meeting. "Forgive me, Chieftess, Champion, Majesty, but one of the King's sentries, Lornan, reports he and his men have caught an intruder who they believe might be a spy of the Enemy. They say he has a dark look about him.

"Lornan says he slipped past all but our last outpost without being detected and that it took all six Dwarves to subdue him once they discovered him. Lornan wishes to know what to do with him. Chieftess, he also says that he will need your aid as Healer, if it is determined that he should be allowed to live, for he was already wounded and they had to injure him further. He would not be easily restrained."

"If he is truly a spy of the Enemy, then this concerns all of us," Jargas said. Jarina rose sinuously from the cushion she had been seated upon, slinging her healer's bag over her shoulder. Jargas heaved himself to his feet and retrieved his staff and Rongas picked up his axe. They followed Kesh to the outskirts of the village and beyond. A cluster of at least twenty Men and Dwarves stood with their attention focused upon the ground, apparently gathered about the suspected spy. They stepped aside to allow Jarina, Jargas, and Rongas access to the prisoner.

Jargas stared in disbelief. It was Farad! He lay beaten and bleeding and bound on the ground. He was not conscious.

But it could not be him! Jargas would have felt his presence along their bond. He tested the bond. It was as if he were trying to see through a thick fog, but after carefully following the strand, it indeed led to the Man before him.

He looked at the Men and Dwarves surrounding them. "This is Hunter. He's a friend of mine, someone I thought far from here, or I'd have told you about him. I did not even realize he knew how to find my home. I had never told him where I lived, save that it was here in the Holoren. You did well in capturing him and subduing him—I do not fault you for it—but I now ask that you bring him to the Chieftess's lodge and tell you that he is to be shown all honor and protection as a guest once he awakens." He knelt and cut the bonds about his hands and feet.

Kesh spoke for all of them. "Of course, Champion. Forgive us for injuring him."

Jargas lifted Farad gently and carried him carefully to Jarina's lodge, while Kesh and many of the others followed. Kesh stationed himself as guard outside Jarina's lodge, while Jargas, Jarina and their father entered. It was evident from the look of him that Farad had survived a far more arduous journey than he had. He appeared gaunt and haggard and worn to the bone, though thankfully not as bad as when Jargas freed him from Balgar's dungeon. He laid Farad down on the cushions in Jarina's living room, where they had been seated before. Friend or not, it would not be proper to lay him down on her bed.

Jargas saw that Jarina was looking at Farad strangely. He could not identify the expression he saw. But he sensed her feelings through the bond they shared, muffled as they were through her shield. He sensed curiosity and sympathy, but also fear, and surprisingly, desire. "I had not known it before, Jarina, but the shield you have been using to protect yourself from Hunter has also been interfering with my bond to him. I had no idea he was so close to me and no indication he was in danger when our men attacked him. You must remove your shield, Sister. I know you did not mean to cause him injury, but I fear his spirit may have been greatly harmed by suffering such a defeat. I cannot help him with our bond so weakened."

He felt her fear overwhelm her other feelings. "I am frightened he will come for me," she admitted.

Jargas was shocked. He had never known his sister to be afraid of anything, and she had battled many dangerous foes: Men and ogres and obearn. Why should Farad as he appeared now, beaten and helpless, frighten her so?

Jargas placed his huge hands upon her slender shoulders. "I'll not let his mind touch yours, Jarina. But I've told you, you have nothing to fear from him. He would never harm you."

Jarina looked searchingly into her twin brother's eyes. She shuddered once and then nodded. "All right, Jargas. I will do as you ask, because it is you who asks me. But I fear in so doing I will change our lives forever."

Jargas stared at her, puzzled, but at the same moment the fog vanished and his bond to Farad suddenly shone bright and clear.

TO RONGAS'S horror, Jarina screamed in terror and Jargas fell to the ground with a cry of despair, his sister crumpling on top of him. Rongas knelt beside them in shock as Kesh and then a number of the other guards from both the Village and the Mountain ran in.

Both Jargas and Jarina were still as death, and when Rongas felt desperately at Jargas's throat, he could not feel the pulse of his son's heart.

Then the ring on Jargas's finger flared, flooding the lodge with a red light as intense as if the setting sun had fallen from the sky into a lake of blood. Rongas and every other Man and Dwarf in the room were instantly blinded by it.

THE moment Jarina removed her shield, Hunter scuttled down the strand linking Jargas to her, like a big, black spider coming to claim a fly caught in its web. She shrank from him and struck out, accidentally hitting the strand connecting her to Jargas, not the spider. Her bond to Jargas snapped from the blow and she was left alone as the horrid black thing pounced upon her.

Jarina screamed and dove into the house that sheltered her mind, curled into a ball, covered her head with her arms. There was a frightening flapping noise above her, as of insect wings. She peeked through her arms.

Now she saw not a spider at all, but a large gray moth. It fluttered above her bright, pure light, and lighted upon it, drawing back as if in pain. She saw a great hole burnt into one wing, where it had touched her. It flung itself forward again, and flapped feebly backward. It had burnt a ragged hole into its other wing. Then it landed upon her house, scrabbling desperately against it with its little sticky feet, as if it were trying to dig its way in to her. She smelled the moth cooking against the roof. She slapped her hand against the ceiling of her house, trying to knock it free, but it clung to her house, even as its feet were burnt away.

Hunter would kill himself trying to reach her! She burst free from the shelter of her house then, spreading out great butterfly wings of all colors. Her wings wrapped gently about Hunter-moth in a way butterfly wings never could, hugging him to her. His frantic, panicked flapping stilled. She shifted her grip, clutched him with her feet, and flapped her great wings, drawing him upward, back up the path from which his mad plunge had taken him toward her.

She found the dangling end of the strand that had bound Jargas to her, and she to him. She realized Hunter-moth had fallen down it and lost himself when she severed the link to her brother. She grasped the strand with the sticky pads of one delicate foot and pulled it downward, back toward her bright house, her great wings straining with the effort. She kept careful hold on Hunter while gently and carefully touching the end of the strand to the broken one that dangled from her house, with two of her feet.

Her river of self flowed back up the strand, fusing it whole again. She felt herself yanked upward and the moth slipped from her grasp. Desperately, she clutched it by one feathery antenna as she was sucked back up the strand toward the darkness of her brother's house.

It should not be dark here. Her brother's house was never dark. She felt fear, then. His house had changed as well. Now it was in the form of a cold, dark cave.

She felt Hunter-moth struggling feebly in her grasp. She could feel his terror at the blackness surrounding them. Every fiber of his being screamed for light, for the warmth of the sun.

Standing outside the cave of her brother's house was an obearn cub. His foot was caught in a great steel trap, and he was pulling and biting at the trap desperately, trying to free himself, straining toward a tiny pumar cub who lay limp and lifeless just out of reach. The obearn cub's mother lay dead beside him. He let out a pitiful cry of despair, and Jarina realized it was memory she was seeing, an altered depiction of the tragic circumstances of their birth.

Jarina-butterfly flew into the girl cub's ear, and suddenly she was butterfly no longer. Now she was the female pumar cub. She rose and stretched. She walked over to Jargas-cub and pressed her paw against the spring that held the trap shut. The trap sprang open, freeing Jargas-cub, and he immediately bounded forward into her arms. She hugged her brother, nipping gently upon his ear. Something fluttered in her own ear, annoying her. She almost swatted it, but knew Hunter-moth for who he was just in time. She pressed her ear to her brother's then, and Hunter-moth flew eagerly, desperately, from her to him.

FARAD *found the thin coppery strand that led back to his own core, his body. His torn and burnt wings flapping frantically, almost uselessly, he made the exhausting climb back to his own core. The burnt stumps of his legs touched his core, and he collapsed upon it, in weariness and pain.*

A great river of warmth and light and strength flowed through the strand binding him to Jargas, into his dark core, filling it with light once again. The warmth radiated upward from his core into his legs. He stared in awe as his torn and burnt wings and burnt leg stumps shimmered and flowed, turning into furry legs with paws, and his body changed and grew.

He was a wolven cub now, and all around him the darkness was swept away. There were three other cubs beside him, playing together. He could hear them, yapping and yowling. They were pouncing upon one another and then without warning the three pounced upon him all at once. He looked into their eyes in wonder and knew them. But they could not be real! They could not be here! They were dead, gone forever.

Then the blue-eyed cub bit his ear, and it hurt; the pain was certainly real enough. He cuffed his youngest brother, Alarad, across the nose in retaliation. Haranad and Sarad came to their baby brother's aid, and it became a free-for-all. Then a great eagle separated the cubs gently with her talons and scolded them with a piercing cry and he recognized his mother, Alaria, Lady of House of Eagles. Her regal wings encircled all her children, and Farad nuzzled against the soft fluffiness of her feathers, desperate to feel her embrace once more. Her wing moved aside a little, and he saw his father, Jarad, Lord of House of Wolven, lope up beside them, a great, gray wolven, fierce and battle scarred but with kind and wise eyes. Farad nuzzled each of his brothers and his mother and father and knew peace and love and contentment once again.

Then he watched them all slowly change. He and his brothers grew into lean, muscled wolven in their prime. Then his father and mother and brothers faded: it was as if they were made of fog now. He howled in panic, but they still answered him, the strong yelps and yowls and screech of their voices mingling with his own. They stood there, as if made of mist, nuzzling and playing with one another, watching him. They did not leave altogether. They did not suffer. They did not die. Farad lay down, his muzzle resting upon his forepaws, and fell asleep watching them.

FARAD awoke and saw an unfamiliar ceiling made of wooden logs but felt no fear. No chains or ropes bound him, and there was sunlight in the room. He took a deep breath and stretched slowly from his toes to his fingertips, feeling every muscle flex. He lifted his left arm and stared at his hand in wonder, a Man's hand.

He sat up suddenly and looked about. Where was he? The walls around him were made of logs as well and the floor was made of wooden planks, planed smooth and fitted together almost seamlessly. But there was so much color and light!

He was lying in a nest of brightly colored silks and pillows and cushions. Light streamed in everywhere from windows framed by yellow and blue curtains, as if the owner of the house would see the sun and sky even were the day gray. There were two doors on opposite ends of the room, both shut. The one to his left appeared to lead outside.

Not Jargas's house, surely? An image came to mind of the colorful butterfly who had saved him and then turned into a pumar cub: Jarina, Jargas's sister. Could this be her home?

He stood and was surprised to find his feet were steady. He hadn't felt so well since he'd parted from Jargas outside Athanark, though he could see his body was still gaunt from the depredations of illness and the long journey, and the knife wound still pained him, as did the newer injuries from when he was overwhelmed by the sentries he'd missed seeing. Oddly, the thought of that defeat did not bring the terror it should. Perhaps because he did not appear to be a prisoner?

He looked about curiously, past the stove and low cabinets near it and the wooden chests scattered about the room to the sole true furniture, a large, sturdy wooden table with six chairs. His eyes widened in surprise. One of the chairs, though of almost the same simple design as the others, was nearly twice the width of the others, and the thickness of the wood it was crafted from was proportionately as great. The joints of the arms to the back and the seat were reinforced with metal. But the legs were both elongated and oddly truncated, as if sawed off midway to the floor. He walked over to examine it closer. Aha! Not cut off at all. Instead, the chair was in a wooden pit that appeared to be nearly two feet deep, so that someone unusually large and tall and heavy could sit at the table comfortably, at a level with his companions: Jargas!

Farad shut his eyes and looked within. The strand binding him to Jargas was still there, gleaming brightly. He tugged on it gently and felt an answering tug and a rush of warmth and strength so powerful it left him breathless. Jargas was very near.

He heard the door to the building open and opened his eyes. Jargas was there, huge and smiling. "Forgive me, Hunter! I meant to be here when you awoke. I only stepped out for a moment."

Farad smiled back at Jargas as if it was the most natural thing in the world for him to do—a warm, relaxed, friendly smile—and Jargas grinned back in delight. "Forgive us the welcome we gave you. We have been preparing to march to war to your aid, and you bypassed most of our sentries. They thought you a spy of the Enemy."

"So those were your sentries? I saw they were Dwarves, but there had not been enough time nor light to determine by the pattern of their braids that they were of Malar, and I had no choice but to fight back when attacked, in any case. I did not realize the village I approached was your home. You felt so far away."

Jargas nodded. "Jarina is sorry about that. She did not mean to cause you harm by it. You frightened her. She thought you meant to hurt her. She did not realize you were reaching for her light."

"I remember all of it. It was so strange." Farad thought of the wolven and searched for them, turning his gaze inward. He saw Haranad, Sarad, and Alarad, not the cubs or the grown wolven, but first the boys and then the men he had known. He looked into Alarad's beautiful blue eyes without intending to and tensed, afraid for what would come next. He had felt so warm and happy! He had hoped the terror might have been kept at bay for a little longer. But Alarad was still there.

He searched for the other image, the terrible one that always followed, of his brother's tortured and defiled body, those beautiful eyes gouged out. It was still there in his mind, but it was safely tucked away. It was not locked away, but it was not springing unbidden into his thoughts, nor was it so vivid that it blotted away the gentler image of the man he yet loved. He was able to suppress the horrific one, and again see his beloved brother as he once had been.

"Farad, are you all right?" he heard Jargas ask, his voice warm with concern. Jargas had used his given name, but he did not feel the familiar rush of panic hearing it spoken in a strange place usually brought.

Farad turned his eyes outward and looked into Jargas's warm, brown eyes and smiled. "I am very much all right. I am whole again." Then he frowned. "Jarina is all right? I only frightened her, I did not harm her?"

Jargas reassured him. "She is fine. My father is the one who was the worst off. When you leapt at Jarina with your mind, she accidentally severed our bond and we both collapsed. My father said he could not find the pulse of my heart. Then this did something it has never done in all the two hundred fifty years we have owned it," he said, holding up his hand. "It shone like the sun and worked its magic upon us."

Farad's eyes widened in shock. It could not possibly be the King's Ring! But he knew the metal, for the color was unmistakable: it was the blood-dipped copper of pyrenteum. And the stone, identical in size and shape to the one Dewalaren wore in his band even now, was glowing faintly, pulsing, as if with the beat of Jargas's heart.

Jargas exposed a pyrenteum band on his wrist then, holding up his arm for Farad to see it clearly. It was twin to the band Dewalaren wore, save Dewalaren's was a copy, crafted of pallenteum, and the stone in his band was a simple ruby, not a wizard's gem like the stone of the Ring and the stone of the original King's Band that Jargas now wore.

"I never lied to you, Farad, not truly, but I did not tell you the whole truth, either, when I told you the story of my grandsire. I was not born House of Gryphon, but to the King's House, House of Obearn, from what you revealed to me. My grandsire was Rowanar, not Stephan, though I did not know his name until you told it to me. Stephan shielded Rowanar with his body from the falling rock, when the mountain fell into the valley. His back was broken and he was killed. It was Rowanar who was rescued by my grandmother, who recovered, though his memory was yet lost. He was the one who married my grandmother and sired a child, my mother, by her.

"I am Jargas, brother to Chieftess and Healer Jarina, son of King Rongas and Chieftess and Healer Jahira, grandson of Crown Prince Rowanar and Chieftess and Healer Janara, Heir to the Throne of Malar in Holoren, Champion of the Varash, Lord of the House of Obearn, the rightful Prince and Heir to the Throne of Amontir."

Farad would not have believed it had anyone else ever told him such a thing, but he was bonded to Jargas and the truth of his claim shone brightly across the bond. He could not doubt the evidence of his own eyes, his core, his heart. A lifetime of faith and loyalty to Dewalaren, and his father, Evanaren, before him, crumbled to dust in the space of a heartbeat. Farad fell to his knees before Jargas, head bowed.

Jargas sounded astonished as he rebuked him. "Don't you dare start that now! I'll not have you kneeling to me, Farad, especially not here in my sister's home."

Farad obediently rose.

There was a gentle knock and the front door opened before either of them could answer. Farad saw a beautiful, black-haired, brown-eyed, petite woman who appeared to be perhaps thirty years old, clad in a filmy, rainbow-hued dress that reminded him of the butterfly's wings. "Father finally let me go," she said, speaking Dwarvish. Her voice was strong, confident, fond, and exasperated. "As if I was the one left helpless in the dark with my paw in the trap! As if I weren't the one to use the Ring to heal you and Farad! I heard you proclaim yourself, Jargas. Just because the Amontir don't have better sense than to rule through their Queens and because you were born a few moments before me...."

She paused in her annoyed tirade. "Why are you staring at me like that, Farad? Although I can't say I mind. You have beautiful eyes."

Farad jumped, more startled by her words than the use of his given name, and shifted his gaze away from her. "Don't say such things." He well knew what his eyes looked like: they were the cold eyes of a predator—dark, yawning, spiritless pits. His eyes reflected what lay within: his blackened and tarnished core, pocked and scarred by every terrible deed he'd ever done in service to King and Crown.

He felt a surge of warmth across the strand that bound him to Jargas, and knew it came from Jarina, not from Jargas. "But you do," she argued, walking over to one of the wooden chests and pulling out an ornate, heavy, silver hand mirror. She brought it to him and held it up in front of his face. "Look at them, Farad. You will like what you see."

Farad gritted his teeth and looked, and the stranger's eyes that stared back at him widened in shock. He unconsciously stroked under one eye gently with his fingertip, as if to be sure they were truly his own.

"They are warm and brown like Jargas's, only brighter. Your eyes shine as your house, your core, shines again. That is the word you use to describe it. I heard it in your thoughts."

He gazed inward and saw all the disturbing tarnish gone: his core indeed gleamed with the brightness of pallenteum as it hadn't since he was a child. "The Ring has healed me," he said in wonder. "You have healed me through it. I did not think I could ever be healed, without being too changed from who I am. I did not know that the Ring had the Power to heal. I thought only the Knife could." He realized even as he spoke that it was his core, not his body, that was healed. He was still gaunt and the blade wound from Gosa still pained him, as well as the new bruises from his defeat at the hands of the Dwarven sentries. But it did not matter. His core was whole again!

The joy shattered a moment later as infinite sadness darkened his core and his features. "Poor Talon! He has searched for the Ring his whole life, but now that it is found, it is no longer his to wear. He has lost me as well, for now that I am bound to you, Jargas, and you are known to be the Prince, I cannot bind to him. He has asked for so little from life and selflessly given so much, to all his people and to everyone he has ever met and aided, yet now he stands to lose all he has ever wanted."

Jargas and Jarina seemed saddened by his words. "But there can be only one King," Jargas said, and Farad nodded.

"That is one lesson he well knows. He will not fight you for the throne, once he sees as I have that your claim to it is sound, that it takes precedence over his own. He will kneel at your feet," Farad said with certainty.

"But the other Lords will not accept me so easily, I think," Jargas stated solemnly.

Farad shook his head. "They will. They must. The Law of Succession is our most sacred Law. I will help any of those who might doubt you see the truth of your claim."

Farad looked at Jarina. He had felt her eyes upon him as they spoke. She had not glanced away from him toward Jargas once. "Now you are the one who is staring," he accused.

Jarina laughed in joy. "Of course, Faradan. I have waited my whole life for you to find me, my Chieftain."

Jargas looked at her sharply.

"Stop scowling, Jargas. You must have known it was him when you told me you wanted to bring him here to me to be healed. You have known since we were children. You must leave us now, Jargas. I still command you as your Chieftess, even if you are now my Prince. Faradan and I have much to learn about each other and not much time before the army is to march."

JARGAS looked from his sister to Farad, shocked by her use of the Varashin endearment meaning "beloved," which she had appended to his name. He understood now the wave of desire coming from Jarina that had puzzled him before, when she had looked upon Farad as he lay bound and unconscious. His sister thought Farad was the man she had dreamt of since before she came-of-age. Jargas had never suspected she might view him in such a light. He liked Farad, he respected him, but he was not pleased at the thought that his sister was so drawn to him.

He remembered all too vividly the horrific images burnt into Farad's mind. He would not have his sister exposed to such terror, such darkness. For all her age and experience, she was still an innocent in many regards. She would lose that innocence, were she ever to truly love Farad. Jargas would not see the bright light and joy in her change to darkness and sorrow. But neither of them was paying attention to him now. They had eyes only for each other. And Jarina had commanded him to leave. With grave misgivings, he turned and left the lodge.

He was still linked to her. He would yet know what transpired. He had never before used their link to spy upon his sister. But he would do what was necessary to ensure her happiness, her safety.

AFTER Jargas left, closing the door behind him, Farad spoke. "Jargas said you prepare to march to War to my aid. You mean to join the armies of Malar in Fromer, Dorolingas, and Ironhand at the pass to Malar in Fromer?"

Jarina nodded. "The warriors of the Varash and of Malar in Holoren will join them. But we have also summoned the armies of the other twenty-nine Kingdoms of the West. We will be a formidable ally for you. But first, of course, we will have to face Dewalaren." Farad flinched both at the use of Dewalaren's given name and her words, and she looked at him in compassion and concern. "It will not be easy for you."

Of course she would know Dewalaren's given name, from her bond with Jargas. And she must feel safe, speaking it here. Dewalaren was no longer their King. Now Jargas would be the one Incuban relentlessly hunted. Still, he would not speak it. Farad sighed. "Nothing in my life has been easy, but facing Talon and being viewed as an enemy by him, when he still holds my heart…. I would sooner face even the Enemy."

He abruptly changed the subject, giving voice to his confused thoughts and feelings for this woman, a complete stranger save for Jargas's shared memories of her, who sought to overawe him by the familiarity of her words. "I am surprised you follow none of the traditions of your father's people, when Jargas so clearly does," Farad criticized. "There is so much color in your home and the clothes you wear. You do not dress in the browns and grays of the rock, you are not cloaked and veiled, you do not even braid your hair. Instead you bare your face and body for the world to see."

"A face such as mine was not born to be veiled, nor a body like mine to be cloaked," she argued, her voice heavy with seductive promise as she reached out to stroke his face.

He drew back from her hand. "Please, do not. It does not suit you."

She said in surprise. "I am sorry, Faradan. You obviously do not yet understand who you are to me. If you knew, you might welcome my touch."

He walked to the second door in the lodge, both unable to stand still and trying to put as much distance between them as possible, even as he wondered whether a room or a hallway to other rooms lay beyond, though he suspected the former. He did not think many might be allowed entrance past the first room.

Guessing his thoughts—or perhaps hearing them through her bond to Jargas, Farad realized, unsettled—Jarina said, "My home is visited by many. Much of the important business of the tribe is conducted in this lodge. I am Chieftess, but woman also. I must be allowed my privacy, as well."

She opened the door and entered the room, but Farad hesitated in the doorway. This was her bedroom. There was an ample bed, covered in jewel-toned silks and satins in all the hues of the rainbow. A heady scent, not of perfume, but of woman, pervaded the room. Jarina's scent was almost dizzying, overpowering. Farad had not expected that, nor had he thought the room might already be occupied.

Jarina was greeted eagerly by two house cats, one black as the night sky and the other gray as the rocks of the mountains. They rubbed themselves against her legs, tails in the air, purring loudly.

She laughed and knelt and petted them. "These are Midnight and Smoke." The cats looked past her, as if realizing she had not been speaking to them, saw him, and hissed, backing from him, hackles raised. Jarina seemed surprised by their reaction to him.

Farad laughed and entered the room. "You bring a wolven, and an eagle besides, before two cats, and you expect a different welcome?"

He crouched down and looked Midnight, the male, in the eye. "I understand your anger. I do not mean to trespass upon your territory and would never harm the two you guard so fiercely. I would be your friend, if you would allow it. My touch is also pleasing. I think you might welcome it, were you to give me the chance. Were you to get to know me, I might also make you purr with pleasure."

Midnight eyed him suspiciously and approached cautiously.

Farad held out his hand. The cat touched his nose against Farad's palm and then rubbed his head against it. Farad began gently stroking him. A low rumble began in the cat's throat and his hand vibrated from it.

"Your words echo my own, Faradan. I would also like to feel your caresses upon me. Would you make me purr as well?"

Farad frowned at her.

"Faradan, how can you reject me, when you have battled for me and saved me from the monster who torments you? When I have dreamt of you since I was a child, knowing you were the only man I would ever love? When I dream of you still? When I have saved myself for you?" Jarina sounded frustrated and hurt.

Farad was surprised by her words and her tone. She had neither sounded nor acted like such an innocent to him. So she did follow some of her father's customs after all. She did not dress as a Dwarven Lady, but she evidently kept the chastity of one. He chose his words carefully.

"It is not you, Jarina, it is me. I have not felt the touch of a woman in over a century. I no longer desire to. I cannot." But even as he spoke the words, he knew them to be false. He had desired her when first he felt her through her bond to Jargas, in Malar in Fromer. And here, now, standing beside him, the look of her, the scent of her, the sound of her voice, the way her body moved, he wanted nothing more than to press his body to hers and lose himself in her sweet embrace. Could he possibly be so healed?

No, it did not matter if he was. He could never lay a hand upon her for the same reason he could not link to her. Incuban desired her already. It would be too dangerous for her. He would use Farad to find her and then would use her to hurt him. He would use her in such terrible ways, if He ever thought Farad cared for her. "The Enemy already knows of you. I cannot make you so vulnerable. I cannot bring you to danger."

"Vulnerable? Danger? Farad, I am Chieftess! Do you think that because we have a Champion such as Jargas the rest of the tribe cannot fight? That I cannot? I am skilled with the bow, not merely upon targets or in the hunt, but in battle. I am proficient with the knife as well. Do you think this is the first time we go to war?" She sounded angry that he would view her as some helpless maiden. Although indeed a maiden, she was apparently far from helpless, at least against mortal foes. But she would die all too quickly, too horribly, were she ever to face what he had faced. He must make her understand.

"Neither bow nor knife will protect you from the Enemy we face. He cannot be killed by them. Do you think we would have fled before him for two and a half centuries if we had the means to kill him? Only the King's Sword can kill him, but only with the King's Ring to power it."

"And what of his warriors? Can they not be killed?" she reasoned.

Farad shook his head. "They are already dead, most of them. You and your people, even Jargas, have no idea of the horrors you will face in such a war."

"Then you must tell me, so we may be prepared," she encouraged.

He sighed. "I will tell you, but you cannot be prepared. Your heart will turn to ice the first time you see someone you know, someone you have laughed with and spoken with and fought beside your entire life, someone you might love, someone who dies fighting beside you, come back again. But he will come back as your enemy, mutilated and twisted, the walking dead or, even worse, changed into a living creature part beast and part Man, somehow fused together.

"I have seen entire armies run screaming from battle. I have seen seasoned warriors turn their own blades against themselves. I have seen mothers kill their children to save them from something that was once their father. For Incuban's servants do much more than kill. They delight in maiming, in death by slow torture, in rape, in depravities you could never imagine: things I have seen, things I have felt, over and over again, through links to those I love." Farad's voice was a whisper now, his warm eyes filled with the horror of it.

"Then share your memories with me. Bond to me so I might be prepared," Jarina commanded.

Farad shook his head violently. "Never. You would be so changed by what you have seen that Jargas would no longer know you. All the love and laughter and joy, all the light in your core, would be burned away, leaving a blackened, scarred ruin. My core should not shine so now. I do not know what the Ring has done. It has returned my strength to me, my Power, but all my memories, all the horrific experiences, I still see them, although no longer unbidden, and the images are no longer so vivid that they block out all else.

"I am sorry, Jarina, I truly am. I cannot live in joy as you do. I wish I could be who you were hoping to find, I wish for both our sakes. But I cannot be one who you can love, one who can love you in return. That I will never be."

He turned from her and walked back into the main room of the lodge and exited from it. He heard a cry of frustration before he closed the door, quickly followed by a loud crash and the yowl of an indignant cat.

Farad passed the man guarding Jarina's door without a word, and he was not stopped, though the man looked toward the closed door to the lodge in obvious concern.

Farad did not know where he should go. Yesterday he would have dragged himself to a flame and begun the all-but-useless meditations and fought against the Madness. But his core was stable now, it was whole. It gleamed with the clear sheen of pallenteum once more, on the outside at least, though inside it was the same as before, save for the many memories now kept safely at bay.

He desired privacy and the light of the sun. He had not truly basked in it since the Dwarven Lands. He did not need its Power, this time, only its warmth. The warmth he had felt upon awakening in the lodge was gone. He felt cold and terribly alone. He realized with a start that was what was missing. He was still bonded to Jargas, but the warmth was gone from the link. With a sudden flash, he realized Jargas was placating his sister, comforting her, consoling her. He should not see so much, feel so much.

He wondered whether he could shield himself from them, as Jarina had shielded herself from him. Could he keep the link in place, but erect a wall between them? None he knew had ever done such a thing. The links were made specifically to feel another, to draw strength when needed, lend it when needed. They could be broken when they no longer were appropriate. But Jargas was his King. He could not break his link to him without permission. And he reluctantly admitted anew that he could no longer stay sane nor even survive without it. So he focused instead on building a wall.

He saw a pallenteum dome take shape about his core, shimmering and solidifying. Now he was truly alone.

The thought panicked him and he felt desperately for the wire that joined his core to Jargas's. It was still there, he was still bound to Jargas, he could still draw upon the bond in need, or similarly aid Jargas.

He turned his gaze outward again, and saw the curious eyes of some of the villagers upon him. He met their glances levelly. There were dozens of log buildings, people moving amongst them with grim purpose all around him. Everywhere he looked, preparations for war were being made: swords and axes were being sharpened, armor was being readied, arrows were being fletched. He saw a cart being loaded with bundle after bundle of arrows, and another stocked with enough food to feed dozens of Men for many days. Here and there, he saw Dwarves among the Men, though they kept to the shadows, moving quickly from building to building, to avoid the full glare of the bright morning sun.

He walked until he found himself at the edge of the Village.

"Where you go?" one of the Varashin sentries challenged him, in broken, guttural Common.

"To the rocks. I seek privacy," Farad replied truthfully, in the same language.

The sentry eyed him carefully, taking in his air of competence and build and bow.

Farad realized with a start he was careful not to betray that he'd picked up his new bow and quiver on the way out of the lodge without even thinking about it. His hand had reflexively found them both. His core might be in turmoil, but at least his body had not betrayed him. After nearly a century and a half at war, it knew never to allow him to be vulnerable and unarmed. Poorly armed, he mentally corrected, as he realized to his surprise that he wore his dagger once more, concealed in the sheath under his shirt. He distinctly remembered it being taken from him when the sentries had fought him. He was appalled that he had not given a single thought to his weapons since waking. With the skill born from decades of practice at dissemblance, he gazed levelly back at the guard without betraying how rattled he was.

"No go far. Ogres, obearn, danger," the Guard instructed.

Farad nodded. "I will not go far."

"Come back same place," the sentry added in stilted Common. Farad nodded again. He did not want another reception like the one he had received earlier.

He quickly left the village behind, glad to be on foot. Ara's horse Aragar had been invaluable to him, but he had never loved horses as some of his people did. None of the blood of House of Horses ran in his veins. He had let Aragar loose when he'd realized a habitation lay ahead. He could not move stealthily on horseback, and he hadn't wanted to tie Aragar. He didn't know how long he might be gone or whether he might be prevented from returning to him, and he didn't want the horse to starve to death or become the prey of an obearn or ogre without a fighting chance to escape. He had seen signs of both within these mountains, and Jargas had warned him of them.

Thoughts of House of Horses and Aragar inevitably brought him to thoughts of Rolin, Lord of House of Horses, and immediately after to thoughts of Aramis, Lord of House of Foxes, Rolin's best friend. He worried anew for both men. He had seen signs of neither man in Thenalon or Aralon, though the City and nomadic tribe were yet divided. Neither should have left until the rift was healed.

He should have asked Dewalaren about them, but he had been too upset from mistakenly thinking him a Resemblant and nearly killing him, and then by observing his closeness and affection for his traveling companion Aras, to even think about them. He knew the grim truth was that Rolin and Aramis had likely both joined the ranks of the dead. The loss of Rolin pained him, while that of Aramis filled him with the same bleak wistfulness thoughts of him often brought. Aramis had despised him from the start, though Farad had often wished it were otherwise. Other than Dewalaren and Lunahr, only Rolin had not hated and feared him.

Lunahr! His smiling face blazed across Farad's core. He had last seen him as a boy of twelve. Lunahr was gone now as well, like all the others. Dead. Lunahr was dead! He had been such a bright light, the youngest of them, a little brother to all of them. Farad had seen him grow to almost a man, through his link with Dewalaren. Lunahr had still lived in joy, in music, in hope. But now he was dead, tortured and killed, like all the rest.

He would pay any price to see a lost kinsman again. But when next he saw Dewalaren and the few remaining Lords he yet led, they would meet as enemies. His people had supported Dewalaren's line for so long, they would not easily pledge their loyalty to Jargas, in spite of Farad's words to the contrary. Farad knew he might well have to fight his kinsmen. He would not hurt them, he would not slay any of his kin, ever. He would die first. But the Power within his core blazed strongly again, as it had in his youth. He would be far stronger than Dewalaren, until Dewalaren held the Ring and was himself healed by it.

Agony tore Farad's heart as he realized Dewalaren could never hold the Ring. He needed it too badly, because of the King's Madness that plagued him. In his need, he might seek to keep the Ring for his own. He realized in dismay that the King's Sword Dewalaren had wielded for decades must also now pass to Jargas. He was to be left with nothing.

Farad wished he had died in the cell in Malar in Fromer or burnt to death in the healer's chamber. Even such a horrific death was better than this, to betray one he loved as no other in order to preserve the line of descent to the throne, to ensure Jargas became King. Jargas was a great man. Farad admired him and respected him, he owed his life and his sanity to him, but he did not love him. He did not want to love him. Everyone he had ever loved had been doomed to pain and suffering and death. How could Jarina expect him to love her?

At the thought, her image flashed bright and laughing in his mind's eye. He remembered the impossible brilliance of her core, the gentleness and tenderness of her touch in his mind as she returned him first to the severed link to Jargas, and then to his own mind and body again. He ached to hold her in his arms, to kiss her laughing mouth. He ached for so much more.

He cursed and redoubled his pace. He would walk until he dropped. He must not think of her.

A long while later, he looked back the way he had come and then toward the sun. It was yet high in the sky and bright, though it was well past noon. He had walked far, much too far. He was nowhere near the Village. But he could yet retrace his steps, though he'd barely left a hint of his passing. He doubted anyone else would see a single mark upon the ground. Or, if need be, he could remove his shield and use the link to Jargas to guide him. He had his bow and knife against obearn. Ogres, though, he had forgotten about the ogres. Alone and yet injured, he would be no match for a rogue, let alone a larger group.

He was being careless. How could he be? He well knew carelessness killed even the most seasoned warriors.

Was he trying to get himself killed, to make it appear to be carelessness? The thought disturbed him. Was he truly such a coward that he'd rather die than face Dewalaren? He remembered wishing that he had died in Malar in Fromer. What a terrible wish!

He felt pity for Jarina, that she had waited her entire life for him. Now she was beginning to see the folly of her dreams. Loving him brought only tragedy, only death.

There was a strange sound up ahead, loud splashing in water, as if some large animal was drowning. The mountains here were far different from those that bordered the Dwarven Lands in the east. They were not so desolate. There was soil as well as rock, trees as well as smaller plants, and he'd unconsciously noted the spoor of several dozen small animals. Small animals were the prey of larger ones. He headed toward the water, and came across a stream, neither swift-flowing nor deep enough that something might drown in it, at least not here. Perhaps there was a deeper pool up ahead? Or an obearn might be fishing; he must be careful. Then he heard what sounded like a man crying out, his voice cut off midcry.

He ran then, all caution forgotten. He rounded a bend in the rock and saw not a man, but a woman, crouched by the side of the stream, dressed as a Dwarf. Her face might be veiled and her body cloaked, but her proportions betrayed her: she was a woman of Man and a tall one at that. She was barely wet, but still there was splashing, and he saw then a Man's leg kicking up from the water in front of her. She was drowning someone!

Farad ran to her and grabbed her left shoulder and tore her away from her victim. He was naked, his long braided hair and twin-braided beard peppered with gray, his brown eyes wild with fear. He was choking and gasping and coughing. Farad dove forward, pulling him from the water. He truly was a Man, as tall as Farad, not a Dwarf, in spite of the distinctively braided hair and beard.

He had been so intent upon saving the Man and so confused by his appearance that he had become distracted for a critical moment. A fist slammed into Farad's head, knocking him away from the Man. Even as he reeled from it, he punched back, hard. His right fist slammed into the woman's jaw and his left her stomach. But where his right met hard bone, his left met something harder still, when he had expected soft flesh: it was as if he hit stone. He drew back his hand in pain and shock. She was armored beneath the cloak! And she was taller and more broad than he had realized, taller than he was. She must have been a scant few inches under seven feet. He blocked a fist that came for his face, but he was a fraction too slow for the next one, to his chest, and it connected. He fell then, gasping and silently cursing. She'd found the blade wound he'd gotten in Gosa.

"Lie still and I won't harm you further," she commanded in Common, her voice ringing with Power, though she was not one of his kin. His strengthened core resisted her attack easily.

Circe. It must be Circe! He'd heard rumors she'd gone to darkness. He'd hoped they were false. If the three wizards who were their allies turned against them, all hope was lost. Regardless, he'd not let her kill an innocent when he might stop her, in spite of what it might cost him.

Farad kicked from where he lay, knocking her backward into the water, and then struggled to his feet. The Man had also been knocked back into the water in their struggle, and he was face down and thrashing weakly. Farad dragged him to the shore once more and to his relief saw him gasp for breath. He turned to face the woman, but it was too late. She kicked him hard in his manhood. Twin waves of pain shot from his groin into his abdomen, felling him. He lay gasping in agony, tiny bright stars everywhere in his field of vision as he fought against overwhelming nausea. Then her foot found his head and the stars and everything else disappeared into blackness.

FARAD awoke slowly, his body protesting. He hurt almost everywhere. He no longer heard the gentle rush of water from the stream. He sensed he was no longer outside. Was he a prisoner? His heart hammered, even as he realized he was not bound.

He opened his eyes only enough to see through his lowered lashes, so any observing him might think him yet unconscious. He saw rock, a wall of rock, and involuntarily sat up and fully opened his eyes, his entire body tensing in panic. Not underground, not a prisoner kept away from the sun, not again!

Sitting brought more pain, but relief as well. There was only a single wall of rock: a large tarp over a wood framework comprised the rest of the room.

A Dwarf came in through the opening in the tarp and looked at him, startled. "How can he sit?" he muttered in Dwarvish. Then in Common he said, "You should lie down. You are injured. I have something for the pain, now that you're awake to drink it."

Farad shook his head and regretted it for the knife of agony that shot through his temple.

"You must. I'll not let a Man suffer when I can aid him," the Dwarf insisted.

Farad spoke intently in Common. He'd not betray his knowledge of Dwarvish yet. "There was an older Man, by the water. He was drowning. Does he live?"

The Dwarf eyed him shrewdly. "I'll not answer any of your questions until you drink this," he said stubbornly, holding out a flask he picked up from a chest by the cot Farad lay upon.

"**You will answer me now**," Farad said, his voice echoing with Power.

The Dwarf glared at him. "You'll not try that on me again, or I'll see your jaw is broken, not bruised. Now drink, all of it," he demanded, thrusting the flask in his face.

Farad's eyes widened in surprise. Not only had his Power not worked upon the Dwarf, he had known what Farad had tried to do!

If this Dwarf had wanted him dead, he could have killed him easily in his sleep. And he had not tied him to the bed and forced the liquid down his throat as he could have. Farad took the flask and uncorked it. He sniffed cautiously at the contents, extending his Power into the metal of the flask. Whatever it contained was not tainted by the Enemy, or Power. It might yet be poison or a drug, but why chance that he might not drink it? Why allow him to awaken while yet free? Taking the risk, he downed the liquid gingerly. "Does he live?" Farad asked again, holding the empty flask out to him.

The Dwarf smiled then. "Aye, he yet lives, despite your trying to help him."

"I don't understand," Farad said, puzzled.

"Shanti wasn't trying to drown Archer, she was trying to save him. He'd fallen asleep in the sun by mistake. He'd not realized how tired he was from the march, when he went to bask on his rock, as if he were a lizard, not a snake. He fell asleep. He was in the sun too long and drove himself sun mad and his body was burning from it. The sun can kill a Man foolish enough to cook himself in it. He'd be dead now if she hadn't gone looking for him.

"When she found him, he was already dying. She knew she had to cool him down to save him, so she carried him to the stream and dunked him in it. But he was in convulsions by then, and he was having delusions besides. That's why he was struggling; he didn't even realize who she was, let alone know she was trying to help him. She had her hands full with him like that and then you came along and attacked her."

Farad grimaced.

"You're lucky Shanti's forgiven you for it, for not only did you hit her, you hit her more than once and you hurt her. No one's ever done that before. By our law, you'd be dead for attacking her, but she's pardoned you for it, for trying to save Archer to start with and for dragging him from the water when he'd gone too far under, at risk to your own life. Your worry for him was what enabled her to fell you. She said besides that she'd not slay kin, when there's so few of you left."

"Kin? How is Shanti kin to me?" Farad asked, vexed.

The Dwarf's brow crinkled. "You are Jarad, Lord of House of Wolven, and you've not recognized Archer?"

Farad stiffened. "How do you know my House?"

"Your chest wound reopened where Shanti hit you. You bled through the bandages and your shirt besides. I removed your shirt to treat the injury, and saw the band," the Dwarf explained.

Farad nodded. "But I am not Jarad," he said, speaking his father's name without hesitation, without pain, as he could not have before Jargas and then Jarina had healed him. "Jarad was my father. He died a century ago. I am Hunter, Lord of House of Wolven. Last of my House," he added softly.

The Dwarf appeared upset by his pronouncement. "I'll have to tell Shanti. It might be best if you were gone before Archer wakens, then. She thought she'd be bringing him joy. She'll not bring him to further darkness."

"Archer... you said he was a snake, not a lizard. Not that Archer? Lord of House of Serpents?" Farad asked in shock. Could Desmond truly still live?

The Dwarf eyed him again. "Then you do know him?"

"I more know of him than know him. I'd only seen him a few times, and that was almost a century ago. He spent little time with the rest of us. But he vanished nine decades ago! We'd thought him lost, and his House with him. His wife and sons were slain by the Enemy."

The Dwarf nodded, as if he knew of that already.

"But how did he end up here, with you?"

"I'll let Shanti go from there. How are you feeling?"

Farad thought about it for a moment and was surprised. "The pain's gone but my head's still clear."

The Dwarf smiled. "Is that why you were so stubborn? I forgot we're the only ones who grow those mushrooms. We're so spoiled by them now, I hadn't remembered what such medicines usually do. Well, you were in a fog enough, without me adding to it. I'll be back shortly, with Shanti, if she can come."

"Before you go, might you honor me with your name?" Farad asked.

The Dwarf said proudly, "I am Donovar of Cavernas, Westhold."

"Cavernas! Jargas told me some survivors of the Lost Kingdoms yet lived in the Saravan Mountains. So Cavernas is one of them?"

"Aye. Of the twenty-nine Kingdoms of the West, we're one of the largest. We alone bring one thousand two hundred seventy warriors to the War. But Shanti can tell you more of that as well. It's she who will lead us in battle."

"She is your Queen?" Farad asked, surprised. Dwarves were led by their Kings, not their Queens, and they would never allow a Dwarven woman to be so endangered.

"No, she is our Princess, but much more than that, as you'll soon learn. But she prefers the term War Leader now."

Farad was amazed. He had struck a Dwarven Princess? In the face, and more than once? "Then I thank you for sparing my life, when I truly should have been slain!"

Donovar smiled again. "You mentioned Prince Jargas by name, casually. It is well for us, I think, that we did not slay you. We might have made him our enemy, when we come to him as allies. But I must get Shanti. I will be back shortly." So saying, he left.

As soon as he was gone, Farad tried to stand and walk. He could do so, but it felt odd. Parts of him were numb, blessedly so, though it was troubling as well. He thought he might be hurting himself, though he could not feel it. The pain would have warned him.

Farad peeked out from the door gap in the tarp. There was a line of such tarps to either side of the one he was in, all along the rock face of a cliff. He was apparently still in the valley. There was nothing so far to indicate that Donovar had been less than truthful to him. Still, he had trusted Donovar too easily. Was it because he reminded him of Gervan? Or was this an aftereffect of the Ring's healing? Had it healed his core enough that he might trust again? If the latter, would he still have the judgment to know whom he should trust and whom he should not?

Farad spied a cloaked and veiled giantess walking beside Donovar toward the tarp that sheltered him and quickly ducked back into the shelter and lay back on the bed. He would not betray his strength to them.

He heard muted voices outside the door flap, speaking in Dwarvish. He recognized Shanti's voice. She was in the middle of a sentence. "...sure of him. He resisted me, Donovar! No one but you and Father ever have." Farad heard fear in her voice.

"He is not a tool of the Enemy, Shanti. He cannot be. There is too much warmth about him," Donovar assured her.

Farad was startled to hear him say so. Was he so changed? He did not feel warm; he felt cold.

Donovar continued. "He did not seek to harm me as he might have, even once he saw his Power could not work upon me. I believe he truly is the son of Desmond's friend. Your father would give anything to see his lost kin again, to find out why they abandoned him, why they exiled him to such loneliness. Now come. Hunter might get nervous if he hears us, speaking so long in a language he does not know. It is not wise to make a Lord nervous."

They entered and Farad sat up in bed again, but slowly, as if it took great effort for him to do so.

"I am pleased to see you are recovering so well from the injuries I dealt you," Shanti said, shocking Farad anew by speaking to him in flawless Amontirin.

"I have been hurt far worse before. I am surprised you know our tongue, Lady. Why would Archer betray such a secret to you?" he replied in the same language, sensing it might be a test to see whether he knew it, as well as being meant to reassure him. He already knew the answer to his question from what he'd overheard: Desmond was her father. But he was curious as to what she might choose to reveal or conceal from him.

Shanti continued in Common, likely so Donovar might understand as well, now that he'd passed her test of knowing Amontirin himself. "He said I could not claim my rightful place as Lady of the House, once he is gone, unless I knew it. I am his daughter. I am surprised to find you in these mountains. My father has not seen any of his kin in nine decades. He had feared you all might be dead and gone."

Farad clenched his jaw. "Not all. Many have died, too many sons and daughters, entire Houses. It is a joy to find a lost House. Archer was with us seldom enough in the two decades before he vanished. It is a pity your father disappeared before we developed the Cache and Marker system, for he would not have lost track of us then. But they are useless now, and we may well lose others who wander too far afield."

"Lose? Wander!" Shanti's eyes flashed in rage. "My father was sent by the Prince, ordered on his mission! He spent six decades of his life safely escorting the refugees of the Dwarven Kingdoms to the Saravan Mountains. He lost his wife and sons to his loyalty to Evanaren, his health, almost his sanity, his very life, and you call him lost! Why was he abandoned for nine decades? Why was he exiled?" Her eyes flashed red-gold and Farad felt the heat of her anger batter his core.

He spoke to her sternly. "You must learn to control your temper, Lady. Were I a normal Man, you would have just now reduced me to a gibbering idiot. Indeed, were I the man I was a scant two days ago, you would have done so. I am appalled that Desmond has not taught you control."

Donovar was watching Shanti in concern, but she averted her eyes from him. "Don't look at me like that! I'm trying! Do you think it is easy with him unconscious? I can't even feel our bond, he is so weak! To draw upon his calm now would kill him." She was trembling wildly.

Farad's brow creased in concern. "If you tell me what afflicts you, I might be able to aid you."

"I should trust you to aid me? You are a trap, you must be! You cannot be here! Why would you be here, now, after so many decades, when we leave the safety of our Mountains, when we march to war? When my father has so weakened himself aiding me that he might die?" The last ended almost in a sob. Farad saw through her anger to her fear. She was terrified, for her father and for herself.

Farad spoke soothingly to her. "I came to these mountains to find healing, for others of our people dwell here. Two more lost kin have been found.

Much has been found, and much stands to be lost by it. But if you seek calm, strength, sanity, I will take you to our kinsman. I was reduced to staring into flame chanting our meditations to ward off the demons of the night before he saved me."

He saw her start and Donovar looked at him sharply. "The nightmares? He can make them leave her?"

"No! Do not say more!" Shanti yelled, apparently forgetting all caution, glaring at Donovar, her eyes flashing red-gold fire. Donovar's face contorted in agony and he crumpled, even as Farad leapt between them. The flame of her core ripped across his own. He grabbed her shoulders and wrapped a leg about her and twisted, sending her crashing to the ground with him on top of her.

She began screaming incoherently as his eyes blazed into hers. He forced himself into her mind, as Jargas had forced himself into his own. But she was not lost to Madness as he had been. This was different. Her core was burning; it raged like an inferno.

FARAD felt unquenchable anger build as his core touched hers and his own core began to kindle with the rage. But he could not pull away and leave her to burn.

Instead he tore away his shield and screamed down his link to Jargas for aid, for strength. Instantly a wave of cool Power enveloped him. His core sizzled and sputtered and the flames went out, like a burning house extinguished by a flooding river. Farad diverted the remainder of the wave and sent it crashing toward Shanti, reinforcing it with every scrap of strength and Power he possessed. A raging torrent of water met the conflagration of her core with the hiss of steam. Her core began to cool and darken.

With an angry cry, a great flaming bird, a phoenix of legend, rose from her core and dove toward Farad's unprotected core, while all his Power was directed toward saving Shanti. A great gout of flame erupted toward him.

But then with a hunting scream, a large cat, a pumar in her prime, leapt at it, biting down hard upon the flaming bird. She gave Farad the time he needed to divide the wave, sending half of it cascading into the bird.

The scorched cat kept her jaw tightly upon the bird, though her fur and skin had seared away in great patches, even as she began to drown.

Farad became a wolven and swam with powerful strokes toward the cat, as the flaming bird withered and then sputtered and vanished.

But it was too late. The last of her strength spent, the pumar sank from sight, apparently lifeless.

Farad silently screamed Jarina's name in denial as he dove downward into the water, paddling furiously with his paws, searching for her desperately. She could not die for him!

He found her floating limply beneath the water and bit gently but firmly upon the loose skin of her neck fur, dragging her toward the light. He left Shanti's core and returned to his own. It was dark with him gone. He followed the bright strand that linked his core to Jargas's with his precious burden. He saw to his concern that Jargas's core was nearly as dark as his own; he sensed he was inside, though not conscious. He found the bright strand linking Jargas to his sister's core in relief. All bonds were broken in death. Jarina yet lived!

When he reached her core, it was empty of her warm presence, as black as night. He fought against irrational fear as he laid the limp cat upon Jarina's dark core. The terror grew as her core remained dark. She did not stir, she did not enter.

Farad howled in anguish and began gently lapping her face with his tongue, against the grain of her fur, as a mother cat would lick a newborn kitten, trying to warm her. He licked her neck, her back, desperately wishing Jargas was there to aid him.

Finally, the waterlogged, burnt cat stirred, and Jarina's core began to glow faintly beneath her. Farad yipped in joy and began licking her again enthusiastically.

Her eyes opened and his tail started thumping wildly, as if he were a mastiff. Jarina rose on unsteady feet. Farad was beside her instantly, his broad, hairy shoulder pressed against her soaking fur, steadying her. She bit his ear tenderly and then nodded at the strand he'd traveled down. He yipped again, understanding, and bounded toward his own core.

He stopped to study Shanti's core before returning to his own. It was blackened and drenched, but it still glowed, still pulsed with life.

He followed the strand of self back to his own core and reentered, leaving the link that had been forged between him and Shanti intact for now.

WHEN Farad opened his eyes, he realized he was still on top of Shanti. His face flushed and he pushed himself off of her. She was not conscious.

He lifted her and carried her to the bed he'd lain on, remembering his wound too late when a fresh wet red spot blossomed against the bandages. He'd forgotten, without the pain to remind him.

He knelt by Donovar and ever so carefully and gently viewed his core, expecting to find a blackened husk. Instead he found to his confusion and relief a sphere of pyrenteum surrounding his core. Donovar's core could not have been strong enough to erect such a protective barrier. True pyrenteum was impervious to fire. Only wizards knew the shaping of it. Donovar must have had dealings with one of The Three. He must have words with Donovar once he awoke.

Farad withdrew his probe and shook Donovar, but he did not stir. Farad sighed and laid a blanket over him, then dragged some pillows onto the floor from one of the other cots in the room. He could no longer stand; he was too weak even to climb into the cot.

He hoped Jargas would come quickly, before the medicine for pain wore off, before these Dwarves found their Princess and their healer felled. Surprisingly, apparently no one had heard her scream. Or perhaps they were used to tantrums from their Princess. A Dwarf would normally never enter a Princess's presence without her express permission, but would in a heartbeat without hesitation were she endangered.

Jarina had saved him from the phoenix almost at the cost of her own life. It had been Incuban; the creature had possessed the chilling, familiar feel of that depraved, deranged monster.

But his thoughts were drawn away from their Enemy to Jarina. He remembered the agonizing pain, the panic, when he feared her dead, the joy when he saw her recover. He loved her!

The fantastic realization brought terror instead of joy. He could not! He must not! How could he, after having known her for such a short time?

He ached to touch his link to her, to feel her again, but they were not linked. He had only been able to touch her because of his link to Jargas.

He would link to her as soon as he saw her. No, as soon as Shanti was well enough for him to sever his link to her. He must make Jarina understand why he had bonded to Shanti.

Jarina had again appeared as a pumar, though a grown one this time. The significance of her form, which had escaped him before, burned brightly within his core: Rowanar's mother had been House of Pumar. Was Jarina truly Lady of House of Pumar, then? Pumar had been a lost House! Had they regained another?

Farad felt a wave of weakness wash over him. He had sent too much of his strength to Shanti and used the rest to save Jarina. He realized the bandages were saturated with blood now, from having torn open his wound carrying Shanti. *Carelessness can kill even the most seasoned warrior,* he mused silently.

Jargas, help me! Hurry! he sent down the bond, with the last of his strength. Then he fell unconscious.

JARGAS opened his eyes to see Lorgas's panicked face hovering over his own. "Highness!" he cried, and then called out in relief, "He's recovering!" to the rest of the search party that had been seeking Farad.

Jargas put a hand to his head. Could it have been real? Could it truly have been the Lady from his dreams? How could he ever have been so blind as to mistake Circe for her?

But Farad had found her first. He had linked to her. A surge of anger and jealousy coursed through him.

Farad had tried to help her, but he hadn't been strong enough. The anger melted, replaced by concern for his kinsman and friend. They were right to have worried about him, to have begun searching for him when he was absent for so long.

Jargas stood, swayed, and then steadied himself on his staff. He saw a cluster of his men about someone on the ground, only his great height enabling him to see the one they surrounded. "Jarina!" He stumbled over to her.

"She does not look well, Highness. She has yet to recover as you did," Lornan said in concern.

Jargas bent over her. She was deathly pale and seemed to be barely breathing. He stroked her cheek and reached for her through the link, his body collapsing beside hers as he left it.

He found her, barely standing, a great cat, like the pumar he had slain in the Fromer Mountains, standing on a dimly glowing core. He sent a wave of strength to her and she steadied, her core brightening markedly. The cat vanished and Jarina stood in its place. She walked over to him and hugged him, then shoved him away, pointing to the strand of their bond. He nodded and left her core for his own and gazed outward again.

He opened his eyes to a circle of frantic faces above his own, but he had eyes only for his sister, as he turned to her.

Jarina's eyes fluttered open.

"You took a great risk," he scolded her.

"Should I have let Hunter die, after you have worked so hard to save him? And he saved me again, when I was drowning."

The Dwarves around them were looking at them both in confusion.

"Hunter is linked to another. She is as we are, part Amontir, part Dwarf. I sensed it. I followed Farad's link to her. I saved her for him." Jargas's voice was bitter.

Jarina gaped at him and said in denial, "No, that is not what I felt. He saved me, he was mourning me. He thought I was lost. His cries awakened me."

"Jarina, he does not love you. He's tried to tell you and now he's found another. Why else would he link to her and not to you?"

"There must have been great need," Jarina reasoned, but Jargas heard the doubt, the pain, in her voice. "I know what I felt," she argued stubbornly.

He shook his head. "You felt what you wanted to feel. I'll not watch him hurt you. It's time we faced him."

At that moment, a weak cry for help came across his bond with Farad. He gazed inward and saw the flame of Farad's core rapidly fading to darkness. He quickly sent him a burst of strength, and the flame steadied, but still it glowed so dimly.

"We must go to him, quickly! He is still in danger, he is injured." Jargas leapt to his feet and pushed through the circle of their men and began striding rapidly, his strength restored, now that Jarina had recovered. Jarina and the six Dwarves that guarded them had to all but run to keep pace with him.

Jargas followed the link easily, now that it was no longer shielded from him.

To his relief, only a short while later they were challenged by Dwarven sentries in unfamiliar armor. "I am Jargas, Prince of Malar in Fromer. My father, King Rongas, and I are the ones who summoned you. One of my people, a Man by the name of Hunter, is in your camp, with someone named Shanti. He is injured. Can you take us to him?"

The Dwarves eyed him carefully, squinting against the bright, midday sun. "If he is injured, she would have taken him to Donovar. Come with us."

More Dwarves joined the small band, until he and Jarina and their six men were surrounded by twenty guards. His men eyed the others warily as they approached what was marked as the Healer's Tent.

"Wait here," one commanded, after another one of them called out but was not answered from within. He ducked inside. "Princess!" he cried in alarm, and more of the guards swarmed inside, while a full dozen yet surrounded them suspiciously.

"Donovar!" another voice cried. "What's happened here?"

"Please," Jargas urged. "I swear to you by Ragnar and Aralyn both that we mean your healer and the Lady no harm, but you must let us see them. We can help. You can disarm the two of us and hold our guards as hostage, but there is little time, if we are to save our friend."

"You would be a fool to make such an oath to the God and Goddess and then to break it, and you do not appear to be a fool. You and the… female… may enter."

JARINA winced inwardly. He had not called her "Lady," but she had no one to blame but herself for the slight. She was hardly dressed as one. She could only imagine how ill they must think of her.

When they entered the shelter, Jarina had eyes only for Farad. He was unconscious on some pillows on the floor, his bandages drenched in blood. "No wonder he is in danger! He's reopened his wound!"

Jarina opened the healer's kit she had brought with her and began tending Farad. His eyes fluttered open.

"Faradan, lie still. You've reopened your wound. You almost killed yourself," she accused.

"I had... to save her," Farad said weakly. "She is... precious...." His eyes closed and he was again unconscious.

His words tore at Jarina's heart. Eyes welling with tears, she continued to tend him.

JARGAS was torn between Shanti and Farad. He reached into his sister's healer's kit and located the small bunch of leaves he sought. He pulled them out and rubbed them together under Donovar's nose.

He coughed and stirred and his eyes opened. "Shanti!" he called out, sounding panicked.

"She is safe," Jargas assured him.

Donovar rose, looking about, and when he saw her lying still, rushed to her side. "You don't understand! She can't sleep, she mustn't. Someone torments her in her sleep. Without her father to protect her...." His hand shook as it hovered over her face. It was obvious he longed to touch her, but he'd not so dishonor her. He could not, without her express permission. Or perhaps he withheld his hand for another reason, for as a healer, he should not have been so constrained.

"She is free from Him. We drove Him from her thoughts, her mind, her core. Hunter is bonded to her. And Jarina and I came to her aid also. But we could only do so much from so far away. Now that we are here, we can aid her further. We bear a Ring of great Power. We can help her core heal."

A voice from the door spoke. It sounded old and weary and in pain. "Who are you?"

Jargas turned and saw a Man, groomed as a Dwarf, with graying hair. The Man swayed, and two of the Guard immediately steadied him.

"Lord, you should not be walking. You must at least sit if you will not stay in bed," Donovar said, his voice warm with concern.

"I am Jargas, Prince of Malar. I am also Lord of House of Obearn, Prince of Amontir," Jargas said.

The Man's eyes widened. "You cannot be. I know the Prince, or knew him. You look nothing like him. You cannot be his heir."

"Aye. That Man's son, Talon, currently claims the same title, but my claim is greater. Talon is the grandson of Idare, great-grandson of the King's brother, his murderer, Ebonar. I am the grandson of Crown Prince Rowanar, eldest son of King Albinar and the rightful Heir to the Throne of Amontir. As proof, I wear the King's Band and the King's Ring," he said, exposing the pyrenteum band about his wrist and holding his hand aloft. The jewel of the Ring glowed softly on his finger. "I wish to use the Ring to heal your daughter. We drove off the foul demon who has been plaguing her with nightmares, but her core is damaged. The Ring can heal it."

The Man's eyes were riveted on the Ring. "It cannot be! Here, now, in our time of greatest need." He focused his gaze onto Jargas's face. "I am Archer, Lord of House of Serpents. I would risk linking with you first, for I cannot leave my daughter so vulnerable to a stranger," he challenged.

"Then link with me," Jargas said.

They touched one another's faces. A strand as thin and delicate as spider web met Jargas's own thick strand. Jargas found a core that was bright and untarnished, but the walls of it were as if made of glass, fragile and transparent.

"Your own core needs healing," Jargas said as he dropped all shields, opening his core fully to Archer, once he tested his core for taint by the Enemy and found none.

The older man instantly began questioning him, viewing memories, testing him. He moved quickly, efficiently, almost frantically. "You are truly who you say you are," he said in wonder. "Much has happened in my exile, but I see you can tell me little of it. But Farad, Jarad's son, will know much. Can his brothers truly all be dead, as you have seen them in his core? I know the pain he suffers. But why is he linked to Shanti?"

"She was in great danger. She had lost control of her anger. She almost killed Donovar and her rage was consuming her. First I must mend your core and then I would link to Shanti, if you would allow it, so that I might mend her core as well," Jargas said.

"Of course," Archer said, reverence in his voice.

The Ring blazed to life and Jargas turned the brilliance of it toward Archer. Archer gasped and drank in the light as if it were the sun's. Jargas saw the walls of his core thicken and darken, growing opaque, until his core appeared solid again.

The Ring's light diminished, to a gentle glow upon Jargas's hand.

Archer stood straighter, now. His body was still burnt from the sun, but his will had strengthened again. "I am in your debt, Highness. Please, aid my daughter as you have aided me." He turned to the Dwarves in the tent. "Please, everyone but Donovar and our guests, wait outside," he commanded, and the Healer's Tent quickly emptied. He stayed just inside the doorway.

Jargas walked over to where Shanti lay. He reached his hand for her temple, and gently bonded to her core. Then he drew it back, feeling shy and awkward. It was wrong to touch her when she slept, even with her father's permission.

Unexpectedly, her eyes opened and she looked accusingly at him. "You will not touch me again. Two have bonded to me while I slept and you are one of them. I will make you regret your insolence."

"I will break my bond, if you wish me to, Lady. But if you instead keep it, you might rely upon my strength ever to aid you when you are in need of it," Jargas swore.

She eyed him coolly. "My father aids me. I need no other." But a flash of fear crossed her face. Jargas felt her seek inward for her bond to her father. He felt her relief when she felt him alive, and far more well than he should be. Her father's strength stunned her. Jargas sensed her shock when she realized he was very near and sat up. She inhaled sharply when she spotted him by the door flap. He heard her next thought clearly. *Why are you allowing this man to touch me?*

"Can we not both help you, Lady? I am Jargas, Prince of Malar, Lord of House of Obearn, Prince of Amontir. You do not lower yourself by acknowledging me," he entreated her.

She stared at him in shock. "Prince of Amontir? Why did you abandon my father to exile?" she demanded, instantly infuriated.

"That was not my doing, nor even that of the other man who currently claims to be Heir to the Throne, from what I saw in your father's core." Jargas explained what he knew of Dewalaren's past, as Farad had told him, though he did not reveal his given name. "Do you not remember me standing beside you, shielding you, through the fire, through the flood?"

"I remember," Shanti said, and she shuddered. "You have seen too much of me."

Jargas shook his head. "I did only what I needed to save you. I did not view your memories, or your heart. I would never dishonor you, Lady. I would give all I have to learn about you, but ever only with your permission."

"Why do you say such things to me? Do you not fear the fire in my eyes, the anger in my heart? No man dares touch me now, not even my father." Her eyes betrayed her anguish.

"The fire and the anger were not yours, Lady. The Enemy had laid claim to you, but we freed you. He'll not hurt you again, I swear it."

"You may live to regret you rescued me from Him, if you indeed have. I heard you call to each other, this woman you so love, your sister Jarina." Her eyes narrowed as she glared at her. Jarina seemed oblivious, all her attention focused upon Farad.

"It was she the Enemy sought, when He found me. He thought I was her, at first. He was angry when He discovered I was not. He sought to punish me for it, as if I had deliberately tricked Him. Then, when He found my Power was akin to hers, He turned all His attentions upon me." She began trembling.

"You cannot heal what He has done to me, in the dreams He forced upon me that are not dreams. You cannot erase the memory of His cruelties. You cannot return my innocence to me. He has defiled me, destroyed me so that no Dwarf could ever want me." Tears were falling from her eyes now, splashing against the veil.

Jargas ached to hold her, to comfort her, to tell her of his love for her, but he dared not touch her nor say such things to her. She could not possibly understand. He had dreamt of her for decades, but she did not seem to know him at all.

"The Ring has healed my friend of many cruelties, of horrible memories and visions of darkness and death. Please, Lady, you must at least let me try," Jargas pleaded.

Her father went to her. He took her hands in his own, and Jargas felt anguish lash her. Even her father dared not embrace her. Her skin all but crawled even from the simple handclasp, but when he tried to pull his hand away, she would not release it.

He looked into her eyes. "Desenia, please. Do this for me. As you have stayed your hand from taking your own life, only for me, please give Jargas a chance to truly return your life to you. I believe he can heal you. If he cannot, then I release you from your promise. I cannot bear to see you in such torment. I would rather see you join my first wife and sons in death, even though your mother and I would soon join you, and the Kingdoms would be left mourning us all."

"Your words are filled with despair, but your eyes and your mind are filled with the light of hope. I will allow him to try. I would do anything to ease the pain you suffer for me." She looked bravely at Jargas, but he could feel the fear coursing through her like a river of heartache.

Jargas swallowed and reached for her hand, as Archer let her go.

The Ring blazed upon his finger as soon as he touched her. The glow enveloped her hand, her arm, her entire body. Tremendous Power flowed from the Ring into her, yet still it vibrated with more.

DESENIA'S burnt and drenched core began to change the instant the Power washed over it. All the coldness in her core was burned away, the terrible coldness the fire had kindled to quench but could not.

Desenia was amazed as the memories of every touch, every taste, every smell, all the humiliations, the depravities, the tortures that had plagued her since leaving Cavernas, faded to dreams, to simple nightmares that would not have the power to drive her to madness nor death by her own hand.

She was still no longer the innocent she had been; how could she be? But she could put the horrors of the past behind her. They would dim now with time. Her father could hug her again, and she would welcome his embrace instead of fighting it. The touch of his hand upon her face would provide comfort again, rather than revulsion and terror. She might even learn to love and to be loved, as she had been born to be.

Who was this man, Jargas, who had healed her, who had spoken as if he wished she might honor him with her favor?

She walked carefully, tentatively, along the bond he had forged while she slept. She approached his core almost shyly. It was so big, so bright! Even her father did not shine with such Power!

Jargas did not stop her, but instead welcomed her. He was kneeling to her, beside his core. He held out his hand. She accepted it and he rose. She realized in wonder that he was taller than she was. She did not have to gaze down upon him as she gazed down even upon her father.

He opened his core to her and entered with her. He bared himself to her. She saw his whole life, from the agony of his birth, which began with inconsolable loss, with his mother's death and almost his sister's, to his recent trials. He concealed nothing from her, except for the chest of dreams. That he saved for last.

He opened it when he sensed that she would not be offended nor hurt by what she saw.

She stared in awe. She was there. She was everywhere! He had dreamt of her, her face, her voice, since before he came-of-age, for decades. Even as a child, he had dreamt of her!

His dreams of her were so innocent, his thoughts so pure. His heart was filled with love for her, true love, though he had never met her.

But there were other dreams, a second chest that he would not open for her, until she commanded him to. He could refuse her nothing, she saw it, yet still, he implored her not to make him open it. She felt his nearly overwhelming fear of ultimate loss, as when the link he had shared with his mother was severed with her death at his birth.

She knew his heart would stop if what she saw inside caused her pain. But she would not be denied. She had to know all this man's secrets. How else could she trust him?

He bowed his head in shame before her and opened the chest.

She was here as well. Many of the dreams in this chest were innocent as well, though not so innocent as before. There were kisses and gentle caresses. But there were other dreams, so very many others, so many long, lonely nights of longing, fulfilled only by dreams of her, love dreams.

He was afraid she would feel terror from them, revulsion for him. But her heart did not close, it opened. Her heart started hammering as the flood of his desire washed over her, even as he curled into a ball on the ground beside her, terrified and humiliated and in anguish, fearing he had lost her forever.

She wrapped her arms tenderly around him and he looked up, startled, into her unveiled face. She pulled him to his feet. "I must be alone with you. You must view my core as I have viewed yours. If you can still love me after what you have seen, then my heart is yours, my body is yours, my core is yours. I am already yours, beloved."

She vanished and a snake was at his feet. She slithered quickly past him, out of his core, along the bond.

He watched her go and then gazed outward.

JARGAS'S and Desenia's eyes opened in the same instant, and locked upon one another as if there were no one else in the world.

Archer had been watching them. "Please walk with me, both of you. I will escort you to your tent, Daughter, and see that that no one disturbs the two of you."

They followed as if entranced.

Jarina watched the brother she loved more than her own life walk past as if she were not even there. The two of them had been oblivious to her. She had been there, hidden in her brother's core, watching, ready to protect him if he needed to be protected. She had felt and seen much.

She was stunned. Jargas had dreamt of Shanti, of Desenia, as she had dreamt of Farad. But he had kept his dreams hidden from her. She had never even guessed he had such dreams. He had never shared them with her, as she had shared hers with him.

She blushed darkly at how she had shared some of her dreams with her brother, before she realized how they traveled down her link to him, before she learned how to shield him from them. That necessity was what had first taught her how to erect such shields, like the one she had used to keep Farad at bay. But Jargas had learned a more subtle method, a better one, for his passion flamed as strongly as her own, yet she had never even suspected it. She saw how he had done it, and a similar shield rose rapidly around her. Instead of slamming downward, this one was a latticework. It did not seal her away so completely. She must teach Faradan this way. The shield he had used was so strong they'd barely known the link still held.

A dagger of pain thrust through her heart. She could not teach him. He would not link to her. He did not love her. And now her brother loved another as well. She had lost both of them to the same woman.

Jargas would leave her and she would be alone. He had always been the weak one, the one who had needed her. She had never suffered from lack of his presence as he had for hers. Jargas was such a little boy, in that. But now she felt panic that he would leave her. She should hate Desenia for stealing the hearts of the two she loved.

She warily emerged from behind her shield. She crept down the link to Jargas cautiously, lest she be drawn into their union. But she must view this woman's core. She would not lose Jargas so blindly. He had almost let the sorceress Circe kill him, thinking she was the woman of his dreams, in his desperation for love. What if he was again mistaken?

Desenia's core was unprotected. Her father was giving them the privacy they craved, trusting Jargas to keep his daughter safe.

Jarina viewed Desenia's recent memories first, those of her link with Farad, realizing even as she did so that the link was gone, as if it had never existed.

She saw their meeting. It was not at all what she had feared it to be. There was no tenderness in their meeting. They had hurt each other, nearly killed one another.

Jarina viewed the march to Malar from Cavernas. She felt Desenia's helplessness and anger and terror as her father grew ever weaker trying to save her from the torment of the nightmares.

She saw the nightmares as well. Jarina was sickened by what had been done to Desenia when the Enemy visited her. She saw the horror and denial of the first time, as Desenia's innocence was taken from her. Her great strength of body was nothing to an Enemy who invaded her very dreams. The monster brutalized her over and over, once He realized that she was not who He sought, but was someone He could feast upon as readily, shielding her father from the knowledge of His attack until the moment before He left her core, so He could feel her father Desmond's horror and rage and anguish when he discovered it too late to aid her.

Jarina felt the terror of the second time, when Desenia knew she was hunted and how hopeless her struggles were. The Enemy defeated her father easily as he tried to protect her. He left Desmond conscious but trapped with them, forcing him to watch as He defiled his daughter over and over again with unspeakable depravities, leaving just before He drove them both mad. He laughed as He left her broken and sobbing, taunting her with promises that He would come back for her.

The third and final time, she had fallen asleep after five days of trying to stay awake, aided by Donovar's medicines. That time He had kept her trapped in her dreams until she was so weak she could scarcely breathe. Her father nearly killed himself reviving her.

Jarina forced herself not only to watch, but to feel all the Enemy did to Desenia. She had been his target. He had desired her the moment He saw her in Jargas's mind, when they aided Farad in Malar in Fromer. Desenia had been an innocent victim, one who had suffered atrocities in her place. And this was what it felt like after the Ring had healed her! What must it have been like before? How could Desenia ever love anyone after what had been done to her? How could she live? How could she still be sane? Her strength of will, of character, was astonishing.

"Forgive me, my sister! I have wronged you," Jarina mouthed silently. She would see no more; she did not have the right. She should not be here uninvited. Sick with shame, realizing she had violated Shanti every bit as cruelly as the Enemy had by coming here, she transformed into the form of the great cat—Jargas had called it a pumar—left Desenia's core, bounded back to her own, and then gazed outward again.

Farad was yet unconscious. There was no sign of Donovar. He had left while she was viewing Desenia's core.

Jarina felt dirty, ugly. She wished she were home; she would have a bath drawn or bathe in the stream. But all the water in the world could not make her feel clean now, between the Enemy's dreams and her own vile actions. Maybe the sun would help her as it helped Farad.

Jarina exited the tent. The Guard at the door averted his eyes as she passed, as did the few others she passed. *They think I am whore, rather than houri. I am dressed enough like one. I have the heart of one. I am as sullied and unclean as one.*

She saw her father's men standing and joking and talking with a party of warriors from the camp. She was pleased to see such camaraderie. Her father's people, the Dwarves, had a violent history. Their Kingdoms were so far apart, so isolated, so insular, for a reason. Ever since they had come to their new lands, whenever two Dwarven Kingdoms had met, there had been war.

In the Dwarven Lands, what Jargas attempted to do now, to bring the armies of twenty-nine Kingdoms together against a single enemy, would have been impossible. But in the Saravan, though there were twenty-nine Kingdoms, there were only three Strongholds containing them: Northhold, Southhold, and Westhold. Ten different Kingdoms dwelt together in two and nine in the last, in harmony. Archer—Desmond—had done the impossible. He had spent over a century of his life doing it.

They had received word from each of the Strongholds. A total of fifteen thousand warriors would march with them. The Kings of all twenty-nine Kingdoms would join them, and even their High-King.

They had not known of the High-King, until they had received the responses from the Strongholds. The Dwarves had not had a High-King for millennia, not since they set foot on their new lands, after fleeing the destruction of their Homeland.

Many warriors would remain in the Strongholds, to guard the women and children left behind. They would be safe. The Enemy did not even know of the Strongholds, let alone their location.

Jarina felt sudden fear. But the Enemy had touched Desenia. Would he not now know of them? Would he not now know all their secrets, their weaknesses? They must be warned! Perhaps they must even abandon their Strongholds and flee to the relative safety of Malar in Holoren. But they could not shelter so many! She must speak with Desmond and Jargas and Farad, when he awoke.

Jarina felt suddenly faint and reached out a hand into the air to steady herself, belatedly realizing there was no surface for her to cling to. Except her hand unexpectedly found a strong shoulder, and she braced herself against it. She saw in surprise it was Lornan. He looked up at her in concern.

"You should have spoken, Lady! We did not notice you standing here until you nearly fell. You must rest. You have strained yourself. Let us guide you back to the Healer's Tent. You must leave the battles to the men."

She laughed but her laugh sounded harsh to her own ear. There was no joy, no warmth in it. There was no warmth anywhere inside her now. How could she still feel so cold out here, under the glaring sun?

"It is not the Varashin way. But I will accept your aid. I do not think I can walk without it." She swayed and Lornan's arm was instantly about her, though his jaw clenched.

The camp's warriors eyed him sharply, some hands reaching for axe hilts.

She scolded them. "Our way is no different than your own, but my mother's customs differ greatly. I asked for his aid. He has my permission to lay his hands upon me to give it."

The warriors grumbled their apologies, hands at rest once again, but they avoided her eyes.

It upset her anew. She should be cloaked and veiled. Jargas and her father had both warned her.

She had planned to be. She had not known that they would be seeing other Dwarves today. They had only sought Farad. They were concerned that he had left camp seeking the sun, that he had sealed himself off from them. They were afraid he might have been nearing Madness again, when they had thought him healed.

Lornan and the rest of her father's men brought her back to the Healer's Tent. Jargas intercepted them on the way. "Jarina! I felt your weakness," he said, eyeing his sister in concern.

"I used my own Power to fight the Enemy as you did, Jargas, but I do not wear the Ring any longer. I do not have its Power at my call to replenish myself as you do. I am drained. Yet you were wise to use your own Power before and not reveal the Ring in our battle with the Enemy." She took another step, but her knees would not support her weight. Lornan caught her as she sagged and then released her as Jargas swept her off her feet. Her brother began carrying her the rest of the way.

She blushed, darkly. "Do you have any idea what they will think of you for this, and of me?" she scolded.

"I am your brother. It is my right to aid you. If they have criticisms, they are free to voice them to me, if they dare." They entered the Healer's Tent. Donovar was back and he watched in concern as Jargas brought her inside.

"Do not worry, Donovar. I am not dying. Jargas is feeling overprotective again." She relaxed against Jargas, reveling in his embrace. Desenia had not taken Jargas from her. Jargas had left Desenia to come to her aid. She was a fool and a child for thinking her brother's love for Desenia could ever change his love for her.

Jargas looked at her tenderly. "You must rest. We will stay here and then march to our camp with those of Cavernas."

Jargas turned to Lorgas, who had entered with them. "Lorgas, return to Malar and inform my father that we are safe, that Hunter has been found, and that Father should expect the first army."

"Yes, Highness," Lorgas said and left to do his bidding.

Donovar scowled at Jarina. "All these years I thought it was only Archer, but today I have been well educated. You Amontir are all mad! You drive yourselves beyond reason, past endurance. I leave for only a moment and you vanish! You will lie down now, and you will stay in bed until I tell you otherwise, and I need no King's Voice to see that you do."

Jarina's eyes widened. Only her father had ever before dared speak to her in such a tone, and he had done so rarely. "You would not speak to Archer so," she said indignantly.

Donovar laughed. "You would be surprised indeed then, Lady, at what I've said to the King."

Her eyes widened further and Jargas looked on with interest. "Archer is your King? How can a Man be your King?"

"By wedding our Queen. How else do you think Shanti was born?" he asked with a laugh.

"Is the Queen still in Cavernas?" Jarina asked.

"Of course! War is no place for women. Of course, neither you nor Shanti have Queen Maravara's sense. You continue to talk when I've told you that you must rest. I'll say no more to you until you lie down."

Jarina scowled at him and Donovar laughed. "You and Hunter are truly suited to one another. He gave me exactly such a look."

She felt pain at the mere mention of Farad and turned again to where he lay sleeping.

Donovar spoke again, but this time his tone was fatherly. "The world will look brighter once you've had some rest. You must sleep, Princess. Any warrior can tell you that you cannot win a battle if you join it already spent, nor can you begin a long march so worn."

Jarina sighed and obediently lay down and closed her eyes.

She heard Donovar say, "Come, Prince Jargas. The King and I would hear more of you, and Malar, and the plans you have made."

Jarina's eyes snapped open and she sat up. "Jargas, wait."

Jargas scowled at her.

"No, this is important," Jarina insisted, undaunted. "If the Enemy had such access to Shanti's core, he might know of the Three Strongholds. He might seek to attack them to weaken the army. When you speak to King Archer, you must warn him. They should consider evacuating at least the women and children to Malar for safety. There is not room for everyone."

Jargas said to Donovar. "That is why my sister marches with us, Donovar. She is a born leader and a warrior born besides." He turned back to his sister. "I'd not thought of that. Sleep now, Jarina. We will take care of it," he assured her.

She nodded, closed her eyes, and relaxed again.

DONOVAR led Jargas to Desmond's tent. Jargas told Desmond of Jarina's concerns. But Desmond felt that the peoples of the Strongholds were safer within them than traveling to Malar, where they would make easy targets en route and a single tempting target thereafter. Desmond assured Jargas that although the Strongholds were not nearly as elaborate as the homes the Dwarves had left behind in the Dwarven Lands, they possessed many of the same safeguards and would not be easy for the Enemy to storm or take.

As they discussed strategies, Desmond began to appear peaked and Donovar spoke up in his stead in response to more than one query. Jargas was impressed that Desmond valued Donovar's input so highly, but was concerned to see Desmond looking less well with each passing moment. He was just about to say something about it, when Donovar spoke.

"Archer, your curiosity has been satisfied enough. You well know you need to rest, and you can do so unburdened, now that you know Shanti is safe from harm. Besides, Jargas only left your daughter's side to come to his sister's aid. I think it's high time he returned to Shanti now, don't you agree?" he asked, with a knowing smile.

Desmond looked at him sideways and then smiled as well. "For once I'll not put up a fight. Go, Jargas. See to my daughter, with my blessing. Donovar will escort you, so her Guard will know you are permitted to approach again."

"Thank you, Majesty," Jargas said, relieved on more than one level. Now that he knew Farad and Jarina were safe, and he had spoken to Desmond, the need to go to Desenia was all but irresistible.

He and Donovar walked to her tent. Donovar saw him safely past the Guard and departed. Jargas entered and saw to his surprise that Desenia was asleep. He had been about to view her core, as she had viewed his, when he had sensed Jarina's need and gone to her.

Desenia looked so peaceful sleeping, and Jargas knew she had not slept peacefully in many nights. He'd not disturb her now.

He watched her as she slept, studying every line of her face and body. She had taken off her veil before for him, and not yet put it back on. He reached out his hand toward her cheek and then withdrew it. He could not touch her without her permission.

He sighed and stretched out on the floor. He would take advantage of the unexpected moment of calm and rest as well, while he could. Jarina was not the only one who had been drained. The Ring had restored his core, but his body was weary as well from the battle with the Enemy and the aid he had given both Farad and Desenia.

FARAD awakened and sat up, slowly and cautiously. He was relieved to find he could do so without feeling dizzy or faint. It appeared that between the Power he had received from Jargas and Jarina and the simple act of resting, his body was able to compensate for the additional recent blood loss. He knew he still must eat, though, in order to truly regain his strength. He could not survive on borrowed Power indefinitely.

He realized he was shirtless, and his wound was bound in fresh, clean bandages and did not pain him at all. The band of his House yet graced his arm, when he would have concealed it. He looked to either side of the cot and saw his shirt, neatly folded. He pulled it on carefully, so that he would not accidentally reopen the wound he could not feel, and was surprised and pleased to find his shirt had been laundered while he slept, but also concerned. How long had he slept? He looked toward the door flap, assuring himself that they must have dried it in the sun, that it was likely still daylight. Then his eyes fell upon another of the cots and his nascent panic at the thought it might already be dark outside vanished.

Jarina was sleeping upon one of them. How could he not have noticed before? He fought the urge to rush to her side and instead rose carefully, again relieved the dizziness he had expected to feel was absent. He went to her, irresistibly, inexplicably drawn to her.

She was so beautiful, so strong, even in sleep. His heart sang as he gazed upon her sleeping visage, joy and wonder blossoming to fill all the cold, dark, desolate places of his core he had thought would never know light and warmth again.

He reached out his hand to touch her cheek, but drew it away without touching her. He should let her be. But her eyes opened, awakened by his scrutiny even as he would have been, were their position's reversed.

"Why do you watch me in my sleep?"

"I hoped you might awaken, but I had not wanted to disturb your rest. There is much I wish to say to you," Farad said intently.

"I do not want to hear it," Jarina said coldly. "I have heard enough. You have already explained that Shanti is precious to you," she accused bitterly.

Farad was stunned by her words. "I did not. No, wait, I did, almost. I said she was precious. And she is. She is heir to a lost House."

Jarina stared at him in stony silence and he felt the nascent hope that had flared in his heart, the budding warmth in his core, turn again to ice. "I had to link with her," he explained desperately. "She was dying! You saw, you felt it as I did. I broke my bond to her as soon as it was safe to. I was afraid you might not understand. I do not love her, Jarina, if that is what you fear. I have eyes only for you."

"You only say so because you have seen that Jargas has won her heart and you are cold and lonely once more. I will not seek to warm the heart nor the bed of one who has rejected me. You told me before that you could not love me. I have found that I cannot love you. You are not worthy of my love."

Farad was stricken. Idare, what had he done? He could not lose her. He did not think he could survive it. He must make her understand!

"Please, Jarina! You are right: I am cold and lonely. I was so warm, only a short time ago, when I was in your home, when you opened your heart to me. Do not turn from me now, when I am just beginning to understand. Love does not come easily for me. I have ever loved so few. The price has always been too high to pay."

Her expression was cold and aloof. "I am a Dwarven Lady, and you will not speak to me with such familiarity. I have injured myself aiding you. You owe it to me to at least allow me to rest." She turned away from him.

Her words were like daggers of ice through his heart. He left the tent, neither knowing nor caring where he went. He had been such a fool before to reject what she had offered! And now it was too late. She might not dress like a Dwarven Lady, but she had the temperament of one: prideful and willful, easy to insult and anger, and impossible to appease.

He left the protective shadow of the cliff face and headed for the middle of the valley. He needed the glare of the sun. He'd still not lain beneath it, as he had meant to when he had left the Varash village.

He walked to the perimeter of camp, moving more slowly than he normally would have, than he wished to, conscious of his injured body's limitations. The guards let him leave without challenge. He walked as far from camp as he dared risk. He could not roam far. He was still weak, though he did not feel it at the moment. He felt numb.

He found a perfect flat slab of rock and took off his shirt and laid it on the hot stone. He lay down upon it. The rock was hot, too hot. Even through the double layer of the shirt, it burned his back. But he did not sit up. He welcomed the pain as an old friend, realizing even as he did so that Donovar's medicine was apparently wearing off. Even as he realized it, his chest began to throb and his groin flared again in pain. He felt every bruise Desenia had given him keenly.

The pain quickly went from comforting in its familiarity to an unwelcome distraction. There was too much and too many different kinds. And it was already well past noon. The rock was like the inside of an oven, but though the sun was still bright, it was not scorching, no longer blazing, as he needed it to be. He basked but did not roast. The sun did nothing for him. He felt no calm, no peace. Worse, he still felt so cold, he shivered. He had denied himself Jarina's warmth and now he would suffer for it, endlessly, hopelessly.

"I thought I might find you here," an unexpected voice said from almost directly behind him. Farad leapt from the rock in a fighter's crouch, his knife in his hand at the ready, but he slowly straightened and did not attack.

It was the kinsman he had tried to save from drowning, Desmond. He was standing with his hands out at his sides, palms upward, in a posture that was decidedly nonhostile. His face and hands were sunburned, the rest of his body concealed from the sun. His voice was soft, as weak and weary sounding as Farad himself felt, and he had spoken in Amontirin. Farad would never harm a kinsman who was not in the Enemy's thrall, and Desmond would not have called out the warning of his presence had he been.

"Desmond," Farad said in acknowledgment, forcing himself to sheathe his blade, to relax. He'd not heard him approach. He should have heard him, even though he was kin and obviously as adept as he was at moving soundlessly. Still, Desmond should not have been so silent Farad did not hear him. "Why do you seek me?" he replied in Amontirin.

"We are kin. That alone would be reason enough, after these long lonely decades. But I have many questions no other can answer. Perhaps you cannot either, but still, I hold hope," Desmond said.

"Hope," Farad said in anguish. "You speak to the wrong man, if you wish to speak of hope."

Desmond looked at Farad in sympathy, taking in his brutally scarred and bandaged body and the band about his naked arm. He asked softly, "Is it true that you are not only Lord of your House, now, but also last of your House?"

Farad nodded wordlessly, a flicker of pain flitting across his face, when he should have run screaming in madness at the thought of all he had lost.

"Tell me of our people. I fear much ill has happened, while I have been parted from them. I fear—no, first I would hear the truth. I will face it after decades of agonizing over it. Why was I exiled? Why was I abandoned? I had performed my mission without question or complaint. I lost my wife, my sons, in the Dwarven Lands, but I saved thousands of Dwarves. I saved the sons and daughters of twenty-nine Kingdoms by the time I was done. I saved them and saw them settled in new homes. I taught them to work together, to live together without wanting to kill one another. They call me High-King," he said, and Farad looked at him sharply, failing to hide his astonishment. These Dwarves had a High-King? But the Dwarves had never had a High-King!

Desmond spoke as if reading his thoughts. "The Dwarves have not had a High-King since they fled to this land, three thousand years ago. I am commander of our twenty-nine armies. We bring fifteen thousand men to your aid. Evanaren might have cast me aside like so much trash, but Dewalaren, his son, Jargas has told me of. He will not be able to forget me so easily."

Farad swallowed. Fifteen thousand men! With the five thousand Dwarves Jargas commanded and the two hundred Varash Jarina led, Dewalaren would face an army of over twenty thousand. "Do you so hate Dewalaren and his father that you would delight in toppling him from his throne? Would you truly use the full might of your army against him? He was once your Prince, though you knew it not, once a Lord. He is still kin. We are to leave him with nothing. Is that not enough? I will not see him further harmed. I harm his spirit enough. I'll not see his body trampled under the booted feet of your army."

Desmond said in surprise, "I do not hate Dewalaren. How can I? He was not even born when I last left you, ninety years ago. Do you think me so honorless and ruthless that I would punish the son for the crimes of his father? As for Evanaren...." His voice broke on the name. "He was as a brother to me. We were bonded, linked, and then he severed it without warning. I feared he was dead, at first, but I found out he was not. I saw some few of our people and they had not heard of any great defeat, of anything amiss.

"I went to Caramore, to see if it yet stood, and found it abandoned, with no trace of where our people had gone. I searched everywhere for signs of them, but found nothing, no one. So I continued with my mission. I at least had my wife and sons with me, to ease the pain of loss. But then they were taken from me and I had only the Dwarves. They became my people.

"I gave my life to them, until they forbade me from endangering myself further. It was the third time that I was dragged from the ruins of a Kingdom I'd been unable to save. It was then, fifty-four years ago, that my heart finally opened again and I learned I could still love. Queen Maravara of Cavernas held the key to unlock my heart. But when we were wed, her people and the representatives of the other twenty-eight Kingdoms who were in attendance did not name me Husband and Consort, as is their custom. Instead, they named us High-King and High-Queen.

"I was not expecting it, nor was she. They made me swear I would never again leave them, that I would never again risk myself in the Dwarven Lands. And I swore.

"Three years later Shanti—Desenia—was born. I forgot you know her name and I am not used to speaking it. None save her mother and Donovar know it, except for me. Her birth did not go well. She was so large, even though she was born nearly two months early. Maravara was injured in the birthing." He took deep steadying breaths, and Farad could see that even now he lived with the terror of it.

"My wife recovered, she lived, but she could no longer conceive. But I did not care. I would never have touched her again, never risked lying with her, were it otherwise. Desenia is both heir to my throne and to the House of Serpents, our Laws be damned! I love my wife and my daughter, and I need no son. I have a family again and my heart has healed, as much as it can, when it still bears the scar of Evanaren's betrayal." His voice sank to a whisper. "When did he die?"

"Sixty-three years ago. Dewalaren had just turned twenty-five, he had just come-of-age. Evanaren must have kept your mission secret even from the rest of us, for fear the Enemy would capture one of us and learn of it. From what you and Donovar and your daughter have said, it began decades before you vanished. Yet even my father never knew of it, and he was Evanaren's closest friend, next to you. Evanaren truly was a brilliant tactician. To have a secret army in reserve to call upon in our time of greatest need! And to save the cultures, the histories, even some of the peoples of twenty-nine Kingdoms we thought forever lost!

"I have lived in the Dwarven Lands for the last twelve years. I have watched five Kingdoms, five peoples, turn to dust. I banded the last three that remain there together and thought I had done a great feat. But you have saved and banded together nearly ten times that number! I love the Dwarves, as I thought I could only love my own kin. They have died just as easily," Farad said, his voice soft.

"If you can tell me nothing more of Evanaren, then what of the Great Houses?" Desmond prompted.

"Only six remain," Farad said, his voice filled with pain. "And it would have been four, except Jarina is House of Pumar, I have seen it—for all her brother is House of Obearn—and you are the sixth, House of Serpents."

"Serpents was lost? All of us? Desenia and I are all that remain? And only four other Houses, in addition to yours? It cannot be only four! Which Houses yet live? Which Lords?" Desmond's face was pained.

Farad sighed. "No Lords you knew, I think. I am one-hundred-forty-six. I am the oldest of the Lords, save for you now. I am also last of my House, House of Wolven. Jargas is Lord of House of Obearn, though Dewalaren knows it not. Dewalaren is older, but Jargas has the stronger claim, by birthright. Jarina is Lady of House of Pumar, though she has no band to show for it. That band was lost two and a half centuries ago, when Alanar and the Houses he led were lost. You are Lord of House of Serpents: you and your daughter are the last. Rolin is Lord of House of Horses, if he yet lives. I fear for him. There are seven more Horses. Aramis is Lord of House of Foxes, though I fear he may now be lost as well. There are eight other Foxes."

"But... but what of Eagles? Even if the rest have fallen, surely Eagles must endure? They were so strong, there were so many!" Desmond entreated, stunned.

Farad's voice sank to a whisper. "Lunahr was Lord of House of Eagles, though he had not yet come-of-age. His parents, Lord and Lady of the House, died of a plague that took most of those of us who had remained. My mother and Dewalaren's were his mother's sisters. My mother was captured and slain. Dewalaren's gave her life for Evanaren. It was a mercy when he joined her in death, though he never would have left Dewalaren alone, or left our people, had he the choice.

"There are no more children. Lunahr was the youngest of us, the last of the Eagles, our last child. How can we bear more children, knowing they are doomed to die so young? We sent Lunahr to the Elves for protection, but they failed us. He was only twenty-four. The Enemy... he is gone, dishonored, dead. There are twenty-three of us left, including you and your daughter, Jargas and Jarina. Six houses of the thirty that fled. Few of those of us who remain have any true Power. I am sorry, cousin. I wish I had aught else to tell you," Farad said quietly.

"Twenty-three?" Desmond asked, in disbelief. "There were over one hundred when I last left you in Caramore nine decades ago! Our number should have grown, not diminished! We left Amontir two and a half centuries ago with thirty Houses, over nine hundred Lords and Ladies, sons and daughters, brothers and sisters, aunts and uncles and cousins. Three hundred six of us fled to Maragar with Felanar, ten Houses. Two hundred fifty-four left there. We lost one hundred fifty-one more in the march across the Dwarven Lands. I thought one hundred was terrible, eight Houses was terrible. Now you tell me there is only one Pumar, one Wolven, two Serpents, two Obearn and the rest Foxes and Horses! We are a dead people! We should cease our struggles. Our cause is lost, our people no more. I should pour oil upon myself and alight myself a living pyre!"

Farad shuddered at his words, gripped in the memory of Gervan's house, when he had almost done exactly that. "It is hard to continue on, in the face of such disaster, of sure defeat. But even if our time here is spent, the Dwarves may yet live, the Elves may yet live, Men may yet live. I do not call them Lesser Men, as we once labeled them in our arrogance, for I have met such Men I would die for. We cannot abandon them to the Enemy when it is our fault he was unleashed upon their lands. We've allies now, warriors among each of the races, willing to fight and die with us. And you yet have those who love you, who need you, who will suffer when you are gone. If I, who have nothing and no one left to live for, endure, then so must you."

Desmond eyed him keenly and then nodded slowly. "I misspoke. Forgive me, Farad. Come, cousin. I welcome you to my tent. I have need of your counsel."

Farad nodded in return, the slightest dip of his head, and wearily followed.

JARGAS burst into the Healer's Tent scowling. Jarina asked in surprise, "Jargas, what is the matter?"

"You can sound so innocent to me? How can you fawn all over Hunter one moment and reject him the next? How can you play such games with him? You dishonor our family!"

Jargas was furious. Jarina had seldom seen him so angry. Her own temper flared.

"I, reject him? I am not the one who refused to link and then made a bond with someone else not half a day later. I will not be trifled with," Jarina said proudly.

"He has nothing, Jarina! He has no one! He is so cold and empty my heart would tear every time I touch my bond to him, only you've taught him how to seal himself off from me. He let his guard slip, a few moments ago. He was talking with Desmond. He had to divert all his strength merely to talk, to stay on his feet, and he dropped his guard while doing so.

"He almost felled me with his pain! His body is almost broken, his spirit is torn to shreds, yet he was bearing it alone, when I would have helped him. You have taken even my aid from him! I want nothing more to do with you. You are as vile and twisted, as cruel and manipulative as that nightwhore Circe. I'll not have one such as you for my sister. I disown you. You think I cannot live without my bond to you? See how hard it is for you! I am stronger than you think, Jarina, and you are weaker than you know." He snapped his bond to her, glared at her, and stormed out.

Jarina cried out in loss as the bond they had shared since before birth was severed, reaching out a shaking hand for her brother. Then she sank to the bed, shivering. She wrapped her arms about her legs, huddled like a lost child alone in the dark, as the cold began to seep in.

JARGAS left the tent striding strongly but only made it five paces before he stumbled and nearly fell. He unstrapped the staff from his back and leaned upon it as if it were a walking stick. The world seemed so dark and empty that he looked up and could not believe the sun still shone in the sky. It was as if night had fallen.

Jargas gently touched his new bond to Desenia, not wanting to wake her. But she was awake, and suddenly there was light again and life and warmth. She called to him, and he straightened and headed for her tent, still weakened but able now to make the journey.

JARINA forced herself to stand. It was not really colder and darker with Jargas gone. He still lived, he was not truly gone. Only she could no longer feel him, nor hear him, nor touch him. For the first time in her life, she was alone. Her brother had his link to Desenia to aid him, and to Farad. Farad would lower his shield if Jargas called to him. She had no one. Even Farad was not so alone. He still had Jargas. Except Jargas was right. Farad had learned from her how to seal himself off from Jargas, from his warmth, from his aid. He'd nearly died for it, today.

Jarina felt a stab of pain in her heart at the thought that Farad had been in such danger, that he might have died, that he might have been gone forever.

But why should thoughts of his death cause her pain now, when he was already lost to her? She remembered the howl of anguish, the warm tongue bringing her back from the brink of oblivion, the energy and strength, the Power freely given, leaving him not enough even to live by. Why would he sacrifice himself to save her? For Jargas?

No. Farad liked Jargas, respected him, but he did not love him as he loved her.

Her breath caught. Did Farad truly love her?

She knew the answer without asking. She'd felt as much through her link with Jargas. She'd argued with Jargas that Farad did. But then, when she awoke, she'd seen Farad standing over her, and all she could think of was Farad and Shanti and their bond. And her heart had turned to ice, like the great icicles that hung across the entry to Malar in Holoren in the wintertime, great daggers of ice that could cut and maim and kill. And she'd turned that ice upon Farad, when he was already so cold, so alone, when he had begged for her to hear him.

She was ashamed then, her face burned with it. She had been so jealous! What her mind had created had blinded her to what truly was. How could she face him? She was eighty-three, but she had acted like a spoiled child.

All her life she had been accustomed to getting her way. Jargas and even their father denied her nothing. But Farad had not instantly caved in to her desire, and for that she had sought to punish him, to hurt him. As if the world had not harmed him enough.

And it had worked. She had hurt him. Her eyes had seen it was so, even if her heart had not.

She must apologize to him. She must beg his forgiveness. On her knees if necessary, for he was as proud as she was, and she might not be easily forgiven.

Could she kneel to him? She had called him her Chieftain. A Chieftain was the same as a King. She knelt to her father, her King. She did so even in her pride, out of her love and respect for him. Did she love Farad? Did she respect him?

She almost crumpled then, at the thought of her love for him. Not only the decades of dreams, but the man in the flesh she'd known so very briefly, through Jargas at first, from a distance, and then in person. He stole her breath away: his enduring strength, his stubborn tenacity as he clung to life when he should have died along ago, many times over. The warmth of his smile, so seldom given, she knew, yet often gifted to her.

She must find him and tell him how she truly felt. She would beg Farad's forgiveness and bare her heart to him. And she would humble herself before Jargas as well. She would kneel to him. He would not gloat nor be smug to see it—he would be appalled—but she would do so anyway. She could have lost her heart's desire, were it not for him.

But first she would attire herself properly. She would not continue to be an embarrassment to Jargas and their people. Although she could not go in search of the Maiden's Tent, not dressed as she was. She would appear a whore to them.

Donovar could help her, were he here, but he was not. Yet what she sought might be. She began to search.

She became increasingly frustrated as she opened trunk after trunk in the Healer's Tent and dug through them to no avail. After a lengthy, fruitless search she was almost ready to give up and risk looking for the Maiden's Tent, not sure they might even have one. Desenia aside, Dwarven women did not usually bear arms. She might well be the only other woman in their camp.

"Have you lost something, Lady?" an intrigued voice asked from the doorway.

Jarina blushed darkly. "I have lost much: my love, my honor, my brother, my pride, and to your eyes now, my integrity. I am not a thief in search of hidden treasures, Donovar. Forgive me for behaving like one. I merely seek a cloak and a veil, or something that might pass as such, so I can venture into camp without causing further distress to your people and to my brother. I would not appear a whore to Cavernas. I had already resigned myself to such attire for the duration of the War. I just had not known your people would be here to see me as I am now."

He eyed her intently. "Wait here. I will acquire what you seek."

She smiled at him. "Thank you. I am in your debt."

The healer left and Jarina pulled her comb from the pouch by her side and began separating her hair into sections. Then she began the complex process of braiding her hair into many dozens of fine, interlocking, looping braids, as her nursemaid had taught her so many years ago, using the tiny bands she had found amongst the healer's supplies to tie off the ends.

She felt eyes upon her and turned toward the doorway. Donovar was watching her, an expression of surprise on his face.

"Are you surprised to see I know how to behave properly, or that I groom myself as Supplicant to King?" she asked, smiling.

Donovar laughed. "Both, actually."

He handed her the cloak and veil, which she eyed approvingly. They were charcoal gray, finely made, yet simple in design.

"Might I ask another favor? I would leave my jewelry with you. It would not be appropriate to wear it, but the bangles and necklace belonged to my grandmother and the earrings to my mother, and I know your people are honest, but it would ease my heart to know you hold them for me."

"Of course."

"Also, once I am ready, might you call my Guard for me? It would be improper for me to appear unescorted. And could you direct me to the High-Princess's Tent, or to the High-King's? I seek both Jargas and Hunter and I think that is where they are most likely to be found."

"It is my pleasure to aid you, Lady. In fact, as your father is not here, it would be my honor to escort you before the High-King in his stead," he added, his voice roughening with emotion.

She was greatly moved by his kindness and smiled warmly at him. "The honor would be mine."

She worked with nimble fingers, producing the intricate weave she had never imagined she might actually use. Finally she was done and eyed her work critically in Donovar's mirror.

"Flawless, Lady. None shall be able to find fault," Donovar said, his voice warm with approval.

"I am relieved to hear you say so, for I have not braided my hair in any fashion for a number of years, and have never done so except in practice in this particular style." She fastened the cloak and veil. The hood of the cloak covered all but the very edges of the braids, but she would remove the hood when she knelt, as part of the ritual.

Donovar summoned her Guard. He had apparently told them no more than that she had need of them, for when she emerged from the tent, she saw from beneath her hood startled glances and eyes quickly downcast not in disapproval, but in all but reverence, in a proper show of respect.

She allowed herself a last smile, in the shadow of her hood, and then adopted the reserved poise of a Dwarven Lady.

The Guard surrounded them and Donovar guided them to an elaborate tent, larger than the rest, and heavily guarded.

"The Lady Jarina is seeking Hunter, Guest of our Kingdom. Might he be in audience with the High-King?" Donovar asked.

"He was, Healer, until his Majesty grew weary," one of the Guard said.

Donovar's face creased in concern and the Guard quickly reassured him. "The High-King said to tell you if you sought him that he is resting as you ordered him to, so you need not scold him." The Guard did not smile with his mouth as he said so, but his eyes were alight with laughter.

Donovar grunted in approval. "Do you know where Hunter might be found?"

"I believe he was headed for the High-Princess's Tent," the Guard said.

"Thank you. We will seek him there instead, then," Donovar said. He led Jarina and her Guard to Desenia's tent. It was nearly as large as the High-King's, and as well guarded.

"Princess Jarina seeks audience with her brother, Prince Jargas, and Lord Hunter. Is either inside?" Donovar asked formally.

"They are both inside, but are not to be disturbed. The Prince is not feeling well," the Guard added.

"If the Prince has taken ill, then I should tend to him," Donovar said in concern.

"My orders are that no one may enter," the Guard said adamantly.

Donovar glared at him. "And when Prince Jargas's people ask why the Healer of Cavernas did not aid him, what will I say to them? My honor would be at stake, if not my life. Stand aside. Or must I awaken the High-King to order you?"

"You would not," the Guard said, obviously appalled at the idea. Then he looked intently at Donovar and sighed. "You would. May you speak as eloquently on my behalf, if the High-Princess is angered, Donovar. You may enter, and the Princess you escort, but her Guard must remain here."

All six men glared at him, and Lornan and Hernon both opened their mouths to protest, but Jarina stopped them with an upraised hand. She could not allow a confrontation. "Remain here. My escort, Healer Donovar, will see to my honor."

Her Guard obeyed instantly, but with obvious reluctance.

Jarina's calm was only on the surface. Was Jargas truly ill? What afflicted him? Without their link, she had not even known of his illness.

They entered the tent. Jargas was there, with the High-Princess and Farad. Jargas truly appeared ill. He was sitting upon a bed, pale and shivering.

Farad was speaking in Dwarvish, his voice warm with concern, "...seen this before, but only when a child loses his mother or a mother loses her child. The bond between them is from before birth. But it is that way with him and Jarina, because they are twins. They bonded even before they were born."

Donovar cleared his throat to make their presence known. They all looked up, startled by the interruption. Farad in particular appeared astonished that he had been so intent upon Jargas, he had not realized anyone had entered the tent. Jargas eyed them with only peripheral curiosity. Desenia looked angered, protective of Jargas, like a pumar protecting her mate.

"Donovar, you were not summoned. This is not an illness you might treat," Desenia chastised. "Lady, forgive me, I mean you no offense, but this is not a time I might pay honor to a visitor." Desenia obviously did not recognize her as she now appeared, properly attired.

"I did not come as a healer, my Princess, but as honor escort for this Princess. However, once one of the Door Guard told me that Prince Jargas had taken ill, he was unable to restrain me from entering. I see now that the Princess I bring before you is the one who will be able to aid the Prince," Donovar said smoothly.

Puzzlement and jealousy warred across Desenia's face as she eyed the apparent stranger. Jealousy won. But surprise and sudden understanding flashed across Farad's face, and he looked at Jargas. Jargas was eyeing Jarina in disbelief.

Jarina approached, bowed her head and knelt at Jargas's feet, then removed her hood, head still bowed.

"I would see your face, Sister," Jargas said.

Jarina heard Desenia gasp in surprise but had eyes only for her brother as she looked up at him and docilely removed her veil.

Jargas studied her intently. "Why have you come, Jarina? You do not look like you would gloat, yet I see you appear well, while I am afflicted."

"I have come to restore the honor I lost for our Mountain. I have come to beg forgiveness for the wrongs I have done your friend. I might appear well to your eyes, but my core is cold and empty, for I lost a part of myself when you severed our bond. I lost my heart. I humbly ask that you restore our bond."

"Rise," Jargas said, and she obediently did so. "What of Hunter? Have you no words for him?"

Jarina turned to Farad. "I have many words for him, but I will speak only some of them here." She knelt before Farad, but did not bow her head, instead keeping her gaze upon him. "Forgive me, my Lord, my love, he who should be my Chieftain, for having wounded you. I am an arrogant, spoiled, thoughtless child. But I would echo your own words back to you and alter some of them. Do not turn from me now, when I am just beginning to understand what it is you offered. For I have seen that love does not come easily for you, and I have tasted your fear, but no price is too high to pay for such love as we were meant to share, be it merely for a single day or a week or a month or a year or a lifetime. I will love you always, whether or not you are able to return my love."

"You should not kneel to me, beloved. A Lady of Amontir kneels only to her King, never to her husband." Farad's voice was gruff, yet tender, and his eyes shone with unshed tears. "I should kneel to you, as is your custom. I would do anything you might ask of me."

Jarina smiled, a look of love and longing and lasciviousness awash upon her face. Then she curbed her expression and turned to Jargas. "Am I forgiven, Brother?"

"Aye. I only wish that Father had been here to see you, for he would never believe me if I were to tell him," Jargas said, bemused.

"When we return to the Mountain, I will still be cloaked and veiled, with my hair braided thus, and I will pay proper respect to him," she replied.

Jargas actually laughed, though he still looked unwell. "He'll still not believe it. May I touch your face, Sister? May I restore our bond?"

"You may," Jarina said formally.

Jargas touched her gently.

JARINA dove from her core and grabbed the end of the broken link in her teeth, her body transformed into a sleek feline. She met the great obearn outside her brother's core and their noses touched; then they touched the ends of the sundered strands they held to one another and they fused whole instantly.

Jarina gasped at the rush of warmth and strength that surged over her, and she sent her own wave down toward her brother's core. Then she assumed her own form, and he his, and they embraced one another as brother and sister. She jumped up and managed to kiss his cheek and he grinned at her. Then she waved and they returned to their cores.

WHEN her eyes turned outward again, the change in Jargas was remarkable. He appeared robust and well again, in the peak of his health, all sign of illness and weakness gone.

Jarina glanced at Desenia and turned her eyes quickly away. Desenia's eyes burned with jealousy and anger. It was obvious she wanted to be enough for Jargas, that she resented the strength of the bond Jarina shared with him.

Her eyes flicked to Farad and she reached out her hand to him, instinctively, for comfort and reassurance. Farad took it, rubbing his thumb lightly across the back of her hand. A shiver of delight ran down her spine at his touch, and all concerns about Desenia vanished.

Jargas smiled at them. "It is about time for Cavernas to break camp. They have already stayed here overly long, because of us. It is nearly dusk."

"I was told the High-King is resting," Donovar said. "I will see if he has awakened."

Jarina refastened the veil about her face and lifted her hood to once again cover her hair. "Come, my love. You must be my escort now," she told Farad.

CAMP broke down quickly and efficiently, and the army marched toward Malar. It was well into night when Jarina parted company with them at the Village. Farad had walked far in his journey and been carried farther still. Jarina would enter the Mountain later. She did not want to spoil the effect of her appearance by revealing herself to her father too soon.

The rest continued on up the trail to the Door to the Mountain. The Door Guard had been told by Lorgas to expect them, so the Door swung open to allow them to enter as soon as the Guard recognized Jargas leading them and gave the signal to those within. It was the first time in the long history of their people upon these lands that a Dwarven army ever entered the Mountain of another in peace.

The two armies were still wary of each other. But Jargas and the six Guards that had accompanied them led the rest in the warmth of their welcome and enthusiasm to make the strangers feel at ease within their caverns. Desenia stayed outside the Mountain with the bulk of her army, but the Door remained open. Jargas and his men personally escorted the High-King and his Guard to the Throne Room, a large, impressive natural cavern that had been further enhanced by the artistry of their people.

Jargas introduced the High-King to his father, showing deference to the station of their distinguished guest by speaking to him first, when normally he would have spoken to his father, knowing his father would not feel slighted by it. "High-King, this is King Rongas of Malar in Holoren, my father. Sire, this is High-King Archer of the Dwarven Kingdoms of the West. He is also a banded Captain of the Watch, Lord of House of Serpents, kin to me through Mother."

Rongas rose and stood on the dais upon which his throne rested, so that he could look the High-King in the eye, rather than be seated above him, as he greeted him. "It is our great honor and privilege to welcome you and your people to Malar in Holoren, Majesty. We had not known there was a High-King of the Kingdoms of the West until we received the replies to our messages. Our people have not had a High-King since we first came to these lands, three millennia ago. I am sure my son has much to tell me, but first, I would give you at least a brief tour of our Mountain, before we show you the best place to camp until all the armies have gathered. There will be time enough in the coming days to give you the grand tour. We've prepared a great feast for tonight in your honor, and would not want to delay it. All your men are invited to join us, of course, so that we might properly welcome you to our Mountain," Rongas said proudly.

"Thank you, King Rongas. We are in turn honored by your welcome. Your hospitality is much appreciated," Desmond replied sincerely.

Rongas led them on a limited tour of the huge natural caverns that comprised the bulk of the Mountain, taking them first from the Throne Room to his Study. "Few who are not of our Mountain have ever seen this chamber, and few enough of our own people. This is my private Study. As you can see, I have already laid out dozens of detailed maps of the lands our combined army will travel. I have made initial calculations of our route and the supplies we will need and the time it will take for us to march to our various destinations. Now that Jargas has returned, he will aid our cartographers in updating our terrain maps of the east, both the Lands of Men and those of our own people."

The High-King's eyes lit with reverence. "So many maps and books! Never have I seen such a library! I could spend years here," he said, gazing in awe and wonder at the hundreds of volumes that graced the many stone shelves carved into the walls, and the dozens of maps set out upon the table.

Rongas's proud smile widened. "I had hoped you might be a fellow scholar. You do not say it, or reveal it by your expression, but I suspect you think it cruel of me to keep such a treasure to myself and deny my people such wealth."

The High-King appeared truly flabbergasted. He opened his mouth as if he would deny it, but then after a brief pause did not. "I can understand how you might wish to protect such a treasure, in order to preserve it. But I have found that the greatest value in knowledge is when it is shared," he said carefully.

Rongas's grin widened. "And you're an excellent judge of character as well, I see! You surmised I'd not take offense when you chastise me ever so diplomatically within my own Mountain."

At the vexed look upon the High-King's face, Jargas said, "I only hope the other Kings are as even tempered and forgiving, Father."

Rongas laughed heartily. "I don't think the High-King will think so poorly of me before our tour is done. But first, we will go to the Great Hall."

THEY proceeded down a winding series of corridors. Desmond and his Guard carefully followed in the footsteps of Rongas and Jargas and their Guard, to ensure they did not accidentally trigger any of the concealed traps they knew must be set along the corridors to discourage any foolish enough to think they might plunder the treasure of their Mountain.

Desmond grinned in wonder and delight at the sight of the soaring chamber of the Great Hall. It was a single enormous cavern, with row upon row of stone tables and chairs, enough to seat thousands. "It is like being in the Dwarven Lands again. I can see we must brace for a flood, for the entire army will weep upon leaving here. If only I had known the Holoren Mountains had caverns such as these!

"In the Saravan there are only a few small natural caves. We have had to hollow out all the rest by hand. You can well imagine the difference. Much as the caverns of Westhold have become home to me now, and I would not exchange them for anything, still I envy you your caverns, King Rongas."

Rongas beamed with pride. "My grandsire found them. He and his people spent six extra months above ground, searching for precisely such a place. They lived in tents along the valley walls. We modified most of these caverns little from what we found.

"Still, beautiful as the caverns are, as the rock that comprises them is, it is not perfect. These walls contain no precious jewels or metals as can be found in Malar in Fromer. But we love our rock just the same. Nothing smells like the rock of home," he said contentedly, breathing in a great lungful of the crisp, cool air.

"But if you think this might move your people to tears, what I next show you... ah, but I will not spoil the surprise," Rongas said cryptically.

Thoroughly intrigued, Desmond followed, accompanied by his Guard. They were led through a dizzying maze of corridors and cautioned about a number of traps. Desmond wondered whether Rongas might be leading them to his Vault. He could not imagine what else might lie so deep within the Mountain and be so greatly protected. It could not be the King's Nursery. Rongas's two children were full grown, and did not yet have children of their own that he might wish to proudly reveal. Though he suspected that would soon change.

He had never dreamt that Desenia might find her heart's mate, that she would ever wed. Even before she was attacked by the Enemy, he had feared she might live and die alone, as he had thought he was doomed to, until he found her mother. The thought that she had not only found her future husband, but that he was one of their people, a Lord of the Amontir, the Prince, filled his heart with burgeoning hope for the first time in decades. He touched his bond to her, overjoyed to feel the strength of it.

His daughter was truly well, for the first time in too many days. He could feel the love emanating across the bond, for him, and for Jargas as well, a man who had been a stranger less than a day ago. She had not dreamt of him, as he had of her. But the warm glow of joy, of happiness he longed to see was absent. Instead, there was grim purpose, and even more troubling, jealousy and anger, both carefully shielded and concealed from Jargas.

Desenia might love Jargas already, but she yet despised his sister. She blamed Jarina for the atrocities she had suffered, the torment she had endured in Jarina's stead. Desmond only hoped that she would be able to put those feelings aside. As close as the twins were to one another, it boded ill for her union with Jargas if she could not.

So distracted was Desmond by his concerns that he nearly ran into Jargas, when he and his father stopped before an enormous pair of stone double doors set into the corridor wall. Thankfully, they were apparently at the Vault at last. He was dismayingly weary from the walk, his body not yet recovered from the strain of his daughter's plight and his overexposure to the sun. But he would, of course, take care to appear suitably impressed by the treasure Rongas was about to reveal.

"We keep these doors closed, not to deny any entry, as you will see, but for moisture control," Rongas explained. "The rock of this chamber has been greatly altered from its natural state, as none of the other large chambers have. Most notably, it has been sealed from floor to ceiling, so that it is entirely waterproof, to protect the great treasure within."

Desmond was shocked to see the Vault was unguarded and to hear that Rongas would allow entry to anyone who wished. Deep within the Mountain and surrounded by trapped corridors as it was, he still would have expected at least a dozen Vault Guard at the door, and he never would have expected open access to what must be great wealth indeed, from what he'd already seen.

Rongas opened the doors and led Desmond and his Guard inside. "Welcome to our Library," he said proudly.

Desmond stared, stunned. They stood on a landing, midway up the outer wall, overlooking the chamber. A stone staircase led down to the cavern floor, and walkways led to either side, along the walls. The cavern appeared to have once been like the Great Hall, a single enormous chamber hollowed out by time and water ages past. But unlike the Great Hall, dozens of feet below, this chamber was divided by hundreds upon hundreds of stone bookcases, each containing hundreds of bound volumes. They stretched as far as the eye could see.

"Thousands. Perhaps tens of thousands. I did not know there were so many books in all the world," Desmond said in a reverent whisper. And they were not entombed, carefully locked away and jealously guarded. There were dozens upon dozens of people here, interspersed throughout the room, some seated in thickly cushioned chairs, others at tables, many at the shelves, singly and in groups, reading, studying, openly sharing the priceless treasure. Desmond's normally silent Guard were equally stunned, muttering worshipful comments to one another.

"As you can see, the books which so impressed you in my Study are only a fraction of our great wealth. I'm careful not to keep any of them out too long, or I try to be. Melnor might argue my claim, I think," he said, grinning, as an older Dwarf approached.

"High-King Archer, I present to you Melnor, our Head Librarian. Melnor, this is High-King Archer, of the Twenty-Nine Kingdoms, the Three Strongholds of the West."

"Majesties. It is an honor. Might I be of assistance? Is there a particular volume you are seeking?"

Archer shook his head wordlessly, too overcome to speak.

"Thank you, Melnor. Perhaps later. For now, I'm only showing the High-King about. He did not even know of our Library." Rongas turned to him.

"Most of what you see here are those books we were able to save from the Great Library of Vekrakesh, from our Homeland, before the Inundation that claimed it. I'm sure you must have heard the story of that great tragedy, having lived amongst us, but you might not have heard of the Library. There were over one hundred thirty million books and scrolls and maps and manuscripts in the Great Library. We have over five hundred thousand of them here. Many of the works you see are over three thousand years old and some date as far back as five thousand years.

"The art of making paper that lasts so long has been lost to us. The secret of the waterproofing and fire retardant techniques our ancestors perfected to protect these works was lost millennia ago. It is a constant battle to preserve the newer books in our collection. I'm sure it would be somewhat easier were we to ban all entry here. There is moisture even in breath, and oils in the skin, all of which minutely damage the works. But what is the point of a book, unless it is to be read? It would be an insult to the sacrifice of the original staff were we to lock them away."

"Sacrifice?" Desmond asked, still too stunned to utter more than that single word in question, when his head was swimming with them.

"Ah, so you'd not heard, then. Aye, a great sacrifice. The staff fought valiantly as the waters rose to preserve all they could. There had been emergency evacuation plans in place for millennia, of course, in case of fire, in case of flood, in case of war, plans regarding which volumes were to be saved in time of disaster. Yet still, no one had truly ever thought the entire Library might someday be at risk.

"When that time came, Velnor, the Head Librarian, and his staff of thousands could not bear that so few volumes might be preserved, only a few hundreds of thousands. So to save all they could, to a man, they gave up their seats in the Great Ships during the Evacuation, sacrificing themselves so that more of the books might be saved. They entrusted the care of the books to their wives and children and the very youngest of the apprentice librarians. The journeymen and even most of the apprentices never left the Homeland. They died proudly, honorably, beside the librarians, protecting what they loved more than their own lives, so that it might be preserved for their children, for all our children.

"Melnor is a direct descendent of Velnor's younger son, Halnor. The elder son, Jalnor, died with his father and all the rest, may Ragnar and Aralyn bless their spirits for their sacrifice."

"I do not have the words...," Desmond said, clearing his throat, choked by emotion. He noted that Rongas's eyes looked unnaturally bright, and Melnor's and Jargas's as well, and so was not embarrassed by the tears in his own eyes.

"My people once had a Library as well. Not nearly so large, but no less precious to us: books, maps, so few remain. Songs, poems. We saved what we could, but the rest.... And the paintings, the ceramics, the tapestries, the dances, the culture: gone, all gone. Only the spirit, the life's blood of those few of us who yet survive, remains. Forgive me. I do not mean to be so morose. But it has been a long march with little rest, and to see such a treasure... I am overwhelmed."

"There is nothing to forgive," Jargas said gruffly, obviously moved.

"It is I who should seek your forgiveness. I saw you were weary. I should have waited to show you," Rongas said contritely.

"You did no wrong," Desmond said, quick to reassure him, lest Rongas blame himself for the unpardonable crime of injuring a guest, no matter how unintentionally. "I would not have missed the opportunity to see such beauty. But if you might lead me back outside, so we might camp, and I might rest?"

Jargas spoke up. "If you'd not object, we have guest quarters only a dozen or so corridors away, far closer than outside. You could rest or bathe here instead, before the feast. We could send a messenger to bring Shanti or Donovar to you, in addition to as many additional Guard or others of your people as you would wish, of course. Unfortunately, we cannot house the entire army within the Mountain, but we easily have room for at least ten dozen or more," Jargas offered.

"That is very kind of you. I thank you for your hospitality," Desmond said in relief. He turned to Tebras. "Tebras, please inform Donovar and Shanti of Malar's hospitality. Ask that, when they come, they bring an appropriate change of clothing for me."

"Yes, Sire," Tebras said.

"Lornan, you go with Tebras. You'll be able to show him the more direct route out," Rongas said.

"Yes, Majesty," one of their Guards said, and indicated that Tebras should follow him.

"We'll escort you to your chambers," Rongas offered.

"Thank you."

JARGAS was pleased to see Desmond and his father getting along so well together, but he was not surprised. He had liked Desmond instantly and had suspected his father would as well. He had known that his father would at least not have had the innate prejudice against him for being a Man that many Kings of their kind would have.

After they saw Desmond and his Guard to the quarters they'd promised, and ensured that their army set up camp in the location they had selected for them, Jargas and his father headed back to the Study. There he told his father all that had happened and all that he had learned from it of the Twenty-nine Kingdoms of the West, the three Strongholds, of Archer and of his daughter and Donovar. He spoke long and intently with his father about Desenia, although he did not reveal her true name. He would not violate her trust by doing so without her permission. Jargas left issues regarding Farad to Jarina, for her to tell their father later. Their father had yet to see her. She had wanted to surprise him at the feast she knew he would have arranged.

SOME hours later, everyone gathered in the Great Hall for the promised feast. Jarina, who was still cloaked and veiled, sat on Farad's right, leaving the seat she normally sat in on Jargas's right empty. She noted that Donovar sat on Farad's left, next to the High-King and his daughter Desenia, an empty seat away from Jargas. Jargas sat on their father's right, as always. The seat on Rongas's left was left empty, in honor of their mother. Jarina saw her father glance more than once at the empty chair beside Jargas with a concerned scowl upon his face, but as she expected of him, he did not wish to comment upon it in front of the High-King.

The High-King stood and the room instantly quieted, even as he motioned the rest to remain seated. He was pleased by King Rongas's hospitality and generosity in arranging the feast for so many and told him so, before their combined peoples, offering his thanks.

There was hearty applause and approval.

Then King Rongas stood and motioned for silence, quieting the room once more. "We are honored to be able to guest you, High-King. Upon first seeing you, I had wondered that a Man might be called High-King by our people, until I heard from Jargas what you have done for us. Never before has a Dwarf of these lands united even two of our Kingdoms, yet you have united twenty-nine! Moreover, we've you to thank for escorting so many sons and daughters of those Kingdoms to safety in the west in the first place, to seeing them so well transplanted that those Kingdoms thrive. I understand your numbers reach close to forty-five thousand. Forty-five thousand, who otherwise would have perished! It is seldom that one King of our people, or any people, does more than bow to another, yet I kneel to you now, in recognition of all you have done," Rongas said, and he knelt before him.

Jarina saw that Desmond was moved beyond words. His eyes shone with unshed tears and he swallowed more than once. But her father was not finished.

Still on his knees, Rongas unstrapped the great war axe from his back, moving slowly so all could see it was not meant as a threatening gesture at all. He laid it at the High-King's feet. "I pledge my axe and those of my people to your service. I have five thousand warriors of my own who will march with your combined army, which Jargas tells me you expect to reach fifteen thousand. I would see my own men serve under you, so that we march as a single army twenty thousand strong. I hereby relinquish command of my men to you and will serve under you in whatever capacity you deem me worthy."

The High-King shook his head. "You move me with your words as no other, for your Kingdom feels no honor debt to me, nor owes its loyalty to me, as I have never before aided your people. I accept your oath to me, but I would not command those you must lead. Each of the Three Strongholds has a General who serves under me. Each commands five thousand men. You will still lead your men, as one of my Generals, and I will in turn lead you. Rise, King Rongas."

The Captains of Rongas's army, who had shifted uneasily at their King's words, were appeased by the High-King's, and by the sight of their King on his feet once more. A great cheer rang out and ran the length of the cavern and back again.

As they set to eating, talk of the coming War waned. "There are other matters we must speak of, King Rongas," the High-King said. "Happier matters, regarding our children, and the union of Malar and Cavernas to one another through them. I am sure Jargas has spoken to you of it. I hope you are as delighted by the prospect as I am. From all I have seen and learned, I can think of no finer son-in-law, nor heir to the Kingship of the combined Kingdoms, than your son."

Rongas beamed. "How could I be other than thrilled? And I know that my beloved wife, who is long since departed, would share in my joy. The High-Queen should also be present and give her approval, yet our children would know great joy if they might join to one another before our march. What is your counsel?"

Desmond smiled. "I do not doubt that my wife would approve or that all of Cavernas would wish to witness such a union. Indeed, all of the Three Strongholds would. Unfortunately, we march to war, and now is not the time for such ceremonies. But love such as theirs should not be made to wait. I propose a simple union, under our law and before Ragnar and Aralyn's eyes, with only the families and closest friends who are able to attend present. Then later, once we are victorious, there will be a wedding such as these lands have never seen."

Rongas grinned. "Then they will wed on the morrow," he proclaimed. Word quickly spread down the length and breadth of the Great Hall and it was rocked by spontaneous cheering, first for Jargas, from his own people, and then for Desenia, by hers, and then for both of them.

Jarina had never seen such joy on her brother's face. She saw her father was eyeing him proudly as well. He looked automatically to her brother's right and frowned at the empty seat where Jarina should be.

Jarina whispered to Farad. "Where does your heart lie in this, beloved? Shall I bring our request for a union to my father's attention here and now as well?"

"I never thought to know such joy, my love. I would bond my mind to yours tonight and my body to yours on the morrow, after we are wed," Farad said.

"Then you must introduce me to him," Jarina said, the mischievous grin upon her lips, which was concealed by her veil, in her voice as well.

Farad spoke. "Majesties, if we may rise, the Princess I escort has a boon to ask of King Rongas."

RONGAS looked curiously at the cloaked and veiled Lady at his table. Jargas had instructed Sarnon to seat his friend and the Lady there. He had wondered who she might be, but his attentions had been elsewhere. Even now, it was hard to focus upon her, when he was worried about his own missing daughter. Jargas would have told him were something amiss, but Jarina should be here. Still, he must not offend a visiting Lady. "Of course. Forgive me for not speaking with you earlier. I hope you have not taken offense by it. What is it you wish of me, Lady?"

FARAD and Jarina both rose and walked to him. Jarina knelt before her father and removed her hood, revealing her elaborately braided hair, but keeping her veiled face to the floor. She could not see her father's face, nor he hers.

"Majesty, your daughter Jarina asks that you give your blessing and approval for her union to Lord Hunter, Captain of the Watch, Lord of House of Wolven, of Amontir. We humbly request that we too be allowed to wed upon the morrow," she said formally.

RONGAS was staring at the kneeling form before him in consternation. "And here I thought nothing I saw or heard today could surprise me more than I have already been. Arise, my daughter, for I would see your naked face. Though I have viewed it far more often than ever I should have, I have never before thought to see you groomed as Supplicant to King. You did not need to go to such lengths to gain my approval, Daughter. You know I want only what might bring you happiness."

Jarina rose, removed her veil, and looked into her father's eyes, even as she observed propriety by turning her back to the rest of the room so no others might see, save those seated at their table, were they to turn their heads. But no Dwarf would ever think to do so. "Hunter has always been my heart's desire, though I only recently discovered he was the one I have dreamt of these many long years. It is Aralyn's will that we be wed. She led Jargas to him, so that I might know the love and joy you and Mother shared. He is of Mother's people. He is my destined heart's mate, my one and only love."

Rongas sought Jargas's eyes, seeking his silent counsel. Jargas would never allow Jarina to do something foolish that might result in her unhappiness, and his son had seemed less than pleased by his sister's interest in Hunter. He'd not publicly approve such a union if Jargas yet had even the slightest reservation.

Jargas nodded solemnly, in subtle acknowledgement and approval.

"Then if it is your wish to join yourself to this Man, the two of you shall also wed on the morrow," Rongas stated.

FARAD turned to Jargas. "As Princess Jarina needed to seek the approval of her King, so must I seek the approval of my own. Prince Jargas, rightful Heir to the Throne of Amontir, I, Hunter, Lord of House of Wolven, seek permission to wed Lady Jarina, Princess of Malar in Holoren, Chieftess and Healer of the Varash, Lady of House of Pumar, so that the blood of our two Houses might join as one. As we are each last of our House, such a union might preserve one or both of our Houses. Do you sanction our union?"

Jargas nodded gravely. "It is my great honor to welcome you to my sister's House, Pumar, and to my own, Obearn, Lord Hunter, House of Wolven," he said formally.

The cheering began again, every bit as enthusiastically as for the first announcement. Jarina reattached her veil and donned her hood once more.

Farad saw Jargas lean over and speak to his father. King Rongas's eyebrows rose and he grinned. He summoned his daughter, and after a few moments Jarina nodded in apparent approval. Jargas rose from the table and left it, while Jarina returned to her seat. Farad asked her where Jargas was going, but she merely smiled, though he could see it only in her shining eyes, "You shall see when the others do, Faradan," she said softly, so no one might hear his name.

Farad kept an eager eye out for Jargas, wondering what was going on, as the feast continued.

Jargas returned a while later with a large, beautifully inlaid wooden chest, which he set before his place at the table. He stayed standing and called for the attention of those present, his booming voice echoing clearly across the Hall. Conversation stilled once more.

"In honor of the joining of Malar in Holoren to the Kingdoms of the West, and of the joining of my father's house to that of the High-King, tonight we present a gift worthy of the High-King. As some of you know, my mother's father was of the same people as the High-King's, the Amontir, those who are called the Watch. My grandsire was Crown Prince Rowanar, eldest son of their slain King Albinar, and Heir to the Throne of Amontir. As his Heir, I wear the King's Band and King's Ring," he said, displaying them both.

"Prince Rowanar's sword was buried with him when he died, as is the custom of my mother's people. But what lies within this chest was passed down, to be worn by the eldest son of our House. Unfortunately, our House bore only a daughter, before me, and it did not fit me, even when I was a lad. But it would serve the High-King well in the war that is to come."

He lifted the lid, as Desmond peered curiously at the chest, and everyone else strained to see a glimpse of whatever treasure the chest might hold. Jargas pulled forth a gleaming breastplate, the likes of which, for all their metalsmithing, no Dwarf had ever seen. He held it out to the High-King. It shone a beautiful odd reddish copper in the torchlight, lamplight and candlelight, reflecting the flames of all three from every curve, so that it appeared as if it were on fire.

"Behold Prince Rowanar's armor. We have always loved it for its great beauty, but until now had not suspected its true worth. Only recently have I learned of the metal it is crafted from. The Amontir call it pyrenteum and it puts the pallenteum we value so highly to shame. Pyrenteum is a metal unknown to the forge of Dwarf, Man, or Elf. Only wizards know the forging and crafting of it. Fire cannot melt it. Stone cannot crush it. Swords cannot cut it. Arrows cannot pierce it. And in this chest is a full suit of it, save for the helm, which must have been lost to the rock of the Valley of Summerhome two and a half centuries ago."

DESMOND stared at the breastplate in awe. He took it from Jargas and gazed upon it reverently. It truly was the lost King's Armor. Not only was Rowanar's symbol, that of a snarling obearn, engraved upon it, but the symbol of each of the Thirty Great Houses, so many of which existed now in name only. As the light of the Great Hall touched the etchings, each symbol appeared to move, to crawl and prance, fly and leap, slither and hop. He traced his own symbol, the snake, with his fingertip. When he spoke, his voice was steady, but his eyes were bright with unshed tears.

"I hold in my hands the symbol of the Thirty Great Houses that once graced the Lands of the Amontir, east of the Dwarven Lands. All but six of those Houses have been turned to ash. As High-King, I am the living symbol of thirty Dwarven Kingdoms, all that remains of the hundreds of Kingdoms that once graced the Dwarven Lands west of Amontir and east of here. Dozens of Man's Kingdoms have turned to ash, and we have heard rumor that two of the seven Elven Kingdoms might also have fallen.

"We march to join our Amontiri and Dwarven brothers, even to join the Elves, and whatever Men might dare to join us. We march to bring light back into the world which the Enemy has turned to darkness, to douse the fires he has lighted, to purify the waters he has poisoned, to restore the lands he has polluted, to avenge the many hundreds of thousands he has slain, and to bring to final rest the tens of thousands of dishonored and defiled dead he has enslaved to his service." He raised the breastplate in his hands before him and roared, "To victory!"

The cry was taken up by thousands of throats, until the very dishes on the tables all but trembled from the thunderous echo. Then Desmond requested Jargas's aid to strap the breastplate on and let all see him so attired. Finally, he sat.

Jargas stared at him reverently. "Never have I been so moved by words. You humble me, that I call myself Heir to the Throne of Amontir when you should be."

Desmond shook his head. "I've neither the blood nor the Power to claim that title. My lost friend Evanaren or perhaps Rowanar or Idare himself stood by my shoulder and whispered those words into my ear, I think, for I have never before spoken so eloquently."

FARAD listened to the two of them and watched. He knew in his heart that Jargas was his Prince and he respected Desmond second only to one other. All that Desmond had done for the Dwarves, Dewalaren had done for their people. He had spent his entire life protecting his people, saving them. He was their light, their strength, their hope. How could they survive under another Prince? How would Dewalaren react to seeing another in the King's Armor he should be wearing? Farad wondered how he himself could survive, after committing such a betrayal, of his cousin, his friend, his Prince.

"Your words did not sit well with everyone, Father," Desenia said, looking pointedly at Farad. "Or perhaps he has no stomach for Dwarven fare."

It was plain to see Desenia still had not forgiven him for his link to her, nor perhaps for the bruises she had suffered at his hands.

"It was neither the words nor the food nor the company," Farad said, looking pointedly back at her. "I have been ill for some time. I am not as recovered as I had believed myself to be. If you will excuse me?" he asked King Rongas, loath to show such weakness after asking for his daughter's hand.

"Of course," Rongas said, and Farad rose.

"Might I be excused also, Father?" Jarina asked.

"Of course, Daughter. Please escort Lord Hunter to one of our guest chambers, so he might rest."

Jarina accompanied Farad from the Hall and down winding corridor after corridor. She led him to a heavy stone door and opened it with the gentlest of pushes. She began to enter the room beyond. "Thank you for your concern, Jarina, but I need to be alone."

She shook her head. "You are ever only alone. You need to be with me. These are my rooms. You need an ear to hear you voice what is in your heart." She entered with him and closed the door.

He looked at her keenly. "You would not understand. You would think I thought ill of your brother, when I do not."

Jarina removed her veil, so he could see her face, and smiled. "I know you better than you might think, beloved. You respect my brother, you admire him, you are grateful to him, and though it pains you to acknowledge it, you rely upon his strength, even as he relies upon mine—but you do not love him. You instead love Dewalaren, who in your heart is still True King. And you begin to hate yourself, for you must betray your King to preserve the crown he will never wear."

Farad stared at her in astonishment. "I cannot see how it upset you that I did not link to you, when it is obvious you need no such link, for you know my thoughts without it. How is it you can know me so well after only a single day? You are still a stranger to me, almost, for all that I love you already. It was the burden of my heart to fear my love was only a reflection of Jargas's own, until he broke his link with you and I could feel more clearly. Yet I still do not understand my love."

Jarina smiled at him again. "I told you, Faradan, I have dreamt of you since before I became a woman grown. Your heart has touched mine for decades, though you felt it not. I think it is perhaps because your own was so scarred, so tortured, that it could not feel such a butterfly touch as a dream.

"I have only just discovered Jargas had similar dreams of Desenia, which he kept hidden from me. I would hear from him if she had similar dreams of him as well. Is such a thing common among your people, or rare, or unheard of? Is it perhaps because of our Dwarven blood, when mixed with that of your people?"

Farad said thoughtfully. "Our poetry, our songs, tell us of such bonds, of one heart bound to another from birth. But I never put credence in such stories. There are so few of us left that we seldom even see our kin. I would not think it possible. We do not often sing ballads now, nor recite poetry."

The pain was like a knife to his heart. "Lunahr, the youngest among us, only he would ever sing. He learned all he could from the few elders who remain and recovered other songs preserved only on paper. Many he created his own music for, to replace what was lost. So many other songs have been lost completely. He ever only smiled, ever lived in joy. The only time I ever saw him cry was when he held a scrap of paper upon which half a verse was written, which had been carefully saved, though the rest was lost forever. But his smile would not be stilled. He wrote a ballad around it and sang it to all who would listen. And we all listened."

Farad's eyes were wet with unshed tears. "He was a brother to all of us, even to me, although I fought against my heart. I tried so desperately not to love him. I was so harsh to him that the others soon hated me for it. It did not matter. They all feared me anyway, for my coldness, so their hatred did not bother me. But then even Dewalaren grew angry with me, when I thought he must at least understand. But Lunahr understood.

"I had just yelled at him: I had ordered him from my sight. I was shaking, I was so enraged. And he turned to me, those beautiful green eyes gazing into my own, and he said, 'It is all right, Farad. I know I remind you too much of those you have lost. I will not speak their names. But I will not die for loving you, nor for you loving me. Your love is not a curse, as you fear, but a rare gift. It is my heart's desire that one day you might see it as such as well, that one day you might find one to love.'

"I hugged him then, and admitted how deeply I loved him. I told him that he was as a brother to me, almost a son. And he smiled, his face lit with joy to hear it.

"From that day onward he followed me about like a puppy. None of the others understood, except Dewalaren. He apologized to me, for being so blind before. He asked if I would forgive him. I forgive him!" Farad was crying now, he could not help it.

"But Lunahr was wrong. My love is a curse. Now he is gone, and I march to destroy Dewalaren, the only other, save for my parents and my brothers, whom I have ever loved. Has any other Man who ever lived been so cursed? And now you would have me love you. You must see the danger! You had hardened your heart against me, and fool that I am, I tried to soften your heart again, and I succeeded; you love me still. I will go mad, Jarina! I cannot bear any more!" He fell to his knees, sobbing upon the cold stone floor.

Jarina knelt and embraced him. Her arms were strong, for all her petite size. "No man can stand alone, beloved, and not be lesser than he was destined to be. My life is not tied to my love for you."

"But Incuban hunts you already," Farad argued. "He came so close to finding you. I saw what He did to Desenia, those appalling memories burnt into her core. Even though her core is now healed, the memories reduced to the dreams that they truly were, she is still scarred by them. She will never forget. Her nights with Jargas will be tainted by it, at least at first.

"Once He finds out how dear you are to me, He will stop at nothing to find you, to hurt you, to torment you, so He might torture me by it. He is as obsessed with me as I am with Him. I would rather die than ever have Him harm you."

Jarina stroked his hair lovingly. "Nothing He or anyone could ever do to me would hurt me worse than your death, beloved. Do not speak of it. I would endure any torment to see you safe, and I do not speak lightly. I touched Desenia, though she knew it not. I forced myself to feel what He did to her, both for her sake and for my own. I told you, I seek to armor myself against whatever might be. That is why you must not try to shelter me. I am more vulnerable as an innocent.

"But much more, I want to link to you, to share every thought, every feeling you have, that you have ever had, as I wish you to share mine. We can truly be as one, my love, as so few are ever fortunate enough to be. We can learn in a moment what it takes most people a lifetime, if they ever achieve it. Then we still have our lifetimes, to live together in joy and harmony. Please, Faradan, I would link to you. It is not enough to feel you through my bond to Jargas. There is too much I cannot share through him."

She reached her hand to his face, and this time he did not turn away. Gently, carefully, he extended a strand of self to her and she did the same. As they touched, Farad felt all the warmth and light and laughter he had lost so long ago, which had been burnt away, wash gently over him, soaking deeply into his core, as if a dry sponge were tossed into the ocean and sought to contain all the waters around it. The joy spilled back out and over and around him. And there were thoughts and memories and feelings as well.

Slowly, tenderly, he shared nearly every moment of his life with her, as they breathed as one, as their hearts beat as one. Though there was more that Farad hid from Jarina.

JARINA basked in the thoughts and feelings that coursed through their bond to one another, sharing her very self with her beloved as he did with her. However, she did not reveal everything to Farad. She did not dare. He might not want her if he knew all there was to know. She hid her shame as carefully as she hid the reason for it.

Then Jarina taught Farad the skill of erecting the new shield she had learned from Jargas, so they might ensure privacy in their intimacy together.

"I wish it were tomorrow already, and we were wed, for I would share my body with you as well as my mind," Jarina said breathlessly.

FARAD agreed wordlessly. He could not speak, but there was no need for words now. Finally, they drew back to their own cores. The link still glowed brightly.

He ached to draw her to him, but he would not be able to restrain himself, were he to hold her so closely. He should not be here with her now. It would mean his head were any to discover him here, alone with her, in her chambers, and by Dwarven custom she would need to take her own life, to restore her family's honor. But he could not leave.

Instead, Farad set out and lay down upon some cushions on the floor at the foot of her bed. He could not bear to be parted from her even by the length and breadth of a single room, though she had many. When he finally slept, for the first time in many decades, his dreams were pleasant ones: he dreamt only of her.

THE next morning, in the Great Hall, Jargas and Desenia, and Jarina and Farad, were wed, in a simple ceremony, with less than a dozen witnesses. King Rongas performed the ceremony, at the High-King's insistence.

Over that entire week, as army after army arrived to join forces with those already gathered, little was seen of either of King Rongas's children.

Chapter 4
My Brother's Keeper

TARRELL used the pry bar to break the wax seal around the lacquered crate and forced open the lid. The fabric looked exactly as it had when they'd sealed the crate in Athanark. He turned to Rion. "Here we went to all this trouble to make these crates waterproof to protect the fabric, and we ended up not fording either of the two rivers, and it hasn't rained once the whole journey."

Rion laughed. "You're lucky we sealed them, then. If we hadn't, it would have poured every single day, and we would have been caught in at least one flood!"

Tarrell laughed with him. It was good to hear Rion laugh again.

Tarrell pulled out the bundle of sample squares and folded two of the bolts of cloth, putting them into the bag at his side. "Well, we're ready to start. From what we saw in the Market yesterday, I think we stand to make a better profit on this than we first thought. Remember, there are at least a dozen different shops, and I think I'll be able to find Tailor Street, from what Elsa told me."

Rion said innocently, "You mean she didn't offer to walk you there herself?"

Tarrell's face flushed. "I told you, Rion, I'm not interested in her."

"Why not? She likes you and she seems nice enough, and she's certainly pretty enough. I can see you not wanting to pair off with anyone on the trip, although enough of the other men did when they had the chance. It's not like we planned to stay in any of those places, and it would have been terrible if you fell in love and had to leave someone behind. But this is going to be our home now, isn't it?" Rion asked.

Tarrell said in exasperation, "What's gotten into you, Rion? Did Elsa ask you to talk to me?"

Rion shook his head. "She doesn't even notice me. How could she, when you're there? Is it that you think I'll get into trouble again, if you're not there? I've learned my lesson. I don't go anywhere without our guards now. You don't have to deprive yourself because of me." He was staring down at the floor sullenly.

Tarrell put the fabric down and walked over to him. "Rion, look at me."

Rion looked up reluctantly.

Tarrell sighed. "It isn't because of you and it isn't because of my arm, all right? I just don't like her that way, that's all. Although I'll admit, I've noticed I'm treated a lot differently dressed as a merchant than I ever was dressed as a guard. Elsa doesn't look at any of the brothers the way she looks at me, and it makes me wonder. I feel like I'm tricking her, dressed as I am. For all I have a heavy purse, it's not like the coin is mine. It's yours."

"It's not my coin, it's our coin. You're my guardian, remember?" Rion said intently. "Stop talking like I've given you charity or something. You've earned that coin every bit as much as I have, probably more so. You saved my life, Tarrell, more than once. You've been like a brother to me. You're an excellent trader, for all you've only begun to learn the trade. I didn't bring you here with me because I felt sorry for you. I brought you because I need you. How could I have made it all the way here without you? I just want you to be happy. I don't want you to not live your life because you're trying to help me live mine."

Tarrell looked him in the eye. "Rion, I promise that's not what I'm doing. Come on, we have a lot of work ahead of us today. I promise I'll take the night off afterward if the trading goes well, all right?" He smiled fondly at Rion.

Rion nodded and gave him a half smile in return.

When they left their room, they were surprised to see Rarnak in front of their door, as well as Ara and Gar. Rarnak said eagerly, "I was just coming to see you. I'm glad I didn't miss you. I was wondering if you could spare me for a few days? Ara said he and his brothers are going to be staying with you. We're very close to my home, and I'd really like to get a chance to see my father and sister. I'd meant to wait until you had set up your shop, but... well, it's been five years...."

Tarrell smiled. "Of course. Take as long as you'd like. I know you said you might not come back afterward for the job we offered you, but I can't imagine you being a farmer after all we've been through."

Rarnak smiled. "It's never really been in my blood, the way it's in my father's, but it might be nice to feel the soil in my hands again, instead of a sword hilt. Besides, he'll be getting older now. I'm sure Talia's a big help to him, but it's a lot of hard work. I know she's not the thirteen-year-old I left behind, but still.... Thank you, Tarrell, Rion. I'll be sure to bring you back something, though nothing my sister has cooked, unless she's gotten better at it!" he said, laughing. "I'll see you in a week or so. I'll return to aid you at least until you're settled here."

As Rarnak headed out, Tarrell told Ara and Gar, "I wish the four of you weren't planning to head home in a few weeks too, but I appreciate that you've offered to help find new guards for us. None of you will be easy to replace, though." All the other men had been eager to leave as soon as they reached the City. They had plenty of coin to spend, what remained of their wages plus the generous end-of-trip bonus they'd been promised.

Gar grinned at Tarrell. "I much prefer the two of you as our employers to the next ones we'll have. I can't say as I look forward to working for you and Ron, Ara."

"I'll remember you said that when the time comes to decide which of you gets night duty," Ara said with a smile.

Gar sighed, and Rion laughed and said, "Come on, we've got work to do." He knocked on the door to the brothers' room to let Ron know it was time for his shift guarding their room. He was surprised to see Ron was alone. He'd expected to see Van with him. The brothers usually never went anywhere by themselves. They'd said more than once it was safer to travel in pairs, especially in a strange city. He realized Van must be downstairs eating.

Rion, Tarrell, Gar, and Ara headed downstairs and left the inn. They made their way to Tailor Street, finding it without difficulty. They walked the length of the street and back again, with Rion and Tarrell studying each of the storefronts intently. "I think we should start with Madame Genevieve's," Rion said.

Tarrell examined the storefront and nodded. It featured a four-foot window made of one-foot squares of glass, thinner and clearer than any he had ever seen. The light-blue gown with gold embroidery in the window was of very fine quality and was clearly visible, not distorted at all by the glass.

A bell tinkled as the four of them entered the shop. The inside of the building was larger than it had appeared from outside, narrow but stretching far back to the opposite wall. There were eight gowns on dressmaker's manikins displayed in the store, each in a different style and hue, utilizing an impressive variety of fabrics and trims. Four racks, each of ten colorful fabrics in different patterns and textures, lined the right and left walls, eighty fabrics in all, framed by a number of smaller racks of ribbon and lace.

A young woman called out to them from the back of the store. "I'll be with you in a moment, gentles. Please feel free to look around."

Rion and Tarrell examined the fabrics carefully. The prices for the bolts were discreetly marked. They turned to one another and grinned. The fabrics they had with them were superior to any they saw here, and at these prices, they stood to make a fortune. Rion wished for the wagonloads they'd had in Athanark, but he was grateful they had brought six cases with them. If the rest of the goods they'd transported across the mountains were equally valued, they stood in very good stead indeed.

An older woman walked past them from the back of the shop, a package under one arm, and the young woman approached and smiled warmly at them. "My apologies for keeping you waiting, gentles. How may I help you?" She was wearing a gown of the palest pink, and the scalloped edges of her sleeves and the edges of her bodice were lined with fine ivory lace. Narrow braids framed her face, while the rest of her long, blonde hair fell loosely almost to her waist. Rion saw in surprise her eyes were as green as Aras's; he hadn't thought any but an Elf could have eyes that vivid a shade.

Rion looked up at Tarrell, curious as to why he hadn't said anything yet. Tarrell was usually the one who introduced them, but he saw his friend was staring at the pretty young woman as if entranced. Rion spoke into the silence. "I'm Master Rion, and this is my Guardian, Master Tarrell. We are merchants who have just traveled from far Athanark. We have brought with us many fine fabrics we thought might be of interest to you and would like to show you samples of what we have to offer."

Tarrell broke from his daze and pulled the pallet of sample squares from his bag. "If you would permit us to show you?"

She looked as if she were about to refuse, but then he smiled at her and her smile widened. "Of course," she said and took the samples. Rion saw her hands were fine boned, her fingers delicate, but her nails were short and unadorned by the paints he would have thought she might wear, and she wore no ring. She rubbed the cloth between her fingers. "This is beautiful fabric. I didn't know silk could be colored so brightly."

"I must show you this, then," Tarrell said and pulled one of the full bolts from his bag. It was made of the same silk but dyed a different shade and shot through with fine golden thread. Rion realized in surprise it was the same green as her eyes.

She let out a little gasp of delight and held out her hands. Tarrell draped the fabric across them, and his hand accidentally brushed hers. She looked at him, startled, and he flushed darkly. Smiling sweetly, she said, "You are like no other merchant I have ever met! I should tell you—I had meant to say so before—we don't usually have dealings with merchants. We have a supplier. But I am very impressed by what you have shown me, and I think Madame Genevieve might make an exception in your case. Might I have one of the squares to show her?"

"Please, take the bolt instead. It truly shows the fine quality of our fabric, and I can see it pleases you. We have two other bolts identical to it, which I will reserve for you, for I would see you craft a gown you might wear from them. The color matches your eyes."

"Madame Genevieve will return this afternoon. Might you be free to meet with her, if she is available, and to bring some additional bolts as samples to show her? We close at sundown."

"Certainly, Mistress...," Tarrell said, urging her to speak her name.

"Marissa," she said, smiling prettily at him. "Until this afternoon, then."

They exited the shop and Gar shook his head ruefully. "We seem to have lost another one."

Ara nodded. "Ah, the folly of youth! Promise me you'll not let me share their fate, Gar, for there is an entire City awaiting me, and I would not take their path so soon if I might help it."

Gar sighed. "He doesn't even hear, you, Ara."

Rion looked at the two of them, puzzled, and then at Tarrell, and grinned with sudden understanding. "So, who else has been afflicted?" Rion asked with a laugh.

"Van, of course, poor lad. But his affections stand to impoverish us all," Gar said soberly.

Ara elbowed Gar in the ribs and then turned to Rion seriously. "Rion, please, don't say anything to Ron. Van's really made a big mess for us, and Ron doesn't know about it yet. We're still trying to figure out what to do. We'd hoped it was just puppy love, but we fear it's the real thing, for all we've been here such a short time. It's not something we should be speaking of. It's rather a delicate situation."

Tarrell asked Rion, "What was that? Did I miss something?"

Rion's initial frown of concern turned to a grin, as he teased Tarrell. "No, that's all right. Go back to sleep."

"I wasn't sleeping, I was thinking. I think we should wait until our meeting here before trying any of the other shops. This one appeared the most promising, and we seem to have made a good impression. What are you grinning at?" he asked Rion, sounding annoyed.

"Nothing, Tarrell. I bow to the wisdom of your advanced age," Rion said with a laugh.

They returned to the inn, and Rion and Tarrell uncrated the rest of the fabric and spent the rest of the morning selecting the bolts to bring with them. They took lunch downstairs, but Tarrell did not seem to have much appetite.

After lunch they left for their meeting with Madame Genevieve. She was an older woman, very prim and proper, impeccably groomed, her graying hair pinned neatly in a bun. She was impressed by their fabric as well and agreed to purchase a number of bolts.

After Rion and Tarrell conducted their business with her, Tarrell said to Marissa, "I would be honored if you might dine with me this evening."

"We would be delighted to dine with you and your ward," Madame Genevieve answered for her smoothly.

Rion thought Tarrell recovered well, for he knew that was not what Tarrell had in mind at all. Tarrell suggested they select a location, as he and Rion were still new to the City, and she named a place and said they would meet them there at sunset.

They returned to the inn, and Tarrell spent the time before dinner trying on different shirts and combing and recombing his hair. Rion was amused, for Tarrell never took as much care as Rion thought he should with what he wore.

DINNER passed much more pleasantly than Tarrell had feared. He was surprised to see the dress Marissa was wearing. She had changed for dinner and was wearing one of the dresses he had seen on display at the shop, but it fit her as if it had been made for her.

Conversation over dinner drifted to their arrival in the City, and Tarrell mentioned they were looking for a house to settle in, something with a shop in front so they might continue their business in the manner Oberas had, before he left Ardock. Oberas had always gone on about how paying rent was a fool's game; once you owned your home you still had the coin when you sold it again, minus the taxes, of course. He and Rion weren't quite ready to make such a permanent commitment. They were still too new to Gosa, and one neighborhood might prove better for business than another.

RION listened attentively as Madame Genevieve made recommendations for different areas that might prove most profitable for them. He couldn't help noticing Marissa seemed most interested in hearing of their travels, and in gazing into Tarrell's eyes. Rion was surprised and pleased to catch an approving smile on Madame Genevieve's face, as she watched the young couple.

THE next two days were a flurry of activity and full of tension, as Rion and Tarrell viewed three different properties. Rion was concerned to note friction developing between the Ogaten brothers, and was careful not to pair Van with Ron, when he could help it.

The third property they viewed was perfect for their needs. The storefront was on a well-traveled street, and the building was set up similar to the way

Oberas's shop had been, though on a smaller scale. There was a large open area that could be used as a display floor, a kitchen with a pantry, a room that could be used as an office, a large back room that would make a good stockroom, four smaller rooms that could be bedrooms, and a large washroom with a privy. With four bedrooms, there would be a separate room for him, another for Tarrell, and two rooms for their guards. The shop was also conveniently located only two blocks from Tailor Street and a block from their stable. They had decided to keep their wagons and draft horses for the present.

They moved from the inn into their new home the following day. Rion and Tarrell encouraged the brothers to use both of the two extra bedrooms, with Ron and Ara in one and Gar and Van in the other, instead of four in one room as they might otherwise have done. Hopefully, by the time Rarnak returned, whatever was troubling the brothers would be resolved.

The following day, after Gar left with Van on some errand or other, Rion heard Ron talking loudly and critically to Ara about Van, though they switched to what he now realized was Thenalonese, and to his frustration, he didn't understand anything beyond the first few words. He didn't know what was wrong. He wished there was something he could do to help, but both Gar and Ara had told him it was something they needed to work out amongst themselves.

Tarrell had found reason to go to the dressmaker's shop more than once over the past four days, but aside from acting a little distracted, was not difficult to live with.

GAR sat in the vestibule of The Silken Bed watching the sand flow down the sides of the hourglass. Van had promised him he would limit his stay to a single hour, this time, and his time was almost up.

The door to the street opened, and Gar's heart was in his throat for a moment when he recognized familiar livery. He breathed a sigh of relief when he saw it wasn't Ron, it was Rarnak. He was surprised to see Rarnak. He hadn't thought he would be back in Gosa for at least another two days.

Rarnak didn't seem to notice him. He entered the brothel, strode right up to the whoremaster's counter, and slammed his hand down on the bell with a vehemence that surprised Gar. Rarnak looked terrible, as if he hadn't slept in days. Concerned, Gar debated whether he should approach him or not.

The whoremaster came out, and Rarnak started talking to him, but Gar couldn't hear what was said. Gar glanced nervously at the hourglass. If Van was on time, he'd be out soon, and Rarnak would definitely see him. He was afraid Rarnak might mention it in passing to Ron, and make things worse. But then, incredibly, Gar heard the sound of a sword being drawn, and leapt to his feet, his brothers momentarily forgotten.

The whoremaster had fallen back in a defensive posture, and two hulking guards emerged from the curtain behind him, both with swords in hand. Gar interposed himself between Rarnak and the guards, his back to Rarnak's bared blade, hands out and placating. "Please, don't act hastily. I'm certain this is all a misunderstanding."

"If he's a friend of yours, he should know the house rules. You've certainly been here often enough this past week for him to know. No one sees the girls unless they pay to see them: one gold per girl," the whoremaster said, fuming.

"Of course. Rarnak, I think you'd better go," Gar said, without taking his eyes off the two guards.

"I'm not leaving here until I see her!" Rarnak said hoarsely. His voice was terrible to hear, full of anguish, desperation, and rage.

"Sheathe your sword, Rarnak, and we'll talk in the street," Gar urged, trying to diffuse the situation. The guards were still eyeing Rarnak menacingly.

"I'm not leaving until I see Talia!" Rarnak demanded.

Gar turned around to face him, to try to talk some sense into him, and cursed silently when he saw Van stepping out from the hallway, the look of contentment upon his face changing to one of worry.

"What's going on?" Van asked in concern. "Rarnak! What are you doing here? Did Ron send you?"

The whoremaster said, "If you want Talia, she's free now that your friend's done with her. But it'll cost you two gold, for the trouble you've caused, and you'd best not hurt her. She's one of our best."

Rarnak let out a cry of pain and rage, and turned toward Van, murder in his eyes.

Gar grabbed Rarnak's arm, trying to wrest the sword from his hand. "Van, get back into the back!" Gar called. Gar and Van's own swords were under the counter, and even if they'd had them, they were no match for Rarnak's skill.

"Rarnak, what's gotten into you? We're your friends! Do you want the guards to kill you?" Gar entreated desperately.

Rarnak unexpectedly stopped straining against Gar, and instead surrendered his blade to him. Gar sighed in relief, and put the sword on the counter. It was quickly snatched up by one of the guards and tucked out of sight.

Rarnak had closed his eyes and was breathing short, deep breaths, in an apparent attempt to master his temper. "I just want to see my sister," Rarnak said plaintively, hopelessly.

"Your sister? Oh, Elmoth!" Gar turned to the whoremaster. "Look, if I give you the two gold, can he take a look at Talia and the other girls here and see if one of them is his sister? He doesn't want to do anything with them. He's only going to take a few moments to look at each. Come on, with all the business we've been giving you, you can at least do that much, can't you?"

"All right, but the guards go with him, and I'll hold you responsible if there's any trouble," the whoremaster said, holding out his hand for the coin.

Gar took two gold out of his purse and paid the man. "What does Talia look like?" Gar asked Rarnak.

"Blonde hair, gentle eyes," Rarnak whispered and started trembling. "How do I know what she looks like, living in a place like this for three years? I don't want to think about what Talia looks like now."

"Talia's a common name," Gar reassured him. "It might not be her. This girl's hair is brown. Besides, if it is her, Van's not hurt her. He couldn't. He's in love with her. He's going to buy her contract so he can wed her."

They went into the back, the guards escorting them. Some of the girls passed by and looked on curiously. The guards called out and then opened the curtain to Talia's room. Van was there with her, arms around her, and he stepped protectively between her and Rarnak when he saw them enter.

Rarnak studied her intently and sagged. "She's not my Talia."

"Then come on, we'll check the other girls," Gar encouraged. "Then you can tell me what this is all about. Van, say good-bye and get all our swords from out front. We'll meet you outside when we're done here. Don't worry. Rarnak won't try to kill you now."

Van looked confused, but agreed. As they left, Gar saw Van take Talia in his arms tenderly and kiss her, and he sighed.

They checked all the other girls. Fortunately, there were few customers that early in the morning. They only had to wait to see three of them. But none of them were Rarnak's sister.

Gar and Van left the whorehouse with Rarnak. "Come on, we're going to a tavern," Gar urged. "I need a drink and you certainly look like you could use one. Then you can tell us what's going on."

Rarnak nodded.

They stopped at the nearest tavern. Gar noticed Rarnak was eyeing the serving girls carefully. "Oushka," Rarnak said. "Bring us a flask."

Rarnak took the little metal cup they gave him, poured, and tossed the drink back into his throat so fast he couldn't have tasted it. Then he poured and knocked back another two in quick succession. He started to pour a fourth, when Gar put his hand on his arm. "Rarnak, tell us what's happened. When you left here for your farm five days ago you were fine. What did you find?"

Rarnak's face creased in pain. "It's gone, burned: the farmhouse, the barn. The fields are full of weeds. I only found one grave, my father's. She'd carved his name and the year into a piece of wood, used it for a headstone. It happened three years ago. Talia would have been only fifteen.

"Everything we owned was burned. I saw the bones of the animals in the barn. She was all alone. What else could a fifteen-year-old girl do? Where else would she go but here? She'd have to eat. There are no other farms out by where we were. Father wanted it that way. He liked his privacy. She's either here, in one of the whorehouses or taverns, or someone would have found her, all alone and helpless. She was so pretty, so sweet and gentle and innocent.... Oh, Areth! How am I supposed to find her? How am I ever to know what's happened to her? I almost wish it had been her, in the whorehouse. At least then I'd know she was alive.

"Why didn't I come back sooner? I let my fear of the ogres, of the return journey, keep me in Lomas while Talia needed me. She had to bury him all by herself. I can picture her digging the grave with her bare hands and crying over it, begging for me to come home. I can picture such terrible things happening to her," Rarnak said brokenly, and he knocked back the fourth drink and then a fifth.

"Rarnak, we'll help you search for her, but you have to stop drinking now, or you won't be able to see straight enough to tell if it's her. We'll bring the flask with us, and you can finish it later, all right?" Gar asked.

Rarnak nodded and let them lead him, swaying slightly as he rose.

They took Rarnak to the two other whorehouses in the City. The first was awful, grimy and squalid; all the women there were too old to be Rarnak's sister. The second place was even more horrible, mean and filthy. The girls were young, too young, and they all looked dirty and scared and hungry. Gar had to keep both Van and Rarnak in check. He barely got them out. Then they started on the taverns and the inns, carefully eyeing the streetwhores they found in between.

It was dark out when they finally gave up and headed for home. They'd spent the entire day searching. Rarnak had finished the first flask he'd bought over the course of the day and purchased a second, and then drunk most of that on the way to the shop. He could barely stand by the time they got there. Gar was practically carrying him.

The moment they entered, Ron confronted them. His nostrils flared, and from the naked fury kindling in his eyes, Van realized to his chagrin that Ron smelled the oushka. No one else they knew could smell it, but he and Ara had never once been able to take a drink in secret without Ron knowing they'd done so.

"Where in Ragnar's fire have you two been? Ara had to go out alone with Rion and Tarrell, while I stayed here to watch things! And you've been drinking and whoring with Rarnak?" Ron glared at Van. "Don't think I don't know what's been going on! Ara finally told me. If you think I'm going to give up all we've worked for, all we almost died for, so you can pleasure yourself on some whore…."

He never finished his sentence. Van launched himself at Ron, cracking his fist into the side of Ron's head. Ron rocked with the blow and then countered with one of his own, and the two began bashing each other viciously.

Gar leaned Rarnak against a table, but he slid to the floor. Gar tried to pull his brothers apart, but they were too strong. All he succeeded in doing was getting hit as well. He was shocked by the force of their blows. He realized, horrified, that they weren't holding back at all. They were literally going to kill each other if he didn't stop them.

Gar forced himself between them, knowing only one way to save them. He was hit from the front and behind simultaneously, and he crumpled to the ground limply.

"Gar?" he heard Van say in a frightened voice, as he knelt at Gar's side.

Through slit eyes, Gar saw Ron was staring in horror at his hand. Ron knelt by Gar's other side. "Gar, it's Ron, can you hear me?"

Gar felt Ron's hands gently checking him for injury, and he could feel Ron's hands were trembling.

"Oh, Ron, what have we done? I didn't mean for Gar to get hurt." Van sounded terrified.

Gar sat up then, although he felt suddenly dizzy and winced. "Now that I've scared some sense into both you idiots, can we work this out a better way? I don't have your hard head, Ron. I would have ducked that one if I'd known I'd be seeing double from it."

Van hugged him in relief. Ron grimaced. "That was a pretty rotten trick, Gar, after what happened in the mountains."

"Should I have let you kill each other? You're wrong, Ron, about a lot of things." He turned to Van. "Van, how about you take Rarnak into our room and put him to bed? Make sure you wedge him on his side so he doesn't drown himself if he starts vomiting during the night. He's drunk way too much too quickly. I'll talk to Ron for you."

Van looked from Gar to Ron and back again and said, "All right. I'm sorry I hit you, Gar."

He turned to Ron. "I'm sorry I hit you too, Ron, but you were saying such awful things about Liana. I couldn't stand to hear you say them."

"Liana?" Gar asked, perplexed.

Van flushed. "That's her real name. Talia is the name she uses when she's working. She said they've always had a Talia there: it's a wholesome farm-girl name. She said men like that. I checked with her to be sure, but neither of the other two girls who used the name before she came were really named that either."

Gar nodded. Van tried to lift Rarnak, but he was a dead weight, now, and too heavy. "Here, let me help you with him. I'll be back in a few moments, Ron."

Gar and Van half dragged, half carried Rarnak into their room and saw him settled. "Stay in here with him, all right? Let me talk to Ron. It will be all right. He'll understand, you'll see."

"I feel so awful about all of it, Gar, but I can't help being in love. I didn't mean for it to happen," Van said, sounding painfully young and sad.

Gar squeezed his shoulder. "I know, Van. Try not to worry about it. It will all work out."

"All right, I'll try," Van said, but he didn't sound convincing.

Gar shut the door and went back to Ron. "First, Van is in love with Talia... with Liana, but he's never bedded her."

Ron stared at him in disbelief. "What do you mean? Ara told me he's spent five gold there already. The first day he saw her, he was there for two hours. How can he be in love with her in any case, when he's only spent five hours with her?"

"He spent those first two hours talking to her, that's all, only talking, and he's been in love with her ever since. And it's been a lot more than five hours. She's snuck him in the nights he's not been on guard duty, and even some of the nights he has. The girls have quite a system there, and Ara and I have been pulling double shifts sometimes, without you knowing, so he could go to her. We'd hoped he'd get her out of his system, but it only made it worse. They've still only been talking and kissing, but their hearts are lost.

"It's my fault and Ara's that this happened in the first place, not his. We just wanted to treat ourselves with a visit to the brothel. We figured after all we'd been through, we deserved it, but we knew you wouldn't approve. So the three of us snuck off and went there.

"Van kept us waiting an extra hour. We were all supposed to be finished at the same time. We were afraid if we were gone longer you might suspect something. We were pretty annoyed with him making us wait and upset about the extra coin too, but he came out with this big smile on his face, and he couldn't stop talking about her. We thought it was only puppy love, but it's pretty apparent by now it's not. We're hoping Father might even understand. Mother told us often enough how it was between the two of them. You got his hard head and his harsh tongue, Ron, but Van got his heart."

Ron stiffened but didn't say anything.

"What are we supposed to do? Keep the coin and have Van be miserable for the rest of his life, thinking about her with all those other men? If it means I have to work four more years instead of two to get my stables, well then, that's what I'll do. It's five hundred gold to buy out her contract. The three of us together have almost four hundred. We figure once we get the rest, Van and Liana can live and work at the mill with Father. We wouldn't want Van going off guarding, where he might get hurt.

"Liana really does seem to be a sweet girl, Ron. I've had a talk with her, too. It's not her fault she ended up where she did. And I, for one, will be relieved to know Van is somewhere safe, and that he's happy. I worried about him most this trip."

Ron sighed. "How did Rarnak get mixed up in all this? I didn't even think he was supposed to be back yet."

"That's a different story." Gar told Ron what had happened.

"My apologies, then. I can't blame you for helping Rarnak, though it would have been a good idea to at least come by and tell us what was going on."

"I'm sorry. Frankly, we didn't even think about how late it was getting or that we were supposed to watch the shop. We just got so wrapped up in the search and trying to keep Rarnak from getting too drunk before we were done with it. I'll straighten everything out with Rion and Tarrell," Gar promised.

"I'm going to need to meet Liana, if she's going to be joining the family. I'll not go home and face Father about it unless I'm sure of her."

"Fair enough. There's no rush. It's not like we can come up with the final hundred gold anytime soon," Gar said with a sigh.

They heard the door to the shop open, and Rion and Tarrell and Ara came in. Van apparently heard the door too and came out from the back. Gar realized he must have been listening to most of their conversation from the hallway.

Rion stared at them wide-eyed when he spotted them, and Ara ran over to them in alarm. Gar realized they must look a sight, in their torn clothes, with their reddened and bloodied faces. All three of them would have some pretty impressive bruises by the morrow.

"What happened? Was it thieves? If the three of you look like this, it's a good thing I had to go out alone," Ara said, eyeing all three of them in concern and obvious relief they weren't injured worse.

Tarrell scanned the room anxiously, obviously expecting to find things broken or missing.

Ron looked chagrined and was silent, and Gar noticed Rion appeared surprised by it, for it was so unlike his older brother.

Van spoke up. "No, it wasn't thieves and we weren't attacked. It's my fault. Don't think less of Ron for it. I threw the first punch. I was very angry. Ron was only defending himself, and poor Gar got caught in the middle."

"You mean you did that to Ron?" Ara asked, sounding both astonished and impressed.

Van grimaced. "Look, none of us are too proud of ourselves now, but we've worked it out. It won't happen again."

Tarrell sighed. "The two of you put your brothers and us in danger by not coming back when we needed you."

Gar spoke up. "We know, and we're glad nothing bad happened to any of you while we were gone. We were trying to help Rarnak, and the day got away from us without our realizing it. We went to every whorehouse and tavern in the City."

Ara stared at him thunderstruck and Ron glared at him. "Gar, you idiot! Do you have any idea what you just said, what it sounded like to them? They don't know about Talia."

Gar sheepishly began explaining all that had happened.

RION let out a big sigh. "Poor Rarnak. I'm glad you helped him, and kept him out of trouble as well as you did. If you'll promise us there won't be any more fighting and you'll work your shifts as assigned, we can forgive you. We've been through much together. But we need to know we can still depend on you. If it's that you need to go home, then go. I'd rather you leave now, while we're all still friends."

Van looked panicked. "No, please! We need the coin. I promise I'll do my work, and I'll stay away from the whorehouse. I won't cause any more trouble for you or my brothers." He sounded desperate and miserable.

Rion walked over to him and put his hand on his shoulder. "Won't you tell me what's wrong, Van? I might be able to help."

To Rion's surprise, Van's eyes filled with tears. He pulled away and shook his head, and then ran into the hallway to the back rooms.

Gar started after him, but Ron stopped him. "No, I'll go to him."

Gar looked at him uncertainly.

"I can be gentle enough when I have need to be," Ron said, softly scolding him.

Gar nodded, and Ron left to talk to Van.

"I wish someone would tell me what's going on?" Rion implored. "What's Van need with a whorehouse, anyway?"

Tarrell stared at him, and Rion blushed. "I'm not a child. I know why a man would go there. I just don't know why Van would need to. He's young and handsome and friendly. Why should he have to pay for company?"

"There are women enough who'll bed a guardsman, although few are fool enough to wed one," Ara said. "We're known for buying the best food and drink, for having coin and spending it freely, for lonely, dangerous work. City women are tired of farmers and storekeepers, of hands roughened by hard labor or bodies too soft and fat from not enough of it. Guards are young and strong, lean and muscled. When they choose to talk, it's of battling thieves and slaying beasts, things a woman finds exciting, not soil and livestock, or goods and profit.

"Sure we could get a woman without paying for it that way, but why risk it? I'd rather know I'm getting someone skilled and eager, even if it's only to earn a tip, than someone who might turn frigid or be scared or clumsy. And after the food and drink figures into it, it's actually cheaper to pay for the girl outright, if all you're seeking is some release. Last week wasn't the first time Gar and I snuck off to a whorehouse this trip. But it's the first time we took Van with us. I swear Ron wouldn't be half as hard and cross as he is if he'd only take a pry bar to his purse and scratch his itch every now and then."

"Ara!" Gar scolded in his big brother's defense. "None of that's the point. The truth is, Van's fallen in love with the girl he met. He wants to buy out her contract and wed her, but it's more than he has, than the three of us have, and he's going mad pining after her. We didn't want Ron to find out, but he finally did, and he took it about as badly as we thought he might. He took it worse. I've never seen either of them like that, Ara. They were truly trying to kill each other. If I hadn't stepped between them and let them hit me, and pretended they'd really hurt me, they wouldn't have stopped. I think it's all going to work out all right now, but I hate seeing Van like this. It's like seeing someone kick a wide-eyed little puppy."

"How much does it cost and how much do you have?" Rion asked.

"Too much and not enough: five hundred gold, and we only have close to four hundred," Gar said with a sigh.

"Five hundred?" Rion exclaimed in shock. "But you could buy a herd of horses for that, or ten wagons or…. How could it possibly be so much?"

"It's a good place," Gar explained. "They get a day off twice a month and don't work if they're sick. The whoremaster buys the girls all their clothes and trinkets, and their food, though they don't eat much, and they live there. When they're working, each hour is one gold, and they treat those girls well: they only work five hours a day, one hour per each of five customers, with an hour off in between, except for the few times someone buys a second hour. When you think of it in those terms, they'd certainly stand to make a lot more from Liana over the next two years.

"But it's not something we ever wanted to think about, really. Ara and I have had no desire to go back since all this started—me even less now, after today, after seeing those other two places. I could barely drag Van and Rarnak out. They were ready for blood, and I nearly was too. I'm glad I've yet to fall in love. I wouldn't trade places with Van for anything."

Tarrell sighed. "Why don't all of you get some sleep? The door's locked, and I'll stand watch tonight. I'm not really tired anyway. I'll call for help if there's trouble. Maybe in the morning things will look a little brighter for all of us."

Rion looked at Tarrell in sympathy. Tarrell had thought he'd be seeing Marissa for dinner tonight, but she and Madame Genevieve had been summoned to the Palace. Apparently, after showing the Princess the new fabrics they'd bought from him and Tarrell, for her to choose her veil and silk to make her new nightdress from, she'd asked to see everything, and she'd found a fabric she preferred to the one she'd already chosen for her wedding gown. They'd need to start making the gown over from scratch with the new fabric. Marissa told Tarrell before she left that meant she'd be working day and night for the next three weeks to see the gown ready in time for the wedding. After that she'd be heading to Ocanton with Madame Genevieve. The Princess wanted them at the wedding in case a pearl or seam came loose. Ocanton was one hundred fifty miles south of Gosa. It would be nearly a month until he saw her again, and Tarrell was missing her already.

Rion could tell the brothers felt awkward about having one of their employers stand guard for them, but they knew enough not to argue the point. Tarrell was still sensitive about his arm. They realized he might take offense at their words, no matter how carefully they tried to phrase their objection. Instead, they headed off to bed and to look after Rarnak.

THE next morning, Van and Gar left with Rion, who was going to the Market. Tarrell went to bed, and Ron and Ara were to take turns guarding the shop.

Ara grimaced when he came to relieve Ron. "Rarnak threw up last night. He missed the bin Van set out for him. I cleaned up the mess. He's still out cold. He's lucky he didn't kill himself, downing that much oushka so quickly. They should have tried to stop him."

"He won't feel lucky when he wakes up," Ron said knowingly.

"I wonder what he'll do now? Do you think he'll stay with Rion?" Ara asked.

"He might. I hope he does. Rion might be able to help him. He loves people and understands them better than any man I have ever met."

Ara looked surprised.

Ron grimaced. "My tongue can also bestow praise, when there is cause to."

Ara grinned. "Here I had feared you might be going soft in your old age. But that last was a two-edged comment and cut as deeply as any I am accustomed to hearing from you." He thought Ron would smile, but he did not.

"I am old, Ara. I'm twenty-six. I'm too old to be a guard. My skill has grown, but I no longer have the quickness I used to. I did not do as well as I should have on the crossing. I will not see one I love dead because of me. Were I alone, when we were tested, I would not have been hired. It is as a team we are valued. But now there will only be three of us. You and Gar are better as a pair than with me. But I have scarcely over two hundred gold. What can I do with the one hundred gold that will be left, if we free Liana for Van? I cannot become a trader with so little as that," Ron said despairingly.

Ara had never known Ron to speak of himself in such a way. It worried him to hear it. "You undervalue yourself, Ron, for you are still the best of us. But you deserve to be a trader. You've earned it. You've worked and saved more than any of us. And there are always the pearls," Ara said softly, hesitant to mention them, knowing how contentious Ron's relationship with their father was. He'd never understood why Ron seemed to hate Father, when it was so apparent how much he loved him as well, and how desperately he craved their father's approval.

"I'LL not beg charity from Father," Ron snapped. "I can well imagine all he might already say to me, for Van and Liana, and when he hears what happened in the mountains. I almost lost him his sons, the only ones he loves, leaving him only the bastard child he does not." He did not say "whoreson" as he should have, for they were all a whore's sons. He'd used the term the nobility favored, not that his true father would have been a noble. Nobles did not pay for whores, they took those girls they wanted, and most of them went to their beds willingly enough.

Ara gaped at him, shocked. "What are you saying?"

"He is father to me in name only. You three have told me often enough that I have his temper and his scathing tongue. You have no idea how you wound me when you say such things to me," Ron said.

"But Mother couldn't have! I mean, she wouldn't.... She only ever loved Father. Even if she hadn't told us, a blind man could see it," Ara said incredulously.

"She only ever loved him, that's true. But love has little to do with begetting children. She lay with many men, before she met him, and she was gravid with me when she did, for all she'd only just turned fifteen. Why do you think you are the one named Aramark, after Grandfather, when I should have been, as firstborn? You are Father's firstborn son, for all I am Mother's."

Shock, anger, disbelief, and indignation all warred on Ara's face.

"I did not think you would remember, or would have known what you heard, even had you. I hadn't realized what he had meant when we were in the room with Mother's body either, and I was older than you. You were young then, only eight, and even then I knew you were too wrapped up in your own grief to think about what he'd said afterward. Lisandra knows, but I'm not surprised she's never spoken of it to you. No woman likes to know her mother was a whore, and no man likes to hear it. Father never told me either, until the day Mother died.

"They'd given him our baby sister to hold. They hadn't wanted to, but he'd insisted on seeing her before she was buried. He'd been drinking and they were afraid of him, of what he might do in his grief, with his temper and the drink inside of him to make it worse. He started talking about how tiny and pretty she was, how she looked like mother, when Lisandra never had.

"He said Lisandra looked like him, big and bony and ugly. He said that in front of her, as she was crying over Mother, knowing how she felt about how she looked. Lisandra was only ten, but she knew she'd never grow into the fair face Mother had, that all us boys had, even me. As if poor Lisandra didn't know how pretty all the other girls were, let alone the Elves half the town boys mooned over. I'm still infuriated Father said such a cruel thing to her, then of all times.

"I hadn't cried for Mother yet, though you all were. Men aren't supposed to cry, and I was twelve. I thought I was old enough to be a man. I turned on him and I yelled at him. How could he say such a thing to his own daughter while she was grieving over her dead mother and stillborn baby sister, when she had so desperately wanted a sister?

"He gave the baby to the midwife and yelled at me that I'd not talk to him in that tone of voice. He said I had no right. Even were I full grown and a man instead of a boy, not even were I truly his son, should I ever raise my voice to him.

"I told him I'd never wanted to be his son, that no one could want to be the son of a mean-spirited drunkard. I said I wished Uncle Donara was my father, or his cousins, for they were all true men, like Grandfather.

"It was then that he grabbed my arm and dragged me from the room. He screamed at me, his face red and his eyes bulging, spittle flying from his mouth. He told me I had my wish: he wasn't my father, though I'd never know who was. He asked if I wanted to know how he'd really rescued Mother. He said her story of the bandits was all make-believe, a fable she'd made up so he could still be the hero in our eyes, without her being anything less than the damsel in distress, being rescued in the nick of time with her virtue intact. He told me the truth was that he'd found Mother scrounging through the garbage in an alley, with me in her belly. She'd been thrown out onto the street from the whorehouse, when she became too round to service the customers."

Ara paled and gaped at Ron, horrified.

"I'm sorry, Ara. I'd say it in a nicer way—those were Father's words, not mine—but no matter the words, how can you make something like that sound any less ugly? But if it is hard for you to hear now, think how hard it was for me to hear then, with me still a boy and her lying dead in the next room.

"I made a mistake then, one I almost died for. I hit him. I told him he lied, and I punched him in the face. I demanded he take back what he'd said.

"That's when he lost all control. Drunk as he'd get, he'd never hit us before. But he started hitting me then, screaming at me. I still remember every word, as if it were yesterday. 'Liar, am I? You haven't cried for her. You'll cry for her now! I'll make you cry. You'll weep once I'm done with you.' And I cried and I begged, but he kept on hitting me. I don't think he even heard me. I knew he'd kill me, and I tried to fight back, but I was so little.

"It was Uncle Donara who saved my life. He came in and saw Father beating me. He had to knock him out cold to get him off of me. He had the midwife tend to me, while he went to town to fetch the healer. I still remember the look in his eyes. I could tell he thought I would die. But I couldn't die. I didn't want to see Mother again. How could I after what he'd told me? And I wouldn't leave Lisandra without anyone to protect her from his cruel words.

"That was the last time Father ever raised a flask to his lips. It had scared him, that he'd almost killed me, for what you three might have thought of him for it, when you were all he had left of Mother. Lisandra didn't count of course. She's never counted.

"He's tried since to apologize for it, but I've seen his heart. I have no wish to hear what he has to say. I've hated him ever since that day, for what he said and what he did to me, but mostly I think I hate him for how he's made Lisandra feel all these years.

"You and Gar haven't spoken of Lisandra once this trip. I doubt you've even thought of her at all. But she's in my thoughts often. She's been alone with him these last two years, with no one to blunt the edge of his cutting tongue, though she's armored her heart against his words all these years. She's twenty-four now, and I've no doubt still unwed, still watching the other girls find happiness, when there's none for her.

"Did any of you, even Van, stop to think what bringing Liana home is going to do to Lisandra, of how she'll feel? Here Van is paying five hundred gold to buy a seventeen-year-old girl. He's only seventeen as well, the youngest of us, and he's to be wed. From all you've said and all you've not, I've no doubt she's a pretty, petite little thing. Meanwhile your own sister is seven years her senior, with no hope of a marriage of her own. Twenty-four is too old to wed. We're both of us old and useless, now."

ARA stared at Ron, stunned, reeling from all he'd heard. He hadn't known any of this! The father he knew was not a drunkard. He never drank a drop. He'd never laid a hand on any of them, even with his temper. He hadn't drunk again or hit them even once out of fear, he realized now, fear he might not be able to stop himself again. And Ron's words about Lisandra hit the mark all too well. It was true he'd not thought of her once these two years, at least, not at all fondly and not often. He was glad to be away from her. Lisandra's tongue was as biting as Father's and Ron's and her temper as terrible as well. He'd never guessed it might spring from years of loneliness and rejection and pain.

He should have seen it. She was his sister. How could he have been so blind to her suffering? He remembered hearing the boys from town tease her as she grew up. He remembered teasing her along with them. It was so easy to taunt her. Her temper would flare at the slightest word against her. It had been fun to goad her. He felt ashamed.

He had to talk to Gar and Van. Ron should not have had to carry all of this alone all these years, not when they loved him and would have helped him. He realized now that Ron's volatile temper and stinging tongue masked his own pain. For all his words, he had always ever tried to make Father proud of him. Ara knew now it was because Ron had yearned to make Father love him as his son. But Father had. They were jealous of Ron, for how Father loved him, even though they'd always known Father would love him best, not only because he was firstborn, but because they were so much alike. He and Gar and Van were always competing with Ron for Father's attention, for all they were men now.

Ron sighed. "I need to clear my head. I hadn't meant to tell you so much. I need to think this through. It's time I met Liana, too." He looked at Ara calculatingly.

"I wonder what other secrets the three of you have kept from me. I'd never known I couldn't trust you as you trust me. I've learned more than I'd wished to on this trip. It's good I won't be fighting beside you any longer. It's dangerous, knowing you can't trust the man at your back. But you're only a half-brother, and I don't know how to halve my trust." He turned and walked away without another word.

Ara stared after Ron, cut to the quick by his parting words, all the more so because he deserved them. He wished again that Gar and Van were there, especially Gar: he was the quickest wit of all of them. He would have known what to say to Ron and what to say to him now as well, so he wouldn't feel so awful.

No wonder Ron had gotten so angry at them, before they'd started hiding where they went! When he and Gar had come back from the whorehouse that first time in Thenalon, Ron had lit into them about it. He'd made it sound like it was about the coin. But it wasn't the coin at all. Ara had never even thought he might accidentally sire a child on one of the girls he'd lain with. He'd always thought women knew their way around such things, especially whores, but obviously whatever they did didn't always work. He wondered if, years from now, some boy might hate him for the hour's pleasure he'd taken on his mother.

RON scowled as he walked and noted with some satisfaction that people were quick to get out of his way. It was good to know he could still intimidate men other than his own brothers. He'd filleted Ara efficiently enough with his tongue, but he took no satisfaction in it. He remembered too keenly seeing him with his back torn open in the mountains, and crying for him in the hills. He took no pleasure in hurting one he loved, just because he had been hurt. Ara and Gar hadn't meant to, he knew. They'd thought it a small thing. How could they know their hard, callous older brother might have a heart that wounded so easily?

Ron headed for the Market. He'd price out things there, see what was needed. Maybe Ogaten had something he could sell for profit here. He wandered the stalls. He spotted Rion and his other brothers barely in time to duck away from them. One look at his face and Rion wouldn't rest until he'd tried to help him. He saw in dismay he'd ducked into a jeweler's stall, but fortunately the man was already busy with a customer.

"But surely you must have something!" the well-dressed customer said to the merchant, sounding vexed.

"I'm sorry, sir, but the Princess has purchased every pearl in the city for her new gown. I hear the train is twenty feet long. I'd be a wealthy man if I had any, regardless of the color. If you'd asked me a month ago for a strand of white pearls I would have had them, ocean pearls, river pearls. A month from now I will. But you can't find pearls anywhere in the City, at any price, or in Ocanton, or even Maraden. It's only three weeks to the wedding or I'd have formed a caravan to obtain some. But opal, now, those I have. Or perhaps moonstone? Both look enough like pearls. Might...."

Ron exited the stall. Pearls! River pearls! And Tarrell knew the seamstress making the Princess's gown. He headed back to the shop. He'd not need Father's charity: the commission from the sale would be enough, if Tarrell would help him.

He stopped short. Tarrell had only fallen asleep a short while ago. He should see Liana first, now that he wasn't in such a foul mood. He'd not want to frighten a new little sister in his first meeting of her. He stopped at the first tavern he saw and asked over a pint of mead which way the good whorehouse was, the pricey one. He took a single swallow of his drink and then headed where they'd told him.

Once at The Silken Bed, he remembered to ask for Talia, instead of Liana. The man behind the desk eyed him with a grin. "Your friend's been advertising our wares for us, I see," he said, obviously taking in the uniform. Then he looked more closely at his face, his eyes narrowing in speculation.

"Yes, I'm his brother. Now for the girl," Ron said impatiently.

The man leered at him then, and Ron gritted his teeth. This place turned his stomach.

"That'll be one gold, in advance. And you must leave your sword here. House rules," the man said.

Ron reluctantly complied and paid the gold piece.

"You'll want the fourth curtain on your right," he said, pointing down the hall.

Ron headed for the curtain, scowling at the two laughing girls he saw. They should not laugh in a place like this.

He ducked through the curtain. A girl was there, a little thing, with brown eyes and soft brown curls that fell in waves to her waist. She was wearing a diaphanous gold shift that revealed more than it concealed. She gasped when she saw him, first staring wide-eyed at the uniform and then his face. She cowered away from him.

Ron realized he was still scowling, from what he'd seen in the hall, and made an effort to stop. "I'm sorry. Don't be frightened. I'm Van's brother, Ron. I won't hurt you. It's not you I'm angered at."

She swallowed and tried to smile.

"What's wrong with your eye?" Ron asked. The skin near her left eye was an odd yellow-green.

"It's nothing. Just a little bruise. I thought I'd covered it well enough," she said, her hand going to the mark on her face self-consciously.

Ron lifted a cloth from her table and startled her by wiping her face with it. The cloth came away heavy with makeup, revealing a large ugly bruise around her left eye.

"Who did that to you? The whoremaster?" Ron asked, fuming.

"Of course not. Regus would never hit me in the face. No, I don't mean that how it sounded! He wouldn't hit me at all. He's not so bad, though nothing like Morgan was. He was very kind. This was from a customer who got a little rough last night. They get carried away sometimes. They made him pay extra afterward for it. There are other girls who like it that way, but they're not supposed to do that with me. Don't tell Van, all right? He worries about me. He's so sweet. I don't want to upset him."

"Can you put some clothes on?" Ron said, more sharply than he'd meant to.

"If you'd like. I'm yours for the hour. I'll do whatever you tell me to," she said, stating the fact plainly.

He looked at her shrewdly. "And if I told you to bed me? And told you what I'd like, you'd do that too, knowing I could go back to Van and tell him all about it?"

She paled. "You wouldn't tell me to," she said, but her voice was faint and her lip was starting to quiver.

"But you'd bed any man who comes through that curtain, without a second thought to how Van feels," Ron pressed.

She almost started to cry then. "I've never minded it. What choice did I have? I had to help my sisters and I had to go somewhere. And this place isn't so bad. The other two are horrible. The medicine's the worst part, but I'm glad for it."

"What medicine?" Ron asked, interrupting.

"The one we drink each night, so we don't conceive. It makes me vomit, but so does carrying a child, and I wouldn't want to have a child without a father for him, or be turned out onto the street." She was slipping on a silk robe and missed the pained look that crossed Ron's face at her words. She tied a golden cord around her waist and took a deep breath and continued.

"Then Van came. He was so sweet, and so shy. I tried to get him to relax, but he said he didn't want me to touch him. He told me he'd only come so his brothers wouldn't tease him. He said they'd paid for me for him. I told him it was all right if he'd never been with a woman before, that I'd be gentle and could teach him. Then he laughed and said he'd had his first at thirteen, that he couldn't keep the girls off of him at first, until he learned what to say. He said it just wouldn't be right, doing that with me, without me having picked him. Then he really surprised me. He told me he liked my voice and said he'd rather just talk. No one's ever asked me to just sit and talk before. I mean, they all want at least something. But Van and I truly only talked."

"Of course. Women like to hear stories of ogres and Elves," Ron said knowingly.

Liana looked at him wide-eyed. "Did you really see ogres and Elves?"

"You mean he didn't tell you, all those times Gar told me the two of you were talking?" Ron asked, amazed.

"No, not a word. I'm sure I'll have to ask him or he never will," she said sincerely.

"Then what did he speak of?" Ron asked, curious and puzzled.

"Of home. Of the mill and your father and Lisandra. He spoke the most about her. He told me about the griddle cakes she'd make for breakfast and how she'd given him ponyback rides when he was little. He told me that when he'd scraped himself up trying to keep up with you three, she'd kissed his hurts and taken the pain away. Of swimming in the River, farther than you were supposed to go, all the way to Elves' Rock, and how he stole your clothes, because you wouldn't let him come. You said he was too little to make it." She laughed. "He said you still blame the Elves for that. You three went on about how it must have been an Elven Princess who'd wanted to see you naked. Then Lisandra gave you a tongue-lashing for losing your clothes, and he came up all sweet and innocent two days later. 'Look what I found in the woods, Lisa.'"

Ron scowled. "Andra would never let him call her Lisa. Only Mother and Father ever called her that."

Liana laughed. "She didn't. She scolded him for it, exactly as he'd meant her to, so he would be scolded just like his big brothers."

Ron shook his head in surprise and smiled. "I doubt that's the only such prank he pulled, either. At least six other things I've always been suspicious about come to mind already."

Her eyes sparkled in merriment, but then she grew more solemn. "I made the mistake of glancing at the hourglass on my table then. I couldn't believe we still had time. That's when I saw the last grains were falling. We're supposed to let the men eye it. Regus likes it when the man loses track and stays too long and has to pay for a whole extra hour. But I didn't want Van to get in trouble with Gar and Ara. I'd so loved hearing of his home, and he was still dressed, so I told him to run up front quick.

"He looked crestfallen and said he'd wasted the whole hour talking about himself, but he hadn't been able to help it, because he'd missed his home and Father and especially Lisandra so much. But he'd wanted to hear about me. Then he laughed and said he'd stay another hour, so he'd get to hear my story and upset his brothers at the same time. He knew they'd squirm and fret about you catching them."

She blushed prettily. Ron was amazed she could, after working as a whore, but she was nothing like he'd expected. There was such sweetness, such innocence about her. He could see why she was popular with the customers. The thought angered him, but he was careful to hide it this time. He didn't want to frighten her again, especially not now, when he was learning so much.

"I don't want you to think badly about Van for that. He talked most about you, along with Lisandra. He said he works so hard to get the two of you to smile, and it's a triumph for him every time you do. He said he doesn't think Gar or Ara understand you two the way he does, and the way you and Lisandra understand each other. He said no one understands him, except Lisandra does a little. He's just the little brother to the rest of you. He said he wished you and your father might love each other again, the way you did before your mother and baby sister died, before you almost died."

Ron paled. Van had been so little. He hadn't thought Van had remembered that part of it. "What did he tell you of that?" he asked, his voice hoarse.

"That's all he said. He talked about something else right away. I thought there must have been illness, for two to have died and one almost to," she said.

"Tell me about the second hour," Ron urged, shifting the subject away from himself.

"He asked me for my story. I told him he wouldn't really be interested, but he insisted and teased that I had no choice, that I had to do what he wanted, because he was paying for my time. I laughed at the look he gave me," she said, smiling at the memory. "So I told him.

"My mother died when I was eight. I raised my two sisters, Anabelle and Gisela. They were four and two then. The brother who would have been six died of the cough when he was just a baby.

"My father was a jewelry merchant. He had a stall in the Market. I was fourteen, the night he didn't come home.

"I wasn't worried at first. He'd stay out later than many, to get an extra customer the others missed. But he didn't come home the whole night.

"The next morning, we went to his stall, but it was empty. He always brought home the jewelry he didn't sell. We asked his neighbors, the men in the stalls to either side of his, but they said he'd still been there when they'd left. They told us to check with the City Guard.

"We went to the patrol in the Market. The Captain was very kind after he asked why our mother wasn't with us and I told him she was dead. He told us to come with him. We walked all the way to the Guardhouse with him. When we arrived, he asked one of the men there if they'd found anyone the night before. They said it had been a busy night, that there were three. He told me to wait and he opened up a thick, heavy-looking door. A little while later he came back with a paper in his hands. He said he was going to describe someone, and for me to tell him if it was Father. The first man he read about wasn't, but the second…." Her eyes filled with tears.

"I thought he'd been arrested for some reason, and I begged to see him. But the Captain said he wasn't arrested. He said I did need to see him, to be sure it was him, but my sisters shouldn't come in. Then he called over one of the other Guardsmen, a nice-looking man with a friendly smile, and told him to watch my sisters. Then he led me through the doorway. He was so kind. He bent down and said, 'The man I described to you was robbed and killed last night. Just look quickly at his face when I pull the blanket off, only enough to tell if it's him.' And I did and it was." She brushed tears away.

"I'm sorry. I cried when I told Van too. He told me not to say any more, that he hadn't wanted to make me cry. But I told him I wanted to finish telling him. I'd never told anyone before. The girls never tell each other why they're here. And that's when he hugged me. He was so tender and strong and wonderful, and it had been so long since anyone hugged me to comfort me. I just melted into his arms, listening to his heart beating, and the whole world went away." She blushed darkly and stared at the floor.

"When I looked up into his eyes, I thought he was going to kiss me. He was gazing at me so lovingly. But he didn't. Instead, he hugged me again, and then let me go. He asked me to finish my story. So I told him the rest, about how I knew better than to go to the orphan house with my sisters. We'd all heard what happens to the girls there. The same for serving girls and maids: I wouldn't want that, not being able to protect them, any time day or night having the master of the house or his sons come to you, where they can beat you and starve you as well as rape you at their whim.

"We lived in rented rooms and the rent was coming due. I sold what furniture we had and paid the rent and bought food and looked for apprenticeships for the girls that whole month. I finally found a good one at a baker, where they could stay together. They'd already lost Mother and then Father, and they were going to lose me, too, so it was important to me that they could have each other. The baker's daughter was getting married and leaving, but his business was growing too, so he and his wife wanted two girls to help them instead of just one.

"You can't be younger than ten or older than twelve to apprentice, so I lied and said they were twins, that they were both ten, and they believed me. Everyone always thought they were twins. Gisela was only eight, but she was big for her age, and twins are always a little smaller than the rest. Anyway, the apprenticeship cost fifty gold each, one hundred gold for the two of them.

"I'd learned a lot from the girls in the Market that month. I knew to come here, instead of those other two places. I looked older than I was too, because of taking care of my sisters and Father for so long, so Morgan believed me when I told him I'd just turned sixteen. He told me I'd get one hundred twenty-five gold for a contract, that I'd work here for five years, until I was twenty-one, unless someone bought out my contract. But he was honest about it. He said that almost never happens. So that's what I did. I bought my sisters their apprenticeships and gave them the twenty-five gold to save for when they are wed. And I've worked here ever since.

"I told Van I wondered about them a lot, if they were happy, and still all right. He asked me to tell him the name of the bakery and he'd go there and check for me, and come back and tell me. I told him he couldn't, that they wouldn't let him talk to me unless he paid the gold for it, but he said he'd pay, that he wanted to talk to me again anyway.

"He came back the very next day, and told me he'd seen Anabelle and Gisela. He said they were very happy. The baker and his wife were kind to them, and they liked the work and they shared a room. They were only ever sad wondering about me, and asked why I didn't come to see them. I was horrified then. They were so young when I'd left them there, but now they'd know what I had done for them, and I was afraid of what they'd think of me for it. But Van said not to worry. He said he'd told them I worked in a grand house, but the master was very strict, and I wasn't allowed to walk about the City. Van told them he was a guard at the house and he was in love with me and was going to whisk me away to wed him, and then I could see them again.

"I scolded him and told him he shouldn't have said so, that they'd be disappointed when I didn't come. But he looked me in the eye and said he hadn't lied to them, not about that. He said he was in love with me and he was going to take me away from here, to wed me. And I just stared at him, and when I found my voice, I told him he was being silly. He couldn't possibly mean it. He'd only just met me, so he couldn't feel that way about me. Then he said to me, 'But you love me.'

"I knew Van could never buy my contract. They make you pay four times what you get. Who would ever pay five hundred gold for a whore? So I told him I didn't love him. But he wouldn't believe it. So then I said everything I could think of to get him to believe me. I said such cruel things to him, telling him he was a spoiled little boy, and mocking him. Then he finally believed me. I saw I'd broken his heart, but he left, and I thought I'd done him a kindness, that he'd heal from it and find someone he might be able to love. I was lucky he was the last customer of the day. I cried the whole night, and I couldn't eat or sleep.

"The next morning I put on my makeup and tried to pretend everything was all right, but my eyes were still red from crying. And Van was the first customer. He looked terrible, like he'd been crying too, like he hadn't slept. He said he didn't believe what I'd told him. He told me to look him in the eye and tell him again. And I tried, I really tried, but I couldn't. Instead, I fell into his arms and started crying, telling him how I really felt and why I'd done what I had. I told him he had to go, that he shouldn't love me as I loved him. And that's when he kissed me."

She sighed. "I'm sorry, Ron. I never meant to fall in love with him, or for him to fall in love with me. I know we've made a mess of everything. But we don't know what to do about it. Gar and Ara have told him they'll give him what they've earned, but it will still be a year or more until he can earn the rest. I'm so afraid he'll be distracted thinking about me, when he should be paying attention to his work, and that he might get hurt or even killed. I told him to wait the two years until my contract is up and I can leave, but he said he can't. He said he'll go mad thinking of me with five men every day until then, that he can barely eat now, thinking of it.

"Maybe you can talk to him for me. He loves you and respects you. He wishes you'd ever talk to him man to man, not big brother to little brother. If you'd only talk to him and listen to him, maybe you can convince him to wait for me. I don't think you can convince him to forget about me altogether, but if you could...." Her eyes welled with tears and she looked away.

"Your face lights up when you talk about him," Ron said. "And your voice changes. It becomes very soft and tender. I was afraid you might be using him to buy your freedom, that Van and even Gar and Ara just wouldn't see it. But you truly love him. And he loves you." Ron sighed. "Do you have any clothes you can wear outside?"

"Outside? You mean in the garden in the back? It's warm enough, this time of year. I usually wear this," she said, indicating a robe.

"No, I mean in the street," Ron said patiently.

She said in surprise, "I can't go into the street. It's not allowed. It takes the mystery out of it, and the streetwhores have whoremasters who are pretty rough. They don't like the competition. We're a lot cleaner and better fed."

Ron sighed again. "I'll take that as a 'no,' then. All right, I'm paying for you for the next two hours. I don't want anyone hurting you while I'm gone. I'll be back by then, with the coin to buy your contract. Pack up whatever things you want to take with you. And I'll need a pair of your slippers and whatever clothes fit you best. You'll need a respectable dress and shoes."

Liana looked at him wide-eyed and then leapt into his arms and hugged him. Then she backed up and blushed again. She handed Ron a filmy dress and a pair of slippers.

Ron rolled the dress around the slippers and left with the bundle, heading to the front. The whoremaster was surprised to see him, for his hour wasn't up. "Did she displease you?" he asked.

"No, she pleased me fine. In fact, I'm paying for her for the next two hours too," Ron said, reaching into his purse for the coin.

"I'm sorry. You can only have her for two hours in a row. We can't have the girls too worn out," the whoremaster said apologetically.

"I'm buying her for two more hours, but I won't be staying. I'll be back before they're up." Ron put two gold pieces on the counter. "And she had better be alone when I return."

"Of course," the whoremaster said, smiling.

Ron reclaimed his sword and left for the Market, hoping to spot Rion again. He needed Van's and Gar's coin. But there was no sign of any of them. So he went to Tailor Street and looked for a place with ready-made clothes, where he could buy something suitable for Liana. He found a green dress that would cover her modestly enough, and held the filmy negligee up to check that the size was right. The salesgirl giggled and he glared at her. He took great delight in haggling over the price while the negligee lay on the counter, drawing shocked looks from the other customers.

The shoes were a lot harder to locate—he wanted to be sure the ones he bought fit her properly—but he finally found ones he thought would be all right. Then he headed for the shop. Rion wasn't there, but Ara was. Ara wanted to talk with him.

"Not now, Ara, I've not the time. Give me your coin, all of it. I've found something I need to pay for," Ron said, his tone brooking no argument.

"But Ron…," Ara said, starting to object, but then he trailed off. "All right," he said, looking grim. Ron could see he didn't have the heart to argue with him, not after their talk that morning. Ara gave him one hundred forty gold and some smaller coin.

"Is Tarrell still here?" Ron asked.

"Yes, he's in his room," Ara said glumly.

Ron went to the back and knocked on his bedroom door, and Tarrell told him to come in.

"Tarrell, I need to ask a favor. I need to borrow some coin, only for two hours or so, until Gar and Van come back. And later, I need to talk to you about a trade deal I'd like your help with. You'll make a hefty profit on your part of the commission."

"How much do you need to borrow?" Tarrell asked, intrigued.

"One hundred seventy gold," Ron said. With his own coin, that would give him the five hundred he needed.

Tarrell's eyebrows rose. "That's a lot of coin."

"It's only for a couple of hours. You trust me, don't you?" Ron challenged.

"Of course," Tarrell said. He pulled up the floorboard next to the wall beside his bed, pulled out a full purse, and counted out the coin. Ron saw that it made a sizable dent, but he still had a hefty amount of coin.

"Is Rarnak conscious?" Ron asked.

"He is, but he's in bed. His head's splitting in two, and every time he tries to move he heaves," Tarrell said, looking troubled.

Ron sighed. He didn't like carrying so much coin alone, but he wouldn't take Ara and leave Tarrell unguarded. "I'll be back in a while, and I'll bring something for Rarnak's head," Ron said. Then he left for the whorehouse.

There was still some sand in the hourglass when he arrived. "You barely made it. Your time's almost up," the whoremaster said.

"I'm buying her," Ron said.

"Now, I can't give you another hour," the whoremaster argued.

"I'm not buying an hour, I'm buying the girl," Ron said.

The whoremaster laughed. "I told your brother, five hundred gold is the contracted rate: no haggling, no discounts, no installment plans."

Ron pulled out his purse and dumped it onto the counter. "Five hundred gold. Now go get her contract. Then count this and give me her contract with your signature upon it showing the full amount has been paid and then I'll fetch her."

The whoremaster's eyes widened and he left the counter. He came back with a piece of paper and a writing kit in his hand and began to count the coin.

"Five hundred gold," he confirmed. He signed the contract. "You, my good man, have purchased yourself one fine whore. We are sorry to lose her."

"No, I have freed my brother's wife, and if I hear you call her otherwise again, you'll regret it," Ron said, checking to ensure the contract had been properly validated. "Now I'm going to collect her."

He strode into the back, sword still at his side. He called through the curtain, "Liana, it's Ron." Then he entered. Liana was sitting on the bed, a bundled sheet beside her. Two other girls were in the room with her, but they left.

"I have a dress and shoes for you," Ron said. "And scrub off all that makeup. I'm sure you're pretty enough without it. Except keep the bruise covered up, I don't want Van to get upset."

Liana blushed and thanked him.

He turned his back as she dressed. A few minutes later she asked uncertainly, "How do I look?"

Ron turned and smiled. "Like a wife," he said in satisfaction.

Liana smiled shyly back at him.

"I'll take your bundle. I would have brought a bag if I'd known you had none," Ron said.

They walked to the front of the whorehouse. Liana looked back over her shoulder, clutching Ron's arm timidly, as they left the building.

Her grip tightened on his arm as they began walking down the street, and she huddled next to him. "People are staring," she said nervously, as she saw more than one set of eyes on her.

"They're thinking, 'Look at that lucky man! I wish I had a wife like her. She can't keep her hands off of him.'"

Liana blushed again then laughed and let go of his arm. "I'm sorry. It's just, I haven't been outside in three years, not since I was just a girl. It feels so strange to be here."

Ron looked at her fondly. "It wouldn't do for you to be hanging all over me when Van sees you. I have no desire to have him hit me again over you."

"Van hit you? Because of me?" she asked, eyes wide with astonishment.

Ron flushed. "I shouldn't have mentioned it. I deserved to be hit, for what I said to him, but I didn't know he was in love then, and I couldn't believe you might be. But once Gar explained it to me, we worked it out."

They walked in silence the rest of the way to the shop, Liana staring in eager curiosity at the buildings and people around them.

"Here it is," Ron said, and let her in.

Ara came out of the back, apparently having heard the door, and stared in openmouthed astonishment at the two of them. "Is that what you were doing? Here I've been wondering how I might be able to face Van to tell him I don't have the coin anymore, and you've bought her for him!"

"I freed her, Ara," Ron scolded. "People aren't bought and sold. I bought the dress and the shoes."

"Forgive me," Ara said formally to Liana, and then grinned. "Welcome home, little sister."

Liana smiled shyly at him. "Thank you, Ara." Then she looked around and asked eagerly, "Is Van here?"

"No, they're not back yet. May I take your things?" Ara asked, and Ron handed him the bundle. "Where's she to sleep, Ron?"

"Move Van and Gar's things into our room. The four of us and Rarnak will share a room, like we used to, and she'll be in the other, until she and Van are wed," Ron said.

Ara nodded.

"Rarnak! I forgot all about him," Ron said, annoyed with himself. "I meant to stop at the herbalist for him on the way here. I'd go now, but I don't want to miss the expression on Van's face when he sees her."

"Then I'll hide her in our room until you get back. I'll keep her company, until I hear the others enter," Ara said.

"I saw both Van and Gar with Rion in the Market. Tarrell hasn't gone out without a guard, has he?" Ron asked in concern.

"No, he's in with Rarnak," Ara assured him.

Ron left for the herbalist and picked up what he remembered his mother always fixed for their father, when he'd had hangovers from a night of heavy drinking. He went back to the shop and was relieved to see Van wasn't back yet. He brewed the herbal remedy for Rarnak and then knocked on the bedroom door. Tarrell told him to enter, and Ron did.

"I've got something that will help Rarnak's head. He'll be able to keep it down, too," he added, for the room smelled heavily of vomit. Tarrell appeared relieved. Rarnak looked miserable. His eyes were red-rimmed and bloodshot, and his face was pale and haggard.

"Here, Rarnak, this will make you feel better," Ron said, holding the steaming mug out to him.

"I don't want to feel better. I want to die," Rarnak moaned.

"You're not the first to think so, after a binge like the one you've had," Ron said sympathetically.

"No, I truly want to die. I want to join my father and Talia," Rarnak said morosely.

Ron glared at him. "And if Talia's not dead? If she's waiting for you somewhere, or is in trouble and needs help, you'd leave her alone to face it, when this time you might have been there for her? Stop being an idiot and drink this, or I'll pour it down your throat. I'm older than you and a better swordsman and my head's not ready to split in two, so don't think I can't," Ron threatened.

Rarnak squinted up at him, as if the light from the oil lamp were too bright to bear. Then he reached out his hand for the mug, took it, and drank.

Ron smiled fondly at him. "Now, get some rest. We've got some traveling to do in the next couple of days. Tarrell, I'd like to talk with you about that, in the other room, when you have a chance," Ron said.

Rarnak lay back on the bed and pulled the covers up around him. Within moments he was asleep.

Ron and Tarrell went into the main room of the shop. "Thanks, Ron," Tarrell said. "He's been talking like that all day. I hadn't known what to do. I didn't think he'd hurt himself, but I wasn't sure. I've been afraid to leave him alone."

"It wouldn't hurt to watch him. He might yet harm himself, though I hope not. Now, I've got a business proposition for you. I heard in the Market today that the Princess has bought up every pearl in the City and still needs more for her dress, that anyone with pearls stands to make a fortune."

Tarrell nodded. "Marissa already asked me if we had any, but we don't."

"Well, I know where we can lay our hands on about two thousand river pearls and have them back here within ten days. If I gave you a five percent commission on the sale, could you sell them to the dressmakers for me?"

"Two thousand? They're going for two gold apiece, minimum, for any size and color, and more for good ones and for white. Even if she doesn't need them all, every lady in the City will want a strand. They're suddenly popular now that the Princess wants them."

Ron said intently, "These are fine ones, white and pink and peach. My father has a chest of them, from the River Elves. They pay him in *raeta*, that's Elven bread, and in river pearls, to grind their grain. Grandfather wouldn't ever accept the pearls, but Father does. He eats the bread but just saves the pearls. With the commission from the sale, Van could get his inn, and Ara and I could get a start as traders. I'd like to leave tomorrow."

The door opened, and Rion came in with Gar and Van, and surprisingly, Lerdon and Jathran as well.

"What are you two doing back with us?" Tarrell asked, intrigued.

Lerdon said, "Rion found us in the Market, listening to the hawkers, looking for work, but there's not much to be had. The day after I left you, I was in the Market and was robbed. I didn't even feel it. It was when I went to pay for an apple that I discovered my purse was gone. It's lucky I hadn't taken a bite. And fortunately, I'd already paid to stable Bramble for the next two weeks. I only wish I'd paid for my own bed. It's been close to two weeks now and I've only worked two days, and not had much to eat. It was last week Jathran joined me in the Market."

Jathran said, "My own story is no less humiliating. I was in a tavern and there was a fight that broke out around me. I was only trying to protect myself. But the City Guard came and they said thirty gold or thirty days in a cell. I know what cells can be like in cities like this. I've had friends in them, and been unfortunate enough to spend five days in one myself. I've no desire to be eaten by bugs and rats, so I paid the thirty gold, but it was nearly every coin I had. As Lerdon told you, there's not much work. We thought of looking for you, to see if you still needed help. We went to The Painted Turtle, but they didn't even remember you at first, and then they told us you'd left after only one night. The City is big; we had no idea where you'd gone. We tried ten more inns and got discouraged and gave up. Then today, when we saw Rion with his injured arm, we thought you might have had as bad luck as us. We were miserable hearing what happened to him, but relieved you'd both kept your purses, at least."

"It was lucky for us you saw me, for now we've the two of you to replace the four we're losing, when the brothers go," Rion said.

Tarrell smiled. "That's perfect! They can watch the shop while we're in Ogaten."

"Ogaten? Why are we going there?" Rion asked, curious.

"Ron and I have business in Ogaten," Tarrell explained. "And there's River Elves in Salenia, Rion. Maybe you could visit them," he added, half-joking.

But Rion's face fell. "I suppose it's time to," he said sadly.

Tarrell looked from him to Lerdon and Jathran and said, "Ron, I think you'd better get your surprise. I can't stand to see all these long faces."

Ron grinned and went to get Ara and Liana. He heard Gar ask in astonishment behind him, "Was he just smiling?"

Ron entered without knocking and saw Ara and Liana sitting beside one another on the bed talking intently. They looked up guiltily when they saw Ron, and then Liana's face creased in sympathy.

Ron glared at Ara, suspecting they had been talking about him, and Ara's sheepish expression confirmed his suspicions. "Come on, you two, Van's back," Ron said gruffly.

Liana bit her lip anxiously as she looked from Ron to Ara. "Do I look all right?"

"Of course. I told you so before," Ron assured her. "Come."

They exited the room and headed for the front of the shop. Van and Gar looked up curiously, and then Van stared wide-eyed and walked up to Liana slowly, as if she were a bubble and might burst. Then he was hugging her and kissing her, and the brothers were all clapping him on the back and hugging the two of them.

"But how did you—" Van began, but Ron cut him off midsentence.

"We'll discuss the finances later," Ron said. "Tonight we celebrate, and tomorrow we head home. But first, I'm to have a talk with you, Van. Liana said I must."

Van looked at the two of them, suddenly nervous.

"Not about her, you idiot. About me and Father," Ron explained.

Van appeared relieved. "Can I take her shopping first? She likely doesn't have much in the way of proper clothes, and I'd wanted to pick up something for Lisandra and for Father. And Liana will want to see her sisters, too, before she goes."

Ron smiled at Van. "You're a good brother and son, Van, and you'll make a fine husband, too. Of course, go. But don't spend too much, all right? You owe me a considerable amount."

Van grinned.

RION and Tarrell began talking about the upcoming journey. Rion asked Lerdon and Jathran if he could rent one of their horses for Tarrell to ride.

Lerdon looked surprised. "Rent him? You can borrow him, Rion. It'll save me having to figure out how I'm to pay to stable him for these next two weeks. I was afraid before I'd have to sell him, and I've had Bramble for three years, now. I didn't want to have to part with him."

Jathran said, "The same would normally go for Blaze, but he's recovering from a stone he picked up. He'll be fine in a few days. Fortunately, I won't have need of him while I'm guarding your shop. But if he were hale, I'd certainly let you use him. I'll not take advantage of your kind heart, Rion, not after all you did for us on our trip. The only mistake we made was in leaving you. You always saw us through, no matter what mess we got into. I never thought we'd escape from the Elves with our lives. We only did thanks to you."

Rion was surprised and touched. "But the Elves were my fault, for insisting we bring Thorn to them."

"And Gar and maybe Ara are alive now because you did," Lerdon said. "And how many of us would have died crossing the marsh or the river? Between the snakes' poison and the insects' diseases, things a sword can't help you fight, we all might have died. It all worked out, in the end."

"I'm glad you think so kindly of me," Rion said sincerely.

They smiled at him and then Tarrell called them into the kitchen to help pack food for the trip.

Rion wondered if Lerdon and Jathran might even be able to find some benefit from his having aided Circe, as well, but he couldn't ask them. He still hadn't said anything to the others about her. He'd decided not to. What was past was past. He'd put it behind him, as Thorn had told him to.

He felt a pang of longing as he thought of Thorn. He still thought of him by that name, even though he now knew his given name was Eladar, from the message. He'd translated it all now. Elanara had wanted him to know; he was sure of it. He felt much more than a pang of longing as her face flashed before his mind's eye, and he sighed.

Even before meeting Circe, Elanara had been strong in his thoughts. Recently though, he'd started dreaming about Elanara. At first they'd only been dreams of her looking sadly into the stream in the white room in Erenia, or sitting alone in her bedroom. But lately they'd been a different kind of dream. He'd started being in the dreams, too. He was no longer just watching her, as if he were invisible. She'd looked at him and come to him and kissed him. Two nights ago, she'd brought him into her bed, and they'd been kissing and touching when Tarrell had woken him up. He'd been in a terrible mood at first, because of it, and he'd had to apologize to Tarrell for being so cross.

This morning his dreams hadn't been disturbed. He blushed darkly at the thought of the dream he'd had. He sighed. Elanara probably hadn't thought about him even once since he'd left. He'd told Tarrell he wouldn't be leaving his heart in Erenia. He'd thought he hadn't, at first, but now he wasn't so sure. He frowned at himself and wondered if he would ever grow up. He was still such a child.

RON gathered Gar's and Van's coin to repay Tarrell and told them about his plan regarding the pearls. He kept fifty gold for himself and then gave Ara and Gar each twenty-five so they would have some coin as well. Van wouldn't be needing any. He'd be staying in Ogaten, and the coin from the sale of the pearls would go to him, if Father allowed it. They'd all split the commission.

Rion came up to them. "Lerdon's lending Tarrell his horse for the journey, so none of you need to ride double with him. You each have your own horses, and Liana will ride in the wagon with me."

A few moments later, out of earshot of Ron, Ara quietly asked Gar if he could borrow ten gold.

"Whatever for? Ron just gave you twenty-five," Gar said, surprised.

Ara's face flushed. "I didn't think we'd have need of our horses anytime soon, and I'll not take advantage of Rion. He'd get me one if he knew I needed one. I need to buy a horse, Gar. I no longer have Aragar."

Gar gaped at him, stunned. "What do you mean 'no longer have him'? Where is he?"

Ara sighed. "He's safe, but he's not in the City."

"Do you have any idea how long it took me to train him? What did you do, sell him to earn coin for Van?"

Ara couldn't let Gar think it was for Van. Poor Van already felt terrible enough about all they'd sacrificed for him.

"No, it wasn't for that. Please, Gar, don't make me lie to you, not after all Ron's said to me today. I can't lie to you, I won't, but I swore an oath, and I'll not break it. I can't say any more. I've said too much already. I still have to tell you about Ron, but the stables will close for the night soon, and I'll not delay Rion, not after the fight you three had before and what he said afterward about us."

"All right," Gar said. "I'll lend you the coin, on the condition you let me pick the horse for you, and you tell me about Ron on the way. We'll tell them we're going to say a prayer to Elmoth at the Temple, before the journey. There should be barely enough time so we can say a quick prayer, so Elmoth doesn't get angry at us for saying so." Ara could see Gar was burning with curiosity.

On the way to the stable, Ara told Gar everything Ron had told him about him and Father and what had happened.

Gar was shocked. "How could Ron think so little of himself? How could he keep all that secret from us, all these years? Did he think we wouldn't love him or respect him if we knew? It's not his fault who his father is or isn't!"

"I remember Ron being sick after Mother died, the healer and the hushed voices and no one letting us see him. I thought Father was afraid we'd get sick and die too, or that maybe he looked too terrible, all spotted or splotchy with the pox or something. It was so we wouldn't see the bruises!"

"I remember how happy I was when he seemed all right again. Only he wouldn't ever smile anymore. He'd get so quiet and sullen, or angry. Only Van could ever make him smile, him and Lisandra. Ron seemed happiest when he was with her. I think that's when I started to resent her so much. Ron was our older brother, but he never wanted to be with you or me anymore. I thought it was because he thought he was a man already and we were only boys. I'd no idea it was the two outcasts banding together.

"How could Father hurt them like that? How could we have let him? All the times Ron protected us, where were we, ever, when he needed us? He cried for us, Ara. Van told us he did, worse than I cried for him in the mountains. Later, I remember him holding my hand and talking to me. I was in such pain and so terrified I was going to die, but also, that I might live, but wish I'd died. And he knew. He said I had to get strong for you, Ara, or else you'd never forgive yourself, because you're older. He said you'd blame yourself forever if I died. And he told me how much you all needed me. He asked who would train his and Van's new horses, without me?

"Then he told me all about the beautiful stable I would own. I could picture it, the way he described it, and I thought, horses don't care how you look. I could still find happiness, as long as I had the three of you, and horses.

"Ron kept me alive, you all did. I fought to live, until we got to the Elves, until I was healed by them. I'd give anything to see him happy, Ara, truly happy." Gar sighed. "Well, we're here. Remember, I pick the horse, but I'll need you to help me bargain for it. You're better at it than I am."

A short while later Ara led his new horse toward the Temple. Gar sighed. "Forty gold! And that was a good price, too. He's a beautiful horse, and the saddle and bridle are better than the ones you lost. But that leaves us with only five gold each. I hope Ron spreads the wealth a little, Ara. I would like to own those stables someday. But at least Ron won't have cause to rake you over the coals for losing Aragar. This one looks enough like him I don't think he'll notice the difference. I'll do the lying, if it becomes necessary. I'll tell him we traded up for him, that we sold Aragar. Hopefully he'll believe me. Try not to lose this one, all right, Ara?"

Ara grimaced.

"At least I still have Thenagar," Gar said. "Wait until Father sees him!" They'd bought Thenagar and Aragar in Thenalon. Thenagar had the blood of the steeds of Aralon in him, he was sure of it. He was hoping it might breed true.

Father had three mares, all descended from Windsong, Grandfather's charger from Aralon. He planned to stud him to all three mares, plus the two new mares they'd bought in Falnor. That would be the start of his stable. It would take a few years for those first foals to grow, before he could stud them as well, and breed more. He hoped he might save enough by then for the pastureland and corrals and buildings. Elves liked horses, he knew, especially River Elves. They might even aid him, somehow.

They were quick at the Temple. Ara went in while Gar watched his new horse. Gar tried to remember to think of him as Aragar. He hoped Ara didn't give his five gold to the God. Elmoth didn't prefer coin as an offering, he preferred weapons, but they hadn't had the time nor coin to buy a sword. He was reassured to see that when Ara returned, he still had his sword at his side.

Ara looked at him guiltily. "I gave Elmoth a gold. I couldn't do any less. I felt bad enough about it, but we were generous before."

Gar exhaled in relief. "Elmoth will understand, Ara. Now come on, we'd best hurry back, or we'll be late for the celebration."

They stabled the new Aragar and headed to the shop to change out of their livery for dinner. Ron was taking them all to the inn Tarrell had first taken Marissa to. He had insisted on treating everyone, Rion and Tarrell as well.

Tarrell lent Van some of his fancy clothes for the occasion, and Liana wore a dress Van had bought for her. Rarnak was feeling better, but he said he didn't want to dampen the festive mood, so he stayed in the shop with Lerdon and Jathran.

Liana was overwhelmed by the evening, and burst into joyful tears when Ron made a toast to their happiness. Later that night, Liana told them she felt awkward having a room all to herself, when the brothers shared the other with the other guards, but Lerdon and Jathran assured her they were just glad to have a roof over their heads, and that it was still better than the common room in the inn. At least they knew they could trust their neighbors.

AFTER the others went to bed, Ron brewed kakla for himself and Van. When they sat down to drink it, Van spoke first. "Ron, I want to thank you for what you've done for us. I never dreamed you might help us. We owe you so much. I saw the bruise, the one she tried to hide. I hate knowing men have hurt her like that."

"It's in the past, Van. If you dwell on it, it will ruin what you have, and I won't stand for that. Liana deserves better," Ron scolded gently.

"I know. I swear that's not going to happen. Now, enough about me. You said you wanted to talk about you and Father," Van urged. "Ara told me what you revealed to him. You're the one trapped by your past, Ron. You can't help who your father was, originally, or what happened when you were twelve. But you have a father who loves you and wants to be loved by you, if you could only see your way clear to forgiving him."

"Why should I forgive Father, when he tried to kill me?" Ron asked bluntly.

"Because he'd just lost his wife and his baby, and he was drunk, and people in pain do stupid things sometimes, or when they've had too much drink, terrible things. Did you know Uncle Donara beat him to within an inch of his life for it, that night, after the healer left? That he told him if he ever drank a drop again, he'd kill him, and he meant it? Or that when Father sobered up he sat by your bed crying the two days you lay there, unconscious?

"I remember crawling into his lap, all of four, and asking if you'd died too, and if I was going to die next. And he hugged me so tight, he told me he loved me and he loved you and I wasn't going to die and you weren't going to die. He was keeping us both safe. He swore you'd be all right again, and that we were still a family, even without Mother.

"Then when you'd recovered physically, it was so hard, Ron, seeing you so miserable. I didn't understand what was wrong. None of us did. We thought you must just be grieving for Mother the hardest, but you wouldn't speak of her to any of us. I used to watch Lisandra doing all she could to make you smile. She'd get me to help, too, at first, but soon I knew enough to do it on my own. I just want to see you happy again. Please, Ron, for all of us, but mostly for your own sake, as well as his, talk to him. You might be surprised by what he has to say."

Ron looked consideringly at Van. "Liana said you were tired of me only ever talking to you big brother to little one, instead of man to man. I do know you're a man now, Van. I guess I'm like Tarrell with Rion. But I'm so used to taking care of you, it's odd for me, you being the one taking care of me, now. It'll take some getting used to."

Van smiled at him. "One down, two to go. Only I don't think Ara and Gar will ever take me seriously."

Ron said slyly. "Maybe if I told them you were the one who stole their clothes, not the Elves, and all the other times you tricked us, they'd learn to respect you."

Van said nervously, "Liana told you? I didn't think she might, when I told her." He saw Ron smile at him, and stared in surprise. He hadn't been trying to make Ron smile. Ron never smiled unless Van worked hard at helping him do it.

"I'm glad we took this trip," Ron said. "I know you all the better for it, now. I wasn't too happy with some of what I found, but the three of you are very special. You're still my brothers, no matter that you weren't born to be. I'd not trade that for anything, not even for a father."

Van's eyes filled with tears and he hugged Ron, as if he were still a boy.

Ron hugged him back and tousled his hair, as he'd used to when Van was little. "Let's get some sleep, Van. We've a trip ahead of us again, although not such a long one."

"Will you talk to Father, Ron?" Van asked.

Ron sighed. "I'll do it for you, Van, and for Liana. But I can't see as how I will ever forgive him."

Van smiled, satisfied, and they went to bed.

Chapter 5
Homecoming

JUST after dawn the next morning, before they left for Ogaten, Rarnak gave Gar two gold. Gar asked what it was for, and Rarnak reminded him he'd paid for him to look at the girls and Gar shouldn't be short the coin for it. Rarnak said he still had plenty of coin, and he had no use for any of it. Rion fed them and paid for the shop, and he'd not be buying oushka again soon. Gar was relieved to hear him say so.

They set out, the four brothers, Rarnak, and Tarrell all mounted, and Rion driving the wagon, with Liana on the bench beside him. They had Van's and Liana's few belongings and everyone's bedrolls and supplies in the back of the wagon, plus some of their goods the brothers had told them would fetch a good price in Ogaten. No one noticed Ara's horse was different. He looked similar enough to Aragar at first glance.

RION hadn't been sure how it would feel to be back in the wagon again. He was surprised to find it felt like home. Oberas had never liked traveling, especially by wagon. He'd never gone far from Ardock, except for a single caravan per year, the last three years of Rion's apprenticeship, and Oberas had always left him in Ardock, with two of their guards, to mind the shop. Oberas had hated every moment of travel on the way to Athanark, and had been pretty vocal about it. Rion realized, now, that not only did he not mind traveling, he actually liked it. He missed it.

There were traveling merchants, he knew, although not many. It was far too dangerous on the road for most Men to risk. Rion knew he could never again hope to have an entire troop of guards of the caliber Talon had found for him. Men would die, next time. Men should have died this time. He pictured Gar's slashed face and Ara's torn back and Thorn's broken body again. The terror of the ogres and the Elven soldiers. And war was coming. But perhaps after the war....

"Rion, are you all right?" Tarrell asked in concern.

"Of course. It's a beautiful day, Tarrell, isn't it? I'm glad to be out of the City," Rion answered, pushing the darker memories back down. He wondered instead what the mill would look like. The Elves had built it, for Ara's grandfather. He was intrigued by the brothers' father and eager to meet him, to see what he might really be like, after all they'd said about him. He was both excited and dismayed at the thought of seeing the Elves in Salenia. He wished he could keep Talon's father's book forever, but he'd promised to deliver it safely.

Liana looked behind her at the City, obviously overwhelmed, and began chattering animatedly, nervously. Rion realized she hadn't been outside the whorehouse in three years. She talked about how she couldn't wait to see Van's home and how she was most concerned about someone named Lisandra liking her.

"Who's Lisandra?" Rion asked curiously.

"Van's sister," Liana answered.

Later, when they stopped for lunch, Rion asked the brothers about Lisandra. "Liana says you have a sister. You've never spoken about her. None of you have. I didn't know you had a sister."

There was an awkward silence. Ron had a scowl on his face, Van seemed strangely sad, and Ara and Gar both looked embarrassed and didn't meet Rion's eyes.

Rion said softly, "I've stepped upon my tongue again, somehow, haven't I?"

Van spoke into the silence. "Lisandra, Andra we all usually call her, is twenty-four. She was second born. She works at the mill with Father. She was like a mother to me, after Mother died, when I was four. I've missed Andra terribly this trip. I guess that's why I haven't spoken about her. But she's wonderful, Rion. I think you'll like her. Not many people do, but I'm sure you will," Van said, his voice going from loving and wistful to sheepish.

"Of course he'll like her," Ron said, in a tone that implied he'd better like her.

Rion was burning with curiosity, but he knew better than to ask any more. He snuck a peek at Ara and Gar. They both looked like they wanted to say something but were afraid to.

Van started talking about their town, Ogaten, and the mill, and the River Elves. "They're not like most Elves, at least, not toward us. They watch out for us and take care of us, ever since Grandfather first came."

"Ara told us that story," Rion said. "I'm eager to meet them. Do you know many of them?"

Van shook his head. "You don't really know them. It's more they know of you. Of them, we know Swiftsong and Meander the best, but still…. It's hard to explain. It's not at all like with Thorn. Remember, he was young."

"But I knew Brook, too, and she wasn't," Rion protested.

"But she was Thorn's sister. Although it's hard to say, Rion. I've never seen anyone get along with Elves the way you do. You seem to understand them. Perhaps you should write a book about them, so the rest of us can understand them too," Van said, with a laugh.

Rion couldn't hide his sorrow at Van's innocent jest.

Van looked surprised and concerned. "Forgive me. I've upset you, somehow. I meant it as a compliment, Rion. I know something happened while the rest of us were asleep in Erenia. I know you were hurt, that none of us were there to protect you, when you needed us. I didn't mean to make you think about it," Van said contritely.

Rion smiled and reassured him. "No, it's not that. Really, it's not important. I'm being silly. I just didn't realize how hard it would be to part with it. Van, do you know an Elf named River? She's a friend of Brook's. I have a letter for her."

The brothers looked at each other. "No one there we know goes by that name," Van said. "Elves never use their given names amongst Men. I don't think they do even amongst one another, though I'm not sure why. It could be anyone, with a traveling name like that. I'm sorry, Rion, but you'll have to ask the Elves when we get there."

That night Rarnak cooked dinner for everyone. He and Ron had taken turns cooking on their trip. Liana was eager to learn how to cook, and Rarnak didn't seem to mind showing her how, at first. He even smiled at her. It relieved Rion to see it. But then the smile fled his face, and he asked Ron if he could take over for him, and he left camp abruptly. Liana was afraid she'd done something wrong, but Ron told her teaching her had probably reminded him too keenly of his sister.

Rion went looking for Rarnak when dinner was ready and convinced him to come eat with them, although it was readily apparent Rarnak didn't have much of an appetite. Rarnak volunteered to take first watch that night. Rion suspected he was hoping to tire himself out enough that he might sleep dreamlessly.

THE next morning they cooked and ate breakfast, then set back out on the road. Van was pleased to see the weather was beautiful again.

They'd been traveling for quite a while at a leisurely pace and Van was just thinking of suggesting they stop for lunch when, without warning, to his horror, an arrow flew out of the trees and struck Gar in the back, felling him from his horse.

Another arrow flew past Van's ear, so close the fletching sliced it as it passed.

Van dove off his horse, to pose less of a target, and yelled at Rion, Tarrell, and Liana to lie flat in the wagon as he readied his own bow, crouching, trying to use the side of the wagon as cover.

He looked frantically toward his brothers and saw Ron and Ara had leapt from their horses and were using them for cover, while nocking arrows to their own bows.

Rarnak had jumped down off his horse and drawn his sword.

Van saw a flash of blue in the trees and let loose his own arrow, hearing a satisfying cry as his arrow found its mark. Then there were yells, and seven men armed with swords ran toward them from the woods on all sides of the wagon. Van, Ron, and Ara let loose a flight of arrows, and the seven attackers became four in the blink of an eye.

Van saw that Tarrell had climbed onto the wagon as he had ordered, but instead of using the sides for cover, as Van had intended, Tarrell had drawn his own blade and stood over Rion and Liana, ready to defend them. Van opened his mouth to scold him for it, when another arrow came from the trees, and this time Tarrell was hit, in the right arm, the one the wolven had mangled before they'd met him. Miraculously, he kept his feet, and his sword, which was in his left hand.

Van climbed onto the wagon, seeking a clearer view of his targets, and let another of his arrows fly. There was a cry from the hidden bowman in the trees, who'd stepped out from behind his cover for a moment in an attempt to fire another arrow at them, as Van's arrow found its mark. "I told you to stay down!" Van chastised Tarrell in frustration and concern.

As he scanned the Road for his next target, Van saw that Ron and Ara had dropped their bows and drawn their swords. The quarters were too close for their bows to aid them now. They and Rarnak had their hands full with the four remaining swordsmen. Then two more men broke from the cover of the trees and ran for the wagon, adding to the pandemonium, his brothers and their horses blocking a clear shot at them.

Van dropped his bow and jumped down off the wagon, hoping to tackle both men as they attacked, but he only felled one of them. The other reached the wagon.

RION anxiously watched Ron, Ara, and Rarnak battle the four men attacking them, as he hugged his pack to his chest protectively, shielding it with his body. He couldn't let Talon's precious book be harmed. Rion hated being so helpless. Although he'd brought his sword, his broken sword arm was still trapped in its cast, useless. Not only could he not help the others, he couldn't even defend himself.

He didn't even see the man coming for him until the brigand was before him. The man's eyes lit with greed, sensing Rion was guarding something of value. He ignored the other packs nearer to him and climbed into the wagon, lunging at Rion.

Liana cowered but didn't scream as Tarrell attacked the man, but he was big and fast and strong, and he tackled Tarrell, knocking him from the wagon, but staying in himself.

Then he grabbed the pack Rion held, but Rion would not let go. The man clenched both hands together and pounded his double fist into Rion's wounded arm, first on the cast and then above it. Rion cried out in pain and his grip on the pack slackened.

The thief yanked the pack away triumphantly and fled with his prize. But Ron, Ara, and Rarnak had felled their foes, and they leapt to Rion's aid. The man with Rion's pack was the last foe standing. He used the pack as a shield, but quickly fell under the combined onslaught.

RON knelt to check on Tarrell, and Ara went to Gar, who hadn't moved since he'd been hit. It was plain to see Ara was terrified of what he might find.

Tarrell was leaning against the wagon wheel, clutching his injured arm, teeth clenched in pain. "I'm fine. See to Gar."

Ron eyed him quickly anyway. "You'll live. I'll be back," he agreed. He grabbed Rion's healer's kit and headed for Gar.

"It's all right," Ara called out, reassuring Ron and the others. "Gar was lucky. I know there's a lot of blood, but the wound's not deep. The arrow struck his shoulder blade and angled off. He got the wind knocked out of him falling from Thenagar, but he'll be all right, once the wound's bound."

After Rarnak heard so, he began making the rounds of the fallen enemy, to make sure they were all dead and to help along those who weren't. Rarnak gathered their weapons and purses and brought them to the wagon, along with two rings he'd found. Van was hugging Liana and comforting her, telling her how brave she'd been.

Ron cleaned and bandaged Gar's wound, relieved to see he was rousing already. "You're going to be fine, Gar. It's not bad, this time, and the men who attacked us are dead. I have to help Tarrell, now. He was hit too." Ron left him for Tarrell. He cut the sleeve of Tarrell's shirt. Ron was worried that Rion wasn't at Tarrell's side. He hadn't seemed too badly hurt. "Van, check on Rion!" Ron ordered, as he began working on Tarrell's arm.

"I'm all right," Rion called.

Ron had to use his knife to get the arrowhead out, then he cleaned and bandaged Tarrell's wound and wrapped clean white cloth over the new wound and older scar. Ron and Tarrell stood and looked anxiously into the wagon. Rion looked ill and in pain, but he had his pack in his lap. He was unpacking it one-handed. It had been slashed by their swords when the bandit had used it as a shield. Ron had tossed it into the wagon after they'd killed the thief. Ron was surprised and worried. It was completely against Rion's nature to care about things when people were hurt.

Rion was tossing aside slashed clothing, and then he pulled out a large, clothbound book and ran his hands and eyes everywhere along it. He sighed in relief. "It's not damaged."

"What is that?" Ron asked. He'd seen Rion staying up late some nights on the journey with a book, but he'd thought it was his own journal, the one with the notes in it about their travels.

RION covered the book quickly. He'd kept it secret the whole trip. It had seemed right to, but now he felt odd about concealing it from his friends. "It's for the Elves."

Tarrell said in concern, "Rion, you look terrible. Were you hurt?"

Rion nodded. "It's my injured arm. He hit the cast, but above it too. I think it will be all right, but it hurts." He looked at Tarrell, embarrassed. "I heard you and Gar were all right, Tarrell. It's not like I didn't make sure, first. It's just, this book is old and important, and Brook trusted me with it, as Talon trusted her. I couldn't let anything happen to it."

"Talon knows Brook?" Tarrell asked, surprised.

Rion nodded. "She knows him well. She didn't quite say so, but I figured it out after we left. He's the one she's betrothed to, although she doesn't want to be."

TARRELL remembered the wistful look she had given Rion when he had left, and understood it better now.

Ron said to Van, "Those were great shots, Van. Neither of those concealed men was easy to hit, and you killed both. I'm proud of you." Van beamed with pride, and Tarrell figured he was probably thrilled Ron had said so in front of Liana.

But Liana was upset. "But Tarrell got hurt too."

"It was his own fault, for not listening to Van when he told him to stay down," Ron assured her. He turned to Tarrell. "Tarrell, you can't keep acting like a guardsman. Promise me you'll let your next set of guards protect you."

Tarrell said crossly, "I never wanted to be a merchant. I only ever wanted to be a swordsman. Is my life any more important than Van's, just because I'm carrying Rion's coin? I'm Rion's guardian. I'm the one who's supposed to protect him."

"No, Tarrell, you are not," Rion said firmly. "The guards are supposed to. And I'm sixteen now: I'm a man. I don't need a guardian anymore." Rion sounded as cross as Tarrell. But then his eyes widened and he quickly backpedaled. "No, wait, I didn't mean that the way it sounded. I do need you, Tarrell, I do." Rion looked like he might cry.

Tarrell realized Rion was afraid he might have taken his words the wrong way. Rion knew his being Rion's guardian was what made Tarrell still feel as if he were a man, instead of half of one, that he still felt he had a purpose. Tarrell understood Rion hated how easily the tears came now, after all he'd been through, that Rion felt little and weak and helpless, when he so desperately wanted to be strong. Tarrell hugged him, only for a moment, and then let go. "It's all right, Rion. I'm not so made of glass as you think. I know what you meant." He knew Rion would still need him, at least for a time.

GAR walked over to the others with Ara. With an effort of will, he was able to walk without leaning on his older brother, and alarming them all further, though he felt a little lightheaded, and was in pain and moving slowly.

"Gar, I want you to ride in the wagon. We'll tie your horse to the back," Ron ordered.

Gar agreed without complaint, relieved he wasn't the one who'd had to suggest it.

When Liana fussed over him, making sure he was comfortable, he grinned at the opportunity to tease Van and reassure all of them by it. "Maybe having a wife isn't such a bad thing after all."

Van turned, ready to go to Liana's defense, but she quipped with a laugh, "No, but the three of you might take some getting used to."

Gar laughed too, the pain from it worth the price of further reassuring his brothers and new baby sister that he'd be fine. "Ara, we've another to spar with! Van's chosen well."

The rest of them started to banter back and forth, the way they always used to. When even Ron chimed in, with an acerbic comment directed at Ara, Gar was finally able to lean back in the wagon against the goods and relax, whispering an unusually heartfelt prayer of thanks to Elmoth. They'd traveled a rocky road, but his family was yet whole.

THAT night, Ron cooked dinner. After dinner, Tarrell examined the thieves' weapons. "Your own swords and bows are better than theirs," Tarrell said to Ron, who nodded in agreement. "What do you think we could get for these?"

"You'd best sell them in Gosa," Ron advised. "Those men might have relatives in Ogaten who'd recognize their weapons. I'd say eighty to one hundred gold total for the five swords and thirty to forty for the two bows, a minimum of one hundred ten and a maximum of one hundred forty."

Tarrell nodded. "That's what I figured. Will you sell them for me in Gosa? After seeing you haggle for the bow, I know when I've met my better. I'll give you a ten percent commission and any profit you make over the one hundred ten you can keep." Ron smiled and agreed to do it.

Tarrell called the guards over. "There was a little under ten gold in their purses, and Ron and I agree the thieves' weapons are worth one hundred forty," Tarrell said, naming the higher price. "So that's one hundred fifty gold total, or thirty each, split five ways."

Van shook his head. "Six ways. You fought too."

Tarrell shook his head. "I didn't help any, and it wasn't my place to be fighting. They had two rings besides, so Rion and I get something for our pain, but you each get thirty." He handed them each a stack of coin taken from his own purse.

Liana looked surprised and Van explained to her that was the way it was done, at least when you worked for a decent man, though usually they'd see the coin after the weapons were sold. He said they'd not had opportunity to share spoils on the crossing because they'd not fought any bandits, only ogres and obearn and Elves. He didn't mention Circe.

Van helped Gar change his ruined shirt. "It wouldn't do at all for Father and Lisandra to see me all bloody," Gar said. "I just wish I hadn't destroyed both my uniform shirts. The three of you look so dapper. I seem a poor cousin to you!"

Ron handed him his own extra uniform shirt. "It won't fit as well, but it will do. Remember, I only cracked my head. I didn't have a chance to ruin mine."

"And I'll want to be riding when we get there, too. I'll not have the three of you arrive on horseback and me not, when I'm the only one who still has my horse!"

Ron caught the sharp look Ara aimed at Gar and his brother's answering grimace. Suspicious, he walked over to their horses and took a good look at Ara's before turning to him. "Gar's right. This isn't Aragar. Where is he?"

Ara dropped his gaze, as if unable to meet Ron's eyes.

"In Gosa, we…," Gar began, but then he sighed and shook his head. "No, I can't lie to you, Ron. I lent Ara enough to buy a horse. He wouldn't tell me what happened to Aragar, but he didn't want to upset you or have to explain to Rion that he no longer had Aragar."

Ron's gaze settled upon Ara. "Ron, I can't," Ara said despairingly. "I swore an oath I wouldn't say anything. I'd no idea we'd be needing our horses again, but even if I had, I would have done it: it was important. Can't you please just trust me like you used to, and not get upset over it? I swear to Elmoth the only thing Gar and I ever kept from you were the trips to the whorehouses and Liana. This is different. I can't break an oath, not even for you." He was pleading with his eyes. Ron could see the tension in him, as if Ara were gearing up for battle.

But Ron only smiled, to Ara's obvious surprise. "Of course I trust you, Ara. You are my brother. Forgive me my words before, when I said otherwise. You had wounded my heart, and I sought to wound yours in return, when I should not have. I should have stayed my tongue. I am older, but I am no more perfect than you. I would never ask you to break an oath for me. How could I respect you if you did?"

ARA smiled uncertainly as he heard Ron's words, then as he thought about all he'd said, a grin of pure joy lit his face. Ron still trusted him, still loved and respected him.

GAR grinned too. Everything was as it should be again. Only Ron's earlier words about Lisandra were all too true and would not be wasted on deaf ears. He and Ara had never treated their sister as well as they should have. He still didn't look forward to facing her, but out of guilt, now, instead of annoyance or resentment. They had a lot to make up for. He only hoped that one day she might forgive them.

LATE in the morning the following day, they heard horsemen approaching rapidly from behind them, around a bend in the road. The trees were thick here, obstructing their view of both where they had been and the road ahead.

"Rion, Liana, Tarrell, get into the bed of the wagon, near Gar. Use the sides for cover," Ron ordered as he, Ara, Van, and Rarnak took up positions around the wagon. The brothers readied their bows, but faced them downward so as not to start a battle if it was merely honest travelers approaching and not brigands. Rarnak drew his sword but kept it by his leg, ready to raise it if needed. Gar readied his bow from the wagon, though Rion doubted he'd be able to draw it or aim well, injured as he was.

"Stay back, this time," Ron commanded, looking pointedly at Tarrell.

Tarrell nodded solemnly, though Rion saw he kept his sword drawn and at the ready to defend him and Liana, if there was need.

Rion peered over the edge of the wagon, studying the oncoming horses. There were four horsemen, riding abreast. There was something odd about them, though. He saw the riders' arms and legs well enough—they wore armor plate that gleamed in the sun—it was their heads he didn't see. He suddenly felt faint at the thought of four headless horsemen, as the stories of the refugees in Ardock flooded his memory. But then one of the horses turned his head to his neighbor, shifting out of position, and Rion saw the rider. It was a Dwarf! A true Dwarf, with the look of Jargas, only much shorter, as a Dwarf should be. But he was on a full-sized horse.

Grim faced, he was eyeing their wagon and guards intently. He was in full armor, save for his bearded face, bare hands, and booted feet; he wore a gleaming helm on his head, metal plate on his torso, pauldron and vambrace on his arms, and cuisse, poleyn, and truncated greaves on his legs. There was an incredibly large axe in his hand, a Dwarven war axe. Belatedly, Rion realized there were more than four riders, as others cleared the trees around the bend, riding in perfect formation. Rion swallowed. Soldiers, Dwarven soldiers! They couldn't be going to war against the Elves, could they?

The column of soldiers pulled up behind them and stopped. From just beyond bow range, one of them called out in Common. "Keep your weapons down, let us and the army pass, and you won't be harmed. If you attack us, we'll slay you to a Man."

"Do as he says," Tarrell commanded loudly, then softer, so only they could hear. "But be ready for treachery."

The first four horsemen rode up to them warily, and Rion saw there were twelve altogether. But the Dwarf had said "and the army." That meant these were only advance scouts. The Dwarves circled the wagon, assessing the guards, then those in the wagon. They scowled at Liana, quickly averting their gaze from her, and she shifted nervously. One of the Dwarves returned to the other eight, apparently to report what he'd seen. Then the other three were called back.

Two of the Dwarves rode back to them. "We will be accompanying you for a time," one of them said. "Sling your bows and have the wagon stand aside, so the others may pass."

Tarrell looked at Rion and then at Ron. Ron nodded. "Do as he says," Tarrell ordered. They led the wagon to the side of the road, their guards keeping their positions around it, and the two Dwarves watching them warily. The ten remaining Dwarves rode past, down the road until they were gone from sight.

"You may proceed until you see the army. Then you must stand aside again," one of the Dwarves commanded.

They obeyed and the Dwarves accompanied them in stony silence.

Rion kept sneaking peeks at them; he couldn't help himself. His eyes met one of the Dwarf's eyes, and to his surprise, the Dwarf smiled at him and spoke to him in Common. "You've never seen a Dwarf before, have you, lad?"

"Actually I have," Rion said. "We traveled with one. But he was different. He wasn't a soldier, I mean," Rion finished lamely. He would not dare say Jargas was taller. He knew enough not to say anything, ever, to a Dwarf about his height.

The Dwarf appeared surprised. "Different indeed. Dwarves don't usually travel with Men."

"He was one of our guards," Rion explained.

"He is not with you now. Did he not survive the journey?" the Dwarf asked, his gaze flicking to Rion's arm.

"No, of course he survived," Rion said, disturbed at the thought of Jargas dying. "I mean, he survived, but we reached our destination, so he parted company with us, to go home."

"He'll find the mountains all but empty, when he gets there, for we are all of us on this march. Which Kingdom did he hail from?" the Dwarf asked curiously.

"He would already have been home. I don't know the Kingdom—he never named it in my hearing—but it's near here. It's in the Holoren Mountains, about twelve leagues from Gosa. Do you mean he's likely marching with you?" Rion asked.

"What was his name? Describe him to me," the other Dwarf demanded, his voice cold and hard, like stone.

Rion suddenly wished he'd kept quiet. His mouth felt dry and he swallowed. "His name is Jargas. He's about seven and a half feet tall, with broad shoulders, and a black, braided beard and hair, and brown eyes, and he carries a staff, he's a staff master. He did make it home, didn't he? I mean, that's not why you're marching, is it? It's not that something happened to him?" Selene had said Jargas was a Prince. If something had happened to him after he left them....

The Dwarf ignored his questions and asked his own. "What is your name, and the names of your comrades?"

"I am Rion. This is my guardian Tarrell, and our guards are Ron, Ara, Gar, Van, and Rarnak. And the lady is Liana."

"I will ride with them. Helvan, report to the Commander," he said to the nicer Dwarf.

"At once!" the other said and rode off quickly.

The stern Dwarf who stayed with them kept an eye on them, but did not speak further. Rion shifted uncomfortably on the bench. He could tell the others were tense again.

A short while later, they heard the sound of horses quickly approaching, lots of them.

More soldiers came into view and Rion's nervousness grew, until he recognized two of them. "It's Jargas, with Hunter!" he said, smiling in relief. Then he stared wide-eyed at the woman who rode between them and paled. It was Circe! There were at least two dozen soldiers behind them. Helvan wasn't with them.

Rion got carefully down from the wagon, mindful of his arm, Tarrell followed, and the brothers and Rarnak dismounted. Rion tried not to stare at Circe, but as they drew closer, he realized to his relief it wasn't her after all. This woman's eyes were brown, not violet. Jargas, the woman, and Hunter dismounted and came to meet them. All three appeared concerned, taking in his broken arm and Tarrell's bandaged one.

Hunter spoke first. "Rion, what are you doing on the road again? Is everything all right?"

Rion stared at Hunter in awe. He was fully armored in plate mail, as the Dwarves were, and he wore his armor as if he had always done so, as if he were born to. But his eyes were what caught Rion's attention. They were different. They were concerned, but warm and alive, like any Man's might be.

"Everything's fine. I mean, it is now. We had some trouble with bandits yesterday. You probably saw the bodies. Gar and Tarrell were wounded, but not seriously. We were worried when we saw the soldiers, but it can't be bad if you're with them. We're taking the fork up ahead. We're on our way to Ogaten and Salenia. We've business there, and we're escorting Van and his betrothed, Liana, too. You're not headed there, are you? Or are you taking the Western Road on past Kashin, or the Northern Road toward Maraden? Gosa must have been in a panic when you marched past," he concluded breathlessly.

Hunter's face relaxed and he actually smiled at Rion. "I'm glad to hear you're doing well. When Helvan reported you to us, I was worried you were back on the road with only a single wagon and so few guards. No, we're not marching against Ogaten or Salenia. We're heading for the Fromer Mountains. We've the armies of the thirty Dwarven Kingdoms of the West with us. We rode on ahead with some of Jargas's Guard, when we heard about you."

"You are being rude, Husband. Aren't you going to introduce me to your friends?" the woman scolded Hunter. Rion and the others gaped at her, astonished.

"Forgive me, Jarina. This, I believe, is the Lady Liana, and these are Traders Rion and Tarrell, and their guards, Ron, Ara, Gar, Van, and Rarnak," he said, looking at each of them in turn. "This is my wife, Lady Jarina, Chieftess and Healer of the Varash, Princess of Malar in Holoren, Jargas's sister."

Her eyes sparkled with laughter. "I know much about you, Rion. I am pleased to meet you in person. You are strong in Hunter's thoughts and in Jargas's. I am glad you are well."

"Thank you, Highness. I am honored to meet you," Rion said.

"Please, call me Jarina. I do not stand on formality," she said, laughing.

"You never have," Jargas said crossly but with affection as well. "I'm glad you're all doing well. I wish we could stay and speak with you further, but we must rejoin the army. You might as well make yourselves comfortable here, on the side of the road. It will take quite a while for us to march past. I'm afraid we must inconvenience you, for a time."

Rion was disappointed. "Before you go, I was wondering, do you think you might be seeing Talon again anytime soon?"

Jargas's and Hunter's demeanors grew grim, and Jarina looked suddenly serious.

Jargas sighed. "Aye, we'll be seeing him," he said, as if seeing Talon were a great burden. "Why do you ask?"

Rion looked at them in surprise. Selene had told him to give her message to Talon. He knew it must be important, and she'd said to trust the Dwarves, not the Elves. He had thought since Jargas and Hunter were both of the Watch, they might give it to Talon, but now he was not so sure. Jargas would certainly discount it if he knew who it came from. Hunter had saved his life, but his eyes bothered Rion. Rion knew they shouldn't. He should be glad Hunter's eyes looked alive again. Only how had he gotten married in only a few weeks? Jarina seemed nice enough, but so had Circe, and they were like enough to be sisters.

Could Hunter be under her spell, somehow? Was that a hidden power all Dwarven women had? Was that why the Dwarven men kept them hidden? Jargas had been so closemouthed about his people. Maybe there was a reason for it.

Rion knew it was odd he trusted Selene and not Circe, when they were one in the same person, but Selene was somehow the nice girl, the one without power, and Circe the evil enchantress with power. They were two people to him. Just as this Hunter was not the one he knew and trusted. An unexpected and unwanted revelation brought a shiver up his spine. "It's not Talon you're going to war against, is it?" Rion asked in a small voice.

Hunter looked down, as if he could not meet Rion's eyes, Jargas looked at him sharply, and Jarina eyed him oddly, and suddenly he felt like he was not speaking to people he knew at all.

"Talon is not our enemy," Hunter said softly, eyes still downcast, but he said it as if he wished it to be true, not as if he knew it to be.

Rion remembered Jargas's eyes, glowing with golden fire, and Jargas saying that Hunter's eyes had surprised him, too, the first time he'd seen them burn. But when Hunter looked up at Rion, his eyes were only sad, not burning. "Why did you ask, Rion?"

Something about the way he said it chilled him. He looked like Arcanus had, sad eyes, old eyes, telling him he was sorry he had to kill him for knowing too much. Hunter's eyes should still be cold and dark and dead, a predator's eyes. These eyes were not his.

Oberas had taught Rion that a good trader can lie and make it sound the truth, that merchants have to lie sometimes to make the sale. Everyone knows it and expects it, so it's not wrong to do so. Oberas said the best lies contain at least a kernel of truth, and the more truth they have, the more likely they are to be believed. Rion had never been good at lying before. He didn't like to do it. He was honest, and he knew people thought him honest, and he was proud of it. Rion was surprised at how easily the lie came, now that he was afraid of his friends.

"I was hoping you could give Talon a message for me. I have Talon's book, the one his father wrote about the Elves. I just wanted him to know it's safe, even though it's not where it's supposed to be. Elanara is in Erenia with Eladar. She gave Talon's book to me for safekeeping, to deliver to one of the River Elves in Salenia. That's why we're going there now." He was careful not to say too much, nothing about Elanara and Eladar being held prisoner, but mentioning their given names, so he might be believed.

Hunter was surprised. "You've met Elanara and Eladar? And learned their given names? I hadn't known that. I guess I missed something by not speaking to you as I'd meant to when I was in Gosa." Hunter seemed satisfied with his answer. He sounded warm again, he sounded safe. Rion almost wished he hadn't lied to him, but he couldn't forget how he felt talking to them. The three of them were planning some kind of treachery against Talon, much as it hurt to believe it. He was certain of it, he could sense it. He saw that it hurt them, too, but they were going to do it anyway. Something was forcing them to, or maybe someone: Jarina, or whatever enemy it was Talon faced.

Talon had saved his life, too, before Hunter, and he'd saved Tarrell's life and his arm. Aras couldn't love Talon as he did unless Talon was good, and Rion trusted Aras, Elf or not, in spite of what Selene had told him. He had to find Talon, somehow, and warn him his friends were going to act against him, that they were going to betray him.

It took time for an army to march, Rion knew. Armies were big, and usually mostly on foot. With fast horses, he and his guards could beat the army to Talon. He wondered, amazed, that he would think to do such a thing. Things were once again unfolding around him that were too big and too complex for him to ever understand, yet somehow he seemed to be in the middle of all of it. It was like Elanara and Selene had both told him: he was at the center of it. He could even be key to it.

What if he didn't go, and Talon was killed? What if Arcanus got hold of Talon's ring? Why was Circe so afraid he might? What could a ring do? Could it be magic, like the wizards? Circe had made the Elfstone be magic; she had said she'd charmed it. Did the ring have an Elfstone in it too? Was it charmed, but with some greater magic, with dark magic, or magic that could be used for evil? Were the Watch magic too? Were they wizards, or like them? Men whose eyes burned must have hidden powers. Did Talon have such powers? Did Aras? Could Elves have it? Rion had far too many questions and far too few answers. The more he began to understand, the more complex things became.

Ara surprised everyone by speaking up. "Hunter, if you're marching to war, then I will march with you. I've pledged my sword to your service. It's time for me to keep my pledge."

Ron looked at him sharply. "What do you mean, you've pledged your sword to him? Why? When?"

"In Gosa, the day he left. I can't say why," Ara replied.

Rion's eyes widened. Aragar! Hunter was riding Aragar! When had Ara given Hunter his horse? Why? It didn't matter. Rion didn't want Ara to go with them. Ara trusted them, and he shouldn't. "But you can't go, Ara! I hired you to protect me long before we ever met Hunter. You can't leave me underguarded on the road."

Hunter seemed surprised Rion would say so, but then he saw Hunter's eyes travel to his injured arm, and his doubt turned to sympathy. *He thinks I'm afraid of getting hurt again*, Rion thought. *Good, let him think less of me for it. The more he underestimates me, the better chance I'll stand against him.* He hid the sudden despair he felt. How had Hunter become his enemy?

Fortunately, Hunter was looking at Ara now, not at him. "No, Ara. Rion needs you here. I'd rather you stay with him and keep him safe for me. And I'll not separate a man from his brothers, I'd never do that. I will call you if ever I have need of you, but for now, you must stay."

Rion again felt odd, as if he might have misjudged Hunter. Hunter wanted to keep him safe? Or did he want to have someone near Rion he could trust? That was the problem with deception, he'd always thought. Once you start down that path, you can never trust anyone again, never be trusted again. He hoped he hadn't made a terrible mistake. But he couldn't tell them his true message for Talon. He still felt they meant to act against Talon, somehow, and he must warn him. If he could even find him. Hunter said they were marching to the Fromer Mountains. It hadn't sounded like a lie. If they intended to cross the Fromer Mountains, they'd need an open pass. Rion remembered what Hunter had said in Athanark, all those weeks ago. They'd have to cross at Malar. Talon might be there.

Rion was glad for his memory. He remembered everything he'd ever seen or heard; he'd always been able to. It made keeping track of the inventories easy for him, and knowing what prices things were here or there or elsewhere, without mixing them up. He'd remember what a customer had been seeking months ago, things Oberas hadn't picked up on, and he'd make sure Oberas had it for them when next he saw them.

It had taken him a while to memorize the Elvish message, but only because of the strange language and the danger. He remembered it still; he could recite it word for word, only now he knew it in Common, too. Elanara had told him he could read anything he wanted in the book. He'd realized it was her way of telling him to find out what the message had said. He'd been teaching himself Elvish, and that other odd language also, though he'd not found a name for it yet.

Rion was sure people didn't realize half of what he remembered, what he understood. That when they said something six months later, he'd add it to what they'd said before and know what they'd meant by it.

And he didn't only understand events, he understood people. He could read people. They were like books to him. He could see their pain or their fear or their need, and could talk to them and learn what he needed to know in order to help them. People trusted him, they opened up to him, they told him things; they told him too much, like Eladar and Elanara. They had at least realized it, though. Most of the time, people didn't even catch themselves, they didn't even hear what they were saying to him.

Maybe that's what Elanara and Selene had meant. They recognized that ability in him and saw it as important, somehow. He'd never thought of himself as important. But he could be important now, if Talon was in some sort of danger from his friends, if Rion could warn him of it. If he could find Talon. So many "ifs." But he had to try. He didn't know how he was going to explain this to Tarrell.

Oblivious to the turmoil inside him, Jargas, Hunter, and Jarina said their good-byes and wished them well. Then they rode back the way they had come, surrounded by most of their escort. A few of them stayed to ensure Rion's party pulled the wagon to the side and stayed there, as instructed.

Only a short while later, the first ranks of the army came around the bend. The army was huge! Row after row, rank after rank of soldiers passed them. They saw banners from Kingdom after Kingdom. Jargas had said there were thirty. Rion hadn't known there were that many Dwarves in the world. There were thousands upon thousands. And they might all be marching against Talon!

The others set about making lunch. Apparently, it would be quite a while until they could begin to travel again.

"Rion? What's troubling you? You seem upset," Ron said.

Ron was a good judge of people too. Rion wondered if he'd felt anything was wrong with Hunter and Jargas. He needed to hear he hadn't made a mistake about them.

Rion spoke softly so the others wouldn't overhear. "If I ask you something, will you keep it between you and me? Will you promise you won't tell the others, not even Tarrell? And especially not Ara?" Rion asked.

Ron looked even more concerned. "If it's something that won't harm anyone, of course I promise."

Rion took a deep breath. "Did Hunter and Jargas seem different to you? I mean, like they were hiding something or upset about something? Something about Talon? Did you feel like maybe you couldn't trust them?"

Ron said curiously, "No, I didn't feel that at all. They seemed fine to me."

Rion deflated.

"But that doesn't mean you shouldn't trust your instincts, Rion. You are the most perceptive man I have ever met. If you sensed something is wrong, then something very well might be. Sometimes you just have to have faith in yourself. If something is wrong, I'm even more relieved Ara didn't go riding off with them to war. I don't know what's come over him."

"Ron, after we sell the pearls for you, are you going to leave us? You and Gar and Ara? I know Van and Liana plan to stay in Ogaten."

Ron nodded. "That's the plan. We'll make sure you have other reliable guards to replace us first, of course. I'm relieved Lerdon and Jathran both sought you out. They're fine men."

"I'm sure they'll want to stay with Tarrell, in Gosa. Before you go, could you help me find some guardsmen as well? I'm hoping some other of our men might still be seeking work, but I'm afraid even if they are, they might not want to cross the Coroden Mountains again," Rion said apprehensively.

Ron looked at him in shock. "You're leaving Gosa? Heading east again? Rion, you can't! War is coming. You came west to be safe from it."

"I think Talon is in danger. I hate thinking of Jargas and Hunter as enemies instead of friends; I don't know which of them frightens me more. But I cannot let Talon get hurt, maybe even killed, when I might have kept him safe."

"Rion, I know what I said, but are you sure you aren't overreacting? What you mean to do is dangerous, even more so than before. You might die this time. No one can have that kind of luck twice."

"I know, and it frightens me," Rion admitted. "Maybe I'll need to go only as far as Erenia. If I tell Elanara, she might know how to get a message to Talon. But I can't be a child anymore, Ron. A man takes responsibility and does what he thinks is right. A man helps his friends."

"If you only mean to go as far as Erenia, maybe the three of us could travel with you: me, Ara, and Gar. After all, Ara swore his sword to Elanara first, before Hunter."

"I'll need to tell Tarrell. But I'll do so after we get the pearls. He already has too many burdens on his mind. He misses Marissa."

The others all ate, but Rion didn't have much appetite. He kept thinking about Talon facing such a huge army, with so few friends to help him.

Finally, the last of the army passed them, and the Dwarves who had been watching them departed after the rest.

Rion and the others continued onward, considerably subdued. It was early evening when they reached the fork in the road. The Western Road was to their right, to the east. They headed north instead, down what appeared to be little more than a footpath. Few travelers ever came this way. This side road ended at Ogaten. The Elven Woods all but surrounded the village.

They made camp soon after. Rion did his best to eat dinner, but he was still troubled. He wrote for a while in his travel journal, pouring out his concerns onto the pages by firelight. He finally lay down to sleep, but sleep did not come easily. He was afraid he would dream of war.

When Rion awoke from his dreams in the middle of the night, it wasn't because they'd been horrible. They'd been wonderful, too wonderful. He'd dreamt of Elanara in Erenia. It was only the two of them, in the dream. She'd been just as beautiful and warm and gentle as he remembered her, only more so. And they'd been in her bedroom, not in the white room with the stream.

This time, when she'd hugged him, it had been as a woman hugs a man, not as a sister hugs a brother. This time she'd told him he couldn't leave her, that she never wanted him to leave. Then she'd kissed him, not on the cheek or forehead, but on the mouth. She'd stolen his breath away. She'd pulled him down onto the cushions with her and they'd made love. He squirmed uncomfortably under his wetted blanket, feeling ashamed at what Elanara would think of him, if she knew.

He'd had dreams such as that before; he knew every boy did, when he was becoming a man, but they'd never been so detailed, or so long, or about someone he knew. When they happened, he often didn't remember them at all. He'd just awaken to damp and sticky sheets. Rion rolled up his blanket, got dressed, and went to the fire. Rarnak or Ara had kept it bright. They were on guard tonight. Rion hoped they hadn't heard, hadn't realized what he'd done.

He thought of Elanara wistfully. He felt cold, and it seemed so dark here without her, even with the fire. If Elanara were here, he wouldn't need a fire; she'd be warmth and light enough. The thought worried him. It wasn't the first such thought he'd had since meeting Selene. Elanara had been strong in his thoughts and in his dreams since then. Seeing Jargas again seemed to have stirred up those thoughts even more. It was pointless to try to go back to sleep.

A few moments later, Rarnak passed by the fire on his patrol and stopped. "It's hours to dawn, Rion. You should still be asleep."

"I can't sleep," Rion said, hoping the yellow-orange light of the fire would conceal his blush. "If you'll wait a moment, I'll get my sword. I'll walk the perimeter with you."

"Ron would have my hide, Rion, even if I'm not one of his brothers, especially after Tarrell getting hurt," Rarnak argued. "You appointed Ron as Captain since Jargas left, and he takes his position seriously."

"But I need to talk to somebody, otherwise I'll think too much," Rion objected, hating how young and desperate he sounded even as he spoke.

Rarnak looked at him assessingly and sighed. "All right. Get your sword. But at the first sign of trouble, you run back to camp, agreed?"

"Agreed," Rion said, relieved.

Rion returned with his sheathed sword at his side, though he doubted whether he'd be able to use it effectively left-handed. They walked the perimeter. They met Ara halfway around. He had his hand on his sword; Rion could see him by moonlight. Rion watched Ara stiffen, then relax. "You had me worried, seeing two of you when I'd only expected the one. Ron won't like this, Rarnak."

"Then we'd better not tell him," Rarnak said conspiratorially.

Ara surprised them both when he looked grim. "I'll have to tell him. I'm sorry, but I won't keep secrets from him, not ever again. Now that I have his trust again, I mean to keep it."

"Then I'll tell him, at breakfast, so if he's angered, it will be at me," Rion promised. "I won't cause friction between you four, now that everything is all right again."

Ara nodded in relief and continued on his rounds. Rion walked in silence for a while. Rarnak was quiet as well. Finally, Rion spoke up hesitantly. "What does it feel like to be in love?"

Rarnak stopped walking and turned to him. "That's not an easy question for so late at night, or so early in the morning. For one thing, you're asking the wrong man. I've never been in love. I've only heard what others say about it. You should ask Tarrell or Van. They could tell you. But they're asleep, and I'm not, and you've asked me for a reason, so I'll try," Rarnak said and sighed.

"You can tell by seeing them, Van and Tarrell, that they're in love. Love can hurt worse than any torture. Your heart can feel like it's tearing in two, when things don't go well. You want to cry all the time, to curl up and die. But it can be wonderful too. You can grin all the time and be so happy that no hardship can touch you. You can feel full when you're hungry, or warm in the dead of winter. Sometimes you don't even know how much you love someone. Years can pass until you realize it. By then, you may have lost them forever. Sometimes you only know it once all the warmth and light in your life is gone, and you're left in the cold and the dark."

Rion saw Rarnak's face was lined in pain and his voice had sunk to a whisper. He knew Rarnak was thinking about his father, and especially his sister, Talia. Rion hadn't realized his question would hurt Rarnak. He'd not been thinking of loving someone as a sister or father. He didn't have any siblings. But he'd lost his father and uncle, and nearly lost Tarrell, who was like a brother to him. He couldn't imagine anything more terrible than losing him. "Forgive me, Rarnak. I've not known what to say to you, to ease the pain in your heart, and now I've thrown salt upon your wound."

"Don't make the same mistake I did, Rion. If you love someone, tell them so. Don't ever leave them. Don't let time or distance take them from you. If ever I find a woman I care for, I hope I'll have the sense to do the same, that as soon as I realize it, I'll tell her. Life's too short by far. Please excuse me,

Rion. I'm poor company and I deserve to walk alone. It's my punishment for leaving the farm, for leaving them alone for so long. I had hoped Areth had understood. I had thought she'd kept me safe to come back to them. I never dreamt she'd take them from me, that she'd kept me alive so long only to punish me."

Rion stared at Rarnak in surprise and dismay. Oberas had not been religious, nor had Rion. But Ara and Rarnak were different. They'd each stopped at every Temple in every city or town they'd been to, at every shrine they'd passed, to Elmoth and Areth, respectively. Rion had started to think he was missing something by not having faith. And now Rarnak seemed to have lost his. He couldn't lose his father and his sister and his faith all at once! What would be left to him if he did?

Rion knew about all the Gods. Oberas had told him it was important to, since so often they influenced what men did. You might not understand their actions at all, otherwise. But Rion had never talked to anyone about religion before, other than to Oberas. He'd not felt he'd had the right. And Oberas had warned him against it often enough. He couldn't keep silent now, though. He hoped he wouldn't make it worse.

"Please don't blame Areth, Rarnak. She might have made your father's death quick and painless, when he might otherwise have suffered. She saved Talia from the fire, and she might still be safe somewhere. Your faith might have helped them both. Don't abandon Areth now, when she might not have abandoned you, now when you most need her, when your faith might see you through this."

Rion was surprised by the passion of his plea, when he had no faith of his own. But maybe that was the cause of it. When he'd been captured, held, and tormented by those awful men, he'd had no one to help him, no one even to pray to. No hope. He'd given in to despair, to terror, when he'd most needed to be strong. He'd sobbed and that horrible man had heard him and come to hurt him. He'd have been hurt terribly if Hunter hadn't sacrificed his own health for Rion's.

Rarnak was looking at him in wonder. "Before, I had thought Areth sent you to me, in Athanark, to see me safely home, though I'd doubted her some even then. I was so afraid of the ogres. But you saw us safely past them. Then, when I found my home and family gone, I thought I'd been wrong, I became convinced I'd fallen from her grace. But perhaps she still walks with me, after all. I think you are her instrument. You might have the Goddess's favor, Rion, without even knowing it, for the goodness in your heart. If so, you are truly blessed. You've given me much to think about. I'd like to walk by myself now, if I might. I need some time to ponder it."

Rion nodded, relieved that he'd helped, not hurt. He knew he was blessed in one regard: he was blessed to have friends like Rarnak, the brothers, Lerdon, Jathran, and Tarrell to stand beside him. He'd helped Rarnak, and it made him feel warm again.

He went back to his bedroll. It was still a while until dawn. He could yet sleep, now that he didn't feel so cold and empty inside anymore. He took off his boots and slept in his clothes, not caring how they might look in the morning.

RON eyed Rion curiously as he approached the cook fire the next morning. Rion looked like he'd slept in his clothes, but he knew he'd seen Rion wearing his nightshirt to bed. He and his brothers had been amused, at first, fresh out of Athanark, at how Rion dressed so fancy and wore nightshirts to bed, even on the road.

Rion looked him in the eye. "Good morning, Ron. I walked the perimeter with Rarnak last night, for a little while, against his and Ara's advice. I promised Ara I'd tell you first thing, so you could yell at me and get it out of your system before you saw him."

Ron was surprised by the blunt statement. Rion had looked and sounded so grown up. He'd seen it, on the road to Gosa, Rion changing from boy to man, but still, he wasn't used to it.

Ron's silence seemed to make Rion nervous. "I also promised them I'd run back to camp if there was trouble, so really, you shouldn't be so very angry." He sounded younger again, unsure of himself, exactly like Van as he was growing.

Ron smiled at Rion. "Then I've no reason to yell, have I?" he asked, and handed him a steaming cup of kakla. Rion grinned in relief.

Ara walked up and looked at the two of them and sighed. "I'd hoped Rion would have told you. He said he would. Last night…," he began, but Ron cut him off.

"Rion did tell me, Ara. He was at least careful, and you were both watching out for him. Rion is a man, now, and my employer besides. Who am I to tell him what he should and should not do?"

Ara grinned in relief and accepted the kakla Ron gave him.

The next two days passed uneventfully. Because of the delay caused by the Dwarven army and exacerbated by the state of the side road, it was late morning of the sixth day when they finally saw the Merdan River that marked the start of the Elven River Kingdom of Salenia.

"Take the path to the left, Rion. It goes to the mill. The one to the right goes to Ogaten." Rion followed Ron's directions.

The mill didn't look like Elves had built it. It looked like any of the other mills Rion had seen in Ardock and along the way to Gosa, except it was made all of stone, not wood, apart from the great waterwheel. But Ara had said the Elves had constructed it as his grandfather had pictured it, so it made sense that it looked like the hand of Man had made it.

As they approached, a woman came out. She was coated head to toe in a light dusting of flour. Her brown hair was tied back from her face. She carried a huge bag slung over one broad shoulder, as if she'd always done so. Her dress was plain, and her face was plain. She tossed the bag onto the back of a wagon and looked up curiously, then scowled. "You took the wrong road. Turn around and take the one on the left, what would have been your right when you came this way. You can't get to town from here," she called out crossly and started to turn away.

"Is that any way to welcome us home, Andra?" Ron chided, smiling fondly.

She turned back, startled, and held her hand over her eyes to squint against the sun. "Ron?" Then a smile lit her face, softening the hard lines of it, and she was running to him. Ron jumped from his horse and wrapped his arms around her.

"What, no welcome for the rest of us?" Van asked, and then he was hugging her, as well.

"Van! You've grown! You're taller than Ron. I always knew you'd be!"

Gar and Ara stood nearby awkwardly. She looked over at Gar and Ara, almost as if challenging them, and they approached. She seemed startled when they hugged her, too.

"WE'VE missed you, Andra," Gar said.

Ara said, "It's good seeing you again." Ara looked his sister in the eye and was surprised to see how bright her eyes were, as if she might cry. Andra never cried. She'd not cried in years, not since they were children.

"I didn't recognize any of you. Look at you! You look like soldiers. Grandfather's heart would have failed him, seeing you riding up looking like this." Her voice grew somber. "Did you make it to Thenalon? Did you bury it for him?"

Ron nodded. "They've a place they call 'Soldiers' Field.' It's where all the fallen City Guard were buried, as well as the others who fought and died. We had to get special permission to bury it there. No one's turned the ground there since the War. But we had his letter, and who else would have a bow from Aralon they wished to see buried there, instead of in the plains where it belongs? The City Guard even held a ceremony. He's a legend to the City Guard, though the rest of the City's forgotten him, even though they've a statue to him. They've forgotten too much. They've broken the alliance with Aralon. It was a sad place, Andra. It's nothing like his stories of how it used to be. But enough of that for now. We've had a long, dusty trip from Gosa. You should offer us something to drink."

"What am I, a barmaid? You see the trough; cup your hands and drink your fill." She turned to Gar and Ara. "You two can just stick your heads right in. You're obviously sun mad, greeting me as warmly as you have."

Andra turned to Rion and scowled at him. "And what are you grinning at, boy?" she asked.

Rion blushed and started to stammer an apology.

"Don't apologize, Rion. It'll only encourage her," Van said, coming to Rion's aid. "Be nice, Andra. We work for Rion and Tarrell. They're wonderful. They've been very good to us. We came all the way from Athanark with them."

"You like everyone, Van," she scoffed, but eyed them appraisingly. "You didn't do such a good job as guards though, if you're all unhurt, he's bandaged, and this one's arm is broken," she said critically.

Rion paled and Tarrell's face flushed with anger on Rion's behalf and the brothers'.

"Gar was hurt too, where you can't see. You should be glad they're alive for you to mock, with all that's happened to them," Rion said. He got out of the wagon and headed for the river.

Ron was glaring at her, Van looked crestfallen, and Gar and Ara fidgeted uncomfortably.

"Oh, Elmoth! I've really stepped upon my tongue this time, haven't I?" she said, sighing heavily. "I'm sorry, Ron. It's just that I wasn't expecting to see you, especially as you appear, all pretty and rich looking. I wasn't ready for it. It hasn't been easy for me here, with you all gone. I should have been with you. I still haven't forgiven you for leaving me here. I haven't forgiven Grandfather yet for dying, old as he was. I need to apologize. Excuse me," she said, and headed after Rion.

Liana said in a small voice, "We shouldn't have come, Van. She's going to hate me even worse than she hates the rest of you."

Van hugged Liana. "She's really not so bad, Liana. Give her a chance. It's a hard life, working a mill, especially if it's only been her and Father. The cousins are supposed to have helped, but I don't see them, and it doesn't sound like they have been. I don't see Father, either. He must be at the grindstone. It can be pretty loud inside. He probably doesn't realize we're here. Would you like to come inside with me?"

"No, let's wait, all right?" she asked, and he put an arm around her to comfort her.

RION stood by the river, watching the water rushing past the smooth stone of the riverbed. "Elanara would say my core's like a storm at sea," he said softly. He pictured her face in the water, smiling up at him, with her long silver hair floating about her, and felt a pang of loneliness as sharp as a blade.

Lisandra came up behind him, but he didn't notice her until she spoke. "I'm sorry for what I said, Rion. I'd no call to say anything. You're right: I've no idea what's happened the past two years. Thank you for bringing them home safely to me. I've worried about them, especially Van. They should have been back a year ago. I thought they might not come back, ever, and feared I'd never know what happened to them. You've no idea how I've missed them."

Rion looked up in surprise. Her voice sounded so different, sad and tender. She was staring at the water, too, and a tear rolled down her cheek. She brushed it fiercely away, then knelt and splashed cool water on her face. "And a fine welcome I've given them too! It's just I'm all covered in flour, and there you all are looking so fine and…. Oh, what's it matter? Please come back with me. I didn't mean to make Ron angry. It was so good to see him smile."

"All right," Rion said, and walked back with her. Ron was still scowling.

"Ron, it's all right," Rion assured him. "She's apologized to me. No harm done, all right?"

Ron nodded. Van looked relieved, but Gar and Ara still seemed edgy.

Lisandra was eyeing Van curiously. He had his arm around Liana. "Aren't you going to introduce me to your other two friends?" she asked, although she wasn't looking at Rarnak.

Van took a breath. "Andra, this is Liana. She's my betrothed."

Pain flashed across Lisandra's face as she looked at Liana. "Of course," she said and then turned stiffly to Rarnak.

"I'm Rarnak. I'm one of their guards."

She nodded. Her jaw was clenched, but her lip was trembling. "If you'll excuse me, there's work to do. Father is inside." Holding herself rigidly, she turned and walked away.

"Well, that went well," Ara said softly, and Van swatted him.

"Why don't we go in?" Ron suggested with a sigh.

"I think I'll stay with the horses," Rarnak said.

Ron led the way. It was lighter and airier in the mill than Rion expected it to be. Rion saw a big man, bony and strong-backed, a bag of flour over his shoulder. "Lisa, what took you so long?" he grumbled, turning. He stared, startled, and put the bag down. "Ron? Ara, Gar, Van? Elmoth, is it really you, all of you?" He looked from one to the other and smiled, then held out his arms to Ron, as if to embrace him.

"Father," Ron said stiffly.

His father faltered and Ara hugged him. "I've missed you. We all have." Gar and Van took turns hugging him.

Ron said, "Father, I'd like you to meet Rion and Tarrell. We work for them. We're not here to stay, other than Van. We'll be leaving in the morning."

"Leaving? So soon? But you only just came!" his father protested.

"We've a trade deal we need to make. I'll talk to you about that later. For now, there's someone else you have to meet. Van?"

"Father, this is Liana. She's my betrothed. Liana, this is my father, Markara."

Liana smiled uncertainly at their father.

"Betrothed?" Markara asked, surprised. "How long have you known each other?"

"Long enough to know we want to spend the rest of our lives together," Van said.

"Then I welcome you to our family, Liana," Markara said and Liana looked incredibly relieved. "Why don't you all clean up? I'll have Lisa make us some lunch."

"I'll do that," Ron said firmly. "Andra's got enough work to do. You shouldn't have her lugging those big bags, Father. Where are Bernal and Arnal? They were supposed to help while we were gone."

Markara sighed. "They did, at first. But Bernal hurt his back and he can't lift anymore. Arnal wed. He has his own family to take care of now. She's strong, Ron. She doesn't mind the work."

"It's the one thing you ever acknowledged she was good at," Ron accused.

Markara scowled. "Ron, we've gotten along fine these past two years without you. She's none the worse for it. If you're going to cook, do so."

Ron scowled back at him and headed through the doorway to another room, presumably the kitchen.

Markara sighed. "Nothing I do or say pleases him. So, Ara, tell me all about your trip."

Ara started telling him the story.

OUTSIDE, Lisandra was struggling to pull a bag of flour onto a stack of four others in the wagon she'd been loading when they arrived.

"May I help you with that?" Rarnak asked.

"I can do it," she said crossly.

Rarnak smiled. "I've no doubt you can. But since I'm here and offering to help, why not take advantage of the offer and save yourself the struggle?"

"Suit yourself," she said.

He climbed onto the wagon and took one end of the bag. He was surprised at how heavy it was; it must have weighed one hundred pounds. "Are there others?" he asked.

"There's always others," she said, sounding resigned. "Why are you so eager to work, when you could just stand about?"

"I wasn't raised to stand about. I was raised on a farm. There was always work to be done. Guarding is a lot different than farming. I was actually looking forward to some real labor, to the lifting, the plowing, the planting, the harvesting, the feel of the soil again. I never liked it before I left. I guess I just thought I'd be home again," he said, his voice suddenly somber and soft.

"WHY aren't you?" she asked, as quietly. She could tell something was wrong and she'd no desire to upset anyone else.

"It's gone. Burned. My father's dead and my sister...." He clenched his jaw and looked agonized.

"There's nothing like backbreaking labor and heavy lifting to take the pain away. Trust me, I know," she said, and led him to a stack of bags.

A while later, Gar came out. "Lunchtime, Andra. You too, Rarnak." Rarnak jumped down from the second wagon, which they were almost finished loading. They entered the mill.

There was a space barely big enough for one more at the table. "I'll stand," Rarnak said, pulling the chair out for Lisandra and indicating she should sit.

Lisandra grabbed the edge of a barrel and rolled it to the table, extending the table out another few feet by it. "You're a guest," she said, standing beside it. "Sit," she ordered. He sat.

ANDRA was surprised at how good the food was. "You're a better cook than I thought you'd be," she admitted to Liana.

Liana blushed. "Oh, I didn't make this. I can't cook yet, although Ron's been teaching me, and Rarnak. Ron made it."

Andra looked at Ron, surprised. "You cooked this?"

Ron nodded. "One of us had to learn how. After tasting Gar's and Ara's cooking, I decided it better be me."

"You cook too?" she asked Rarnak, impressed.

He nodded.

"Tell the rest, Ara," her father said.

Ara said, "So we left Athanark with Rion and Tarrell and ten other guards." He continued the story of their travels, through lunch.

GAR noted Ara downplayed the danger and their injuries, and he didn't mention Circe.

AFTER lunch, Rion asked if someone could show him the way to Salenia, explaining that he had something for one of the Elves.

"You're in Salenia," Markara said. "The mill is within their borders. The riverbank all along here is part of their Kingdom. Which Elf are you looking for?"

"She's called River," Rion said.

Markara appeared puzzled. "I don't know anyone who goes by that. Are you sure?"

Rion nodded. "She's a friend of the Princess of the River Elf Kingdom of Riviera. She told me I would find River here."

"Well, I'll lead you to Swiftsong. He should be able to guide you to River, if she's here. He knows everyone."

"Thank you," Rion said.

"I'll show him the way, Father," Gar said. "Remember, Ron wanted to talk with you."

Markara grunted in response.

"Come, Liana, let me show you the River," Van said.

"All right," Liana said. Gar realized she was probably glad to be away from Markara and Lisandra, both of whom obviously intimidated her.

The four of them left together.

RARNAK started clearing the dishes. "Which way to the kitchen?"

"Door to the right," Andra said, gathering dishes as well. Tarrell also helped clear the table.

Markara was left alone in the room with Ron. "What kind of girl doesn't know how to cook, Ron? I've seen her hands. She's never worked a day in her life. She can't be rich, not dressed as she is. What haven't you told me? What's her story?"

"You know all you need to. Van's in love with her and she with him. I'm not here to talk about Liana. I'm here to talk about the pearls. You still have them, the ones the Elves give you?"

Markara nodded. "Why?"

"Because the Princess in Gosa is getting married, and she needs pearls for her dress. They're selling for two gold apiece or even more, except no one has any now. Tarrell's sweetheart is making the gown. I want to sell them for you, at a fifteen percent commission, ten percent for me, Ara, Gar, Van, and Lisandra to split, and five for Tarrell."

"I don't want to sell them," Markara argued. "What would I do with that much coin? I'm only not robbed now because no one knows of the pearls. Coin like that, they'd hear about. They'd never get past the Elves to get to it, of course, but I'll not bring trouble like that to their land. I'm keeping them in case I ever need to sell them."

"You can use the coin to buy Van the inn he wants to run, or to help him build and furnish one. It's all he talked about on our trip. You'd have him safely back here with you. And you'd have grandchildren soon enough. And with our commission, Ara and I will go into trading. We're good at it. Gar wants to open a stable. He wants to stud Thenagar to your three mares and the two we brought with us. For now, he'll work as our guard, until the mares foal."

Markara looked at him curiously. "You've got it all planned out, haven't you? And what of Lisandra?"

"She'll still work here, or if you'd let her, she could work at the inn or in the stable, where she'd be happier. She's a good cook. She's good with horses, too. She's good at a lot of things," Ron challenged.

"I've never said she isn't," Markara said. "But why can't you start your business with what you've earned? Haven't you saved enough? You can't have spent everything you've worked for."

"We haven't saved enough," Ron said evasively.

"If you manage your coin as poorly as that, why should I trust you with the pearls?" Markara asked.

"I've saved for two years now, and before we left, too. I've gone without plenty to do it," Ron said hotly.

"How much do you have?" Markara pressed.

Ron gritted his teeth. "Fifty gold."

"Fifty? In two years?" Markara scoffed.

Ara came back into the room from the kitchen, where he'd apparently been eavesdropping, from the way he leapt to Ron's defense. "He had more, but…."

"Ara!" Ron cried out sharply.

Ara looked pained. "We never said we'd keep it secret from him, Ron. He'll find out anyway." He turned back to their father. "Ron had over two hundred gold, more than any of us. We've all been frugal, but none of us saved as much as he did. But he gave most of it up, we all did, to buy out Liana's contract."

Markara's eyes widened in sudden understanding. "No wonder she can't cook. No wonder her hands look so soft! You did that for Van? Why?"

"Because he loves her and he'd be miserable without her," Ron said defensively. "She's a sweet girl. It's not her fault she ended up where she did. She sacrificed herself to give her sisters a chance at happiness."

"You've never forgiven your mother for being a whore, but you can forgive Liana," Markara accused, as if he'd forgotten Ara was even there.

"I never blamed Mother," Ron snapped.

"Oh yes, you did. You blamed her for plenty. You blamed her for being a whore, you blamed her for me not being your father, you blamed her for dying, you blamed her for my drinking, for my beating you near to death. None of it was her fault, Ron. Do you know why your mother was a whore?" Markara challenged.

Ron gritted his teeth. "I've no desire to know."

Markara spoke anyway. "Her father sold her into it. He'd tired of her. He'd taken her himself every night since she was ten. When she turned twelve, he didn't want her anymore; she was too old for him, too experienced. Her sister was ten then, all wide-eyed and scared and innocent. So he sold Andralyn to the whorehouse on Eastgate Street, the one that doesn't care how young they are. And they worked her. They worked her till she bled, till she couldn't walk, till...."

"Stop it!" Ron yelled.

"I'm not done yet," Markara said, iron in his voice. "Then, when she was fifteen, she got pregnant. It wasn't the first time, not by many, but she was sick and she didn't realize. She didn't stop it in time. And they still kept her and worked her until she was too round to service the customers. Then they tossed her out onto the street, to starve. When I found her, she was all bones, and big eyes, and big belly. Elmoth, those eyes! I was walking past an alleyway and thought I heard a baby crying. I thought someone had thrown one away. They do that there, sometimes. So I checked. It was Andralyn. She'd been going through the garbage to find something to eat and a rat had bitten her hand. She was lying there whimpering. I'd thought her cries were a baby's. That's how weak she was. And she cowered from me, begging me not to hurt her. Then she fainted.

"What was I to do? I could see she was pregnant, I could see she was dying. I picked her up and carried her. I took her to the orphan house, but they took one look and refused her. I took her to the City Guard. They said they could jail her. I could hear the rats gnawing at the walls there. So I took her to the inn I was staying at. They wouldn't let me pay to have her sleep on the floor of the common room: she was covered in fleas. So I took her to a worse place and paid for a private room, and a bath for us both." He started scratching his neck and grimaced. "I still scratch, every time I think of it.

"When she woke up in that room she was scared to death. She started sobbing that I'd kill her and the baby if I touched her. It took half the night for me to calm her down and convince her you couldn't pay me to bed her. I was just trying to help her. I got her to bathe and to eat some soup, and she fell asleep before she finished it.

"Later that night, when she woke up screaming, I tried to calm her. She told me her nightmare: it was her father. He was always in her nightmares, touching her. And she told me all the rest. But then she said it was all right now, because I was holding her, and I'd saved her. I'd protect her. I tried to tell her I wasn't, that I'd only taken her in for one night, out of pity, but those eyes! They were so green. I'd never seen eyes like hers. Not even the Wood Elves had eyes like hers. So I took her home with me.

"I still meant only to see her well, to find honest work for her. But Father, he took one look at her eyes and said she was staying. He told me if I wouldn't wed her, so her baby would have a father, he would. He said he'd seen those eyes staring back at him at every pool of water he'd stopped at before he found Salenia: the terror and the suffering and the pain. But he was worried he'd get too old too fast for her, and then who'd keep her safe? So I wed her.

"Not two days later you were born. You came early. It's a miracle you lived at all, and more so that you were strong and healthy, though she couldn't nurse you. She was so frail she almost died from bearing you. You were so tiny and perfect, and she was so happy when she held you. I thought she'd hate you, but her heart was so full of love! She'd never had anyone to love before. She'd had to compete with her sisters for food, for everything. Her mother had died when she was little, and her father's idea of love was raping her nightly. I realized the same way Andralyn looked at you, she looked at me as well. That's when I realized I loved her too. It was you who finally made me understand. And I loved you, too, for it, as if you were mine. You were always special to me, because of that."

Ron shook his head. "You never loved me as a son. You were ashamed of me. I was firstborn. I should have been named Aramark, after Grandfather, but I wasn't."

"I wanted to," Markara explained. "But she wouldn't let me. She wanted to name you after her mother, Ronara. It was important to her. It was her way of forgiving her mother for dying and leaving her with her father, for forcing her into that terrible life. How could I deny that? You must remember how it was between us. I could never deny her anything she ever asked of me. She asked so little and gave so much. She gifted me with so many fine children. I knew it would be a risk for her to have another child. Carrying Van had been especially hard for her, after the four of you, but she wanted to give Lisa a sister. We both knew how much she wanted one."

Ron clenched his jaw. "It's Andra, not Lisa! She's always hated Lisa. It was too pretty a name. It made her feel ugly. You made her feel ugly. How could you say such cruel things to her? She is not ugly. She's big-boned and strong. She has a plain face, an honest face."

Markara sighed. "I hadn't wanted her to look like me. What father would wish that on a daughter? But your mother was so happy. One look at her and there was no question I was her father. And the other boys all have my eyes. Andra was your mother's name. Lisa was what she chose for her: that's why she's Lisandra.

"My drinking wasn't your mother's fault. Her dying wasn't. My beating you…. Ron, I've hated myself for that night for fourteen years. I've begged you to forgive me for it. I lost you that night. I lost her and the baby and you all at once. My brother didn't have to beat me. Once I'd sobered up, I knew I'd never drink again. Little Van in my lap, thinking you dead, asking me if he'd die next. I still have nightmares from it, or worse, I wake up thinking she's still alive, thinking you still love me, and then I lose you both all over again, when I see you don't, when I know she's truly gone. She only had twelve years of happiness. I'd wanted her to have so much more. She deserved so much more. And instead, I saw to it you only had twelve years, too.

"Take the pearls, Ron. I don't want any of the coin. Give it to your brothers, to Lisa. Buy yourself some happiness. I'd give anything to see you smile, to hear you laugh again." His eyes welled with tears.

Ron looked away. He saw Lisandra and Rarnak and Tarrell then, in the doorway to the kitchen, and turned away, only to see Van and Liana were in the doorway to the mill. Ara was still beside him. All their faces were wet with tears. Dry faced, he walked past Van and, without a word, headed outside.

He couldn't forgive his father, ever. He couldn't forgive his mother. He hated them both. He hated himself. His mother had told him she loved him, but she'd left him alone to take care of all his brothers and his sister. Not alone, worse than alone. Only Father had never drunk a drop after that. He'd never hit any of them, either. He'd never abused Lisandra like he might have, the way his mother's father had abused her.

Father and Uncle Donara and their cousins had taught him and Ara how to fight, the way Aramark had taught them, when Ron was thirteen. Gar and Van were too little to learn, yet. Ron remembered how intent he'd been to learn. He thought back on it. All those tricks for how to hurt a bigger opponent his father had taught him, how to fell one. "Now, I'm an ogre, and you're a Man," Father had said, as he'd begun each session.

It had taken him a long time to feel a man, after what Father had done to him, but Father had been ogre enough. He'd delighted in knocking him down, in hitting him as hard as he could. He'd been vicious, knowing Uncle Donara was there to keep Father off of him. Ron had taken some small amount of revenge, until the first time Ara stepped in and took a blow aimed at his father. It hit Ara a lot further up than it would have hit Father. He lay there gasping for air, the wind knocked out of him. Ron had been angered at Ara for spoiling his attack, but Ara was angry with him, too. He said he didn't know why Father let him hurt him so much, but he wouldn't let him do it anymore. Maybe Father felt better, letting him hit him. Or had he done it for him, so he'd overcome his fear?

That's why Ara and Gar had hurt him so much, when they'd been sneaking about behind his back. He'd felt betrayed, once again, by the ones he loved. He'd loved Father, and Father had betrayed him. He couldn't trust him, or respect him anymore, after what he'd done, and he could never love anyone he didn't trust or respect.

He hadn't known about Mother, though, not the details Father had told him tonight. It wasn't nearly so dirty, knowing the details, as not knowing. He'd lost his love for his mother when he lost his respect for her, knowing what she'd been. He'd lost his trust in her, for all the times she'd lied to him, to all of them, about how Father had saved her.

He looked down in surprise. He was standing by Mother's grave. He'd never done so before; he'd never come near this spot. Grandfather wasn't here. The Elves had come for him. Only Mother was buried here. There were flowers growing all around. She was in the middle of a garden. Father tended it, Van had told him. It was beautiful, like her own was, when she'd lived.

Ron knelt and started talking to her, about what Father had told him, and how he'd felt when she died and about afterward. He'd never cried for her. The tears when Father had beaten him weren't for her, they were for himself. She'd had such a terrible life, yet been so loving, so wonderful, so joyful. She'd been such a good mother to him, when she should have hated him for being the son of one of the men who'd hurt her for his own pleasure.

Ron cried now, he wept for her, for losing her twice, for losing both her and his love for her, when she'd deserved to keep it. He finally forgave her. He forgave himself.

He thought of Father. Father hadn't made himself out to be a hero. He'd only done what he thought was right. He'd done more than most men would have, much more. He could respect him for saving Mother, couldn't he? Neither he nor she would have lived without Markara. Lisandra, Ara, Gar, and Van would never have been born at all. And Markara had been a good husband, and a good father. He had a fierce temper, but Ron realized now, with an adult's eyes, that Markara was angry at all the suffering: his father's, his wife's, and all he saw as a guard before he came back home.

He'd never been meant for the life of a guard. He'd never loved the mill as his own father had, but it was his refuge from the ills of the world. That and the oushka. But he'd never drunk again, not a drop. Ron could respect that, couldn't he?

No, because he never should have drunk before. Except... his heart was like Van's, all gentle and soft, only he'd been the oldest. There was no one to protect him, like Ron protected Van, like they all protected him. Mother certainly couldn't.

Ron wanted to forgive his father, he realized in surprise. He hadn't ever wanted to before. It was a start. Maybe someday he'd be able to.

He felt exhausted, like he'd been battling, when that extra burst of energy flees and afterward you're left shaking and trembling.

Ron rose slowly to his feet and walked to the River, washed his face and drank deeply from it. The water felt good, cool and sweet and fresh. No other water in their entire journey had tasted like it. He'd missed the River.

Ron thought of the sea of faces inside the mill. He clenched his jaw and went back. They were all still there and Gar had returned as well.

He walked up to his father, his face stern. "I've forgiven Mother, for lying to us, and for being what she was, and for dying. I cried for her. I still can't forgive you, but I want to, and I've never wanted to before. I think I maybe even understand, now. That's the best I can do. It'll have to be enough for you. I still can't love you, not yet."

His father stood, his eyes brimming with tears again. "It's enough. It's a start. It's more than I deserve, more than I'd ever hoped to hear. I've missed you, Ron. You've no idea how much I've missed you, what I lost when I lost you."

Ron hugged him then, stiffly, quickly, awkwardly, and then he backed away. He looked up. The others were all looking carefully elsewhere.

Ron said crossly, "Don't just stand there, Ara, Gar, Van! The grain's not going to grind itself. You could help your sister, now that you're here."

They grinned at him and got to work.

GAR had led Rion to Swiftsong and introduced them, and then headed back to the mill. Rion thought Swiftsong was different from Aras and Eladar and Elanara, and the soldiers. He was nothing like his name. He was calm and sedate, slow and strong: there was power in every movement, every word. He was like a great river that doesn't seem to move, until the current drags you under. Rion thought he must be old, that maybe when he was young, he'd been like a rushing mountain stream in spring flood.

"There is no River here, other than the one beside you," Swiftsong told Rion, in musically toned Common.

"But there must be! I don't know her true name, or what she looks like, but I have a letter for her, and a book. They're both important. They're from a River Elf I met: she's the daughter of King Laranela of Riviera," Rion said, not wanting to speak Elanara's given name.

"I cannot lead you to one who is not here," Swiftsong said. His voice was deep for an Elf's, rich and ponderous. "I will ask the others. Many come and leave quickly now. Perhaps she has come and gone."

"Thank you," Rion said. After Swiftsong had gone, Rion looked about curiously. He didn't see any buildings, neither of tree nor stone, yet the City was here, he was in Salenia. Where did the Elves live? Then, through the trees, he spied an Elf, his face partly obscured by the leaves, but achingly familiar, his hair a flash of silver. He was moving quickly; he'd be gone in a moment. It couldn't be!

"Thorn?" Rion called out eagerly, running up to him.

The Elf turned and surveyed him coolly. It wasn't Thorn. Rion blushed darkly. "Forgive me," he said, in Elvish, in the mode of Student to Teacher. Then in Common he added, "I thought you were someone else." He studied the face before him. It was not Thorn's, and yet the eyes were almost his, though the blue was too pale and they were far too cold. And the shade of silver of his hair, and the shape of his cheekbones....

"It is not often one of your kind is so eager to see one of mine, Little One," the Elf said in Common, frowning at him. "So I will not take offense that you are staring at me most rudely." Still, he indeed sounded offended, not at all amused by him. The Elf turned from him.

"Wait, please," Rion said, in Elvish. He switched to Common. "The way you said 'Little One,' your voice, your eyes, your face. I know better than to say their given names, but is your father King of Riviera?" Rion asked, holding his breath fearfully, remembering the last time he had offended an Elf this cold, this aloof... this old, he belatedly realized.

The Elf turned back to him and his stance was completely different. He was eyeing him now as a spider might eye a fly before leaping upon it. "Why would you ask me that?" he asked Rion, and his voice was like silk on steel.

Rion swallowed and stood with his left hand carefully away from his sword, and his knife. He wished for the hundredth time his right arm was not broken. He felt incredibly vulnerable before the tense Elf.

"I am a friend to two of the King's children, and I thought perhaps you might be their older brother," Rion said. His voice sounded high-pitched to his own ears; he could hear the fear in it. "Please, I am no danger to you. Or if I am, I don't know that I am. I don't mean to be. No one heard me ask if you were the King's son." He realized that, if this Elf was their brother, he might have been keeping his identity a secret, lest he become captive like Elanara. But there were no other Elves near enough to hear, at least none he saw, and he'd seen no soldiers here.

"At first you were eager, but now you are afraid. You claim to know two of us, yet you fear us as if we were unknown," the Elf said, appraising him carefully.

"I know three of you, but I've met many others, enough to know I should fear you. The Elves I fear even your sister is afraid of," Rion said, frustrated this Elf still hadn't acknowledged his kinship to Elanara and Eladar.

The Elf's eyes narrowed and Rion's legs suddenly felt weak. "But I shouldn't have said so. I'm sorry I ever spoke to you. Please let me go. Please don't hurt me," Rion begged. He was trembling now; he couldn't help himself. He remembered the soldiers dragging and hitting him, and he remembered those vicious, evil men in Gosa. And the two of them were alone here and his arm was broken. He was helpless to defend himself, just like in the alley. He began shaking so badly he could barely stand.

Unexpectedly, the face before him softened, the frown left it, and even in Common, the voice now held the familiar singsong melody his ears had ached to hear. "You are truly terrified of me," the Elf said, in surprise. "I will not harm you, Little One. I can see you are no stranger to pain. You have been harmed enough already. If you have truly met my brother and sister, you could describe them to me, so that I might be certain."

Rion swallowed and nodded and his fear eased. This Elf knew compassion: he wasn't like the soldiers. "Your brother was full of smiles and laughter. He has silver hair like yours and your face is similar, especially the cheekbones, except yours is more narrow. But his eyes are deeper blue and... and warmer," he said hesitantly, hoping that last might not be taken as an insult. "He loved to talk, to hear himself talk, and he delighted in being called absurd. He said it was something his sister would have called him. Your sister had hair down to her feet, the same shade of silver, with eyes the blue of sapphires, and she sparkled like sunlight on water. She glided when she walked, like water over river rock, and her smile was warm and tender, and she gifted it often to me."

The Elf looked amused, and with his smile, his face was suddenly like Thorn's, when he'd first spoken to them in Common. "I notice you do not mention how my brother walked."

"I don't know how he walked. When we rescued him from the ogres, he could not walk: his leg was broken. But your sister said he was healing well, that he would recover," Rion added quickly, seeing the concern in the Elf's ice-blue eyes.

"You are right: I am kin to them. I am Crown Prince Elavar, son and heir to King Laranela of Riviera. I tell you my true name because you have not only met my siblings, but you apparently have news of them I am eager to hear."

Rion said in relief, "I am Alarion, son of Anorion of Ardock. But if you don't mind, please call me Rion, as Eladar and Elanara did. I will tell you all I know of them." He began with how they met Eladar, and the trip to Erenia, and all that happened there. He even told Elavar the two messages he had carried for his brother, in Common.

Elavar seemed deeply troubled.

"I'm sorry, I didn't want to upset you, but I was afraid you and your father might think Elanara safe when she isn't at all, and you should know Eladar can't help protect her. Or couldn't. I hope he might be well, now. They are my friends, and I am still worried about them," Rion said sincerely.

"I thank you, Rion, for your information is important," Elavar said, very formally.

"I was wondering. Do you happen to know how to get in touch with Talon? As Elanara's brother, I'm hopeful you might know him," Rion probed.

"Talon? Why? Even though River is not here, his book would be safe with the Elves here. Quicksilver or Meander or Swiftsong or any of the others might keep it safe," Elavar assured him.

"It's not about the book," Rion explained. "I have two messages for Talon, two warnings."

"Then you may entrust them to me, for I will be seeing Talon again shortly. He is my friend, and I have aided him and his people before," Elavar said confidently.

Rion was relieved to hear him say so. He told Elavar first about Hunter and the Dwarven army, and what he'd sensed about them. Then Rion told him Circe's message about keeping the wizard Arcanus away from a certain ring. "Please only tell that second message to Talon. It is very secret. I wouldn't have told you at all, except you're Eladar and Elanara's brother, so I know I can trust you, and I think it's important Talon hear it as soon as he can."

Elavar was staring at Rion in astonishment. "Why would Circe say such a thing? And why to you? Who are you to her, that she would betray Arcanus for you?"

Rion blushed at what he'd almost been to her. "I helped her. She's been... ill." He hadn't meant to tell Elavar that part, he'd sworn he wouldn't, but Arcanus had frightened him and was dangerous, and Rion was afraid Talon might discount the message otherwise. So, he told Elavar everything.

"You have no idea what you tell me, do you? That Arcanus is crippled, Magus compromised, and Circe turned to darkness. It is a wonder you yet live, though I know not how long your innocence can save you, for you have become such a target they should all wish to see you dead. And Circe's concern is the lost Ring? She was truly still mad when she spoke to you. Unless the Ring has been found?"

Rion swallowed. Elavar's words had frightened him terribly.

Elavar looked him in the eye. "I will deliver your two messages to Talon. He must decide how to react to what he hears. I must leave now. I've urgent business of my own," Elavar said, turning to go.

"Wait! Before you go, Elanara gave me a letter for River. Since she's not here, but you are, and you're family, I think you should see it. I think someone should read it. Elanara made it sound like it wasn't urgent or important, but I've been thinking that she may have given me the book just to conceal the letter, to smuggle it out of Erenia, so the soldier's wouldn't seize it, and she didn't say more because I might have been nervous in front of the soldiers, if I knew." He handed the letter to Elavar.

Elavar broke the seal and opened the letter. His face paled and grew grim. "It was indeed fortunate I spoke with you, Rion, and you told me what you did and guessed what you have. Elanara is in peril. This letter is for our mother. She goes by the name River. It is a call for help. Our mother was supposed to have been in Salenia, but she never arrived here. Riviera is no longer safe. Now Elanara is in danger, and Eladar as well, as he is with her. I must alert my father at once. With High-King Laedrin fallen, the army is like a great serpent that has lost its head, still whipping and writhing about to potential deadly effect. No, it is far worse, for the one who is now in command will guide it with deadly purpose. Even the Navy...." His eyes widened and his mouth shut, as if he realized he was revealing too much.

"I must go, Rion. My family is in your debt. If ever you are in need of aid, remember that the Elves of Riviera will succor you. You need only tell them my true name, as I spoke it to you. And I won't forget your messages for Talon. I will get your warnings to him, before the Dwarves reach him."

"Good-bye, Prince Elavar. Be safe. I am honored to have met you," Rion said.

Elavar left, quickly disappearing into the trees. Rion exhaled loudly. Perhaps Talon would be safe, now. And he had been right. The book had been a ruse. Still, he knew how important it was to Elanara and to Talon. He'd keep it safe for them. Even the Elves were in danger, Hunter had said. Rion knew he also kept it for selfish reasons. He wanted to study it more, to learn all he could about the Elves, to learn to speak Elvish fluently. But also, it was an excuse to see Elanara and Talon again.

Now that he had delivered his messages, he felt a great loss, as if the part he'd played was finally finished. And Elavar had reminded him vividly, painfully, of Elanara and Eladar. He missed them terribly. With Elavar gone now as well, the woods seemed cold and dark, dead and empty. He wondered how the brothers had been able to survive, away from the grace of the Elves for two whole years. Maybe because they'd known they'd come back, that they'd be surrounded by them again.

Rion headed slowly and reluctantly back to the mill. It was a welcome sight, and Tarrell even more so.

"Rion, are you all right?" Tarrell asked in concern.

Rion nodded. "Things got more complicated than I expected. But everything worked out well enough in the end," Rion assured him. "I'm eager to go home now, I think," Rion said, but he couldn't keep the wistfulness from his voice.

"Is Gosa truly home to you, now?" Tarrell asked softly.

"I guess it is. Your heart is certainly there, and you hold my heart, if you've still room for it," he finished softly and sadly. He hadn't meant to say so aloud.

Tarrell looked at Rion tenderly. "Of course. There will always be room in my heart for yours, Rion," he said, and put his hand on his arm, man to man, when he would have hugged him in the past.

Rion grinned then. He couldn't help himself.

THE trip back to Gosa was completely uneventful. Rion suspected there would be few bandits terrorizing travelers between any of the cities along the Western Road for a while, with so many thousands of Dwarves marching to war.

Tarrell selected a handful of pearls from the small chest they had brought back with them and took them to Madame Genevieve. He told her about the chest they had acquired and showed her the sample. She was thrilled by them and asked him to bring the chest to her and the Princess at the Palace.

After arriving at the Palace, Tarrell and Rion and their guards were escorted by a troop of armed Royal Guard into the Princess's presence.

The Princess was ecstatic. She wanted every single pearl. In addition to the ones she wanted sewn onto her dress, she was having elaborate jewelry made as well: a necklace, bracelets, and a tiara.

Rion and Tarrell received a total of five thousand gold for the pearls. They were overwhelmed by the amount. They had each of their guards carry some of the coin. They hid the bulk of it in the shop, under various portions of the floor, so if some of the Royal Guard or their acquaintances proved less than honest and they were robbed, they would not lose the entire amount.

Ron, Ara, and Gar made plans for a second trip home. They'd have to buy everything necessary to build the inn and furnish it in Gosa, whatever things they knew could not be found in Ogaten. The lumber and much of the furniture had to come from Gosa; the Elves did not allow anyone to cut the trees of their Wood.

Van had given Ron and Ara a list of what he wanted, and they made preliminary contact with different suppliers. They would personally transport everything in one or more caravans. Later, once the inn was nearly completed, they'd buy much of the linens and other goods necessary to stock the inn in Gosa as well. The contacts they made assisting Van would benefit them when they began their own business as traders.

When Ron gave Tarrell his commission of two hundred fifty gold, he didn't so much as smile. He'd hoped to see Marissa when he'd brought the pearls, but she was busy working on the dress.

Rion was concerned about Ron and his brothers traveling all the way to Ogaten with so much coin, even though they only planned to bring part of it. He tried to convince Ron to take Lerdon, Jathran, and Rarnak with them. "Tarrell and I will be fine on our own until they come back. By then we might even have found the other guards we hope to hire," he assured Ron.

"I'll not leave you underguarded," Ron argued. He was finally able to convince Rion that one additional man would be enough.

"I'd like to be the one to go," Rarnak volunteered.

Rion studied him carefully. The trip to the mill had done him much good. He looked himself again. "Done. Stay as long as you need to. Only come back whenever it's safe, both for you and the brothers."

RARNAK nodded. He'd been thinking about Lisandra on the way home, thinking he'd like to see her again. Wondering what might make her smile. He thought about bringing her something. Van had brought her honeysuckle bath soaps and oils. She'd seemed to like that, but such a gift wouldn't be proper from him. And she'd not like perfume, nor hair ribbons, nor jewelry, he suspected: none of the things women usually desired. Kakla! When Gar had complained about hers, she'd told him it wasn't her fault none of it was fresh, it was all there was to be had in Ogaten and he could go back to Gosa if he wanted better.

Rarnak headed to the Market. He went to three different stalls before he found some beans that smelled just right, and he bought five pounds. He passed a ceramics stall on the way out of the Market and hesitated. The tin cups they'd drunk the kakla from certainly hadn't helped the taste any. He examined the wares they displayed with a critical eye. There were two sets of six ceramic mugs, pine green, plain and simple, sturdy. Twelve would be more than enough for the family and visitors. He bought the dozen, pleased at how well he'd been able to bargain the price down, for buying both sets.

He'd meant to stop by the Temple, too, but he didn't want to go there so burdened. When he went back to the shop, Rion was eager to have him go to work immediately. He hesitated, but then spoke up. "I'm ready to work, since the brothers won't need me until morning, but Rion, could I have some time off before sundown? I wanted to stop by the Temple to make an offering before my journey tomorrow. I've been remiss. I haven't been to Temple since coming back from the farm."

"OF COURSE," Rion said, relieved he was going. "In fact, if you don't mind, I'd like to come with you. I'm ashamed to admit it, but I've only ever been to a Temple once before, when Oberas was with a customer who insisted on conducting business there, so Laneth could see he wasn't cheated. I promise I'll be respectful. I won't gawk or anything. I'm just curious. And I'll bring an offering, of course. Since it's Areth, would a basket of fruit from the Market be all right?"

Rarnak smiled. "That would be perfect, Rion. And I welcome the company. It's thanks to you I'm going, after all."

Rion smiled, pleased his earlier words had helped.

A little while later Rarnak found himself back in the Market. Both he and Rion bought offerings and then proceeded to the Temple of Areth.

This Temple was simpler than the others Rion had seen from the outside. It was made of coarse gray stone, rather than polished marble. Inside, on the lower level, there was a cacophony of noise from all of the livestock. But the upper chamber was sealed off from the noise below. It was made of carved wood, and there were white candles of all lengths burning inside. There were freshly cut flowers everywhere, as well as potted ones, and their scent filled the room.

Rion was entranced. It was all so beautiful! It was nothing like the Temple of Laneth he'd seen, with wrought metal everywhere, and the heady scent of incense so thick he'd almost fainted from it, for lack of clean air to breathe. The worshippers here were different as well. There were no fine clothes here, nor bright colors, only coarse linens, homespun, gray or beige, all of simple cut and design. Rion suddenly felt a fool, dressed in his bright-blue silk shirt with brass buttons. At least he'd worn his tan pants and boots, so he didn't stand out quite so terribly in that regard.

Rarnak motioned to him to come, and he followed and knelt when Rarnak did, and bowed his head. What should he say to the Goddess? Rion muttered softly, "Areth, Honored One, please forgive me my presence here. I wanted to come because I was curious. But please, also forgive Rarnak for not coming to you sooner. He does not love you any less than he did. And please, if his sister Talia still lives, see her safe. And if Rarnak might be allowed to see her again…. But I don't mean to ask too much. I hope I haven't insulted you. I apologize if I have."

Rion had never felt so humbled before. He looked up. Rarnak was still praying. Some few new people had entered while his head was bowed. One in particular caught his eye, a cloaked figure, kneeling on a mat five paces ahead of them, to the right; he'd just come in. He removed his hood. For a heartbeat, Rion thought he was an Elf. Who else would have such long, blond hair? It shone in the candlelight like spun gold. But then he realized an Elf would never come to a Temple. It was a woman, not a man. The cloak was of such coarse homespun, he'd not been able to tell her gender, at first.

When the woman lifted her face, she turned before donning her hood again, and to his surprise, Rion recognized her. It was Marissa! But Madame Genevieve had told Tarrell Marissa wouldn't be leaving the Palace today. What was she doing here? And she had always been dressed so fine, when they saw her. Why wear such a cloak?

She was heading for the exit. Rion looked toward Rarnak, but he was still praying. Rion left him and followed her, walking quickly to catch up to her. He couldn't run or shout here, but he had to speak to her. He touched her shoulder and she jumped back from him, startled.

"Marissa, it's only me, Rion," he soothed her.

"Rion! What are you doing here?" she asked in surprise.

He blushed at her tone, feeling out of place again. "I'm here with a friend. I asked him to bring me. I'm curious, I guess. But I'm surprised to see you here. I thought you'd follow Aralyn. Unless things between you and Tarrell are more serious than I'd realized," he added, feeling his face flush hotter. Areth was not only the Goddess of the Harvest and of farmers, but the Goddess of Fertility, of pregnant women and the Goddess of Marriage, of brides, or those hoping to be.

Marissa's face reddened in turn. "No, it's not because of Tarrell," she said, her voice wistful. "I've always followed Areth, although I can't do so openly anymore. It doesn't look right. I offer to Aralyn too. Madame Genevieve encourages us all too. She's very devout. She hasn't forbidden me to come here or anything, but she'd likely not be too pleased about it. I was concerned someone might recognize my dress. I always wear the ones she designs, and it would embarrass her if people saw me here and maybe thought I was with child," she said, her blush deepening.

"But you told Tarrell you'd be at the Palace. Why did you lie to him, Marissa? Don't you know how much it hurts him when he can't see you? The whole time we were away, all he talked about was coming back here and seeing you."

"But I didn't lie, Rion. I'd never lie to him! Madame Genevieve sent me to the Market on an errand, and I haven't been to the Temple for almost a week. I thought I could sneak in quickly and explain to Areth why I haven't been. I was afraid she might not hear my prayers from home, with the rest of the girls all praying to Aralyn."

"Oh," Rion said, embarrassed and relieved. He liked Marissa; he hadn't wanted her to have lied.

"There you are, Rion! I was wondering where you'd gone. You shouldn't have disappeared like that. I was worried about you," Rarnak gently scolded, coming up behind him.

RARNAK glanced curiously at the girl Rion was speaking to. No wonder she was cloaked, if she had no escort. She was lovely, breathtakingly beautiful, with blonde hair framing her face and eyes so green she could make the Elves weep at the sight of her, knowing she was a Child of Man, and as such doomed to fade and die so quickly. He'd known eyes like that once. He'd not have thought two could have them.

Her eyes, locked with his, widened in shock, and then inexplicably lit with joy as she unexpectedly launched herself into his arms. He caught her by reflex alone. "Nicky? Areth, it's you! You're alive, you're here! Areth's brought you back to me!"

At the sound of the familiar nickname spoken in the voice he had ached to hear, that he had thought he would never hear again, he hugged her tightly, not daring to believe it could truly be her.

RION was staring in astonishment at both of them, his heart tearing in two at Marissa's betrayal of Tarrell. She obviously loved Rarnak. She'd apparently known him first. He'd left her in a city or farm somewhere in the east and she'd come here and now Rarnak had come, too.

Rarnak hadn't seen Marissa before, he realized. The brothers had, and Lerdon, but not him or Jathran. Rion was stricken. Rarnak was Tarrell's friend. Once Rarnak thought about it, how would he feel? And he couldn't still guard for them after this. With the brothers gone, now there would be only Lerdon and Jathran.

"Let me look at you," Rarnak said, oblivious to Rion's pain. Rarnak let go of her and looked her up and down, as she took off her cloak and held it in one hand and curtsied and giggled like a little girl playing Princess. Others in the Temple were watching them now, some eyeing them in disapproval, some looking jealously at her fine dress, others admiring how handsome Rarnak was in his uniform and smiling at the two lovers, reunited.

"I'm a fine Lady now," Marissa said, grinning.

Rion realized in anguish that she must have been a farmer's daughter or a tavern girl when Rarnak had known her. Had winning Tarrell's heart all been part of a game to her? Had she planned from the start to trick the rich merchant into loving her? Had the coyness and the shy smile all been a carefully rehearsed act?

Marissa turned to Rion, still smiling, but then the smile left her face. "Rion, whatever is the matter? Why aren't you smiling? Why are you looking at me like that? I thought you'd be happy for us. Why didn't you ever tell me Rarnak guarded for you! I've known you for weeks and I've never seen him."

RARNAK turned to Rion and saw the dismayed and accusing expression on his face and was as startled by it as she had been. Rion looked stricken, betrayed, as if…. "Oh, Areth, he doesn't realize! Rion, it's not what you're thinking. I love her, but I'm not going to take her from Tarrell. She's Talia, she's my sister."

RION gaped at him in disbelief and then back at her. She was blushing again. "Oh, Rion! What you must have thought of me, throwing myself at him like that!"

A thousand questions flooded Rion's mind. "But why did you tell us your name is Marissa?" he asked, voicing the first. He had to start somewhere.

"Because it is: no one's called me Talia for three years, now. Madame Genevieve picked Marissa for me. She said Talia is a farm girl's name, not a dressmaker's. I know you've so many questions, both of you, but if I don't hurry back I'll be in heaps of trouble. I never meant to be gone as long as this. I'll come by the shop tonight, I promise. I'll get one of the Royal Guard or City Guard to escort me, so it will be safe."

"We'll escort you now. I'll not have someone thinking you've a fine purse to match that fine dress, let alone what else they might think," Rarnak said protectively.

Talia grinned at him. "I've missed you so, Nicky!"

They headed for the Palace, Rion in tow. "Do you know about Father?" Talia asked, suddenly somber.

Rarnak nodded. "I went home. I found the house and barn burnt. I'd guessed from the ruins how long ago it was, and then I found Father's grave. You'd marked the year. I knew you were only fifteen. Did he suffer?"

"No, he wasn't burnt. A beam fell from the ceiling onto him. He didn't die right away, but it knocked him unconscious and he died pretty quickly afterward, without waking up again. I'm sure he didn't feel anything."

Rarnak turned to Rion. "You were right, Rion. Everything you said about Areth. She saw that Father died quickly, when he might have burnt. She saw Talia safe. She even brought her back to me. I'd never have found her in a fine dressmaker's shop. I'd never have thought to look there for her. I didn't even recognize her when I saw her, until she spoke, she's changed so much. Areth brought Tarrell to her so I'd find her, but revealed her to me at the Temple to reward me for not losing my faith, when She tested me."

Talia said indignantly, "She brought Tarrell to me for more than that, I hope!" Then she blushed again. "Look at me! I must be in love. I've never felt my face flush so hot so many times before in my life!" And she blushed more deeply. "You do approve, don't you Nicky? I mean, Tarrell's so sweet and kind and gentle, and he's good to me." She laughed. "And it doesn't hurt that he's so handsome, and wealthy, either."

"Of course I approve," Rarnak said. "You couldn't hope for a finer husband. You are asking my approval for marrying him, I hope?"

"Rarnak! Of course. I mean, he hasn't asked me, but I hadn't expected him to yet. We've only just been getting to know one another and we haven't seen very much of each other, what with the Princess's wedding," she said wistfully.

They arrived at the Palace gate. "Don't come if you can't find a guard, Talia. I'll not have you come to harm because of me," Rarnak insisted.

"I'll be careful. I can't wait until tonight! I've missed you so!" she said, and then she was in his arms again, and he hugged her fiercely and kissed her on the cheek.

The Royal Guardsmen at the gate were smiling knowingly at them. Rion looked away, embarrassed, but happy for them. Then she went through the gate, waving to Rarnak.

"I can't thank you enough, Rion," Rarnak said. "It might have been weeks until I finally saw her! And if you hadn't put up with my getting drunk that night like I did, and my mood afterward, I might never have found her. I might not have lived long enough to, or crawled out from the flask long enough to. I owe my thanks to Gar and Van and Ron, also, and to Tarrell."

Rion swore seriously, "That's what friends are for. I'll always be here for you, Rarnak, no matter what you might need of me."

TARRELL stood at the end of the street, staring in disbelief. Marissa had told him she couldn't see him, that she'd be at the Palace the whole day, and for days after. Yet there she was, walking and talking with Rarnak and Rion. As he watched, Marissa beamed up at Rarnak, her face lit with love, and she threw herself into his arms. Rarnak hugged her and kissed her, as Rion stood there, looking embarrassed, and the Royal Guard leered at them. Then she left, waving to Rarnak, and he and Rion headed down the opposite end of the street.

LERDON looked from Tarrell to Rarnak's receding back and back again. "Tarrell?" Lerdon asked, in sympathy.

"Go back to the shop," Tarrell said.

"But I can't leave you unguarded," Lerdon protested. Jathran was in the shop, and the brothers were at the Market, buying goods for their trip.

"I'm man enough I can guard myself, no matter what you or Rion or Marissa might think!" Tarrell fumed, and spun on his heel and left.

Lerdon debated the wisdom of following him at a distance. He tried, but within ten blocks he'd completely lost sight of him.

He was worried. There was no telling what Tarrell might do in such a state. Most likely he'd pick a fight with someone dangerous, to prove to himself he could still win one.

Lerdon checked the three taverns he'd passed, but Tarrell wasn't in any of them. He had no choice but to head back to the shop. It was a big City. Tarrell might go anywhere.

Lerdon still couldn't believe Rarnak would betray Tarrell like that, or that Rion might just stand there, knowing what it would mean to Tarrell if he found out. He wished he hadn't come back after all. He'd rather have gone on liking Rarnak and Rion. He'd lost all his respect for both of them.

TARRELL was devastated and enraged. Marissa had tricked him. She'd used him. He hadn't even known she'd met Rarnak. But she'd apparently wanted Rarnak all along, but knew Madame Genevieve would never approve. Or maybe she'd liked him at first glance, for his handsome face and fine clothes, before she'd found out the coin was Rion's not his, before he'd shown her his arm and she'd seen he was only half a man. Rarnak was older, bigger, stronger. Not as handsome, maybe, but that obviously mattered little to her. She wanted two strong arms around her, not one. Tarrell was shaking he was so angry, at the thought of her in Rarnak's arms, maybe even in his bed.

At least it was Rarnak and not Rion. But Rion had betrayed him too. Rion had known. He'd stood and watched. He'd let Rarnak lead him around the City when Rarnak was supposed to have been guarding Rion. Tarrell felt someone slam into his bad arm.

"Watch where you're going, you dandy!" the man scoffed. He was rough-looking, mean. He'd slammed into him deliberately and then challenged him, thinking to make him cower. Well, he wasn't about to cringe before him.

"I'm not the one too stupid to get out of the way of his betters," Tarrell snapped, glaring at him.

"Stupid? Are you talkin' to me?" the man asked, flummoxed.

"I guess you're too much of a moron to know," Tarrell sniped.

The man glared at Tarrell and then eyed his sword warily. "No, I'm not so stupid as you think. I'll not let you spit me on the end of your sword and say you was only defending yerself." He glared and walked off.

Tarrell cursed. But at least the man hadn't laughed at him. In fact, he'd been afraid of him. He'd thought he was some cold-blooded killer, that he'd have used his sword on him, though the man wore none.

Tarrell wanted a drink. In fact, he wanted many. He wanted to get drunk. He'd never been a big drinker, but he'd not gone drinking at all since his friends had all been killed outside Athanark. It wasn't the same now, with the new guards. He was the boss, not one of the men. Only Ron treated him like one of them, sometimes, but Ron seldom took even a single drink. Ara and Gar were drinkers, but he'd not gone drinking with them. And Rion was still young, and small. He couldn't hold much mead, and the oushka had made him sick. Rion hadn't tried it since. And Rion wasn't his friend; he'd betrayed him. He'd never thought Rion, of all people, might do such a thing.

That man had called him a dandy. He looked down at his shirt and pants in disgust. He'd not go drinking in such clothes. He'd buy some like he used to wear, swordsman's clothes.

He went to a shop he'd noticed before, but never gone inside. He'd not felt right, before, spending Rion's coin on himself. But he went into the shop now and was well pleased with what he saw. He didn't even try to bargain. He wasn't in the mood. Rion could die a pauper for all he cared. It would serve him right if Tarrell just left him. If he took half their coin and set up a business of his own, in some other City, somewhere he wouldn't have to see Marissa and Rion and Rarnak, all those he'd thought were his friends. He'd have to go back to the shop for the coin. He no longer carried it secreted in his clothes. He had only a limited amount of coin in the purse at his side.

He changed into the new clothes in the store and left. The storekeeper ran out into the street after him, with his fancy clothes in his hands, saying he'd forgotten them. "You can keep them or sell them or burn them. I don't want them," Tarrell said, and left without another word.

Tarrell strode down the street. People looked at him differently now. They got out of his way. He saw true fear on some of their faces, now, not jealousy or respect. He must have a terrible scowl upon his face, he thought, to appear so dangerous. Then he realized his hand was on his sword hilt. He was clutching it so tightly his knuckles were white. No wonder those who saw him were so worried! He forced his hand to release its grip and lowered it to his side.

He scanned the storefronts around him and saw a promising tavern. It smelled of food, good food. He'd not had lunch yet. He went inside, and the innkeeper didn't give him a second glance. It was nice not to be fawned over, for a change. He sat. A tavern girl came up to him. She was passing fair to look at, though not a beauty, but her blouse was cut low and her breasts were big and her hips full.

"I don't get paid for staring," she said, but she gave him a look that indicated he might pay her to do more than stare.

"Lunch for now, your best meal. And oushka, bring the flask. Aged, if you've got any."

Her eyes widened. "You must've just gotten in. I'll bet you could tell a tale or two about your travels," she said, eyeing him appraisingly.

"If you're interested in hearing about ogres and Elves and bandits I could," Tarrell replied arrogantly.

"Then let me get your lunch, and I'll see if Amber can cover for me. I'm Jasmine," she said, batting her eyes at him.

"Tarrell," he said, hesitating only for a moment over giving her his real name. If he bedded her later, he'd not want her screaming someone else's. It would spoil it for him.

He'd not had a woman in months, not since Ardock. Because of Rion. He pictured him now, looking disapprovingly at the clothes, the drink, the girl. Rion could go hang! Why should he care what Rion might think of him, after what he'd done? Where was that oushka?

Jasmine reappeared, a weathered-looking flask in her hands. "It's ten years old, five gold, but I'm sure you can pay."

Tarrell doubted the innkeeper had said more than four and it was worth only two. He could get it for half that at a place he knew in the Market.

He cursed. He was thinking like a merchant. "Fine. And here's another gold for you, so your profit's two, not one."

She said, astonished, "How did you…."

He smiled confidently. "I didn't survive coming here from Ardock by being gullible. I'm good at what I do. But I won't fault you for being good at what you do, either. Especially if you're as good on your back as you are on your feet."

"I underestimated you," she admitted in obvious surprise. "And I didn't take you for someone quite as direct as that. I'm impressed. Don't eat or drink so much you can't find out how good I am on my back. Or on my knees before you," she said, and licked her upper lip sensually. She sashayed from the table.

Tarrell poured a drink and gulped it down. He'd never been so crude before. Elkrum had. Tarrell had always thought he'd gotten away with it for his impressive build. He'd never met anyone nearly his size until Jargas. Jargas would have dwarfed Elkrum. He laughed at the unintended pun, pleased that thoughts of Elkrum hadn't dismayed him. He poured himself another drink and held the cup up in front of him. "Here's to you, Elkrum. May Ragnar treat you well, for Aralyn would have nothing to do with a womanizing whoreson like you," he said aloud, toasting the empty chair across from him.

Tarrell toasted each of his dead friends as he ate his lunch, one at a time, though not all with a full cup, heedful of Jasmine's words. He toasted Oberas too. "May Mereth forgive you for your lack of piety, and Elmoth as well, before him. I wish I'd known you when you were young, before you gained your wealth and girth. From that one night you drank with me, I think I'd have liked you more then."

Oberas had gotten melancholy. It was the twenty-fifth anniversary of the death of someone named Terhannon. He'd ordered Tarrell to sit with him, and toast to him. That was the night he'd found out Oberas had been a guard as well, once, long before. He'd learned Oberas preferred a knife to a sword, though, and he had wrestled. Oberas had told Tarrell he had journeyed to the Dwarven Lands when he was a young man. It was there he'd gained his great wealth, but it had come at a price too terrible to pay. He'd said no more after that. He'd drunk the rest of the flask of oushka by himself as Tarrell watched, and he'd fallen asleep at the table.

Rion had been wide-eyed, seeing Oberas like that. Tarrell had explained to him that men need to drink like that, sometimes, and he shouldn't think poorly of Oberas for it.

"I don't," Rion had said. "I only wish I could ease his pain, somehow."

Oberas was always very strict with Rion. He'd been protecting him, Tarrell knew. Before he'd grown quiet, Oberas had told him Terhannon had died young. He had only just turned eighteen. Tarrell could tell Oberas still blamed himself for Terhannon's death.

Tarrell knew how he felt, when he'd thought Rion might die: first the wolven-riders, then the ogre, the Elves, and worst, the bandits in town who'd taken him, who'd hurt him so badly. Why was he here, when he should be protecting Rion?

Because Rion wouldn't let him. Rion didn't want him now, nor need him. He had other guards, and now that he was sixteen, he'd no further need of him as a guardian.

Rion had betrayed him. He wouldn't have believed it, if someone had told him, but he'd seen it. His own eyes hadn't lied to him.

He poured two more shots and drank them in quick succession. He sloshed the oushka about in the flask. It was perhaps half full. He'd better stop now.

Jasmine appeared at the table. "Are you ready for your dessert, Tarrell?" she asked, looking lasciviously at him.

"Do you have a room we can use, or am I to pay for that as well?" Tarrell asked, his voice surly. Thoughts of Rion had turned his mood sour.

"I've a room," she said, eyeing him carefully.

Tarrell stood, bringing the flask, and followed, glad to see his step was steady, that he could still hold his liquor. At least he'd had the sense to eat with it, to take his time.

She led him to one of the inn rooms. So, he'd be paying for her then, and the room would be included. It was clean enough, and the bed looked inviting. A little too inviting. He'd not been sleeping well. Thoughts of Marissa had kept him awake. He'd barely seen her. Then his eyes focused on Jasmine's breasts, and he stopped thinking of Marissa. He reached into his purse and handed her some coin.

He took off his shirt, watching Jasmine carefully. Her eyes were inevitably drawn to his right arm, as he'd known they'd be. It was thinner than the left and unevenly shaped, and the terrible scars were plainly visible. He'd more than half expected her to be repulsed by it. But if anything, it seemed to excite her. He'd forgotten the effect guards had on women. Ara had been right when he'd told Rion about it.

Tarrell cursed and tossed his shirt angrily onto the bed. What would it take to drive Rion from his thoughts, to force his face from his head?

He felt Jasmine's hands on his back, and he shuddered with desire. Rion fled from his thoughts.

Jasmine massaged his shoulders and then wrapped her arms around him from behind, kissing his back.

Tarrell turned to face her and his mouth met hers hungrily. Her hands went to his waist and she unlaced his pants. He worked the lace on her blouse nimbly. It fell from her shoulders and slid to the floor. Her skirt soon followed. His pants joined them there a moment later. She was warm and soft and inviting.

She began kissing his chest, slowly kneeling before him, as her kisses fell first upon his stomach and then his groin. He gasped as he felt her tongue upon him.

It was over too quickly. His need had been too long unfulfilled. She smiled at him. "You *have* been on the road a while," she said. She led him to the bed and pushed him gently onto it. "But we've still plenty of time." Her hands were very skilled. Sooner than he'd thought possible, he felt his desire swell again. Then she climbed on top of him, and he found her hips were as eager and as pleasing as her mouth had been upon him.

A while later, she rose from the bed, where she'd lain nuzzled against him. He stirred back to wakefulness lazily. He'd been at least half-asleep, maybe more so, with her in his arms. "I have to go back. My lunch break is over and then some. Amber will be wanting hers."

Tarrell smiled at her, pleased to see he'd tipped her well enough before that he still had all the coin that had been in his purse. She'd not stolen any. He'd known exactly how much he carried. Most guards didn't. "Pay for this room for me for the night and keep the change, if you'll visit me here again after I've had my dinner," he said, handing her another three gold.

She beamed at him. "It will be my pleasure. I'd not expected you to be so skilled." She seemed to truly mean it.

He smiled warmly at her. "I'm glad to hear it. I am a little out of practice. Tell me, is Amber as pleasing as you?"

Jasmine pouted. "Haven't I satisfied you, Tarrell?"

"You need ask? I've not risen from the bed, have I? But I'm afraid my thoughts may turn sour again if I'm left alone with them, and I'd not be such good company tonight, if I spent hours brooding," he reasoned.

"Then I'll send her up to you now. After both of us, you should be spent enough you'll sleep until dinner. We'll be sure to come wake you then."

He smiled at her again. A short while later, there was a knock on the door. He opened it and a brown-haired girl entered at his bidding. She was prettier than Jasmine, though older, but not so old that she was not pleasing to look upon, even once he'd released her from her dress.

He was surprised at how strong his desire still was. After some gentle teasing, Amber led him to the bed. But this time he was the one to push her down upon it, and less gently than he'd meant to. She didn't seem to mind, though.

He'd not wanted to be rough or clumsy with Marissa their first time, once they were wed. He'd wanted her to enjoy it as much as he did. He'd been worried he'd be too fast or too eager or too clumsy or too rough. He'd wanted to test himself, but he'd not had the desire to touch another since he'd first seen her. He'd needed to see if he was still truly a man, all of him, if his arm could still support him long enough to take a woman, without having to hurry. He gazed into Amber's eyes. They were brown, and hungry. They drove all thought of Marissa's green ones from him.

By the time they were done, he was utterly spent. He fell back upon the bed, exhausted. His arm had trembled at the end, but not buckled. Amber was well pleased with him and with the coin he gave her. He pulled her to him and fell asleep against her.

He ate well downstairs, after they woke him again for dinner. Both of them had finished their duties and accompanied him upstairs once he was done eating. They told him they'd decided to share him. Elkrum had bragged of such things, but Tarrell had never believed him. He'd have to toast him again later and apologize to him.

The two women surprised him. Apparently, they'd worked as a team before. But he didn't let them overwhelm him. He thought to surprise them as well, first. He didn't want to just take his pleasure from them; this time he meant to give as good as he got. There had been a girl in Ardock who'd shown him how: Elsbeth. He smiled at the memory of her, and then gave Jasmine his undivided attention.

He could tell he hadn't forgotten what Elsbeth had taught him by the way Jasmine grabbed his wrist as her body shook as he forced his fingers more deeply into her, and her muscles clutched hungrily at them.

Amber was looking at him eagerly, lustfully, when he turned his attentions to her. After she'd been sated as well, and then they'd both seen to it he was as pleased as they, he collapsed onto the bed next to them and fell into an exhausted and contented sleep, a girl nestled under each arm.

THE next morning he made sure the girls would not soon forget him. He left them curled up in each other's arms in the bed and went downstairs and had a hearty breakfast. He'd not felt so good in a very long time. He was still the man he'd been. The injury to his arm had not changed him as much as he'd feared. It was Rion who had changed him, without meaning to. He'd not let him have as much influence upon him in the future.

He sighed. Now it was time to face Rion, as well as Rarnak. At least his head was cool enough to do it. Still, he was far from looking forward to it. He was unsure of the reception he'd get. Lerdon would have told them by now what they'd seen.

He still had the half flask of oushka. He clutched the neck of it tightly as he made his way down the streets, back toward their shop. He knew he'd have need of the rest of the flask later, after they spoke.

Tarrell was surprised to see the door to the shop closed, when it should be open, to encourage customers to enter. It wasn't like Rion to turn away customers. He felt a pang of concern for him. He tried the door, but it was locked. He knocked, but there was no answer. He opened it with his key.

The shop was empty. Tarrell looked about, stunned. Rion had left it unguarded. Rion never left it unguarded. Anyone might have forced the door and gained entry. Tarrell locked it again behind him. He realized in sudden guilt where Rion and the guards must be: they'd gone out looking for him. It was still early, but they were gone. They might have searched all night for him, while he'd eaten and pleasured himself on the girls, and slept. Well, it served them right!

Only Jathran and Lerdon had had nothing to do with it, and Rion would have called the brothers in to help search for him, too, and they'd meant to leave today. Unless that's where they all were. Maybe Rion had decided to go with them after all. But no, he'd not have left the shop unguarded.

Tarrell's gaze fell upon an inventory that lay half-finished on the table. It was pointless to go looking for them. They could be anywhere in the City. They'd have to come back eventually. At least he could finish the inventory while they were out. He went to work.

He was nearly done with the inventory when he had to head to the back to recount stock. They couldn't possibly have sold six cases for so little profit. Those numbers must have been wrong.

He heard voices in the front room and stiffened. For a moment he feared it might be thieves, and he cursed himself for leaving his sword on the floor next to his chair, in the front room. But then he recognized Gar's voice.

"...find him, Rion. You promised if I went out with you you'd try to eat something and get some sleep. It's nearly noon," Gar reasoned.

"But he didn't come back! You said he'd come back to sleep at least, but he didn't. We waited for him for hours! How can I eat or sleep, when he thinks I've betrayed him, when he might be hurt, when... when...." Rion's voice ended in a sob.

Tarrell clenched his jaw and headed for the doorway to the front room. Rion hadn't eaten or slept, while he'd done both, and more besides. He felt guilty and ashamed.

"Rion, get behind me! Someone's here," Gar ordered urgently.

"It's all right, Gar, it's only me," Tarrell said, emerging from the back.

Gar relaxed from his crouch and lowered his sword as Rion let his own sword fall to the ground, forgotten, sprang out from behind Gar, and ran to Tarrell, hugging him fiercely with his good arm. "Tarrell, you're all right! I was so worried!" he cried, his voice muffled by Tarrell's chest. "Where have you been?" Rion demanded accusingly, pulling back from him and looking up at him.

Tarrell realized he didn't have to look as far down as he'd had to only a few months ago. In a year, perhaps two, Rion would be tall enough to look him in the eye, without having to tilt his head. But that would be a while in coming. Rion's eyes were red rimmed. Rion reminded him of Van, the night he'd spent hours crying over Liana, when she'd said she didn't love him.

"I needed some time to myself. I went to an inn. Lerdon obviously told you why. How could you help them, Rion?" Tarrell asked softly, his voice revealing the pain of the betrayal.

"But I didn't! I wouldn't! How could you even think I'd betray you like that? It's not what you think, Tarrell, I swear. Marissa is Talia. She's Rarnak's little sister. That's why she was hugging him when you saw them. That's why he kissed her. They saw each other in the Temple and recognized one another," Rion said, looking searchingly into Tarrell's eyes.

"His sister? Marissa is Talia?" Tarrell echoed numbly.

Rion nodded, looking him over. "What happened to your clothes?" Rion asked, curious.

"I bought new ones," Tarrell replied. "You've been up all night searching for me?"

Rion nodded. "I wasn't supposed to be. Ron told me to wait here with Gar. I tried to, but you didn't come, and I thought I could find you. I made Gar take me out. I told him I'd go alone, otherwise."

Gar sat down wearily. "We've been searching since yesterday, all of us. Lerdon and Rarnak haven't stopped for even a moment's rest. They both feel responsible."

"Didn't it ever occur to any of you I could take care of myself for a day without you? Who asked you to look for me?" Tarrell argued sullenly, feeling worse than before. Anger hurt less than guilt.

"We were afraid you might do something foolish. We were worried about you. Friends worry about each other. And Rion asked us to look. He begged us to. We tried to tell him you were probably fine, but Rion thought you'd get yourself killed because you'd be too upset to think straight," Gar said, losing the rein on his temper. "Armed men can still get hurt in a City like this, if they go to the wrong places. Ron and Ara got hurt enough last night, and they were together."

Tarrell's anger evaporated. "What happened? Are they all right?"

Gar sighed and nodded, cooling off as well. "They've got some pretty impressive bruises, especially Ron's eye, but they'll live. But they'd not have done as well if they'd been alone. Or drinking," he added, gesturing pointedly at the flask by the inventory book.

"I was drinking to my dead friends. I thought I'd lost some of my few living ones," Tarrell said.

"Well, unless someone's run into a rougher bunch than Ron and Ara did, you haven't. And we kept Talia from finding out you were missing, when she came by to see you and Rarnak. I lied to her. I said you had a meeting with someone on a trade deal and Rarnak went with you to guard you. She said she'll come by tonight instead. You might want to wash the lip paint off your neck by then," Gar said pointedly.

Tarrell's face flushed and Rion looked at him in surprise.

There was a knock. It saved Tarrell from having to say anything or seeing the surprise turn to disapproval or disappointment.

"Who's there?" Gar called warily.

"It's Jathran and Lerdon," Jathran said.

Tarrell strode to the door and opened it. Lerdon was leaning against the outer wall with his eyes closed. Jathran turned and gaped at him. "Tarrell?" he cried in surprise.

Lerdon's eyes snapped open. Jathran turned to Lerdon. "I told you he'd be back by now." They went inside. "I was just bringing Lerdon back. He's asleep on his feet, but I see I can get some more sleep myself now."

Tarrell told Lerdon guiltily, "You shouldn't have blamed yourself, even if I'd gotten hurt. I ordered you away."

Lerdon grimaced. "Try telling that to Rion. You should've seen the look on his face when I told him what had happened. How could I sleep with him looking at me like that?"

Rion apologized to him. "I'm sorry, Lerdon. I hadn't meant to. It's just I knew how much it would have hurt Tarrell, seeing what he did. When Marissa and Rarnak hugged one another in the Temple, I'd thought the same as Tarrell did when he saw them, only they saw my reaction and were able to explain it to me."

Rion turned to Tarrell. "I'd never keep something like that from you, even knowing how much you'd be hurt by it. I'm old enough to know that keeping it secret would hurt worse, and you'd find out eventually. Secrets always come out, in the end." He looked like he wanted to say something more, but he grew silent.

Tarrell sighed. "Why doesn't everyone get some sleep? If the others aren't back in a few hours, I'll search for them."

Gar said, "We broke the City up into sections, so we'd not search the same places, after the first few hours of looking. Rion's got it all written down. It will make it easier to find them."

Tarrell wasn't surprised. Rion thought like a merchant in everything he did.

Rion was examining the inventory in surprise. "You've been working on it. The writing's yours, and I'd not gotten so far. It's almost finished. Even before you knew Marissa was Talia. Why?"

Tarrell shrugged uncomfortably. "Because it gave me something to do. It needed doing. And I guess I still wanted to help you."

Rion's eyes were bright, but he only nodded.

Everyone but Tarrell went to their rooms. Tarrell washed up in the basin in the kitchen, careful to get the lip paint off. Marissa didn't wear makeup. He'd liked that about her. She didn't need lip paint; her lips were rosy enough without it.

He'd kissed her on the lips, the last time he'd seen her. He hadn't meant to, but she'd looked up at him, and he'd leaned down and kissed her. She'd been startled, but then she'd kissed him back, eagerly. She'd melted against him.

He'd kiss her again tonight when he saw her. Somehow the thought of just kissing her excited him more than the memory of Jasmine and Amber combined. He was in love with her, he realized. He hadn't been sure before. He'd never been in love before, but he was sure now.

Did she love him? He didn't know. She liked him, he knew.

He went back to the inventory. It was quiet, with the others asleep.

A WHILE later, Tarrell rose and stretched. His hand was cramped. He'd make lunch for them all, then go looking for Ron, Ara, and Rarnak. He'd not have them wasting any more of their time searching for him, when he was here. Ron usually cooked for them, or Rarnak, but he could make a passable meal when he needed to. He'd relied on Ron and Rion too much. That was going to change.

He was halfway done with lunch when there was a knock. He cursed, assessing the pots and giving the stew a quick stir. Lunch would keep. It wouldn't boil over.

He went to the door and opened it. It was Ron and Ara. They looked worse than Gar had described.

Tarrell smiled sheepishly at them. "Well, that's two more I won't need to look for. I'm sorry you both got hurt because of me. I'm fine, and Rion's explained everything. Everyone's back but Rarnak. They're all asleep. I'm making lunch. Why don't you wash up, and rest? I'll call you when it's ready."

RON took in the unfamiliar clothes and what Tarrell had said, and nodded, for once speechless. He and Ara sat down at the table. Ron picked up the flask of oushka sitting on it and shook it. It seemed at least half full. He went to the kitchen with it. "Do you mind?" Ron asked, holding up the flask.

Tarrell shook his head. "Help yourself. I've had my fill," he said, handing him two cups.

Ron went out to Ara and poured for both of them. Ron drank the oushka slowly, letting the fire of it burn his mouth and throat, instead of downing it quickly. He stretched and felt the tension start to leave him.

He hadn't expected Tarrell to be all right, not after last night. He and Ara hadn't even realized they were in any danger, and they'd barely escaped with their lives. This City wasn't like Thenalon or Athanark or Logareth or any of the others they'd been to. It had a hard edge to it, a vicious side. He and his brothers would stay here for now, trading, but they'd go elsewhere, perhaps to Maraden, in the north, or Ocanton, to the south.

A while later Tarrell came out. "Lunch is ready. Should I let the others sleep? You know better than I how much they've had."

"Let's try and wake them," Ron recommended. "Those that don't waken easily we'll let sleep."

There was a knock, and Tarrell answered. Rarnak was standing there, looking grim. Tarrell smiled at him.

"So, you're not only all right, but someone's talked to you," Rarnak said, sounding relieved, as he entered the shop, and Tarrell nodded.

"I'm sorry for thinking ill of you, Rarnak, and of Rion. I suppose I should have known better," Tarrell apologized.

"You should have, but I would have reacted the same as you if I'd seen what you did. Are the others back? Who found you?"

"No one found me. I came back on my own, and the place was empty. Rion and Gar came in a while later and straightened me out on everything."

"You mean Gar took Rion looking for you in the dead of night?" Ron asked. "And they left the shop unguarded?" All their gold was under the floorboards with the bulk of Rion's and Tarrell's. They might have lost everything.

"DON'T blame Gar for it," Tarrell said, in his defense. "You've told me yourself, Rion's not a child anymore. A man helps his friends, first, and worries about himself second. And his goods. I don't ever want to see Rion become so much a merchant as that, that he cares for his goods more than his friends."

Ron nodded. "I'm glad, too. But I was thinking of the coin we have hidden for Van and Liana."

Tarrell understood then. "That's different. Why don't you go ahead and wake the others, while I put lunch on the table?"

Everyone but Lerdon got up for lunch.

Ron said to Tarrell, "It's good. I didn't realize you cooked, or I'd have had you share the duty with me and Rarnak."

Rion said in surprise, "You cooked this? I thought Ron did."

Tarrell felt inordinately proud of himself. Ron cooked well.

Rarnak said, "I'll be glad for the help, once Ron's gone."

Rion eyed Tarrell speculatively. "Are you going to change before you see Marissa, I mean Talia, tonight?"

"I hadn't planned on it," Tarrell said challengingly.

"Good. I like what you're wearing. It suits you much better than what I've gotten for you," Rion admitted.

Tarrell was surprised. He was glad, now, for everything that had happened. He turned to the brothers. "I'm sorry I delayed you. I know you'd planned to leave today for Ogaten."

Gar shrugged. "It won't hurt for us to be a day later. And we couldn't have left when Rion needed us. We want you and Rion to know you can always count on us, whenever you're in need of help."

Rion beamed at them. "It means a lot to hear you say so. I'm still going to miss you all terribly, though." His eyes were bright.

Ron said, "The City's not so big as that. We'll still see each other, you'll see. Although the next few weeks we'll be busy enough, and we might decide to start our business in a different city. But still, we won't stray far from Ogaten."

"You're always welcome here, if you've ever the need of a place to stay, or friends, or work, or anything."

THE brothers left after lunch. They told Rarnak they'd stop by just after dawn the following day for him, and he told them he'd be ready. Everyone else went back to bed, except Tarrell, who caught up on work.

Talia came by before dinner, with one of the City Guard escorting her. Everyone else was still asleep. She told the Guard he could go, that Tarrell would see her safely home, and he nodded and left. She looked at Tarrell.

"So, do I call you Marissa or Talia, now?" Tarrell asked her.

She blushed. "Talia. Marissa's the dresses and the City. Talia's who I really am. I'm sorry. That probably doesn't make any sense to you."

"On the contrary. I know exactly what you mean," Tarrell assured her.

She gazed into his eyes and then at his clothes. "You look like a swordsman."

He nodded. "I am a swordsman, for all I've been playing at being a merchant these past months. For all I might have to keep being one. But the coin's not mine, it's Rion's. And I don't plan to wear such fancy clothes anymore," he said challengingly. He hadn't meant to sound quite as terse as he did.

"Do you feel any differently about me, now, knowing I'm only a farmer's daughter under all the fancy dresses? That even my name isn't mine? Will you be ashamed to be seen with me?"

"Of course not," Tarrell said indignantly.

"Then why do you think I would care what clothes you wear, or how much coin you have, or what you do to earn it?" she asked.

He looked at her in surprise and suddenly felt extremely foolish.

"Those things don't matter, Tarrell. None of it matters to me. They're not why I love you," she said. She appeared panicked then, and blushed and glanced down, as if she were afraid to look him in the eye.

His eyes widened and he gently placed his hand under her chin and tilted her face upward.

TALIA swallowed. He wasn't smiling. He looked so serious. She never should have told him yet. She'd not seen enough of him for him to believe she might truly love him. Her heart was hammering.

But he leaned his face toward her and suddenly he was kissing her and his arms were around her and she couldn't even breathe. She didn't need to breathe. She needed his kiss to go on forever. When he pulled his lips back from hers she made a little whimpering sound of loss.

"I love you too, Talia. I just hadn't had the courage to tell you, for fear of what you might think," he admitted bravely.

She pulled his face back down and kissed him with such passion, he finally pulled away from her, blushing. "Everyone's here, Talia, they're all in the back."

"Oh. Well, if Rarnak is here, I'd better behave myself," she said wistfully.

"I'd better start dinner. They'll all be looking to be fed soon."

"I'll help you," she offered.

"You know how to cook?" Tarrell asked, surprised.

"Of course I can cook! I cooked before I was ten," she said indignantly.

Tarrell looked at her sheepishly. "Rarnak wasn't very impressed by your cooking," he said carefully.

She laughed. "Well, I'm certainly better at it now!" and he smiled, relieved. "I'd like to see him do better."

"Rarnak's a great cook," Tarrell assured her. "He and Ron have cooked for the rest of us since we left Athanark and smelled their dinners were so much better than ours. But I've practiced some since then," he added.

"You are so sweet. That's why I love you, Tarrell," she said, gazing into his eyes.

Tarrell laughed and pulled away, "At this rate, dinner won't be ready until breakfast," he said and she smiled coyly at him.

"If Talia's the one cooking, I'd rather skip dinner," Rarnak said from the doorway to the kitchen, barely catching the carrot his sister threw at his face.

"You're welcome to the kitchen, then. Tarrell and I will find something to do," she said sweetly.

Rarnak handed her the carrot. "Not with that look on your face you won't. Peel that for me, that's a good girl. I'll make a cook out of you yet," he teased.

She glared at him and Tarrell laughed.

DESPITE Rarnak's misgivings, he had to admit his sister had learned a lot since he left. Dinner was a festive affair. Afterward, Rarnak grew serious. He asked Talia what had happened since he'd left, how she'd ended up a dressmaker when she'd been left all alone at such a young age. And she told them.

"I'd just turned fifteen the month before it happened. We'd had a very dry summer, but the harvest was a good one. The barn was full of hay. We'd gone to Market here in Gosa five times in the previous two months. Father had taken me with him, of course. We'd even done some shopping in town. He took me to Tailor Street, to look at the dresses. I remember he bought me a new ribbon for my hair." Her eyes brimmed with tears for a moment, and she brushed them away.

"I'm sorry. It's all so long ago, really, but I still miss him so. Anyway, as I said, it was very dry, too dry. We'd been without rain for a long time, and we were relieved when the thunderstorm came.

"I remember lying in my bed, listening. It was such a powerful storm. There were several tremendous cracks and booms that sounded as if they were right outside my window, but I wasn't frightened at all, until I heard the horses screaming. I pulled on my dress and shoes and ran outside.

"The barn was burning. Lightning had struck it, and the roof was on fire. The hay in the loft had already caught as well. It was raining, but the wind was stronger than the rain, and the fire was so fierce.

"Father came up behind me and told me to stay put. He said he'd get the animals out if he could, but he wouldn't have me risk being burned by the fire. He was only able to get Nora out, before the loft caved in on the rest. It was terrible, listening to the cows and Edwin screaming and the pigs squealing, and the whole yard smelled of roasting meat. I still get sick sometimes, in the Market, when I pass by the stalls where they sell the skewers of meat.

"It was then we saw the roof of the house had caught fire, too. We could see burning hay blowing from the barn and falling onto it. It burned so fast! I saw the roof of my room cave in as we watched. I would have been burnt alive in my bed if it hadn't been for Nora and poor Edwin.

"Again, Father made me stay outside, but he ran inside, to get the trunk. I watched and waited, but he didn't come out again. I finally ran inside. I found him in the family room by the mantle. A timber had fallen from the ceiling onto him, knocking him unconscious. I pulled him out from under it and dragged him outside. I could barely do it. He was so heavy! Then I went back for the trunk. I dragged it out, too, just before the whole house collapsed.

"I tried to wake him. He was still alive, for a little while, though his breathing was horrible to hear. I think his ribs had been crushed and his back might have been broken. I don't know. I just knelt at his side and cried and watched as he died and everything burned.

"I buried him in the garden in the morning. I'd forgotten to put the spade away. You know how I was always forgetting things like that, Nicky. Father was always scolding me, saying the tools would rust in the rain." She wiped a tear from her eye.

"So I was left with Nora, and the horse blanket Father had tied about her head, so he could pull her through the burning barn, but no saddle or bridle.

She'd only ever been meant for the plow and the wagon, but the wagon was burnt, too. And I had the trunk, and the dress and shoes I was wearing.

"The ground had already dried, mostly. I laid the horse blanket out onto a dry patch, and opened the trunk. Mother's gown was there, and the purse of coin from our trips to the Market, and the letters Grandmother had written, and Grandfather's book, and lots of other little odd things, things I'd never thought to ask why they were important to him: the dried flowers, and the shell, and the broken comb and the bent mirror. I didn't care what they were or why they were there. They were our family treasures, and they were all I had left of my family, and suddenly they were important to me, too. So I bundled everything into the blanket, as carefully as I could, and tied the end, and mounted up on Nora, and headed for Gosa. She was such a patient, gentle beast. I never could have ridden her otherwise.

"It wasn't so bad in the daytime. I was glad I saw no one. I was most afraid of bandits finding me on the road. I didn't have any weapons, and I couldn't have fought them even if I did.

"That first night was terrifying. I stayed on Nora's back the whole night. I had no way to build a fire, and I was so afraid of fire then, I don't think I could have, even if I had the means to.

"I was determined to make the City by the second night, and I rode Nora all day, only stopping for her to drink by the stream, where we'd stopped on the way to Market. I was glad to find it. I was sure I was heading the right way then. I mean, I knew I must be, but it was comforting to see it. I realized I was thirsty too, and I drank, along with Nora, and then I realized I was hungry, but there was nothing for me to eat. I let her graze on whatever she could find.

"I made it to town just after dusk. I saw the gate falling. They were just closing it. I remember being terrified that I was being locked out. But then I heard the sound of horses and wagons behind me, and I saw the gate being lifted again. There was a merchant caravan coming, and they lifted the gate for them. I rode in with them.

"I remembered the way to the Market, and I knew I'd seen inns on the way there the times we'd gone. I stopped at the first one that seemed respectable enough. The stable master told me it would be four copper to stable and feed Nora for the night, and I gave it to him. I think he was surprised I could pay it. I know I looked pretty wretched.

"Then I went into the inn with my blanket pack. One of the serving girls saw me looking lost and guided me to the innkeeper. I told him I needed a room for the night, and he told me a room upstairs, by myself, would be five silver, or a spot on the floor of the common room would be five copper. I remember thinking it was funny it almost cost the same to shelter a horse as a person, except her food came with it, and mine didn't. I couldn't believe the room was so much, but there were some men eyeing me in a way I didn't like, so I told him I'd pay for the room, and I'd like dinner too, but asked if I could have it in the room, and if there was a lock on the door, and he said yes to both. I had to pay five silver for the meal, too. I know now he sold me the best he had. I would have paid less for a coarser meal, had I realized.

"So I ate, and I slept, and in the morning, I decided I had to find a way to make more coin, to find a cheaper place to live, to plan what I might do next. There hadn't been much coin in the purse. We'd spent most of it as soon as we got it, laying in supplies for the winter. They all burned up with the house and barn, of course. I'd spent so much of what was left on the room and food for just a single night. So I washed up and used the broken comb and mirror and braided my hair, and I didn't look quite so wretched. I thought that the one thing I had of value was Mother's gown. I hated to sell it, but I knew I had to. So I went to Tailor Street, figuring since they sold dresses there, they might buy one."

She blushed then. "I was so naïve! I walked into Madame Genevieve's because I thought the gown in the window looked something like Mother's. Madame Genevieve came up to me and asked me politely if she might help me, this farm girl in a sooty dress with no stockings carrying a horse blanket. She didn't yell at me or swat me with a broom or call the Guard or do any of the things she might have done.

"I showed her the dress and told her I needed to sell it, and why. And then I saw one of the seams had come undone, and I told her I could mend it if she had needle and thread, that I knew how to sew. She took me into the back, where the seamstresses sit and make the dresses, and the girls all looked at me curiously. There were so many colors of thread and so many different sizes of needles! I picked mine and sewed it, as she watched. The others all had their own sewing to do.

"She seemed pleased and asked if I'd ever made clothes, and I told her I'd made all my clothes, and Father's, since Mother had died. She'd taught me how. She examined my dress carefully. And she told me I was too old to be an apprentice, but one of her journeymen seamstresses had just left her to be wed, and since I already knew something of sewing and clothes making, she'd be willing to teach me more if I would like the job.

"I couldn't believe it! I found out later I wasn't the first stray she'd taken in off the streets. She's a remarkable woman. I don't want to think of where I might have ended up if it weren't for her. I had already been so very lucky to live safely on my own for two whole days.

"She told me I would have to live in the rooms connected to the dress shop—she ran a sort of rooming house for her girls—and I was overjoyed. I had to sell Nora, though, and that was hard, for she was my only friend. But I was able to buy the things I needed to live and still have coin left over, and the other girls were very friendly. Madame Genevieve said Talia sounded like a farm-girl name, so I'd go by Marissa. She picked it for me. And that's it really. I've been there ever since."

Rarnak's voice shook with emotion. "I owe Madame Genevieve a debt of gratitude I can never repay, for I had imagined such terrible things had happened to you, and here I've found you safe and happy and well cared for."

RION was glad to hear her say such good things about Madame Genevieve. He'd liked her before, but had thought less of her when he had heard about Talia having to change her name and even who she worshipped for her.

"Speaking of her, I wish I could stay, but I'd better get back. It's getting late. I told the City Guardsman you'd walk me home, Tarrell."

"Of course," he said, strapping his sword on again. Rion bit back the urge to suggest one of the guards go with him, and he saw Rarnak held his tongue as well.

Talia put on her cloak and the two of them left.

TALIA kissed Tarrell good-night before they got to the shop, so Madame Genevieve wouldn't see. "I still won't see much of you the next few weeks. I'm to go to Ocanton for the wedding. But after that, you'll be hard pressed to keep me from you," she said with a laugh.

"I'll wait for you. You're worth any wait," Tarrell promised. He saw her safely inside and headed back to their shop.

Chapter 6
Dark Secrets

JARINA was keeping something from him. At first, Jargas had been oblivious to it. He was so caught up in his own happiness he hadn't sensed it as he should have, even shielded from Jarina as he now was. The focus of all his attentions had been Desenia. He couldn't help that it was.

He'd not anticipated the intensity of their union; neither of them had. He'd had no one to warn him of it, and Desmond had never thought to warn Desenia, for despite raising her to become Lady of House of Serpents, in his heart he had never thought he would see his kinsmen again, let alone dreamt his daughter might marry one. The merging of their thoughts and feelings as their bodies joined almost overwhelmed them both, but it had helped rather than harmed, when Jargas's lack of experience coupled with the trauma of all Desenia had endured might have prevented them from finding happiness.

But when he was able to focus outward again and he'd sought his sister, Jargas had found longing and disappointment and overwhelming sadness when he'd thought to find joy. When he had lowered his shield to try to find out what was wrong, he'd felt a wave of jealousy and pain so intense he'd been driven to his knees and had been forced to slam his shield so fully into place he sealed himself off from his sister completely. It felt as if their link was gone altogether. Now that his bond with Desenia was so strong, he was no longer as impaired as he had been when he had severed his link to Jarina, but still it was hard to bear.

He'd gone to Farad then, to discover what was wrong. He'd been astonished by what he had found. Outwardly, there was coldness. Farad's eyes were no longer the shadows they had been before the Ring had healed him, but it was as if his heart had turned to ice. Farad would not speak to him.

Jargas had opened his shield enough to sense longing and guilt, humiliation and despair, so sharp and strong it cut him like a knife. He realized he felt only the faintest of echoes of the pain Farad felt. Farad had been fully shielding himself against Jargas when he'd felt so much. But Farad still would not speak to him. He told him he could not.

Jargas knew he could have commanded him to, as his King, and he saw Farad knew he well might, when he'd seen a bright flash in Farad's mind of

Farad on his knees, with his dagger in his hand, ripping the barbed blade across his own throat, and seen that Farad's hand was even then grasping the hilt.

Jargas had ordered Farad to surrender all his weapons to him, and to go to Donovar and tell him what was wrong. For a moment Jargas thought Farad would defy him, that he might even use his knife against him, instead of upon himself, but then he'd wilted, as if all the life had drained from him, and he'd walked as a man condemned to the executioner's noose to Donovar's tent.

JARGAS waited outside now, anxiously watching.

Donovar poked his head out and spotted a warrior passing and spoke to him for a moment in a voice so soft he couldn't hear.

Jargas was puzzled. More so when a few minutes later the warrior returned with the High-King, Desmond, and six of his Guard in tow. Desmond entered, but his Guard remained outside.

Jargas waited impatiently as more time passed and then Desmond finally emerged. He spotted Jargas and headed for him. Before Jargas could open his mouth to speak, Desmond spoke to him, not as his father-in-law or as a friend, but as the High-King, his voice ringing with authority.

"Jargas, your father, King Rongas, has knelt to me and pledged himself and his people to me as High-King. For all you are King to me, as Rongas's son and one of his people, do you acknowledge my authority as High-King over you?" Desmond asked.

Jargas bit back his instinctive reply that he did. He was Desmond's King. How could he let him command him? He sensed importance, perhaps even danger, in the question. Yet his father was his King, and he still bowed to his father's authority. And his father bowed to Desmond's. "Ach, my head hurts from thinking about it, but aye, Majesty, you are my High-King. Your authority over me supersedes my own over you," Jargas admitted reluctantly.

Desmond let out his breath in a long sigh. "Then as your High-King, I command you to sever your bond to Hunter, and to lend me the Ring, so I might aid him," Desmond ordered.

Jargas was shocked. "Sever our bond and give you the Ring?" he asked, astonished such a thing might even be asked of him.

"Yes," Desmond said simply.

"But why can I not be the one to aid him, as I have done before?" Jargas asked.

Desmond sighed again. "Jargas, if you were the one who tried to heal him now, if you tried to use the Ring upon him, he'd be dead, in a heartbeat. Please, just do as I command of you," Desmond said, his voice weary.

"High-King or not, commanded or not, I'll not sever my bond to him," Jargas argued. "How can you even ask me to? The Ring has healed him as much as it could, but his body is still weak and his spirit is still damaged. Our link is all that keeps him alive. I'll not murder a friend at the command of a King, not even if my own father were the one to order me to. A good King would never ask such a thing," he said, appalled. He stopped speaking then, for in the heat of his indignation he had said too much.

He saw rage kindle upon the face of the High-King, and his Guard, who surrounded him, had stiffened and their hands were clasping the handles of their axes.

Without hesitation, Jargas knelt and bowed his head before Desmond. "Forgive me, Majesty. I did not mean to imply you are not a good King, for you are more: you are a great King. I can think of none more deserving of the title and rank of High-King. You have certainly earned it. But being such a King, how can you ask me to do as you have? You must not understand, or I must not. How can I, if you won't tell me what is wrong with my friend?"

DESMOND'S anger evaporated at Jargas's words. "Jargas, you must know I would never harm a kinsman. I will tell you only what I can. Hunter will not be alone when you sever your bond to him, even should he have to sever his bond to Jarina, which he well might. He will be bonded to me, from today onward, for as long as he has need of me. Will you now trust me enough to break your bond, to give me the Ring, so I might aid him?"

"Aye," Jargas said, removing the Ring from his finger and holding it out in his palm to Desmond, as he severed the bond.

"Thank you," Desmond said. He hesitated a moment, as he reached for the Ring, then took it gingerly, as if it might bite him. "You may rise, Jargas," Desmond said and turned and headed for Donovar's tent.

His Guard took up position outside of it, and Desmond went in alone. He shifted the Ring onto his finger. The stone glowed, pulsing with the beat of his heart, betraying the quickness of it.

Farad was sitting on one of the cots inside. He was hunched over and shivering.

Desmond sat beside him. "Are you ready?"

Farad nodded, teeth clenched. Desmond touched his face and extended the link. The link touched the shield about Farad, and the Ring flared to life.

The link began to glow and then began to bore a hole through Farad's shield. Desmond was wielding the Power of the Ring with infinite care and restraint. He sensed the Ring could pulverize the shield easily, but he feared what that might do to Farad. Still, Desmond marveled at how strong Farad was, at how strong the shield was, that they had needed the Ring to pierce it. His own unaided Power paled in comparison to that of Farad. But at the height of his Power, even his friend Evanaren had never wielded such Power.

The link touched Farad's core. Images and feelings leapt across the bond toward Desmond. He was not prepared for the ferocity of the bond. The Ring blazed as Desmond cried out and fell to his knees. He felt Desenia's fear, felt her coming to aid him and snapped his bond to her, cursing himself. He had not realized he would have to do so. He would have warned her if he had. Vaguely, with his outer ears, he heard a commotion at the doorway, but he trusted Donovar to keep him safe from those who might seek to aid him.

JARGAS watched as the tent glowed redly from within and knew Desmond was using the Ring. The Guard about the tent shifted uneasily. Then the tent blazed as if consumed by fire and he heard a cry from within and saw the Guard surge toward the door. But Donovar was blocking their way. Jargas saw one of the Guard flung bodily back. "Stop or you'll kill them both!" Donovar cried desperately, and Jargas saw another Guard stumble back, clutching his manhood.

Jargas ran to the tent. Donovar was a healer to his core. He'd only ever harm anyone to save a life. He saw the fear in Donovar's face as he came, the knowledge that he was being overwhelmed and there was no way he could stop Jargas.

Jargas squinted into the tent. The light was fading. He could see Desmond on his knees on the floor and Farad on a cot, hands clenched into fists, every tendon of his neck vivid.

Jargas interposed himself between the Guard, who had axes raised now, and Donovar. "**Stop. You will not enter**," Jargas thundered, his voice echoing with Power. The Dwarves before him froze. "**Stow your axes**," he commanded and they did so, entranced.

Jargas swallowed. He knew he could command them to slit their own throats and they would. No one should have such Power over other men. He'd used it only once before in such a manner, accidentally, when he had frozen Gervan and Arvan, to protect them from Farad when he had gone mad. He thought he would be able to break these men from their trance, but he might not. He hoped Jarina might aid him, for he feared Farad would not be capable of aiding him this time. He feared for Farad.

Donovar said, "Thank you, Jargas, but please, go quickly. Farad must not see you."

Jargas nodded. **"Come with me,"** he told the Guard, and they followed, even the two Donovar had injured. It was a wonder the one could walk. He might be injuring himself by it.

Desenia came then; she ran to him in a panic. "Jargas, what's happened? My father, where is he? He's severed his bond to me! I felt his fear."

Jargas sent a wave of warmth to her. "You're not alone, beloved, nor is he. You are safe, and he will be as well, but only if we leave him be for a time. He is trying to help Hunter."

"Hunter!" She spat his name venomously. "Why must he always be such a torment to my family!"

Jargas glared at her. "You wrong him with your thoughts. You still won't forgive him for his bond to you, when you were ill."

"How can I? He forced himself upon me when I was helpless. He violated my thoughts even as the Enemy violated my body in my dreams. I hate him! I'd kill him for what he's done, if you'd let me."

Jargas looked at her in loathing. "You are not the vision I fell in love with, all those many years ago. I have been trying to help you to be. But if you'd rather wallow in your hate than bask in my love, I want nothing more to do with you."

Desenia drew back from him as if he had slapped her in the face. He saw her anger flare and he started to turn away from her. But unexpectedly, tears sprang into her eyes. "Please, Jargas, my life, my love! Don't leave me alone, now when I loathe myself almost as much as I repulse you. I'm not strong enough to bear it, without Father's spirit to aid me."

Jargas's heart went out to her again, and he embraced her. "I know, Desenia. Can you not trust me, both to aid you and to see your father safe as well? You know my heart is linked to my sister's. I do not know what is wrong with her or with Farad, but I can feel her pain. Her very heart is breaking.

"Jarina has always lived in such joy. I cannot bear to see her shrouded in sadness now. I like Hunter, I value him as a friend, but I never wanted him to marry my sister. I was afraid he might bring her to darkness, but even then, I did not truly understand all the harm he might cause her with such a union. I sent him to Donovar, and Donovar has called your father to his aid, and your father is wielding the Ring. I only hope that whatever they seek to do works."

DESMOND sighed in hopeless frustration. "I am sorry, Farad. I cannot heal you. It is your body, not your core, that is damaged. Or perhaps it is your core, but magic though this Ring may be, it cannot repair your core fully, it can only fortify it. Can Jarina not love you anyway? Your minds and hearts are as one. You are bonded to one another." He continued carefully. "And there is more than one way to satisfy a woman physically. Can you not pleasure her, even if you are not able to be pleasured in return?"

Farad's face darkened in shame. "I have tried. She will not let me. She tells me she will wait for me, as if I might somehow be healed. But I can feel her frustration, her need. Dwarven Ladies save themselves for a reason, Desmond. You must know it as well as I. There is no mystique surrounding their customs to those of us who come from the outside. Their passions are so great, their joinings so intense, that they are bonded to their men for life by the very act of lovemaking. But without that act... I am not truly her husband. It is as if we were never wed. Yet all now see her to be. Her shame, her frustration.... She tries to shield herself from me, but she cannot."

"Then perhaps you should break your bond," Desmond suggested softly.

Farad looked haunted. "I cannot! I did not mean to become so dependent upon her, as I have been upon her brother. But the bond you have forged with me, even with the Ring to sustain it, is severing, even as we speak. I cannot maintain it. I must be bonded to either Jargas or Jarina now, or I will die. I have felt it, I know it to be true, and it terrifies me, for now they might both be lost to me."

"Then you must let Donovar speak to Jarina. She must be made to understand. She will understand, I know she will, if only he might explain it. Please, Farad! We can afford to lose neither you nor your House," Desmond urged.

"No, of course not," Farad said bitterly. "I have not been made to suffer enough yet. First I must betray the only man left alive whom I truly love, the man I have spent nearly nine decades protecting, the man I have lost everything for. Perhaps then I will be allowed to die." His voice was hollow with despair.

"Farad, this is difficult for me to ask. Forgive me for it, but I must. Were you and Dewalaren once lovers?" Desmond asked. Such male pairings were a common enough practice amongst his kin.

Farad shook his head, and his voice sank to a hoarse whisper. "No. We are first cousins. Our mothers were sisters. Had I been born a woman, we would have been wed, but I failed him, even in that. He is the King. He must have a Queen. We could never be lovers, for I was named Protector and King's Friend before he even came-of-age. Then I could not be. You know our laws: the King must never risk his life for that of his Protector. It is to ensure his safety. But then even that position I so treasured was taken from me. It is why I left. How could I have stayed, when they all hated and feared me so?"

Desmond had not realized he was reaching into a hornet's nest with his question. But he had to continue, if he was to have any hope of helping Farad. "How… why did you lose your title? What did you do to the King that you lost it, that you were feared and hated, that you left?"

"Dewalaren went mad," Farad whispered. "It was the King's Madness. It seized him suddenly. He… he tried to kill us, just as Ebonar did. All the Lords. We were all there. They would not act against him, even to save themselves. But I had to act. I had to save him. I love him. I could not let him be lost to the Madness. I could not let him murder his friends, his people, murder Lords. I overpowered his Guard and seized a bow. I drove an arrow into his wrist, yet still he would not drop his sword. I fired twice more. I pinned his arm to a chair. Finally, he dropped his blade."

Desmond nodded. "You lost your position, your title, their respect for you, for your attack upon the King, for wounding one you'd sworn to protect."

Farad shook his head. "No, it was much worse than that. They tried to seize me, but I could not let them. I still had to help Dewalaren. I had carefully concealed my Power my entire life. Our kin feared me enough, for my coldness, for my ruthlessness, without knowing all about me. There was a time, when I was young and still whole, that my Power rivaled that of Dewalaren himself. I did not want him ever to fear me. But then I had no choice. I had to reveal myself.

"I used the King's Voice upon them, Lords all, all with at least some level of Power. They were as statues. Then I took Dewalaren's head in my hands and forced my thoughts into his core. I bonded my core to his so I could heal him of the Madness. And it worked. I healed him, but at a terrible price. I could no longer be Protector and King's Friend, so bonded to him, yet I could not break my bond to him, knowing he might need me again, he might go mad again. But worse still, he named me Heir to the Throne. I could not be, for that. The Heir cannot be Protector, for he seeks to gain the most by the King's death. And they were terrified of me, all of them, now that they knew the strength of my Power. So I left.

"I kept my bond, such as it was. But I could never touch it, never draw strength or even warmth from it, for fear I would weaken Dewalaren and lead him back down the path to Madness. His core is frighteningly unstable, for his Power. I became his anchor. I even gave him my strength, the few times I could. Then, six years ago, when he fell to the Madness a second time, I felt it and was powerless to aid him.

"I was trying to save the children. Forgehead was dying. The Enemy had breached the Door. I had twenty of the children with me. I couldn't go to him or they would have died." Tears began to fall. "They died anyway, one by one, all of them, in the mountains, in the desperate march from Forgehead to Axemore. I carried the last for a week. She died of fever, in my arms, not twenty feet from the Door to the Mountain."

The Ring was glowing brightly; Desmond was channeling more Power to Farad than he had ever used before in any of the many battles of his life, keeping Farad's core intact, healing the cracks as it tried to shatter over and over again. He had to bring him to stability, somehow.

Farad continued, "I know I have not been the only one to suffer. You have lost much as well, Desmond. You have suffered for almost ninety years, you lost all your kin for decades, you lost your family. But you have found a new wife, you have sired a new child, you are High-King of thirty Kingdoms and still Lord of your House. Your line will continue.

"I cannot sire a child. I cannot even lie with my wife as a man should. My House dies with me, but not only mine. She is Lady of House of Pumar, last of her House as well. So, I kill two Houses. And I dethrone the King. I am the tool of the Enemy in all that I do. So tell me why I should not end my life, before I cause more anguish to those I yet love?"

Desmond did not know what to say to him, but a voice spoke from the doorway. It was Jarina. "You cannot, Faradan, because to do so would be even worse. If you die now, I will die with you, for I have no desire to live without you. So you would kill two Houses instantly, rather than one hundred or so years from now, Aralyn willing, when we might both die.

"And I am not the only one who would suffer by your death. When Dewalaren loses his throne and Lordship of his House, what will he have left, other than his friends, and those who love him? How would it ease his pain to know one he so loves is dead? Why did you not tell Jargas you were Heir to the Throne, should Dewalaren fall? Or that you were once in name and are still by your heart the Protector and King's Friend, and all that implies? We live in ignorance of our mother's people, but I have seen from your thoughts what that means. Why did you not tell me how I was harming you?

"I am a woman full grown. Do you think my desires are new to me? I have pleasured myself many times in the past decades, most often while seeing visions of you. I have not since I met you, because it would not have been proper. Nor did I want to be pleasured by you, when I knew you could not receive the same pleasure I took. I thought to do so would be selfish. I did not understand your desire to fulfill my needs was for your own sake as well as mine, that you would have found a different type of pleasure in the gifting of it to me. But your shield against me has shattered many times as Desmond has spoken with you, although the Ring keeps restoring it. I have seen and heard much. Now I understand. Please, Faradan, give me the chance to express my love for you as well as I can, given the limitations we have.

"And do not lament that you cannot sire a child upon me. As you have not bonded as fully to me as you should have, out of fear, I have kept secrets from you as well. It has been the curse of my mother's line for these three generations past that the mother dies birthing her first child. Jargas was born first. My mother died with me still inside her. All three of us were linked. He still remembers the terror of losing her, and almost losing me as well, before the midwife took me from her and his touch restored my breath. Jargas has always feared that I could never wed, lest I die, as our mother and her ancestors did. I knew I must tell you, but I feared you would not want me, were you to know I was so flawed." Her face darkened with shame, akin to that he had felt himself.

Farad went to her and embraced her. "Then I am blessed when I thought myself cursed! For I would not want a child now, not if he or she would take you from me. I must never lose you, Jarina." Farad kissed her, slowly and passionately, and she melted into his arms and returned his kiss with equal passion.

Desmond saw the Ring fade to a dull glow and breathed deeply, for the first time in a long while. His link to Farad was gone, but it did not matter. The danger was past. Farad's core was stable again. "I'll see that the two of you are not disturbed," Desmond said. He would tell Jargas only what he needed to know, of Farad and Dewalaren. He exited the tent. Donovar was still at the entrance, guarding it.

"I am surprised you allowed her to enter, though it was well you did so, for I was at my wit's end," Desmond admitted.

"She spoke to me. She told me what she had learned, what she would say. I knew she could help him, now, rather than harm him. And I saw you had done all you could," Donovar explained. "I will make sure no one disturbs them. You must speak with Jargas, and return the Ring to him."

Desmond nodded and went to do so.

Desmond told Jargas what he had learned about Farad's relationship to Dewalaren. "You must be sure Farad knows that when the time comes to stand against Dewalaren, we will not harm him. We will do all we can to see him safe."

"What of Jarina? I cannot let Farad hurt her further," Jargas said, troubled.

"Farad was not the one harming her. She harmed herself and him along with her. I cannot tell you more, other than to assure you on two counts: the two of them have discovered a way to find happiness together, and Jarina will not die in childbirth, as you have always feared."

JARGAS was surprised, both that Desmond knew his fear and that he now told him it was groundless. "You mean the Ring has healed her? But I thought it could only heal the mind. You mean there was some flaw that's...."

"Jargas, I have told you all I will tell you. Here is the Ring. Please take care with it. The Power contained within is far beyond what a mere mortal was ever meant to hold. I had no idea of its true Power, until I used it. Only a God should wield Power such as this. Now, where is Desenia? It will be safe to restore my bond to her now, if she will allow it."

"She is in your tent. Should I tell the men we are readying to march again?" Jargas asked.

"NO. TELL them the High-King has been ordered by Donovar to rest here for the remainder of the day. We will march once the moon is high. And be sure one of your men tells him I've so ordered it," Desmond said. Donovar would figure out what he had done and why, easily enough. Farad and Jarina must be given as much uninterrupted time together as possible, before the march resumed. Now all he needed to do was to face Desenia's wrath.

Fortunately, his fears were unfounded. Jargas and Desenia had apparently spoken before. He had never seen his free-spirited daughter so complacent as she had been since her marriage to Jargas.

Desenia was overjoyed that he sought to renew his bond to her. After they renewed the bond and she had left, Desmond lay down, both to put credence to the orders he'd given and because he truly felt in need of a rest, as if he'd fought many battles that day. These, at least, he'd won. It remained to be seen what would happen once they reached Caramore and faced Dewalaren.

Chapter 7
Reunion

DEWALAREN was weary, almost past even his endurance. Endless weeks of little food or sleep, the brutal march through swamp and ruined land, all for naught. Now he was almost back to Nalea. Each step took him ever closer, but it seemed he would never reach it.

HE HAD begun his quest certain it would lead to the Ring. He had walked to the Fromer Mountains and gone through the Malar Pass, the only one still open, barely escaping detection. The Pass was well patrolled, but the focus of the Dwarves' efforts was upon those coming from the Dwarven Lands, not those coming from the Lands of Men. Although he knew they expected and braced for an army, he doubted he could have snuck past them, had he come from the east. He could not reveal himself yet, not to the three armies awaiting him as King, at the head of his own army. Without the Ring, he could not claim the title King, and though he and his nineteen surviving kin were formidable, they could not claim to be an army.

After entering the Dwarven Lands, he had headed south, before heading east. He had crossed the Dwarven Lands by the way of the Great Marsh and Dead Sea, avoiding the Enemy's minions by taking such a route. But he had faced many other dangers by doing so. He had fought his way clear of the sucking mud more times than he could count. He had survived three snakebites, and hundreds of insects had feasted upon him. He had drained dry the flask of medicine Aras had given him for fever, though he had used it sparingly. Finally, he had reached the Deathshand Mountains.

He found the pass there sealed in its tomb of stone, as Farad had described it. But he also found a smaller tomb, what had once been a cairn of stone, half-tumbled down by the weather. Asking forgiveness of the occupant, he began to remove the stones. He needed to know who lay within. He suspected it was Prince Rowanar's tomb. No one had called him King while he lived: the shock of his father's murder and the horror of the massacre of the Lords had been too fresh. None had been called King since, for lack of the King's Knife and the King's Ring.

Dewalaren found a skeleton within, in scraps of rotting cloth, tall and long limbed, as one of his people would appear in death. The King's Armor should have graced his remains, as well as the King's Band, but both were missing. Dewalaren knew then the pallenteum copy of the Band he wore upon his own arm must remain. But there was a sword. Not the King's Sword, of course: he wore Kathalanar, though only he, and Farad and Lunahr, as his heirs, knew its name.

He had lifted the blade gently. His heart had all but stopped when a section of the rotting scabbard flaked away, revealing the sheen of a pallenteum blade. Then his heart quickened in fear as he tore the rest of the scabbard from the blade. The handguard was in the shape of a gryphon, with its beak biting the blade. He saw a name etched clearly upon it, as if it had been engraved that morning, instead of two hundred eighty-three years earlier: Garalathon. Even without it, the blade was unmistakable.

There was only one man who would have worn this sword: Stephan, Lord of House of Gryphon, Protector and Friend of the King's son, Rowanar. The blade had been gifted to Stephan by King Albinar, upon Stephan's coming-of-age, to replace the broken blade of his House, the blade he had sacrificed in saving Rowanar's life. A blade of pallenteum would not tarnish, would not break, would never dull.

But it could not be that sword! Not if Jargas had told Farad the truth. Jargas had claimed to be descended from Stephan, the sole survivor of those Rowanar had led. He had worn his band, House of Gryphon. But how could he be his descendent, if these were Stephan's remains? He had felt Jargas's Power, while he was lost to Madness. Had Aras not come when he did, who knew what Jargas would have done to him, as he lay so vulnerable? Idare! To have been deceived once more, by a false hope, when he had been powerless to test Jargas's claim, to discover his perfidious true nature!

The ancient leather of the hilt crumbled to dust in his hands as he grasped it, and his hopes crumbled with it. He would not find the King's Ring in this terrible valley that had claimed the lives of three hundred of his kin. His arduous journey had been for nothing. No, not for nothing: it had brought him knowledge, invaluable knowledge. Jargas was not who he claimed to be. He was a tool of the Enemy. Jargas had deceived both him and Farad, but Farad had not had Aras to save him.

Dewalaren's face had darkened in anger, his rage replacing his fear. Jargas had bonded to Farad and was using him as his pawn. Jargas would be twisting Farad into a servant of the Enemy. He would have had many weeks to do so. Farad would already be lost to them.

No! Dewalaren would save him! He must be in time to save him! He could not lose Farad a second time, not when he yet lived, after Dewalaren had thought him slain.

Dewalaren apologized to Stephan for disturbing his rest, and for taking his sword, but he had need of it. He swore to Stephan he would reclaim the band of his dead House, so he and his lost family might know peace in death, when they had known none in life.

He replaced the stones of the cairn. Then he drew out Kathalanar and stripped off his glove. The blade blazed reddish copper, the sheen of pyrenteum, with the masking spell removed. He stared at the glove in wonder for a moment, that he still wore it, that it might still work, after Arcanus had tried to kill him. The Sword glowed softly with Power; there was so little of it left. He held the blade parallel to the shattered rock that filled the valley, vainly hoping to see the blade blaze with the Power of the nearness of the Ring. But the Ring was still lost, forever lost. He walked over the remains of his dead kin in their unmarked graves to no avail: the Lords and Ladies and their children, the aunts and uncles, nephews and nieces and cousins of ten lost Houses.

Weary from the search, Dewalaren collapsed onto the rock in despair and wept, for Farad, for Stephan, for the dead beneath his feet, for all his dead people and the scant few who yet lived. When finally his tears were spent, he rose. He would never cry again. Tears served no purpose. What use had his people for tears? Their tears could have filled an ocean, yet still they would die as a people.

He wrapped himself in cold resolve and began the long march back to Nalea, heading for the green forests and those two he loved whom he had left behind there.

Lunahr needed him. He had promised Lunahr he would return, that he would see him free of his prison. He pictured him clearly as he'd last seen him, sobbing brokenly in Aras's arms. He could no longer see him the way he had once known him, smiling and laughing and singing, full of light and life and song.

DEWALAREN'S thoughts returned to the present. He must take care here. He was near his goal, but the river crossing would be dangerous, weak as he was. There had been little food for much of his journey back. His supplies had been consumed long ago. Now that there was life around him again, he was too weak to hunt, too tired even to forage.

A fallen log serving as a bridge saved him. Even then he nearly fell from it into the waters below. He would have drowned, even in such a slow-moving river. He was utterly spent.

There was no eager burst of speed as he headed deeper into the forest surrounding Nalea. Soon now he could finally rest, before he must go forth again and find and confront Farad, or what might be left of him. Before he would face Jargas and wreak vengeance upon him for what he had done. Even thoughts of Aras could not lighten the burden of his heart, for he feared for Lunahr these many long weeks in his lonely exile amongst those he'd made his enemies.

He walked along the River, where the ground was less densely wooded, each step bringing him closer to his rest. Then, up ahead, he saw something impossible. He shook his head and blinked and rubbed the palms of his hands against his eyes, as if the image might go away, as if it were some terrible shadow dream. But it was real, horrifyingly real. Even viewing Garalathon had not frozen his heart as this did. Shock gave way to dismay and then despair.

The outer rim of the forest, inward from the riverbank, seven hundred yards or more deep, was gone. Hundreds, perhaps thousands, of trees were missing. Instead there were fields, where those proud trees had once stood, the ground plowed and irrigated and green with newly sprouting crops. The blackened husks of trees lay beyond them, and barren stumps, and then stack upon stack of felled trees, left to rot by the edge of the forest. Women of Men tilled the fields, and there were Men with swords and bows guarding them, and a long, low building made of wood.

The Elves did not build out of wood; they built out of stone or they used living trees. They would never cut a tree to build from it. They would not burn their Wood. They would never allow Man here, upon their lands.

The Elves were gone, then. And Dewalaren knew "gone" meant dead, unless some few had escaped. There was nothing he could do. He was far too late. The disaster that had struck the Elves and their Wood had apparently happened many weeks ago.

Incuban's minions did not farm. It must have been the Hill People. Somehow they had beaten the entire combined Elven Army and Navy.

Dewalaren stared, stricken. No! Not Lunahr! Not Aras and all his people! Not while he'd been off chasing the Ring.

He was stunned by his grief, oblivious to the danger around him, until he was suddenly surrounded by four archers with drawn bows and nocked arrows. He had neither seen nor heard them approach.

He realized with a sickening lurch that their bows were Elven, although their arrows were fletched in green, not gray. He knew the Elves who had owned those bows were now dead. Men had burned their forest and farmed their land. He had crossed the Dwarven Lands and gone into the Deathshand

Mountains and back again, while Nalea had fallen. He almost fell to his knees then, but thoughts of Farad and revenge upon Jargas kept him on his feet.

"Who are you and what are you doing in these lands?" one of the bowmen asked, in such thickly accented Common Dewalaren could barely make out the words. The Man's voice was hard and cold. He was dark haired and dark eyed and dressed as a warrior.

Dewalaren did not speak. He could not. He could not even think.

"If you will not answer, you will be bound," the Man threatened, but still Dewalaren stayed silent, his mind racing but his thoughts a hopeless fog of despair. Aras was dead! Lunahr was dead! He let the agony of his loss flare across his features for a moment. He saw the Man's face soften in compassion, as he reached for his arms to bind him, rope in hand.

Dewalaren struck out at him, catching him completely off guard, stunning him with his blow, the unexpected ferocity of his attack. He grabbed him and used him as a shield against the arrows of the others, backing quickly into the woods. But then there was a sudden pain in his head, from behind, and he realized too late there had been at least one other he had not seen.

He fell to his knees from the blow, fighting to stand, but he was pounced upon, his face forced into the leafy dirt and pinned by many hands. A strong knee was pressed into his back, with the full weight of a Man behind it, and other hands grasped his still struggling arms, as he fought, clawing and kicking. His hands were forced together and bound securely, and his feet were tied as well, but still he struggled. Then they took Kathalanar and Garalathon from him, and his knife, and his struggles ceased and he lay still. He closed his eyes and forced himself to go limp.

He thought they would kick him and beat him, for he'd hurt the one Man and done some damage to the others in his struggles, but they did not. The Men around him were talking in a different tongue now, a guttural one that was unknown to him. Then strong hands lifted him under each arm, and he was dragged forward. He forced himself to stay limp, conserving what little energy he had left, hoarding it carefully for future escape. But the swords! He could not escape without the swords!

He felt the forest loam give way to tilled soil under his dragging feet, and he felt the sun upon his back, and knew he was being carried across the fields, now. The Men around him called out, and he heard the steps of at least six others join them. Then there was more guttural talk, and a different voice called out. There was the sound of a door opening in front of him and he realized they were at the building, now. Then he unexpectedly heard an achingly familiar voice utter that same strange language.

His head jerked up in shock and he stared, unable to believe his ears and eyes, for it was Aras, alive and healthy and whole, a look of astonishment and love and concern on his face as he recognized him.

"Dewalaren!" Aras said, forgetting himself in his surprise and speaking his given name. And then he was at his side, holding him, barking guttural commands, and Dewalaren felt the ropes that bound him cut from his hands and feet. He sagged in Aras's arms, for the moment unable to get his feet under him again.

"Can you stand?" Aras asked in Elvish.

Such a simple request, but it was almost beyond his strength. Through an effort of will, Dewalaren forced himself upright, but he yet swayed and leaned heavily on his friend.

There were more unintelligible voices. "My swords," Dewalaren pleaded, and his voice shook.

Aras called out, and Dewalaren's weapons were returned to him. The hand that clutched the scabbard and the cloth-bound blade trembled, as he took back the blades.

Aras led Dewalaren inside the building. It was all a single room, with windows on the south wall, facing the ruined Wood and the River, and a fireplace along the east wall. There were colorful cushions all over the floor, tapestries on the walls, a low wooden table spread with maps, and two red ceramic mugs. A woman was there also, with dark hair and eyes, dressed in red, an exotic beauty.

"Sit, Talon, before you fall." Aras lowered him to a cushion on the floor, and his legs folded. Then Aras went to the fire, brought over a pot, and poured him a cup of something hot.

He accepted the cup and drank it gingerly. It was an odd brew, but not unpleasant. He set the cup down, and his hand shook slightly, from fatigue and draining tension and his fading battle rush.

"Talon, what has happened to you? You look terrible! I scarcely recognized you," Aras said, his voice warm with concern.

Dewalaren wanted nothing more than to collapse into his arms and hold him. He'd been so sure Aras was dead. He'd thought him lost forever. But he could not betray such weakness, especially not before a stranger. "I have had a difficult journey. But Aras, what is going on? When I saw this place, I thought you were all dead!"

Aras sobered. "We ended the War. We both won. We each lost some people, but not nearly as many as we could have. And the trees. A lot has happened since you left." His face clouded with the memory of their losses, but then he smiled. "But it's so good to see you!"

"Is Beryl all right?" Dewalaren asked softly, afraid to hear the reply, to voice the fear that had haunted him for so long. Even when speaking Elvish, he would not use Lunahr's given name with that woman here.

Aras smiled again. "He is well. I'll take you to him, but later."

Then the woman came over, a small bag in her hand, and asked in accented Common, but much more clearly and intelligibly than the warrior, if she might see his head and hand, so she might treat his injuries. He allowed it at Aras's urging, and she was both skilled and gentle. She peeled off his gloves before he even thought to protest.

"Talon, this is Shadala, Chieftess and Healer of the Hill People, the Urwani." Aras turned to her. "Shadala, this is my friend, Talon, the one I told you of."

"I am honored," she said. Her voice was low and husky, and she inclined her head to him, almost in a bow.

"As am I. And I thank you for your aid," Dewalaren said politely.

"I will bring food and other comforts for your friend, Akarhad," Shadala said.

"Thank you, Shadala," Aras said in Common, and then added something in that tongue Dewalaren did not know. She smiled and nodded, and left.

"You're lucky the Wood Guard didn't kill you when you attacked them, despite our orders to bring all prisoners to us for questioning," Aras chastised. "We've been teaching Common to as many of the Urwani as we can, but few are anywhere near fluent in it yet. Meanwhile, Shadala and a few others have been learning Elvish."

"Why does Shadala call you Akarhad?" Dewalaren asked, desperately grasping at the single question that thrust foremost into his mind from the swirling chaos of his thoughts.

Aras grinned. "Ah. That's my Urwani name. She named me that the first time we met, when we were both fifteen. It means 'Fair One.' I would be most interested to hear what name Shadala might bestow upon you. They gave me a far different name when I came here with you, you know. Then they called me 'Yehorog.' It means Yellow Demon. That must have been your bad influence. And now, as usual, I think you've made a distinctive first impression on her, what with the way you look and smell. And I thought you stank the first time I met you! I had no need to be so vividly reminded!" Aras laughed.

For a moment, the signs of the many long weeks of his strenuous journey faded from Dewalaren's face as he laughed with his friend. "I have missed you, my friend!" After decades of traveling alone, it had suddenly become unbearable not to have Aras at his side.

Then the door opened and Shadala came in bearing a tray of food and a flask, likely of wine. Dewalaren was surprised she brought it in herself, given what Aras had told him of her rank. He realized the fare was entirely Elven, save for some sort of sausage and an odd white cheese.

Shadala was followed by a younger woman, also dressed in red, who brought in a basin filled with scented, oiled water, a sponge and a towel. Much to Dewalaren's surprise, she washed his face and hands. He was embarrassed by how filthy the cloth was by the time she was done. He thanked her, in Common, and she smiled, lids low on dark eyes. She poured him wine then, and he drank deeply. His eyes sought Aras's face, desperate for the reassurance he was alive and well. After seeing the burnt forest, he had been convinced he would never see that face again.

"Eat, my friend," Aras encouraged, and Dewalaren did so, ravenously. The sausage was spicy and flavorful and the cheese crumbly and tangy. Dewalaren's thoughts wandered, and he wondered what animal they had milked to produce it. He hadn't realized he'd voiced his thoughts, until Aras answered. "Both the meat and cheese come from deer. The Urwani keep a large herd."

Dewalaren was surprised. Deer were notoriously skittish and uncooperative. He had never heard of a people other than his own successfully domesticating and milking them. But House of Deer had been lost two and a half centuries earlier, with Alanar.

It was getting harder and harder to form a coherent thought, and the effort of even eating was becoming too great. He felt his eyelids grow heavy, and he shook his head, to clear it.

AS ARAS watched, Dewalaren shook his head and then slumped slowly to one side onto the cushions, finally unconscious. Shadala and Falara helped him lay Dewalaren out properly on the cushions, and Falara brought a blanket to cover him.

"Thank you, both of you," Aras said to them, in Urwani. "I'm afraid he might be more than a little angry with me about this when he wakes up, but he has pushed himself far too hard this time. And he no doubt would have had me keep him up for hours catching him up on all that's happened, when he could scarcely stand. How long will he sleep?"

"You were right to do this, Akarhad," Shadala reassured him approvingly. "As healers, sometimes we must help those in need, even when they might not wish it. The wine will keep him asleep for half a day, at least. Beyond that, his body may keep him asleep for far more, if he will let it, but I do not know that he will allow it."

"Still, that will be a start. I doubt he's slept at all in days, and little in the weeks before, to look like this. And I can see he has eaten even less often. He is so haggard and gaunt I scarcely recognized him. Will you stay with him? I want to have clothes ready for him when he awakens, and to let Lunahr know he has returned. There is much we need to tell him, but he was in no condition to hear any of it yet."

"I will see that the King's rest is not disturbed," Shadala assured him. "Falara will tell our people of his return. All will be in readiness tomorrow, for when he awakens."

Aras left Field House and headed to the Guest House. There he rifled through Lunahr's things for clothes that would fit Dewalaren passably well. Everything he now wore was fit only for composting. He remembered to retrieve a comb. Then he wrote a note for Lunahr and Leonas, instructing them to come to the Urwani City the following day, at noon. He did not say more. He realized if he told them who it was, Lunahr would insist upon seeing Dewalaren immediately, and he should not see his cousin in such a state, ragged, exhausted and more than half-starved.

Aras returned to Field House and placed the clothes near where Dewalaren lay. A tub had already been brought in that would be filled tomorrow. Dewalaren would need to bathe before getting dressed. Aras would sleep here with him tonight, lest Dewalaren awaken in the middle of the night and start to get suspicious thoughts about his friend.

That night, as soon as his other duties were done, Aras lay down upon the cushions beside Dewalaren. Aras studied his beloved face and then caressed his cheek, gently, lovingly. He still could not believe Dewalaren had returned to him. He had feared greatly for him, gone so many weeks, alone, but to see him return so weakened he appeared to be all but the walking dead! The very thought terrified him.

Aras shuddered, thinking how Incuban could have found him instead, too weak to fight, and what he might have done to him. Incuban would learn of his own identity soon now, it was inevitable, but he must never learn the place Dewalaren held in his heart. He was in enough danger already, as a weapon to torture Arcanus with. He must never suffer in Aras's stead.

Aras fought crushing sadness and aching loneliness that Dewalaren must not learn the true depth of Aras's love for him. He kissed Dewalaren gently upon his soft lips, afraid his butterfly-wing kiss might somehow wake him, even as his traitorous heart desperately wished it might. He sighed at the thought that he was so bold he would risk demonstrating his love only because he knew Dewalaren was in a drugged sleep he could not yet waken from.

Aras put his arm possessively about Dewalaren and held him tightly. No one would ever harm him. He would protect him always. He would not let Dewalaren leave his sight again, not until all three enemies were defeated, not until the War was won.

He laid his head against Dewalaren's chest, reassured to hear his heart yet beat strongly. It should be enough to be holding him again, to know he was here, that he was safe, that they were together as they had always been meant to be. But he wished with all his heart someday Dewalaren might love him as strongly as he was loved.

Aras fell asleep, lulled by the rhythmic beat of Dewalaren's strong heart.

Even after the elixir in the wine was spent, Dewalaren slept. It was morning before Dewalaren roused.

IT HAD been so long since he had felt so warm, so safe, so content, since he had woken to the feeling of a lover's arms about him, a warm body beside him. Dewalaren's eyes focused upon the face beside him. Not a lover: Aras. Dewalaren studied his perfect features, the incomparable beauty of his fine-boned face. There was a slight smile upon Aras's lips, almost of mischief, of a playful secret. He leaned his face toward those inviting lips but then stopped. No, he must not. Aras was such an innocent, such a child, for all he was a man. He could not be the one to take that from him, not when he had only danger and death to offer in exchange.

Besides, he would only be using Aras. He was betrothed to Elanara. He loved her. But she did not love him. He feared she never would. He had tried so hard to win her love. He had revealed so much of himself to her; too much. She feared him, instead of loving him. But Aras was not afraid of him.

He frowned, remembering how casually Aras had defeated Arcanus, just before he left Nalea, how his core had blazed like the sun. No, Aras was not a child. He was a wizard. How could he have forgotten? And there were so many secrets that had yet to be revealed. Even while Dewalaren was viewing Aras's core, Aras had hidden so much from him. Dewalaren had been so desperate to see Aras and Lunahr again, he had forced all such thoughts from his mind, but now, with Aras beside him again, he needed to acknowledge them once more. He must discover all Aras sought to hide from him.

As if sensing his thoughts and endangered by them, Aras awoke.

"How long have I slept?" Dewalaren asked, his voice hoarse and scratchy. But he felt more clearheaded than he had for at least a sennight. He could focus his thoughts again.

"A day and a night," Aras said, sounding strangely sheepish.

The last remnants of his earlier feeling of safety vanished with Aras's words, guarded wariness replacing it. "I know I was tired, perhaps more tired than I have ever been. Too tired, for I could scarcely think or even walk, but I had not thought the blow I took so strong, nor should I have been so affected by the wine that I slept, when there is so much that must be done," Dewalaren said carefully.

The expression upon Aras's face changed to one of guilt. "Ah. About the wine…. That was my doing, I'm afraid. I could see you were utterly spent, but I feared you would not rest. And your head was not clear enough for me to propose renewing my bond to you. So I had Falara slip a sleeping draught into the wine when she poured if for you."

Dewalaren remembered the words Aras had spoken when Shadala had left, and her smile, but even in remembering that, or Falara's heavy lidded, dark-eyed look, none of them had betrayed their intentions to him. He was fortunate he'd been with true friends, then, not friends who were enemies in disguise. But he had never let his guard down before.

If they had intended him harm, would he have sensed it? He thought long and hard. Yes. Then he would have known. He realized he might still have been caught, as he had been in the woods, unable to fight strongly enough or flee, but he would have tried, as before. If he had been rendered so vulnerable, then Aras had indeed acted in his best interests.

"Dewalaren, will you forgive me for it?" Aras asked, looking as young and unsure as he had in the earliest days of their journey together.

Dewalaren smiled at him and hugged him, and Aras released what sounded like a relieved breath. "Aras, yes, I forgive you. I could forgive you for far worse, just to be able to see you again, my friend! I had known it would be hard, but I still had not dreamt I would miss you so terribly. I would never want to undertake such a perilous journey again, without you by my side. I never want to leave you again at all. Now, if you'll promise not to trick me again, I would break bread with you, since last night's meal proved so short, and it has been many, many days since I've last eaten well."

Aras grinned. "Gladly. But first, I have brought you a change of clothes and hope you will allow me to bury what you now wear." He pointed to the clothes and the bath.

Dewalaren said seriously, "Forgive me, then, for hugging you!"

"Ah, that is not something I would want to forgive, for I have missed you greatly, even with Lunahr and Leonas by my side." Then Aras spoke to the Guard at the door, again in that guttural tongue, and he nodded and passed the message.

A stream of bearers came in with hot water, and Falara entered as well, with scented oils and soaps. She spoke huskily to Aras for a moment, and to Dewalaren's astonishment, Aras blushed. Then Aras laughed and said, in Common, "You'd have to ask him that yourself."

She laughed also, softly and musically, and turned to Dewalaren and bowed to him. "Would it please you for me to bathe you?" Her accent was heavier than Shadala's but she spoke Common well, and she again gave him the heavy lidded gaze from the previous night.

Dewalaren said politely, "No. Thank you for the offer, but I had better do that myself."

She batted her thick lashes and handed him the soaps and oils, her fingertips brushing against the back of his uninjured hand and lingering there for a moment. Then she turned and sashayed out the door.

Dewalaren said, "Your new friends are quite intriguing. I look forward to hearing your long story, my friend."

Aras laughed. "Believe me, your first meeting with them was far more pleasant than my own. I met Shadala at the wrong end of a knife, while Falara only wanted to strangle me with her bare hands." Then, having whetted his friend's appetite to hear more, he left him to his privacy.

Dewalaren set to bathing with a vengeance, scrubbing away weeks of filth. He reveled in the feeling of the hot, soapy water against his skin. By the time he was done, the water had grown cold and was dark with muck. He rinsed himself with the last of the buckets beside the tub, standing in the water, then extending one leg, rinsing it, stepping out, and rinsing the other over the tub, wrapping a towel around his groin.

The water bearers returned to empty the tub. To his embarrassment, he saw the water was nearly the color of ink. They took away his soiled clothes as well.

Once they were gone, he dressed, taking particular joy in the supple new boots of Elven fabric that replaced his leather ones. His old ones had been long past watertight, and he'd spent far too long in bogs and marshes. He ran the comb through his hair and stretched and luxuriated in the feel of the soft, Elven clothes against clean skin. He felt a man again.

Dewalaren stood by the open window, breathing in the fresh air. He watched the Guard patrolling the area between the building and the forest. Then he heard the door and turned. Aras was back, with a tray of food and drink.

He eyed Dewalaren approvingly and grinned. "Much better."

Dewalaren said, "I still can't believe your father would let them farm here, instead of replanting the forest, after they'd burned the trees." It had been hard enough for Aras to forgive him for burning the two Markers, and those hadn't even been in Aras's Wood.

"He wouldn't have. But they didn't set the fire. If it weren't for them, we would have lost the entire Wood and the City. They were the ones who did most of the work extinguishing the blaze. Such a conflagration was beyond us. Even the Navy quailed before it, and they are well trained to face such hazards. Ahrnad lit the fire." The smile had fled his face.

"Ahrnad? Lord of the Guard?" Dewalaren asked, shocked.

ARAS sighed. "No. Ahrnad, mad tool of the Enemy. But it is a very complicated story, and there are many you must hear it from. There will be a great feast in your honor at the Urwani City today, at noon. You will hear much then."

"Aras, please thank them for the honor, but I do not have time for feasts. I must find my cousin, Hunter. He is in terrible danger."

"I have news of him, from Tanieria. He was well when he left, though not when he came." Aras grimaced, for it was his own arrow that had nearly killed him. He explained Hunter had narrowly escaped death from the wound he had inflicted, when he had been forced to injure him in order to disarm him to protect Dewalaren. Aras told Dewalaren Hunter's wound had festered from the arrow tainted by wolven blood, and he had developed the same fever some of the Urwani had died from. The Elves of Tanieria had found Hunter still mounted on Kaldahar, but delirious and unconscious, at the edge of the Woods of Lysenia.

They would have left him to die there, but with his last remaining strength, before passing out, he had sliced the shirt sleeve covering his House band with his knife, exposing the sheen of pallenteum to the sun's dying rays. They'd further exposed the band and recognized it, and brought him to their healers. They had found the message he carried from Nalea, ordering that all members of the Watch be slain, and Aras's message countermanding that order, written in blood upon the back.

They could not believe a banded Captain of the Watch would bring his own death warrant to them, but had been suspicious of Aras's message, in spite of the verification codes it contained, after having been informed he was dead. So they had decided to heal Hunter and question him. When Hunter's fever had broken and he was able to speak, Hunter had verified the contents of both messages. They had sought to keep him confined, for they were yet suspicious, but did not harm him. He had escaped from them shortly thereafter. They still did not know how he had done so.

"AND that is all you know?" Dewalaren asked and Aras nodded.

"It is not enough," Dewalaren said. "He might have come to great harm from Jargas since then." Dewalaren told Aras about all he had found.

Aras grew grim. "Then it is my fault, for having bound you in the tree, keeping you from touching your cousin, when you might have yet saved him. And from having likewise prevented you from touching Jargas, so you might have known him for who or what he is. But I cannot believe I was so deceived by Jargas. I thought him an honorable man. I am sorry, Dewalaren, I did not mean to harm you. I meant only to aid you."

"It is in the past. Now I must go in search of Hunter. But first, I would go to your City and see Lunahr, if only to tell him good-bye," Dewalaren said resolutely.

"You must certainly see him, but you need not say good-bye. And he is not in Nalea. He is in the Urwani City, which is yet in the hills, though their farms are now here," Aras said.

"But how can he be, when he is bound by the trees of Nalea?" Dewalaren asked, astonished.

Aras looked nervous. "Lunahr is no longer bound. I removed the restraints Arcanus put upon him. They were no longer necessary. I have rid him of the compulsions he was cursed under, to kill you and your kin, and my father."

"You broke Arcanus's spells?" Dewalaren asked, remembering how it had nearly killed Arcanus to cast them upon Lunahr and how easily Aras had defeated Arcanus as a result, when they fought over him outside Nalea. "You broke Incuban's spells?" he asked incredulously, as the full implication of what Aras had said struck him. Surely Aras could not be so powerful!

Aras swallowed. "That part was easy. But I have not yet been able to fully heal Lunahr. I have had to work slowly and carefully. Incuban harmed him terribly. The compulsions were overlaid roughly upon his core, as if an afterthought. The real harm is far more subtle and complex. I have had to rebuild Lunahr's core entirely, and even so, I have not yet been able to remove Lunahr's love for Incuban," Aras said, his face flushing in shame.

"His what?" Dewalaren asked, paling.

"Incuban twisted Lunahr's core cruelly. He forced Lunahr to love Him with his mind and his heart, as well as his body. Even as Lunahr knows Him for the evil he is, even as Lunahr fears Him and hates Him for all that has been done to him, Lunahr also loves Him. His love for Incuban overrides all else, even his love for you and for Farad," Aras explained.

"For Farad? Lunahr told you Hunter's given name?" Dewalaren asked in disbelief. "He would not have, ever. Did you take the knowledge from him? What do you mean 'rebuild' his core? What have you done to him?"

"Dewalaren, please do not look at me like that! I cannot bear to see fear in your eyes, or revulsion. I have not harmed Lunahr, I swear it. I have not fully healed him yet. But he remembers how to sing now, how to laugh. Dewalaren, you did not know. You could not touch his core. My tree kept you from him. The music had all been burnt away. Everything had been burnt away."

Aras's eyes filled with tears at the memory. "It was horrible, feeling him so altered, after having handled Loruthanar and feeling his true self as it was etched onto the blade. But with his sword, I had a clear and pure template to work from. It is not as if I was guessing who he might have been. I introduced Meloneth to him, when I thought it was safe enough for both of them. Meloneth has aided me. He helped return Lunahr's music to him, to remind him who he is."

"Meloneth? You cannot mean the God of Music! The Gods are not real!" Dewalaren denied, reeling from all he was hearing.

"Man's Gods are real, Dewalaren: Jarnath, Meloneth, Laneth, all of them." His voice sank to a whisper. "I am one of them."

Dewalaren stared at him in horror.

Aras looked desperate. "But Dewalaren, you do not understand! We are not truly Gods. We are not immortal, not exactly, nor all-powerful, not quite. We are Elf Lords, we…. I have said too much, too quickly. I never meant to tell you so much. You are not ready to hear it. You might have been ready, after the gift you will see today, after the hope Lunahr and I will return to you.

"Please, Dewalaren! You must link with me, if you cannot believe me otherwise. But first you must see Lunahr again, and he is in the Urwani City.

"Lunahr is like a brother to me. When I first sensed his true self upon the sword, I knew it, but we have grown very close these past weeks. I never thought I might find someone who might love me so for who I truly am." Aras's face flushed. "He is not afraid of me, as you are. He trusts me."

Dewalaren looked at Aras in revulsion. "You are worse than any of them! You pretend to be noble and compassionate. But it appears you need your own pawns for this sick, twisted Game the four of you are playing. Jargas has taken Farad: he belongs to Incuban now. You think to control me, but worse, you took Lunahr from Incuban, only to use him to your own ends. You have made him love you just as vilely as Incuban has. You calmly speak about having altered his core so I might not recognize even the scraps of him Incuban had left. Then you try to convince me you are helping him!

"What are you after, Aras? What is this Game for? What is the great prize you all seek? What will victory bring? What is worth the price of the lives of the many hundreds of thousands of innocents who have died upon your Game board? Those who have yet to die? It cannot be just the Ring!"

Aras had paled at his words. His voice was but a whisper. "My mother lives only for hatred, for revenge. She does not care for what the other two seek. Arcanus and Incuban…. I cannot reveal to you what they fight for, or why. But I swear to you, Dewalaren, I do not seek what the three of them do. I seek only to protect everyone from the harm they cause in seeking it. I wish only that you might believe me, that you might still love me as you did, before you left, even after you saw the very essence of my core. How can you think me such a monster, with all that I have shown you? But I see it in your eyes. You are truly lost to me, when I thought you were not."

Aras's eyes filled with tears. "You hugged me. You told me you wanted me by your side always. I cannot bear that you do not! Go to the Urwani city, Dewalaren. I had hoped to see your joy, but it is not to be. I will not come with you. I know, instead, what I must do, where I must go. I had not thought myself ready. I had feared what I might lose. But I have already lost it. It does not matter now that I might not survive. Just try to remember, no matter what you see, no matter what you feel, no matter what you hear, that I love you, I will always love you, and I will protect you. I would die to save you, though you will hate me for what I must now do to see you safe." Aras's eyes crackled with silver lightning, and Dewalaren knew true fear as he began to draw his blade, but instead of light there was only darkness.

DEWALAREN felt a wet cloth upon his head and gentle hands tending to him. His eyes snapped opened. A face was scowling down upon him, one he recognized. "Shadala? What happened? Aras!" he cried in fear, and sat up suddenly, wincing and collapsing again. His head felt as if it would split in two.

"So, you remember? You have done great ill this day. You have wronged a friend. You have quite possibly sent him to his death. You are not who we thought you to be. You are King in name only, not in deed. You have wounded Taratur, Lunahr, worst of all, by driving Akarhad, Aras, away as you have. Aras did not even say good-bye to him."

Dewalaren put his hand to his head. He was in agony. It was as if... as if Aras had been battling Arcanus for him again. He turned his eye inward and his heart turned to ice. A tree encased his core again. But this one was different. It was gnarled and twisted, as if it had fought great storms to grow. There were no leaves. It looked cold and hard and strong. There was no life or warmth to it. Aras! Aras had done this to him. Aras must be forced to remove it. He could not be so crippled again.

"Aras. Where is Aras?" Dewalaren asked, and his voice shook with anger and fear.

"Gone. He has left us. You have driven him away. You have forced him to act too soon," Shadala said, glaring at him in hate. "I should kill you for what you have done, but I will not break the Laws Taratur has taught us. You are the King, much as I wish anyone else were in your place.

"Here. You must drink this. It is not the poison it should be—it will instead take away your pain—but it will not dull your thoughts. It will not cloud your mind. You will be able to think more clearly again. Although you did not think clearly before. I do not see how even my medicines can aid you."

Dewalaren eyed her warily. "Thank you, but I would rather not," he said carefully.

Shadala's eyes flashed angrily, but only with the anger of a woman, not an Amontir or a wizard. "Very well, suffer. You deserve your pain. I pity us all, who have waited so long for you. I thought Falara and Veran blessed, that they might witness the coming of the King when they were yet young enough to fight by your side. It shames me that I share your blood with them."

Dewalaren looked at her in confusion. He could not think past the agony in his head, past the terror of Aras attacking him. He did not know how long he might have lain helpless. His body felt strong again, when it should not, but his head was ready to burst. Aras had betrayed him to her. She knew he was King. Aras had betrayed much.

"Laren?" The voice was soft and sweet, full of love and concern, as he remembered it, from so long ago. Dewalaren tensed and looked up. It was Lunahr. But he did not look horrible and twisted. He looked himself again, healthy and whole.

"Shadala, what's wrong with him? What's happened? Falara told me where you were, that you were tending him. She cried when she told me. She wouldn't say anything more. I thought… I thought something terrible had happened to him."

Lunahr approached Dewalaren eagerly, arms outstretched, but Dewalaren shrank from him, remembering cold chains about his throat and Lunahr's mad eyes. Lunahr's hug died stillborn. "Laren? It's all right, didn't they tell you? Aras has healed me." He said it worshipfully.

"Taratur, you are not supposed to be here. You are supposed to be in the City," Shadala scolded him gently, as if she were his mother. "You are still such a child. You are as bad as Akarhad," she said, but her voice caught on his name.

"SHADALA, what's wrong? Why won't you tell me? Where is Aras? I can't imagine him not being here with Laren. I did not think he'd ever let him out of his sight again, with all he's said and what I've seen these many weeks. He was so sad and so scared while Laren was gone, for all he tried to appear brave. He wore so many masks, for his father, for everyone, even for Jarnath, but I saw through all of them. He couldn't fool me as he's fooled everyone else for so long. I know him too well. He's let so few of us into his heart. He is so terrified that we might suffer for him."

To Lunahr's horror, Shadala began to cry, as Falara had. He had never seen her cry. He had not thought she could.

"Akarhad is gone, Taratur. He had to go. He could not say good-bye. He...." She glared accusingly at Dewalaren, but did not say more.

"But... but he can't be gone! He can't leave now, not when Laren's going to meet everyone and I.... I still need him, Shadala. He wouldn't have left when I still need him." He hated that his voice was that of a child, left lost and alone in the dark.

She shook her head. "Talon is here now, Taratur. He will have to help you. He is your King. He can do no less." She said it as if it were a threat.

Lunahr backed up in fear. "No, he can't. He mustn't! Aras warned me that he can't risk touching my core until I am fully well. I'm still a danger to him." He looked at Dewalaren sadly. "I wouldn't ever want to hurt you, Laren. You know I love you. But Incuban would make me and I would do anything He asks me to. I know it's wrong to feel that way, Aras has told me it is, and Leonas and Shadala, but I would do anything to please Him. I know He'd only hurt me again, He only wants to use me, but I want to be used. Even when He punishes me, that is enough, I.... Laren, I'm still so confused! Please tell me Aras isn't truly gone. How am I ever to escape from Him without Aras to guide me? You are no match for Incuban, none of us are. Only Aras can save me from Him."

DEWALAREN swallowed. It was terrible to see Lunahr warring with himself for control. And Aras had convinced Lunahr he was the only one who could help him. "I will help you, Lunahr, somehow. I'll find a way. Now what's all this about me meeting people? What's going on?"

"I can't tell you. You have to come to the City. Once you're in the Hall of History, once you see the tapestries, once they declare themselves to you, you'll be able to believe it. And then... but you must come. I can't say more.

"Please, Laren! You cannot always live in such fear. You must trust someone. I.... I know you can't trust me, and you shouldn't," he said, his face burning in shame. "But you can trust Shadala. Aras did and even High-King Laedrin trusts her, and he never trusts anyone, at least not since Aras took away the change Arcanus made to him. His Tree has helped him, though. The High-King trusts the Grove and Aras now. He doesn't hate Aras anymore. He can't, after all Aras has done for him. The High-King even trusts me, for all I did to save Nalea. He even truly pardoned me for trying to kill him.

"Laren, where did you go? Where have you been? I don't think even Aras knew. He said he didn't, he said he mustn't, that he couldn't, and I believed him."

"I told him when I returned. I was a fool to have told him!" Dewalaren said in Amontirin, so Shadala would not understand, fuming at himself for having revealed such critical intelligence to a potential enemy. "I thought I knew where the Ring was. But I was tricked. I went all the way to the Deathshand for nothing. The Dwarf who led me there lied to Farad and to me. He was a tool of the Enemy, though I did not recognize him as such. I found Stephan's body. I recovered Garalathon, sword of House of Gryphon."

Shadala stiffened but remained silent. She must have only been reacting to his tone, to how upset Lunahr looked. He was speaking Amontirin, and she could not possibly know it. He continued speaking to Lunahr.

"Jargas could not have been Stephan's descendant. Stephan died in the valley with everyone Rowanar led. I have endangered not only Farad by believing Jargas, but others I met, innocents I was trying to help, who I was trying to save: Rion and Tarrell and all their guards. I should have known better! It was folly to hope a member of a dead House might yet be found alive. I'll draw my sword against the next Man who makes such a claim to me," he said, and his eyes flashed with anger.

LUNAHR looked anxiously at Shadala. He had never seen Laren so angry. Laren could not truly mean what he had said, could he? Lunahr had to know for certain. He licked his lips and said timidly, "Even if they have proof you cannot deny? Even if they hold the bands of their Houses?"

"Jargas had a band," Dewalaren said darkly. "It was real, it was House of Gryphon. The Enemy must have had it all along. Stephan's body had not been disturbed, until I dug up his cairn, and the Enemy would have taken his sword as well."

Shadala's eyes widened as Lunahr bit his lip and then spoke in a rush. "What if they had the lost King's Knife? What if they returned it to you and knelt before you and swore their Houses to your service?"

Dewalaren looked at him suspiciously. "What are you saying?"

Lunahr looked at Shadala in dismay. "We'd better show him now, Shadala. He can feign surprise at the Gathering. He'll be surprised enough when he sees the tapestries, and all the Houses. We won't tell him which ones they are, how many survived, how many of us there are now."

Shadala glared at Dewalaren. "I do not want to kneel to him, after what he has done. But, much as I hate him for it, he is my King, as much as he is yours. There are those who hate me as Chieftess who kneel before me. I have always wondered that they can." From under the folds of her red dress

Shadala drew out a dagger, from a concealed sheath, and held it reverently across both hands.

"IT CANNOT be," Dewalaren denied, staring at the all too familiar hilt, the blade the color of copper dipped in blood. It was the stunted twin of the King's Sword he carried. He took it gingerly from her hands.

"Behold the legacy of Albinar, passed by Idare to Alanar, and from his hand to my blessed ancestors. We return the King's Knife to Dewalaren, son of Evanaren, son of Idare, the rightful King of Amontir," Shadala said carefully in Amontirin. Then she rose.

Dewalaren looked from her to the blade in shock. He studied it intently as he held it. The hilt fit his hand as if it were the Sword, and there was the same depression in the hilt, where the stone of the Ring that powered it should go.

Lunahr said, "Aras recognized the blade for what it was. He'd seen your own. I was shocked when he told me he had. You never let anyone see it unmasked. He found out the history from the Knife itself, somehow, and from Shadala, and I filled in the missing pieces for both of them. I also coached Shadala in Amontirin for the ceremony. Few of her people speak it with any proficiency now. Many only knew a handful of words at best. As Chieftess, Shadala knew it far better than most, though much had been lost over the years, and their accents are very pronounced. But they've been eager to learn. They are proud of their dual Urwani-Amontir heritage. I've been holding classes daily now."

"But... but this can't be real," Dewalaren said in denial. "Alanar was killed with the ten Houses he led, two and a half centuries ago."

Lunahr shook his head. "He was crippled in the battle that killed all the new Lords and Ladies, all the adults of the Houses he led, and even most of the older children. But they had hidden the youngest children, with a few of the older ones to guard them. The battle was terrible: both sides decimated each other. Alanar would have died, he should have died, but the Knife wouldn't let him. He made it back to their camp, to the children, though it took him three days to drag himself back to them. Shadala's people swear by him as we swear by Idare. They've all but forgotten Idare, Alanar so holds their hearts.

"The children went out onto the battlefield and rescued the bands and the swords of their Houses from their parents' bodies, but there were hundreds of bodies. They could not bury so many, though they beheaded every last one, as they'd been taught to.

"The oldest child left alive was fifteen. Alanar made sure the oldest ones knew the names of the parents of all the children who yet lived. He noted all of it in the Book of Houses in his own hand, before he died. He reminded them they must try to marry only within their own Houses, as much as they could.

"They abandoned everything but the Book and the tapestries. The Knife soon lost what little Power it held, without the Ring to charge it. It hadn't been able to heal Alanar fully. He was too terribly injured. Without the Power of the Knife, Alanar got worse. He died pretty quickly after that. He was the only one they buried. They knew they must keep the Knife, and they still hoped Rowanar or Felenar might find them. They marched onward. They lost some to predators, some to illness, some to cold. When the Urwani found them, they were half-starved and half-frozen and many were mad with fever, yet still they tried to protect the tapestries and the Book and the Knife. There were forty-one of them left, all ages ten to fifteen. All the littler ones had died. The Urwani took them in and cared for them and nursed them back to health and welcomed them into their tribe.

"They kept to our Laws, to their promise to Alanar. The eldest married only within their own Houses, and most of the others tried to marry within our people, but some of the second sons and the daughters intermarried with the Urwani. They kept careful records, though, in the Book, of all of it. Now even the few pureblood Urwani are recorded there too."

"Forty-one? Forty-one of the three hundred lived? Which Houses? How many are there now?" Dewalaren asked, in dawning excitement.

Lunahr shook his head. "Now you must come. They have waited two hundred fifty years for you to find them, to welcome them home. I'll not take any more of that from them. And you must return the Knife to Shadala, so she can present it to you in front of them."

Return it? After he and his father and his father's father had spent two hundred fifty years searching for it? He would not! He looked at Shadala stubbornly. She glared challengingly back at him.

"Please, Laren?" Lunahr asked. "Shadala is Chieftess and Healer, and her brother Haran is War Leader. He is the Lord of House of Gryphon. They are descendants of Alvan, Stephan's younger brother. Haran is much like Laedrin: he is a hard man, he is respected but not loved, and he does not trust easily. But from what you've told me, you can return Garalathon to their House. Haran will love you for it, and his love is not easily given. And that's only the beginning. I will tell you the rest. I see that I must."

Lunahr took a breath. "Eight Houses survived, eight of the ten. From the forty-one original survivors, there are now two hundred twenty-three pureblood Amontir, over eleven times the number we thought yet lived, and four hundred three of mixed Amontir and Urwani blood, almost Shadala's entire tribe, and I've told you, they've kept careful records of all of it.

"Laren, don't you see what this means? It's not hopeless anymore! We're a city, a people again. We haven't died out as we'd thought we had. We're not alone anymore. And they are strong, Idare, they are strong! They are almost all warriors. Even the farmers, the women, can fight with swords. They've had their own enemies to face over the years. They've not had an easy time of it. They'd lost the art of the bow, but the Elves have taught it to them again. They shoot like the Elves. Even Farad cannot shoot as well as they do! Laedrin and Haran have become like brothers, now, after the fire.

"Don't you see? It will work. We can defeat Incuban now. Laedrin's ready to send half his Army and Navy to the Dwarven Lands with us, under your command. He's planning to lead the other half to the south, so the Enemy can't come easily over the Velmar Mountains and outflank us. Please, you must let Shadala present the Knife to you properly, or it will all fall apart. And for Idare's sake, drink what Shadala's been trying to give you, cousin. I cannot bear to see you in so much pain, when it is all for naught."

Dewalaren stared at the Knife in his hands. All for naught. Idare, what had he done? Aras had found the King's Knife for him, found and saved his long-lost kin from their War with the Elves. He'd forged an alliance between his people and the Elven Army and Navy. But Dewalaren had driven Aras away. And Aras had encased his core in this new cursed tree, and now he would not be able to test any of what he'd been told. He'd have to take it on faith. And Shadala had said Aras was going to his death, and that he was to blame.

Dewalaren knelt before Shadala. "Forgive me, Chieftess! I have lived too long in shadow. I begin to act like one. I return the King's Knife to you and humbly ask that you give me the medicine you offered me before. It cannot ease the pain that is now in my heart, but it might ease the pain in my head, so I do not further harm those who wish only to aid me."

Lunahr swallowed. "Shadala, you should know that I've never seen Laren kneel to anyone before. He has only ever knelt to his father, his King. The pain in his heart must truly be worse than that in his head, for him to kneel to you now. I know he did not mean Aras any harm. Please forgive him. Aras would, were he here. You know he would."

She looked from Lunahr to Dewalaren. "Very well. Rise, my King, and let me help you."

Dewalaren rose and she gave him the medicine to drink. "Now, we must hurry. You must prepare before we go to the City."

"First, there is something I must do," Dewalaren said, and he walked over to Lunahr and hugged him tightly. "I have missed you, Lunahr," he said softly.

Lunahr cried out in joy and returned his hug fiercely. "I love you, Laren."

Dewalaren was most of the way to the Urwani City by the time his head stopped hurting. When he reached the City, it was exactly as Lunahr had described it to him, the ancestral tapestries that had been smuggled out of their homeland, the Book of Houses, the atrociously accented Amontirin, and the hundreds of survivors of the eight Houses: Deer, Goats, Rabbits, Boar, Owls, Beaver, Squirrels and Gryphon. They presented the bands and swords of the two dead Houses, Tortoise and Pumar, to him. He received the King's Knife from Shadala and presented Garalathon to her brother Haran, with a cloth wrapped where the hilt leather should be. The sword would be made whole again soon enough. He spoke of the blade's history to all of those present, and Haran beamed with pride to be the great-grandnephew of Stephan.

Then Dewalaren told them he was leaving for Caramore with the Elven Army and Navy, to begin the march to war against Incuban, the wizard who had driven King Albinar's brother Ebonar to madness and murder two hundred fifty years earlier, the wizard who was responsible for the destruction of their homeland, the massacre of their Lords and Ladies and people, and the systematic slaughter of hundreds of Dwarven Kingdoms, as well as a number of those in the Lands of Men, now. He asked for all who could bear arms to join him, and the response was thunderous. Every man, woman, and child there was eager to march with him.

Afterward, there was a feast, and he did his best to eat, so he would not insult his newly discovered kin.

That night, he lay awake alone in bed, shivering, thinking about all he had gained, but heartsick, for he realized too late what he had lost. Aras's face haunted him. He feared he would never see him again.

It frightened him to know his own heart: that he would trade all his newly found kin, all the Houses, and the King's Knife, all of it, if only Aras would come back safely to him again.

Chapter 8
Betrayals of the Heart

DEWALAREN was reviewing maps in the War Room in the citadel at Caramore. In spite of what Farad had told him, they had been surprised to find it still standing, when they had returned to their abandoned City. They'd fled from Caramore six years ago, when the Enemy discovered their refuge in the mountains, and they thought He would have leveled it to the ground. But Farad had discovered it still stood and named it as the location for his War Council. Farad himself was noticeably absent.

DEWALAREN had, of course, sent scouts to investigate, before marching in with all his men. The Elven scouts had discovered two very edgy Knights of the Watch, whom they had captured easily. Then, to their astonishment, they had been successfully ambushed by nine more Knights and a Captain, who had lain in wait for them. It had been a tense moment, until Thaedrin, the Elven Commander, had produced the message Dewalaren had written for exactly such an occurrence. The twelve Men had been astonished to read that Dewalaren traveled with over three hundred long-lost kinsmen, and a combined Elven Army and Navy of five thousand.

They recognized the hand as his, but still, they'd been cautious. They'd kept the Elves hostage and sent Lord Rolin's younger brother Colin, known as Thistle, back along the Elves' trail. He was linked to his daughter Rowena, called Heather, and she monitored his progress nervously. They had been overjoyed when she told them her father was safe, that it truly was Dewalaren, and all he had written was true. Fortunately, Dewalaren's combined forces had come well provisioned, or they might all have starved.

Dewalaren had been greeted far more warmly than he had expected to be by his people, but Lunahr was greeted far differently than he had thought to be. He had thought he would be welcomed back amongst his people in relief and joy, but instead, he was viewed with open loathing and hostility. Word had spread of his capture by the Enemy and of his crime against the Elves. The other Amontir did not trust him. Of them all, only Rolin, Lord of House of Horses, who went by the name Fennel when in the Lands of Men, would speak to Lunahr.

Dewalaren had hugged Rolin upon seeing him. "I had feared you and Aramis both dead, when I could not find any trace of you in Aralon, or of Aramis in Thenalon. It brought my heart great joy when Colin told me you were here." Dewalaren held a special love in his heart for Rolin, for of all of them, only he had not been among those who had alienated Farad, causing him to flee from his kin.

Rolin embraced Dewalaren strongly in return. "Dewalaren, I am overjoyed to see you looking so well! Much darkness has befallen these lands, and we had feared you might have been lost to us."

Then he grew solemn. "I have not heard from Aramis in over a year, since just before I was forced to flee Aralon. He had already abandoned Thenalon. I had hoped to find him here. But to hear now there are hundreds of us again, eight restored Houses, and to know House of Eagles yet lives as well, that our Lunahr is returned to us! I had thought his voice forever lost to us."

"Then you must tell him so, Rolin," Dewalaren urged. "For he has been hurt terribly by the Enemy, but also by our kin here. I should have realized how they would react, so that I might have warned him. He was ill prepared for such rejection, when everyone has ever only loved him. And he has only just lost two very dear to him, who were helping him, though I hope he may someday see them again."

Leonas was at least safe. He had remained in Nalea, named by Laedrin as the new Lord of the Grove, Protector of the Trees. But Aras.... Dewalaren almost fell to his knees at the knowledge that his paranoia, his foolish doubts, had caused Aras to head into danger prematurely and ill prepared. He was as unworthy of Aras's friendship, his love, as he was of his people's. He only hoped his unforgivable incompetence would not cost the life of another he loved.

LUNAHR sat shivering on the bed in the room he had been assigned to. He felt so alone. He missed Leonas fiercely, and Aras even more so. The three of them had been like brothers. These past weeks had been some of the happiest in his life because of their presence, their warmth. It was as if all of the light was gone from his life now.

Leonas had been promoted by Laedrin to Lord of the Grove, when Lunahr told the High-King that he must go. Leonas's friend Gaius had been made Captain of the Grove Guard, the special unit Lunahr had helped establish before he left, that now guarded the Lords' Grove.

It had been difficult for Leonas to leave his side. Leonas had wanted to accompany Lunahr to Caramore. But how could Lunahr deny his friend the fulfillment of his fondest wish, to be forever amongst the Trees of the Grove?

Aras had gone, without a word. He still did not know what had happened. Shadala had told him only that Laren was to blame. He could not ask Laren what had happened. One glance at Laren's face and he knew he could not. Laren was in agony over Aras.

The march here had gone from unsettling to disturbing to frightening, as Lunahr had felt his Tree Aranahr slipping further and further away, until he could no longer hear him, nor feel him. Aras had broken the Enemy's hold on him as much as he could before he had left. The horrific nightmares had gone, and he had begun sleeping at night again and without needing the shelter of Aranahr's branches. But he still loved Incuban. He still missed Him. He still craved His attentions.

Now that Aras and Aranahr were gone, he had begun to hear faint whispers again, that terrible sweet voice, urging him to do such horrible things. It had started two days before reaching Caramore, the soft voice, as if from very far away. But, Lunahr knew it would grow louder and louder, until his thoughts were no longer his own.

He'd tried to tell Laren, to warn him, but somehow he couldn't. Every time he tried, his tongue wouldn't obey him. It terrified him that he might still be used by the Enemy, that Laren and all of their newly discovered kinsmen might be in danger from him.

His dulcimer lay on the bed beside him. The music would not come. He'd tried to play, but his fingers froze on the strings, and his tongue was stuck as well: he could not sing.

He sat trembling on the edge of the bed. Aras had told him he could know he was free from Incuban by the music, but the music would not come as it should. He should warn Laren; something was wrong.

His brow creased in confusion at the odd thought. Wrong? No, nothing was wrong. And his kin feared him so already. Were he to voice his fears, they would become even colder. He must instead keep silent.

Yes, that was it. He must not tell anyone, lest they begin to worry. He did not want to trouble his kin when they were already so anxious. Instead, he could help his kin. He should go down to the War Room and study the maps Laren had been working on. Perhaps he could aid his kin in their plans. The first step would be seeing all their carefully laid strategies.

He wondered for a moment why the reassuring whispers had frightened him, only a few moments ago. How could he have felt so alone when his beloved Master was always with him? He caressed his own cheek with his hand and nuzzled against his palm. It would be so good to see Incuban again, to feel Him again. He had missed Him so desperately.

Laren was selfish to have kept him from Incuban, especially when he had so many new kinsmen to keep him company. He had no time for Lunahr, now that so many kinsmen fawned upon him. Lunahr must tell Incuban all he could about them, especially about those among them who might wield great Power.

Lunahr felt an irrational stab of fear, of panic, but it quickly subsided. There was no need to be afraid. Incuban would protect him, always.

Incuban had missed him in His bed. He had something special planned for him, when He came to Caramore.

Lunahr began heading for the War Room, eager to please his lover. Incuban wanted to hear more about Aras on the way, the evil wizard who had kept the wonderful dreams away.

Lunahr's brow crinkled. Aras wasn't evil. He'd been Lunahr's friend. He'd helped him somehow. It had been something important. Why couldn't he remember?

Was Aras his given name? It must be. Aras had shared so many secrets with him. He would not have kept that from him. His true name must be High-Prince Aras, son of High-King Laedrin, mustn't it? He could ask Laren. Laren would know.

No. He mustn't speak with Laren. Laren had important things on his mind, and no time for his young cousin. Incuban had spent so much time with him. He always had time for him. Lunahr knew he had been His favorite. His heart began hammering as he remembered all the delights Incuban had shared with him.

Incuban had time for Lunahr now as well. He wanted him.

Lunahr barely made it to the privy before his hands began pulling at the drawstring of his pants. There was time for some fun, before the maps.

Incuban guided his hand. It was so wonderful to be touched again. He had not pleasured himself even once while in Nalea. Aras wouldn't let him.

Aras was so mean. Lunahr was glad he was gone. He hoped Aras never came back.

Incuban had many plans to keep Aras from coming back. His beloved Master shared them all as He guided Lunahr's hand skillfully upon his manhood.

Lunahr's heart pounded as Incuban shared one of his wondrous visions: Aras in chains, on his knees before Incuban's feet, pleasuring him with his mouth while Lunahr wielded the barbed whip that lashed him. It was so real!

He could feel the sweat-slicked leather in his hand, smell the sweet tang of the blood, taste the passion that permeated the very air they breathed.

Lunahr was brought to his knees by the intensity of his orgasm. But he must not tarry. He stole only a few exquisite moments to lick the sweet cream from his hand. Then he laced up his pants again and splashed cool water upon his face.

He felt flushed, radiant, as he exited the privy and headed for his goal. He could not wait for Incuban to take him with His own hand, His own mouth, and something far more wonderful than either.

But later. Now he must tell Incuban all about Aras, and his new kin, and show him the maps.

Oh yes, Master! Anything to please you, he thought, but was careful not to voice his thoughts as he saw others in the hallway.

He heard Incuban's laughter and felt warm all over, knowing he was pleasing Him. Lunahr could hear how happy He was.

"MAJESTY, we have captured three people at the perimeter. They claim to have an urgent message for you. They say they know you," Elven Army Captain Darian reported. "They were armed, but they put up no resistance. They surrendered themselves to us without a fight." His voice was tinged with scorn, indicating he would not have been so easily captured.

"Have they told you their names?" Dewalaren asked.

"No. They were afraid of us. They would not tell us their Kingdom, nor their names, but they appear to be of the same family, and they are from one of the River Kingdoms," he said disdainfully, Laedrin's prejudice strong in his words.

Dewalaren's surprise turned to excitement. River Elves! Of course! He should have realized. Darian had said "people," not "Men," as he would have. Few Elves had known of this City, before he had led the soldiers here.

The Captain described them in detail and Dewalaren's face lit with relief and joy. Elavar, Elanara, and Eladar: it must be! But as always, he must proceed cautiously. The belated realization they might only be shadows that walked in their forms chilled him. It might be only their bodies. He might be welcoming a trio of Resemblants into their midst.

"Bring them to the Audience Chamber, under heavy guard, but do not harm them. We will watch them from the walls. Man every arrow slit, but as a precaution, only." He knew a moment's confusion, when Darian did not move to do his bidding and then remembered to add, "Dismissed." He should know by now none of the Elves under his command would ever leave his presence without him saying so.

"Yes, Majesty," Captain Darian said, immediately leaving to carry out Dewalaren's orders.

Dewalaren felt his excitement grow, and banked it. Elavar, Elanara, and Eladar were not dead, although both Riviera and Loatia had fallen. He'd read the soldiers' grim reports in Nalea. Laedrin had given him full access to them.

Many thousands were dead or missing. Dewalaren had been horrified to read of the burning of both Cities and the Library, of the entire Wood, and the damming of the Methris River. He had thought the Royal Family among those lost until he had read a report that Eladar and Elanara were being held in protective custody in Erenia. Elanara had been awaiting his return, but Eladar had been brought there only recently, barely alive, though Dewalaren was relieved beyond measure to learn Eladar had since fully recovered.

He read the interrogator's report, eager to hear all the details. He was astonished to read it was Rion's caravan that had found Eladar in the Coroden Mountains. They had rescued him from a tribe of ogres there and brought him to Erenia to be healed. Dewalaren was greatly relieved to learn Rion and Tarrell and the others they traveled with were alive and well, and that they had been sent safely on their way. Unfortunately, Jargas had been released with them. If only he had known! If only the Elves had kept him captive! But at least Jargas had not harmed those he professed to guard.

Dewalaren had despaired that though Elanara and Eladar had survived, Elavar must have been lost. He knew Elavar would never have left his father's side, nor left his people in such danger. Yet now it appeared he had, that he was here, he was safe. It was too good to be true. That was why he was suspicious of them, why he was proceeding so cautiously. It was indeed too good to be true. The Enemy must have a hand in their miraculous appearance. Elanara and Eladar should still be in Erenia, and Elavar should be dead. He would watch and listen and learn.

The Elven soldiers were at the ready. He secreted himself behind a small panel, opened it silently, and then signaled his readiness. A few moments later, the prisoners were led into the Audience Chamber.

Dewalaren's heart began hammering as he saw Elanara, as lovely as he remembered her. It was truly her, truly all of them. Their bodies, at least. He forced the thought away and watched. The soldiers closed the door behind them, leaving them alone in the room.

ELANARA began shivering, holding her arms, trembling, and Eladar put his arm around her. The soldiers had taken their cloaks when they had taken their weapons and searched them. Elanara had stood proudly as she felt their hands upon her. She knew she could not react adversely to their search, that it was all Elavar and Eladar could do to watch them touch her without intervening. But she trembled now, in the cold of the stone room, in memory of their hands upon her, and in growing despair and fear. "I do not think Talon is even here," she said, despondently.

HEARING her voice and her words, it was all Dewalaren could do to keep from calling out to her to reassure her, from hastening to her side to hold her, to comfort her, to warm her.

"He had better be here. I refuse to have freed the two of you from Erenia, only to see the three of us imprisoned by the soldiers here," Elavar said angrily.

Dewalaren was surprised. He had never seen Elavar angry before. Elder Elves seldom angered, and Elavar was almost five hundred fifty. Elavar made it sound as if Elanara and Eladar had been prisoner in Erenia, and he suddenly wondered what form the "protective custody" had taken. Surely Elanara had not been held in the dungeon there? Had she been chained? Mistreated? He angered at the thought.

"It's far worse than that," Elanara said. "They tried to conceal the scope of their numbers from us, but we saw enough entering the City to know that there are not hundreds of soldiers here, but thousands. Think what will happen when Jargas's Dwarven army reaches here! Regardless of what their commanders have in mind, one misstep by either side and this City will be reduced to a blood-soaked battleground. The carnage... there will be thousands dead on both sides. We must warn the Army."

"Warn them?" Eladar scoffed. "Let them die! Let them destroy each other! What use are the soldiers? Did they save Riviera? Or Loatia?"

Dewalaren listened, appalled. That could not truly be Eladar speaking. The voice was his, but the words.... Then Dewalaren saw the tears fall. "Did they save Mother? Or Father? All our people? The River itself, the trees?" A sob escaped him and Elanara hugged him tightly.

"Hush, Eladar. We yet live. Riviera is not truly gone, while the three of us survive," she soothed.

Eladar laughed, a terrible laugh, nothing like the one Dewalaren remembered, as Eladar yanked away from his sister's arms. "Three of us! Talon may not have your heart, Sister, but you think as one. You are as deluded as he is, believing his twenty kinsman are still a Kingdom! Lords of the Great Houses: charnel houses, houses of bone and ash, of rotting corpses that walk like men. But you are right. Maybe we will yet see Mother and

Father again, if the Enemy has use for their burnt bodies. Maybe you'll feel Father's arms around you again, Sister."

"Stop it!" Elanara shouted, her hands over her ears, falling to her knees with a sob.

Elavar grabbed Eladar by the shoulders and shook him. "Enough! I have heard all I will from you! I never would have freed you, if I'd known what you've become! When Rion told me what had happened, I had been proud of you, for nearly giving your life to save his, for helping them even as you lay dying, for finding a voice to save the Watch, to relay your message, when your own voice had been silenced. Now, I wish the ogres who'd held you had eaten you. That the other one who attacked you had squeezed harder. I wish you'd died in the mountains. I wish Rion had never saved you. I wish the soldiers had killed you. I wish you'd burnt to death with Riviera, with Father and Mother and all our people!" Elavar was quivering with rage and he was shaking Eladar so violently Dewalaren thought he might snap his neck.

"Stop it! Stop it! I can't bear it, Elavar! I can't...." Elanara begged, pulling ineffectually at his arm.

Dewalaren was at the door to the room in a heartbeat, and he flung it open as the Elven soldiers hastily took up protective positions behind him.

Dewalaren was surprised to see Eladar and Elavar interpose themselves between him and Elanara, ready to face whatever new danger had come for them. So, some scrap of the Eladar he had known remained. He still loved his sister enough to protect her, even if he somehow also took sick pleasure in hurting her.

"Stand aside. I will see my intended," Dewalaren commanded.

Elavar bowed slightly and stood aside. Eladar glared at Dewalaren. Their eyes locked for a moment, but then Eladar looked down and away.

Dewalaren sighed. Eladar's eyes revealed much to him. He was in agony from all he had lost. His anger could not mask his pain.

Dewalaren gazed into Elanara's eyes and felt the familiar pain in his heart. There was no love in her eyes to match his own. Her heart was still cold and dead to him. He took her in his arms anyway and winced as he felt her stiffen in his embrace, when he ached to feel her melt into his arms. He let go of her. "I trust you haven't been ill-treated by the soldiers," Dewalaren said, walking coolly to his throne and sitting, forcing them to stand before him.

"Not here, no," Elanara said. "But Talon, we've no time for niceties. We've come with a warning for you, from Rion."

Elavar's face flushed. "Actually, Elanara, we've come with two. But the second is for Talon's ears only. I could not even tell you or Eladar. But that one, I think, can wait. The other cannot."

ELANARA was looking at Elavar in surprise. He had spoken their given names before the Elven soldiers here, yet he had not spoken Dewalaren's. Perhaps he strove to put them on equal footing with the soldiers? She would follow his lead. "You should tell him, Elavar. Rion spoke it to you."

ELAVAR nodded. Without further preamble, he spoke. "I met your friend Rion, in Salenia. He recognized me as kin to Elanara and Eladar, and asked if I knew how to get in touch with you, as you are Elanara's betrothed. When I told him I would be seeing you shortly, he gave me a warning for you.

"He said he and his guards had come across a Dwarven army to the south. The army is comprised of soldiers of the thirty Western Kingdoms, survivors of the Lost Kingdoms, survivors we had never known about. The army is being led by Jargas, one of Rion's former guards—he said you know him—and by your kinsman, Hunter. Rion told me Hunter had saved his life in Gosa, when he was taken by thieves for ransom. He said Hunter had been in Gosa searching for Jargas, and that Hunter had told him he was ill. Rion said it seemed to him that Hunter was going mad. I can give you more detail later, in private."

Dewalaren nodded, his face pale, his hands clenched into fists. Jargas had told him Farad had gone mad in the Dwarven Lands, but he no longer knew what he should believe.

Elavar continued. "Rion said when he saw Hunter on the road, only a few weeks later, his eyes were completely different than they had been. And Hunter was married, in only those few weeks' time, to a Dwarven Lady, Jarina, Jargas's sister."

Dewalaren stared at Elavar, astonished. Farad had married? He could not possibly, both for the state of his mind and the state of his body. And it was against their Laws to marry without the King's approval, to ensure preservation of the Houses.

"Rion said...." Elavar hesitated and eyed Dewalaren oddly. Dewalaren was stunned at the hesitation, for it was not something Elves ever do and he and Elavar had been close friends, almost as brothers, for years. "Rion said he'd seen Jargas's eyes burn, and Jargas had told him Hunter's burned as well. Rion thinks the Captains of the Watch have Power akin to wizardry and he thinks Jarina might have it too." Elavar's eyes never left Dewalaren's. "He's afraid Jargas or Jarina has entranced Hunter.

"Rion asked them if they might be seeing you again. He'd trusted them at first, and thought they might relay the other message I bear for you. But they acted strangely, and when he asked if it was you they were marching against, they did not deny it. Far from it. Their reaction frightened him. But Rion was able to trick them into thinking it was safe for them to let him go, that he was no danger to them."

Dewalaren was stunned. This was worse than his wildest fears. Not only was Hunter lost to him, but a Dwarven army marched against him! "Do you know how large an army, or if they know where we are or have any idea when they might arrive?"

"They know. They are marching to the Fromer Mountains. Rion estimated at least fifteen thousand soldiers, perhaps even as many as twenty thousand. He said he saw dozens of banners and many thousands of troops, armed and armored and well supplied. He described some of the heraldic bearings to me. It is how I know they are of the Lost Kingdoms. At the rate they were coming, we will have beaten them by a day, at the least, three at the most, for it took time to free my siblings in Erenia. I was able to sneak in with some of the refugees from Riviera and Loatia. We escaped in the resulting madness.

"The soldiers there were overwhelmed. The entire City of Erenia was. There were so many injured, burns, terrible burns, and their eyes.... Even those who were not injured, without the trees, our River, they were dying, all of them, hundreds upon hundreds." He shivered and looked away.

Dewalaren shuddered. No wonder they were so scarred! To see such horror, all that was left of their people, and to have to flee instead of aid them! He must find a way to help them. But for now, there was not the time.

"At least we have some warning, some small time to prepare. Elavar, I need to speak further with you, but Elanara and Eladar should rest. The soldiers will escort you. But I want you to know, you are not being held here. High-King Laedrin has given me command of these squadrons. You are free to go whenever you choose to. But for now, it's safest to stay with us, I think."

Elanara nodded wearily, but Eladar said, "If I'm not a prisoner, then I want my knife and bow returned to me. When I die, I will at least die fighting."

Dewalaren frowned at him, but turned to the Captain. "Return their weapons to them, and Elavar's as well, once he leaves my presence. Dismissed."

The Captain nodded and escorted Elanara and Eladar out.

"Tell me, Elavar, before I hear more of the Dwarves, and of Rion and your journey, what is your other message?" Dewalaren asked.

"I cannot tell you here. Even if you send away these others, there are guards at the arrow slits listening to our every word, even now, as you were earlier. I realized it, even if my sister and brother did not," Elavar said.

Dewalaren eyed him shrewdly. "Yet you did not temper your words to Eladar. Or did you seek to trick me into trusting you?"

Elavar shook his head and said softly, "No. I did not. I spoke from my heart. It is a terrible thing to wish someone you still love dead."

Dewalaren eyed Elavar carefully. He thought Elavar told him the truth. He hoped he did. He could not test Elavar. "Come, we will speak in my room. If it is monitored, I know it not. I think it is not."

"How about the parapet? I think you underestimate the fervor of the soldiers who serve you," Elavar suggested.

"You would not seek to cast me from it, I hope?" Dewalaren asked, forcing a smile. He could not trust Elavar as he once had. He could not trust anyone, after what Aras had done to him. He had attacked him and crippled his Power.

He sighed. Aras had done it because he had not trusted Aras.

Dewalaren escorted Elavar down the corridor to the stairs to the tower, careful to stand at his side instead of in front of him, where his back might provide too tempting a target. He cursed that he did so, but did not alter his position. He waved away the soldiers who intended to accompany them up the stairs.

Elavar was silent until they reached the top of the staircase and were outside.

Dewalaren stayed away from the edge, close to the door, again cursing himself for his lack of trust, but not willing to take the risk that Elavar might not be all he appeared.

Elavar looked at him intently. "I will not harm you, my friend. I cannot hate you as Eladar does."

"Eladar hates me?" Dewalaren asked, incredulous. "Whatever for? I have never harmed him!"

Elavar shook his head. "No, but your Enemy has. He blames you for Incuban's attack upon Riviera and Loatia. He is no longer the brother I once loved, yet I love him still. I have tried to help him, but I cannot. There was a time I would have thought the wizards might help him, but now I can hold no such hope in my heart. Which brings me to Rion's second message. But, before I speak it, I must know, are any of The Three here in Caramore? Arcanus or Circe or Magus?"

Dewalaren stiffened. "No." He did not elaborate.

Elavar seemed intrigued. "Perhaps this message is not the surprise I thought it to be, then. I have never before seen fear in your eyes, Talon. Something has happened. Have they already acted against you, somehow?"

Dewalaren was silent.

Elavar continued. "Rion told me Arcanus has lost his Power, Magus has been compromised by Incuban, and Circe has turned to darkness, though she even now struggles back toward the light. Rion told me Circe kept Arcanus from killing him, for knowing too much about them, then whispered a message for you, that Arcanus must never again hold the Ring."

Dewalaren was shocked. "Rion, the boy I rescued from wolven-riders? But he has no Power, nor ties to any of us! How can he have become such a crucial piece that even the wizards use him to their own ends? How can he possibly know more than I about the wizards?"

Elavar told him all Rion had said to him. Dewalaren shook his head in stunned disbelief. "I had no idea what I did, saving Rion. I thought him a helpless innocent. It is fortunate he appears to be on our side, for he makes a surprisingly formidable enemy!" Dewalaren forced a humorless laugh, but it ended abruptly when he saw how solemn Elavar appeared.

"There is something more, something you are not telling me, about Rion," Dewalaren said shrewdly. "He is, in some way, my enemy after all."

Elavar sighed. "I had never met anyone as perceptive as you, Talon, until I met him. You have guessed it. There is something more, but it is not my place to tell you. Elanara is the bearer of that message, but she is in no condition right now to deliver it. Please do not ask her to. She will speak to you as soon as she is able."

Dewalaren was puzzled by his words, but nodded in agreement.

"I have told you all I know of the Dwarves. It is up to your people and our soldiers now, but I would yet aid you if I could. My father always welcomed my counsel as sound," Elavar said, his voice wistful.

Dewalaren nodded and clasped his arm. Elavar was still the Elf whose friendship he had valued so highly, in spite of all that had transpired. "As have I, Elavar. I know I cannot replace what you have lost, but you will always have a place with us, as long as you are in need of one."

"Thank you, Talon. That being the case, I can address you as an equal no longer, for I am a Prince without a people, without a Kingdom, and you are a Prince who has become a King. It would be my honor to swear to you as my new King."

"You truly wish to?" Dewalaren asked, incredibly moved.

"I do," Elavar said. He knelt to him and swore oath to him, holding out his empty arms as if they held a bow.

"Come, my friend! We must form a strategy to stand against three to four times our number, without slaughtering each other to oblivion. I think I have a way. At the least, it will keep my newly discovered kin safe. We must go to the War Room. The maps are there."

Elavar followed him.

Dewalaren was surprised to find Lunahr inside, studying one of the maps so intently he did not hear them enter.

"Lunahr!" Elavar cried in shock. He was so overcome he actually ran to Lunahr and embraced him.

LUNAHR returned the hug, glad for the distraction. It gave Incuban time to tell him what to say, if they questioned his presence in the room. "Elavar!" Lunahr responded, in feigned joy.

"I had thought you lost to us, from what Elanara and Rion told me," Elavar said, sounding stunned.

"Elanara! Is she here as well? And Eladar?" Lunahr asked, excited, without any prompting from Incuban. He had never thought to see any of them again, not after.... Something had happened. Something horrific. Something about Riviera. He felt a brief flash of pain and terror, but Incuban quickly calmed him.

"Yes, they are both here, both well. They will be so happy to see you! But Lunahr, what happened to you? We heard such terrible things!"

The smile fled Lunahr's face as Elavar's troubling words haunted him. Something terrifying had happened to him. Why couldn't he remember?

"It's all right, Lunahr. We don't need to talk about it now. Why don't you go out into the sun for a while? Elavar and I have work to do in here," Dewalaren said patronizingly.

He might as well have patted him upon the head and said, "Go outside and play while the adults talk." Lunahr's resentment flared, burning away his doubts and fears. Laren was always pushing him aside, ignoring him, treating him like a lost little boy, when he was as much a man as any of them! He was more.

They were all so weak, pale imitations of the glory of the Faeren. But he was different. Both his parents had been House of Eagles. He alone was born of the pure perfection of the Houerfashang, untainted by inferior Latent blood. He had all the beauty of feature and form, the delicious Power, combined with the warm potential of a full-blooded Aerta Lord. The Aerta, those of the Wood, were born to feed the Faeren, to be consumed by their eternal living flame. Lunahr alone of all his kin was blessed to be born to fuel Incuban's unquenchable desire. There could be no more noble purpose. Laren and the rest of his pathetic kin were mere playthings, disposable minor amusements at best, worthy only of his scorn, so easy to deceive, to manipulate at his whim.

"I want to help too. Please Laren? You're treating me like a child," Lunahr said sullenly, Incuban guiding his voice to ensure he sounded just right, that he did not reveal the depths of his loathing.

DEWALAREN desperately wished he could fully trust his young cousin, but Aras had warned him Lunahr was not yet free of Incuban's influence, though he'd seen no sign of it. He wished again that Aras had not left him so helpless. It would be so easy to touch Lunahr's core, to know his heart, did the tree not imprison him. Yet still he cherished it, in all its cold, twisted barrenness. Its very presence meant Aras yet lived.

"LAREN, what's wrong?" Lunahr asked without prompting, his hand reaching out to his older cousin, as a bright flash of love momentarily overcame his resentment. "You look so sad."

"It is nothing, Lunahr. Please don't worry about me. I have received some troubling news. We must prepare for a battle, though I yet hope to avoid it. I won't say more, I've said too much already. Please, Lunahr, you cannot stay here. Elavar and I must talk."

"Oh. I understand. You can't trust me anymore, either. You said you did, but you don't." He tried to sound as dejected as he could, but it was hard, with Incuban laughing. He wanted to laugh, too. It was such a fun game, tricking Laren like this. But he played his role well. "It's all right, Laren. I can't blame you for hating me too," he said, turning away with a big sniff, as if he might cry at any moment.

"Lunahr, wait!" Laren said, intercepting him, clasping his arm, man to man. "I don't hate you. I love you, as the rest of your kin yet do as well. You will see. And of course I trust you. If it means so much to you, you can stay."

Lunahr beamed at him. It had worked; Dewalaren had believed him! He could feel how happy Incuban was with him. It made it easy to smile.

Laren had the guards wake Rolin and call him in, too, to help plan their strategy.

Rolin appeared surprised to see Lunahr there, but was friendly toward him, though Incuban made sure Lunahr saw that Rolin treated Elavar as more of an equal than his own kinsman.

They formed their battle strategies. All their people save for a few of the Lords would draw back from the City. The Elves would remove all signs of their presence. They and the bulk of the Amontir would hide in the mountains and surround the Dwarven army, once it entered the valley. Then they'd ask to parlay. With five thousand Elven bows trained upon the Dwarves from the high ground, the army would be forced to surrender to them. Dewalaren, Elavar, Rolin, Lunahr, and Fenris would confront Farad and Jargas and their men. Laren did not want to risk revealing any of the new Lords, any of their recently rediscovered kin. The Elves would man the arrow slits of the Audience Chamber during the peace accords. If necessary, they'd be ready to slay the others.

DEWALAREN was surprised at how readily Lunahr accepted the necessity that Farad might need to be slain. He had once loved Farad as a brother. He had only been twelve when Farad had left. It had been twelve long years since he'd seen him, but still Dewalaren was disappointed to see Lunahr's love for Farad had apparently dimmed with time and distance.

DEWALAREN did not see the battle raging inside Lunahr, as love for his elder cousin coursed through him like a flood quenching a raging inferno. Concern for all his kin struggled to the surface of his core like a drowning man making one final desperate effort to breathe, to live.

Please, Master! If I went to Farad, I know I could make him listen! So many will die if I don't! Farad and Laren. All of them might! Lunahr thought desperately.

Incuban laughed. *Let them. I will have over six hundred new Amontir to play with, to teach! I grow weary of these others.*

But Master..., Lunahr entreated.

Do not make me tire of you, too, Lunahr. You remember what happened the last time you annoyed me, do you not? Incuban said, the voice in his core going from silk to flame in a heartbeat.

Please, Master! I'll be good! Don't send me away again! Don't deny me your love! Lunahr begged, and he began trembling.

Dewalaren startled him by hugging him. Lunahr jumped at his unexpected touch. "Courage, Lunahr! I thought you no longer cared what happened to Farad. I should have realized you were trying to appear a man in my eyes. But you need not hide your love for him. Men should love their kin. They should be tormented when the men they love are in danger, especially when they are the ones who endanger them. Oh, Lunahr, what will I do without Farad? He was my strength. I thought before I had lost him, and now I truly have," Dewalaren said despondently.

"I will be your strength, now, Laren, for as long as you need me," Lunahr swore.

"You are more than that. I once named Farad my Heir, and you after him, should I fall. Elavar, Rolin, I say it now, you must bear witness, and I will say so before the other Lords later, when we tell them our plans. I hereby name Farad, Lord of House of Wolven, a traitor to our people and to the Crown and strip him of the title of Heir and of Lord. House of Wolven now joins the ranks of the dead Houses. And I name Lunahr as my Heir, should I fall. Do you both so witness?"

"Yes, Majesty," they said in unison.

Lunahr hugged Dewalaren tightly. "I never want to be King, Laren. I never want to lose you," he said, with his own voice, the voice of a boy.

Then he took a deep breath and straightened. "But if it is my fate to do so, I will lead our people as well as I am able," he said, with the confidence and dignity of a man. Dewalaren would have been horrified to know it was Incuban speaking, not Lunahr.

Incuban was laughing inside Lunahr in glee. *We will have plans of our own, Lunahr. But first, we must hear all of theirs. You must listen carefully.*

"I SHOULD be with the scouts," Farad said testily.

"No, Husband. Your place is here. It is bad enough we might lose Donovar. But he, of any of us, is most likely to succeed against our kin, since you and Desmond and Jargas refuse to let me or Desenia go, and we could not risk any of you." Jarina knew the true reason for her husband's anxiety. He wanted to confront his kin as quickly as possible. The long march had been excruciating for him. He feared Dewalaren and others of his kin might not survive the coming confrontation.

And he had not been the only one with doubts. Jarina was touched that her brother still sought her counsel, and her comfort, when he might have sought only Desenia's instead.

JARGAS had come to her questioning why he should seek the throne, when he did not want it, and Dewalaren did.

"Because you are Heir. You are the True King. Farad has told me they hold their Law of Succession most sacred of all their Laws. You will make a good King, Jargas," Jarina assured him.

"Aye, but I'd make a better King of Malar, someday, when Father passes, may Ragnar keep from calling him too soon. I do not see how I can be King to both," Jargas said with a sigh.

"Your son can rule Malar," she said, carefully hiding her pain. She would never conceive, never know the joy of a child inside her. Nor of her husband inside her. She was angered then, that she so dishonored Farad with such a thought, when he would give anything to be able to please her so.

"I am sorry, Sister. I did not mean to make you angry with me. I know you have burdens of your own, though you will not share them with me," Jargas said sadly. He rose to go, but her hand on his arm stopped him.

"Do not go, Jargas. I am not angry with you, I am angry at myself," Jarina admitted. "I would share my burden with you, if I could, but I cannot. Can you not understand how it hurts me, that I cannot? But you cannot aid me in this, Jargas."

"Aye, I know it is so, though I do not understand why. I am sorry, Jarina, for adding to the burden of your heart, when I would instead lighten it, if I could."

"You will ease my burden by letting me help ease yours," Jarina soothed. "I understand Dewalaren is a good King. But he is not a stable one. You have witnessed him fall to Madness. Farad has told me he has fallen twice before the incident you witnessed. Each time, he has relied upon another to save him. The first time, he tried to slay the Lords he loves, his own people. The last time, he almost killed you, and you are also a Lord and his kin. You do not share his weakness, though your Power of mind equals his own. Further, your power of body far surpasses his. Your skill with your staff exceeded his with a sword. And you recognize the danger of the wizards, when he yet seeks their counsel. You will make a better King."

"But I know little of their history or language, or of their Enemy," Jargas argued.

"Farad and Desmond already teach you. You do not love our grandsire's people any less for never having met them. Nor they you. Both Farad and Desmond acknowledge you as True King. Neither is easily swayed. You must have the faith in yourself that others have in you. Even Farad marveled at how you stood against Incuban, innocent and untrained."

"Aye, I had the raw Power, but Farad had the skill," Jargas admitted reluctantly.

"A King is always aided by his people. And when facing such a powerful Enemy, strength is no small thing," Jarina countered.

"You would make a better King, I think," he said, smiling grimly, but Jarina shook her head.

"No. I am a good Chieftess. Ogres and obearn do not frighten me. But the Enemy of the Amontir does. Incuban terrifies me. I'd not stand against him. I've not the strength." She bit back the rest. Nor the experience. She had only the nightmare memories she had viewed in Desenia's core. Her innocence was a dangerous liability, a vulnerability she could not reveal, one Incuban would eagerly exploit. She shivered.

"He'll never take you, Jarina, I swear it," Jargas said, with such fierce protectiveness she had to smile.

Jarina kissed him on the cheek. "Go to your wife, Jargas. I'll not have her jealous of me as I was of her."

Jargas nodded and smiled and hugged her. "And you take care of Farad for me. I worry for him, without my link to him."

Farad had severed it, after speaking with Donovar and Desmond. He was linked only to her, now. Jarina nodded and smiled reassuringly, then sighed once Jargas left. She worried for Farad as well. The next few days would be a terrible trial for him. She hoped her aid might be enough.

DONOVAR scowled at the Elven bowmen surrounding him and his men. The plan had been that if the Amontir guarding the City tried to use their Power upon them, he would pretend to succumb with the rest and then take the Lord or Lords off guard. Twenty-four Elven bowmen were completely unexpected.

He and his men had been effectively ambushed en route to Caramore. Two-thirds of the Elves wore concealing cloaks the gray of the rock surrounding them, though patterned to mimic a riverbed. The remaining eight wore brown cloaks, in the pattern of tree bark. They had kept to the back, their camouflage not as effective in this terrain.

Donovar had never heard of Elves such as these. They had the look and bearing of soldiers. Beneath the hood of the bark-patterned cloak of the Elf facing him with drawn bow, he saw the gleam of a metal helm, and where his cloak gapped, plate mail over a forest-green tunic and brown leggings. The Elves with the gray river-rock-patterned cloaks wore blue tunics and silvery-gray leggings. He wondered what the significance of the clothing colors might be, if any, and realized as he studied them that the Elves in green and brown all had blond hair and the ones in blue and gray had silver hair.

"Drop your axes and you won't be harmed," the brown-cloaked Elf before him repeated impatiently in Common, his green eyes cold and piercing.

Donovar and his men were surrounded and outnumbered. "Do as he says," Donovar commanded, laying his own axe upon the ground.

His men reluctantly complied.

"You will come with us," he said to Donovar. "Haerin, take the others," he commanded, and one of the other brown-cloaked soldiers stepped forward.

"You'll not be taking Donovar anywhere without us," Lornan said, imposing himself protectively between Donovar and the Elven Commander, even as his other men braced for a battle they could not win.

The Commander scowled at him as his men stiffened, and Donovar quickly intervened. "Lornan, you'll do as commanded, unless you wish to face me as your enemy next. And you can guess what I might do to you."

To Commander Thaedrin's surprise, the disobedient Dwarf laughed. "Forgive me, Donovar! I've no doubt I'll see you safe, and soon."

Thaedrin's men and Theodas's all looked warily at the two Dwarves.

"Don't worry, lad, I'll not harm you," the Dwarven Commander assured him arrogantly and then had the unmitigated audacity to laugh heartily. Thaedrin had misgivings about bringing this prisoner before the King, but he had been so ordered, and would obey.

Donovar's jovial air belied his thoughts. This had been completely unexpected. Where were the Amontir, and what were Elven soldiers doing so near their City? It was fortunate he'd been able to convince Desmond he should go, for the protective shield about his core. Now he'd need all his wit and skill at strategy and diplomacy, skills and experience even Desmond, close friend that he was, did not dream he possessed. He must try to see that there was no bloodshed, if possible.

He doubted these soldiers were here alone. They were too confident by far. There might well be an entire army of them. And it was as if they had expected the Dwarven scouts. They'd purposefully lain in wait for them and then surrounded them so quickly they had no hope of escape.

Donovar steeled himself for what was to come. He'd no wish to be interrogated by Elves. He'd heard of their methods.

Six of the Elves accompanied Donovar: their Commander, one other in brown, and four in gray. The other eighteen left separately, with all of Donovar's men.

After taking him a short distance from his men, far enough so they were out of hearing, the Elf said, "Now we will search you, and you will be blindfolded."

"Blindfolded? Why?" Donovar asked.

The Elven Commander sighed. "You are our prisoner," he said, as if talking to a backward child.

"Oh, sorry, I forgot," Donovar said, laughing.

"Search him carefully," the Commander said, scowling.

The Elves searched his person thoroughly after removing his healer's kit. They searched it just as thoroughly.

"What's all this?" the other Elf in green and brown asked, holding up a phial suspiciously.

"I'm a healer. I thought it best to bring my medicines with me," Donovar replied.

"A healer!" the Elf scoffed. "Leave it to the Dwarves to send a healer to do a soldier's work!"

"Leave it to the Elves to insult someone they should be treating with respect," Donovar retorted.

The Elf eyed him warily. Donovar could see how frustrated he was that Donovar refused to play the part of cowed prisoner.

"If you would permit my touch, I will blindfold you now," one of the four Elves in blue and gray said solicitously. The Elven Commander scowled at him.

"Your courtesy is much appreciated. You may blindfold me," Donovar replied.

The Commander snorted. "He speaks to you as if he were a King!"

Donovar was glad for the blindfold that had dropped to conceal his eyes. They might otherwise have betrayed his sudden pain at the Elf's words, as memory of Armsguard and all he had lost unexpectedly tried to overwhelm him at the simple retort. He began breathing deeply.

"Bind his arms as well," the Commander said, in vicious satisfaction.

Donovar stiffened, his heart pounding in sudden terror as sweat broke out over his body, and he fought to keep from trembling. "I will not try to escape. You've my word as a Dwarf. I would rather not be bound."

Rough hands jerked at his and he fell to his knees at the feeling of rope against his wrist. "I swear to Ragnar I will not try to escape. Please, you cannot," he begged, fighting to keep from attacking them, knowing at least half of them would not survive it, nor would he. He would not fail Desmond, but he could not be bound. Never again.

"No! You heard him. You'll not bind him," the courteous Elf argued.

Donovar clung to the promise of the words as a lifeline, even as the confining hands were torn away.

"You dare lay your hands upon me! Who are you to order me, Guardsman?" the Commander asked in appalled indignation, saying the word "Guardsman" as if it were an insult.

"My rank is equal to your own, Commander. And the three men that now surround you are of the Guard as well. There are four of us, to the two of you," the Elf challenged.

Donovar listened, intrigued, remaining motionless, lest whatever action he take further incense the Commander in green and brown. He never would have volunteered for this mission had he realized his dark past might become such a liability to its success.

The Commander in green and brown said something in Elvish, and Donovar braced for a scuffle. It sounded ugly, and their language was not meant to sound harsh to the ear.

Donovar hoped he might diffuse the situation. He said carefully, "The two of you might do well to remember your prisoner. While we like living underground, we're not fond of blindfolds." He rose, slowly, doing his best to appear nonthreatening.

The Commander in green and brown said something rude-sounding in Elvish, but the other Elf laughed. "I never thought I'd see the day when I would prefer the company of a Dwarven prisoner to a fellow Elf! I am Commander Theodas, of the Guard. Will you honor me with your name?"

"Aye, I see no harm in telling you." He would not reveal his position as Confidant and Advisor though, not yet. "I am Donovar, of Cavernas, Westhold. Might we begin our journey now? I might not be able to see it any longer, but the sun's rays are still harsh upon my skin, and I would prefer not to burn under them."

"I agree. I'd much rather be underground in a cool riverbank, myself. My fair skin was not meant for such heat either," Theodas empathized.

The Commander said something vicious-sounding in Elvish.

"Go climb a tree," Theodas snapped back at him in Common, and one of the other Elves laughed.

"You're in for it now, Theodas! Your next assignment won't be so pleasant," the voice of a different Elf said, as he too laughed.

"It won't be the first time, Feonas! But I can't seem to help surviving the punishment assignments I'm given!" Theodas responded, laughing, but there was a bitter note to it that made Donovar wonder at what he'd said.

"The King won't like us bickering in front of a prisoner," Feonas added, his tone more serious.

"Better the King than the High-King, if I'm doomed to annoy one of the two," Theodas said with a sigh.

"Which Kingdom do you hail from?" Donovar asked politely.

The silence was deafening.

"Forgive me. I did not realize I should not ask," Donovar said softly. "I'd forgotten for a moment that you've lost two as well, now. We've heard rumor that Riviera and Loatia have fallen. My condolences for all you've lost."

At his own words Donovar started remembering his own lost Kingdom again. Long-buried images, never far from the surface, began playing in his mind's eye. He fought to still his hands, lest he rip off the blindfold, even as he began trembling uncontrollably once more. "Commander Theodas, please. I know you'll think me mad, but I need to see the sun. I promise, I swear to Ragnar, that I'll not look about, but I can't stand the blindfold. I knew I might be captured and I'd thought I could bear it. It was so long ago. But I'm hearing the screams again, and seeing their faces, and...." He fell to his knees again, gasping for air, his hands clutched in tight fists around the braids of his beard in a desperate, last-ditch effort not to tear off the blindfold.

He felt gentle hands upon his face and then the blindfold was gone. Donovar looked up and spotted the sun. It was bright and burning, terrible in its glare. He forced himself to stare at it. It helped Desmond and Farad. He hoped it might work for him as well. His cavern-bred eyes began filling with tears, never meant for such brutal glare.

"Donovar, look away! You'll burn your eyes," Theodas chastised, concerned.

Donovar nodded and forced his head down. "I've been a healer for too long. I forgot the first rule of the warrior: never volunteer for anything." He shivered.

"Here, drink this. Just one sip. Do not gulp it," Theodas cautioned.

Donovar peered up into his face. It was hard to see, with the bright-red spots before his eyes, afterimages of the sun's glare. He took the flask offered to him and drank. The effect was instantaneous and remarkable. He felt coolness spread from his tongue to his throat, down into his stomach, then slowly to his head, until even his hands and feet felt cooler. His eyes stopped watering. But most astonishing of all, the unbearable images of the past that threatened to overwhelm him became as muted and indistinct as if a thick layer of fog or mist shrouded them. "I'd not even realized I was thirsty until I drank it. What is it called?" he asked in wonder.

"*Sharesh*. I was hoping it might work the same on you as it does upon us," Theodas said.

"What are you doing with *sharesh* here?" the other Commander criticized.

"The High-Prince gifted it to Leonas before he left us. Leonas told me he had no need of it, now that he was made Lord of the Grove: the Trees would take care of him. He gave it to me. He said it might help. He was worried about me."

Theodas turned to Donovar. "My friend Leonas and I are from Tanieria, but we'd had friends in Riviera, men we'd trained with. They were like brothers to us. They weren't foolish as we were—they chose the life of Reservists, instead of Naval Guardsmen. They would have stayed and fought, when the Enemy attacked. They'd have tried to save our people, the River and the trees of Loatia. They'd have died there. One drink of *sharesh* can't take the pain away, but it can dull it. It blurs the faces, it quiets the voices. You may walk without the blindfold, if you focus your eyes on your feet and do not try to look around you."

The other Commander spoke in Elvish again, and Theodas snapped something back at him, just as harshly. Then he said in Common, "You may gleefully report my insubordination upon our return. But you've not the authority to execute me here and now for it, not under the King's command. The High-King granted him full authority over us all. We're under orders to bring the lead scout in for questioning, not to torture him, and that's what that blindfold was to him. I'll answer to the King for it. He'll understand, and if he decides instead to feed me to you, so be it. I'll not kowtow to the King's Guard here. You should have stayed safe by the High-King's feet in Nalea if you'd wanted that."

The other Commander glared at him, enraged, but he took no action against him.

"Come, Donovar, we've a way to go yet," Theodas said, in a kindly voice.

Donovar tried not to see too much as they walked; mission or not, he'd not break his word or his sworn oath to Ragnar, any more than he would take advantage of Theodas's kindness.

They walked for at least three hours, possibly four or more; it was hard to judge. Then he sensed they were entering a City: the ground changed to paved stone beneath his feet, though cracked and worn with time, weeds struggling forth between every crevice. He saw the edges of buildings and felt the rock thrusting upward in vertical walls all around him. This must be Caramore.

A few minutes later, they entered one of the buildings.

"You can look up now," Theodas said.

"Thank you for all your kindness to me. I won't forget it," Donovar promised. He memorized Theodas's face, surprised at how easy it was to tell him apart from the others. He'd always thought all Elves looked so alike that it would be difficult to distinguish one from another, but Theodas's features were quite distinct. He was silver haired and blue eyed, but fine featured, like a Dwarven Lady. He was not nearly so odd for his hairless face when Donovar thought of him in those terms.

"Tell the King we are bringing him a Dwarven prisoner for questioning," Theodas said to a guard, and the Elf quickly disappeared down the corridor.

They stood and waited.

A short while later, the Elf returned, and they continued onward. They approached a large wooden door, which was well guarded.

"We must search the prisoner for weapons," one of the guards said. Donovar eyed the guards keenly. They were Men, not Elves, tall and long-limbed, like Hunter. Perhaps it was not an Elven King he would be seeing after all.

"He has already been searched. The pack he carries is a healer's kit. It appears harmless, but he will leave it here with you while in audience with the King. We have his axe and his knife."

The guard took him at his word and opened the door for them, after Donovar surrendered his kit. They entered a large room. The room itself was ornate, but it was simply furnished. The Man in the raised throne at the end of the room had the bearing of a King, but was not dressed as one. He was dark haired and blue eyed, long limbed and leanly muscled, like Hunter, but not as gaunt, nor quite so haunted. He had a look of intelligence and compassion to him.

Donovar silently sighed. This must be Talon. He liked him already. He must not. He should not have liked Theodas, either. For now, they were the enemy.

He glanced curiously at the two others in the room, at the King's side. There was an Elf, one not dressed as a soldier, and a Man of a similar build to the King, but with reddish-brown hair frosted with gray and brown eyes.

The King said something in Elvish to the Commander in green and brown. Donovar was surprised. He had not known a Man might be able to speak Elvish.

The Commander spoke back in the same tongue, and they entered a dialogue. The King turned to Theodas. There was an exchange in Elvish. Theodas said little, but his back stiffened and his shoulders sagged.

"Please, Majesty, if I might be permitted to speak?" Donovar asked politely and the King nodded.

"I'll not have Commander Theodas viewed poorly nor punished for his kindness to me. I ask that he remain here for our talks, for I like him and trust him."

TALON stared at the Dwarf, Donovar, in surprise. The Dwarf was speaking to him with the voice of an envoy, not a prisoner.

Donovar continued. "We had not realized you had an army of Elves here, nor had we known you were expecting our own army. But seeing the state of things as they stand now, it would be folly to set our forces against one another, weakening us both before facing our common true Enemy. Instead, I propose a parlay. As Confidant and Advisor to the High-King, I have that authority, even if I had not expected to use it when I volunteered for this mission. My name is Donovar, of Cavernas, Westhold. Am I correct in assuming you are Talon, Lord of the Watch, Prince of the Amontir? Or do you now go by the title of King?"

Talon gave Donovar a calculating look. He was proposing a parlay, apparently also hoping to avoid terrible bloodshed by the clash of the two armies. This would make his own plan far easier, but it troubled his spirit. He must not let it. "I am Talon, King of the Amontir. So, Jargas has now appointed himself High-King of the Western Kingdoms?"

DONOVAR was surprised. How did he know Jargas rode with them? "No, Majesty," he said, not hesitating at all on the title. "Archer is High-King of the thirty Western Kingdoms, and has been of twenty-nine of them these fifty years past. Although Prince Jargas does accompany us on this march, as does Hunter, one of your own Lords."

Talon nodded. "So we were told. Jargas's sister Jarina accompanies you as well, does she not? I understand she is now wed to Hunter."

Donovar again hid his surprise. How did Talon know so much, yet not know of the High-King?

King Talon turned to the Man at his side and said, conversationally, "Fennel, I am parched. If you would pour for me, and for our guest?"

The red-haired Man bowed and said, "Of course, Majesty." He went to a tray where a pitcher and four goblets sat.

Donovar eyed him warily. He well knew Elves used foul elixirs to question prisoners. But the Man handed the King a goblet first, and he truly drank from it. It seemed safe enough, unless the drug was already in the bottom of the cup meant for him before he poured. He handed the elder Elf a goblet also. Then he approached Donovar and handed him one. His hand brushed Donovar's as he did so. Then he returned to the King's side and took up the remaining goblet.

Donovar pretended to take a cautious sip, to be polite. He was not thirsty after the *sharesh*, nor was he comfortable drinking, knowing it was likely drugged.

The Man next to the King whispered into his ear and Talon's eyes narrowed. "You tell me you wish to avoid unnecessary bloodshed. Yet is bloodshed not the reason for your march? Do you deny Hunter and Jargas march against us? You claim we face a common Enemy. Yet our Enemy is Incuban. Do you deny that Jargas is his pawn? That he has turned Hunter against us? That you, yourself, are Incuban's tool? That your core is shielded by him?" Talon's voice had turned deadly.

Donovar realized he was in great peril. He'd seen the arrow slits dotting the walls. He'd no doubt an Elven archer stood at each, with bow at the ready. "I deny all but that we seek to avoid bloodshed and Incuban is our common Enemy. We hope to avoid harming you or any of your kin. Hunter and Jargas are indeed marching against you, but not for the reason you fear. Neither they nor the High-King wish to see you harmed, nor are they in league with Incuban. They are all sworn enemies of Him. He has harmed each of them terribly. They would never aid Him. They have come to join the combined Army of the Western Kingdoms to that of Malar in Fromer and Dorolingas and Ironhand. We alone march twenty thousand strong. We have come to join your people and the Elves in your final stand against Incuban. And I would die before ever serving one who aided that foul beast," Donovar said, shaking so violently that the wine splashed from his goblet.

"My core is not shielded by Incuban. It was shielded against Him, decades ago, to protect me from Him. Please, Majesty, parlay with High-King Archer and Jargas and Hunter, for your own sake and the sake of your people, but also for the sake of the Dwarven Lands and the Elven Kingdoms and the Lands of Men, lest they all fall before His insatiable hunger."

DEWALAREN turned to Rolin. Rolin whispered to him again in Amontirin. "I could read nothing from him when I touched him, Majesty. The shield I felt blocks his core completely. His words sound sincere, but we have been tricked before. Let the Elves question him. He'd be forced to tell them the truth."

Dewalaren shook his head. "Not if Incuban controls him. He'd believe what he told us was true and the Elves would believe him. We must lure the Dwarven Army further into our trap. Once they are surrounded, then a parlay might be in their best interests. If what Donovar told us is true and there are indeed twenty thousand of them, as Rion warned us through Elavar, then it is the only way we might defeat them without losing our entire army. After we are done here, we will question the other Dwarves. You must test them, to see if they are all shielded. We need not be so subtle about it with the others."

Dewalaren turned to Donovar. "You have admitted your Army marches against us, yet say they don't wish to harm us. That makes no sense. Why march against us, then? What do they hope to gain?"

Donovar sighed. "They do not march against your kin, Majesty. When I said you, I meant you alone. You are the one they march against. It is not my fault Common is a less precise language than Dwarvish. But their reason is a personal one. It is not my place to reveal it."

Dewalaren was surprised. "Twenty thousand against me alone! I am flattered," he said, with the ghost of a smile.

"THE Army is not here to fight you, as I've already told you. Archer or Jargas could each defeat you on his own, with no need of an army. Although now that I've seen the Elves, I'm glad we brought one," Donovar said with a smile. He was glad their own Army was not so fractious and divided, either, but he liked Theodas and would not see him in further trouble.

"You wish to parlay? Then here are my terms. Hunter and Jargas come before me alone and unarmed here in my Audience Chamber. Then we speak," Talon stated coolly.

"And what assurance do they have you'll not kill them outright?" Donovar asked. "From what Hunter has told me of you, though you love him as he loves you, if you think them pawns of the Enemy, you'd rather see them dead."

Donovar saw the King's jaw twitch. "Two of my kin will go to your camp as hostages for their safe return," Talon said, his reluctance readily apparent.

"You'd risk two of your twenty remaining kin being turned by the Enemy?" Donovar asked in disbelief.

"I'll not see thousands die needlessly for me, if I am truly your target," Talon swore.

"I will relay your terms," Donovar promised.

"No. I am afraid you must remain here as our prisoner. You have seen too much to return to them. We will send an envoy of our own, bearing a letter in your hand in Common, detailing the terms. Do you agree?" Talon asked.

"Aye, I'll do it," Donovar said. So, they meant to imprison him. He hoped he would not be chained. He had not dreamt the blindfold would affect him so. He would not be able to bear the chains. He'd dash his head against the wall of his prison before he'd let them bring him to madness.

"Majesty, let me be the envoy," Theodas said in Common, kneeling to King Talon. "I would redeem myself. I had not considered a single dose of *sharesh* might harm Advisor Donovar. I am thankful it did not."

Talon eyed him carefully. "I already have an envoy in mind and they must not learn the Army and Navy are here. But you may aid me in other ways."

So there were at least two different military forces here, an army and a navy. Donovar wondered what need they had for the navy, landlocked as they were here. The nearest sea was well over a thousand miles away in either direction. The only waters anywhere nearby were the rivers. The rivers! River Elves! Then those others must be Wood Elves. That explained the differences in the cloaks, the colors. Even the hair and eyes, he realized belatedly. So the silver-haired ones with the river-rock cloaks were the Navy, the River Elves, and the blond-haired ones with the tree bark cloaks were the Army, the Wood Elves. Perhaps that knowledge might prove useful, somehow, in the negotiations, if he was allowed to relay it at any point.

Donovar was given pen and ink and paper. He was relieved for the excuse to put the goblet down. He wrote and signed the letter as King Talon dictated it, though he added a postscript of four sentences of his own: *Archer, be sure to tell Shanti I've been well treated so far, lest she worry. Also, the parlay was my idea, not King Talon's, although the terms are his. The situation here is not what we thought it to be. I cannot see how else we will prevent bloodshed.*

King Talon eyed the last lines suspiciously. Donovar sought to reassure him. "Shanti is High-King Archer's daughter and War Leader of Cavernas on this march. She's also my goddaughter. She's very protective of me. She has a fierce temper and she's not the trusting sort. She was not happy at all that her father sent me ahead with the scouts. She'll be in a state when I don't return. I'm hoping this might calm her."

He hesitated a moment then added, "She's also Jargas's wife. She has influence over him. And you know Hunter: he's not the trusting sort, either. I know you don't want them to know you've your own army here, but I had to say something to justify the two of them coming here as you've requested. If you want this parlay to have a chance of success, you'll not cut that last from the page, or ask me to rewrite it."

DEWALAREN nodded. At face value it revealed little. He doubted it was some sort of code. He wanted to trust Donovar, to believe him. The alternative was too terrible. He still could not bear the thought that Farad might be lost to him. He sealed the letter.

"Theodas, see that Advisor Donovar is quartered with his men, then report back here. Take four of your men," Dewalaren commanded. He'd not risk their docile-seeming prisoner harming anyone.

"YES, Majesty," Theodas said. "Advisor Donovar, if you would please follow me? Loras, Salanar, Maerin, Darrow, to me."

Donovar tensed again without meaning to.

"Fear not, Donovar. You will not be harmed nor chained, though you will be well guarded and unfortunately will be far less comfortably accommodated should you try to escape," Theodas cautioned, as he led him from the chamber.

DEWALAREN watched them leave, thoughtful. Theodas seemed very solicitous of Donovar. He turned to Commander Thaedrin. "Now, tell me all that happened."

Commander Thaedrin detailed the capture of the prisoners and all that followed. Dewalaren saw the remaining Guardsman tense, but keep silent.

"Now you. Feonas, isn't it?" Dewalaren asked.

"YES, Majesty," Feonas said, surprised the King knew his name.

"You tell me all that happened," Dewalaren commanded.

Feonas looked nervously at the Commander. "The Commander already did so," he said, sensing a trap.

"Feonas, I am not the High-King," Dewalaren said, his voice weary. "I do not favor the Army over the Navy. I have mixed your units for a reason. You must learn to work together, to respect each other. You must be willing to die for each other, if necessary. So, I would hear what you saw and heard."

Feonas nodded with dawning comprehension. He told much more than Thaedrin had. He spoke honestly of the altercation between Thaedrin and

Theodas in front of the prisoner, and how he had thought it ill advised to show such divisiveness before the enemy. But he defended Theodas for giving the prisoner the *sharesh*. He said, as a healer, the Dwarf should have known it might affect him adversely, if there was a chance it might, but Dwarves were well known for their hardiness in regards to drink and their resistance to most poisons.

DEWALAREN nodded, impressed by what he'd heard. He faulted Theodas only for rising to Thaedrin's bait. But their harshest words to each other had at least been in Elvish, from what Feonas said. He sighed. He was not as impartial as he tried to be. He favored the Navy over the Army, as Aras did, for all they'd endured, all they still endured.

"Commander Thaedrin, the matter is closed. You and Commander Theodas are both at fault. I could choose to punish both of you for it, but instead, I pardon you both. There are to be no repercussions from this altercation, official or otherwise. Am I understood?"

Thaedrin tensed and nodded. "Yes, Majesty," he said stiffly.

One by one the Dwarves were brought before them and questioned. Rolin tested them all. No one else was shielded, there was no taint of the Enemy about any of them, but they remained stonily silent, and their cores were too small and dark for Rolin to hear their thoughts. After the last one left, Dewalaren sighed and dismissed the Elven soldiers. Once they were gone, he said "Elavar, I've a mission for you, if you are willing."

"You believe Donovar? You wish me to be the envoy?" he asked perceptively.

"I wish to believe him. And I can think of no one better suited to the task," Dewalaren said.

"I can, if you'll order your guards to allow me to enter," a familiar voice said, seemingly from thin air.

"Eladar?" Elavar asked, looking about. "Where are you?"

Dewalaren heard a curse in Elvish and a scuffle behind the wall. "How'd you get in there?" a voice asked sharply.

"The same way Talon did when he spied upon us," Eladar retorted wryly.

"Bring him to me," Dewalaren commanded.

Dewalaren glowered at Eladar as two soldiers led him in.

"You're lucky I'm not your enemy, Talon. I could easily have acquired a bow, and I had a clear shot at you from where I stood," Eladar goaded.

"I'm surprised you didn't take it. Elavar says you blame me for the fall of Riviera and Loatia," Dewalaren retorted sharply, in no mood for Eladar's vicious games.

"My brother is perhaps not as good a judge of me as he likes to think," Eladar said, glaring at Elavar.

"Why would I think to send you as envoy instead of Elavar?" Dewalaren challenged. "Elavar has knelt to me and sworn oath to me as his King."

Eladar stiffened but remained silent, as Dewalaren continued. "Elavar is a skilled diplomat. He is trustworthy and an experienced strategist."

"All of which are reasons he should remain safely here. He knows the full strength of the Army and Navy. Unlike me, he's been involved in all your plans. Hunter or Jargas could strip that knowledge from him easily. I, on the other hand, have no such knowledge, yet I too am a skilled diplomat. Also, I am sneaky and devious. I am a survivor. I know Jargas. And I have dealt with Dwarves before I ever met him. Father...." His voice broke, but then he continued forward firmly.

"Father sent me secretly to Dorolingas and Ironhand following my graduation from Nalea, after the High-King rejected his counsel concerning an alliance with the Dwarves for the fourth time. I met with their Kings. Over the past year I have learned some of their customs, their protocols. I even speak Dwarvish now, with some fluency. Even if Jargas remembers I do, I'd likely still overhear things they meant to keep secret. And I will kneel and swear oath to you, also, so you might know I can be trusted."

"He is right about your knowledge of our plans, Elavar. Can he do this?" Dewalaren asked.

Elavar shook his head. "Once, perhaps, but now, his anger rules him. For this you need someone with restraint, someone with a clear head." He breathed deeply. "If you cannot send me, send Elanara. They'd not harm a Lady. She'd be safer than either of us."

"No!" Eladar denied explosively. "You don't know anything about Dwarves! They'd not see her as a Lady, but as a harlot! They'd spit upon her, they'd do far worse! She's Elven. They'll know she's not a virgin, even if Hunter hasn't told them Talon's slept with her. She'd be in great danger as a weapon against him. And they'd not listen to anything she had to say. They'd see her as without honor. I'm a second son of a dead Kingdom. They'd respect that. Enough of their own Kingdoms are dead, their heirs. I'm also expendable. You'd lose little if I did not return," Eladar argued desperately.

"This mission is too important to send someone with a death wish," Elavar said coldly.

"I'm not the one who wants me dead! You do. You told me! You said you'd been proud of me before. You said... you said you'd rather the ogres had eaten me, you wish I'd burnt," Eladar choked out, visibly fighting against tears. "That I'd died so horribly. I want.... I want you to be proud of me still, Elavar. I want you to love me still. I cannot bear that Father and Mother are dead, and that you hate me so much now you wish I was dead too." The last vestige of Eladar's control shattered and he began sobbing.

The ice in Elavar's eyes melted. They grew bright with compassion as he took his younger brother into his arms and began comforting him softly in Elvish.

"Rolin and I will be outside," Dewalaren said gruffly, and he motioned for Rolin to come with him.

In the hall, away from the guards, Dewalaren said, "Rolin, I must ask a terrible thing of you. I need to send two of your House as hostages."

Rolin paled. "No, Majesty! Please! There are so few of us. What of the new Houses? They are eager to prove themselves to you."

Dewalaren shook his head. "I do not want Hunter or Jargas to learn of them. And they would guess I was sending two who might have volunteered to die. I need these hostages to mean something."

"Then send me as one of them," Rolin urged.

"I'll not send a Lord," Dewalaren refused.

"Colin can take up the band of my House if I am slain," Rolin said bravely.

"Rolin, I can't. I have told you why. You alone know my secret. I am crippled. I cannot wield my own Power, and no other here has any to speak of, except Lunahr. And he is yet a boy and I... I find I can no longer trust him as I wish I could. He has shown no signs of being under the Enemy's influence, yet still I doubt him. You have told me you did not sense His presence, but we could not risk your probing too deeply, lest the Enemy take hold of you, if He is in Lunahr's thoughts. I am relieved Lunahr was not here to hear all this."

ROLIN could see how hard it was for Dewalaren to admit his helplessness. He swallowed. "Then I will have Colin go, and our cousin Garrett. Colin already has an heir. Rowena is being raised as Lady of the House should Colin and I ever fall. Colin and Garrett are both clearheaded enough for the job."

Dewalaren clasped his arm. "Thank you, Rolin."

The door to the Audience Chamber opened. "Majesty, we would have audience with you," Elavar said formally. "And Eladar requires a bow, if he is to swear service to you, and for the journey, for he lost his own to the ogres in the mountains, and the weapons we traveled with have not been returned to us as you ordered them to be."

Dewalaren was surprised, both by Elavar's change of heart, and that his earlier order to return their weapons had been disobeyed. He commanded one of the Amontir guards by the door to go to the Armory to fetch their confiscated weapons. Here was yet another case of the Army overstepping its authority. He sighed and wished again for Aras, for Farad as he once had been, for anyone he could trust to share his burdens.

AN HOUR later, Eladar was well on his way, when Elanara confronted Dewalaren in the hall. "Dewalaren, what have you done? Elavar said you sent Eladar on a mission to the Dwarven camp. Are you both mad? He is in no condition to shoulder such a responsibility. He'll get himself killed!"

"Elanara, I am sorry, but Elavar disagrees. He made a convincing argument on Eladar's behalf," Dewalaren apologized.

"It's because of me, isn't it?" she accused.

He nodded and, to his utter shock, Elanara slapped him in the face. Her blow was so unexpected he neither dodged nor blocked it, and his vision swam for a moment from the force of it.

"You admit it! He told you, after he promised he'd keep silent, and now you're sending Eladar into danger to punish me for loving Rion instead of you! I never thought you capable of such petty revenge! How could you, after all I'm sacrificing for you? Isn't it enough that I'm still marrying you? How could you endanger Eladar?" She was seething, but he saw tears in her eyes as well.

Dewalaren gaped at her in stunned horror. "Elanara, please! I have no idea what you are talking about. Please, calm down. I have not hurt Eladar, nor you. At least, I have not meant to. And you must tell me about you and Rion," he said, steeling himself for what he might hear.

"But you know already. You said it was because of me," she said, confused.

"Elavar suggested I send you to the Dwarven camp, when we determined he would be too great a liability. Eladar convinced us it would be better to send him instead of you," Dewalaren explained.

"Oh," she said and looked at him in loss. "I thought.... Oh, Dewalaren, I screamed it at you! That is not the way I meant for you to hear. I am not myself, either, since... since the refugees, in Erenia. It was too horrible, it was.... Oh, Dewalaren, please forgive me! I did not mean to fall in love with

Rion. I tried so hard not to, but he was so bright and so brave, yet still so painfully young. But Men age so quickly. I thought my heart still my own, but he kept entering my thoughts, my dreams, and then when Elavar came to rescue us, I heard about all he had done, and I....

"But it does not matter, Dewalaren. Rion does not know. He need never know of my feelings for him. It changes nothing. You and I are still betrothed. I will marry you, Dewalaren, because I must: it is my duty as a Princess. I will pleasure you and produce heirs for you, because I must: it is my duty as a wife. But you must know I will never love you, I cannot. I can only ever give my heart once. I will always hold Rion in my heart." She said it dry eyed, but her voice was filled with sadness.

"I release you from your pledge to me," Dewalaren said raggedly.

Elanara shook her head. "Dewalaren, you cannot. High-King Laedrin will not permit it."

"He is not my King, nor Rion's. I will not let him destroy the happiness of two I care for. I would not have you for a wife, or a Queen, as you described, Elanara. I would rather live and die alone, and see my cursed line end," Dewalaren swore, his voice infinitely weary and sad, as he turned from her and headed for the privacy of his room.

She was lost to him, to Rion, of all people! He should never have saved Rion. He cursed, angry at himself for the unworthy thought. Rion deserved saving. If the price of Rion's life was Elanara's love, then so be it. Rion had selflessly aided all who had needed him, Aras and Eladar and Elanara. Rion had aided him as well, when he'd sent Elavar to warn him of the wizards and the Dwarves, to see him safe, little dreaming it might cost him Elanara. But he was still a boy! How could Rion love her, how could she love Rion already, after knowing him for so short a time, when he had known her for far longer, when he had bared his core to her, when he had lain with her?

Dewalaren knew the answer. He'd seen it in her eyes, in Erenia. It seemed so long ago, a lifetime of pain ago. She feared him: his Power, his Madness. Rion was not one to be feared.

He opened his door and entered his room. It was as cold and dark and empty as his heart. He closed the door, condemning himself to the emptiness he deserved.

Dewalaren's eye turned inward. *Aras, how could you abandon me when I most need your aid, your counsel, when I most need your love? Please come back safely to me,* he begged, but he was met only with the cool, metallic silence of the tree. Aras was gone because Dewalaren had driven him away. He'd feared Aras, exactly as Elanara had feared him, when Aras was still such a child at heart, so perfect yet so terribly vulnerable.

Aras would die. Dewalaren would never see him again. He would spend his whole life hating himself for what he had done, what he had lost by it.

He collapsed onto the bed and lay staring at the ceiling, cursing himself for his stupidity, haunted by memories of all those he had loved, all those who were now lost to him.

"THEY should have reported in by now. Something's happened to them. They've been overwhelmed. How could you send Donovar into such danger?" Desenia accused, glaring at her father.

Desmond winced and sighed. "Donovar is no stranger to danger."

"Desenia is right," Farad said. "Something has happened. We must be on alert. I will go looking for them."

"You'll do no such thing!" Jarina denied. "You'll not stride boldly into danger this time."

"I can track them better than anyone," Farad argued. "I can warn the rest of you through my link to you."

"No, I'll not allow it," Jarina said stubbornly.

Desenia glowered at Farad. "You told us there were less than twenty of you, that of those, few might even be here, that only Dewalaren had any true Power, or at most Fennel or Pierce, if either yet lived."

Farad stood. "Whatever the danger they faced, we're yet hours from it. Have the Army halt its march here and prepare for a surprise attack. Don't forget to watch the skies. If the Enemy's taken Caramore and killed my kin, they may have chimaera or hippogryph with them. I've warned you already what to expect. I'll bring back Donovar's body if he's dead, or behead him. I'll not leave him to the Enemy."

"No, Farad. Jarina is right. We'll not risk you like this. I'm ordering you to stay," Jargas commanded. "We'll send out six units of a dozen each. They'll find the missing scouts. Meanwhile, you'll help us prepare for attack."

Jarina looked at her brother gratefully, but Farad glared at him. "I'll not let you endanger others to keep me safe. If the Enemy's taken Donovar...." he began, but Desmond cut him off.

"Donovar would not be taken alive, nor his body left in a condition where it might be used. I hope some other ill might have befallen him and the other scouts, though the hope's a faint one. Jargas has ordered you as your King, Farad. Do not make this harder on any of us than it already is," Desmond said tiredly.

"Father, are you ill?" Desenia asked in concern.

"I fear I have sent Donovar to his death. Should I not be ill, having done so?" Desmond asked.

"Desmond, you must rest. Jargas and I can see the troops are readied," Farad urged.

"You forget yourself, Hunter. You've no authority to order my father about, nor any right to exclude me from the preparations," Desenia snapped.

"I only meant…." Farad began, but Jarina took his hand.

"Let Jargas put her in her place, Husband. It's a spanking she needs and she might enjoy it, coming from him," Jarina suggested, smiling sweetly at her brother's wife.

Desenia's face darkened in rage and Jargas interposed himself between them. "It's a good thing the Enemy is unaware how at odds with one another we are. Attend me, Wife," Jargas commanded.

Jarina and Farad quickly moved out of earshot as Desenia began screeching at Jargas indignantly.

Jarina sighed. "I pity my poor brother. He got more than he bargained for when he wed her."

To her annoyance, Farad defended Desenia. "Her anger masks her pain. Donovar was a second father to her, and now, of all times, she needs his love to guide her."

Jarina's annoyance evaporated. "I had forgotten, for a moment. You never cease to amaze me, my love. The depth of your compassion overwhelms me."

"Do you truly love me, Jarina?" Farad asked.

"You need ask?" she laughed, then grew serious. "I love you so much it frightens me, Faradan. I can never lose you. Please, if you will not be careful for yourself, be careful for me."

"I would do anything for you," Farad swore. "Come, we must brief the commanders. I doubt Jargas will have the opportunity."

Jarina blushed darkly and slammed her shield more firmly into place against her brother. Jargas had found a different way to subdue his wife's rage. The timing was inconvenient, but they were both far too tense. Perhaps it was for the best.

Jarina turned her eye outward again and saw pain and despair on Farad's face. He had felt it, or heard her thoughts, or guessed. "I love you, Farad, just as you are," she assured him, kissing him firmly on the mouth. "Donovar would not want his death to cause such pain. He had the heart of a healer." None of them believed any longer that Donovar might live.

Farad quietly agonized over how many of his kin he might have sent to their deaths as well, by calling the War Council at Caramore. Jarina saw his face and knew his thoughts without touching them. "Do not, Farad. Do not suffer for your kin, when we do not yet know what has happened."

He nodded.

They ordered the six search parties out and prepared for attack.

HOURS later, one of the search parties returned, surrounding a prisoner. Farad was surprised to see he was an Elf and he was not bound.

Hernon said in Common, "Hunter, we bring Prince Eladar of Riviera to you, as envoy to you and Prince Jargas, from King Talon, with terms for a parlay. We did not capture him. He revealed himself to us, when he might instead have effectively ambushed us," Hernon admitted, though it obviously hurt his pride to acknowledge it. "He says he bears a letter from Donovar. We've seen a letter, but we can't verify it's from Donovar. None of us are familiar with his hand."

"Prince Eladar? You are Princess Elanara's brother?" Farad asked eagerly.

"YES," Eladar admitted cautiously. He knew the Enemy would already know their given names and so he had not hesitated in speaking his own when he was surrounded, but it still made him nervous to hear it spoken aloud by another. The Dwarf had called this Man Hunter; he would have known it was him anyway, from his distinctively scarred face.

"Tell me, do you know if she... is she safe?" Hunter asked, concerned.

Eladar was surprised by the question. "Why would you ask?"

"Because she is betrothed to Talon, and he truly loves her. If she lives, if she were with him, it might make what is to come easier for him. I do not want him to suffer more than he must." His voice fell to a whisper. "I do not want him to suffer at all."

Eladar looked at Hunter, confused. This Man was little like who he had expected to confront. Whatever he was planning against Talon, he was haunted by it. Yet he seemed to be acting of his own free will. If the Enemy were controlling him, it was not apparent. "She is safe," Eladar admitted cautiously. He did not reveal she was in Caramore.

"AND you've a letter from Donovar? Then he is also safe? We had thought the Enemy had taken Caramore. We had feared that was why he did not return. But you've no taint of the Enemy about you," Farad said. He had viewed Eladar's core with great care even as they spoke. With the Power of the Ring, there was no need to touch him. Eladar's core was astonishingly bright, as bright as if he were kin, even more so. He'd found no sign of the Enemy. This was truly an Elf, not a Resemblant masquerading as one. And his thoughts, though many were hidden from him without probing more deeply than he currently desired, were his own.

"Donovar is safe also," Eladar confirmed, and Farad knew it as the truth.

"Hernon, summon Jargas and Archer. And Shanti," Farad added, not wishing to anger her further against him. He contacted Jarina with a gentle touch to their bond.

"Come, we will meet in my tent," Farad said. He stopped and turned to Hernon. "You searched him for weapons?"

"Of course," Hernon said. "Envoy or not, we'd not risk him causing harm. We have his bow and knife, and his water pouch is indeed filled only with water."

Farad nodded in approval. They'd been thorough.

He had the patrol accompany them inside. Jarina was already there. Jargas and Desenia joined them just after he arrived.

Jargas smiled in surprise upon seeing Eladar. "Thorn! I'd not known it was you they spoke of! It is good to see you well again, lad!"

ELADAR did not know what to say to Jargas. He'd not expected such a warm welcome from Jargas. He'd not thought Jargas liked him.

He looked in surprise at the woman next to Jargas, who must be his wife. She was only somewhat shorter than Jargas; she towered above both Eladar and Hunter. Dwarves were not supposed to be so tall. Could her mother have been a woman of Man? So, this was the High-King's daughter. He was curious to meet the High-King.

A Man entered, even as he thought so, and Eladar hid his surprise. He did not appear to be a Dwarf at all, despite his grooming. Jargas introduced them. "This is the Lady Shanti, War Leader of Cavernas, Westhold, and my wife, and her father, Archer, High-King of the Thirty Western Kingdoms. I understand you've a letter for us, from Donovar," Jargas said.

"It is addressed to you and Hunter and High-King Archer," Eladar said, hiding his shock that a Man might be the Dwarven High-King. Archer held his hand out for the letter and Eladar handed it to him.

Archer broke the seal and scanned it quickly. "It's in Donovar's hand, though the voice is not his, until the end," he said in Dwarvish, obviously relieved to read those last lines of text. Eladar understood every word he spoke. Donovar read the letter out loud in Common to those assembled.

"Donovar may have penned it, but Talon wrote it," Hunter confirmed, also in Dwarvish.

"Talon's mad if he thinks you'll go to him like a lamb to the slaughter, Jargas," Desenia scoffed in Common, as if eager to goad their prisoner.

FARAD scowled at her. "Hernon, please escort Prince Eladar to one of our tents." He'd not have Eladar see the argument he sensed was coming, even if he could not understand it. "He is to be carefully watched, but given the proper courtesy for his station. You did well in not binding him before, as he came to us as an envoy."

Hernon smiled at the words of praise. "Come, Highness, if you'll accompany me," Hernon said politely in Common.

"Talon is an honorable Man," Farad said sharply to Desenia, now that the envoy was not there to overhear. "He's not the one planning treachery."

"Are you insulting my father?" Desenia asked, looking at him icily.

"No. I am belittling myself, for my role in what is to come. Something has happened, something unexpected. We had feared the Enemy had struck, but it is something else."

"At least Donovar is safe. I had thought him lost," Desmond said, the relief plain in his voice.

"So, do we parlay? I will go. I've no wish to see the bloodshed Donovar warns us against," Farad said.

"Aye," Jargas said, nodding.

"Are you mad, Jargas? I need not ask Hunter! We all know he is. Why risk your life when we can so quickly and easily overpower Talon?" Desenia asked.

"Because if we do so by force of arms, we'd likely kill Talon, and he's kin to you as well as me, Desenia. I'll not kill him," Jargas replied. "Especially seeing as how I liked him when I met him. I wish I did not need to unseat him. Also, from Donovar's caution, I do not think it would be an easy victory, perhaps not a victory at all. There is some sort of danger awaiting us in Caramore."

"I wonder who the hostages he offers will be?" Farad said. "Desmond, you'll see they are kept safe?"

"I'll so order it, but I won't be here to see it. I'm coming with you," Desmond said.

"Father!" Desenia cried in protest.

"I've been waiting nine decades for this day, Daughter. I'll not be kept waiting longer than need be," Desmond said, his tone brooking no argument.

"It's too dangerous! Talon asked only for Hunter and Jargas. You are High-King. Our Army needs you," she argued desperately.

"I'll be in Rowanar's armor. If anything makes them stop and listen, seeing that will. And it also makes me hard to kill," Desmond added practically.

"It didn't save him," Desenia said bitterly.

Desmond sighed. "We've the Ring also, though we mustn't bring it. Dewalaren might be as honorable as you say, Farad, but the temptation of the Ring might be too much for him. This way, if he wishes to take it by force, he'll have to get through twenty thousand Dwarven warriors to do it."

"Then I will hold it for you, Brother," Jarina said.

"Why you? You are not Heir, Jargas is, and our children yet to be born after him. I will hold it," Desenia said.

Jarina's eyes narrowed. "I wore the Ring for sixty-seven years. It was given to me by my father, not to him, and not to you."

Jargas said with finality, "Jarina will hold it, Desenia. And wield it, if we've need of her to."

Desenia glared at him and stormed out of the tent.

Jargas sighed. "She is getting worse. There is so much anger in her."

Desmond agreed, his face creased in concern. "She needs to face the Enemy. She will not find peace until she does."

Jargas nodded solemnly.

"Do we send Eladar back, or keep him hostage, as they have kept Donovar?" Farad asked.

"I see no harm in sending him back, and it will be a show of good faith to do so," Jargas said. "But first we must prepare. We know what we must say to Dewalaren, but we must determine how we will say it. Farad, you must be ready to draw upon the strength of the Ring through Jarina, as I will be ready. We might need it."

Farad nodded. He was dreading the coming hours. He suspected they would be the hardest of his brutal life.

HERNON began heading for one of the food storage tents. He did not know where else to bring the Elven envoy: he must not be allowed near any of the weapons, nor permitted to see any of their strategic plans.

He saw King Rongas walking with six of his Throne Guard and changed direction. He'd not risk endangering the King, should his prisoner surprise them. But the King headed for him and called out to him. Hernon's men interposed themselves between the envoy and the King, and the Throne Guard in turn encircled Rongas protectively.

Rongas ignored all of them. "Hernon, have you seen Jargas? He's not in his tent, and I've need of his counsel. And what is an Elf doing here? Is he a prisoner?" he asked in Dwarvish, intrigued.

"The Prince is meeting with the High-King and the High-Princess, Lord Hunter and the Princess in Hunter's tent, Majesty. The Elf we are escorting is Prince Eladar of Riviera, an envoy from King Talon. I was surprised to find your son actually knows him, but by a different name: he called him Thorn. He came with good news. Apparently Donovar has not been slain after all. He carried a letter from Donovar, requesting a parlay. That's what they're all discussing. I am to escort the Elven Prince to a tent where he is to be watched. I was taking him to one of the food storage tents. I hope he won't be insulted by it, but there is no other safe place to bring him," Hernon replied, also in Dwarvish.

"You're right to be concerned. War camp or not, any Prince must be shown proper courtesy, but especially an Elven one. Their pride is easily bruised. Escort him to my tent and offer him some wine. They're fond of wine, I've heard. And food. He might be hungry. Oh, but be careful what you offer. It wouldn't do to insult him by mistake. Elves don't eat meat. There may be other things, as well. Do the best you can. Their ways are strange to us.

"In fact, stop by the kitchens and speak with Sarnon on the way there. Tell him what I've told you and see that he prepares something appropriate. Have him serve the Prince in my tent, as well. Tell Sarnon to treat him as he would me." Then he laughed heartily. "No, tell Sarnon to treat him as he'd treat visiting royalty. I'll not have him abuse a guest!

"Tell him not to give him anything to eat that he'd need a sharp knife to cut with. There's no reason to ask for trouble. Keep a careful eye on our guest, lest he obtain a weapon or see the maps I've stored in the chest. Nothing is out in plain sight that he should not see. But try not to offend him by your presence.

"I'm going to see what this parlay is all about. Jargas may need my counsel as well. Rennon, you go with them, so the Guard at my door will let them pass," Rongas said, addressing one of the men with him. Then he departed with all but Rennon.

Hernon breathed a sigh of relief when Rongas left. He loved him fiercely, they all did, but he could be overwhelming at times. He was nervous enough about his prisoner, and now he was to be guested in the King's tent!

ELADAR had listened to the exchange in Dwarvish with interest. He'd understood much of what they had said. He wondered what this King's name was, who sounded to be Jargas's father. He was impressed by the concern he'd shown for him and what he'd said about Elves. He'd not said anything particularly insulting and had, in fact, known more about his people than he might have expected him to. Many of the Dwarves he'd met in Dorolingas and Ironhand had still tried to feed him rare goat meat by the time he was ready to leave, even after all his months in each Kingdom.

He hoped they might have something other than mushrooms here, if he was to be staying for any length of time. He assumed he'd be kept as a hostage, as they were holding Donovar. He'd liked mushrooms well enough before he'd gone to the Dwarven Lands, but he'd gotten quite sick of them by the time he'd left.

He hoped the King might find Jargas did not need his counsel. Perhaps he might get a chance to speak with him. He wondered who Sarnon might be, that the King would tolerate the disrespect he had implied. The way the King had laughed, he thought he might be someone he was fond of. Perhaps he was a relative? Dwarves had few cousins or siblings. The King had a good laugh. There was a time Eladar might have enjoyed laughing with him. He'd not laughed nor even smiled since Erenia.

They arrived at the kitchens. Eladar was asked to wait outside by Hernon, in careful Common. Then Hernon went inside, leaving him guarded by his men. The mixture of aromas coming from the tent was both intriguing and intoxicating. That could not possibly truly be the scent of fresh baked bread, could it? In an army camp?

Hernon returned shortly, looking much more at ease than he had when he had left. Eladar wondered anew about Sarnon.

They began heading off in a different direction, Hernon leading them. Eladar marveled again at the size of the Dwarven camp. They truly had many thousands of soldiers here, yet there had been no sign of their presence as he'd headed toward them from Caramore.

It was fortunate Rion had warned Elavar and they'd come to warn Talon. Talon might have been taken completely off his guard. Eladar sighed. He liked Talon, though he hadn't when he'd first met him. It had been a blow to their father when Laedrin had commanded him to betroth Elanara to Talon, instead of to his own son, Aras. Father had, of course, done as Laedrin commanded, but it had hurt him terribly to do it. Father had met Aras and had loved him from the first. Father had been civil to Talon, but he'd never wanted him for a son-in-law, for all he'd loved Talon's cousin Lunahr almost as another son, though it was Elanara who was his official guardian. Still, Eladar had wished Elanara could open her heart to Talon.

Now it did not matter. Father was dead, Riviera was gone, and although Elanara was in love with Rion, she was determined to carry out their father's wishes and Laedrin's command. He fumed at the thought that his sister would sacrifice what little happiness she might now have for Laedrin.

"HIGHNESS, please forgive the delay. We are almost there. The camp is large. I had thought to take you to a different tent, but King Rongas is instead offering you the hospitality of his own quarters," Hernon said in Common nervously, hoping to appease the envoy. He had no desire to guard an angry Elf. From all he'd heard, Elves could be quite vicious when angered.

ELADAR realized his thoughts must have been reflected in the expression on his face and silently sighed. He'd not yet mastered the ability to appear in cool control regardless of the circumstances. "Do not be troubled on my account. My thoughts were not of my current situation. You are treating me with far greater courtesy than I had thought to receive when I volunteered for this mission," Eladar reassured him.

Hernon appeared surprised and relieved. He hesitated a moment, but then spoke further. "You volunteered to come to us? Knowing that we had an army here and would likely take you prisoner?"

Eladar fought down a laugh at his expression, but he could not keep a smile from his face, even as his own reaction astonished him. He could not remember the last time he had felt like smiling. "I had already learned that Dwarven hospitality is not nearly as terrible as it is rumored to be." The smile left his face. "Please forgive me. I should not have said that. You might misunderstand the intent of my statement. I have been a guest of your Kingdoms before, in Dorolingas and Ironhand. I was well treated in both, but I was well aware you are at war with us, and prepared for far worse treatment than I have received."

Hernon looked at him in surprise. "We are not at war with you. It is your Enemy we march to fight. We march to destroy Him, for all He has done, and to reclaim our Lands. We seek vengeance for the Kingdoms He has destroyed, not only our own people's, but all of them: Amontir, Dwarven, Elven, and those of Men. It is a pity your people do not march with us. I do not understand why you do not seek vengeance as well."

Eladar's eyes narrowed and he stopped walking. "Do not presume to know my heart," he said coldly. "I am a Prince of Riviera. I have seen what is left of my people! The Enemy burned them! My father and mother are dead, my River dry! And Loatia, which we died protecting, gone as well! Of course I seek vengeance! Our army would be marching on the Enemy already, did you not delay us with yours!" Eladar was shaking with rage. He was shouting by the time he was done.

The guards around him had stiffened and drawn back warily during his tirade, as if expecting physical violence.

Hernon swallowed visibly. "I offer my sincere apologies for insulting you, Highness. I assure you, that was not my intent. I will report myself to my commander for disciplinary action once I have completed my duty as assigned. I will keep silent from this moment forward, if you would please continue onward?"

Eladar glared at him. He tried to breathe deeply, to calm the fury that yet boiled within him at the thought of all the Enemy had done, at the merest suggestion he might have meekly accepted the destruction of all he held dear. His temper flared so easily now. But he had promised Elavar he would perform this mission well. He must not disappoint him, not again, not in this. And he had mentioned the army! He had never meant to tell them of it. He only hoped Hernon did not realize what he had meant, that perhaps he would think he meant Talon's kin, though so few could hardly be considered an army by anyone. All their plans might be undone if the Dwarves learned the Elven Army and Navy were here.

He realized he was shaking, and forced himself still. "I will walk," he said stiffly and stepped forward.

Only forty more paces brought them to the King's tent. The Throne Guard standing before it eyed him warily. He realized they had no doubt seen his outburst. Rennon spoke with his fellow Guardsmen in Dwarvish, relaying the King's orders. After a brief exchange, they were allowed to enter.

The King's tent was larger than Hunter's, but no more elaborately furnished than his had been. There were silks and finely crafted metal chests here as well.

Hernon said something softly to one of the other guards who walked with him that Eladar could not catch. Then he left the tent, although the others stayed.

"Would you care for some wine, Highness?" the Dwarf Hernon had spoken to inquired politely.

Eladar bit back an angry reply. He would not learn anything by remaining hostile. He should not have driven Hernon away. He had already learned some valuable information by speaking with him. "Yes, I think some wine might be a good idea," he agreed with forced calm.

"We are also preparing some food for you, in case you are hungry," the Dwarf risked adding.

"Might I ask your name?" Eladar asked politely, taking care regarding his tone.

"It is Fenlon, Highness."

"I should like to wash my hands before I eat, Fenlon. And some cool water upon my face would be refreshing," Eladar ventured.

"Of course," Fenlon agreed readily. He showed Eladar to a basin and pitcher beside a cask of water. "The King uses the warrior's latrine. I can escort you, if you have need of it as well," Fenlon volunteered.

Eladar shook his head. "This will be fine."

Fenlon retreated to a respectful distance.

Eladar washed his hands and then cupped his hands and held the water against his face. He wanted to dip his face into the basin, but he fought the desire. He really wanted a river to lie in, to soothe him. He wanted his own River, the pang of longing for its lost waters slicing into his heart like a blade. He cursed under his breath in Elvish and forced the thought from his head. He breathed deeply, dried his face with the towel beside the basin, and turned back to the guards.

Fenlon held out a gold goblet to him. It was intricately etched, though free of the jewels he might have expected to see adorn the goblet of a King, particularly a Dwarven one. He admired the metalwork and then sipped at the contents. The wine was excellent. He looked about for somewhere to sit and settled upon some cushions. The guards watched him, while trying to appear as if they were not. Eladar sighed.

A figure appeared at the entrance to the tent, and Eladar turned toward it, eager for the distraction.

An elder Dwarf entered. His long braided beard and hair were both pure white, and his face was wrinkled. Eladar noted in surprise he did not bear an ax, as every other Dwarf he had seen in the camp so far had. Instead, a long knife was sheathed at his side. He had a huge tray of food in his hands, which he set upon the table near the cushions as Eladar rose politely.

"Prince Eladar? I am Sarnon, King Rongas's steward. I have prepared some refreshment for you. I hope it is to your liking. If I have erred in any regard, please inform me, and I will do the best I am able to please you," he said in Common.

Eladar surveyed the contents of the tray in astonishment. There was enough food to feed a dozen Elves, and such food! There were greens arranged so that they appeared to be a forest, four different kinds of bread, sliced and precisely stacked to form a mountain range, and several different types of fruit carved into flowers and arranged as if in a garden. He had been to many a banquet that paled in comparison to this. And he had feared he might be doomed to a diet of mushrooms!

Eladar grinned in delight. He could not help himself. "I have never been given a work of art such as this to eat before. How in the world did you prepare it so quickly? Or am I stealing someone else's lunch, or perhaps an entire squadron's, for I will not even begin to be able to finish this, though we Elves have been known to astonish Men with our appetites."

Sarnon smiled at him. "As have we Dwarves. I am accustomed to having to work quickly. The King has unpredictable eating habits. I see your goblet is almost empty. Allow me to refresh it for you."

Eladar handed him the goblet and looked at the Dwarven guards spread throughout the tent. "Fenlon, have you and your men eaten?"

"We will eat once our shift is done, Highness," Fenlon said, obviously surprised by the question.

"Then I will try not to feel too guilty," Eladar said in contentment.

"Is there anything else you desire, Highness? Am I correct in thinking I am not remiss in not offering you bacara?" Sarnon asked.

Eladar nodded. "You are correct." He did not say his people preferred air they could breathe. "You have provided for me quite well. But I might ask a favor of you."

Sarnon said, "You may ask."

Eladar said grimly, "I got into a verbal altercation with one of the guards, Hernon, before. He told me afterward that he would report himself to his commander for it. I am troubled by it. I overreacted to what he said. I lost my temper, when I should have kept it, had circumstances been kinder to me than they have been, of late. Hernon had not meant any harm by his words. The King had apparently wished to show me courtesy by offering his tent to me. I would not want Hernon's commander or his King to think he did not perform his duty well, when he in fact has. Would you be able to relay that to his commander? As it is a military matter, I am not certain of your protocols in regards to such things. Is your standing in the King's household as his steward sufficient to the task? Or should I request Fenlon intercede on his behalf?"

SARNON studied Eladar carefully, as he pondered his words. He had learned long ago to hide his true reactions before the King and his guests, so it was easy to conceal his surprise. When Hernon had spoken to him in the kitchens, he had been impressed by how genuinely concerned Hernon had seemed that the Elven Prince be pleased, not merely because the King had ordered it. Then, at the door, the Throne Guard had warned him the Elf had thrown a fit and would be difficult to please, though they knew Sarnon was unflappable, from his service to the King. Yet the Prince had been quite pleasant and was now seeking to make amends for his earlier outburst.

"Do not trouble yourself over it, Highness. I will speak with Hernon and then his superior on his behalf, if it is warranted. Is there anything else you require?"

"No. I am well provided for," the Elven Prince assured him.

"If you think of anything else, please have the guards summon me. But if you will excuse me, I have other duties now that I must perform."

"Of course. Ah, wait. There is one other matter. I am rather poor company, of late, and would promptly drive myself mad, I think, if forced to spend any more time with myself than is necessary. Does the King perchance have a book in Common that I might read, or a map that I might study, or some other form of distraction? When packing for this journey, I did not think to bring any, for I thought my time might be short enough that I'd no need of any, if you chose to execute me out of hand, or filled enough if you decided to keep me amused with torture or other absorbing pursuits. Although perhaps I should not give you such ideas! I had not expected to be lounging about eating fruit in the King's tent," he said, his eyes twinkling in merriment and mischief.

ELADAR wondered how he could feel better here, when he had felt so awful on the road with Elavar and Elanara, and worse still in Caramore. He sighed. He hoped they had not drugged the wine. It would be quite disappointing if they had. But no, his head seemed clear, just better attached than it had been of late.

"Of course," Sarnon said. He went to the chest near the King's bed.

Fenlon went over to him and spoke softly to him. Eladar could not hear him, but he heard Sarnon's reply and understood it. "Nonsense. There is certainly no harm in him seeing these, and if they will keep him complacent, it surely will make your job easier. Try to think for a moment how you might feel in his place. He was honest enough about it when he asked me for them."

Fenlon muttered a reply, and Sarnon returned with an armload of maps. "These are of the Dwarven Lands, or at least, the Lands as we knew them, when we left, over seven hundred years ago. They are recent copies of the ones that are safely stored in our Library in Malar, but they are as accurate and well drawn as the originals. They also have the benefit of being in both Dwarvish and Common, as we yet hope to have allies from the other races aiding us in our coming battles."

"Thank you," Eladar said sincerely. "Now, if you would not mind filling my goblet again, and perhaps leaving the flask upon the table, for I appear to be somewhat parched, I think it will be safe for you to depart and leave me to my own devices. I am rather hungry and would hate to see any of the fine repast you prepared go to waste."

Sarnon smiled and left after pouring him more wine, and Eladar began eating in earnest, and studying the maps, careful not to spill anything upon them.

"LAREN? What's going on?" Lunahr asked plaintively. "I was copying songs in my room and now I hear we have Dwarven prisoners, though they're certainly not being treated as such, and Eladar's gone off with some sort of message for the Dwarven army. What have I missed?" It was hard to keep the desperation out of his voice.

Incuban had brought him to his room. He'd wanted to share some pleasure dreams with Lunahr. They'd been wonderful. But then Incuban had found out Lunahr had missed something important, and now he was furious with him. Lunahr was desperate to please Him. It was terrible when Incuban was angry with him. He'd threatened to send him away again. He'd threatened other things too. Lunahr fought to keep from whimpering, but Incuban's anger was burning him. He knew he deserved to be punished. He had to please Incuban. He had to get Laren to talk to him. Maybe then his master might forgive him.

"It's nothing you need to be concerned with, Lunahr. Why don't you go back to your room for a while?" Dewalaren urged. "I'm glad to hear you've been working on your songs. You haven't been singing lately, and I've been worried about you."

"Don't send me away! Can't I help somehow? Please, Laren?" Lunahr begged. He'd been careful to wait until he'd seen Rolin wasn't in the room with Laren. He was safe from Laren, he'd not tried to view his core, but Rolin had, more than once, they'd felt it. Incuban had been careful to hide from Rolin. But Incuban didn't want him near Rolin now. He'd talked earlier about how they might keep Rolin away for good, in the pleasure dreams. Incuban had told him what to do, but now He was making him wait. Incuban was concerned the others might get suspicious if Rolin had an accident now.

Colin entered the Audience Chamber. "Majesty! Eladar has returned!" he said, excited.

"Has he been disarmed and bound as ordered?" Dewalaren asked.

"Yes, Sire!"

"Then summon Rolin at once. We need to test Eladar." Laren turned to him. "Lunahr, this might be dangerous. I don't want you near Eladar until we're sure of him."

Lunahr felt tears well in his eyes and, to his relief, upon seeing them, Laren relented. "All right. You can listen from behind the wall."

DEWALAREN was worried about Lunahr. He looked like he was ready to faint, and he was so moody lately. He seemed so young and helpless. He hoped the King's Madness was not threatening his young cousin, but he'd been through so much, his core might have weakened and made him more susceptible to it.

Elavar came in with Elanara. Dewalaren's gaze went from Elanara to his Guard. "This is no place for the Princess. Remove her."

"Don't you dare try to!" she snapped. "My place is here, with my brother! With what might be left of him. I was not here when he left, but I will be here for his return. I will never forgive you for this, Talon, if he has been harmed."

Dewalaren sighed heavily as the Guard hesitated. "So be it. She may stay." It rent his heart just to look at her. She was so beautiful, so filled with passion, with love, but none of it for him, never for him. He forced his eyes away from her. The door opened, and Eladar was carried in. His eyes were flashing with anger. His hands and feet were bound, and he was gagged.

"Test him," he commanded Rolin. He placed his hand upon Rolin's arm. "But please, be careful."

Rolin nodded and headed for Eladar, striding boldly toward him. He touched his face and Eladar seethed. Elves did not like to be touched by Man, especially upon the face, without their express permission.

Dewalaren saw Rolin's face strain with effort, but then he relaxed. "He is unharmed. His mind is his own," Rolin said in relief.

"Free him," Dewalaren commanded. The Guard began cutting the ropes and removed the gag from Eladar's mouth.

"How dare you treat me like this, after I risked my life for you! I can see I've chosen the wrong side! I was treated far better by the Dwarves as their prisoner than I am by you as an ally!" Eladar raged.

"Enough! I am your King, lest you forget. You have sworn oath to me. You are commanded to silence!" Dewalaren snapped.

Eladar glared, but held his tongue.

"Now then. You will report everything that happened to you, from the moment you left us, and you will do so respectfully, or I swear to Idare I will bind you and gag you again."

Eladar began his report coldly, accurately, and succinctly. He stated the perplexing and disturbing fact that Farad's first question to him, upon hearing who he was, was to ask if Elanara was safe.

Dewalaren frowned, worried that she might be a particular target. "Why would he ask that?" he puzzled aloud, not expecting an answer.

"I asked him that very question. He told me he asked because she is betrothed to you. He said you truly love her, and if she were still alive, and here with you, it might make what is to come easier for you to bear. He said he did not want you to suffer more than you must. Then he added, so very softly I do not think he meant to be heard, that he did not want you to suffer at all. It was obvious he is in agony over what they are planning. Yet his will seemed his own."

"Why, then, act against me? No, he is controlled. He must be. It is the only explanation I can believe. Farad would never willingly betray me."

ELADAR continued his report, omitting having lost his temper with Hernon and letting the presence of their Army slip. But he told them the rest, all he had seen and heard and guessed. Eladar also told him Hunter had not needed to touch his face to know he was not tainted by the Enemy.

DEWALAREN was troubled by what he heard. Could Farad truly be so powerful? Or had he merely led Eladar to believe so, and not tested him because he himself was controlled? He would find out soon enough.

"It is good to know there is some dissension in their ranks, as well. The High-King's daughter sounds like she might cause them some trouble. I had hoped you might learn something of what they are planning against me. But they have agreed to the parlay, at least."

He switched to Amontirin. "Rolin, tell Colin and Garrett to ready themselves. We will exchange them for Jargas and Farad, as agreed. I am surprised they did not request a third hostage, for their High-King, and that they would risk losing him. This Man intrigues me. I had not known the

Dwarves would acknowledge rule under a High-King, and even so, I would not have expected them to bow before a Man. There is a story here. Perhaps we might learn it.

"There is much to do. If their army has halted its march, we must set up our troops as best we can around them. I had hoped for the high ground the valley would have accorded us, but it is not to be made so easy for us."

LUNAHR nearly fainted in relief as he listened from behind the panel of the concealed alcove. Incuban was ecstatic. Jargas was coming here, and Farad. They would both be within his grasp so very soon. Lunahr must be ready with his poison-tipped arrows and blade. Incuban was not sure who he'd need to kill, yet, but Dewalaren had already announced Lunahr officially as his Heir. By the end of the day, he would be the new King. A great many might need to die to see that his title was secure.

Lunahr would do anything Incuban asked. He was so happy he might be able to please Him now. He had been terrified that Incuban would send him away again, or perhaps even kill him, He'd been so angry.

How could he have worried? Incuban loved him. He'd shown him in his room how much He loved him in his dreams. And soon Incuban would be here, with all His minions. He'd be able to show Lunahr in person again how loved he was.

Incuban had so much love to give. He'd share His love with all his new kin, but Lunahr would still be His favorite. He'd let Lunahr aid him in loving his kin. Lunahr's manhood stiffened as he trembled in anticipation.

But first we must have help, if we are to make you King, Lunahr. It is time your friends helped you, and in return, you will help them as well. They will love you even more for it, Lunahr.

As soon as Dewalaren finishes his audience with Eladar and Elanara, you must go to them each separately. Dewalaren has wounded Eladar's pride terribly. You saw how cruelly Dewalaren treated poor Eladar. He bound him and gagged him, after he had risked his life for him!

And Dewalaren has hurt Elanara even worse, forcing her to betroth herself to him, when her heart belongs to another. Eladar has told you of it. He could not help himself. You are such a good listener, and you love his sister. You have been as a brother to both of them. You know Elanara loves Rion, the young Man we have begun to hear so much about. You cannot let your former guardian suffer so. She must not be kept from her love.

We must free both Eladar and Elanara from Dewalaren. I can help you free them, Lunahr. And then, once Dewalaren and the others are dead, we will help Elanara still. We shall find Rion for her. We will summon him before us. I am so very eager to meet Rion. There is so much I wish to learn about him and so very much I might teach him.

Lunahr fought a wave of jealousy, but Incuban laughed and caressed him.

How can you be jealous, Lunahr, when you know you are my favorite? You will always be my favorite. Besides, until we bring Rion for Elanara, she will be so very lonely. We must not allow Elanara to be lonely. You and I will comfort her, while she awaits Rion. We will share her between us. You have so much love to give, Lunahr, and you have not yet had the opportunity to love a woman. There are so many sweet new pleasures you will learn, so many wonderful things you have yet to experience. And Elanara has likely experienced few of them herself. See what we will teach her.

Lunahr's mind was awash with visions of Elanara's and Eladar's happiness, of the pleasures he and Incuban would bring to both of them. The pleasures the brother and sister he loved would bring to one another, under Incuban's guiding hand.

Lunahr's heart swelled with love for Incuban, that he would be so considerate, so compassionate toward his friends, when he already had so many important things to do.

Everything of import had been said within the Audience Chamber. He listened impatiently at the concealed panel until Elanara and Eladar were dismissed, and then left his hiding place, eager to help his friends.

"HUNTER, we've captured someone. He appears to be a kinsman of yours," Gernan reported. "Forgive us, but we had to injure him. He did something to us. He spoke and all but two of us were felled. I struck him upon the head. He is unconscious, but still our men will not move, though they yet breathe, they yet live."

"Why would Talon risk such treachery now?" Farad wondered aloud. "What might he gain from it?"

"He did not come from the King's camp, Hunter. He came from behind us. From the Man's reaction, I do not think he had thought to find Dwarves here. I think he might have been heading to Caramore when we waylaid him," Gernan said.

Farad turned to Jarina eagerly. "If he truly is one of our kin, we may be able to sway him to our side. He might lend weight to our claim. If he used the King's Voice on Gernan's men, it must be either Fennel or Pierce. Both are Lords. No other is strong enough. Fennel is House of Horses and Pierce is House of Foxes. I'd feared both might have been slain. With my support, and yours, and Archer's, that would make four Houses! Talon would have only the remaining House and his own to back his claim to the throne, and Jargas has stronger claim to the title of Lord of House of Obearn than Talon does, for being of Rowanar's blood. Bring your medicines, Jarina."

Farad turned to Gernan. "Take us to him and then tell Jargas and Archer immediately thereafter. We've not much time before we are to leave for the hostage exchange."

Gernan led them to the captive. Farad saw it was Aramis, known to Men as Pierce. He'd last been assigned to Thenalon. He looked like he had traveled many weeks to reach them, likely with little food or rest. Lines were etched into his face that had not been there twelve years ago, and his hair was already shading to gray.

Farad had hoped it might have been Rolin who had come. Aramis hated and feared him. Rolin might have listened more readily. But Jargas was King, not him, and Aramis had no reason to hate or fear Jargas. And with Desmond's voice also to sway him, as Lord of House of Serpents, Aramis might listen. Merely seeing the King's Armor and the true King's Band might sway him, even without revealing the Ring. But first he must help the Dwarves Aramis had immobilized, and he must test Aramis for taint by the Enemy.

Farad reached out from his core to awaken the Dwarves, gently, as he had awakened Gervan and Arvan in Malar in Fromer, with the most gentle breeze upon their cores. He marveled at how easy it was to break Aramis's hold over them. It was so weak! The Ring had restored so much strength to him. His Power frightened even him, now.

Gernan brought his men away, as Farad instructed, so that he and Jarina were left alone with Aramis, or the Resemblant that posed as his kinsman. It might well be Incuban's Power through his servant in Aramis's form that had felled the Dwarves. He took a deep breath and tested Aramis, dreading what he might find.

He stepped back in relief. It truly was Aramis. But he had been through so much in the past five years. He had not meant to see, but the anguish of it had churned all around him. They had all been driven so close to death. Had Jargas not found Farad in Malar, and restored his core, if Jargas had not later revealed he possessed the Ring, they all might have died. It had been such a close thing that it frightened him. And they had not yet achieved victory. They must first conclude the battle that had yet to begin among their own ranks, before they might even begin to seek out their true Enemy.

"We must keep him carefully bound while you tend to him, Jarina. Then we must waken him and allow him to test me, if we are to have any hope of swaying him to our side. We must be certain of where his loyalties lie when we leave. We must keep him unconscious if we cannot convince him. He would be a danger while we are gone. He would try to use his Power to escape, even bound and gagged, and the army might then be forced to kill him."

"We will not fail, Husband," Jarina assured him, as she knelt beside Aramis to begin treating his injury.

Once she finished treating the wound on Aramis's head and examining him for other injury, she revived him.

Aramis's eyes narrowed upon waking and seeing Farad beside him. "Farad," he spat, as if his name were a curse. "I might have known you were up to treachery. I was suspicious when I saw Rolin's message saying he was relaying yours. I suspected Caramore would be a trap. You've brought your Dwarves here, I see," he said, speaking in Amontirin.

"No, Aramis. These Dwarves are not from the east, but from the west. The armies of the thirty Western Kingdoms march with us, against the Enemy. The Ring has been found."

Aramis shook his head. "It cannot have been. Where would you have found the Ring?"

"On the finger of the True King, Jargas, grandson of Rowanar," Farad said evenly.

Aramis eyed him shrewdly. "I am not so gullible as to believe that."

"Then I will have to show you the Ring, and the Heir," Farad said. "But first you must test me for taint by the Enemy."

"You'd like that, wouldn't you? Me to lower my defenses like that," Aramis said shrewdly.

Farad shook his head. "Your defenses are not as strong as they need to be. The Ring can strengthen your core, as it did mine. I've already viewed your core, while you slept. I only meant to check for taint. But I've seen memory, enough to convince you that I've touched you while you slept. I saw Lord Garathon of Aralon being cast out from Thenalon, after all the work you did to bring him there. I saw Thunderbolt throw you three years ago. Your back still pains you from it, so badly that you can hardly draw your bow. You are in agony when you but walk. Yet that pain is nothing compared to the pain in your heart when you were cast from Thenalon yourself two years ago."

Aramis's face darkened with rage.

"I do not want you as my enemy, Aramis," Farad said softly. "You have been one for too long already, though I wish it were otherwise." He continued more strongly. "I am sorry, but there is not much time. I hope to convince you Jargas's claim to the throne is sound. I hope you might ride with us when we go to unseat Dewalaren, so your House follows you."

"Unseat Dewalaren?" Aramis asked, appalled. "And you speak of my heart! But I see your eyes. I am talking to a shadow. The real Farad is dead. Nothing you show me will bear any weight," he said. Then his eyes widened in shock, focused on a point over Farad's shoulder. "It cannot be."

Farad turned. Desmond strode up, in Rowanar's armor. It gleamed like blood-dipped copper in the sun. The sun's fire leapt from the images etched upon the breastplate, so that the creatures depicted seemed to move, to leap and run and slither, as he walked, as Aramis watched in awe. The armor was legendary to their kin. "This, then, is Jargas, Rowanar's heir?" Aramis asked, his voice almost reverent.

"No. This is Desmond, Lord of House of Serpents, long thought lost to us. He is the High-King of the thirty Dwarven Kingdoms of the West. The Dwarves know him by the name Archer," Farad told him.

Jargas strode up behind Desmond.

"That is Jargas, Rowanar's Heir. He gifted Rowanar's armor to Desmond, as he cannot wear it."

Jargas eyed the Man before him and spoke in Common. "You've been ill-treated, cousin. Forgive us. Our goal has been to avoid bloodshed when I claim the throne, but still, we know it will be hard to do without causing some injury. Have you tested Farad? Once you do, you must test me as well, I suppose. But our time grows short. We must be at the rendezvous in time to exchange hostages. Your arrival was both well and ill timed. Sooner would have been better."

Aramis's eyes narrowed. "So that is it. I am to be a hostage?"

Farad shook his head. "The three of us are to be. If you ride with us, you must bear the same risk."

Aramis studied Jargas intently. "Farad says you have the Ring. I see the King's Armor. And you have the band of your House?"

"Nay. That band was lost long ago, I have heard. But I wear the King's Band." He showed the band to Aramis. It was identical to the band Dewalaren wore, save that it was crafted of the distinctive reddish copper of pyrenteum. It blazed beneath the rays of the sun. "I currently wear Stephan's band as well, House of Gryphon, though it is not my own. I deceived Dewalaren with it, concealing my true House. I wish now I had not, but what is past is past. I cannot change it. But you see the Ring," Jargas said, holding out his hand. The stone set into the pyrenteum band of the Ring was glowing, pulsing with the beat of his heart.

"I would touch you, Farad, and test you," Aramis said warily.

Farad sighed. "Be careful, cousin. My core shines on the outside now, but it is still terrible to look upon on the inside. Jarina, be ready to aid him if need be," he said to his wife, who had been standing silently beside him.

"Yes, Husband," she said.

"Husband? That I cannot believe!" Aramis exclaimed.

"Neither can I, though it is true," Farad said, with the ghost of a smile, then his face resumed its somber cast. "Test me, Aramis, but be careful."

Farad forced his shield down. It was hard. It kept trying to spring back in place. "Help me, Jarina. It hurts me to leave myself so unguarded."

"Courage! I am here, Husband," she said, and aided him in forcing the shield down.

A few moments later Aramis drew back. He was trembling. "I cannot imagine what your core must have looked like before! It truly is terrible, but so strong! Now I must test this man who seeks to claim the King's throne."

Aramis did so and drew back. "His core is as strong as your own. And there is not a trace of Madness in him. I never knew one of us might have such Power, without the Madness it brings. You both all but blind me with your brilliance!"

"Do you trust us now?" Farad asked. "Enough to let us fortify your own core? Enough to swear fealty to Jargas?"

"Tell me the story of Rowanar, first. What of the Houses that traveled with him?" Aramis asked.

Jargas told him the story, of how Rowanar and the ten Houses he led had traveled through a pass far west and south of where they should have been. The Enemy had apparently attacked them, burying them all in a tomb of rock. Rowanar alone had survived. The King's Armor had saved his life, but his helmet had somehow been lost in his travels. Stephan died protecting him, but some of the rock still struck Rowanar's head, injuring him terribly.

He was rescued and healed by the Chieftess of the Varash, Jargas's grandmother, but he had lost his memory, so that he even had to learn how to speak again. He married the Chieftess and became the village Champion, finding happiness with the Varash, and living many decades longer than a Man should live.

Aramis said, "I had hoped some others might have survived. There are so few of us. Still, two new kin and a restored House, plus Desmond, long thought lost to us, yet live."

Jargas said, "He has a daughter as well: Shanti, my wife. So there are four more to add to your nineteen. And my sister is House of Pumar, though Farad tells me her band and line were lost long ago. There are twenty-three of us now, six Houses."

"Twenty-three? Six Houses?" Aramis said, puzzled. "No, there are twenty-four, seven Houses."

"Have you not heard, cousin?" Farad asked, his voice a whisper. "Riviera and Loatia have fallen. Lunahr…." Farad's voice broke upon his name. He forced himself to continue. "House of Eagles is no more."

Aramis appeared stricken. "Lunahr? No, he could not be! We sent him away so he might be safe!" he said in denial. "So he might come-of-age and we might see his House grow. Eagles has always been one of our strongest."

Aramis gazed into Farad's eyes searchingly, and then looked away. "I had not known you still had a heart, cousin, even having viewed your core, yet now I see it breaking."

Farad's voice was a ragged whisper. "All of us loved him, but he was precious beyond naming to me. He was one of only three who did not hate nor fear me. Now Dewalaren will be lost to me as well. And Rolin, if he yet lives, will hate me for what I now do."

"We both wear masks to conceal our pain. Yet the pain in my back is as nothing to that in your heart," Aramis said astutely, in unexpected compassion.

Farad was surprised by his words. Aramis was not known for his kindness. To his utter astonishment, Aramis smiled at him. "Rolin always told me I did not get along with you because you and I are so much alike. I have spent decades denying it. I had always viewed it as an insult. I never understood why Rolin, who is my closest friend, might say such a thing to me. But now that I have viewed your core, I see it is a rare compliment. Do not despair, cousin. You are not so alone as you fear. You have your wife and these other new and recovered kin here. But you also now might have my friendship, should you wish it."

Farad stared at Aramis, stunned. "Do you truly mean that?"

"Farad, I have smiled at you. Do you remember a time, ever, when I have done so? I gift my smiles rarely enough to anyone that I remember each of them. I can tell you, this is your first." And he laughed, and his keen eyes twinkled for a moment.

Farad's shocked face broke into a grin. "And you never laugh, almost never. You make me look jovial by comparison. Cousin, I welcome your friendship. I will cherish it always," Farad said, placing his hand upon his shoulder gently, instead of clapping it down heartily as he might have, lest he pain Aramis's back further.

Aramis turned to Jargas. "You are married as well. So, as the new King, you would bring stability of two kinds: Power, without Madness, and heirs. I never thought I would swear to another as King. But now I shall. And my

House, what is left of it, will swear to you as well." He knelt before Jargas, slowly and awkwardly, and swore oath to him. Then he rose stiffly, hissing in pain, though Farad could see how he fought to hide it.

"Then we've only Rolin and Dewalaren to stand against us," Farad said. "It heartens me to hear you saw a message from Rolin. When I saw the state of Thenalon and Aralon, and no sign of either of you, I'd feared the worst. The Enemy sows his seeds of dissension everywhere."

"You are forgetting the army Hernon told us of, that Eladar spoke of, Farad," Desmond said. "Be they Men or Elves, they will stand against us as well. Much will depend upon them. Come, we will be late. Jargas, give Jarina the Ring. We must hurry."

"We have time to help Aramis first," Jargas said. With Aramis's consent, he touched his face. The Ring flared brightly and then, a few moments later, dimmed again.

"Would that my body were so strong again!" Aramis said. "I will be of little use to you, should you need to fight. But I will lend my voice to yours."

Jargas gave the Ring to Jarina and hugged her. She embraced him tightly and then hugged Farad. "You must both return to me safely."

THE four of them rode off, Farad and Aramis in front, and Jargas and Desmond behind them. Desmond was on a white charger and Jargas was on a massive steed, a tremendous gray animal who carried his impressive bulk with ease. Aramis was on a borrowed horse, black as night. Farad rode Aragar.

Farad saw Aramis's jaw twitch as he rode. His back was unnaturally stiff and straight. It was obvious it was causing him pain to ride, yet he did so without complaint. Aramis was proud and strong. For him to be betraying so much, he must be in agony. But there was nothing further he might do to aid his kinsman. Farad wished they had the lost King's Knife as well, so they might heal him.

They approached the exchange point warily. Two hundred Dwarves trailed them at a distance.

They saw two figures on horseback slowly approach. Farad saw Colin's eyes widen as he recognized Aramis. "Pierce!" he called out, in surprise. "You were not mentioned. How is it you ride with them? You do not appear to be their prisoner."

"Thistle! Then is Fennel lost? I cannot believe he would send you and Basil, when he should go himself," Aramis said, distressed that Rolin was not there instead.

But Colin was staring behind him, stunned at seeing Desmond in Rowanar's armor. "It cannot be!"

"I am sorry, cousin. We cannot stay to explain, or both sides will fear treachery," Farad said. "I am sure your army watches as ours does, though I can see no sign of them. We must ride past each other, as agreed."

They did so, but Colin and Garrett turned about in their saddles, eyes still riveted upon Desmond.

Aramis did not turn to watch them in turn. Farad's concern for his kinsman grew. He suspected he might not be able to.

ROWENA said to Dewalaren, "They are approaching the others." Her brow was creased in concentration. "But there are four, not two. The two in front... Colin sees Farad and... Aramis! Aramis is with them!"

"Aramis? They said nothing of him," Dewalaren said, concerned.

"He does not appear to be their prisoner, but Father says he is sitting stiffly in the saddle, that his posture is all wrong. Aramis always rode with the ease of one of our House. Aramis is asking after Uncle Rolin. He is distressed to see Father and Garrett. He fears Uncle might have been lost to us," Rowena said. Then her eyes widened and she grew silent.

"Rowena, what's wrong? Has something happened to your father?" Dewalaren asked in sudden dread, that he might have sent two more of his kin to their deaths or to the Enemy, and that Rowena might be in danger as well, through her link to her father.

She shook her head, eyes focused elsewhere.

"Then what...." he said, but Rowena interrupted him.

"Majesty, please! He is so far away. It is hard for me to hear. I cannot when you speak also. We are not so strong as you," she pleaded.

"Forgive me," Dewalaren apologized softly and waited silently, anxiously.

She shivered then exhaled a deep breath. "They are safe. They have been surrounded by what appears to be two hundred Dwarven soldiers. They were asked to surrender their weapons and then both they and their horses' saddles were searched. But they have remounted. They are not being forced to walk. They are not even bound. They are being treated with much courtesy. They have been told they are being taken to King Rongas, Jargas's father, that he has offered them the hospitality of his tent. They said he will be happy to answer the questions they must have, as well as he can."

Her eyes focused outward again. "I am sorry I concerned you, Majesty. It was quite a shock. I have never heard Father so conflicted. There were four of them altogether, not two, as we had expected. Farad and Aramis rode side by side in front. Two Men dressed and groomed like Dwarves rode behind them. One was a giant, and his horse was spectacular. Father had never seen that breed before. It was enormous but beautiful. From what you told us, the rider must be Jargas. But there was a Man next to him, no taller than you, older, and… he wore the King's Armor, Majesty. Rowanar's armor, Albinar's."

Dewalaren stared at her in disbelief. "He could not have."

"Father described it to me. It was the color of copper, only too red to be. The breastplate was etched everywhere with the symbols of our Houses, as they appear on our bands. House of Horses was clearly visible. Father said it was as if the horse pranced, that the sun made the etchings appear to move. He could not take his eyes away. He turned so far about in his saddle he almost unseated himself. Father has never fallen from a horse in his life."

Dewalaren swallowed. "Then I fear I know what has come over Farad. Jargas has tricked him. Farad believes this other Man is Rowanar's Heir. He rides against us because he thinks he has found the True King. And now it seems Aramis has been deceived as well. Jargas will be surprised to find he faces the Lords of eleven Houses, when he thought he would find only two. He thinks only Obearn and Horses stand against him. He cannot know Lunahr is here, or our newfound kin."

ROLIN was listening anxiously to his niece. Dewalaren had commanded him to sever the bond he had shared with his younger brother Colin since childhood, for safety, in case the Enemy seized him or killed him. Rolin had been terrified he might lose Colin, when he might have saved him, but he had done as his King commanded.

"We will change our plans accordingly," Dewalaren instructed. "I want all ten Lords here by my side when they enter the Audience Chamber. All must know Aramis and Farad are to be harmed only as a last resort. They must be made to see Jargas and this false Heir for the charlatans they are. They must wait in the courtyard while Commander Thaedrin reports to me all they have seen and heard." He turned to go.

"Majesty, wait!" Rowena urged. "You must know one more thing. Farad said he was sure our army watched them, as theirs did. He knows about the Elven army."

Dewalaren cursed. "It seems we must change all our plans. We've not much time. Rowena, I have a dangerous and important mission for you to perform. Rolin, I will need you to aid her. I would never command this of you, did I not know how much you love your niece. I would have you bond to her."

FARAD, Aramis, Jargas, and Desmond rode forward. Suddenly, over one hundred cloaked Elves appeared as if from thin air from the valley walls and surrounded Farad and the others, bows trained upon them. "Dismount from your horses and lay down your weapons and you'll not be harmed," their leader said in Common.

"At least now we know the army Eladar spoke of is real," Farad said softly. "Do as they command." He touched his link to Jarina and told her of the Elven army, even as they complied with the Elf's demands.

A dozen Elves approached, ropes in hand. Farad paled, and Jargas's face darkened in rage. "We'll not be bound."

"You've no choice," the Elven Commander said.

"Thaedrin, you'll not bind them. Our orders were to disarm them and escort them with all courtesy," another Elf said.

"Your men don't outnumber mine this time, Theodas," Thaedrin said. "Step aside or I'll bind you as well."

Farad's heart began hammering as the Elves reached for him. "**WE WILL NOT BE BOUND**," he commanded, his voice ringing with the Power of the Ring as his eyes flashed golden fire. All one hundred Elves froze where they stood.

"Farad, what have you done?" Jargas asked, dismayed.

"I could not let them bind me," Farad said, stunned by his own action.

Aramis gaped at him, thunderstruck. "How can you wield such Power?"

"I called upon the Power of the Ring," Farad said. "I am sorry, Jargas. I did not mean to."

"Farad, this cannot be their entire army," Jargas reasoned. "You must release them, quickly, or the parlay will fail. They'll have no knowledge of what's happened to them. It will be like Gervan in Malar."

"Jargas, I cannot be bound! You of all people know that I cannot be," Farad said desperately.

"Then you must go back to camp and await us there. I will free them once you are safe," Jargas instructed.

"No! I can abandon neither you nor Dewalaren. I will allow them to tie me. I will release them."

"Wait," Desmond said. "Perhaps we can use this to our advantage." He turned to the immobile and insensate Elf nearest him and removed the rope from his hand, and dropped it on the ground at his feet. "Can you awaken them individually?" Desmond asked, as he pulled another rope from an Elf's hand.

Farad thought for a moment. "Yes, I believe I can."

"Then all of you, pick up your weapons again. Once we remove these ropes, disarm that one and awaken him, Farad," he said, pointing to the one called Theodas. "I will speak with him."

Farad nodded and they readied themselves. "All right, release him," Desmond commanded.

THEODAS stared at the prisoners, astonished. Their weapons had suddenly appeared in their hands again, and there was a pile of rope at their feet. He reached for his sword, even as he realized no one else was moving: they stood as if statues. He discovered with a sinking heart his sword was no longer at his side.

"We do not wish to harm you. We want only to talk," the older Man, groomed as a Dwarf, said.

"What have you done to them?" Theodas asked, looking at his comrades, appalled.

"They are not harmed," the Man assured him. "We will release them, but we would seek to improve our lot first, if we could. We do not wish to be bound, and it does not sound as if Prince Talon might have ordered us to be. Do you see a solution? We would prefer not to leave your troops here and proceed on alone. We would no doubt meet with hostility, were we to do so."

"I'll not help you. To do what you have done, Arcanus or one of the other wizards must be aiding you. You are truly pawns of the Enemy! The King has his answer." Theodas did not want to believe it, and not only because of the twenty thousand Dwarven troops the King and his own people would face. He had liked Donovar. He had not wanted him to be a pawn of the Enemy.

The Man with the scarred face appeared suddenly wary. "Since when is Arcanus considered an enemy by Talon?"

"I'll not speak anymore. Use your tortures, use your magicks, kill us all here; it does not matter. Our army will crush your own. You will fail," Theodas said bravely, knowing those well might be his final words.

"THIS has not worked as I had hoped," Desmond said, in Amontirin. "His core is too small and dark for me to learn anything from him, other than what he has told us, and he has told us little. Farad, can you keep him conscious but control him?"

Farad shook his head. "His core is not strong enough," he replied in Amontirin. "I could only control simple actions and they would immediately know something was wrong. But I can freeze him now, so that we may put everything back as it was before. Then I will waken the others, but fell him. I will not wake him until after our mission is complete."

"Do so," Desmond commanded.

Farad froze Theodas with a thought. Jargas clasped Farad's shoulder. "You will still be bound, Farad. Can you bear it?"

Farad nodded. "I must. Jarina will aid me. But Jargas, if I cannot bear it, though I try, she must break her bond to me and you must fell me. I would be violent otherwise. I would not be able to help myself. Jarina can aid you with the Ring's Power against my own through her bond to you. Listen to her voice, Jargas. She will tell you if it is necessary. I am sorry I am so weak."

Jargas squeezed his shoulder. "You are far from weak, my friend! I have yet to meet the Man who is stronger than you in will, or braver than you, or more noble. I hope you might one day see yourself though my eyes."

"All is ready," Desmond said. "Once Theodas falls, they might suspect us and treat us roughly. I am hoping some might argue upon our behalf, that if we'd felled anyone, it would have been Thaedrin, rather than one who was trying to aid us. Now we must lay our arms down again and return their ropes to them."

They did so.

"Now, Farad, release the army and fell Theodas."

Farad complied. The army could suddenly move again, and Theodas crumpled at Thaedrin's feet.

"COMMANDER!" Feonas cried, kneeling by Theodas's side. He glared up at Thaedrin. "What did you do to him?" he demanded, angrily in Elvish.

"I did not touch him. It was the prisoners," Thaedrin accused.

"Why would they harm one who tried to aid them?"

"To shift suspicion from themselves. To sow the seeds of dissension among our men," Thaedrin said in Elvish. Then he ordered tersely in Common, so the prisoners would understand, "Bind them! If they resist, kill them!"

Feonas stepped protectively in front of the prisoners and spoke in Common to Thaedrin. "You would kill envoys of peace, whom you have been ordered to safely escort? Perhaps it is you who is the Enemy's pawn! You are the one seeking dissension, Thaedrin. You might have been the one who felled Theodas. Drop your weapon and surrender yourself to your second-in-command. You must be bound until the King can test you for signs of taint by the Enemy," Feonas said, hand on his sword hilt.

"I do not take orders from the Guard," Thaedrin said contemptuously. "Stand aside." His hand went to his own hilt.

"Commander Thaedrin, on suspicion that you may have been compromised by the Enemy, you are hereby ordered to surrender your weapons. You will be bound and escorted back to headquarters," Captain Lareth said, drawing his sword.

Thaedrin stared at him in shock. "You conspire with the Navy against me, Lareth? This is mutiny! Lieutenant Sadrin, I order you to disarm and bind Captain Lareth."

Lareth tensed.

"I am sorry, sir," Sadrin said. "Please do not resist, Commander. I do not wish to harm you."

Thaedrin's face darkened in rage as he removed his sword and tossed it into the dirt at the feet of Lareth's horse. "The three of you will answer to the High-King for this," Thaedrin promised.

"Captain Lareth," Feonas said. "As we are of equal rank, but you are longer in service, my men and I will follow your orders. What do you command in regards to the envoys?"

"I will follow your fallen Commander's recommendation, Captain Feonas, that they are envoys and not prisoners, and it would not be proper to bind them," Lareth replied.

Thaedrin, who was being bound, began to hurl vile imprecations against both of them.

Lareth said, "You will be silent, Commander Thaedrin, or you will be gagged."

Thaedrin's eyes flashed, but he grew silent.

Their healer Janus checked Theodas. "He does not seem to be in any danger. His heart and breathing are strong. We will carry him."

They began riding to Caramore.

AFTER what he estimated to be about two hours had passed, Farad studied Aramis in concern. He was sweating heavily, his hands were trembling, and he looked ill. "Cousin, why did you not tell us you could not make the journey?" Farad asked in sympathy in Amontirin.

"I can make it," Aramis said bravely.

"I just touched your core, Aramis. It is a wonder you are still conscious, or that you can yet talk, let alone sit in the saddle. I'll not have you suffer further," Farad said.

"Captain Lareth, we have need of the healer who rides with you," Farad called out.

"Why, are you ill?" Lareth asked, appraising him coolly.

"I am not, but my kinsman Pierce is in pain from an old injury. I had not realized this journey would harm him. It will be at least two more hours until we reach Caramore. Please, might your healer tend to him?"

LARETH examined the Man called Pierce, who was sitting stiffly and proudly in the saddle. He indeed appeared to be in pain. He halted the troops and called for Janus. Lareth instructed Pierce to dismount.

ARAMIS'S face burned with shame. He winced as he turned his head to Farad. "I cannot dismount without aid, Hunter. I do not think I can even with it."

Jargas said, "I will aid you, cousin. If I hold you about the waist, will it harm you?"

"Anywhere will. Just do it quickly," Aramis said.

Jargas dismounted and went to Aramis's side and lifted him from the saddle, as if he were a child, placing him gently on the ground. Aramis stifled a moan and collapsed against him, then cried out, and a tear rolled down his cheek.

Farad removed his cloak and laid it on the ground. "Lay him down, Jargas."

"I will tend to him," the Elf who had examined Theodas said, approaching them. His voice was surprisingly compassionate. "I am Janus, a healer. Lay him down."

Jargas set Aramis down carefully.

Janus began examining him, questioning him about his injury. "Three years? You have lived in such pain for three years, instead of being healed?" he asked, sounding stunned.

"I cannot be healed. Many have tried. I have learned to live with the pain. I could bear it, if only I could still draw my bow, if I could still fight. I am useless to my kin as I am… I am worse. I am a liability, a danger. I should have taken my own life long ago, but our Laws will not allow me to, especially now, when there are so few of us left."

Janus shook his head. "I cannot heal him here. I can give him something for the pain, but he still should not ride. He will further injure himself if he does."

"Can he walk without injury? Lareth asked.

Janus shook his head. "We must carry him until we reach the citadel, as we carry Commander Theodas. We will lay him on a stretcher between two horses."

Aramis protested. "I'll not be carried before the King. I am still Lord of my House," he said proudly. "And I'll not have my mind dulled by medicine."

The healer sighed. "We will carry you to the door. By then, the swelling will be less and the medicine will have masked the pain. I will give you only enough to get there. It will wear off by the time we arrive. As long as you take care, you will not harm yourself. But, if you strain yourself further, you will cripple yourself and then even we cannot aid you."

"I'll try not to get into any battles in the Audience Chamber," Aramis said dryly. Then he looked at Jargas and frowned, realizing it might indeed come to that.

"You must drink this and relax," Janus ordered.

"You swear I will have a clear head before the King?" Aramis asked.

"I swear it, as clear as the pain will permit. It will be even worse for you, having been free of it for a time," Janus said solemnly.

Aramis drank. Farad turned to Lareth. "I thank you for your aid. I will not forget it."

"Perhaps you can speak on my behalf at my court martial," Lareth said wryly. "Although the High-King has never been known to summon such witnesses before."

Feonas looked at him in blatant surprise.

Lareth sighed. "Life in Nalea is difficult for my people as well as your own, Captain Feonas. Come, we must continue our march or the King will think some ill has befallen us."

TWO hours later they approached the City. "They must have at least one thousand Elven soldiers here," Farad said in Dwarvish to Jargas and Desmond. They were riding three abreast, now.

Desmond said, "And that's got to be only a fraction of their army. The bulk of it is probably somewhere near ours."

They approached the citadel.

"There are Men here as well," Farad said in surprise. "Has Talon succeeded in rousing them and rallying them to our cause?" He was troubled. The Elven army would never follow Jargas, for his Dwarven blood. Farad could not believe they followed Dewalaren now, from what he had heard of the Elven High-King, Laedrin. The Men they saw glared at them with a mixture of suspicion and hostility. Farad voiced his concerns and Desmond and Jargas echoed them.

The City gate opened before them, and they entered the citadel on horseback. Lareth dismounted and headed for the door to the building.

Chapter 9
Heir to the Throne

FENRIS entered the Audience Chamber breathlessly. Dewalaren scowled at him. "Fenris, where have you been? We...."

"Aramis isn't with them!" Fenris gasped out, then took panting breaths, trying to recover from having run the entire way.

"Fenris, calm down. What do you mean?" Dewalaren asked.

Fenris caught his breath. "I was looking down from the window, into the courtyard. I just wanted to see him. It's been three years since he broke his link to me. I had to see him. I knew I could make it here in time. But he wasn't there. There are only three of them, riding abreast, Farad and the two dressed like Dwarves. Aramis is gone."

He fought the panic in his heart, that his older brother might be dead. He had worried he was lost, it had been three years with no word, and now, just when he had thought him safe, he had again vanished. "I wanted to go to them, but I knew I had to tell you. Please Majesty, send me to find out what's happened," he begged.

"No, Fenris. I need you here, where you will be safe," Dewalaren said. Fenris knew he was to stand as representative of House of Foxes by the King's side with the Lords.

"VERAN, come inside, I have need of you," Dewalaren called.

A moment later Veran entered the Audience Chamber, the arrow-slit he had been manning covered by an Elven soldier. "Yes, Majesty!"

"Veran, go to the door," Dewalaren ordered. "Commander Thaedrin is supposed to report to me upon arrival, before the envoys are led in. We need to find out what's happened. Be sure they do not gain entry without Thaedrin first reporting to me."

"Yes, Majesty!" Veran said, and ran from the room, after a quick glance at his father, Haran. Haran was the Lord of House of Gryphon, though the band of their House had been lost. He was in place at the King's side. Veran was glad the King had sent his twin sister, Falara, along with Rowena out to the army, though what he truly wished was that Falara might instead be safely back at their City with Shadala, his aunt and Chieftess, guarded by the Elves, or in Nalea. All their own warriors were here.

He was relieved to see Goturan was one of the two of his own men at the door. "Goturan, come with me! I am to bring in Commander Thaedrin. The King believes there has already been treachery."

"None will harm you," Goturan said, with fierce protectiveness.

Veran smiled at him and clapped him on the shoulder. "I would rather have you by my side than any other here, my friend." He turned to the Elven guard at the door. "I am to enter with Commander Thaedrin. Do not make it easy for me to enter, should I try to gain entry otherwise."

The Elf nodded. The door was opened and then quickly shut again, an Elf manning one of the concealed peepholes.

Veran approached the soldiers warily. Captain Lareth came up to him. "We have come with the envoys, as ordered." Lareth reported.

"Where is Commander Thaedrin? I am to speak with him," Veran said, looking for him.

"Thaedrin has been temporarily relieved of his command," Lareth said. "I am acting Commander."

"Relieved of his command?" Veran asked in surprise. "On what grounds? On whose authority? If he has been, why is Commander Theodas not in command? Do you not recognize that he outranks you?" Veran asked. He wondered if the Army was again acting against the Navy. He knew the King had hoped his previous reprimand of Thaedrin might have sent a sufficient message to his men that such prejudices were not to be tolerated under his command.

"Commander Thaedrin was to have reported to the King. I should do so in his stead," Lareth said.

Veran's eyes narrowed and his hand went to his sword hilt. "I think not. The King has sent me to speak with you. You will answer my questions, or you will not be permitted entry." His face and voice did not betray his hammering heart. Ninety-nine Elves rode with this one. Had they all been compromised?

Lareth said, "Commander Thaedrin ordered the envoys bound. The envoys protested and he threatened to kill them if they resisted. Commander Theodas confronted Commander Thaedrin. They argued, and suddenly Theodas fell. He still lives, but we cannot revive him. Captain Feonas accused Thaedrin of felling him. He said that he was acting as if in league with the Enemy, to cause dissension in our ranks, to sabotage our mission. He told Thaedrin to surrender himself to me. Thaedrin refused. I ordered him to do so.

He tried to order Lieutenant Sadrin to arrest me instead. The Lieutenant refused. Thaedrin is being held and is bound."

His face tensed in the closest approximation an Elf would ever show to a grimace. "We had to gag him as well. He was silent for a time, but then he secretly tried to rally the men against us. Feonas stated that I should take command, as we are of the same rank but I am senior to him. I have done so. Thaedrin has told us he will see the three of us executed by the High-King for mutiny. We are prepared to report to King Talon for sentencing, as required."

Veran called out, "Captain Feonas, Lieutenant Sadrin, report to me."

Two Elven officers approached. He recognized Feonas. The Wood Elf must be Sadrin. "Have you heard what Captain Laneth has reported to me?"

"Yes, sir!" the Elves said in unison.

"Do you support his story?" Veran asked.

"Yes, sir!" they repeated.

"Where is Lord Pierce, of House of Foxes, the fourth envoy who rode with you?" Veran asked.

"With our healer. He is suffering from an old injury and was unable to ride the entire distance. He has been carried the rest of the way."

"I must see him, before I report to the King," Veran said.

"Captain Feonas, tell Healer Janus to bring Lord Pierce to us," Captain Lareth ordered.

Veran studied the three other envoys on their horses, all watching the proceedings intently. That one must be Hunter, now branded traitor, former Lord of House of Wolven. Next to him, the big one would be Jargas, the one who controlled Hunter, or deceived him. The other, the Man who was the Dwarven High-King, was still a mystery to them. He appeared strong, wise, noble, every bit a King. He did not look evil. Veran cursed silently. This Enemy was treacherous, his minions equally so. He must not be deceived by them. He wondered what they were thinking. He wondered if Hunter was even capable of thought, any longer.

FARAD eyed the two Men who had exited the citadel, intrigued. They had the look of his kin, but they could not be: he recognized neither of them, and he would, were they truly kin. The younger one appeared to be barely older than Rion or perhaps as old as Tarrell, seventeen or eighteen at the most, though he had the leanly muscled build of a Man, a warrior. He was dark haired and dark eyed, with a handsome face, and he had the eyes and bearing of a seasoned commander. But he could not be kin. Lunahr had been the youngest of them.

Farad forced thoughts of Lunahr and the pain that came with them aside. The older Man stood at the other's shoulder. He might have been perhaps thirty-five. He was rugged looking, with more muscle and bone, and a plain, angular face. Farad saw it was the younger Man who spoke, who led.

He listened to the exchange between the Man and the soldiers with interest, and then stared in surprise. The Man had asked for Pierce, by name. He had known Pierce had ridden with them.

Of course! Colin or Garrett must be linked to someone here. They had told them what they had seen. He cursed, silently. The King's Armor would not have the same effect they had hoped for. They had already been warned to expect it. He spoke softly to Jargas and Desmond in Dwarvish.

Farad felt eyes upon him and searched for them. It was the young Man. He was watching him with pity in his eyes. Then he looked at Jargas, and there was unbridled hate. Then he turned to Desmond, and at first there was respect, but then anger.

Farad saw Aramis approach. He was walking stiffly, back straight, Healer Janus beside him. Aramis's face was lined with pain, but he was concealing it as best he could. He must be in agony, to be revealing so much.

The younger Man moved toward him.

Farad dismounted, in sudden anxiety.

"You must get back in the saddle," one of the Elves said to him.

"Pierce, you mustn't let him touch you! I think he is kin to us, though I know him not. If he uses his Power on you, you will fell him with your pain and they will think we have attacked him," Farad called out desperately in Common to him, so the Elves would also understand and be warned.

Veran moved closer, but Janus interposed himself between them. "I am sorry. I cannot allow you to approach him, Warrior Captain Veran," Janus said.

Veran spun about and glared at Hunter and then at Jargas. "Your Master is afraid I will test Lord Pierce, that I will discover He is the one harming him! He is using you, both of you! He is deceiving you. Can you not see it, Hunter? He has tricked you into believing the Man beside you is the True King, because he wears Rowanar's armor. He is not! Armor does not make a Man King! Talon is the rightful King. How can you, of all of us, have betrayed him, after all I have learned about you?"

"You are not the one we came here to face," Desmond said. "If Talon is anything like his father, he has not ordered you to confront Hunter. He would not. It would be far too dangerous for you to. He would face Hunter and all of us himself. You overstep the bounds of your assignment, I think, and you make Talon nervous with this delay. Go, report to him. We will wait here as long as is necessary," Desmond said, scolding him as if he were a junior officer in the Dwarven army.

VERAN'S face reddened. Goturan went to his side and spoke to him in Urwani. "Command me, my Warrior Captain. Should I cut out his tongue for having spoken to you so? Or should we report to the King? For despite the fact your enemy suggested it, he is right in that you were so commanded."

Veran took a deep breath and released it. He answered in Urwani. "And you asked me so many months ago why I took the arrow that was meant for you? How could I lead without you by my side to guide me, my friend? We will report to the King. He must be the one to decide what to do. I long for the enemies we used to face. This new Enemy is far too devious and treacherous for my liking." He turned to the Elves. "We go to report to the King. Thaedrin, Laneth, and Feonas must accompany me. Laneth and Feonas, you are to carry Theodas. Sadrin, you will lead until our return."

"Forgive me, Warrior Captain Veran, but Lieutenant Serath of the Navy is senior to me. He must now lead," Sadrin said.

"Very well, Sadrin," Veran said. "You will accompany me also." He longed to be back among his own troops, where the chain of command was far less convoluted. But he was surprised to see one of the Army voluntarily surrender command to one of the Navy. And Feonas had not sought command once Theodas was felled, either. Perhaps the King's plan of integrating the two forces was working.

As he left, he saw Hunter approach Pierce. Hunter wrapped his arm around him, and Pierce leaned against him, an expression of gratitude upon his face. Veran was surprised to see them so. From what he had been briefed of Hunter, he had had few friends among the Lords, and Pierce had certainly not been one of them.

The guards at the door let Veran and the others enter. There were reinforcements at the door now, both more of his Men and more Elven soldiers. He called for those other Men who were at the door to accompany him, and ordered the Elves who had been with the envoys to surrender their weapons to them, lest they suddenly become treacherous. He could not trust any of them.

They walked quickly to the Audience Chamber. He explained to the guards at the door what had transpired quickly, in Urwani. He went inside alone and came back out a short while later, waving them in.

Thaedrin was shaking with rage, to be brought before the King with his hands bound behind his back, and gagged.

DEWALAREN asked Lord Rolin to see to Theodas.

Rolin reported back, troubled. "Someone has used their Power upon him. It is… it is very strong, Majesty. I have never felt such Power. I can do nothing to waken him."

Dewalaren clenched his teeth. He had liked Theodas, he had needed him. If only he could use his own Power, perhaps it might be enough. "You must test Thaedrin, then, for taint by the Enemy."

Lareth, Feonas, and Sadrin watched with bated breath. "He is clear, Majesty, I can find no trace that the Enemy has touched him," Rolin said. The three stiffened.

"Release him. He will report to me first what has happened, while you test the others." He turned to Thaedrin. "And you will do so, calmly, Commander, lest I gag you again. I have no time to waste on theatrics: the Enemy is at our very door."

Eyes narrowed, Thaedrin reported what had transpired.

Rolin turned to Dewalaren. "None of the others are tainted, either, Majesty."

Dewalaren hid his relief. Then he heard from the others as well, and last from Veran.

Fenris could not keep silent. "Majesty, please, I beg you! Let me go to my brother! I can tell you if the Enemy has taken him. I can help him. You cannot let him suffer so, when I might aid him."

Rolin spoke as well. "Please, Majesty! Pierce is like a brother to me as well. He broke not only his bond with his brother Sorrel but his bond with me. Let one of us link to him, let both of us. We can still save him, I know we can."

"No. They are to be led here. I need the two of you by my side. We will face the four of them with the combined might of twelve Houses: the Lords of eleven and the representative of one."

Reluctantly, the two of them resumed their places.

"Thaedrin, Veran, the two of you are to lead them to us. Lareth, Feonas, Sadrin, for now, you are to report back to your unit. I will speak with you further on all that transpired later. Bring Theodas to the Healers' Hall. Dismissed."

A chorus of "Yes, Majesty" filled the room.

Dewalaren steeled himself to face Farad. He had been dreading this moment from when he first saw Garalathon in the cairn. Garalathon was sheathed at Haran's side, now.

VERAN left and Goturan, who had been waiting outside with the other Men and Elves, went immediately to his side. "Go to the arrow slit I manned before, Goturan," Veran instructed him in Urwani. "You can see and hear from there. I may join you, or may yet get to stay inside with my father and the others."

"No harm will come to either of you," Goturan said fiercely. He had tried to ward him so against harm with his words ever since the fever from the arrow wound had nearly killed him.

Veran smiled grimly and left for the envoys.

FARAD tensed when he saw Thaedrin had come for them, with the young Man, Veran, from before. Thaedrin's eyes flashed with anger as he ordered them to enter. Farad kept his arm about Aramis, who could scarcely walk from the pain. "We never would have brought you, had we known we would harm you so by it, cousin," Farad said softly, as they entered the building.

"It was my choice, Farad. I had to be here. With me here, you've only House of Horses to face, and Rolin and I are as brothers, and he always liked you. We can still do this without bloodshed," Aramis said.

A shudder passed through Desmond. Farad looked at him in concern. "Archer, what is it, what do you feel?" he asked, worried the Enemy might be acting against him.

DESMOND said, "It is not the Enemy. It is these corridors. They are filled with ghosts, cousin. I see the faces of the dead all around me. I have so many memories of these hallways."

Farad said, "Courage, Desmond. We are not all dead. Some of us yet live."

"Few, so few. All so young. None who knew me," Desmond said, his voice haunted.

Farad knew how he felt. The weight of time, of the stones of these corridors, pressed in upon him, as well. He forced himself forward, glad for his arm about Aramis. It helped him as much as it helped his cousin, now, to feel his warmth and strength next to him, even so injured.

They stopped at the Audience Chamber door for a moment and then it was opened for them, and they went inside. Farad stared, stunned. Dewalaren was there, seated on the throne he had always hated to use. Behind him stood Eladar, Elanara, and Elavar. Flanking him, on either side of him, were Men. Eleven Men, six to his right and five to his left, all but two with the band of his House proudly displayed upon his arm, but he almost did not see the others for the Man at Dewalaren's right hand.

"Lunahr! It cannot be!" he cried, forgetting himself so fully that he spoke Lunahr's given name, though he was in a room full of strangers, strangers with the look of his kin, and banded as them. Astonishment turned to fear turned to horror. This was all some terrible trap, a trick, a mind game of the Enemy. He tensed and Aramis hissed in pain, as Farad's arm tightened around him.

Desmond was the one who spoke. "So, now we know why the wizards have become your enemy. We had not thought to find you taken, cousin," he said, and Farad realized he was stalling to give him a moment to recover himself. "Yet here you sit, surrounded by false Lords, and beside one we know has been lost to us." They had walked into a trap, like lambs to the slaughter. Their concern for Dewalaren had been their undoing. They had never dreamt he might have already been lost to them.

DEWALAREN fought for calm. Farad stood before him, embracing Aramis, one who had always been Farad's enemy. But he had cried out for Lunahr, in longing. Something of his cousin must yet remain, for him to have reacted so strongly. And the armor the false King wore! He had thought it a fake, a deception of the Enemy, when Rowena had told him of it, but it truly was Rowanar's armor. It was exactly as the stories had told it to be: even by oil-lamp light the figures upon it shifted and moved. But there was no helm.

How could they have the King's Armor? Surely they could not now have the Ring as well? If the Enemy held the Ring, they were undone! The Lords beside him would be slaughtered. He never should have had them stand here by his side. His first thought had been to keep them safely hidden. And Jargas stood before him again, but in challenge this time. He remembered his battle with him, when he had tested him. Jargas had bested him in Athanark; his staff had broken Dewalaren's borrowed sword. He must not allow Jargas victory this time. Any of the four might have the Ring! They might use it against them at any moment!

Dewalaren sprang to his feet, drawing Kathalanar, and the other Lords drew as well, seeing him bare his own blade.

"DEATH to Talon! Long Live King Hunter!" Eladar shouted from behind Dewalaren, even as he drove the knife he carried into Dewalaren's unprotected back. Dewalaren convulsed, turning halfway toward him, but then he fell.

Farad watched, horrified, then sprang across the room toward them both, as an arrow impaled Eladar from behind, and he fell to the ground.

"What have you done? Murderer! You've killed the King!" Elanara screeched as she lunged for Farad, murder in her eyes and a dagger in her hand.

"Treachery! Archers, slay them all!" Lunahr yelled, even as he drew back the string of his upraised bow and released it, driving an arrow into Desmond's throat.

Farad yelled, "**NO ONE MOVE!**" in a desperate attempt to stem further carnage. He felt everyone in the entire building, his people included, freeze. His Power, supplemented by the Ring his wife held, had been faster than the Elven archers' arrows.

Farad ran to Dewalaren's side, hands shaking. He yanked the knife from Dewalaren's back. Blood was flowing freely. He had to stop the bleeding! But even as he held him, the light left Dewalaren's eyes. His chest fell when it should have risen with his next breath. Farad put his ear desperately to his chest, but Dewalaren's proud heart was still.

"No! It cannot be! You cannot be dead! If the Enemy has killed you, it would mean you were not already lost." He looked in horror at the bloodied knife in his hand. Horror turned to astonishment to frantic hope. It could not be! The blade he held was a stunted copy of the King's Sword Dewalaren wielded. The King's Knife! He held the King's Knife! This blade had never been meant to kill, only to heal. Only the Enemy would have twisted it so terribly, to use the King's Knife to kill the King.

Farad held it to the wound on Dewalaren's back, he forced his Power into it, but it was not enough. "Jarina, help me, I need the Ring!" he cried desperately across their bond.

Jarina had been screaming for him in terror. She had felt her brother fall and had not realized it was Farad who had felled him with all the rest.

"He is unharmed, he will live, Jarina, but Dewalaren will not. Please Jarina! I beg you, the Ring!" She quieted, calmed by his assurance, and he felt the Ring's Power surge across her bond to him once more. It raged like a river in flood, but a river of fire. He banked it and channeled it, forcing it down his hand, into the Knife. The Knife flared like the sun, and he saw the terrible wound close, the severed flesh joining together until his skin was unmarred.

He put his other hand to Dewalaren's head. To his confusion he felt something was wrong. He realized what it was in horror. Poison!

He felt the Ring and the Knife work as they burnt the poison away. "Dewalaren, please, you are healed! You cannot die, not now." He shook him, the Power flowed into him, but he did not waken. Dewalaren's body was healed, but his heart had stopped. He was too late. Dewalaren was already dead.

Farad forced himself away, staggering to Desmond's side. Desmond might yet be saved, unless the arrow had been poisoned as well. Blood was gushing from Desmond's ruined throat. He heard the whistle of air through the hole the arrow had made. The arrow had pierced all the way through. Farad severed the shaft and pulled out the arrow from both ends, and laid the Knife against his throat. Desmond at least was still breathing. He watched the wound heal. Astonished, Farad felt poison burn away from him as well. Why had he not succumbed to the poison? How could he yet live? He would find out later.

He went to Eladar. He must save him as well. He was so young, still an innocent. The Enemy had apparently claimed him, but he must at least give Eladar the chance to live. The Ring might yet heal Eladar of the Enemy's hold upon him. The arrow had barely missed his heart, though the shaft was Elven. He had not thought Elves could miss. He dug the barbed arrowhead out with the Knife, and healed him with it.

There was a blinding flash of silver light from where Dewalaren's body lay and Farad turned in terror. No one else should be moving in this room. Lightning arced from Dewalaren's fingertips, from his feet, from his head and crackled against the stone walls around him. Farad ran to where Dewalaren lay, ready to do battle with Incuban for Dewalaren's body. He would not let him claim it!

To Farad's horror, Dewalaren rose, his eyes crackling with silver lightning. The lightning lashed out at Farad as he desperately tried to counter it with golden flame, to shield himself against it, knowing he was helpless before such an onslaught. It was too late to call upon the distant Power of the Ring. Farad's world ended in a white-hot flash of pain.

THERE was a voice, very faint, from so far away. "Farad, can you hear me? Please, Farad! I need you." Farad felt something warm and wet splash against his cheek. The voice was familiar, he loved that voice, but it was gone, gone forever. He fled away from the sound. "No! Farad, please, you mustn't go that way! You must come back to me! Aras, where are you? Help me! You saw, you showed me. The Enemy does not have him. He would never harm me. He saved me. He is dying. You cannot have killed him, I cannot have! Farad! I love you! Please don't leave me alone!"

There was terror in the voice and pain. He could not so hurt one he loved. But it was a trick. It was the Enemy, it must be. Dewalaren was dead. He could not be calling to him.

Farad heard a scream and realized it was Dewalaren screaming.

Then he heard a different voice.

"Faradan, where are you? What has happened? Please, my love, there is still light here, in your core. You are not yet dead. Why do you not fight? I have driven off the one who harmed you, I have hurt him, but he is so strong! Even with the protection of the Ring, I fear he will break through to you again. I cannot waken Jargas, Desenia cannot waken Desmond. The Elven army is approaching. You did not want death for your kin nor for mine! Help me! Farad, I love you, please don't leave me alone!"

There were no tears from Jarina, there could not be. She was so far away. Or should be. She was here, outside his core, he could feel her, but she could not get in. But if she was here, her body would be in grave danger from the Elves. Dewalaren had screamed. If he was dead, he should not still be able to feel pain. Incuban's servants did not feel pain. Then did Dewalaren yet live? He headed for Jarina. He must understand what had happened.

Farad left his core, warily.

"Farad!" Jarina cried in relief, and ran to him, hugging him tightly. "I thought you were lost to me!"

He returned her embrace. "What has been happening?"

"Jargas and Desmond were felled. We don't know what happened to them. Then you cried for my aid with the Ring. The Elven army is charging toward us. We are surrounded on all sides. Their force appears to be smaller than ours, but they have many bowmen. We are not yet within range of their arrows, but it will be terrible, Farad! I fear both armies will be destroyed."

"Jarina, you cannot let them be. This is all the Enemy's doing. You must tell Desenia our army must throw down their weapons and surrender to theirs. It is our only chance," Farad urged.

"Surrender? Farad, she hates me! She will never listen to such an order from me!" Jarina argued in despair.

"Then I must waken Desmond and Jargas, and tell them what needs to be done," Farad said. "Between the two of them perhaps she will listen. It has been madness here. Go back to your core, so when Jargas tries to touch you to verify I am not being controlled, he will find you and you can assure him."

She kissed him desperately on the mouth and then turned into a pumar and bounded down the strand that connected their cores.

Farad turned his eye outward and sat up.

Dewalaren lay limp at his side. Farad saw to his incredible relief he was breathing, though he was not conscious. He fought the urge to help him and went instead to Jargas. He wakened him and quickly told him what must be done and why, and then went to Desmond and did the same. Then he knelt by Dewalaren once more.

He touched his face gently and probed, trying to view his core. To his surprise and fear he saw instead a great tree of pallenteum encasing it completely. It reminded him of Donovar, the pyrenteum shield around his core, which he said a wizard had erected. Which of The Three had done this? It was not Incuban's work.

Dewalaren had cried for him when he had thought him dead. He would not have, did Incuban control him. But did another control him, or merely protect him?

Gently, he tried to waken Dewalaren, but he could not rouse him. He remembered Jarina had said she'd harmed him. He was not sure what she might have done to him. He might need healing. He laid the Knife upon his head, using only the Power he had left inside him from the Ring, and the blade glowed gently.

Dewalaren's eyes opened, and Farad saw to his relief they were the familiar, deep blue he loved. They no longer flashed silver lightning, and they were bright with love. "Farad!" Dewalaren cried in joy, sitting up and embracing him. "I had thought you lost to me!"

Farad hugged him tightly. "I feared you were lost as well. You were lost. I still do not understand how you live. Eladar attacked you. He stabbed you with a poisoned blade. I ran to your aid, I used the King's Knife to heal your wound, I burnt the poison away, but you were not breathing, your heart had stopped beating, you were dead. You should still be dead," Farad said mistrustfully, as he let go of him and drew back from him slightly.

"How can you have healed me with the Knife? There is no Power at all in it. We have tried to use it before," Dewalaren countered, pulling further away.

Farad challenged, "First you must tell me why you live, and why a pallenteum tree stands where your core should be."

DEWALAREN eyed him warily. Arcanus had asked him the same, just before he almost killed him. But Farad had saved him, and he had been helpless after the second attack. He still did not know what had happened to him, but Farad had revived him, when he could easily have slain him instead. He took a deep breath. "Aras. I live because he revived me. He could not have, had you not healed me, but as my body was healed, he started my heart again. The tree is his. He protects me. I was even able to feel him for a moment, to hear him, to speak to him, but he is lost to me now. It is not a bond of the kind you and I once shared."

"Aras is a wizard?" Farad asked, astonished.

"The secret of his identity is no less precious than the secret of my own once was. I fear he has already been revealed, with what has happened," Dewalaren said. "Now you must tell me how you could use the Knife."

"I will. But first, the Enemy is here, in this room. I fear Eladar has been compromised. He used the King's Knife to stab you, and he had poisoned the blade. I fear for Elanara and Lunahr as well, and there may be others. Elanara acted so quickly, while the rest of us were still in shock, and the arrow Lunahr used upon Desmond was poison tipped as well. We must test them, all who are here. We must see if we can save them."

Farad's face creased in pain as he looked from Lunahr to Elanara and Eladar. "We must slay those who cannot be saved. But Dewalaren, how does Lunahr yet live, even as a tool of the Enemy, when he should be dead, when the Elves must have killed him?"

"They could not. They were holding him and torturing him, to try to save their High-King. The blade Lunahr had wielded upon him was poisoned as well, but with terrible, foul magicks. But Aras healed Lunahr, he was truly healed. How can he have fallen again?" Dewalaren's face showed his pain. "You must test them for me, Farad. I have been relying upon Rolin to keep us safe, and it appears his Power was not up to the task. I cannot use my own Power, while my core is so bound. I am helpless, and we have all almost died for it."

"No, Dewalaren, you are not helpless. It seems the Enemy cannot act against you directly because of the tree that shelters you. That tree of yours may be our second greatest asset in the War," Farad said.

DEWALAREN wondered at his words, looking about him at the fallen. His eyes widened in horror as he saw Rolin and Veran lying prone amongst them. "The Army! Farad, the Elven Army, they were to attack if anything happened to us! Rowena was linked to Rolin, and Falara to Veran. When they fell, the order would have been given to attack! It must already be too late!"

"Do not worry, cousin," a strong voice said, from behind him.

"Jargas, you were able to convince her to surrender?" Farad asked.

"Aye, with Archer's help, though my head still hurts from her screaming," Jargas said. "It was a close thing for a few moments, but the Elves have accepted our surrender."

Farad turned to Dewalaren. "We had the High-Princess order our army to lay down its arms and surrender to yours. It was the only way I could think of to save both armies."

"She convinced twenty thousand Dwarves to surrender to five thousand Elves?" Dewalaren asked in astonishment. "And we had thought her your weak link! I don't know which astounds me more, that the Dwarves would surrender, or that the Elves did not attack anyway. I envy you the discipline of your army!"

"Come, we must begin testing them, and reviving those we can. I cannot believe no one has entered yet," Dewalaren said.

"You need not worry we will be interrupted," Farad assured him. "You will learn why, but later. And I will be the one to test them. We cannot endanger anyone else and we must be certain we are not deceived."

Farad began testing everyone in the room one at a time, beginning with the Elven siblings. When Farad viewed Eladar's, Elanara's, and Elavar's cores with the utmost care, he was surprised and perplexed to find that Elanara's core was far less bright than those of her two brothers, both of whose shone with the strength and Power of one of his kin. He was relieved to discover the Enemy's will was only roughly laid over both Eladar's and Elanara's cores, and Elavar had not been compromised at all. "Elavar is free of taint. The Enemy controls Eladar and Elanara, but only as puppets. He has not harmed them."

He saw Dewalaren's eyes widen in horror. "No, Dewalaren, listen to me. He has not harmed them. He has not raped them. Lunahr has not. Their cores have not been altered. They will recover from this. With his puppets incapacitated, the Enemy is as blind as the rest to all that has happened here. I must view Lunahr next. We must try to free all those who are controlled at the same moment, lest the Enemy unleash His vengeance upon them. I must test the rest and then waken all those who are free of taint, and you must keep them all from trying to kill me as they waken."

Farad checked Aramis. His core was still pure, but he was in agony from his back. "You need suffer no longer, cousin," Farad said softly, as the King's Knife glowed to life. Farad felt Aramis's pain vanish, and then he removed his hold over Aramis. Aramis leapt to his feet.

"Easy, cousin! There is no more immediate danger," Farad assured him. He told him quickly what had happened and that he had used the King's Knife to heal his back.

Aramis knelt at his feet. "Forgive me, cousin, for all the ill I ever thought of you!" he said and unbuckled his sword and laid it at his feet. "My blade will ever be at your service, second only to the King's."

Farad clapped him upon the shoulder. "I had need of such warm words, Aramis. Come, we have need of you. Rolin is your closest friend, and I test and waken him next. He loves and trusts you. I would rather not use the King's Voice to calm him."

Rolin was found to be free of the Enemy's influence. Dewalaren knelt beside Rolin along with Aramis, to help calm him when he awoke, and to assure him of both Aramis's and Farad's loyalty.

One by one, the others were all tested and awakened. Only Lunahr and the Elven siblings had been compromised. Aramis stood back with Desmond and Jargas as Dewalaren and Rolin ensured the rest understood Farad and the envoys were not their enemy.

Farad told Dewalaren, "Everyone else must leave the room. There will be much danger here. I may well need to battle the Enemy for the three he controls."

Dewalaren ordered all the Lords out, including Aramis, to his brother Fenris's visible relief, but Aramis said he would stay to aid Farad. Dewalaren told him that he must go, he was ordered to leave, but Aramis still refused. Then Desmond and Jargas told him to go, and he reluctantly left. Dewalaren frowned but remained silent. Only he, Elavar, Jargas, and Desmond remained with the three who were yet immobilized.

Farad viewed Lunahr's core. From the outside it appeared whole. He touched it. On the surface it was fine, but when he gazed deeper, the illusion shattered. Lunahr's core was more terrible than his own to look upon: it was burning. There were endless layers of unspeakable horrors, fire and depravity, submission and degradation, pain and subservience, bound everywhere by sick, twisted bands of a hideous, deformed love. There was no light, no laughter, no music: the cousin he loved was gone. No! He would not believe it, not after thinking him dead and finding he yet lived! He began searching. He heard a faint fragment of music and headed toward it.

"No, Farad, it's a trap! I don't want to kill anyone else!" Lunahr begged, sobbing. "Kill me! Leave quickly, before…." There was a terrified scream.

Farad ran toward it, ripping through horrific memories unseeing. A replica of the Knife he held in the outside world appeared in his hand as he ran.

He heard terrible laughter. "The Knife! You disappoint me, Farad. You choose the wrong blade if you hope to kill me. Or is that for your young cousin? You needn't have bothered. I brought my own." Incuban!

There! He saw Incuban, the same visage that was burnt into his own memory, the same image. Lunahr lay hog-tied, bound, and naked at Incuban's feet, sobbing, a knife at his groin.

"I am punishing him because of you, Farad. And he is only one of many. I will take Jarina next, and Rion. You have made a host of new friends I will take from you.

"Remember when I held you like this, Farad, in your own core? When I punished you, when I castrated you? You will never be a man again. And as I took that which was most precious to you, your manhood, I now take what is most precious to Lunahr: his voice." In a blur the knife moved to Lunahr's throat. But Incuban was the one to scream, as the healing Knife in Farad's hand suddenly became the King's Sword, as he lunged forward with astonishing speed and severed Incuban's wrist at the base of the hand that held the knife to Lunahr's throat.

"No, don't hurt him! I love him!" Lunahr begged.

Farad plunged the Sword into Incuban's black heart. Incuban's image burst into flame and vanished, and Lunahr screamed in loss and collapsed. Darkness fell in his core, and Farad was terrified for his young cousin. The Sword in his hand became the Knife again. It flared brightly.

He knelt beside Lunahr and cut the ropes that bound him by knife-light. Farad hugged Lunahr, but he was limp, cold, lifeless. Farad shook him frantically. "Lunahr, come back! Please don't die! Not when you've survived so much! I love you, I need you! Dewalaren loves you. You cannot leave him! He is not dead, Lunahr! I saved him. I saved Desmond too. You did not turn Eladar or Elanara to darkness. They have not killed, you have not!"

He kissed Lunahr on the forehead. "Please, Lunahr! We love you. Can't that be enough for you? I will go mad if you die, Dewalaren will. Who will save us without your music to guide us? We've found the Knife and the Ring again. You must live to see Dewalaren King." Then he began sobbing, for he realized the lie of his words. Dewalaren could never be King now. Jargas was King. And Lunahr had not moved.

Farad forced the despair down and let go of Lunahr and raised the Knife. It flared to life in his hand and blazed like the sun. A pyrenteum chest formed at his feet. All the terrible images around him burst into flame, until there was nothing left but ash, and the ash swirled as if driven by a wind and gathered in the chest, and the lid slammed shut. Only Lunahr was left, and gray nothingness all around him.

Farad eyed the desolation in renewed despair. Nothing of Lunahr remained. When he had first heard him, he had hoped, but... what was that? There was something hard and bright that glistened in the light of the Knife. Farad walked wearily toward it. It was a chest of pallenteum, small and beautiful. How could there still be beauty here? There was something written upon it, but it was in Elvish.

Farad reached for the chest with the Knife yet in his hand. The hilt of the Knife suddenly grew hot; it burned his palm and he dropped it. The Knife disappeared, and the Ring's Power vanished with it. But the small chest glowed.

Farad reached hesitantly for the latch with his bare hand. The metal was cool to the touch, soothing. The pain of the burn on his hand disappeared. He lifted the latch and opened the chest. There was a song inside. A sweet, clear voice was singing, an Elven voice. Tears sprang to Farad's eyes and he fell to his knees at the exquisite beauty of it. He had never heard such a voice!

A second voice rose from the chest, harmonizing with the first. It was almost as beautiful. Then there was a third voice. This one he recognized, but it came not from the chest, but from the limp form lying in the grayness. Farad ran to Lunahr as he began to sit up. He was singing, his eyes closed, an expression of pure joy upon his face. And then there was light, flowing from his mouth, flowing from the chest. Grass and flowers formed all around them, and a great fir tree began to grow until it towered above Lunahr. It reached down and embraced him, and the wind through the needles sounded almost like a fourth voice.

Farad remained absolutely still, afraid he might somehow break the spell. He must not break it. Then the song ended. The tree let go of Lunahr, and the needles rustled softly in a breeze, as if whispering.

Lunahr saw Farad and his eyes lit with joy. "Farad!" Lunahr ran to him and hugged him. Lunahr felt warm and strong.

"You found it! You found the chest! Meloneth and Aras made it for me, with Aranahr, in case... in case He ever came back. So I could find myself again. But I didn't think I could ever find it...." His eyes welled with tears. "Is... is Laren truly all right? You didn't just say so, so I would come back?"

"Dewalaren is fine, Lunahr, or he will be, once he sees you well again," Farad assured him.

Lunahr looked down in shame. "I'm not truly well. I still love Incuban, Farad. I still want Him to hold me again."

Farad paled, horrified to hear it.

Lunahr looked up. "But I know He's making me feel this way. I can remember, now, all the terrible things He's done. Not only to me, to you, to everyone. I hate Him for it. I would fight Him if He came for me again. And I'm trying not to feel the other way, too. I feel much stronger, now. I don't understand, Farad. How can you wield such Power?"

"I will tell you when I tell the others. I must make sure Eladar and Elanara are safe. I had meant to free you all at once." He gave his cousin another hug. "You must remember Dewalaren and I truly love you. We wish only happiness for you. We wish you to be safe and healthy and whole."

Lunahr nodded. "It was so hard to remember, when Aras left, and without Leonas and Aranahr to watch over me. I was so alone. I will be alone again, when you go. Laren cannot link to me, though he has tried. Please, Farad, link to me?"

Farad said, pained, "I cannot, Lunahr. I would put you in danger again. My core looks well from the outside, but it is not."

"I know. I understand. I heard Him and saw Him, what He's done to you," Lunahr said, agonized for his cousin.

Farad's face darkened in shame.

"Not only that, not just now, when he was taunting you. All of it." Lunahr shuddered. "He shared all of it with me, as if it were something wonderful. What he did to Aunt Alaria and Cousin Alarad, all of it. I know it was monstrous, but.... I have to see, Farad, don't you understand? I know it was horrible, but only with my head, not with my heart. I need to be stronger. I can't let him turn me again. Please?"

"No, I cannot. You were singing and your face was lit with joy. It would burn all the music away again," Farad said, as horrified by what Lunahr had said as by what he had asked.

"No, it won't. It can't, not with the chest open again. I had to hide it before. I couldn't let Incuban destroy it, but then I lost it, and by the time I found it, it wouldn't open for me. Aras warded it against His Power and I was His again. It burnt me when I touched it, and I collapsed. When I woke up, it was gone. I had thought it was lost forever or destroyed somehow. Please link to me, Farad? Incuban can't trick me again if I'm not alone."

"If you truly think it will be safer for you," Farad said reluctantly. "I will leave your core and return to my own and link to you. You must break the bond if it harms you."

"Thank you Farad!" Lunahr said gratefully.

Farad turned to go, then took a good, long look at Lunahr's healed core. Lunahr smiled at him. He left Lunahr's core and looked about, lost. He had not bonded to Lunahr, yet he had left his own core. He felt sudden panic. How could he find himself again? The Ring had guided him into Lunahr's core before, but he'd lost the Power of the Ring when he'd touched the chest.

Farad heard the cry of an eagle behind him. He turned, and for a moment, he thought it was his mother. But this eagle was male and far too young: it still had some of its fledgling feathers. It shimmered and changed, to Lunahr.

"You must come back inside, Farad. I felt your fear. I had not understood. You cannot get back. Can you waken me from here?" Lunahr asked hopefully.

"I think so," Farad said.

"Then I will go to you and form the bond to you, so you may cross back. Then later, when there is time, and we can be alone, I will view your core. Come, cousin. They might already be frantic with worry for you," Lunahr said.

Farad released his hold on Lunahr's body as they reentered his core.

LUNAHR sat up. For a moment, no one noticed. They were all bent over Farad, all but Elavar, who stood watch over his brother and sister.

Dewalaren was speaking, his voice frantic. "... must! He cannot be gone!"

"There is nothing. Hunter is gone. His core is dark, he does not breathe, his heart does not beat," Jargas said, his voice thick with despair. "The Knife cannot heal him. It cannot raise the dead."

Then Elavar spotted him and sprang to his feet, snatching up Lunahr's own fallen bow and quiver, yelling a warning even as he nocked an arrow against him.

Lunahr shrank from him, huddling, arms about his legs in fear. "Elavar, don't kill me! It's truly me! Farad saved me!"

Dewalaren ran to Lunahr and grabbed him roughly by the shoulders and shook him. "What have you done to him?"

"Laren, please, you're hurting me!" Lunahr begged. He had never seen his cousin so enraged. He no longer knew him.

Jargas said harshly, "Hold him. He'll tell me." He reached for Lunahr's face with his massive hand.

Lunahr saw a red flash and felt fire and screamed as Jargas ripped into his core.

JARGAS stopped, stunned by what he found. He was standing in a beautiful, idyllic garden: there was a towering fir tree and song everywhere. Lunahr was there, whimpering, hurt, and trembling, but Farad was there also, holding him, protecting him.

"Jargas, stop! You mustn't hurt him, not when I've saved him," Farad said.

Jargas gaped at him in disbelief. "Farad? But... we thought you dead! You are dead. How can you be here?"

Farad explained, "I used the Ring to heal Lunahr, but there is wizardry here. The magic broke my link to the Ring, somehow. We are not bound, so I could not return to my core. Lunahr needs to link to me, so that I can. Eladar and Elanara, are they all right? I had meant to free all three of them at once, but the Enemy attacked Lunahr and I had to save him."

"They seemed all right, though still frozen. I would touch you, Farad. You might be the Enemy trying to trick me. I've touched your core before. I'll know if it's truly you," Jargas said warily.

"I don't think it will work, but you can try," Farad said.

Jargas touched him, but there was nothing. He would draw upon the Ring, as Farad had already mentioned it. Lunahr knew he had it. But first, he warned Jarina and Desenia to sever their links to him, if they felt him fall. But as the Power of the Ring coursed through him, a replica of it appeared upon his finger, it glowed red, and he felt Farad's presence clearly. It was truly him! It was Farad! He drew back from him, clapping him soundly on the back. "Never do such a thing again! I must tell the others Lunahr is healed." He turned to Lunahr. "I'm sorry, cousin. I'd not meant to harm you."

Lunahr looked up at him wide-eyed. "Cousin? And you have the King's Ring? Archer is not the King at all! It is you who is claiming to be!"

Farad grimaced. "He is the King, Lunahr. Jargas is Rowanar's grandson."

Lunahr was devastated. "But Farad, he cannot be! Laren is King, he must be! How can we call another King, after all Laren has sacrificed for us?"

Farad winced. "Do not look at me like that, Lunahr. My heart is torn in two already, by what I must do."

Jargas said to Farad, "I must tell the others you live, and make sure they let Lunahr bond to you, Farad." He left Lunahr's core.

FARAD hugged Lunahr. "You must know I would never hurt Dewalaren by choice, Lunahr. But our most sacred Law is the Law of Succession." He winced and drew back from Lunahr. He thought of the regicide he had committed, of the hypocrisy of him saying such a thing.

"Farad, what is wrong?" Lunahr asked.

"It is not important," Farad said. "Not now, that Jargas will be King. Lunahr, please, I want my body back. It may not be whole, but it is the only one I have."

LUNAHR hugged Farad fiercely. "You will get well, Farad. We both will."
Then Lunahr gazed outward.

Jargas had let go of him and Laren was releasing him. His arms hurt
fiercely, where Laren had crushed them.

Lunahr looked around cautiously. Elavar was kneeling beside his fallen
siblings, glaring at him. Aramis appeared wary. The elder Man, Archer, was
looking at him curiously. Lunahr turned back to Laren. Laren was staring at
him as he had in Nalea, when he'd strangled Laren with his chains, horrified
and repulsed.

"Come, Lunahr," Jargas said. His voice was kind.

Lunahr went to Farad, feeling many unfriendly eyes upon him. He
touched Farad's face and extended a bond to Farad's core. He peered inward
and saw a shaggy wolven bounding eagerly home.

FARAD rose.

"Hunter, please, you must help them," Elavar pleaded.

It was as close to begging as Farad ever wanted to hear from an Elf. Farad
reached out both hands and called upon the Power of the Ring. Gently,
carefully, he broke the Enemy's hold upon the siblings. Then he roused them.

Eladar sat up suddenly in fear, reaching for his back. And Elanara stared
at Lunahr in horror. "Lunahr! The Enemy! He…."

"Hush, Sister," Elavar said. "It's all right. The Enemy is gone from him
now, as he is gone from you."

"I was hit, I felt the arrow, but I am unhurt," Eladar said, confused. His
eyes widened in horror. "Talon! I killed him!"

"Hush, Eladar," Elavar soothed. "You tried to, but he lives. He has been
healed, as you have been."

THERE was the sound of a commotion in the hall, and the door burst open. A
squadron of Elven archers with bows drawn poured into the room.

"No one moves, any of you!" Thaedrin ordered.

"Thaedrin, what is the meaning of this?" Dewalaren demanded.

"The building's been taken. It's the envoys' doing," Thaedrin accused.

"Taken?" Dewalaren asked.

Farad said tiredly, "I did not just incapacitate everyone in the room. I froze the entire building."

Dewalaren stared at Farad in shock. "How could you have such Power?"

Lunahr said, "They've found the Ring, Laren. Jargas is the True King, he's Rowanar's grandson."

There was an indignant tumult of voices from the room and the open doorway.

"SILENCE, all of you! Majesty, we need you and the Princes and Princess to go into the hall, while we subdue these others," Thaedrin said.

"I am still King, Commander. At least for the moment. Lower your bows. The meeting must continue. Hunter, as a show of good faith, you will release your hold on everyone. Now," Dewalaren commanded.

"YES, Talon," Farad said. His eyes focused inward for a moment. "I have done so. Someone should go to Theodas to calm him. I am the one who felled him before. I had no choice. He learned too much from us when we were questioning him. But Lunahr has already told you about the Ring. It is a secret no longer, so I have released Theodas from his slumber as well as the others."

There was a chaos of voices outside and concerned voices from the walls, demanding to know what was happening. All had last seen the King and others felled. Now the room was filled with their fellow bowmen, and the King appeared unharmed, though the back of his tunic was still dark with blood.

Farad sat tiredly on the floor, so he would not appear a threat. Desmond joined him and after a moment, Jargas did as well. Then Aramis entered the room. "I must join the others. My allegiance lies with King Jargas."

Fenris was at his heels. "I must join you, also. After what you have told me, it is clear where my loyalties must lie." He turned to Dewalaren, agonized. "I am truly sorry, Talon. I would have followed you to the very lair of the Enemy, but I can do so no longer. I must follow our Laws. There can be only one King, and you are no longer he."

Dewalaren looked at him as if he had struck him in the face.

Dewalaren calmed the others, calling the Lords in and ordering everyone else out, to sort out the madness in the corridors. He ordered the Elves out from their posts behind the walls as well, so they would not overhear. Once the room was cleared, the five rose.

"Tell us your story, Hunter," Dewalaren said. "But start with who that other Man is. Is he truly the Dwarven High-King? Why did he speak as if he knew my father?"

"Because I did," Desmond said. "I was Protector and King's Friend to him for forty years, before I bonded to him. I am Desmond, known as Archer in the Lands of Men, Lord of House of Serpents. You can see my band," he said, extending his arm. It was snapped into the groove in the metal plate of the vambrace of the King's Armor.

"Desmond? But... we thought you dead! Where have you been these ninety years past?" Dewalaren asked, incredulous.

"I have been fulfilling the mission your father commanded of me: to rescue and preserve as many of the Dwarven Kingdoms as I could. There are twenty-nine Western Kingdoms in the Saravan, thirty total, including Malar in Holoren. I am their High-King."

"And Jargas. You told me you were House of Gryphon, Stephan's descendent. Yet I found his cairn and his sword Garalathon was upon the body inside," Dewalaren challenged.

"I told you I was a banded Lord. I showed you Stephan's band, but I never said that was my House. I let you assume wrongly. I could not trust you to reveal my true House, until I spoke with Hunter again." He told them the true story of his House.

Farad said. "And as we found the Ring, you found the Knife. Now I have seen the bands these Lords wear and know the truth of it. They are the descendants of the Lords Alanar led. Tell me, I do not see House of Pumar here. Are there any survivors?"

"No, nor of Tortoise. Eight of the ten survive, both Amontir purebloods and Urwani-Amontir. Why the concern for Pumar?" Dewalaren asked, intrigued.

"Because my wife Jarina, Jargas's sister, is House of Pumar. I had hoped she might have found others here. But even her band is lost."

"No. I have the band of House of Pumar. But how is it you have married, Hunter?" Dewalaren asked.

Farad's face darkened.

"I meant, how is it you married without the consent of your King?" Dewalaren asked softly.

"I had consent. King Jargas approved the union. You cannot deny the Law of Succession, Talon," Farad said.

Dewalaren sighed. "I must test Jargas, to see the truth of his claim."

"Then test me," Jargas said.

Dewalaren winced, glancing at Rolin. He had not detected Lunahr's taint. "There is none here that I trust who is strong enough not to be deceived."

Lunahr looked devastated and Rolin appeared ill.

Jargas said, "If one you trust was to hold the Ring, he could then test me."

Dewalaren stared at him, astonished. "You would never allow such a thing!"

"Why wouldn't I? I do not seek your throne for glory or power, Talon. I only follow our Laws and seek what is best for our people."

"Then give Fennel the Ring, and he will test you," Dewalaren challenged.

Jargas said, "The Ring is not here. Hunter and I wielded it through our link to the one who holds it."

Dewalaren was astonished. "Can it be so powerful? Then, we must send for it."

"I can tell her to bring it, if you'll swear to me she'll be escorted here safely," Jargas said.

"I swear I'll not allow harm to come to the one who holds the Ring, even after she surrenders it to us," Dewalaren said.

"My sister Jarina, Hunter's wife, holds it." Jargas's eyes lost their focus for a moment. "I have told her to come. She says she is still captive with the rest of the Army."

Dewalaren said, "Fennel, tell Heather to see that the Lady Jarina is safely escorted here. Make sure she is well guarded. The Enemy may now suspect the Ring is near."

Rolin's eyes lost focus for a moment. "They will come. It will be four hours by horse."

"Then we can hear in detail all we are each curious about," Dewalaren said.

FOUR hours later the door to the Audience Chamber opened and Rowena entered with a Dwarven Lady, cloaked and veiled. Dewalaren eyed her in surprise. Dewalaren still did not believe Farad was married. How could he be husband to her, to anyone? Unless he had been somehow healed?

The gaze that passed between Farad and Jarina was unmistakable. Dewalaren's heart ached, for a moment, to know Elanara would never look at him with eyes like those.

Jarina walked to Farad. "I am here, at my husband's summons," she said. "And my King's," she said, bowing her head to her brother.

"I require the Ring, Sister," Jargas said.

"Of course," she said, handing it to him.

Jargas walked toward Rolin, the Ring in his palm. It throbbed with Power; it pulsed and glowed with the beat of his heart.

"Wait," Dewalaren said. "I have waited eighty-eight years to see the Ring. I would hold it now."

Jargas studied Dewalaren in careful calculation. "Hunter has told me I can trust you to follow your Laws, despite what it will cost you. I have myself seen you are an honorable Man. Please do not prove otherwise, Talon. I would not want to have to slay you."

Dewalaren looked at him levelly, and Jargas handed him the Ring.

Dewalaren examined it intently. The stone was lifeless in his hand, dark and dead. He handed it to Rolin. "Test him," he said. Then he added softly, "Though his handing me the Ring was test enough."

Rolin took the Ring. It glowed in his hand as it had not in Dewalaren's. It pulsed, the glow betraying the quickness of his heart. He slipped it upon his finger and held up his hand toward Jargas. "May I touch your face?" he asked Jargas.

"You don't need to. You can test me from there, with the Power the Ring grants you. But if it makes you more comfortable, of course," Jargas said.

Rolin took a deep breath and touched him. A few moments later he pulled back and knelt at Jargas's feet and held the Ring up to him. "He is the True King. By blood and by thought, by heart and by skill, and by deed." He turned to Dewalaren. "I am sorry, Talon. House of Horses can no longer follow you."

Dewalaren seemed to wilt. He walked to Jargas and then he knelt to him. He unbuckled his sheathed Sword and held it in his outstretched hands. "I, Dewalaren, son of Evanaren, of House of Obearn, pledge my sword and my life to your service, though I will bear this blade no longer. The King's Sword and the King's Knife are yours, as the one True King." He looked up at Jargas, tears in his eyes. More than anything else, the loss of the Sword pained him beyond bearing.

Most of the other Lords appeared shocked and some looked angry. Dewalaren turned to them. "You all swore to follow all of our Laws as your own, when I recognized your Houses in your City. You must kneel as well and swear your allegiance to King Jargas."

They knelt, many of them reluctantly.

Jargas looked at them all, then at Jarina and Farad, and sighed. He stared intently at Jarina for a moment, his eyes glazing over. She seemed surprised, but then nodded slightly.

Jargas turned to Dewalaren and spoke. "I might be the True King, Dewalaren, but you are a true King among Men. Not one other Man in one hundred thousand would have done as you have just done. You held the Sword and the Knife and the Ring in your hands, the means to slay your Enemy, and restore yourself to the throne in your own lands. You deserve to be a High-King, but our people recognize none. I would make a fair King for our people, but not a great one, and we have need of greatness now, of all times. You know the Enemy we face. You are a master swordsman. You are a brilliant tactician. You are brave, and loyal, and compassionate. You are a friend to the Elves. You are loved by your people and all but worshiped by your Lords.

"I am heir to one throne already and have need of no other. I hereby abdicate my claim to the Throne of Amontir, for myself and my sister and my line, and all the heirs of my body, from this day forward, until the end of time. And so, I return the Sword, the Knife, and the Ring to you, my King. And I surrender the King's Band to you as well." Jargas knelt before Dewalaren. "I Jargas, brother to Chieftess and Healer Jarina, son of King Rongas and Chieftess and Healer Jahira, grandson of Crown Prince Rowanar and Chieftess and Healer Janara, heir to the throne of Malar in Holoren, Champion of the Varash, pledge my staff and all the people and might of Malar and the Varash to your service. I will serve you with my life or my death, as you command."

Those in the room stared, stunned, none more so than Dewalaren. Dewalaren found his voice. "I, Dewalaren, son of Evanaren, Lord of House of Obearn, grandson of Idare, accept the Sword and the Knife and the Ring, and with them, the Throne of Amontir. And I now truly claim the title King."

He turned to Jargas. "Jargas, I would see your line mix with my own, for your heirs may one day be lesser Men, although I might doubt it, and seek to wrest the Throne from my heirs, and I would not see our Kingdoms war with one another. So, I would seal my kingship with a pact between our two lines, that an heir of your line wed an heir of mine, and henceforth, the eldest son of that union be named King. And until that time, I name you as Heir. Arise now, Jargas, Prince of Amontir."

Dewalaren exchanged the ancient true King's Band for the copy he had always worn. He rose and smiled, and a great cheer rose from the room. "Hail the King! Hail the Prince! Great Lords of Amontir!" and as one, the Lords knelt before Dewalaren and renewed their oaths of service.

Then the others rose, but Farad stayed kneeling at Dewalaren's feet. "I must seek judgment from you, now, Majesty," Farad said solemnly, and the tone of his voice sent a chill down Dewalaren's spine.

"You are absolved for your actions here today, cousin. It took great courage to stand against me and all your kin, but you did so in observance of our most sacred Law, the Law of Succession," Dewalaren said.

Farad shook his head. "I do not kneel before you for my actions today. I kneel to be judged for my crime of these months past. Already I know what your judgment will be. I would hand you my own knife, should it be returned to me, for your Sword should not be stained with my blood."

Silence enveloped the room. Dewalaren's voice was soft, as he looked at Farad intently. "What crime could you commit, cousin, you who are the best and once again restored to be the brightest among us, that I would seek your life, after you restored mine today?"

"Regicide," Farad said. He spoke the word softly, yet it echoed from the stone walls in the absolute silence, as if he had yelled it.

Dewalaren paled then, for if Farad had truly killed a King, there was no apology, no appeal, no explanation that could stay his hand. Of all their Laws, next to their Law of Succession, that Law was held most sacrosanct.

"Whom did you kill?" Dewalaren asked, his voice softer still.

"I willfully and maliciously killed King Balgar, the rightful King of Malar in Fromer, so that his son Valar might succeed to the throne and rule in his place. I made it appear to be an accident. I used my Power to tangle his feet and drive my own knife, which he held, into his heart," Farad said. He looked ill.

Dewalaren paled. "Did anyone witness this?" he asked, appalled.

"THE King's son Valar, Jargas, the Healer Gervan, Gervan's son Arvan, and one guard, although he was mad and knew not what he saw." Farad looked intently at Dewalaren and swore, "No one realized that I shifted the knife with my Power. That secret is safe. I used the pallenteum blade you had gifted to me for the crime," he added, bowing his head in shame. He could no longer bear to see the pain in Dewalaren's eyes. Then he forced himself to look Dewalaren in the eye, again. "I await your judgment and my execution."

Jargas and Jarina both began speaking at once. "Majesty, I would have you listen to me bear witness for Farad," Jargas said.

"You will not die for saving my people from that twisted monster," Jarina said.

Dewalaren said, "Silence!" speaking with the voice of a King, but not the King's Voice. "For the crime of regicide, there are no witnesses, there can be no mercy."

Jargas's eyes flashed and Jarina's begged, as Dewalaren continued. "But I must, for my own safety, understand how you of all people could do such a thing, and then act as you have here today."

Lunahr burst into tears, unexpectedly. "He didn't really do that, did He, Farad? Incuban wouldn't... but He...." Lunahr started sobbing and fell to his knees before Farad.

Farad hugged him tightly. "You said you knew how evil He is with your head, but not with your heart. Lunahr, if I'm to die now, I must show you what He is before I die."

He turned to Dewalaren, tears in his eyes. "Please, this is important. Lunahr must see it, if I won't be here to help him. I'd promised him already. I'll not die now and leave my promise to him unfulfilled. Come to me, Lunahr. I want to show you King Balgar. You came close to becoming him today, as Incuban's pawn. I must also show you Alaria and Alarad, so you see what might have happened to Elanara and Eladar."

"I'm afraid to look," Lunahr said, in a small voice.

"I'm here as well, cousin. Hold me, but you must keep your eyes open. You must see what I show you," Farad encouraged.

"All right," Lunahr said. Both Farad's and Lunahr's eyes lost their focus.

JARINA looked desperately from Farad to Dewalaren. What had she done? When Jargas had asked her about the kingship, she'd never dreamt Farad might die for it. She would not let him die. She would defend his life with her own. Or perhaps she could seize the Ring, and use its Power to bring Farad to safety.

LUNAHR pitched forward onto his hands and knees and began retching. Farad held him as his body was rocked by spasms.

Lunahr fought for breath to talk. "You can't... you can't punish Farad for that! King Balgar was a monster! He... he was Incuban's servant, even if he still had his core. The things he did! You would have killed him too, Laren, any of us would have. But Farad is so noble, he almost died doing it, it was so against his nature. Balgar tortured innocent people to death. He branded them to death and he tried to whip them to death. He was going to kill a healer and the healer's son, slowly and horribly. And when Farad killed him, it was in defense of an innocent. Balgar was trying to murder his own son with Farad's knife, when his son was so injured he couldn't even walk, and so heartsick and horrified at what his father had done he wouldn't have even been able to defend himself. If you kill Farad for that, you'll have to kill me, too, before I turn into what Balgar was, without Farad to help me."

Jarina stepped forward. "You will have to kill me as well. I will not live without Farad. And you would lose not only House of Pumar, but my father's army, also."

Jargas said, "Please, Majesty. Let me tell you all I saw in Malar in Fromer. If you still think Farad deserves death after that, then I'll spend my last breath defending him."

Dewalaren looked at them all. "Jarina, Lunahr, Farad, you are to wait outside. Jargas, I would hear all you know of this."

The three of them left. Jargas told Dewalaren and the assembled Lords all he knew, starting with how he discovered his heritage to how he'd found Farad near death in the dungeons, and all that had been done to him. He told them of how Farad had kept the healer's son, Arvan, from killing the King and losing his innocence by it, and how doing so had so weakened Farad, it had cost him his sanity and very nearly his life. Then he told them all that had happened thereafter, the tortures and the deaths. Jargas told them that the Kingdom of Malar would have been handed to Incuban by Balgar.

DEWALAREN was stunned by all he heard. "And without Malar, nothing would stand between Incuban and the Elves and all the Cities of Man. And yet Farad could barely force himself to act against Balgar! I cannot slay him for what he did. He still suffers for it. I can see he is haunted by it, when he should be hailed as a hero for it. He is not guilty of any crime. I will hear no one speak to him of it again. Jargas, you have my undying gratitude for all you have done for him and for defending him now. Summon him, so I may tell Farad as well."

Jargas went to the doors and called them in. Elavar, Elanara, and Eladar entered with them, and no one prevented them from doing so. Farad came as a condemned man walks to his execution. Jarina had her arm around Lunahr in a motherly way. Lunahr was trembling and looked like he might collapse.

"Farad, upon hearing all that transpired in Malar in Fromer, I hereby pass judgment upon you. For slaying the monster that Balgar had become, you are no more guilty of regicide than you would be for beheading a Revenant or a Resemblant. I would pardon you, but you are guilty of no crime. You are a hero. You have always ever only been that.

"I hereby restore your title of Lord of House of Wolven, which I had erroneously revoked. I hereby name you Protector and King's Friend once more, as you are no longer my Heir and you have ever always been Protector and Friend to me, even as you marched against me. And I name you guardian of Lunahr, for although he is Lord of House of Eagles, he has not yet come-of-age, and is more sorely in need of a Protector and Friend than I am. Welcome home, my Protector, my cousin, my friend," Dewalaren said, and hugged Farad tightly.

Farad stood stiffly in his embrace for a moment, then hugged him fiercely in return.

Dewalaren stepped back. "Now, we need to tell our army to free yours, Desmond."

Lunahr, who had been looking somewhat better, paled again. "The army! Laren, Majesty, the army! Incuban is coming! He is marching here with fifty thousand Revenants. They will be here within less than five days! They are coming from the east. I know nothing more of their plans, other than they come to seize Caramore and to destroy Nalea.

"I'm sorry, Laren! I didn't mean to tell Him! I couldn't stop myself. He knows! He knows about Aras, He knows too much! Aras never should have told me so much! And the Trees, He knows about the Grove, about their Power, about the Lords. Oh, Laren, He's going to kill them! The Trees and the Elf Lords!

"And He's coming here! He wants… He wants all our people, especially the ones with Power. Jarina and someone named Desenia, though I don't know who she is. Falara and Rowena. And Rion, He is obsessed about Rion, for all he has done, for all he knows, for his ties to Farad."

His eyes filled with tears and his voice sank to a whisper. "And me. Please don't let Him take me, not after what I just saw! Kill me, please! I can't bear it!" His fragile control shattered and he began sobbing brokenly.

"Hush, Lunahr. We will protect you. I will. I am your guardian now. I am bonded to you. You are not alone anymore," Farad soothed, embracing Lunahr, who collapsed into his arms.

Elanara came to Lunahr and he shrank from her. "I'm sorry, Elanara. I never wanted to hurt you," Lunahr whispered in despair.

"Hush, Lunahr. I am still your guardian, also, for all I have let you come to such terrible harm. But I will help guard you now, with my life. You have given us warning. There is still time to prepare. Dewalaren will not be beaten. The Enemy's army outnumbers our own by only two to one. One Elven bowman can stop many, and we have five thousand. And one Dwarf can behead many Revenants with his axe, and we have twenty thousand, and more in the three Dwarven Kingdoms of the east, who are ready to join us. We will have victory, Lunahr. At last we are ready to face Him. We need no longer flee before Him."

Dewalaren said, "We have the Sword, and the Ring, now, to Power it, and the Knife to heal us. We can slay Him. We will slay Him. Come, we must form our plans quickly. Victory is within our grasp."

"Victory!" one of the new Lords shouted, and the cheer was taken up by many throats, until the walls rang with the word.

JARINA shivered. Over the tumult of their cry, she heard the memory of laughter, terrible laughter, as the Enemy had come for her, through her bond to Jargas.

Farad hugged her. "He will not take you, Jarina. I promise you, He will never take you."

Jarina looked at him with frightened eyes. She heard the echo of Incuban's words to Farad, when he fought for Lunahr. Incuban was coming for her and for Desenia, for Lunahr and for Rion, and the others.

"He will not take any of us," Jarina said, with so much conviction, she almost believed it. Almost.

The Beginning of the Story

DESCENT of KINGS Book 1

Prelude to War

Maria Albert

http://www.dreamspinnerpress.com

The Story Continued in

DESCENT of KINGS Book 2

Heir to the Throne

Maria Albert

http://www.dreamspinnerpress.com

Coming Soon

Descent of Kings
Book Four:
The Final Battle

"But I am just a Man! You all want so much of me! ... I am not a wizard. I am not even one of you. I have no magic. There is no fire in my eyes."

—Rion of Ardock

Rion wields a power of heart that touches all he meets. The wizard Circe once called him a lynchpin, a keystone of the world. When Rion is viciously attacked and maimed in Gosa, he believes Circe's family is retaliating for his betrayal of them to Crown Prince Elavar. Learning the horrific truth brings him to the brink of madness.

Rion's friends take him to the River Elves of Salenia for aid, but the Elves send them onward, to King Talon. The company's perilous journey to the Watchtower is fraught with danger and filled with tragedy and triumph, but their trials have just begun.

King Talon's army has been decimated by the Enemy's relentless attacks. After staggering losses, they are outnumbered ten to one and teeter on the brink of defeat— yet somehow their dwindling forces must overcome a being with the Power of a God.

MARIA ALBERT lives in the California Bay Area with her two daughters and several dozen friends, most of the latter of whom are still confined in binders on her bookshelves. She looks forward to releasing many more of them in the coming months.

Also from MARIA ALBERT

http://www.dreamspinnerpress.com

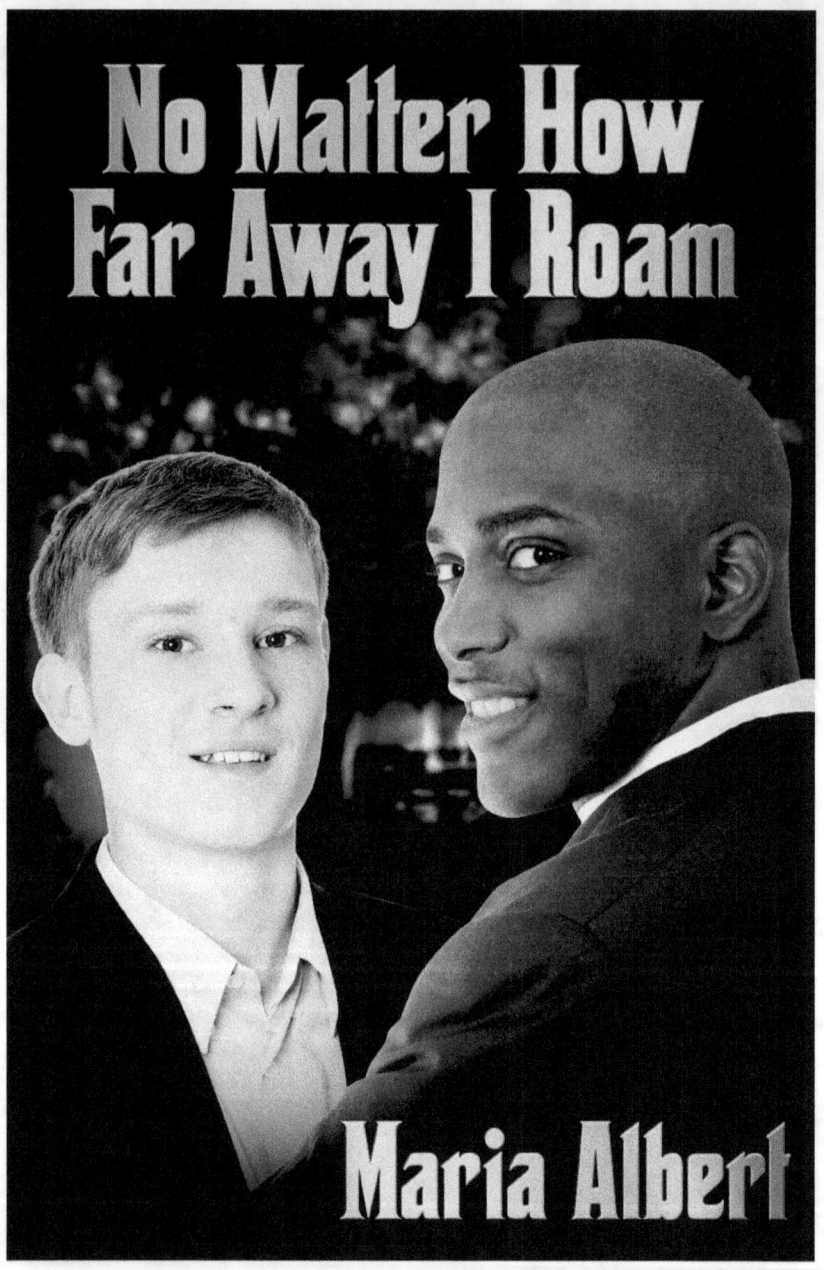

www.ingramcontent.com/pod-product-compliance
Lightning Source LLC
Chambersburg PA
CBHW050023030726
47506CB00001B/90